I0760563

Fatgirl

THE COMPLETE SERIES

○ ○ ○ ○

C. S. Johnson

Contains a Bonus episode of *Date Night*, a bonus prequel episode of the spin-off series, SPYGIRL.

ISBN for Hardback: 978-1-948464-94-9

Fatgirl is a serial, episodic work of fiction, meant to be read in shorter sittings. The story itself is a blend of satire, superhero fiction, and contemporary genres. It is meant to be enjoyed with a tongue-in-cheek kind of innocence.

There's no trigger warning here, but if you're offended, chances are you didn't read it.

This is a collection of all of my Fatgirl stories, from the very beginning to the series' end.

AUTHOR'S NOTE

Dear Reader,

Thanks for checking this book out. When I toyed with the idea of writing this series, I thought it would be a fun sort of thing, something that I could fail at, especially in the serial form.

But I'm grateful to say I don't think I failed. Kallie grows from a very self-centered, hurt little girl into a wiser and more compassionate young woman with more of a sense of her individual worth. While I can say I safely managed to avoid radioactive doughnuts in my high school days (so far as I know), I had to come to terms with much of what Kallie faces, too, and I hope in that way, I've honored her character as much as she's redeemed mine.

So while the book may seem designed to offend people, I hope you will give Kallie's story the same grace we all hope for as teenagers, just as much as I hope you will cheer for her growth.

One of the best things I've come to see as I've written my books and stories is that change is always possible, and that is one reason hope for this world—and whatever you may be facing—is real. And I think it's great to have stories that not only remind us of that, but help us aspire to become better, too.

Until We Meet Again,

C. S. Johnson

Dedicated to all my beloved readers and supporters, but especially to two fellow writers this time: C. O. Bonham and Cathy McCrumb. To the first, your remarks on my work have always encouraged me, and I hope to do the same for you; and to the second, Kallie and I would be up the creek without a waddle if it weren't for you.

My special thanks also goes to Spencer Baculi, for his Fatgirl artwork that always made me smile, and for Paul Hair, without whom this "Appalling Story" and its series would never have been brought to life.

Fatgirl

ORIGINS

PART ONE

○ ○ ○ ○

C. S. Johnson

FATGIRL
ORIGINS: PART ONE

○ ○ ○ ○

My stomach rumbled, and I tried not to think about how long it'd been since I'd allowed myself to eat. Instead, I thought about the day my mother left, and that took care of any appetite I might've had.

There was a sudden lump in my throat, and as I remembered the poisonous joy of swallowing food, it only made my stomach grumble again, this time much more loudly.

"Achoo!"

Thankfully, the sweaty, fat kid sitting behind me sneezed at that same moment my gastrointestinal tract declared mutiny, so no one else in my super-boring computer class heard me or my rebellious gut.

Everyone, including me, was now watching Sweaty Fat Kid.

I didn't exactly know who he was; he was a new student around Cuttingham City High School. That was all I knew about him, other than what I could see before me. He was a big kid, and dressed in an even bigger hoodie, so it was almost laughable how he shrunk down in his seat. If I'd been feeling better, I might've made a snarky comment of some kind, but, things being what they were, I said nothing.

It was actually nice there were others who were willing to offer Sweaty Fat Kid some comfort. There were a few muffled, "Bless you," remarks—and then more softened snickers.

However, soon enough, the silence of the room resumed, the *clack-clack-clack* of the keyboards its only accompaniment.

That was when I let myself relax, if only by the tiniest degree.

Thank God.

Contrary to what everyone else thought, it was hard being popular. If the least little embarrassing thing happened to me right now, I'd face a firing line of highly-scrutinized, unforgiving judgment, courtesy of my high school peers. And this week was even harder for me.

So *of course* I had to get awful stomach pains along with terrible gas issues today, of all days.

I was due to appear on *Model Middle America*, to earn my chance at a modeling career. To prepare, I'd been on a restricted diet, with only a limited amount of liquids and proteins. Egg whites and milk had been the only thing I'd consumed in the last two days, and I would be committing social suicide if I let myself fart in public.

I would get exactly zero sympathy if it happened. No one really cares about beautiful people suffering, because they believe that people really only suffer if they're ugly.

That's why Sweaty Fat Kid had no trouble ginning up sympathy for his loud sneezes, but if someone heard me fart, it'd be all over the school like weaponized wildfire in a matter of moments, thanks to social media.

Since I had my *Model Middle America* audition coming up later, today was the day to avoid the negative limelight. There could be nothing but good vibes and positive energy. I *had* to become the Next Top Heartland Teen Heartthrob Model.

I *had* to win.

I *needed* to win.

And frankly, if anyone *deserved* to win, it had to be me, Kallie Grande-White.

What would my mom say if I didn't?

Honestly, I didn't even want to think about that. It was entirely possible she would say nothing at all, and there was nothing I feared more than disappointing her.

Thinking about her again, my nose prickled.

Quickly, I bit down on the inside of my cheek until my swelling tears subsided.

I had good reasons to fear getting mocked by other students, but between getting racoon-eyed over my mother or shutting down guts full of fuming gas, I had literally no idea which would cause me more embarrassment.

It was probably good that I was having this sort of trouble during computer class. Everyone was too interested in watching their screens to notice me sitting here, feeling depressed.

And I hated feeling depressed; it made me hungry and tired and hopeless.

For a moment I closed my eyes, shutting out my surroundings and allowing myself to remember my mother. I breathed deeply, as if I could pull myself into the past, before Mom decided she wasn't happy enough living with me and my dad.

I mean, I couldn't exactly blame her. She was a famous model, known throughout the world for her beauty and grace. Cuttingham City, Arkansas was nothing compared to Los Angeles, New York, Milan, Paris, and London. Last month, she'd even been in Beijing, shooting a feature for *FEMME Magazine.*

She lived exactly the kind of life I wanted. For as long as I can remember, I'd studied her movements, trying my best to imitate her. I could still clearly picture her in my mind.

I smiled, thinking of how she used to put on her lipstick. She would study her reflection in her mirror before carefully and smoothly painting down both sides of her mouth. When she was finished, she would rub her full lips together, smooshing the ruby-red gloss to perfection before she would blow herself an adoring kiss.

If anyone deserved unabashed adoration, love and kisses, it was my mother, Katalina de la Carte Grande.

I smiled again, picturing the last time I saw her. Her stomach rumbled then, too.

"There's nothing that will cure an empty stomach like a broken heart, Kallie."

Suddenly, I wondered how long she'd been planning on leaving me when she'd said that.

"Kallie?"

My eyes blinked open. I'd been eager to block out my surroundings, but my surroundings were not as apt to let me go. My teacher, Mr. Embers, called my name again.

"Kallie, did you hear me? I need your homework," he said.

I hate that he drew attention to me as I was wrapped up in my mother's memory; I felt somewhat violated, forcibly ripped from my mom once more.

But there was a time and a place to worry about my mother, and it would come later, after I made it to the Cuttingham City

Amphitheatre. That was where *Model Middle America* and its crew was working hard to get ready for the show later on.

I pushed down another rumble of hunger as I gave my teacher a bright, brilliant smile. "Yes, Mr. Embers. I'll get it."

He nodded nicely and waited patiently as I reached into my backpack, looking for my homework.

Another thing my mom taught me: Always suck up to your superiors. Teachers were the ones who gave out the grades, whether you learned things or not, and it was their opinions that had to be changed in the end. Dad was a little more on the other side of that argument, saying it was best to learn what they were teaching.

Frankly, I was smart enough to know both my parents were right, even though I was only in my junior year of high school. It also helped that most of my teachers were nice enough, too, and that included Mr. Embers.

He was an older man, with short, wheat-colored hair and a lanky, computer-nerd body. He even wore a pocket protector and aviator-style glasses, as if it was some kind of package deal as a professional nerd, but I had a feeling he and my dad would get along well, agreeing on the all-important man-questions of which sports teams and trucks were the best.

As I handed him my homework, he gave me a thumbs-up—seriously, didn't he know that was racist now?—but I knew he was a little out of the cultural milieu, so I didn't take it personally.

I would've taken it personally if he was one of the teachers I didn't like. Any anti-Hispanic sort of remark or reaction could be used to my advantage, and when I needed to use it, I used it well.

How could I not? I was, just like my mother, such a pretty crier.

"Thank you," Mr. Embers said. "Now, get to work. I know it's a big day for you, but the AP test is coming up soon, too, and I want you to be ready for it."

"You got it," I replied, already grabbing my assignment checklist.

Mr. Embers was nice enough, but he was also one of my favorite teachers because he had a clipboard by each computer, and when we logged onto our stations, we just had to finish the assignment he'd given us. If there was a lecture involved, there was a resource video of Mr. Embers giving the lecture.

I appreciated the ingenuity of a man who figured out how to do ten years of work in one go.

My stomach growled again, but this time, I dropped one of my textbooks onto the floor to cover up its rampant howling.

"Ope," I exclaimed coyishly, twirling a stray lock of my black-brown hair in a cutesy manner as I picked it up. I saw several of my classmates smile as they looked over at me. To them, it was adorable when I acted as midwestern as they were. They liked the idea that someone as beautiful as me could really be one of them.

The rest of the class passed slowly, as my attention straddled itself between my coding assignment—who knew wire frames could be so simple, yet so complicated?—and the growing beast in my stomach.

Thank God it was the last period of the day.

Come on, Kallie. You can get through this. And then you'll be able to get to the audition, and maybe Mom will see you, and she'll be proud enough she'll finally come home …

That was my fantasy, of course, and the reason I was able to make it through life in addition to my classes.

Still, it seemed like an eternity later when the bell rang and class ended.

I glided to my feet, carefully balanced on the heights of my strappy heels. A model was only as good as the clothes she wore, and that included her shoes.

"Don't forget to finish everything on your checklists before you leave," Mr. Embers said. I pushed past the sea of forgetful students as I handed in my clipboard.

And that's when it happened.

My heel snagged a stray patch of worn carpet, and I hurried to catch my balance. My stomach, overwhelmed with gas and pressure, let out a loud *rarugh!* in response. As the pain in my torso twisted, gas came blaring out of my behind with more fanfare than a pack of homemade fireworks lit up inside an old toilet bowl.

My face blanched over before it was dyed crimson red with shame and fear. If I'd had any food in my stomach, I would have barfed it all up out of sheer embarrassment.

"What in the world was *that*?"

I knew I was in trouble at the sound of Uli Winters' voice.

Uli was my friend, but more importantly, she was Amory Franklin's second-best friend. As the most popular girl in school and my best friend, Amory wielded a considerable amount of social power. Uli had everything to gain, like I had everything to lose, from my humiliation.

All she had to do was send out a message into the sea of social media, and I was doomed.

"Jesus." My voice was a whisper, though whether it was a desperate prayer or a request for quick damnation, it was hard to say.

"It was Jesus?" Uli came up beside me and latched onto my arm as she turned around to glare at the kid behind us. "Oh, my gosh, Jesus, you're so disgusting! First that snozzy sneeze-balling, and now this? Ew!"

Who is she yelling at?

I looked to see the tall boy who'd been sitting behind me. It was indeed Sweaty Fat Kid standing there, the one who, as Uli said so eloquently, had sneeze-balled and covered up my earlier gas.

I stared at him, my face still stricken, and I barely noticed how repulsive he was. I mean, okay, so I noticed, but I didn't *feel* like I noticed it. His curly hair was darker and oiler than mine, and pimples dotted his face like constellations across a campground sky. I wondered if he hadn't failed a grade or two, given how tall he actually was, but the geeky glasses pushed back on his flat nose suggested that this was not the case—not unless his classes were all about fashion. His oversized hoodie added to his girth and lazy slacker-appeal, and it was almost a relief to study his face just so I didn't have to look at his clothes.

His eyes made me look twice, especially since he was staring back at me. From behind the thicker-than-fashionable frames, I saw he actually had nice eyes. They were a deep, deep blue, and as we looked at each other in that long, eternal moment, I waited for him to mock me, too.

So I was surprised when he only shrugged.

"Can't help it if I've been sick lately, you know?" He rubbed his arm over his face, wiping off a layer of sweat. "It's a natural part of life."

"So gross, either way," Uli scoffed. "Come on, Kallie. Amory's waiting for us. You'd better move out of the splash zone."

She tugged me again, and I gave Sweaty Fat Kid—whose name I guess was Jesus—a quick, grateful look.

He gave me a small, shy smile back.

My earlier half-prayer had actually been answered. And by a literal Jesus, too.

A sense of divine validation covered me as I walked out of the classroom and into the tide of teenage life.

Now if only God would let my mother come home.

I forgot everything that happened with Sweaty Fat Kid and my horrible, horrendous gasball the minute Uli and I met up with Amory and our other friends.

Part of this was because I loved my friends, and part of this was because the hallways of Cuttingham City High School were so constricting. The whole student body moved as slow as a fat snake forced to wear a corset; I had to pay attention if I was going to avoid death by stampede, and that meant leaving all my almost-humiliation behind.

Amory spotted Uli and me first and waved. "Kallie, oh my gosh, I just *love* your outfit!"

Both Uli and I know she's purposefully saying nothing to Uli.

"*Gracias*," I replied with a smile, giving Uli's arm a stealthy pat. Uli gave me a quick, grateful look, and then we shifted away from each other. We both knew it was never wise to give Amory cause to complain about something, especially since she found enough to complain about on her own.

Amory was known for her well-honed perfectionism, and that was the way she liked it. She always carried a coffee tumbler around with her, because according to a movie she saw when we were younger, caffeine stunts your growth, and she was desperate to stay at her current height. At five feet, seven inches tall, she was the perfect height to be a model, and she was determined to keep it that way.

"Any taller and I wouldn't be able to wear heels," she would say if someone asked about her coffee, and I was content to believe her, even if I'd seen science articles that refuted her caffeine claims.

I guess it was something to set her apart from the rest of us, although I didn't know why she felt like she needed that. She was our group's African-American, just like I was the Hispanic. But then, I guess it made some kind of sense; I was the one who used Spanish words and downplayed my father's excessively white heritage—seriously, even our last name was "White"—so it was more difficult for me to stand out if I didn't flaunt my more foreign features. I guess it made some kind of sense.

And it really was for the best if we all just played our given parts. Uli was the "Hot German," since her family was from Germany; June Hideko was Asian-American; and finally, Lizzie Myers was the designated white girl of our group of friends. Of course, we all had our "other" special features that made us stand out from the rest—Lizzie had these wide, gray-blue eyes and always wore the most fashionable glasses; June had this flat, little pixie nose; Uli had her bright blonde hair, which was almost platinum in its color, and she didn't even have to dye it. I, of course, have the totality of my mother's looks, and with her height, Amory carried herself like a queen—which was actually probably the real reason why she was our leader. She looked the part and acted accordingly, and the rest of us never met her expectations if we tried to mimic her.

"Are you girls ready for tonight?" Amory huddled us together in the crowded hallway.

"More than ready," Uli replied with an excited giggle.

Lizzie adjusted her glasses. "I don't know," she said, before someone bumped her from behind, and she stumbled into the middle of our group.

The rest of us caught and steadied her, before glaring at the responsible party.

It was a girl, one I almost-recognized from some of my advanced classes. Her name escaped me, but she ducked her head as her face burned red, and that was something I'd seen plenty of times before.

Still, I scowled at her, because she should've known better. It was a little irritating that so many people could bump into us like that, but

I knew the boys liked to have an excuse to be near us, and the girls enjoyed getting to tell others they were "rubbing shoulders" with my friends and me.

But *he* suddenly appeared, and I changed my tune at once. For a long, slow moment, my breathing stopped along with my heart as I saw him approach.

A familiar scent of body spray wafted up to my nose; it was the smell of clean cotton and fresh air, layered with Grinding Ax's latest scent, "Teenage Phere-Gnomes," giving off a harshly intoxicating scent of freshly-cut grass and sandalwood.

Blake Turner.

He brushed up next to me, and I let myself waver in my footing enough that he moved to assist me at once. I let him hold me as I watched, amazed, as his perfect hair did a perfect blonde swoop over his perfect forehead.

"Oh, sorry, Kallie," Blake said in his perfect voice, before giving a nod to the rest of our group. "Ladies."

"Oh, Blake, you tease," Amory replied with a laugh. "If you wanted to hang with us, there's no need to knock poor Kallie down from her two-inch heels. She's so thin, the fall could've easily snapped her in half."

I tried not to frown at Amory's compli-hating, that thing she did where she would give me a compliment, but it wasn't really meant as one. I smiled instead, envying how easily Amory kept chatting with Blake.

I couldn't remember how long I'd had a crush on him. Probably since we were just kids in elementary school, since I was at least ten and an awkward girl trying to feel like a lady. Now, seven years later, I was grown up—and almost a model—while he was our high school's equivalent of a demigod.

All of that made it even more of a tragedy that no matter how popular we were, it was getting harder and harder for me to talk to Blake using a normal-sounding voice. If I wasn't stuttering, I was shrilly; and if I was speaking at all, I stumbled over my words. I would have to work on my poise if I was going to ever get him to date me.

Blake gave me another smile, and I felt my heart flutter as much as the gas in my stomach. I tried to hide how much my teeth were gritting in my mouth as I hid the rising gas. I took great comfort in knowing I only had to starve myself a little longer. Once the audition was over, I could eat again.

That reminder comforted me as Amory and Blake kept talking.

"How's the team?" Amory asked.

"Good. We've been working really hard for today's game. The Crossville Cougars have a good rank this year."

Blake was the midfielder for our lacrosse team, and thanks to his prowess, our school's varsity team defeated the Appleseed Mountain Mountaineers in the state championship last year.

He was handsome, he was talented, and he was a star.

Who wouldn't be smitten over him?

"Well, we hope you have a good match tonight," Amory said. "We're only sorry we'll miss it."

Blake blinked in surprise. "You aren't coming?"

"Maybe we can stop for a short time," I said, before I realized I was contradicting Amory.

"Really?"

Amory cocked her eyebrow at me, but I looked back at Blake and completely forgot about the integrity of the high school social fabric; I was lost in the glory of his gorgeousness.

"Sure," I said. "You know, to wish you luck."

"I'd like that," Blake said, before he turned back to Amory. "For all of you to come and wish us luck, that'd sure be great. Where would Cuttingham High be without its best-looking bleacher babes?"

June wrinkled her pert little nose. "Babes, Blake? Really? We're not 'babes.'"

"I was hoping you'd be happy with the 'best-looking' part," Blake said with a charming grin, before he tipped his head to her and giving me a wink.

"What time does your game start?" I felt empowered and brave, speaking to him without stuttering or shaking nervously. Nothing could bother me at that moment—not Amory's flaccid smile, nor June's derision, nor even Lizzie and Uli's inattention.

"Game's at five," Blake said. "I've actually got to go suit up now."

"Already?" My voice nearly squeaked, but I managed to clear my throat and correct it before anyone seemed to notice. "You have two hours until it starts."

"You know how it is. Coach wants us to be ready and warmed up," Blake said. He ran his hand through his hair before giving us a quick nod goodbye. "I hope to see you ladies there."

My heart pounded as I watched him leave, and I loved and hated how I loved looking at him. If we weren't perfect for each other, nothing I knew about life, the universe, and everything could be anything close to true.

"What was that all about, Kallie?"

Amory's voice, sharp with impatience and irritation, cut through my Blakedreams.

"Oh, well," I floundered, "I just thought—"

"Kallie! Please, this isn't math class," Amory snapped. "There's no need to think when I'm in charge around here. You just have to follow my orders, *comprende, chica*?"

I sighed. My daydreams about Blake would have to wait. "Yes. Sorry."

"You're fine. I forgive you. Now, *we are not* going to make to it to the lacrosse game today, because we have to get to the Model Middle America audition downtown."

"Ooh, I can't wait for the contest." Lizzie giggled with excitement. "We're sure to win."

"We can't *all* win," June reminded her. "There's only going to be one winner from our city."

"So four of us won't win?" Lizzie looked shocked, as though we haven't known this for literally months now.

I was proud of my group of friends; we weren't some whiny, backstabbing clique like in some high school Hollywood TV show. We genuinely cared for each other, and that was never more clear to me than at times like these.

I linked my arm through Lizzie's, leaning my head against her shoulder in a friendly manner.

"That means that four of us will get to cheer on the winner," I said, spinning Lizzie's ditzy comments into bright jewels of optimism and hope.

She smiled brightly at me. "Yes, of course, you're right. Thanks, Kallie."

"That's only if we all manage to get there on time," Amory said. Her eyes darkened as she glared at me. I shifted away from Lizzie, pulling out my mirror and looked over my face, happy to avoid Amory's line of sight.

She'd said I'd been forgiven earlier, but that didn't mean my fawning over Blake would be forgotten.

"The registration information said we need to be there at six," Amory continued.

"Are you sure? That seems late. I heard we should be there as early as possible if we want to get selected." June took out her phone and began typing on it.

"If we have to get there early, we should just go now," Amory said.

"No, wait," Lizzie said. "I don't have my outfit."

Amory sighed. "They're going to give out clothes to wear based on this week's chosen theme, remember?"

"But if I have a super-cute outfit on when I get there, it'll help me get picked."

As Amory began to argue with Lizzie, I carefully positioned my phone inside my pocket.

I had my own special outfit I'd selected to wear to the audition. I'd left it at home to keep it safe, both from the school and my friends. I didn't want them to copy me, after all. I wanted to embody the full grace and loveliness of Katalina de la Carte Grande for the judges tonight, even if that meant dumping my friends to go home and get it.

Lizzie huffed behind me. "Fine, then let's just go," she said. "But if I lose, I'll know it's because of this God-awful high school stink on me."

It was time to put my escape plan into action.

I hit a button on my phone in my pocket. My ringtone, some Spanish song from the famous, top-chart Hispanic singer, Pata, rang out. I ignored it for a couple of rings so my friends could all hear it, which was harder than I thought we were still inside the school. To help, I leaned up next to Lizzie, knowing I could count on her dumb-foolery.

I began to mumble along with the lyrics to my ringtone. I didn't actually know what the song was saying, so it was the perfect cover.

By the time I hit the song's bridge, Lizzie took the bait.

"Kallie, is that your phone?" she asked.

"My phone?" I let my eyes go wide. "Oh, you're right. Let me answer it."

I stopped away from them, before I pulled out my phone and put it to my ear. I silenced the ringtone playback and began talking to myself. "Hello?"

As Amory and the others looked over at me, I immediately corrected myself. "I mean, *Hola*? Hi, Dad."

I turned off to the side, keeping my face hidden from them as much as possible while I had a fake, one-sided conversation with my dad, loudly objecting to his imaginary demands and stomping my foot as I listened to his imaginary pleas.

After an award-winning performance, I slammed the phone into my pocket and crossed my arms.

"Kallie?" The uncertainty in Lizzie's voice almost made me smile, but I quickly composed myself.

Time to work the crowd.

My friends were all looking at me expectantly, and at once, I gave them a large, teary-eyed pout.

"My dad just called," I said. There was another lump in my throat, and swallowing it helped my stomach rumble dangerously again. Thankfully, the pain allowed my tears to swell more realistically. "He wants me to come home right away."

"Oh, no!" Lizzie came up to me and held my arm, trying to comfort me.

"But we don't have time," Uli said. "Can't you just ignore him?"

"I think I can make it really quick," I said, trying to sound weak and thoughtful. "He was very insistent about it."

"Do you want us to be late, Kallie?" Amory was no doubt trying to knock me down another peg or two or cast my situation as selfish before the rest of our friends. "Not all of us live three blocks away from the school, remember?"

"Why does your dad need you home?" Lizzie asked. "He's not really even there a lot, right? I mean, that's why you spend the night at my house so much."

I crossed my arms and ducked my head, disguising my sudden anger. Lizzie was a fool, and I needed her to stay a useful one.

"He said he had a surprise for me," I said. "That's why he's home early today, for once."

That actually wasn't a lie. My dad had texted me earlier to let me know he would be home, and early enough he should be home by the time I got home from school.

"My dad's just getting a little sentimental. He has been working so hard and everything since my mom … you know, left."

I paused here, letting the pain of my mother's heart-rending choice between worldwide adoration and simple family life resettle into their minds. That was my secret weapon, and I'd pretty-cried enough in front of my friends for them to know it.

"Maybe that's his surprise," I said. "Maybe she came back!"

I didn't believe this for even the smallest measure of time, but it was good to let my friends think I did.

The truth was a lot more depressing. My dad was a truck driver for several local companies, and because of that, he was constantly on the road. Since Mom left, he tried to make sure he was home every night, but more often than not I was left alone for days at a time. I knew that Dad had to make ends meet, and I knew it was hard. I mean, my own shopping ventures proved how expensive all the must-have clothes and brands were, and Dad had been aiming for a promotion with his company lately. I had a feeling that was actually the surprise he had. It was either that or he got fired, and I didn't really want to think about that at all.

The only thing I did want to think about was the *Model Middle America* audition. I needed Dad to take me to the Amphitheatre tonight. If he got the promotion, I'd put on a proper show of enthusiasm and cheer, and then I'd shuffle him out the door.

My friends were watching me still, so I gave a heavy, tragic sigh. "I can go home by myself. You girls can go on ahead. I'll get a ride with my dad."

"You're not going to make it if you don't go with us," Uli said. "You're always late when we don't drive you, Kallie."

At that, I had a hard time not gritting my teeth. Uli was right, but I didn't want that to deter me.

"Oh, no," I said. "Go on ahead. I'll just be a little late. You girls can hold a place in line for me, right?"

"Oh, of course we can, *chica.*" Amory gave me a bright, encouraging smile as she gave my arm a friendly pat. "We wouldn't dream of going in without you. Just come and meet us there as soon as you can."

I nodded, but I didn't think Amory was entirely sincere with her kindness.

"Don't forget, the Amphitheatre's going to be crowded," June said. "Get your dad to leave quickly. Traffic will be terrible. We'll have to plan for that, too."

"We'll all be fine," Amory insisted. "We're leaving now, aren't we?"

"You don't know what traffic is like in Cuttingham City this time of day, and we'll have to get there early if we want to compete."

As Amory and June argued about time and traffic in their friendly-catty way, I waved a silent goodbye and struck out on my own.

I was glad I was able to make my escape when I did; I didn't want to admit June was both right *and* wrong.

From what I knew from my mother's experience with open-call type auditions, it was better to show up early if you wanted to be *seen.* But if I wanted to be *chosen,* I knew it was best to show up as late as possible without missing the actual audition. With open auditions, there were so many people that all the worker-bees production managers would always send the extras home and then last-minute changes would prompt the need for more models.

With something like this, in a smaller Heartland-area city like Cuttingham, I was willing to bet anything that showing up late would increase my chances of being selected.

My phone beeped a moment later, and I checked my messages.

Amory was already texting me to tell me that it wasn't a problem that I'd had to run away, and there was nothing shameful about it at all, and how they would look for me when they made it to the stage.

I cringed. It was too saccharine to be sincere, that was for sure.

Another text beeped at my phone, asking me for the address to the Amphitheatre once more.

"It figures," I muttered to myself, as I turned down another hallway. From my location, I could see the sports field, where Blake and the rest of the lacrosse team would be playing in another two hours.

I tightened my fingers around my phone. Now that I was away from Amory, I reasoned, it would be easy to go and see Blake. For the warm-up, at least. Maybe I could get him to ask me out on a date, and maybe I would even say yes.

Glancing at a clock, I figured I'd have enough time, even if I went home and showered.

Beep!

My phone had a new text message from Amory, asking for the address again, followed by a passive-aggressive text-slap: *You're not going to let the rest of us lose, are you?*

I rolled my eyes. I thought about it for a long moment, and then I smiled. I decided I was glad she texted me, actually.

I was my mother's daughter. Surely, I would win the audition anyway. But there was no harm in helping the odds lean more in my favor, right?

Quickly, I texted Amory and the other girls the address of the Amphitheatre—purposefully leaving off the right street direction.

And then I turned off my phone and pulled out my mirror, freshening up my makeup.

Everything was working out even better than I'd planned. I had everything to look forward to—my audition, watching Blake play lacrosse, and auditioning for my first real modeling gig thanks to *Model Middle America.*

As I walked outside, I grinned. *Can this day get any better?*

My stomach, still empty of food and full of angry gas, growled ferociously as if in reply. I ignored it as much as I could, determined to focus on the life-changing events ahead of me.

It was close to four when I made it to the lacrosse field. After leaving Amory and the other girls, I'd worked on finishing my homework before heading outside to the game.

Since it was still pretty chilly for March, I didn't mind delaying my arrival, even if I knew it would cut into my time watching Blake. I was actually a little glad for the slight frost on the wind, though; it numbed me enough that the tumbling gas in my tummy didn't bother me as much, and I was more than okay with that. It would do me no good if Blake heard me farting up my bleacher section any more than he saw me shivering on the bleachers like some desperate fangirl. I was able to even both ends out nicely, so Blake would get to see only the best parts of me. Or at least the non-farting and non-desperate sides of me.

I wanted him to be in awe at my presence; I didn't want him to think I was such an easy touch when it came to getting me to come to his games, like he said he'd wanted.

Social politics are hard in high school, but if you know how to work the system, you'll be able to work it in your favor.

I found a seat at the front of the bleachers, down by the visiting team's goal. All I had to do now was wait. I pulled out my phone; it was still turned off, but I could pretend to play on it while I secretly watched Blake. Looking at the clock on the scoreboard, I suddenly hoped I wouldn't have to resort to any unrealistic trickery to get him to notice me; I needed to leave no later than five if I wanted to stick to my plan.

It was four-thirty when Blake finally caught sight of me, and frankly, thank God for that; I was at the point where I was debating about whether or not I should get up and "trip" across a few rows of bleachers, like I'd fallen against him earlier.

But it was just then I saw Blake wave at me from the field, as the whole team was finishing up on their warm-up drills. Even though I was watching him out of the corner of my eye, I kept my pretend focus on my phone's dark screen.

Blake actually waved at me several times, but I didn't make a move to acknowledge him. There was nothing that made a prized specimen like Blake Turner more frustrated than inattention.

As the warm-up concluded and our school's cheerleaders, band members, and twirlers began to stir up the crowd, Blake jogged toward me.

I kept my gaze firmly on my hands as he approached, forcing myself not to blush. I was more than pleased when he came up to me, and I was more than determined not to let him know that.

"Hey Kallie," Blake said. "What're you doing here?"

I glanced up at him and blinked in feigned surprise. "Oh, hi, Blake. Nice to see you."

"You didn't answer my question." He leaned in a little, trying to see my phone. "I was trying to get your attention out there, but you were too busy with your phone."

"Oh, you were waving at me? How sweet." I gave him a bright smile as I tucked away my phone, grateful he didn't have time to notice it was turned off. The last thing I needed right now was Amory calling me, demanding to know why she and the others were lost in the city as they headed toward the wrong address.

"I thought Amory said you and the girls couldn't make it today."

"Well, you seemed so sad earlier … " I let my voice trail off as I tried to seem compassionate but still blasé.

"Did the others come, too?"

Blake didn't seem to notice how coy I was being—but I guess men are not known for their ability to detect subtlety, or so Mom had once told me.

"Oh, no," I told him. "Since I live so close to the school, I'm able to drop by for a little bit. After this I'll have to meet up Amory and the other girls. Tonight's our big audition for the *Model Middle America* program."

I was desperate for him to ask about it or tell me I was sure to win. I would've literally died for him to say something even remotely close to the fact that I was beautiful and it would be an atrocity of boundless proportion if I was not selected to be their model for

Cuttingham City. Or if I wasn't picked, the judges had to be the biggest bigots this side of the Mississippi or something.

Anything. Please just say anything to me, Blake. One word of encouragement, and I will have everything and more to be a real winner.

"Oh. Well, I'm glad Amory let you come," Blake said. "I know I play better knowing when y'all are watching, and tonight's a big game."

My stomach dropped, its already stewing anger fueled even more by Blake's disappointing comment.

But I couldn't hold that against him, right? He was getting ready for the game, and he was really focused on that. We were juniors; it was time to start thinking about college and scholarships and sports and all those things with growing up that made my devastatingly specific wish to seem unfair.

I thought about giving him another hint to tell me how he felt about me, before I just let it go.

"I'll make it a point to show up for the rest of the games, then," I said instead.

"Cool. Tell Amory and the others to come, too." Blake ran his hand through his hair in that way of his, and I instantly forgave him for his inattentive transgressions.

A whistle blew behind us, and Mr. Withers, the lacrosse team coach called Blake over to huddle up with the team.

"I guess you've got to go? But then, the team can't win without their star player." I twirled a loose lock of hair around my fingers. It was a flirty move, and *finally, finally,* Blake noticed.

"Yes," he said, staring at my hand. He looked back at me, sizing me up, as though he was making a mental calculation. "Hey, come with me. I'll find you a better seat."

I didn't have to think twice as I followed him. Blake took my hand, and I let him, trying not to freak out I was so excited.

We came to the middle of the field before Blake stopped. There was a familiar hoodie on the seat, one that looked too large for even some of the goalies to wear.

"Jesus," Blake muttered with a sigh.

"What is it?" I asked.

"Nothing." Blake picked up the hoodie, used it to clean the seat, and then offered me his hand. "You can sit here."

It was like watching Prince Charming offer Cinderella her shoe, and I was content to be the princess. Amory might be the queen—and a somewhat wicked one at that—but I was sure to win the heart of my one true love.

After I sat down, Blake tossed the hoodie onto the ground. I thought about chastising him for his rude behavior, but our eyes met, and I forgot about how rude he was and focused on how handsome he was instead.

Before I could say thank you for my seat, I was interrupted by a familiar voice.

"Hey, what did you do with my sweatshirt?"

I turned around, first surprised and then angry, as I saw who interrupted us.

It's him again.

I thought I'd recognized that hoodie. But then, maybe I didn't want to.

Sweaty Fat Kid from computer class was back, apparently, and he'd managed to mess up my chance to properly thank Blake for his chivalry. I nearly choked as I looked at him now, and in some ways that was for the best. I needed the time to think of a way to tell him to go away.

But before I could compose myself, Blake did it for me.

"You shouldn't leave your stuff in my way, Jesus." Blake stood in front of me. "This is the lacrosse team's section. It's not for a Bigboy Baggypants knockoff like you."

"I think you mean Bilbo Baggins, and that's not really how insults work," Sweaty Fat Kid retorted. He held up his hand. "Bigfoot jokes might've worked better with a guy like me."

I let out a compulsive giggle, but quickly stopped when I saw Blake frown.

"What're you doing here, anyway?" Blake asked. "Coach need someone else to wear the mascot tonight?"

"As much as I'd enjoy donning the mantle of the Mighty Cuttingham City Crusader, I'm here to film the game." Sweaty Fat Kid pulled out a camera from the bag hidden behind his bloated belly. "Coach Withers asked me to tape it so he'll be able to help you guys develop new strategies against the Cougars."

"That's pretty smart," I said. "Like from *The Art of War*, right?"

"It's kind of an update to Sun Tzu, but same principle," Sweaty Fat Kid agreed.

He gave me another small smile, just like the one he'd given me earlier, and I almost felt sorry Blake had been mean to him. My aching stomach groaned, but it was hard to say if it was out of disgust or agreement.

Blake coughed. "Come on, Kallie, you're not agreeing with Lard Boy here, are you?"

I felt a little bad for making Blake seem like a dumb-butt, so I shook my head vehemently.

"Of course not. I was just thinking that we should just let him sit here. I mean, it's fine with me," I said. "I have to go soon anyway. Remember, I'm going to that modeling audition at the Amphitheatre tonight."

"You should've already left for that if you wanted to be on time," Sweaty Fat Kid said. "The Model Middle America people wanted everyone there by six, and you're going to be too late now. It'll be an hour till you get there, if not more with the traffic."

I glared at him. Just as I opened my mouth to tell him off this time, once and for all, Blake interrupted me again.

"Kallie's here to see me play." Blake picked up the discarded hoodie and tossed it to him. "Something you wouldn't understand, clearly."

At that, I tugged on Blake's uniform. For all I hated how Sweaty Fat Kid was right, I didn't like seeing Blake turn into a douchebag just to defend my honor.

"It's fine, Blake," I said. "I'll just move, okay? He'll be able to film everything from midfield, and I'll head out once kick-off is over."

"Face-off," Blake corrected.

Ignoring his haughtiness, I gave him a hug. Blake seemed surprised, but then he tentatively wrapped his arms around me, letting his hands settle on my back in a too-friendly manner.

Over Blake's shoulder, I looked at Sweaty Fat Kid, nodding my head to the side. I was telling him, in my own way, to back off while Blake was around if he didn't want any trouble.

I didn't really want any trouble, either.

The coach's whistle blew again, and it was time to start the game.

Blake was smiling when he pulled back from me, and I was relieved.

"Good luck," I said. "I know you'll do great."

"Well, I will now. I wouldn't want to disappoint you or the rest of your girlfriends," Blake said as he stepped back from me. He scowled at Sweaty Fat Kid again. "Jesus, you're ugly," he said, and then he ran back to his teammates.

I rolled my eyes and scooted down a little. It was time for me to forget about everything else, except for the face-off, and then finishing up here so I could go to my audition.

"I prefer Zeus, if you really want to know."

"Huh?" I looked back over at Sweaty Fat Kid, confused.

Were we having a conversation?

He apparently thought so, since he repeated himself. "My name is Jesus, but my family's Latino, so it's actually pronounced like 'Hey, Zeus.' But I just go by Zeus."

"So you're Latino, using a Greek god's name?" I forgot for a moment how he'd made me mad, and I giggled. Zeus was kind of funny, after all, and Blake had been a bit of a jerk.

"That guy's a jerk, you know," Zeus said. I flinched; it was almost as if he'd known what I was thinking. "This isn't the first time we've run into each other."

"Well, it's hard not to run into Blake," I said. "He's so popular and so gorgeous. People are just drawn to him, literally."

I watched as Blake took his stance in the midfield area for our school's side of the field. Zeus continued talking but I didn't really hear him until he said my name.

"You're Kallie White, right?"

"It's Grande-White," I said, straightening up a little. "I'm Hispanic myself. Or at least half."

Zeus nodded. "I'm in your computer class."

I did not want to talk about that. "You're new around here, aren't you?"

"Yeah. I've been here since January."

It was March, so that must've meant I'd missed him in the last two months of school.

Oh, well.

I crossed my arms and shrunk into myself. "Cool."

"You know, if you want, I can just send you the video of the game when I'm done," he said. "You can get going to your model thing. I know it'll take a while to get there."

"I don't have to be there until seven," I told him. "I'm going home first, so I can change and get ready."

"I think you look good enough like that. Really, you should be fine." Zeus blushed, making the pockmarks of his pimples stand out even more against the redness of his cheeks. "I mean, it might be better for you to go now, so you'll be on time. You're not a wizard, you know."

"Wizard?"

"You know, like the saying of how a wizard is never late or early, he just comes when he means to?"

I blinked again, and he laughed. "You know *The Art of War*, but not *The Lord of the Rings*?"

I bristled.

Thankfully, another whistle rang out, and the face-off commenced. The game began, and I had the perfect excuse to leave. I would have to deal with Sweaty Fat Kid—Zeus, I guess—another time. I did not bother to say good-bye as I stood up and walked away, but when I reached the end of the bleachers, I looked back to see Zeus was watching me.

I grimaced. *Gross.*

I did not need Sweaty Fat Kid crushing on me. He was nice enough, and he'd done me a favor earlier. But that didn't mean I wanted to hang out with him or be seen with him.

I was not sorry I had to leave.

As I walked home, I could still hear some of the cheering and the band music from the school. It was comforting in some ways, almost like walking home with a friend, but I was glad it didn't take me long to get to the house.

Dad and I had a big house. It was three stories, with two floors above ground and a basement, built with a Tudor design. When Mom had lived with us, there had been a beautiful garden in the back, with a well-kept lawn. Every year, we would get a new layer of paint on the paneling to make it stand out against the other houses on our block. Mom liked having the best house on the street. My dad had always done so much to keep her happy with everything here, it made it so much more tragic that the grass needed to be mowed and new flowers would have to be planted to replace the withered ones from last year. I tried not to think of this as I walked up the walkway to the front porch. I paused as I put my hand on the doorknob, and then I looked around.

Something seemed … off.

There was a large, old, white car on the street, just in front of my neighbor's house. I didn't think anything of it, really, just that it was old and one of those classy, antique type of cars. It was different enough to make me wonder if the neighbors had a guest, or maybe some kind of timeshare gurus were going door-to-door.

I did notice my dad's car was missing, and I bit back an angry growl. He was supposed to be home; that was what was wrong.

Where is he?

Zeus had said there was a lot of traffic. Maybe Dad was just running a little behind schedule.

I wanted to scream with frustration, but as I pursed my lips, gritted my teeth, and tugged at my loosened tresses of hair, I forced myself to calm down.

"Get your shower, get ready, and *then* we can yell at him for not being here on time," I said to myself.

My plan was still in motion, and everything had worked out fine so far. And I did still need to shower. Perhaps this was a good thing, I told myself. If this was the worst hiccup I faced, it was nothing.

It was nothing, so long as it worked out in the end.

I tried not to think about that as I walked inside and immediately headed for my bathroom upstairs. As pretty as I was, I needed to work on myself, and I didn't have a lot of time.

When I was finished, I stood in the bathroom, looking at the mirror before me, obsessively but quickly checking over every inch of my skin and every last inch of my outfit.

My mother's dress, with its empire waist and sexy minimalist design highlighted my perfect figure. The dress was a scarlet red, bringing out the brown in the long waterfall of my nearly-black hair. I was walking tall with my strappy heels, my pedicure touched up and shiny.

I looked perfect—almost.

There is just one thing missing. I pulled out my lip gloss and added another layer to my lips, before blowing myself a kiss. For the first time in a long time, I felt like I deserved it.

"*Now* I look perfect," I whispered. I walked out of the bathroom, ready to go.

But there was one problem.

Dad wasn't there.

I felt my nose prickle with oncoming stress tears, and my stomach rumbled, desperately hungry after nearly two days with nearly nothing to eat.

"Where is he?" This time, there was no mumbling to myself. I screamed my question, as if my voice alone would summon him to the house.

I ran back to the living room, digging through my backpack and school stuff looking for my phone.

Why hasn't he called, if nothing else?

The answer to that particular question became clear a moment later, as I held my phone and stared at the empty, blank screen.

"Oh."

I'd forgotten I'd turned off my phone while I was talking to Blake. Groaning, I turned it back on.

Almost as if on cue, the phone rang, and my dad's number lit up the screen.

"Daddy!" I cheered as I answered it. "Are you close? I need you to take me to the Model Middle America audition and it's getting—"

"Hi, Kallie." Dad interrupted me with his flat-toned voice, and I immediately backtracked. He didn't like it when I assumed he would just bow to my wishes, even though he usually did.

"Sorry," I said, trying not to sound flustered as I walked into the kitchen. For some reason, it was more of a mess than I'd remembered when I'd left for school earlier. "I *am* eager to see you, too, so tell me where you're at."

"I'm on the highway—"

"Good." I grinned. Everything was working out well, after all, it seemed.

Silly me for worrying!

"I'm ready to go, so when you get here, I'll just come out and we can go right away."

"Kallie, wait—"

No, I thought. This was not the time for more stress, more pressure, more sadness.

I *had to win.* Which meant I *had to be there. And my dad had promised me he was okay with me going!*

"Come on, Dad," I pleaded. "You've already said I could go. I know it's a modeling thing, but this is *my* dream, not Mom's mess. Just come here, and quick, and we'll go, please."

My patience was gone, especially as I looked at the clock. It was nearly six, and I would be late for sure if I didn't get out of the house in the next few moments.

"Kallie, would you let me finish my—"

"No, no please, no," I continued, as my dad started sputtering. "Just get here, please. We can talk then. I've already heard that there'll be some traffic."

"Kallie." Dad's voice cut through me. "I'm not going to make it home tonight."

I didn't know if I died or not in that moment.

Dad kept talking, explaining to me, seemingly in some made-up language that sounded just like English but meant nothing, that he was still in Louisiana.

His words were too unreal, almost as if I was in a dream or nightmare of some kind. Or worse—maybe I'd been hit by a car on the way home from school, and I was actually dead, and this was my formal entry into Hell.

I mean, I had to end up in Hell, didn't I? My own mother didn't love me enough to stick around, and this was just me finding out my dad was leaving me, too, right?

Pain pierced me as I dropped to my knees. Tears began to stream down my face—my perfect face!—as Dad told me he wouldn't be able to make it.

I threw the phone away, not even caring that it smashed into the wall in the next room, likely leaving a dent.

"No, no, no, no!" The words started as whimpers and ended up as screams.

Uncontrollable sadness and rage crashed inside of me. Everything—*everything*—had been for nothing.

My mom had left me, knowing I was a failure. My dad had abandoned me to fight off financial ruin. My friends were barely that, and even God himself thought it was amusing to send Sweaty Fat Kid as some kind of bogus, ironic knife in my back.

Before I knew what was happening, I threw my backpack down onto the floor, and then followed it with several other things. When the living room was trashed, I headed for the kitchen.

There, I found a framed picture of my mom and dad, together at their wedding. They were surrounded by their friends and other family members, so happy and cheery that I felt an extra flood of repulsion in the face of my own reality. I flung the picture aside, feeling a perverse pleasure in shattering something that had shattered a long time ago.

I shoved a pile of dishes onto the floor with a sweep of my hand, before kicking a cabinet as hard as I could. The pain stung, but it was freeing, too—a manifestation of everything I'd hidden in my soul for the past year, since Mom left, and maybe even longer, as she drifted away from us.

It was only when I banged my knee into our oven that I finally stopped. The metal was hot, as though it had been recently used, and in that moment, I feared a burn mark more than I felt rage.

"Ow, ow, ow." This time, I started out screaming, but finished in a sob. I was just about to fall over into a fetal position and cry forever.

But that was when I saw them.

A small pile of powdered doughnuts, so elegantly shaped and molded to perfection.

Darling Donuts?

I almost couldn't believe the sight before me. I looked back at the wedding picture of my parents, wondering if I was hallucinating again or something.

Mom and Dad had met thanks to Darling Donuts, a local company that made the most delicious doughnuts I'd ever tasted. My dad had been one of the first truck drivers to take them to different states, while my mother made her modeling debut as the model for "Darla Donut," as they called her. She was my city's answer to Aunt Jemima and Little Debbie and the Pillsbury Dough Boy.

I reached out and took hold of one, just to see if in fact it was real enough to touch.

One second my hand was just touching the doughnuts, and then next, I was tasting them.

My angry stomach lurched in gassy happiness as I ate the whole plate, stuffing them into my mouth. I barely even chewed as I inhaled them, breathing them in like they were the essence of life itself. Sweetness and warmth, fluffy cake and speckled sugar coating ran over my tongue, more powerful than a passionate kiss and infinitely more intoxicating.

I was crying and bawling, all while eating them. My mother's dress had smudges of the white powder all over it, and my makeup was clearly running down my cheeks along with my tears. It was probably for this reason that I didn't notice someone approaching me until just before I shoved the last bite of doughnut into my mouth.

"Oh, dear!"

I nearly threw up, realizing I suddenly had an audience, but my stomach had been too empty for too long to just give up what I'd haphazardly stuffed in.

The heat of the oven and the warmth of the doughnuts was nothing compared to the furnace blazing on my face as I looked up to see the flustered old lady before me. It took me a long moment to recognize her, even though there was no mistaking her.

"Abuela-Blanca."

It was my grandmother, the one from my dad's side of the family, in the flesh. Briefly, I recalled her first name was Margaret, and Mom had referred to her only as "Dr. White" when she had to talk about her, and Mom had laughed when I said I'd call her "Abuela-Blanca," saying it was perfect for a racist like her.

I didn't really know for sure if AB was a racist or not, but I did know she didn't get along with Mom. Dad said we didn't see her a lot because Abuela-Blanca had a very demanding job.

It was a literal miracle that her old-lady visage—her blue eyes, pale face, and white-gray hair, styled the same way for more than two decades—had stuck so securely inside my memory.

But just like the doughnuts, she was real.

And she was apparently real angry, too.

Her brow wrinkled over several times as she scowled at me. "What in God's green earth have you done with my doughnuts, young lady?"

I coughed, spitting out a small cloud of powdered sugar, as if to answer her.

"Oh, this is *just great.* Just absolutely *great*, let me tell you!" Her expression soured as her voice dripped with sarcasm. She scuttled over to the oven, scouring the counter, likely looking for any other sign of her precious doughnuts as she ignored me. Meanwhile, I sat there on the kitchen floor, still covered in tears, running makeup, and powdered sugar.

She let out an old-lady huff. "Goodness gracious, I take one call in my room from the Director of CERN, listening to her beg me to come work for them, repeatedly, and this is what I get?"

With her old-style designer dress and fancy black shoes, she reminded me of a housewife from the fifties, terrified her dinner was ruined and her husband would come home and beat her or something.

"What're you doing here?" I finally asked.

I shouldn't have had to ask. It all came together in my mind.

Dad had a surprise for me. Abuela-Blanca had a "room" here. That could only mean …

My eyes blinked as I looked back up at her.

"Yes, Kallie." She must have seen my shock. "I have come to live with you and Johnny. He clearly needs some help, and I have decided to take a break from working while your mother decides to go play her dress-up games for money."

My earlier anger-fueled tirade was still processing, but it was swiftly changing into outraged confusion. My stomach reacted for me, letting out a growl even louder than the ones I'd felt at school.

The doughnuts had spiked a sudden, demanding joy inside of me, but now the rumbled churning of my gut made me sick.

"You didn't eat all my doughnuts, did you?"

My grandmother's self-centered concern made me even more angry.

"If you didn't want someone to eat them, you should've put a sign up," I snapped. "And Dad should've told you when I was coming home."

"I arrived here this morning after you left for school, and I have been working ever since. You'll have to excuse me for such egregiously bad manners." She put her hands on her hips. "But that's a discussion for another place and time. We need to get those doughnuts out of you before Johnny comes home. I'd hate to think he'd want me to leave after I've only just arrived."

A new realization struck me. "That was your car outside by the house, wasn't it? Oh my God, Abuela-Blanca, this is amazing. Come on, we have to go now!"

"It's not very proper to address me as 'Abuela-Blanca,' Kallie." She smoothed out her dress. "Don't you think it's a little racist? And it's so unbecoming on a lovely young lady like yourself."

I coughed, and a little more powdered sugar wafted up out of my mouth.

"Perhaps 'lovely' was being too generous." Abuela-Blanca frowned. "Oh, that was you screaming earlier, wasn't it? When I was on the phone with Carol?"

"Who's Carol?"

"The HR director from—"

"Never mind," I said. "We can talk about this in the car." I grabbed her by the arm and pulled her after me.

"What do you think you're doing now?" Abuela-Blanca was surprisingly resistant.

"It's a long story, but I have this modeling audition tonight, and it's only for tonight, and it's down at the Cuttingham City Amphitheatre, and I need you to take me there."

"Modeling? Oh, please, Kallie, no. Not after your mother—"

"Come on, please?"

"We have more important things to attend to," Abuela-Blanca insisted. "Those doughnuts—"

"Look, I'm sorry I ate them, okay? Sorry. But it'll fine. I can buy you some more," I insisted. "Just get me to the audition. Please?"

I dragged out the whine. I'd learned from dealing with my dad and teachers that I didn't have to outsmart anyone to get what I wanted. I didn't even have to argue very well half the time. I just had to keep pushing and pleading until their patience collapsed.

Abuela-Blanca was stubborn, but I could see signs of her weakening. For a long, long moment, she frowned at me, studying me carefully. I didn't know if I should try to make myself look more pathetic or more presentable. But in the end, she sighed.

"I don't think this is a good idea," she finally said. "But if this is really what you want, and you won't listen to me, you'll see what I mean."

"Oh, thank you!" I hopped up and hugged her, making her stiffen.

"You'll need to sit in the back. There's a seat cover there, so you won't make my Imperial into a mess," she said as she pulled away from me. "Do you know how rare the red fabric is in car seats today?"

Despite the fancy car and her primness, I was surprised—and thrilled—that Abuela-Blanca was a mean driver. She cut across lanes at a time, muttering angry, properly horrified phrases like, "What in the world could that poor man be drinking that he's driving so terribly? Oh, never mind, it's a woman, so that explains it," and "My, my, it's awful to see how driving standards have fallen." After I told her to drive more carefully so I could fix my makeup, she clicked her tongue at me.

"*Tsk, tsk,* Kallie, I'm the one doing you a favor, remember?"

"Okay, but you should drive better so we don't wreck," I said, flying forward as she changed lanes and slowed to a halt behind a van.

"I've never gotten into an accident in my life." Abuela-Blanca huffed as I had to swallow the fearful lump in my throat. "Where do you think your father got his excellent driving skills? I'm only sad he never acquired my good business sense."

I gripped onto the armrest as she swerved off an exit ramp. I didn't know what she was talking about; my dad was working hard to make sure we had enough money. I decided I didn't care, especially as my stomach raged again, this time much more violently.

"Please, can you just slow down a little? I think I'm going to be sick." I thought of how much more mortifying it would be if I barfed or farted while I was modeling, and I decided I would literally die of embarrassment if that was the case. A person could only take a certain level of terrible luck in one day.

Everything is okay. We're sticking to the plan. Right now, I am going to fulfill my destiny.

My stomach roared again, as if it agreed—in the worst possible way.

Abuela-Blanca looked back at me from her rearview mirror. "Oh, I have a feeling you're going to be more sick than you realize."

I was going to ask her what she meant by that, but the Amphitheatre came into sight. The analogue clock on the dash seemed to say it was six-forty-five. I reached for my phone to double-check, before I realized I'd forgotten my phone at the house.

"We're almost there," Abuela-Blanca said. "What do you want me to do?"

"Go around back, as far as you can, and I'll hop out, and then you can go park. You have money, right? You can park in the Amphitheatre's parking lot if there's room."

Based on what my mother had told me from her stories, that was my plan. Go to the back, slip inside, find the stage director, and never let them see that you're not supposed to be in there. I knew I would have to improvise some in this case, but I was prepared for that.

"I don't think that's wise, Kallie. I shouldn't leave you." Abuela-Blanca held up a bag. "I brought my portable lab."

"Portable lab?"

"For the doughnuts."

I groaned. "I said I was sorry, but you're not seriously going to make me toss my cookies before my modeling audition, are you?"

"Think of it as tossing your doughnuts, as that is technically truth." She glared at me through the mirror again. "I told you those were my own recipe, Kallie. Believe me, you don't want them inside of you."

"I'll have you know, bulimia is way down in the modeling community. And I'm already perfectly underweight, so I should still make the cut, AB."

"That's not it," Abuela-Blanca grumbled. "And what is this 'AB' nonsense now?"

"You said 'Abuela-Blanca' was too racist for you, so I've shortened it."

"Goodness, you're just as vapid as your mother, aren't you?"

"She was smart enough to know you're an old white lady racist," I shot back, visibly shaking now. I was so glad we were pulling into the Amphitheatre. As quietly as possible, I unlocked the door. I decided it would be better for me to slide out as quickly as possible.

"I am not a racist," Abuela-Blanca argued.

"Look, if you have to argue that you're not, you probably are."

"So my options are for you to go uncorrected in your assumptions, or I can try to correct them, and that will supposedly prove you correct?" She shook her head. "I guess I should be grateful you didn't eat the plate along with my doughnuts if you're using that kind of logic."

"Hey, I am smart. I've got good grades, and I actually read for fun sometimes, even though it might wrinkle my brow early."

"That's not—"

"And also, I'll have you know my mother is better than you'll ever be," I said. "She wouldn't insult me like this. She would be proud of me for being here, and she would be so supportive, and I will not stand for you ruining my night!"

At that, I pushed open my door, causing her to slam on her brakes.

"Oh my goodness gracious, what are you doing *now*?" AB whirled around in her seat just as I hopped out of the car.

"Thanks for the ride," I said, waving goodbye as I ran off for the stage entrance. It was hard to balance on my heels, and my stomach pain quickly made its reappearance now that I was no longer on a car ride with Lady Death, but I was determined to get to the audition.

I will do this, no matter what gets in my way.

"Kallie, wait, it's dangerous," AB called, putting her own window down. "You shouldn't leave me."

"No, I'm pretty sure I should," I yelled back, smothering a laugh as I watched her try to drive and keep up with me. There were a lot of other cars, and plenty of barriers. I looped my way through one, turning around to briefly show my face in triumph. There was nothing to stop me now.

"You don't understand." She finally pulled over and got out of her car. AB smoothed down her top again, trying not to look as frantic as she sounded. "Kallie, those were radioactive doughnuts!"

I stared at her for a second, and then I laughed.

I laughed so hard my stomach crippled me with pain, and I had to limp as I walked away.

"It's the truth!" AB yelled after me. "You'll see soon enough."

I didn't pay any more attention to her as I hurried into the Amphitheatre, letting myself get swallowed up into the large crowds. I'd been the Amphitheatre more than a few times as a kid. When I'd been younger, Mom had signed me up for ballet and gymnastics and acting, and I had spent more than one summer stuck in the Amphitheatre for a performance of some kind. *Model Middle America* didn't know who they were dealing with when it came to me. I knew this place well enough that slipping into the green room was a piece of cake.

My stomach felt bloated and gassy. I clenched my butt cheeks together. Radioactive doughnuts or not, I would not make a fool of myself tonight.

Radioactive doughnuts.

AB must've thought I was pretty stupid indeed, if she thought I'd believe *that.*

"What are you doing here?"

A voice cut through my thoughts, and I turned to see a stage manager. I could see from her harried expression she was stressed. Her headset bobbed on her head as she ran a critical eye over me.

"I was told to come here tonight for the modeling," I sort-of-lied. I straightened my shoulders and stood tall. "They needed another girl for the walkway."

"Did Joe send you?"

I had a feeling this was a test, so I shrugged. "It was a lady, actually."

The lady chewed on her bottom lip. "Let me check. Everyone selected was supposed to go get dressed backstage."

"I just assumed this is where I had to go," I said. "I mean, my mother's a professional model, so it's only natural they selected me to walk for them."

The lady cocked her brow at me, and I knew I would have to back down some—not demurely, but cautiously.

She pushed a button on her headset. "Joanna, I have a contestant here in the green room."

Joe, Joanna … I almost rolled my eyes. Close enough, really.

I was gratified a second later when the manager nodded to me.

"Okay. I'll send her to Azure for dressing," she said into her headset, before turning it off and focusing on me. "You're lucky that we need another girl. You're not supposed to be here at all. This area is off-limits to contestants. I could've had you sent home for this."

"Well, thank you," I said, this time with much more graciousness. As we walked, I hid my excitement, and it was a chore to force myself to calm down. My stomach was still aching in pain, and I was getting more bloated by the minute.

When the stage manager opened the door to the backstage changing area, it was as though I'd been swept up into fashion heaven. From the acerbic smell of hairspray and various fruity and smoky cosmetics, to the crowds of long-haired women and chiseled-chested men with their glacier-faced, smoldering-stillness, it was all a sea of chaos and harmony, and I was a captive whale released into its wildness.

A tall, thin man came up to us. He had the wide shoulders of a gladiator, the elegant arms of a ballet dancer, and the soured look of a displeased food critic. I could feel my eyes shine over as I faced him.

He was, undoubtedly, my designer.

"There you are, Bernice." The man put his hand over his heart in fake, stark relief. "The judges have been waiting for my last couple of contenders."

"Don't worry, Azure, you know the MMA wouldn't let you down," the stage manager replied. "This is … another girl. Get her ready. I know Dan is getting ready to start rolling soon."

Azure turned his attention to me, frowning critically. We take a moment to look over each other. He had cut and cropped hair, with half his ebony head shaved. For the life of me, there was nothing about him that suggested he had anything "Azure," on him. As he watched me, I arched my brow at him and strike a pose. He let out a sour "Hmmm," before he sighed.

"What's your name?" he asked.

"It's—"

"I'm thinking it's something like 'Arlanda,' or 'Mary Josephine,' right?"

I wasn't sure how to respond to that. My mouth flubbed open and closed a few times, before he waved his hand at the stage manager.

"Okay, Arlanda here will have to do," he said, pulling me away. "Thanks, Bernice."

"It's Bernadette," the stage manager muttered, before she scuttled off, and I felt a little bad at the sadness in her voice. After all, I was Arlanda now, wasn't I?

Azure led me towards his territory. I didn't see any of my other friends, and most of the other girls I saw were not as pretty as me. I was happy about both of those things, and as I remembered I'd left my phone at home, I rejoiced once more: Amory could be calling me, and my phone would just be endlessly ringing off the hook.

"You're lucky we had a last-minute opening, Arlanda. One of the girls here got sick and ruined my outfit." Azure narrowed his eyes at me. "You would never do that, would you?"

"Uh, no, of course not," I said, crossing my arms over my stomach as more pain ran through me. I felt my stomach bloating out underneath my arms, and panic began to settle inside of me.

"Hmmm."

The "Hmmm" was back. I watched as he shifted through different racks of brightly colored clothes.

"Now," Azure said, "you're here, so you know how the show goes. Every chosen girl by our team gets an outfit and a chance to walk the runway. Tonight's theme is superheroes, so yes, the outfits will be absolutely atrocious because if you're going to be caught dead wearing them, you might as well actually die, right?"

Azure tore through his designs, muttering on about how talented he was, because it took skill to make outfits this awful. For my own part, I was instantly more than horrified by the clothes. There were several patches of neon on nylon, some polyester, and some shining gems and jewelry sewn into the cloth. I felt more than a little sick looking at them, and I was pretty sure it had nothing to do with my own gut issues. The outfits all looked a little trashy.

Perhaps that's the point?

I thought of the girl who'd gotten sick earlier. Perhaps she had faked being sick. Did anyone really want to make their modeling debut wearing ugly outfits like these?

Before I could ask, Azure thrust on a navy mask across my eyes.

"Hey," I yelped. The inside of the mask was sticky and uncomfortable, but I could do nothing but remain silent as he began listing off instructions and pointing in a variety of locations letting me know where to go for his stylist team.

Before I could check to make sure I had it all down, another girl came up to Azure.

"Azzy, we're missing my Flashy Femme makeup set," she said. "Can you help me?"

"My stars!" Azure sighed. "The downside of being perfect is that everyone else is utterly incompetent."

"But we love you more for it," the girl replied in a gushing voice.

Azure seemed to take this in stride and kissed the girl on her forehead. "I suppose it's the least you could do since you need my help so much."

Both of them took off, and I was left with a pile of hot pink, magenta, and navy stretch suits—and my horrendous stomach cramps.

Oh my gosh, I'm not having my period, too, am I?

I'd heard that was the cause of death for more than one professional woman, and at the thought, I glanced around for a bathroom. There was a line of makeshift stalls in the back of the room; I hurried toward them, pushing my way through the other models, whimpering as my body coursed with undeniable agony. The pain in my stomach launched out from my core, wrapping its way around my limbs, spinning a web of pure terror and throbbing torture.

"Ouch." My yelp drew some quizzical, superior-than-thou looks from some of the other would-be contestants. Remembering Azure's sick girl, I wasn't surprised to see plenty of smug looks and haughty smirks; they thought I was going to be sick, even though I would've said it felt like I was going to die.

I took a deep breath and held my head up high.

"I will perform here tonight if it kills me," I grumbled through tear-filled eyes and gritted teeth. It seemed like a long time later that I made it to a changing room, just barely more than a cubicle. I managed to shut the thin door. There was a mirror hanging up on one of the walls, but I couldn't bear to look at myself as I took off my mother's dress.

To help with the pain, I bit down on the inside of my cheek hard enough to draw blood, just to keep myself from crying out as I pulled on the least-dreadful-looking clothes I'd been given.

"Ladies, it's almost time for the show!" Azure's voice called out.

My heart began to race.

I clenched my fists into balls, digging my fingernails deep into my palms.

I need to do this … come on, focus!

I finished putting on the hot pink and navy-blue-or-black suit, my legs rang with stinging awareness. And then, all of a sudden, they were straining against the nylon, and pushing it out even more as the rest my body expanded and hardened in horrifying ways. My legs expanded out from sexy calves to full-blown cankles in a matter of seconds. My hand went over my mouth in shock—surely, I was hallucinating?—only to find my fingers ballooned out into carnival-sized hot dogs.

What is going on?

Was this some kind of revenge for setting up my friends for failure? Perhaps some kind of cosmic joke, as if I'd been given a chance to be here, only to have my victory taken from me at the last possible moment, in a way that was divinely and bizarrely appointed?

As my body rounded out and stretched out the silly fashion pieces I wore to their thinnest point, I peeked at myself in the mirror hanging in the thinly-walled room.

My mouth dropped open, and I nearly screamed at the sight before me.

I'd managed to squeeze into the superhero suit, but my entire body—my legs, my arms, my stomach, and even my butt—were now super-huge. The navy and black lines were stretched, sliding over my body like horizontal lines over a watermelon; the matching mask was burrowed into the fat-lines of my face, while the rest of me was covered in hot pink spandex, looking like a severely pink gumball princess. There was a hood on my back, hanging limp, like a roll of toilet paper caught on an unsuspecting shoe.

When I realized there was no way the mirror in front of me was originally from a funhouse, I nearly screamed again. Only knowing that would-be models and fashionistas like Azure and the *Model Middle America* people would be the first ones to see me stopped me from making any audible noise. I could only dry-heave, feeling the sick slurpage of my stomach contents.

Radioactive doughnuts …

AB's comment came to mind as I burped and tasted the satanic sweetness of powdered doughnuts again.

Was she serious? Seriously serious?

A bell rang outside, calling the models to their positions.

"Where is Arlanda?" Azure's voice cut over the crowd, calling for me. Not that anyone would know, given that "Arlanda" was not my actual name.

I slumped against the door, using my newly-blossomed girth to keep anyone from coming into the room. Remaining there, standing overly still as my body kept bulging out, I held my breath waiting for him to leave. I could hear the *Model Middle America* theme song music behind him.

"Belinda! Belinda, go find me another girl. I can't find Arlanda."

There was a flutter of footsteps as the rest of the room cleared out. I stood as still as stone, terrified someone would find me as much as I was afraid I would be alone like this for the rest of my life.

I've never been this alone and afraid before.

I leaned harder against the door, weeping silently, my hands covering my once-perfect face.

If I'd thought my breakdown earlier in my family's kitchen was hard, it was nothing compared to now. At least earlier I'd been thin and pretty.

I was even closer to fulfilling my dream of worldwide fame and adoration, of making my mother proud enough to come home, of making myself into someone that people could love—and yet here I was, fat and getting even fatter, my once-perfect body covered in rolls of flesh and fat and probably muscle, stuck in a superhero costume probably concocted up by hippie with a bubblegum fetish.

Outside of the room, a whole other world was going on, one that had no idea how much I was weeping and crying and blubbering.

My body started to slow down as it ballooned out. I suddenly wondered if I was going to explode, and it wasn't the worst fate in the world.

There was a collection of explosions outside, coming from the stage area. Everyone was having a gay, old time, and I was suffering beyond human capability. I could hear their cries and shocking silence, no doubt in awe of the other models that I was supposed to have been upstaging.

"Secure the area," a man's voice called out.

That was when it hit me.

I might have been fat, ugly, caught in a spandex uniform only Super Pink Princess would wear, but *no one else had seen me.*

If I didn't clear out of the backstage area soon, I would be worse than dead: I would be humiliated, on a scale even more unthinkable than farting in front of my class.

"All clear back here, boys." The man's voice was right on the other side of the door from me. I flinched, surprised at the proximity, before it happened.

The cheap, wooden door I'd been leaning on cracked, cracking from my weight.

"Whoa!" I fell backwards through the doorway, my sides screeching with splinters.

The man was in the wrong place at the wrong time. I landed hard on him, knocking him over as I rolled onto him, smooshing him into the floor.

"Ouch," I grumbled, as I wobbled between my feet and hands for balance. He was caught underneath me, as I lay on top of him, with my big belly holding him down. As I breathed heavily and tried not to cry from my rush of deadly embarrassment, he began to shout.

"Get off me!"

I was about to apologize when I saw the rifle next to us.

His radio chimed beside us.

"Boss, you okay? We've got the audience held hostage and we're ready for phase two when you are."

Miraculously, I forgot about my fatness and shame as I looked down at him.

The man was wearing part of a black mask, almost like a handkerchief over his face. He was wearing gloves and there were some straps of ammo hanging around his shoulders.

The explosions and music and silence earlier … all of it made a new, terrible kind of sense. Now that I was focused on what was happening around me, I could tell something had gone horribly wrong for other people, too. From the other side of the Amphitheatre, my ears perked at the sound of sirens and a police bullhorn. A helicopter whirred its blades fiercely outside.

"You're a terrorist," I realized, looking down at the man I was sitting on.

"Get off," he said, his voice huffy. "I can't breathe. You're too heavy."

The gunman tried to squirm and slide me off of him, but there was no moving me unless I wanted to be moved, apparently. His radio chimed and there were knocks at the back doors, and all I could think was I had to keep him down, or he would shoot me.

I didn't want to be caught dead looking like this, like some kind of magenta-blob monster, but I didn't want to be literally caught dead, either.

The door burst open, and my world might as well have ended at that moment. Police charged through in their SWAT vests.

"Hold it right there!" One of the armored guards pointed his gun down at us, and I sheepishly held up my hands in silence while the SWAT Team surrounded me and the gunman I'd trapped underneath my slobbish body.

As more troops come in, I hung my head, unwilling to look any of them in the eye.

This is the worst day ever.

And the worst part was, it wasn't over yet.

Fatgirl

ORIGINS

PART TWO

○ ○ ○ ○

C. S. Johnson

FATGIRL
ORIGINS: PART TWO

○ ○ ○ ○

Before I found myself surrounded by a SWAT team, sitting on top of a wanted terrorist while wearing a traumatizingly ugly superhero costume after my body had swelled up to thirteen times its usual size, I used to think that the worst day of my life was the day I found out my mother left.

To be clear, it wasn't the day she'd actually left. I was used to my parents leaving me for a few days at a time. Dad was a truck driver, and Mom was a former model who constantly wanted to visit family, go to the spa, or just leave town. It was almost part of a routine that one or both of them wouldn't be around. I am still not exactly sure how many days it took me to realize something wasn't right, and it doesn't help that Mom left while I was still at school.

So the day I found out she'd left for good, not necessarily the day she left, was literally the worst.

The worst.

Literally the worst.

Period.

At the time, I was in tenth grade, and I was worrying about my gym grade, since my teacher, this ugly lady named Coach Keelson, didn't like how I never changed my socks into generic white socks for class. I'd tried arguing that she was being racist with her obsession with white, but she wasn't willing to change the dress code.

It was a real bummer for me, too, because cute socks were big last year. Like, really big. It was this huge thing to get socks with shoe patterns on it, so if you took your shoes off, it would still look like you had shoes on. Amory and I were in an informal competition to see who could have a different pair on each day, and who would repeat themselves first. So Coach Keelson's tyrannical "you-must-change-out-of-your-fancy-socks-Kallie-or-you-could-end-up-with-colored-feet" speech was extra grating, especially since the sweat my feet supposedly produced literally never happened; I was too pretty to exert myself too much in gym class.

The day I found out about Mom, I was prepared to have my parents wage war over Coach Keelson's systematic racism and her atrocious use of the word "colored" in her socks-related comments. Instead, I came home to find Dad was home, drinking scotch—the good kind, too, the kind that looked like refined blood and seemed too smooth when it was poured from the bottle. The fancy stuff that looked like a wedding gift.

As a truck driver, Dad doesn't drink on principle, so I was shocked. "What's wrong?"

Dad hesitated, and I sat down across from him. I was fully prepared for him to tell me he'd lost his job.

"Your mother … took a modeling job … in LA."

"Oh, that's it?" I sighed. "What are you upset about, then? That's great."

It didn't hit me right away, the implications of what he'd said.

Dad patiently tried again. "No, it's not."

"What do you mean?" I frowned. "This is a good thing for her. She's always wanted to get back into modeling, and it's not like she's got a lot of opportunities here in Arkansas. I mean, really. This place sucks."

"Kallie."

"I'm just saying, if I were her, I'd've started working again a long time ago—"

"Kallie!" He was clearly upset, but I still didn't understand why he was so ticked off.

"What? It's not like she's never coming back." I crossed my arms, indignant I had to reason with my own father. "I mean, most modeling jobs are with companies, and they have vacations and time off and everything, don't they? And it's not like it'll be that much longer till she comes home, right?"

Dad said nothing. He just took another sip of his scotch.

That was when I started to worry. Dad continued to say nothing for an egregiously long moment, and I finally ran out of patience.

"Well, when *is* she coming back?" I asked. "I wanted to see about throwing my birthday party early this year, and I've got to talk to both of you about the sock situation with my gym class teacher."

"Kallie … "

"What?" I snapped. "Just tell me, would you?"

"She's not coming back." Dad made a little bit of a choking noise, and then hung his head.

The unspoken words hung in the air between us. I could've sworn he said them, but I didn't see his lips move.

She's not coming back. Not ever.

And I'd just admitted I didn't want to be in Cuttingham City, either, didn't I? I could understand, couldn't I?

Turns out I couldn't.

I didn't say anything else. I stood up slowly, my sock fiasco already forgotten along with my other concerns.

As I ran out of the room, Dad called after me.

"I'm sorry, Kallie."

I didn't know if I hated him or not in that moment. Mom had the power to leave, sure—but Dad should've had the power to convince her to stay, too.

And what about me?

Dad's apology was the worst part of that whole night. It told me that Mom had left us of her own choice, and not even the adoration of her husband and the love of her daughter were enough to make her stay.

I walked to my room, flopped down on my bed, and then just fell over.

I don't remember when I started to cry, but I remember crying for a long, long time. It was hard to tell if it seemed longer or shorter than it actually was, since I was still awake when morning came the next day.

I didn't want to go to school, and thankfully, Dad didn't make me. He came in to check on me and tell me he had to go to work. He said if I was feeling well enough, I could invite a friend over if I wanted.

"I'll be fine," I told him, keeping my voice clear and stoic.

He nodded and kissed my forehead, promising me I could still have my birthday party early and that he would call the school about Coach Keelson.

I was lonelier than ever with no one other than the old cable TV and my cell phone to distract me from my pain. My friends were mostly all at school, so there was a limit to my texting capabilities, and while the Internet might love a victim for the day, when they get tired of you, they forget you—or worse, they mock you. Sympathy only goes so far before it runs out.

By the time lunchtime rolled around, I put on my clothes—mistakenly putting on a repeated pair of shoe-socks—and went to school late. Amory was quick to claim her victory, and even my mother's departure didn't stop her from squawking around like a peacock in heat before me and the other girls were tired of her show.

So yeah. The day I found out about my mom leaving was the worse day of my life.

Until, of course, the day I found myself swollen to the size of a sumo wrestler, dressed up like a diet company's super-plus superhero, stuck on top of a terrorist who'd been planning on gunning down an entire auditorium full of innocent people on live television.

"I don't think I can breathe!"

The gunman underneath my stomach was flapping his arms and feet around, doing anything he could to wiggle free. His gun—a long, scary-looking black stick of a thing—was just out of his reach, and it honestly looked heavy enough I don't think he would have been able to shoot me even if he'd been able to grab it. Still, I was glad my huge girth held him down. I was also a little glad he was having trouble breathing. It was hard for me to even move, considering this had never happened to me before, and he was really only thinking of himself. It wouldn't bother me if he stopped talking.

"Uh … Miss?" An officer came up beside us, looking the both of us up and down, obviously trying to figure out what was going on. "Can you tell me what happened?"

"No." It hurt to shake my head, but it should've been obvious I didn't know what *had* happened, let alone what *was* happening.

And as God as my witness, neither would they. I was *not* going to tell the officer *anything*, *ever*, and I was smart enough to know this was where I would need a good lawyer if I didn't escape soon.

"You do realize that this is Frank Whitey … Miss?" The officer was still looking down at the man underneath me. "He's on the FBI's most wanted list."

"I can believe it," I said through gritted teeth.

"Help me," Frank begged.

He managed to gasp out a putrid cloud of his breath right in my face.

"Ew, gross!" I coughed at the smoky smell and taste that suddenly flew up into my mouth. It was like vaping vomit, and I nearly retched at the intrusion.

"I'm begging you, help!" Frank said again.

"Oh, would you just shut up?" I snapped down at him, glaring through the mask drawn tightly over my floppy-fat face. "You weren't worried about killing a bunch of people, and all of a sudden, you're worried that *you're* going to die?"

Frank Whitey glared up at me. "I'm worried I'm going to die being crushed by an ugly fatso like you!"

"Come on, break it up." The officer scowled down at Frank. "You're lucky to be squashed by this heroine of the night. She saved a bunch of people. Perhaps even yourself, Mr. Whitey."

Frank spat up at the officer, only to have the spit fall back on his face. "I wasn't going to kill anyone who didn't get in my way."

"Yeah, well, the government doesn't look too kindly on hostage situations, either."

The officer reached down and looped his arm with mine, getting close enough to me I could see the name "Powers" on his badge. As he pulled me to my feet and his other partners closed in and cuffed Frank Whitey, I cringed; between "Whitey" and "Powers," my situation had all the hallmarks of a cheesy teen movie.

What can possibly happen next?

I didn't really want to know. Already behind me, I could hear the *click-click* of crime scene photographers, and if I ever wanted to get my dignity back, I would have to get out of here, find Abuela-Blanca, and make her give me some un-radioactive doughnuts to change me back to my normal, regular, devastatingly beautiful self. Then, I wanted to go home and hit my head so hard that I would never, ever think about this night ever again.

Officer Powers looked me up and down. He was a nice-enough looking man himself, with his no-nonsense sort of face which juxtaposed with the patient sparkle in his brown eyes. He had his cop shirtsleeves rolled up underneath his armor, and I took a moment longer than needed to appreciate how neat and strong he looked.

"I'm not sure what I should ask," he finally said.

"Nothing," I said, shaking my hair loose. Thankfully, it was still its long, gorgeous form, and I could use it to help hide my eyes. "I don't know if I'd have any answers for you anyway."

To his credit, Officer Powers chuckled.

"Sorry, Miss, perhaps that's a little rude," he said. "But let me thank you, ma'am, for your services today. We captured a wanted criminal thanks to you, and no one was even injured."

"Hey, I got hurt, you tool!" Frank snarled.

I heard him spit again, and I looked back to see he was getting fingerprinted at one of Azure's beauty stations.

Officer Powers grinned. "Hazards of the crime. What can I say?"

Frank was not amused, and several more officers had to close in on him as he unsuccessfully and stupidly tried to fight off his captor.

For a guy who had a team of people working underneath him to commit mass murder on a reality TV show, he sure seemed violent and stupid.

I was a little grateful for it, though.

While Frank distracted the SWAT team and the others, I tested out my legs. Earlier, I'd fallen over, surprised as the changing room door had broken underneath my new weight, but now that I was back on my feet, I didn't seem to have any balance issues.

Now is the time. I need to run away.

But where would I go?

I glanced around, looking for some feasible, semi-logical path out of there.

There was nothing.

Nothing … except the runway.

No! I do not *want to do this.*

But I had to, didn't I?

I could jettison out of there, bowl through the crowds, and get out to the parking lot. Once I was there, I'd have to find a way to hide, even wearing the hot pink mess I was stuck in, but between all the cars and the people, I could probably at least get enough of a head start it wouldn't matter so much.

That was assuming I could get away from the crime scene. I was a witness, after all.

But when I saw the back doors burst open, and a bunch of brightly colored microphones, boom guys, and cameramen came pouring into the room, I knew it was time to high-tail it out of there.

It was bad enough I was super fat and stuck in a beachball-like costume—no matter that I'd stopped a gunman from killing a bunch of people probably, or holding them hostage, or something like that; I'd saved a bunch of deplorable people who would have no trouble laughing at me now.

I mean, if I was in their (probably ugly) shoes, that's what I would've done to a bloated bubblegum hero like me.

So I did *not* need to talk to the media, and I did not need to let them see me, either.

Thankfully, it seemed the cops and Frank Whitey had the same idea about that as I did.

But between the cops and the media, I didn't know who was worse. The SWAT team moved to push the media personalities back outside, calling for order and asking for cooperation.

That was when I hobbled away. My knees cracked as I began to run, but my new mass appeared not to be just fat. The muscles around my former self began to faithfully crank like a machine, and I managed to run faster than I'd ever run before as I bolted out of there.

"Whoa!" I didn't mean to scream quite so loudly as I bounded out from behind the stage curtain and hurdled down the runway. I didn't even have time for bittersweet angst as my legs continued to move me forward mechanically.

People screamed as they saw me. Fingers pointed at me, and then whispers and catcalls of an inappropriate and shocking nature followed. Stumbling, I curled and rolled myself off the stage and into the crowds.

My body was too big to be crowd-surfing, but it might've made me feel better about myself if people tried to catch me; instead they began running away, bawling and crying at the huge pink hippo lady. It was almost like being Cinderella at the ball, running away and scaring a bunch of people into running away too. Except I was the pumpkin changing back instead of the princess.

I tried not to think about it as I ran. It was only when I reached the door that I heard the police calling out, telling the people around me to try to stop me.

Officer Powers' kind, steely voice cut through the crowds: "Stop her! She's a witness!"

I'd always thought I'd come face to face with the cops over something silly, like breaking curfew for my junior license or texting and driving at the same time, or even shoplifting if I found something tempting enough. I wasn't worried about it before, because I was pretty and a good crier, and most of the people in the town knew of my mother, even if they didn't know her personally. I was content to believe I'd be able to use my looks to get out of a ticket.

That wasn't going to be possible now, I thought with a grimace.

That's why I pushed open the doors with a powerful thrust and then propelled forward, carelessly shoving people out of my way as I run by them.

As I came up to the curb, I tripped and ended up rolling into the line of cars. My body lurched in dulled pain as I knocked off a bumper and crushed in a headlight before hitting the side of a large van.

Honk! Honk!

I winced at the noise.

"Hey, Fatgirl! What do ya think you're doing?" The driver yelled at me, hanging out of the window of his now-dented vehicle, but I was only too grateful I'd been able to stop rolling after hitting him.

"Sorry!" I yelled back, before sprinting off to the side of the parking lot; it was a lot less crowded, and there was a lot more space for me to run between the rows of cars.

I didn't even want to look back, because I wasn't lying when I apologized to that man.

I *was* sorry.

I was sorry I'd ever thought coming to the *Model Middle America* audition was a good idea.

I was sorry I'd eaten my stupid grandmother's doughnuts.

I was sorry my mother had left me and my dad, and that I couldn't seem to get over it.

I was sorry this whole mess had happened.

I was sorry I'd been born at all.

The tears dampened my mask before streaming down my fluffy cheeks. I rubbed them away until I saw a small wooded area, hidden largely by the shadows. I made my way over there and flopped my fat bum down into the cold, March mud, and then I cried and cried and cried.

Like the time I found out Mom had abandoned me and Dad, I didn't actually know how much time had passed before I stopped crying. I just seemed to stop at some point, and I guessed several hours had passed, although no sliver of sunlight peeked across the horizon.

It was still nighttime. A bunch of light pollution cast an additional sense of dread as I looked around.

Maybe not a lot of time had passed at all, but I didn't like to think I was used to disappointment enough it stopped traumatizing me so quickly, especially at this extreme level.

I had enough sense to make sure I wasn't making a lot of noise. The police cars and the media vans and the amphitheatre security golf cars all blinked their different colored lights like alien starships, each holding people who would grab me up off the face of the earth and then poke and prod me until I gave them all the answers or laughs they could take.

So in some ways, it'd just be like high school.

Despite my poor mood, I sobbed out a laugh at the thought. While I was in with Azure and Bernadette or Belinda or whatever her name was, I hadn't recognized any of the girls I knew; perhaps I'd managed to make Amory and the other girls miss the event all together, just like I'd planned.

Maybe I deserve this … this Fatgirl thing.

I wasn't a particularly nice person, after all. I'd done my best to undermine my friendship with Amory by going to see Blake at the lacrosse game. I'd just assumed Dad would be home to take me to where I wanted to go, and I'd lied my way into a spot for the runway at *Model Middle America.*

My own mother didn't want to be around me, either.

Why would anyone want to be around me at all? It was a hard question, and one I didn't know if I wanted an answer to—especially since the only sure answer I could give was that I was pretty, and I wasn't even that anymore now that my size rivaled that of a small elephant.

I dug my fat face further into my hands and moaned softly. "Oh, God … this is terrible."

I shook my head and smiled wryly. *Where is Jesus when I need him?*

Zeus' pimple-pockmarked face swam to the surface of my mind, and I decided when I got out of here, if I could ever be my normal, pretty self again, I would apologize to him for being petty at the lacrosse game. And for letting him take the fall for my fart in Mr. Embers' class earlier.

"At least I didn't fart on TV," I told myself, and my attempt at self-deprecating humor only made me cry again.

My blustering whimpers softened again at a small *chime-chime-chime* noise coming from behind me.

All at once, I went absolutely still and silent. I could hear my probably-enlarged heart as it thundered.

"Kallie?"

I let out a long, slow sigh.

Abuela-Blanca had found me.

The chiming noise continued, the cadence and volume increasing as her footsteps approached. I didn't dare make any noise at all, not until I was certain she was alone.

"Kallie, this is not funny," AB said with a huff. "I'm a respectable doctor, even with my past employment history. I shouldn't be wandering out here in the mud wearing my good shoes."

I almost preferred the gunman whining about how he couldn't breathe as I sat on him. Before I could yell at AB and tell her off, she began to grumble again.

"I've worked with blood samples every day for ten years; why are bugs and germs so much worse?"

There was a small *splosh* of mud.

"Oh, no." A wrangled moan ripped from her throat. "Oh, this is appalling!"

Finally, I snorted. "If you want to see appalling, just shine a light in my direction."

"Oh, there you are, Kallie. Finally." AB cleared her throat and fiddled with her device. I couldn't see her clearly through the darkness, but I could see enough of her movements to know she was alone, and she carried a large handbag over her shoulder.

Seriously? Is she that much of a white lady?

That was probably the wrong question to ask. We'd already established that earlier with her fancy car.

"Yes, it's me. It's a whole lot more of me than I'd like, too," I snapped.

"Oh, my." A small, bright light flashed over me and I could see my grandmother's shadowy face. Her scientific gaze was cold, impersonal, and downright dehumanizing.

"Well, do you believe me now?" AB asked. "Those were my radioactive doughnuts."

"That's probably not the best thing to say to me right now," I snapped. "I'm strong enough I could sneeze and snap you in half."

"I'm almost curious enough to see if you could, given your girth." AB's voice cracked in a strange way, and I took another hard look at her.

She stared at me for another long moment, and I stared back at her.

Then her face crinkled, and her eyes lit up with pure mirth. She let out a loud, cackling laugh and put her hand over her mouth.

I almost killed her on the spot.

"Shut up!" I shouted, my voice loud enough to shake the nearby trees. "This is *not* funny!"

AB coughed and sputtered several times before she got herself back under control. "Yes, yes, you're right. I'm sorry. But you have to admit, that outfit is terrible. I wouldn't be surprised if the big twist in this American reality TV show is that it's all a ploy to embarrass you and all the other would-be models."

Her assessment was close enough to some of my earlier thoughts that I slumped over even further into my mudhole.

"Don't look so down," AB said. "That 'sad-clown' look is hardly appropriate here."

"Should I look like an angry villain instead?" I shot back.

"I can fix this, Kallie. There's no need for your anger right now. And the sadness, while I understand it, might actually be good for you in this case. Remorse is a precursor to change for the better."

"Which is why I can assume you've never felt it?"

AB ignored me as she squatted down and pulled out her purse. She was surprisingly agile for a grandmother. I didn't know her exact age, but Dad was at least in his thirties when I'd been born, so she had to be pushing at least mid-fifties. And from her hairstyle, I could easily assume she was much older.

"Ah, ha," she whispered. "Here it is."

She pulled out a large needle, and I scuttled back.

"What's that for?" I shrieked, then immediately tried to muffle my voice.

"I need some of your blood, Kallie. Hold still."

Before I could object, she stuck me with the blunt needle. I went reeling back, screaming at the shock more than the pinprick of pain.

"Oh, my," AB muttered. "You're lucky this is sharp. It barely went in your arm at all."

I grimaced. "Can you just stop talking? Your talking is making this worse?"

"I just need a bit of your blood to reverse-engineer a cure."

"Are you done yet?" I wriggled in embarrassed pain. "How long will it take?"

"Longer if you squirm." She pulled the needle from my arm with my blood sample, she scrubbed it down with alcohol strips and then pulled a lighter and a couple of other items out of her purse. I knew enough from AP Bio to identify the centrifuge and a small, collapsible microscope. Her "portable lab" comment struck me as astoundingly accurate from earlier, especially as I recognized other things she had on her, like litmus strips and small vials of chemical solutions.

It struck me that I didn't actually know AB very well. From her quick, smooth movements, it was clear that my grandmother was apparently a good scientist.

"Why did you come to live with me and Dad?" I asked.

"I told you, I've come to help you while your mother's out of the picture." She picked up a small twig and lit it on fire. "I'll need to dispose of my materials in an unorthodox manner. The downside of a portable lab, you know: no haz-mat help."

I watched as she blew on the small brush fire and dropped the alcohol swabs. Nothing seemed to phase her.

Aside from me eating all her doughnuts and unexpectedly jumping out of her car.

I cleared my throat. "I was upset when I came home."

She waved her hand at me. "You're a teenager, and your mother, no matter her skill level of parenting, is gone. I shouldn't expect much discipline from you."

My nose wrinkled with disdain. "You know, that's kind of judgmental."

"What? It's not racist, you mean?" AB arched her brow as she laced her words with sarcasm. "Well, what do you know? The remorse is kicking in already."

"The only remorse I feel is that I have to deal with you to get this solved." I glared at her. "If you hadn't made those stupid doughnuts, I wouldn't be in this position at all."

"There are a thousand and one steps that can take us off the straight and narrow path, Kallie," AB replied. "This is not my fault."

She said it with such a softness to her usually brusque tone that I faltered for a moment. Then I felt my suspicion rise.

Whose fault does she think this is, I wonder? Aside from my own, of course. Because she would never, ever do anything that would cause this sort of trouble, would she?

"You're right," I said a moment later. "I suppose you think this is my fault, and my Mom's fault, too."

"Partially," AB agreed, not seeming to realize my growing rage. "But this is, unfortunately, much bigger—no pun intended—than either you or me, or even your mother."

"Ha, ha." I laughed bitterly, and then jolted with fear. "You can fix me, can't you?"

"I can fix *this*," AB assured me, gesturing to my body. "But the other problems of the night will be harder to clear up."

"What do you mean?"

"Well, you were caught on TV body-slamming a wanted terrorist, for one," AB said, making me ball up into a fetal position on the ground all over again. She held up her gloved hands and counted off her fingers. "You're a witness to a federal crime. You're a hero to the press, and you've managed to gain more attention in the last two hours than you'd ever imagine. People are looking for you, and I'm not the only one."

"How did *you* find me?" I asked, suddenly curious.

"My Phi-ger," AB explained, showing me the small crackling device that had been chiming earlier. "It's a Geiger device, but its frequency is tweaked to a particular radioactive isotope I created. It's in my doughnut recipe." She looked pointedly down at me. "And since you've consumed them, I figured it wouldn't be hard to find you that way."

"Gee, thanks."

"You can thank me later. I'll have to monitor you for the next few weeks to make sure it doesn't affect your system in a negative way," AB added.

"It's already affected me in a negative way," I nearly shouted, gesturing down my body and its more-than-voluptuous form.

"I can see." AB chuckled again. Before I could hit her, she held up her hand. "Forgive me for my laughter, Kallie. I can assure you, this is not exactly what I had in mind when Project: SERUM was approved by the higher-ups in the NAH."

"Project: SERUM? NAH?"

"National Association of Healthcare," AB explained, focusing on the latter half of my questions. "They do a lot of rather unethical stuff, but if there's a way we can make it ethical, we do it."

"I don't understand."

"Sure you do. If you lie to someone, you can rationalize your actions in saying that it's for their own good to be lied to."

"White lies." I rolled my eyes. "Figures."

"Yes, Kallie Grand-*White*," AB snapped, reminding me of my own connection to the "white" part I hated to hear. "White lies. And you'll be thankful for those in the coming weeks, especially since I'm going to need your help if we're going to take care of this mess."

I was dumbstruck, flabbergasted, and appalled—not just that she would need my help, but that she would assume I would give it to her.

"Tell me what happened in there," she said. "I'll need to know the details so I'll be able to make the right calls. I might not work for the government right now, but calling in favors is an older tradition, so we'll have to be precise in making the right ones."

"You don't work for the government anymore?" I nearly choked on the words.

"Of course not. I'm living with you and Johnny now, aren't I?"

Her machine blinked and beeped a few times, and then she pulled out a small bottle of solution. "Got it," she muttered, before using a plunger to suck all the liquid out of the jar and into another needle.

I gritted my teeth. "Oh, come on—"

The needle slipped into me before I could prepare myself. I felt the solution bubble up underneath my fat. Instantly, I felt my stomach start to soften, and my body's tension eased back. I felt like a balloon, blown up to its extremes, slowly leaking air.

"It won't be an instant cure," AB said. "I'll have to take you back to my lab for further testing."

"There's more I have to do?"

"Yes." AB smiled at me with her prim, evil smile, before her eyes darkened with something that reminded me of sympathy. "There's much more you'll have to do, I'm afraid."

Escaping from the police and various other SWAT officers shouldn't have been as easy as it was, but somehow, blaming Abuela-Blanca for all my trouble was harder than it should've been.

I mean, sure, yeah, I was the one who'd eaten her precious doughnuts. But I'd been angry at the time, and it could've happened to anyone.

As we drove home—me in the backseat, now shrunken down to half my hippopotamus-level size, wrapped in an old, smelly blanket AB had in her Imperial's trunk—I thought about what AB meant when she said I'd have much more to do after tonight.

Her phone rang, blaring out its last-generation ringtone.

"Hello?" She picked it up before I could tell her she wasn't supposed to be driving and talking on the phone. I ducked further down into my seat, fervently hoping and praying that no cop would pull us over.

"Yes, Johnny, things are fine," AB said. "Kallie and I are having a wonderful time. We are actually having a girl's night out right now, just getting reacquainted after all these years."

From the backseat, I glared up at the rearview mirror. She caught my eyes and smirked. "Oh, Kallie's just an absolute hoot, don't worry. She took the news that I was moving in much better than we expected."

I nearly choked.

"Oh, gotta run, Johnny. My other line is ringing. Love you."

I thought about accusing her of being a liar when she pressed another button—right as she made a sharp swerve around an eighteen-wheeler—and answered the phone again.

"Dr. White here," she said. This time, she shot a warning look back at me, telling me in her own way to stay quiet. "Thanks for getting back to me so soon, KP. Bless your heart."

I wondered who KP was; AB sounded much more authentic as she exchanged the common "Southern Pleasantries" on the phone. One of her contacts, maybe?

I leaned forward to listen for the voice on the other end, trying to get a sense of what was going on when AB's tone darkened.

"This is exactly what I'm doing," she argued. "And don't use that tone with me. I need your help. You owe me, especially after the business with Geneva."

I perked up my ears. There was a nasty-sounding voice on the other end of the line, and I saw my grandmother—normally so calm and sharp—weaken with vulnerability.

"This is my life's work," she said. "It is not my fault we're in this position."

I almost felt sorry for Abuela-Blanca as she sat there and talked quietly and angrily with the nameless voice on the other end.

"We'll see that it's taken care of," she finally said. "I deserve this. If anyone deserves this, I do, do you hear me?"

She quickly ended her call and then dropped into silence.

I just stared at her again, wondering what on earth she was talking about.

She swerved off the Interstate and headed toward our exit, saying nothing.

Finally, I dared to ask her the question. "Who was that?"

"No one you need to worry about," AB said. "Let's just say I was able to call in some favors to get you off the hook with the Cuttingham City cops, and there's a bit of a price to pay for it."

"What is it?"

"That's nothing you need to worry about, either," AB said. "At least, not right now."

I sat up in my seat. "When will I have to worry about it?"

She ignored my question. "Your father called to say he'll be back Sunday. Thank God for the traffic delays in the South, for once."

"Will I be back to normal before then?"

"Yes."

Oh, thank you God. Thank you so much.

At that moment, I felt all of my relief soar through me, as though I could fly if I wanted to, I was so happy and light. My heart swelled with joy, and I felt all the weight of my sadness slide away.

"But according to KP, we're going to have some problems," she added, making my stomach do a seismic drop back into reality's harshness. "We'll have to see."

"See what? What problems?" I crossed my arms.

"I'll explain what I can later. But I need your help, Kallie." AB glared back at me in her rearview mirror. "Just like you need mine."

○ ○ ○ ○

The next morning couldn't come quickly enough. I didn't sleep well at all; it was nearly three in the morning when I finally made it back to my room, and thanks to the whole "FBI caught a wanted terrorist while he was planning on shooting up America's most popular TV show" thing, I found out I didn't have school the following day. And since Dad wasn't home, and my phone had busted when I'd chucked it across the kitchen, I had the rest of the weekend to myself.

Well, mostly myself.

AB was still at home, too—and that prompted questions to burn inside of me with relentless fervor.

It was probably those questions that kept me from sleeping soundly that night.

Unlike the day I found out my mother left, I had literally no idea what could possibly drive a woman like my grandmother to leave her cushy, high-powered, demanding job with the government, come and live with my dad and me, and suddenly indulge herself in the urge to make a batch of homemade, radioactive doughnuts.

It was quite a conundrum, and I hated how curious I was.

When I did manage to doze off, dreams of doughnuts attacking me while a giant bubblegum balloon tried to squash the city kept me from finding any semblance of peace. Some part of me didn't want to wake up either, thanks to my fears that I would be stuck being a fat butterball for the rest of my life.

At that, I eased open one eyelid, letting my long eyelashes cloud my vision as I nervously looked down at my body.

"Oh, no!" I shot upright, my eyes bugling out; and then, immediately, I let out a small chuckle of relief. I'd worn the costume to bed, and the pink and navy fabric hung over my body like a stage curtain thrown over a stick.

I was back to normal.

Thank you, thank you, thank you, Jesus.

"This is amazing." I wanted to cheer even though I wept as I ran my hands down my hips and legs, marveling at their once-more perfection and slimness. "Whatever AB did, it worked."

Carefully and curiously, I ran my fingers across my stomach, relieved and amazed to find it was flat again. Even the extra skin I'd grown was gone!

For all I knew looking at my body, I could've just been dreaming that whole "radioactive doughnut" mess happened. Maybe I'd gone to Blake's lacrosse game and Sweaty Fat Kid—Zeus, I mentally corrected myself—had sat on me by accident, or maybe I'd been knocked out by a random lacrosse ball and been in a coma, dreaming away in a hospital.

Of course, there was the matter of the ugly superhero outfit I found myself in. That quickly proved my hopes were useless.

"Kallie, are you up?"

Speaking of useless …

AB was calling me, and I didn't want to answer. "Come down here," she said. "I'm afraid we've got a problem."

The sense of dread I felt slowed my heart, but quickened my steps as I headed to the kitchen.

The oven was on, and something was baking. The coffee pot was warm, and there were dirty dishes in the sink.

My stomach rumbled pathetically, but I didn't know if I wanted eat anything ever again, thanks to the doughnut fiasco.

"I wouldn't eat anything if I were you." Abuela-Blanca walked into the room. She was as calm and collected as ever, dressed in one of her regal pantsuits, with her hair styled back in a fashionable knot. She held a teacup in her hand, although the distinct scent of espresso wafted through the air between us.

"Why?" I gripped my now-flattened stomach with my hands. "Will it make me fat again?"

"No, on the contrary, you'll probably be sick," AB said. "Just check the news. It seems you've stolen the show, Kallie."

All the joy I'd felt before was instantly sucked away, as if I were a floor speckled with happiness and some kind of universal vacuum made sure that never lasted.

I almost didn't look.

But then I did, and I instantly regretted it.

All over the place, I could see my blurry-faced picture, some awful black-and-white security camera footage, and posters with

"Thank You, Fatgirl" written in different ways with large variety of bad grammar flying high across the city.

Several well-known city officials and our own small social media stars were all on the news, gushing about me—some with genuine, hick-loving, backwater-pride sort of love—and others with that *politically correct*, "you-go-Fatgirl" sort of admiration that just made me cringe. They were clearly glad to have a meat puppet to represent their fake-virtuous, vice-filled fantasies—a *fat superhero! A fat female superhero! One who actually saves people!* I gagged as they talked; it was like listening to gold-digging women comment about how handsome poor men are, even if they still won't date them.

Honestly, between the country lovin' Monster-Truck-Theatre-Heroics and the city life's "Stunning and Brave" Standing Ovation, I didn't know which was worse.

Gas rumbled in my stomach again, just like it had at school the day before. I was pretty sure if it wasn't for the fact I had to hold in farts again, I would've fainted at the horror of my fate.

"This is awful," I said, nearly choking on my words.

AB took another calm sip of her espresso. "I'm afraid this isn't even the worse part. Come with me to my lab."

"What could possibly be worse?" I gritted my teeth, instantly regretting the question.

I had only been reacquainted with my grandmother for a day, but I already knew I should be glad she wasn't in my life any more than she was. She seemed like the kind of person who enjoyed telling kids that Santa Claus wasn't real, or that unicorns died every time a baby cried.

I didn't know AB that well, but from all the movies and TV shows and most of the books I've read, I imagined my grandmother's room should've been like a little cottage from the past, complete with the gag-worthy violet powder perfume sprayed all around, cheery lace decorations hanging on her dresser, and maybe even tiny ceramic figurines or photos of all her grandchildren and family placed all around. Any little sign of humanity would've comforted me, at least giving me a reason to think maybe I could get along with her.

Needless to say, her room was nothing like that.

Not at all, believe it or not.

Walking into the room felt more akin to walking into a time machine than a small cottage. Large computer screens and humming boxes of electricity and lights cluttered her desk and her dresser. All of them twinkled with flashing lights and little numbers, doing things I couldn't even begin to imagine or ever guess.

"Don't touch anything," Abuela-Blanca warned, marching down behind me. "I'm working on some delicate projects down here."

One device made a chiming noise like the one I'd heard last night, and despite her warning, I reached for it. "Is that your Phi-ger?"

She slapped my hand down. "Yes, and it's crackling off its radioactive isotope music, so it clearly knows you're here."

"What's the radioactive isotope like?" I asked, glancing around again. I might not have liked AB, but her work interested me. I mean, really, I wasn't just a dumb, pretty face the way Lizzie was. I had an avid interest in books and learning and most everything caught my eye—such as the poster of the periodic table of elements hanging up, with one of the bottom rectangle highlighted.

"The radioactive element of my doughnut recipe comes from an isotope of Protactinium," AB said. "It's very rare, and the extra neutrons make it more dense, but it also makes it more flexible."

"I don't know what you mean."

"Of course not. I know how bad public schools are," she said. "But as basically as I can say, the recipe is mainly designed to turn the consumer into his biggest fear."

I looked down at my flat stomach. "So I became fat because being fat is my biggest fear?"

AB laughed. "You can see why I was so amused last night, can't you? Imagine being fat as the thing you fear most."

I bristled. What did AB know about being a teenager in today's world? She'd grown up before the Internet could be so effectively weaponized, and she could sit back on her rocker and count her blessings for that. And it wasn't as if AB actually knew the main reason I'd desperately wanted to win *Model Middle America.* If I won, Mom would come back home and finally love me. Losing the show's competition meant that I would lose Mom all over again.

"There are more specific questions I have for you about what happened with the doughnuts," AB continued. "I was surprised you could keep your mind so well when the effects started happening. I'm willing to bet it has something to do with your metabolism, but I'll need to do some more tests on it if I'm going to perfect my recipe even more."

"Eh … what?" I put my hands on my now-perfect hips. "We're not actually going to test that, are we?"

"We'll have to. Oh, don't give me that look, Kallie," AB scoffed. "You don't have the mind of a scientist, do you? There are questions that need to be answered."

"Like why I was able to stop that gunman guy?"

"Oh, no. That's easy to explain. The serum is supposed to work more as a defense mechanism."

"But why?" I asked. "If the serum turns you into your worst fear, why would you need to defend yourself?"

"It's meant for our enemies, Kallie. We don't actually want to save them." She sighed. "I don't expect you to understand geo-political strategy here, but suffice to say, we need to be able to kill our enemies without our other enemies knowing that we're the ones behind it."

"We?" I asked.

"It's complicated. Don't worry about that." AB pulled on a thick pair of reading glasses, hiding her blue eyes behind the half-moon lenses. "Anyway, that was the purpose of my research for the last decade or so."

"Isn't chemical and biological warfare illegal under the Geneva convention?" There was a large lump in my throat as I suddenly looked around. Was it actually possible that I was an accidental superhero standing in the middle of an intentional supervillain's lab?

And if AB was racist, it had to be said: she wasn't *that* far from genocidal, was she?

"That's where the tricky part comes back up," AB said. "Don't worry about that either."

"This … doesn't sound good." I took another step back.

Maybe I should call the cops …

But I had a nasty feeling if I did, I would only get laughed at or thrown in the crazy house.

"This is my work, Kallie." AB pursed her lips and then sighed. "And more importantly, it's been stolen."

"Stolen?"

"I mentioned earlier that we had worse problems on our hands," AB said. "And that's true. But it's also true that it's worse than you could possibly imagine."

I didn't know about that; I'd bloated up like a parade balloon and nearly flattened a terrorist only the day before.

"I worked for the NAH," AB explained. "This recipe is part of my research. It's what I've been working on for the last decade and even before that. It's a weapon that we've made to have our enemies destroy themselves."

"Why can't you just kill our enemies?" I asked. "And who are these enemies, anyway?"

"We can't always just kill people," AB said. "That's preposterous. Someone would get suspicious."

"And someone won't get suspicious of suddenly fattened people rolling over gunmen?" I cocked my eyebrow at her.

"That's *your* fear," AB said. "Do you know what terrorists fear most, Kallie?"

"No. Death, I imagine."

"No." AB shook her head, her eyes narrowing into darkened slits. "Powerful men—or women—fear the loss of power, respect, and dignity on the world stage. They hate to relinquish their command to others. Sometimes they have accumulated enough power that we can't just jump in and bring it all down at once. More than one American war has been needlessly prolonged because we hit our enemies too hard and too fast. The number of innocent people who have suffered and died because we wanted to 'just go in and kill everyone' has exponentially increased."

I didn't honestly know much about that.

"Hmm." AB rubbed her chin. "Come to think of it, they aren't so different from your mother, to be honest."

"Hey!" I scowled. "That's not true!"

"Not exactly true in practice, but the theory is similar enough." She walked up to her largest screen and began typing. "That might explain why we didn't get along though."

"Dad told me you'd had a high-pressure job," I said, watching as AB pulled up diagrams and other files written in codes and languages I didn't recognize.

"Please, your mother never cared for me." AB rolled her eyes. "But we're not going to be able to worry about that now. Right now, you just need to know that the recipe is mine, and it was stolen. And then I was fired from my job last month."

Well, *that* was surprising, I had to admit. "You were fired?"

"Imitation serums were found being sold on the black market, and I was framed."

"Imitation serums?" From where I was standing, I saw AB's fist furl up on her desk.

"Yes. Project: SERUM requires testing to refine it," AB explained. "Once the original recipe was stolen, the project file was cancelled, and the Alterants we were already testing were destroyed after I was fired. Or so they told me."

Alterants? My head was starting to hurt. There was something so incredibly wrong about all of this, and I didn't know where to start. I had enough at this point.

"Why are you telling me this?" I asked. "Isn't there some kind of secret government code that I can't be allowed to have certain knowledge of without some kind of clearance?"

"This is the kind of stuff that can get you killed, Kallie, not to mention ruin your father's life and everyone else's as well."

I gulped. "Then why are you telling me? I know I'm the one who's ingested your poison stuff, but I didn't mean to. And now I'm fixed, and you know not to make Darla Donut lookalikes. So we don't have to worry about it ever again."

"We have to worry about it, I'm afraid." To my personal horror, AB was not joking around. Her face was stark, and her eyes were clear, and she was looking at me in a deadly serious way.

"I don't want to," I said.

"You don't even know what I'm asking of you."

"I know it's asking too much."

"Kallie."

"No, don't you 'Kallie' me."

"Would you prefer your new nickname, *Fatgirl*, then?" AB's mocking voice was edged with impatience.

"Shut up!" I started to storm out of her room. "I don't owe you anything."

"Excuse me, but who's the one who made sure to blur your face over in those pictures in the media? The one who's had all the security tapes destroyed?" AB scoffed. "You don't realize how much potential trouble you can get into now that you've made a spectacle of yourself."

I stopped moving, filled with dread.

I didn't want to ask how many favors my grandmother had called in last night; I had a feeling she wouldn't have a problem lying about how many she actually did call in if she thought it would convince me to go along with her plans.

"It's not my fault the FBI's most wanted showed up at *Model Middle America*," I argued back, desperate not to lose this battle.

"No, it's not."

"He's in jail now, so I should be fine. I saw him with the Officer who caught him."

AB paused. From the expression on her face, she seemed torn between pleasure and perversion, and then she pressed down on one of her keyboards. The mug shot of Frank Whitey lit up a nearby screen like an ugly clown-in-a-box. "While they were moving him to the city's jail, he managed to escape police custody."

"What?" I leaned forward, looking over the file, doing everything I could not to spiral into morbid rage. "How could they lose him?"

"There's no official report, because they think Frank's got a man on the inside," AB explained. "From what one of my contacts told me, they're unable to move. Since my contact was able to get a hold of the files with your face on them, we owe him something."

She didn't have to tell me what the biggest part of her plan was. From what she'd told me, she was essentially blackmailing me into helping now.

She straightened her jacket with obvious pride. "Don't worry. I have a plan."

She pointed up to the roof of her room, and then I heard it: a small buzzer went off upstairs.

The oven.

"Oh, no," I whimpered. "Please, no. I don't want to eat anymore doughnuts."

"Why not?" AB asked. "They're hot and ready for you, Fatgirl, as is your adoring public."

She took me by the arm—right at the top of the elbow, where the pressure point is, and dragged me out of her high-tech room, pulling me up the stairs as I tried to fight back.

"Stop," I yelled.

"Come on, Kallie, you have the entire day off school anyway," AB insisted. "And you have the weekend to recuperate from engorging yourself."

"I don't want to be Fatgirl," I argued. "Haven't you seen me? I'm gorgeous. I'm radiant. I'm ravishing! I'm not a superhero. I'm a supermodel!"

"No you're not," AB said. "You didn't make the finals last night at your show."

"All thanks to your freaking doughnuts!"

"I'll have you know that my *freaking* doughnuts—and inventions like them—are responsible for the safety of the free world."

"That's not true, or you wouldn't be in this mess," I shot back as we made it back into the kitchen.

At that, AB finally let me go.

"All right, fine. I can't reason with you. Let's talk instead." She shook her head. "What do you want?"

"I just want to be a normal teenager—"

"No, you want many things," she corrected me. "But I already know you don't want to be normal. No teenager really wants to be *normal.* There's nothing special about that."

"Okay, fine, I guess I do want to be a model." I threw up my hands, exasperated. "But there's no going back in time and stopping me from becoming Fatgirl at the Model Middle America audition, is there?"

The thought of the lab equipment in her room stopped me, and I put my hands on my hips, glaring at her with suspicion. "Or is there?"

"No, time travel is too big a task right now." AB shrugged noncommittedly, before she brightened. "But I could do something else for you. Something I know you desperately want."

"Oh, yeah?" I rolled my eyes. "What's that?"

I was expecting money or a maid, or possibly even some secret knowledge of Blake Turner's family that would allow me to date him. I blushed as I thought of that, hoping that wasn't the case; I didn't really want Blake to date me because of AB's interference … her direct interference, anyway.

"Your mother."

My tongue grew thick; this time, it was not because of any radioactive doughnuts. "What?" I asked, dumbfounded.

"You want your mother back, don't you?" AB waved her arm around, looking at the once-spotless kitchen I'd messed up the day before. "You want your mother to come home, and you want me to leave. Well, if you help me with this, I can make that happen."

"You have that kind of power?"

AB nodded.

I looked over at AB, looking her over carefully, checking her for any sign of deceit or desperation.

"Are you telling me the truth?" I finally asked. "You'll get my mom to come home, if I help you get your job back and find the bad guys and stuff?"

"I promise." AB held out her hand to me. "As much as it might pain me to do so, you have my word, and my word is my bond."

I didn't want to think about all the ways this could go wrong. All I wanted to think about was getting my mom back—and getting my record as Fatgirl scrubbed from history, while also not getting killed for knowing top secret government information.

"Please," AB said quietly. "I need your help. And the sooner you help me find the person who stole my formula, chase down the buyers, and catch the bad guy, the sooner I can go back to work, and you'll have your mother back."

While I went quiet, AB looked down at the floor—the first time I'd ever seen anything that looked remotely like humility and desperation on her face.

"Please, Kallie. I don't have anyone else I can really trust. Whoever framed me knew me well. As much as you want your mother back, I want my name cleared."

An uncomfortable amount of sympathy bubbled up inside of me like a bout of bad gas.

I knew what it was like to be alone and afraid. Amory and Uli, June and Lizzie, and even my dad and teachers were just people to me. I didn't actually have someone—maybe anyone—I could truly ask to help me if I needed it. AB might've been a sexist, racist, somewhat wily old woman who acted too white and drove too chaotically, but here she was, betrayed by an unknown, possibly would-be ally, off on her own, and in a new place and in a situation she definitely didn't want to be in.

I really didn't want to do this.

She was asking a lot of me, and I *didn't* want to do it.

I mean, I *really, really, really* didn't want to do it.

Fatgirl was the biggest mistake of my life, and even though somehow she was already a beloved hero to the public and a mystery to the media, that didn't mean I wanted to take up her mantle ever again—especially since said mantle might as well have been the saddle a mutant pig would wear at a carnival.

But I did, despite all of that, want to help my grandmother. I hated what I would have to do for her, but I didn't want her to feel the way I did: so hopelessly alone. Only able to really rely on myself.

So after a long moment of consideration, I finally gave in. "Okay."

I didn't like what was happening here.

I didn't like it at all.

But Mom…

At the thought of getting Mom back, I couldn't really say no.

Not right now, anyway.

"All right." I couldn't believe I was agreeing to this. I stuck out my hand, and AB took it at once. Her hands were old and pliant, a little papery to the touch. But there was a fire that I could feel inside of her, too, and for a moment, the bad gas inside of me waned.

"Well, look out, Frank Whitey." AB grinned. "We're about to meet at last."

She reached into her pocket and handed me my dark blue mask from the night before.

I didn't need any other hint to know she'd been planning this whole thing out since she'd heard of Frank's escape.

Seeing nothing else to do, I reluctantly pressed it down onto my face, hoping that the silicone stickiness would last just a bit longer.

"I'll make you a new suit," AB said as she reached down and opened the oven. At once, the smell of heavenly doughnuts wafted up to my nose, sending a tingling of delicious awareness through me. My mouth was already starting to water as she handed me a doughnut.

"I think I have a friend who can whip us up something really nice," she added. "He's done some great work with fabric."

"Don't worry about it," I said with a reluctant sigh, looking upstairs where my circus tent of a superhero costume was located. I tightened my fingers around the doughnut in my hand crumbling it a little. "This is a one-time thing, right?"

"We'll see."

I decided to ignore that. What else was there to do?

I glanced over to the side of the room, where the picture of Mom and Dad's wedding was crumpled on the floor in its shattered frame. If I wanted to get my mom back, I had a bad guy to catch, a favor to repay, my identity to hide, and a freaking doughnut to eat.

I looked at the doughnut in my hand, and my eyes nearly blurred over in tears.

I'd never thought a doughnut would betray me like this.

My fingers clenched the arm rest in AB's Imperial as we sped through Cuttingham City traffic again. *The Old-Bat-mobile*, I thought with a pained grimace. I was already starting to bloat up again, thanks to Abuela-Blanca's freaking doughnuts, and trying to find any bit of humor in this situation proved to be too much work.

"Frank has a few known hideouts, so if we want to avoid trouble, we'll have to catch him quickly. Kallie … Kallie, are you listening?" AB tried her best to keep my attention as she swerved dangerously close to another motorcycle; the rider honked at her, clearly irritated.

"This is my side of the road, so find another way to almost kill yourself!" AB yelled, shaking her fist at him as she sped up past him. "Kallie? Did you hear me?"

I squeezed my eyes shut as she slid over in front of an eighteen-wheeler. "I heard you just fine, but maybe we can get off the Interstate first?"

"You'll have to learn to multi-task sometime," AB said. "It's practically required of all women these days. Now, let me tell you what I know about Frank's whereabouts."

"Why do we need to catch this guy again?" I nearly shouted the question as I squeezed into the back of AB's Imperial. "Why can't the police do it?"

"He's seen you up close," AB reminded me. "It's better if I talk with him first and alter his memories—or something, you know. Work some taxpayer-funded magic on him. I just need you to catch him. That'll take care of the favor I owe my contact, and then they'll further be indebted since they don't have to publicly admit to their failures. So your identity will be safe, and I might be able to find out some information on who framed me."

"How is that related to me again?"

"Don't worry about that. Just keep him alive while I ask him questions, and then we'll get him to a drop-off zone where some other interested parties will be eager to pick him up."

"What do I do if I … hurt him?" I asked, remembering how I'd almost smothered him to death before.

"Don't worry about that, either." AB grinned as her Phi-ger started to chime. "Perfect! I've locked onto his frequency. It was lucky you almost killed him earlier, you know. Some residual radioactivity managed to get stuck to him."

If I didn't know any better, I'd have said AB was enjoying herself. As we followed the signal on her Phi-ger, heading down to the old city streets of Cuttingham City's present-day slums, I had an uncomfortable feeling I had to trust her—for now. She was clearly a lady who was determined to get done what needed to get done, and she would damn the world if it got in her way.

Which spoke volumes to me, belatedly, how dangerous what we were doing was.

Someone had managed to get AB fired from her job and frame her for selling the recipe for her radioactive doughnuts. Her own investigation had led her here, to Cuttingham City, right when my mother was out of town on a years-long business trip and my dad was struggling to raise me and work more than full-time.

"Can I change my mind on this?" I asked.

"No," AB snapped. "I need to talk to Frank. He's highly connected, and enough so that he might be able to help me find out more about where my recipe went and who sold it to whom."

I barely listened to her explain what happened with black markets and the dark web and other stuff. Between her criminal knowledge and her criminally bad driving, I just wanted Mom to come home again—and soon, before I got into more trouble.

I'd already embarrassed myself on national television and my fatty face was famous all over the Internet. Helping AB was the easiest way to solve my problems and get what I wanted.

Maybe if I'm good enough, AB will get me some modeling contracts, too.

She probably didn't want to do that, considering what she thought of my mother, but it wouldn't hurt to have something pop up close to Cuttingham City so Mom will be more eager to stay with me and Dad again.

The Phi-ger crackled brightly as we turned down the street.

"We're getting closer," AB said.

"How do you know?" I asked. "It could just be reacting to me, since I'm fatting out here."

"I've set it to lower-dosage frequencies for the isotope," AB explained. "You're putting out too much radiation for it to currently pick up on your emissions. There's also a little bit of a change in your radioactivity levels since your decomposition rates of the isotope have been accelerated by the reverse-serum I gave you before."

"Oh." I nodded, unsure of what she was talking about. "Okay, then. Good to know."

AB slowed her driving down. There were plenty of spray-painted symbols on the street signs, and there were several pairs of shoes draped over tree limbs and cable lines. There wasn't a lot of traffic—thankfully—but there didn't seem to be a lot of anything here. Just lines of old-looking shops and broken down brick apartments.

The Phi-ger clicked again, and I could see the little lines on its screen hurriedly jumble up and down, up and down. It was chiming like crazy, just as it had before.

"He's within twenty feet of us," AB said. "Perfect. I'll find a place to park while you go look for him."

"If he's so close to us, shouldn't we be able to see him?" I asked, suddenly uneasy. There was no sign of anyone remotely resembling Frank Whitey, and as much as I knew we needed to find him, I was glad we didn't see him.

Where could he be? Is it possible AB's device isn't working right?

"Remember, I will need him in *my* custody," AB said, ignoring my question. "Just find him, sit on him, and hold him down until I catch up to you. Don't let the police take him if they get there first."

"What police?" I scoffed as I glanced out the window. Already my widened girth was forcing me against the window; if we didn't move quickly, I would be stuck in the car. But even with my face smooshed against the window, I could see this was clearly a "no-snitch" area. I doubted the cops would come, unless I could give them a limp body.

At the thought, I looked down at my hot-dog-sized fingers, wondering if I would have to kill someone. Quickly, I firmly shook my head. I'd already sacrificed my body to help AB here. I didn't want to have to sell my soul, too.

"Stop rolling around," AB said. "You're bouncing the car around."

"Sorry," I muttered, slumping down.

"Oh, it's fine. You should get out though. You're getting too heavy for the car." She pointed to her dashboard. "My gas mileage plummeted about ten minutes ago."

"Gee, thanks for letting me know." I tugged at the blue hood I'd pulled over my head, straining the fabric over my face as I blushed with shame.

"I'll turn down this alley," AB said. "Get out at the corner, and make it look like you're entering the street from above, okay?"

"Sure, Captain Crazy."

"Excuse me?" In the rearview mirror, I saw AB cock her brow. "What was that?"

"What?" I sniffed. "If I have 'Fatgirl' attached to me, you might as well have a nickname, too, and 'Captain Racist' might be too spot-on."

"Just go," AB snapped, swerving the car into a hard left. "I'll join you as quickly as possible."

I didn't have time to tell her that it wouldn't be a bad idea if she had a costume anyway; as Old White Lady Extraordinaire, she and her bright white Imperial already stood out like a sore thumb in this part of town.

As soon as she jerked the car into the small alleyway, I unlocked the car and burst out, my girth already back to the size it had been the night before.

AB revved her engines and sped out of there, leaving me. I rolled onto the ground, squealing with disgust as my face hit the cement—no physical damage, but the smells were pungently overwhelming.

"Oh, yuck!" I coughed and sputtered, hurrying to use my momentum to roll myself into an upright stance. I wobbled a bit, but I finally managed to fix myself.

"Don't you dare let your face turn red," I grumbled under my breath. Hot pink and red didn't match, and I was already making enough of a spectacle of myself. Thankfully, I didn't have much of an audience, especially when I thought of the large crowds at the Model Middle America audition.

Here, out in the slums and in the streets, there was practically no one.

There were a few shadows that seemed to disappear into the walls as I left the alleyway and looked around the surrounding streets.

Some guys in hooded sweatshirts glanced over at me and laughed, pointing at me.

"Hey, Fatgirl," one of them called. "Looking for some action?"

Catcalls were nothing compared to fatcalls, I thought bitterly.

But at least I knew how to deal with both.

"Sure am, boys," I said instead, using their taunting as an invitation to use them as volunteers to practice out my supposed superhero powers.

○ ○ ○ ○

Several moments later, it felt good to watch my catcallers run away. I looked on their loud crying faces while they gripped their swollen retreating backsides with a sense of pride and accomplishment, even if beating them was not the job I'd set out to do.

"I hope you think about that backlash next time you're tempting to fat-call someone," I shouted after them, enjoying the feeling that I could do no wrong after I'd set out to make the world right. "I'll send your mother the spanking bill!"

It was intoxicating, and even more of a thrill to realize models were only ever supposed to look pretty; they never got cool catchphrases and no one really ever asked for their opinions on important things unless they were dating someone related to those important things.

I brushed off my hands, and then I remembered I was supposed to be looking for Frank Whitey.

Turning around, I stared around the street.

Several buildings were boarded up; brick buildings didn't seem to house anyone.

Is this really where a wanted criminal would hang out?

"Yes," I said, answering myself.

I looked through some of the dirty glass of some of the businesses, the ones which didn't have wooden panels boarded over up over them.

I made it to the end of the street with no leads.

A loud sigh escaped me.

It figured that I would eat more of AB's freaking doughnuts, only to end up just sitting on a sidewalk, fat, lonely, and made fun of. I sat down on the curb, depressed and annoyed I'd done anything at all.

That was when a familiar smoky smell made my nose twitch.

Frank Whitey's breath.

"Ew,"I muttered, trying to wave the smell away, even though I knew I should've tried to find the source. "He must be a smoker."

Or just a guy who didn't brush his teeth. Or both.

I shuddered at the thought. Either way, it was disgusting, and I wanted to get away. My hands slipped on the ground as I wiggled my way back up to my feet. I tripped and fell forward onto my stomach, feeling the roughness of the cemented streets through my superhero suit enough that I could suddenly empathize with a beached whale to the point where I didn't move for a long moment.

It was only the thought of AB coming around as Street Whale Rescue that made me attempt to right myself.

That, of course was when I managed to lodge my arm in the sidewalk drain instead and get my sleeve stuck.

"Of course," I muttered. If I managed to get a hold of any street camera footage of me, I could add a laugh track with some "whoo-whoo-whoo" sound effects and break the Internet.

I pulled hard, but my sleeve only started to rip; I stuck my head under the street gutter, ready to see how I could pull myself free.

Only to see a familiar face in the sewer staring back at me.

Frank Whitey.

Through the darkness, I could see his eyes glaring up at me.

"It's you!" we both exclaimed aloud at the same time. The cigarette he'd been smoking fell to the ground and fizzled out in the dank puddles.

The strangeness of our surprised song echoed throughout the sewer passage.

Frank was the one who was much more seasoned when it came to shock—of course, I'd never seen a so-called superhero like myself before, so my estimates of my own shock value were going to be way off—and he quickly pulled out his gun.

"No, don't," I yelped, reaching for his arm. I missed, and I knew it was over.

It had to be, right?

I was a stupid teenager going up against a crime boss,

My lips trembled, and I let out a small whimper and squeezed my eyes shut. The last thing I saw was the black barrel of Frank's gun and all I could think about was how much I wanted my mom.

There was a small *click*, and then a shuffle.

My eyes opened up tentatively, slowly peeking around.

I saw Frank run off into the darkness, and I breathed a prayer of thanks.

I—not without some trouble—dislodged my arm. I hurried over to the manhole, but came to a sudden stop when I realized I wouldn't be able to fit inside …

"Ugh." My hands run down over my flabby face, dragging down my skin.

A bridge…

I vaguely recalled a nearby bridge. There would be openings in the drainage system I could get through. I should be able to climb in there.

I start running down the street, wishing I had a new cell phone. AB had her Phi-ger to find me if she needed to, but I wouldn't be able to tell her

I can't believe I am doing this.

The thought crossed my mind once more as I made a dash for the bridge reservoir, gritting my teeth as my knees buckled under my increased body weight.

I didn't like it, but I knew why I was here.

I would do anything for my mom to come home, and I would do anything to remain safe while I waited for her—even comb through the city's slums and sewers to find a terrorist.

Getting into the sewers should have been harder. It wasn't easy, sliding down an overpass, climbing into drainage pipe, and even breaking through a weakened, rusted grate—but it really should've been harder.

Despite all that, it was the big mess that the mud and sewage lines made that made me struggle the most.

Well, that and the running.

I was never much for running, and as I huffed and puffed, the smell and stitch in my side forcing me to breathe through my nose, it looked like Coach Keelson would have her revenge for my gym sock rebellion.

"This … is … awful," I gasped.

My voice echoed loudly back at me, forcing me to realize how bleak and dark my whole surroundings were.

Oh, great. This is just great.

I pulled my hood tighter around my face, desperate to keep the stench in the air. I glanced down, realizing that my legs—now these thick, tree-like limbs of power and muscle underneath my body—were wet up to the middle of my thighs.

I didn't actually *want* AB to make me a new suit. I wanted this to be the absolute last time I was forced to do this or even think about this.

That's why you need to get Frank. He saw you up close and he could identify you. AB will wipe his memory or something and get the info she needs to find out who stole her recipe.

It suddenly struck me how very Southern the whole thing was. If we'd been a hundred years in the past, it'd be like Granny would be on a rampage for the person who stole her church potluck recipe.

The image made me smile a little, at least, and that gave me some comfort as I moved slowly through the sewers. My eye were narrowed and my ears were perked, ready to jump on any sounds that sounded more human than rat or sludge monster.

Thinking of monsters, I wondered how Amory and my other friends would react hearing I was Fatgirl.

I guess I didn't really wonder how, so much as how badly.

My life would literally be ruined. Forever. And not just on the legal level, the one AB could apparently handle.

An almost-famous model like me couldn't have a bad hair day with my reputation getting called into question. Gaining weight was a big fat no-no, especially if it was clearly obvious despite any attempts to hide it with a waist trainer or make up or even blaming my period.

I wouldn't be able to walk into school without people whispering about me, pointing at me, never leaving me be until they've drained me of all possible hope for any speck of self-esteem and my soul has bled out, and I die quietly curled up in a fetal position, probably licking doughnut powder off my fingers as my only source of comfort in this cruel, cruel world.

No.

I would never eat doughnuts again, I decided. Not even Darla Donuts.

My parents' marriage was over, wasn't it? What good was there in eating the doughnuts that had brought them together?

A grunt reverberated from up ahead; I could barely hear it as the water around me began to run faster. I was heading back toward the slums where I'd seen Frank hiding.

The sewers seemed like such a fitting place for a guy with the FBI after him to hide. I cringed at the dark, dank, and dreary atmosphere. The cement walls were black and dirty, and there were rats that scurried around my feet as I turned corners and skipped over service lines.

I did my best to keep my hand over my mouth—to protect myself from tasting the putrid air any more than I had to, and to keep myself from crying out in disgust. I walked around, wondering how long it would take for either AB to find me, or for me to find Frank.

This whole thing is like an ADD game of hide and seek. I reeled back as I walked into a spider web.

"Ugh!" I batted at the web, skirting forward quickly, coming upon a place where the sewer lines opened up to a service area. There were floors' worth of machines, all buzzing and lit up with power as they cleaned and processed the incoming flow. I gazed down, seeing a waterfall-like operation set up.

That was when I saw him.

Frank Whitey's familiar form was walking along a crosswalk, passing over a large water tank.

"Got you," I hissed under my breath as I moved forward

I skirted after him, keeping my steps as silent as possible. It was when I managed to get on the same walkway—making it rock horribly, thanks to all my weight—that Frank finally saw me.

"Not you again, Pinky," he grumbled, pulling out his gun.

I waddled onto the walkway more forcefully, messing up his aim. It was a risky gamble, and I nearly screamed as the bullets sounded out in all directions. I didn't know where he'd ended up shooting, but I saw a few lights shatter by the top of the waterfall. An alarm went off, hiding the exact words of Frank's sudden storm of cussing.

He ran toward an exit, but I managed to follow. The walkway shuddered under the pressure of my feet.

"Whoops!" I tripped and stumbled forward, rolling into Frank as he tugged on a locked door.

I slammed him into the wall harder than I'd meant—really, I hadn't meant to do that at all—and he grunted in pain.

"Get off me," he shouted. "I'm tired of being flattened by you and all your fat."

My face flushed over in embarrassment, but I held my head high. "If you'd just come with me, you don't have to worry about it ever again."

"What do you want?"

"I want you to go to jail," I said. "But I need to talk to you first. Or, well, someone I know needs to talk to you first."

"The Feds sent you?"

"No," I scoffed. "Please. They don't want someone like me doing a better job than they are. I'm embarrassed to be me, so I imagine they'd be even more embarrassed if I outmatched them."

Frank started inching back away from me. "I'm not going to jail. My ride will be here any moment, then you'll be dead."

"Well, plans might change," I said, trying to feel clever if I wasn't going to be pretty at least.

When his eyes closed and he laughed menacingly, I lunged for him.

He'd been waiting for me to move; he launched himself upwards and down another sidewalk. I hurried to catch up, but he pulled out his gun again.

I hurriedly reversed, ducking into a crevice in the wall as he climbed up the exit ladder.

When he moved to reload, I hurried and reached for his foot.

I didn't think about what the slime on his shoe was as I pulled him down, hard, and he dropped his gun as he fought to shake me off.

He let go of the ladder a moment later, allowing himself to fall halfway down the length of it. His body slammed into mine, and I fell back.

"Ow!" I yelped, standing up and rubbing my sore behind.

Frank laughed. "Just go home. You don't have to do this, you know. If you're worried I'll say something about who you might be, you can trust me to keep quiet on who you could be. Not a lot of fat chicks out there as gargantuan as you, but either way, I've a reputation to uphold. Getting flattened by someone like you isn't going to evoke sympathy or even amusement among my crowd."

AB had told me before that my mother wasn't too different from a terrorist when it came to motivation; was it possible that, as grotesque as Frank was, he and I weren't that different, either?

Angry at the thought, I reached over and tentatively grabbed the fallen gun; I was either going to prove that I was nothing like him, or I was going to stop him.

Of course, Frank likely had more years of experience with guns. I held his weapon the way I'd seen in movies, and it turned out movies didn't really portray guns realistically. It was heavy and hard, and I didn't even know if there were bullets in it still or not.

I aimed the barrel up at him and squeezed as hard as I could on the trigger, just to see if *something* would work.

I was as shocked as he was when it fired. The empty round nearly hit me in the face as it went flying, and I squeaked out a shout as the bullet rammed into the ladder near Frank. I could see little sparks as they showered down, and I almost smiled at my luck.

"Put that thing away," Frank yelled. "It's clear you don't know how to handle it."

I didn't argue with him. I was probably breaking the law, shooting a gun when I didn't have a license. Vaguely, I remembered that Dad had mentioned once about taking me out hunting in the country, and Mom had promptly shot that idea down.

Hurriedly, I tossed the gun down into the water stream nearby.

Frank was right about me, so I would have to get him with my own power.

He resumed his trek up to the top of the ladder, and I quickly followed. The ladder buckled dangerously under my weight, and I let out a sigh. Frank groaned as the ladder shook as badly as the walkway had, and he hung on for dear life as I sped up after him.

"Wait," I called after him, as I saw him reach the top.

"You really don't know how this business works, do you?" Frank snorted down at me.

I scowled, but I said nothing as I used my weight and muscle to pull myself up even more quickly.

A second later, I gripped the final rung firmly, silently cheering at my accomplishment.

And then it broke, and then I fell.

I grabbed at another rung and dug in my heels. The weight was too much, and the ladder broke underneath my feet.

"Help!" It was my turn to scream as I clung to the broken ladder. The metal bar holding me crumbled in my hand as I tightened my grip. My legs were swinging wildly as I panicked, kicking and pressing against the wall to find some kind of foothold.

Frank suddenly stood over me. "You shouldn't have come after me, big girl."

"Hey, you're the one who shouldn't have tried to shoot up a TV show," I said. "Funny how you never think of what you're supposed to do."

Frank's foot slammed down on my fingers.

"Ouch," I yelped, before he ground his heel against my knuckles. My grip along the ladder rung weakened.

The metal creaked and I knew my time was limited.

But what can I do?

I frantically looked around, but there was nothing. I had no idea how to save myself.

The rung began to splinter, and I looked down below me. Would I be able to survive the fall? It couldn't have been more than twenty feet …

I gasped as Frank shifted his aim. His foot collided with my head, and I yelled in protest.

"This is it," he said. His breathing was heavy as he raised his knee and prepared to strike again.

"No," I whimpered.

Frank shook his head. "Not this time, Fatgirl."

My fingers slipped on the ladder rung; it snapped, and one of my hands dropped. Frank laughed triumphantly.

It's over. This is over.

I squeezed my eyes shut to prepare for the coming blow; The last thing I saw before everything went dark was Frank's ugly, dirty shoe as it headed toward my face.

"No!"

Fatgirl

FANDOM MENACE

EPISODE 3

○ ○ ○ ○

C. S. Johnson

FATGIRL
FANDOM MENACE

○ ○ ○ ○

"No!"

Despite its ferocity, my scream was drowned out by the sounds of the sewer around me. A flowing waterfall and leaking pipes emitted hissing wisps of air, and in what was sure to be my last moment of life, I took in every inch of my surrounding ugliness and reluctantly marveled at it.

After all, it's not every day you find yourself hanging from the top of a ladder, leaning against a sanitation filter, in the middle of a sewer, under the ghetto parts of your home city, getting kicked around by the FBI's most wanted, all while musty, moist fumes waft into your nostrils and you have to wonder if it's from the atmosphere or the home-grown terrorist standing over you.

I'm going to kill Abuela-Blanca.

She was the reason I was here, after all—right along with her radioactive doughnuts that had the body-altering ability to bring about a person's worst fear.

Remembering that, I almost snorted; if death was suddenly what I feared most, thanks to my grandmother's radioactive doughnuts, perhaps that meant I would become invincible? Or maybe immortal?

Well, if I did, it would be just in time to die of embarrassment.

I snapped back to attention as the bad guy's shoe smacked into my face.

My enlarged cheeks absorbed the blow, but the jolting pressure made the rung of the ladder I was hanging creak horribly. I held my breath, anxiously praying it would hold.

The slimy shoe hit me again.

"Nosy brat."

Notorious bad guy Frank Whitey's voice was quiet enough I could barely hear him, but loud enough I knew he was fed up with me. In that long, eternal moment, I looked up at his gruff, middle-aged face and felt nothing but anger and irritation.

Only yesterday, Frank had tried to take the whole audience of the Cunningham City Amphitheatre hostage, holding them up with his goons and his guns while I—along with a good portion of other girls who longed to be a model—competed for the title of America's Next Top Heartland Teen Heartthrob from the *Model Middle America* TV show. After accidentally becoming Fatgirl, I'd accidentally stopped him, and now I had to re-capture him, make sure he wouldn't be able to recognize me, and get some information about the whereabouts of a radioactive doughnut recipe.

So far into this mission, Frank had insulted me, shot at me, and now he was repeatedly slamming his filthy, slime-covered foot in my face, trying to get me to fall even faster.

It was time to do something, I decided.

And that's when something else happened.

Snap!

The ladder broke just as my face stung, and I found myself falling.

Desperately, I reached out, clawing for anything that would save me.

I managed to grab hold of the only thing I could—Frank's foot.

"Let go!" he yelled. Frank stumbled and fell back, while I only kept climbing, practically rolling over him thanks to my surprising strength.

Seconds later, I blinked to find I'd slammed down on top of him again, much like I had at my audition.

Fatgirl was sitting on her target, hurray.

I grimaced, even as adrenaline pumped through me; my hands were too thick to really be shaking. I panted, trying to steady myself, and looked around.

I was on top of a small balcony, where there were old, dirty exit signs, half-lit, were hung on along the wall. Below me, I could still hear the trickling water of the sewers, and I could even feel its churning power held back by the sturdy pipes.

I cheered silently as I saw little beams of barely-there daylight, shyly poking through a manhole cover.

"Thank God," I muttered, even though Frank was once more yelling and screaming at me; his cussing and curses were interrupted by pants for breath and choking noises; I ignored him, straining my ears for any indication I was not going to be stuck in this position for long.

"Stupid girl, get off—!"

Apparently, Frank was just as concerned about that as I was.

"Just shut up, would you?" I leaned forward and stuffed my arm across his face, making sure his mouth was unable to move but he could still breathe through his nose.

What else could I do at this point?

I can't believe this.

I literally couldn't believe this. I mean, I'd barely managed to capture him, but I did it.

An unfamiliar thrill of accomplishment ran through me, as I basked in my momentary victory. How many teenagers my age could say they've captured a criminal—especially one as clearly vile and disgusting as Frank Whitey? And not just once, but twice in the last two days.

The adults had screwed up, and I had to pick up their slack.

I grinned. Maybe there was somewhat of a financial reward with this, too! Maybe I could get enough to go visit Mom in LA and tell her all about—

Oh. Right.

My feeling of accomplishment dimmed as I remembered I wouldn't be able to tell anyone about this. I mean, I didn't really *want* to tell people the details, but it was still something new for me. The hardest things I'd had to overcome usually involved starving myself or beating Amory at one of our friendly fire social media competitions, where we had to passive-aggressively or backhandedly compliment each other until there was a clear winner.

The rush of physically taking down a real-life criminal was truly satisfying, and in a way I'd never felt before.

As I basked in my newfound glory, there was a movement in the shadows, and I looked up to see none other than Abuela-Blanca appear out of the darkness.

For once, I could see where all my grandmother's white-ladyness came in handy. She looked more than a little ghostly and malevolent as she came forward. I could see the small revolver in her gloved hand, completely mismatched against her Chanel-like outfit. A small, beeping noise sounded out from the bag on her shoulder.

The Phi-ger was still working.

"Hello, Frank," AB said as she approached us. "I suppose I must apologize for my informality, but I feel as though I know you. I studied your profile in my post-graduate studies on criminology."

At that, I decided Frank's muffled words were better left to the imagination. I could feel him literally shaking with rage underneath me.

"I'll admit my associate is a bit surprising, and that doesn't help you at all, clearly," AB continued, moving forward. She dropped her bag next to him and began pulling out different items, many of which seemed unnecessarily frightening.

"What're you going to do?" I asked, watching as AB flicked a switch on the Phi-ger.

"Does it matter?" AB arched her brow at me as the beeping stopped. "I'm a scientist first, remember. I'd love to do some experiments."

"I'd really rather you didn't," I said, unable to stop myself from groaning.

"I'll wager you'll like this one. Hold your breath and move away, Fatgirl," she said, and before I could tell her off for calling me *that name*, I remembered she was here to prevent him from recognizing me in the future, and that probably entailed not using my actual name.

AB dropped a cloth over his nose; I could smell traces of it as its scent drifted past me. It was a violently sour smell, but also an intriguing one, like day-old cabbage boiled in hot sauce-flavored lollipops. Once I moved, Frank began to call us vile names again. But the instant he breathed in, everything about him slowed.

Despite his very best attempts—including an instance of flipping AB the bird—the rest of his body went limp a moment later.

"That's a special toxin called Agent Iris," AB explained. "It's designed to act like a muscle reboot system, specifically inhibiting voluntary movements while it forces the brain to reconnect its sensors. It doesn't last for long, so watch him while I get started, Fatgirl."

"Shut up," I muttered darkly.

"There's the charm. No wonder you're a sensation already."

I scoffed and folded my arms over my chest, silently fuming while trying to ignore how much funnier I probably looked.

AB hummed as she worked. It was almost like a strange dance, watching her. Her movements were both mechanical and methodical, but also majestic. Her hands were a white blur as she pulled samples and organized her testing tubes. I'd done some science class work before, but I'd never seen a real scientist work. Not unless you counted Mr. Pineda, my Biology teacher, which I'll admit, I didn't, since he was only a teacher, and not someone who worked in the field.

I wondered all over again if I was in the presence of a terrorist *and* a mad scientist as AB pulled out her another device.

It was a strange-looking device, a little like the Phi-ger, with a boxy shape and a readout screen. This one had a couple of wires lopped around and attached to two sticks, one red and the other black, both covered in a clear plastic mold. It made me think about the battery jumper in Dad's old car, and the resemblance didn't stop as the device crackled with electricity.

I pointed at it. "What's that?"

"You don't need to worry about it," AB said.

That was quickly becoming her standard reply to me, and I had a feeling she was doing her NAH type of work, something that wasn't completely ethical, but she could justify in the moment.

"Okay." AB stepped back a moment later and took me aside. "I'll get the info, alter his mind a bit, and then I'll need you to carry him to a drop-off sight. While you take him there, I'll meet up with my source on the squad. We'll be able to pay him back from altering the tapes with your face on it. And once I'm done with Frank here"—his eyes bulged fearfully underneath his lids—"we don't have to worry about him anymore."

"Those are the only videos of me, right?" I asked. "The ones the police have?"

"If we fulfill our end, my source will take care of his. But one step at a time." AB pulled out her gun again. "First, I have questions."

Before I could stop her, I watched as she shot her gun. I shrieked as it went off. Earlier, I'd thought the gunshots had been loud. This time, just from being closer to the source, it was a hundred times worse.

Bang!

"What are you doing?" I yelled, torn between grabbing my ears and strangling AB. "Don't do that!"

"Let me handle this," AB warned. "I'm a trained professional."

"*Professional* what?" My heart pounded loudly between my ears, pushing back against the sound of the bullet being shot.

I clamped my hands over my ears as AB raised the gun again, and that's when I saw Frank's expression. His eyes were dilated and he seemed desperate to breathe faster, almost as if I was watching him have a panic attack in slow motion. He'd clearly heard the shot.

"Who're you? I can't see." His words were slurred.

"There's no need to worry," AB said, her voice much more calming and mesmerizing as she spoke. I stared at her, terrified as much as intrigued. "You're safe, Frank. Completely safe."

"Whattya want?"

"You'll see." AB glanced over at me. "How squeamish are you?"

Before I could answer her, she took the battery charger sticks and jammed them into Frank's temples.

"Hey!" I gasped as Frank tried to scream. His tongue lapped out of his mouth and his voice cut off at different times.

While I was freaking out and Frank was probably soiling himself, AB calmly continued on.

"If I'm going to alter his memories, I need to be able to work," AB hissed at me. "I know what I'm doing. Trust me."

"What if I don't?"

AB looked sadistically amused. "I can always alter your memories."

I went silent after that, focusing all my concentration on making sure I would remember that moment for the rest of my life, no matter what.

AB talked with Frank, asking him regular questions, periodically adjusting the small knobs and buttons on her device.

All while this was happening, Frank was lying flat on the floor, his blinded irises shaking. I could see his fingers were twitching, and his voice had gradually become more clear.

I didn't particularly care about anything they discussed—favorite colors, politics, family, etc. And then Abuela-Blanca asked the question I could tell she'd been waiting for.

"Frank, what do you know about Project: SERUM?"

"Only whispers. Edible fear." Frank's response was strange and chilling.

"Who's whispering?" AB asked. "Tell me. Who told you?"

"Not told. Invited." Frank cleared his throat. "ZZ's retiring. Wants to auction it off."

I turned my attention to AB. There wasn't a wrinkle of surprise on her face. Perhaps this—all of this—was more of a confirmation than anything else?

I'll kill her if this is for nothing.

AB pushed another button on her device. I watched as the earlier electricity crinkled up again and zapped Frank, rendering him unconscious. I winced as the little sparks made his hair stand on end, and after a good minute, I finally grabbed the device out of AB's hand.

"That's enough, don't you think?" I snapped. "You've already drugged him up."

"Agent Iris' influence is almost gone." AB frowned but turned off her device. "If you are inclined to give mercy to others, you'll be surprised when they object to justice."

"You got what you wanted from him, didn't you?" I nudged him with my boot.

"I did." AB began to put her gear away. "Now we need to get him to my contact before Frank's minions find us. He was here for a reason."

Now she tells me. I glanced around, looking to see if we were being watched. I didn't see anyone, but I could feel the hair on the back of my neck start to tingle.

"The police will be headed toward the drop-off zone I've selected soon." AB tucked her revolver back into her purse. "You'll take him there and make sure the police pick him up."

"Didn't you say there's supposed to be a mole on the police squad?" I asked. Now that the hard part was done, I wanted to make sure it would *stay* done this time.

"Yes, and that's why we will make sure he gets picked up. I'll be able to follow his progress to the police station thanks to the Phiger." She pulled out the familiar beeping device.

"What if he gets away again?" I asked.

"That's why we watch him," AB repeated, rolling her eyes. "Frank's a seasoned fugitive. He's been doing this a long time. He's getting old, clearly, and he'll need to learn a lot of new tricks when he feels better. But let's go. If he doesn't rendezvous at the pick-up location, his allies will come looking for him. We'll worry about the rest of your questions after he's back in custody."

Roughly an hour later—after I hauled Frank out of the sewers, dropped him off in a back alleyway twenty blocks away from where we found him and the police, including the familiar Officer Powers, successfully picked him up—I allowed myself to worry about those other questions.

I was in the back of Abuela-Blanca's Imperial, thankfully deflating. She'd given me the anti-serum only moments before, and while I was still pretty bloated, I could feel my skin starting to constrict. I was sitting on my hands, trying not to itch myself; it wasn't a pleasant feeling, even though I looked forward to the results.

Looking around me, I was amazed all over again how I'd survived all of that.

And it was another miracle that I wasn't dead from AB's driving, either. I held in my breath—and my breakfast—as she whirled the car in front of the van ahead of us and cut another driver off.

"If you're going to drive the speed limit in the left lane, why not just retire to a nursing home, you dingbat?" AB scoffed, slamming her foot down on the gas hard enough to make it rev.

After the other driver honked at AB, she leaned on her own horn in reply. She exhaled almost like she was blowing out steam through her nostrils.

"Are you okay?" I asked.

"It's nothing. Nothing out of the norm, anyway." She wrinkled her nose, making the rest of her face even more wrinkled. "I should've figured ZZ had her hand in the honeypot."

"Who's ZZ?" I tried to keep my voice calm, but it was hard as we swerved into another lane. *Maybe if I talk as calmly as AB did with Frank earlier, she'll slow down some.*

I didn't think it was really going to work, but I decided to try—for my own semi-peace of mind, if nothing else.

"Hmmm." AB's blue eyes were frosty in her rear-view mirror. "Do you really want to know?"

I paused. In truth, I was curious, but it was a lot easier to squash down my curiosity than to keep asking questions that I knew would likely get me into trouble. And I'd literally had enough trouble today for two lifetimes.

I mean, really, the only upside to this was that I would have a lot more confidence as I walked through my school hallways. I'd taken down an experienced terrorist. What could mere high schoolers do to me?

AB turned onto the exit ramp, cutting off a truck. I bit down on my lip to stop from screaming as it nearly hit us.

Ask the question. You won't live otherwise.

"Yes," I said. "Tell me who ZZ is."

"She's the daughter of a former KGB agent and a talent agent from LA. Her real name is Zina Morozova. She also goes by Zina Zova, hence 'ZZ.' Frank's likely known her for years." Abuela-Blanca frowned and slammed on the brake as we came to a red light. "A lot of men like her."

"So she's very popular, I take it?" I clutched the armrest.

"That's one way of putting it." AB coughed delicately. "The feeling is mutual, even if the motivation is not. She's the kind of woman who'd infect herself with AIDS just so she can say she's the one responsible for taking down James Bond, literally living up to her *femme fatale* title."

"Why hasn't anyone stopped her before?" I asked.

"She's a master of disguise, for one," AB explained. "And the other is that she's made a lot of connections over the years."

"So she's the one who has your recipe?"

"Frank said she was auctioning it off. I don't really mind that, but I need to know who gave it to her."

"But what if it gets into the wrong hands?" I asked. "Maybe you should try to figure out who else wants it."

"Everyone *wants* it, Kallie. US-issued developments are in huge demand around the world. But I don't care about that right now; I *can't* care about it. This is not a 'save the world' type of assignment for me. This is a 'clear my name, restore my honor' mission. We have to be focused on that goal as much as possible."

What was with this "we" stuff?" I frowned. And there were other things to consider, too. "But if something bad happens to others—"

"Something bad has *already* happened." She glanced back at me, looking up and down my bright pink deflated hot balloon of a super suit. "But I still don't regret making my recipe."

I could understand AB's perspective on this, but it was a little infuriating to think she didn't care too much about any potential victims that might come from her invention. And I guess that was the trouble with innovation. Unknown costs and sacrifices were sure to happen, and some people somewhere would suffer in the name of progress.

If radioactive doughnuts that transform you into your deepest fears can be considered "progress"…

"So." AB cleared her throat and curled her fingers around her steering wheel, clearly satisfied. "That means we'll have to find a way to crash ZZ's party."

"We?"

There was that *we* stuff again. I didn't like the sound of that.

I mean, I thought it was cool and everything, but only I *could* think it was cool and everything *because I was finished with my end of the bargain.*

I'd helped AB get Frank back to the police, so she didn't owe her inside guy a favor anymore; we even found out who had her recipe. AB, in turn, altered Frank's memories with her little car battery charger device and no one could know my identity any longer.

I didn't have to be Fatgirl anymore, and more importantly, I didn't want to be.

And the best part was, AB now owed me.

And I knew what I wanted more than anything else in the world.

I was just about to ask AB about bringing Mom home when AB turned the car down the street where we lived. My fingertips clawed the armrest. At the sharp turn as I wondered how a car as outdated as AB could handle corners without tipping over.

"I'll get started on the plans for ZZ. There's likely going to be some travel involved with that one. She's known for her eccentricity."

"It sounds like you'd get along."

"Please, I have standards, Kallie. Not to mention some morals."

Well, *that* was a surprise to hear.

AB turned off the car. "Well, either way, you don't have to worry about it just yet."

I crossed my arms. "That's easy for you to say."

"Exactly," AB agreed. "It's easy to say, and people who hear it think it's easy to achieve. It's a good thing to say if there's trouble."

"But it's not true."

"Sure," AB said with a huff. "Not necessarily, anyway. But if a man is having a panic attack or needlessly scared or borderline violent, you have to admit getting him to negotiate and talk will likely make things much better than if you let him go all crazy."

"Was that what you did with Frank?"

"Mostly."

I didn't like her tone.

"Is there a recipe for everything you do?" I tugged at the slightly loosened wrinkles of my superhero suit. "Like how you managed to turn people into their biggest fears?"

"That's not quite what Project: SERUM does. I explained it poorly before," Abuela-Blanca admitted. "There are other serums, several still under testing, but this was my project. And I loved working on it."

From her expression, it was clear she was wrapped up in the warmth of her memories, like a mother recalling the early hours after birth.

"When you deal with fear, you are dealing with a very visceral part of the human psyche, and a rather delicate part of the brain, too.

The idea behind Project: SERUM was that it would trigger the 'fight or flight' response, but it would stymy it enough that the Alterant would be paralyzed with fear and refrain from significant action."

I thought about the terror I'd felt in gaining mass; how heavy and muscular and also round I'd gotten. It seemed that AB had a good point, and I could agree with her based on my experience now.

"Fear has a powerful effect on a person," AB continued. "By triggering the deepest, darkest reality a person can face, suddenly, and rather unexpectedly, the serum ideally would distract them and give us time for our forces to act. Or, even better, it would cause the internal collapse and ruin of our enemies."

"Forces?"

"You know, like espionage or military agents, or even regime-change forces. Like what we did in … oh, never mind. I guess you don't need to worry about it, Kallie."

I wrinkled my nose. Apparently, there was a lot that it was better I didn't know. "Good to know."

"The point is, it's a very powerful serum, and I need to track it down, take care of the people who are using it or have used it, and find out who it was who framed me for its loss." AB got out of the car and headed for the house. "And that means finding ZZ and the one who gave her my recipe."

"Well, good luck."

I didn't want to think about how uneasy AB's speech made me feel, especially after all the triumph I'd felt in taking Frank down.

"We'll need it."

"*You'll* need it," I corrected her. "I have other things to do.

AB arched her brow at me, and I huffed indignantly.

"What?" I asked. "I'm a teenager, remember? A minor. You can't drag me into danger like this."

"It's easier since you don't have a record—"

"Seriously?" I grabbed a large blanket and covered up my still-largely-enlarged-self, toppling out of the car after her. "You're insane."

"Come on, Kallie. I might need your help again."

"You mean you need Fatgirl's help, and like your friend ZZ, she's retiring."

AB clasped her hands together in front of her, looking every inch the proper lady as we glared down our noses at each other. A long moment passed as I forced myself to breathe normally; AB could be intimidating even as her dainty old-lady self, and I hated it.

I hated it, but I also wanted to know how she managed to do it.

"Unlike ZZ, Fatgirl doesn't have the proper leverage to retire."

"Fatgirl doesn't need leverage," I insisted, even though I still squirmed. How did AB manage to make me feel so angry and afraid at the same time? She was supposed to be a harmless grandmother with pockets full of lint and pieces of gum in her purse. Instead she could just grab her gun and she carried around a portable science lab.

I jutted my chin out as defiantly as possible. "Right now, all 'Fatgirl' needs to do is go to bed and sleep this nightmare of a week off."

"You do that, dear. I think you've earned that." AB gave me a sugary smile and patted the large bag at her side. "I've got work to do in the meantime."

I gave her a mocking salute, and then headed to my room and buried myself in my bed.

I didn't want to think about my serendipitous foray into the superhero schtick ever again. I was done, wasn't I? I could burn my hot pink and navy-blue suit, bury the ashes, and dance on its grave. And since I managed to deflate back to my normal, model-ready skinny self, I could even dance like a rock star instead of a sports team mascot. I was safe now.

Wasn't I?

Yes, I was, even if I had to remind myself that truth, over and over, all weekend long. I managed to scare myself into oversleeping by recalling that if I stayed up without sufficient distractions, I would end up obsessing about Fatgirl again.

When I did finally resume my normal life on Monday morning, I was found that I had—excuse the pun—bigger problems to worry about.

My phone was still busted.

I touched the cracked screen with care. My splintered portrait reflected in the broken glass, and even more than the Fatgirl schtick, I hated seeing my face fractured into tiny little slides.

It was too easy to remember the pain and sadness I'd felt from my whole breakdown, when I'd basically torn up my kitchen while screaming in unbridled rage and inner angst, both over the loss of my mother and the loss of a chance to get to possibly see her and make her proud again. I'd thrown my phone across the room, hard enough to smash it up.

I wasn't that complicated of a person when it came down to it. I didn't like thinking about how small and afraid I felt, now that Mom was gone. I would never admit, publicly, how I wasn't really sure I liked my friends, and I didn't know where I truly belonged. I didn't like thinking how all those little breaks and cracks in my reflection could easily reflect the existential teenage torment tearing me up inside.

I was pretty and popular, and I was smart and I could even be kind, but I wanted what I wanted, and I didn't apologize for it.

And now I wanted a new phone.

A new phone was a safe thing to worry about.

And I needed one, didn't I? How else would Dad get a hold of me when he was on the road? Especially now that AB was here with us, he would need to make sure he could get a hold of me, and that I could get a hold of him.

Not that he would really believe his mother was some kind of ex-government agent doing selectively unethical work and I'd accidentally eaten one of her projects in a moment of emotional weakness, or something like that.

But still, I needed a phone so I could contact him.

And all my friends had one, there was a new updated phone that had just come out, and if I had a phone I could maybe get a proper job. Plus, my dad had never denied me a phone before, and if he did now, he was an irredeemable jerk and I would be forced to act out in a form of uncivil disobedience. That's what Americans do, really—I mean, 1776 and all that. And it's just a human right at this point in time, isn't it?

Finally, there was also the simple matter that I didn't just need a phone; I *deserved* one.

By the time I was ready for school, I had all my arguments prepared.

Only to forget them all as I walked into the kitchen and see the news report streaming live on a tablet.

My mouth dropped open so quickly I felt my jaw sprain.

"What … in the world … is *this*?" My mouth flopped the words out, my body seemingly torn between shock and outrage. I could've sworn I'd wanted to scream, but gasping and panting seemed to be the reaction of choice.

My eyes bulged as "FATGIRL FAND-A-MONIUM!" scrolled across the bottom of the screen. The news anchors were talking about the new "Local heroine" and how she was a champion for the "common people" and she was a "true hero for America," uniting people of all walks of life.

My face burned over with scorching heat as they showed a blurry picture of me running out of the Amphitheatre, running into that guy who called me "Fatgirl" as an insult.

Great.

I shook my head furiously. How stupid could people be? I mean, the guy was clearly *insulting me*, and I was a fat, grotesque monster who only by the sheerest of luck managed to stop that gunman from taking the Model Middle America audience hostage on live TV—and that was *last week*.

"Well, I hope you're ready for today, Fatgirl."

I turned around to see AB sitting at the table behind me. She was wearing another one of her fancy pant suits and sipping down her espresso. The weather report could've been on, for how much she was reacting to the news.

"Why is this still a thing?" I pointed at the TV. "The news cycle should've blown over. We had a whole weekend since the *Model Middle America* audition!"

"Somethings don't just go away so quickly," AB said. "Remember how Epstein didn't kill himself?"

"But he lived a long time ago," I argued. "And it's *Einstein*, not Epstein, genius."

AB sighed and rolled her eyes. "How could I be so silly?"

"That's not silly." I pointed toward the news anchor again, as she was showing the new official Fatgirl Fan website, which was apparently now offering membership subscriptions. "*That* is silly!"

"It's actually not." AB pursed her lips thoughtfully. "I imagine whoever's running the site will make a lot of money off your name, and if you want to take him to court or get a cease and desist letter, you'll have to admit who you are. In fact, you might want to be grateful for this; an official website is a good thing."

"What are you talking about? This was not supposed to happen. None of this was supposed to happen! Ugh!" I tossed my still-busted phone down on the counter and slumped down into another chair. "This is awful."

"Awful things happen no matter what your life is like, Kallie," AB said, still calmly sipping her espresso. "Having a tantrum won't make anything better."

"At least maybe I'll feel better if I do." I stood up and grabbed my backpack again. "I'll burn more calories."

"Stress doesn't burn calories. It just makes the sugar turn into body fat."

"Just shut up, would you?" I stood up, glumly aware she was right about the tantrum part. "I need to go to school."

I glanced over at my phone on the counter. "And I'll need a new phone. I think you should get me a new one, since it's your fault I broke it."

She arched her brow at me. "Didn't you break it before the whole Fatgirl mess was started?"

"I would've gotten it replaced sooner if it hadn't been for you."

"Let me see it. I can probably fix it," AB said.

"No, I need a new one." I huffed as I straightened my shoulders. "I wanted the latest smartphone model. I'll need it in pink, and a bright shade, too, since Amory, my best friend, says that's the best color for me."

"Best friend?" AB snorted. "You know she's lying, right?"

"Of course I know she's lying," I assured her. "But if I get a neon pink color, other people will see it more, so I'll get more attention, *and* Amory can't complain if I never wear pink clothes again because I'll have the phone as part of my permanent wardrobe."

"Hmmm." AB looked impressed. "What did you tell her in response when she was supposedly complimenting you?"

"I told her that her hair was perfectly fine when she braids it."

"And it's not?"

"She's the prettiest African-American in her class. Of course her hair looks perfectly fine when she braids it."

"So she's lying to you, and you're telling her the truth, so she thinks you're lying?" AB picked up my phone and looked at it, before drinking more of her espresso. "Clever, but thank the good Lord I'm out of high school. I thought government agents were petty."

"You just don't understand," I said. "In fact, you don't understand anything else about me or my life, and hopefully you won't have to pretend to try for very long."

"I'm well aware of what social media is, Kallie," AB said. "That's why I think you'll be in for another couple of rude awakenings when you get to school."

She wasn't wrong about that. I bit my lip, quickly stopping once I remembered my lipstick. I looked back at the news screen, which was being interrupted by an ad for Darla Donuts, of all things. I would have to deal with more Fatgirl gossip, and then there were likely several hundreds of social media tags and messages from my friends I had waiting for me.

I grimaced; Amory and the other girls will be angry with me about *Model Middle America*, especially if they figured out I'd given them the wrong address for the Amphitheatre.

"With this whole website mess out there, why not just embrace it?" AB asked. "I've got some feelers out for ZZ's current location. You could help me some more."

"No." I'd have rather faced a hundred days in school without my phone than help her.

"Perhaps I could even leave faster if you were to help me again. The city is very big, of course, and I may need more help navigating it. Especially if I'm going to get your phone later, and assuming you'll be able to finish your work and be able to get through the school day unscathed."

"What do you mean? Is there something else I should worry about from your doughnuts?" Fear trickled through me again, and I did everything I could not to give into its poison. Surely, I didn't have to be afraid of fear now, apparently, just if there some kind of weird side effect that kicked in … right?

That thought made everything worse than it already was, and things were already so much worse than I ever could've possibly imagined. *Again.*

I put my hands on my hips, staring down at AB and all her smug contentedness. I had to be strong. I was about to face the day knowing there were pop culture nerds out there who were trying to get my face plastered on t-shirts and bumper stickers, and I was going to have to do without my phone.

I didn't know if I could handle it. But I did know there was nothing to be gained—gosh, I had to stop with the fat puns—by admitting that out loud. AB was a racist and probably a psychopath and a half, and she acted too white and her taste in cars was archaic, *but as God as my witness, I would not let her see me as weak.*

Shallow and petty I could handle, but not weak.

"In case you've forgotten, I took down a gunman twice last week, and I fulfilled a promise for you. I'm not going to fall apart over your doughnuts again. If anything, you owe me, and you should be worried about finding my mom now and nothing else."

"Good to know you've got some fight in you after all." AB smiled bitterly, clearly upset at my show of spirit. "Well, then, you'd better hurry. You're almost late."

I still felt hugely embarrassed and annoyed about Fatgirl's large and growing fandom, but I felt triumphant at besting AB.

I should've learned from the last time how that would backfire.

The several blocks it took me to walk to school was not enough to rob me of my emotional irritations. If anything, I was even more furious with Abuela-Blanca by the time I got to school. I'd mentioned the phone, but I'd forgotten to ask when AB would get moving on getting Mom back here.

AB was probably happy about that, too.

She had gotten all *she* wanted, didn't she? Oh, except she wanted more now. What a soul-sucking monster.

But I'd beaten her, too, hadn't I?

Remembering that, I carried myself proudly, having both survived the *Model Middle America* fiasco and AB's terrorist hunting adventure. I was also back to my regular self, thin and gorgeous, with my brown-black hair washed and brushed to a shine, my face covered in a layer of makeup, and my feet adorned with my newest pair of fashionable boots.

Sure, I didn't win the title of America's Next Top Heartland Teen Heartthrob, but I was also not outed as Fatgirl and AB wasn't kidnapped by government officers for her radioactive nonsense.

Of course, that last thing could've been different and I wouldn't have minded so much. But I was still proud of myself, even if I couldn't tell anyone—and if I'd been changed into Wonder Girl instead of Fatgirl, I might've been tempted to leave clues or make inside jokes about the whole thing. I'd taken down a wanted man, survived a battle in the sewers, and been entrusted with criminal information.

I was proud of myself.

It didn't take me long to realize how much I'd underestimated the world and its capacity for cruelty.

"Kallie!"

Lizzie's voice was the first one I heard, and its startling clarity made me realize that it'd been several full days since I'd heard from any of my friends.

My shoulders sagged slightly; I would need a good story for them.

"Oh, I'm so happy you're there," Lizzie said, practically clawing me as she grabbed my arm. "I've been so worried about you! We were worried you were captured by that terrible gunman guy last week."

"Oh, no." I put on my best teary-eyed, dead-puppies-dying expression. "My father ended up grounding me last week so I didn't make it to the audition at all. He was just so awful. You should've heard him. I really should call CPS on him. He even took my phone away from me."

I didn't like lying about my dad. He was actually a good guy, even if AB was probably right about his lack of ambition. But I had enough ambition for the two of us, and in this case, that meant throwing him under the bus. So I did.

"Well, that's good you weren't there," Lizzie said. "Amory and the rest of us were still on the road. Apparently, you'd given us the wrong address for the Amphitheatre—"

"And so conveniently, too."

Amory's voice was sour as she came up beside me. On the other side of her, June and Uli were also there; Uli looked fearful, while June seemed to be wary as she studied me.

I was about to be called out for my trickery, I realized. I held my breath, waiting to see what Amory said.

"Yes, that's right." Lizzie curled up to me. "And thank goodness, too, or we could've ended up dead."

All of us looked to Amory, waiting for her response as I tried not to turn blue.

"Yes, it seems it worked out for the best," Amory finally said. "It's good to see Kallie's carelessness saved all of us."

I slowly let out my breath. I was about to assure her it was nothing less than the divine providence of God himself when Amory spoke again.

"Although, thanks to what I've seen about that whole Fatgirl debacle, I doubt we would've been killed."

Uli and Lizzie dissolved into laughter, while Amory still glared at me, and June was pulling out her phone.

"OMG, Kallie, did you see that whole Fatgirl thing?" Uli's giggles only grew louder.

"Uh, no," I lied. "I was grounded. No phone and electronics."

"You've got to see this then," June said, shoving her phone in my face.

It was nice she seemed to warm up to me a little, so I took her phone and looked down at it. I was fulling expecting to see the Fatgirl fangirling website, so I was not as surprised or nauseous as I had been earlier when I saw it on the news.

"Oh, you'll get a kick out of it," Lizzie agreed. "It's freaking hilarious!"

I blanched. The last thing I wanted to do was remember any part of my life as Fatgirl, especially in front of my so-called friends. "Oh, no, that's not necessary right now … We have to get to class—"

"Come on, Kallie!" Lizzie nudged me. "I want to hear you make fun of this. You're so smart and you have the best take-downs."

"Hey, mine are actually quite smart, too," Amory insisted. "You just aren't smart enough to understand them."

I fell into complete silence, letting them chat away about how fat Fatgirl was, how ugly Fatgirl's outfit was, how hilarious it was that her super power was sitting on people, and how it was a hoot that Cuttingham City was her hometown, apparently.

June cleared her throat. "Given the nature of the internet—"

"Talk about world *wide* web, right?" Amory brightened at the sight of the fat superhero girl on the screen. The rest of my friends all broke down in laughter at her comment, and I struggled to smile and nod.

But inside, I was reeling. My legs were numb and my face felt feverish as I realized there would be no support for Fatgirl among my friends.

I didn't know why I'd maybe secretly hoped someone would appreciate her. I mean, plenty of people on the news had been supporters, hadn't they? And there was that person who'd started the website. Even if it was all for money, and none of it was very good, surely *someone* out there would love Fatgirl?

I frowned. *Why would they? I don't even like her, and she's me!*

While the rest of my group stood around making fun of Fatgirl, I silently cursed AB to a quick and lonely grave, one stuffed with all the exploding chicken turds she'd suddenly dropped into my life.

If I'd seen the whole show from an outside perspective, I would've joined in with the others; even more so, perhaps. I would've howled with laughter at the idea of a fat and most likely ugly superhero, trying to save the day at a fashion show.

"I can't wait to see her in action again," Uli said. "I'd love to see if her thighs jiggle as much as I think they would."

"Ew, that's disgusting." Amory crossed her arms. "Gross, Uli."

If I had my way, Fatgirl would *never ever ever* show her fat face in public ever again.

No matter what the people on the Fatgirl's fansite wanted.

"Well, Kallie, tell us," Lizzie said. "What do you think?"

"Oh, uh … " I decided it was best to change the subject. For the first time, I noticed Amory was carrying a large box.

"Wait, what's that for?" I asked.

"It's our Pi Day assignment for Mrs. Bakersfield's class." Amory arched one of her newly-waxed eyebrows at me. "Remember? It was due today since it's March fourteenth."

"Um … no."

As if I need more bad news right now.

I tore through my memory, trying to recall anything about last week. Most of the memories involved were centered around my attempts to flatten my flatulence and the whole Creepy Sweaty Fat Kid—I know, I know, it's Zeus—having a crush on me while I was watching Blake Turner warm up for the lacrosse game.

But yes, now that I think of it … there was a small corner of my mind I'd forgotten about, and in it, practically thrust into the crevasse, was the reminder that Pi Day was coming up, and I had to make a pie to bring into math class.

Maybe I can just leave.

The thought struck me like lightning. School hadn't started yet, after all. Maybe there was time to go home. Or maybe I could go to the nurse.

I wished I had my phone so I could text my dad. He was already on the road again, but he would be understanding.

He would understand, and I wouldn't feel so alone right now.

"Kallie?" June leaned in close to me. "Are you feeling okay? Your eyes look glassy."

"Uh … "

I could even play the sick card without trying, apparently.

"Oh, please, June, give your doctor routine a rest. Kallie's just faking," Amory said. "She forgot about Pi Day, so she's trying to think of a way to worm out of turning it in today."

June, Uli, and Lizzie all looked at me, and I had no choice but to clear my throat and straighten my shoulders.

"Well, it was worth a shot," I said.

"You forgot your Pi Day assignment, too, Kallie?"

I'd had a really hard time with life since my mom left, and an even worse time since my grandmother came to live with us. I was content to blame my dad and myself, and especially God, but as I stood there and I heard Blake Turner's voice behind me, I was more than tempted to break into a Hallelujah chorus.

"Blake!" I whirled around to see Blake with his blond locks tousled oh so carelessly—and oh so attractively—across his forehead. It was murder to stand there and try not to brush them off to the side like a good girlfriend would do, especially since I was so grateful he'd shown up. "Hi! How are you?"

He gave me a smile. "Unlike my upcoming math grade, I'm pretty good. With all the excitement of this past weekend, I forgot all about Pi Day."

"You mean all that Fatgirl stuff?" I asked, my throat suddenly thick.

"Oh, not her," Blake said. "Me and the team won another game on Saturday. I'm surprised none of you were there, actually."

"We were busy with our pies," Amory said, playfully elbowing him as she held out her box. "I made little pie-lettes today for the class."

"Ooh, looks fantastic." Blake gave Amory a warm smile. "You always think of the coolest twists on projects like these. Maybe you should help me make up this assignment."

"Oh, I can do that!" My voice squeaked just a little at the end, and I know I sounded desperate, but I was, okay? I'd had the hardest weekend of my life, and here was a perfect chance to hang out with Blake without my friends and his teammates coming between us. I *needed* this.

"Kallie forgot her pies, too," Amory said. "That would be a good idea, Blake."

I shot Amory a pathetic look of gratitude.

"Okay, cool," Blake said. "And maybe once we're done with that, we could have a party at my house. Sounds fun, right? What's the point of making pie and not having any one else to eat it with?"

"Oh, that would be great—"

Blake pointed behind me. "I mean, unless I could use it to hit ugly nerds in the face, right?" He started laughing, and the rest of my friends began to giggle.

I glanced around to see Zeus Evans walking down the hall toward us. Just like before, I didn't find it in me to laugh with my friends. He was wearing one of his baggy sweatshirts again, and his face seemed extra-oily today, as if he hadn't slept much in the last few days. From behind his thick glasses, I could see he saw us, and I knew the second he realized they were all laughing at him, too.

Then Zeus looked at me. Our eyes met as the others were laughing at him. I knew Blake was just joking in that goofy way of his, but I also knew how it felt to be unable to control how disgusting you are and how awful it felt that other people out there who wouldn't leave you alone to hide away in peace.

I wanted to say something to Zeus, but I wasn't sure what I could say. Certainly nothing he would believe—such as how my friends weren't that bad, and they weren't really laughing at him so much as the way they perceived him.

"What's wrong, Kallie?" Amory waved her hand in front of my face. "Hello? Earth to Kallie, come in!"

"Don't tell me you're worried for poor Jesus," Blake said with another laugh. "He's got a lot of thick skin."

I shrugged, pushing my hair back over my shoulder. "Oh, I was just thinking about what I would do for my pies," I lied. I was angry at all of them at the moment, so I didn't mind antagonizing Amory. Especially if it would help me score points with Blake. "Something much more creative than smaller pies."

"Oh, really?" Amory frowned, and I knew she'd taken my bait. "And what's that?"

"Oh, you'll just have to see," I bluffed. "It'll be real fun, too. Now, I have to get to class. It's almost time for homeroom."

I walked away from them, using my sexy walk in case Blake was watching—he wasn't, he was talking to Amory again—and headed off to class, never more grateful that I had to focus on schoolwork.

Even if I had to deal with an angry Mrs. Bakersfield.

If there was ever a math teacher who was made for Pi Day, it was Mrs. Bakersfield. My mother had gotten her break-out modeling role as Darla Donut, but Mrs. Bakersfield could've easily been that mom from that "mom and apple pie" adage. I didn't know her first name but if her name had been "Jane," I wouldn't have been surprised. She was a middle-aged plain Jane alright, with dull brownish-hair that she always seemed to wear pulled up into a strict bun. She wore floor-length skirts like a time traveling Anabaptist, and she never wore makeup. Frankly, I didn't really know how anyone did *that.*

Of course, I also didn't know how anyone chose teaching math for a career, either.

But on the other hand, if there was anyone who was going to do it, Mrs. Bakersfield was a great fit.

"Oh, Kallie." She shook her head sadly as she passed my desk. "You didn't bring in your pie for the class today?"

Her thin lips were slightly turned down in what I assumed was a pout. I clasped my hands together, trying to put myself together and present myself as a strong person.

"I—" I coughed, trying to buy myself time as I tried to think of a way out of this.

Seriously, I have stared down a terrorist, why is my math teacher so hard to lie to?

"I, um, was just so busy this weekend," I said. "And I forgot to—"

"Saying you forgot is enough of an excuse, Kallie," Mrs. Bakersfield said. She shook her head again, making her bun whip from side to side. "I'll send an email home tonight."

I bit the inside of my cheek and nodded, trying to ignore all the others in the class who looked at me. Apparently, it was easy as pie for them to judge me and think I was stupid for forgetting my homework.

The instant the bell rang, I zipped out of there.

"Well, thank God that's over," I muttered.

I wasn't *stupid.* I knew there were bricks with a higher IQ than some of my peers. I wasn't really a nerd, but I did all my work, and I did what they wanted me to do more because it was *easier* to do what they wanted me to do. If I did it, they would lay off me when I failed like this. Even Mrs. Bakersfield's disappointment had been relatively easy to bear.

Of course, there were a lot of worse things in the world.

After all, I didn't have my phone. And Fatgirl had an online fandom. And Mom was still off in LA or somewhere else, getting admired by millions of people while she got free clothes and a large paycheck.

"Hey, Kallie!" Blake called as I passed by his locker.

I cheered up at once. I'd almost missed him since I was too focused on wallowing in my own misery and grievances, but there he was, like an angel of light, ready to give me something good among the crap being thrown around me today.

"Hey, Blake." I gave him my most charming smile. "What's going on?"

"Nothing much."

"Same here, although I just got out of math class. Mrs. Bakersfield can sure be brutal when people forget their pies, huh?"

"You'd think lunch would calm her down some, huh? My guess is she's after the pies herself." Blake laughed. "Hey, can you help me with this?"

He handed me his phone, and I was just about to say what a shame it was I didn't have a new phone as cool as his when I saw what he was signing up for.

"You … want to subscribe to the Fatgirl website?" I asked.

"Yeah, sure. Why not?"

My soul felt like an overstuffed toilet bowl, unable to wash away all the crap I was being forced to accommodate.

Never mind about that good stuff, I guess.

Blake Turner was signing up for the Fatgirl fan club.

This was officially the worst.

"I just was surprised," I said. "I mean, you're doing this ironically, right? Seems like a lot of unnecessary effort."

"Nah, Fatgirl's cool," Blake said, surprising me.

"Oh. I guess you like heroes, then?" I said, looking down at his phone.

"She's our town's first real hometown hero, you know? I figured I'd sign up to show my support, but the website's not letting me subscribe for some reason." He gave me a smile. "I know you can help me. You're better with computers than me. Mr. Embers says you're one of his top students."

"One of his top students who doesn't care about computers," I said with a snort. I didn't want to have to explain to Blake I just did the work and learned the stuff so I could get by without being bothered by anyone, but he was more content to talk about Fatgirl, clearly.

"But you can fix this, right?" Blake grinned. "Me and some of the guys are hoping we'll be able to get her to come and sing the national anthem at one of our games sometime. That would be so cool."

My fingers were shaking as I finished signing Blake up for Fatgirl's website notification, trying not to feel even more sick as I finished typing in his email, which he apparently had misspelled earlier.

"There," I said. "You should get a confirmation email."

"Thanks, Kallie. I knew I could count on you," he said. He ran his hand through his blond hair again, giving me something of a sheepish smile. "You never let anyone down."

"You're welcome." I brushed my own hair behind my shoulder, trying to look blasé. I wanted to ask him if I could email him about the make-up Pi Day party he'd mentioned earlier when I heard another voice behind me.

"I wouldn't say she's got a perfect record of helping people," AB said.

I flinched, but I covered it up by turning around to see her. Yep, there she was. Abuela-Blanca was here, wearing her classy pantsuit with her expensive low-heeled pumps and her bag-lady bag wobbling back and forth as she walked.

"Who's that?" Blake asked.

"That's … my grandmother. I mean, my Abuela." I glared back at AB in warning. If looks could kill, my grandmother would've been dead four or five times over and the HAZMAT crew would need back up to come and clean her up off my high school floor.

"How do you do?" AB reached out her hand to Blake, who clapped it like she was reaching for a high five, before trying to do some currently-trending hello dance along with it.

I didn't know who I was more embarrassed by in that moment, and that was a new tragic low.

They say crying doesn't help, but I'll bet crying loudly enough to get sent to the psych ward in the local hospital would've at least made me feel better based on a change in scenery.

"I've been looking for you," AB said to me.

"It's in between class periods." I shrugged. "What did you want?"

"I have a favor to ask," she said. "And I thought I'd bring you your phone."

"You got my phone?" I blinked, once more filled with hope.

"Yes," she said. For the first time, I noticed AB was carrying a shoe-box-sized parcel. She handed it to Blake as she reached into her purse. "I have it in here somewhere."

"Did you get me the new pink color I wanted?" I asked, nearly jumping forward as she rummaged through her bag.

Only to be *really* disappointed when she handed me my own phone from before. The screen was still cracked but it was held in place with a new screen protector.

"Uh … thanks." Considering how disappointed I was, it was *really* hard to be grateful.

"All your apps were open when I turned it on," AB said. "So I checked your messages for you and everything else. I saw you had Pi Day today, and Amory and the others were asking after you. I responded to them saying that you'd been grounded."

"What?" I grabbed her by the wrist. "You went through my messages? Those are mine!"

"And now you don't have to worry about them," AB said. "I took care of them for you. So you're welcome."

"That's not how that works," I hissed.

"Hey, at least she brought your Pi Day assignment in," Blake said. "And they taste great."

AB and I both froze as we looked over at Blake.

Beautiful, dumb-headed Blake.

He was halfway through eating one of AB's Darla Donut lookalikes.

There was powder on his cheeks like an overzealous cocaine addict, and a big smile on his face as he licked it up.

"Really great, actually," he said. "You could give Darla Donuts a run for their money."

AB and I exchanged a glance. Clearly, we didn't know what to do.

Hurriedly, I tucked my broken phone away and grabbed the box back from Blake, even grabbing the half-finished one he was eating right out of his hand. "I've got to get these to Mrs. Bakersfield. See you later, Blake!"

"I'm going to her class now," he called after me. "I can take them with me if you want."

"No, thanks!"

It was pure agony, trying to ignore him as I sped off, jerking AB behind me. Thankfully, the hallways weren't too crowded since next period was about to begin, and I was able to make it to an empty classroom before the bell rang.

The instant we were alone and it was quiet, I turned on AB.

"What is your problem?" Tears welled up into my eyes as I looked at her. "Are you trying to kill me?"

"What is my problem?" AB huffed. "What is your problem? I was going to ask if you wanted to go to Los Angeles with me. ZZ's there and I'll need your help getting into her auction."

"You mean you need *Fatgirl's* help," I shot back. "And I already told you no!"

"I've worked in government and STEM fields for the last four decades! I don't take 'no' for an answer."

"Well that explains the 'questionable ethics' part of your job description."

"Come on, I'll help you with something in exchange," AB promised. "You have your homework assignment for Pi Day, right? I can help you with that. You already know I'm good at baking sweets." She gave me sidelong glance. "Even your cute little friend Blake seems to think so."

"You think that offering to help me with homework is going to make me change my mind?" I scoffed. "You know, for a nuclear scientist or whatever you are, you're pretty dumb."

"Well, you're in high school, so I guess it's natural for you to think you're smarter than you are."

"Why is it that you're better at negotiating with terrorists better than you are talking with teenagers?" I asked, genuinely curious.

And then I remembered—*Blake!*

I gasped. "Oh, my Lord, you poisoned Blake!"

"Excuse me, but he took *my* doughnuts and didn't think to ask if he could have one. I wanted to go to the airport after getting you today, but *no,* now we'll soon have a rogue Alterant running around," AB hissed.

"How are we going to fix this?" I asked. I looked at her bag; it was hard to say just what she had in there. "Do you have your lab with you?"

"I'll need a sample of his blood and about ten minutes to reverse-engineer a cure," AB said. "Here."

She reached out and handed me another doughnut.

"I can't be Fatgirl *here,*" I whispered, desperately hoping that there was no way I would have to do this ever aga—

Then AB pulled out the familiar hot pink and navy-blue uniform. "I've had it updated a little," she said. "Here."

Ugh.

She had this entire thing prepared. She literally wasn't going to take 'no' for an answer at all.

"I have some other things in here," AB said. "I don't know if you'll be able to use them. Take a look."

She started pulling out different items—some bottles full of different solutions, including some smelly ones, a pocket knife, a gun—

Hey!

"What the heck are you doing with a *gun*?" I could barely breath right. "This is a *gun-free zone.*"

"Well, they're just asking for trouble then, if you ask me."

"Put that away."

"Fine. You don't know how to properly shoot people anyway."

"There's no need to insult me. I'm the one who's doing you the favors here." As proof, I started eating the powered doughnut she'd handed me.

I hated how delicious it was. It was the taste of my childhood, wrapped up in my mother's love, with the security of a home my father provided. There was a warmth to its texture that made me want to cry, both for the pain I knew was coming as well as the pleasurable taste it left on my tongue.

"I wanted to go to LA." AB rolled her eyes. "If that idiot hadn't eaten my doughnuts, none of this would've happened."

"You leave Blake out of this."

"It's too late for that, remember?" My grandmother smirked down at me, as she put her hands on her hips. The smug superiority in her eyes made me want to punch her—anything to prove she might've been right, but she wouldn't win our arguments without a price. "Good Lord, Kallie. No wonder you're obsessed with him. He's as terribly rude and self-centered as you are."

"Yes, I'm the self-centered one." I glanced down at myself, as I changed into the circus tent that was my so-called superhero costume. "Just watch me be self-centered as I go and save an innocent teenager that you inadvertently poisoned."

"The Protactinium is not poison."

"That's a terrible comeback."

"It's a terrible comeback because it's replying to an ignorant come-front," AB muttered.

"Come-front isn't a word."

"It's *comedy*, Kallie. Good heavens, you complain about me being white all the time, and then you get upset at me for using English-like words in a comedic and nonsensical way? Do you know how much writers in New York and LA get paid to write good material?" She shook her head. "I'm trying to make this bearable for you."

"I don't need bearable," I muttered back, hurrying to change my clothes. "But I could use a new phone after this, by the way. I think this should qualify me for one. Especially since you've been poking around with my other one."

"I told you I could fix yours!"

"We'll go get it later," I said. If AB was going to manipulate me, I would have to learn to do it right back to her if I was going to get anything out of this. "Right now we need to save Blake. I know he's got Mrs. Bakersfield's class this period, so he'll be there."

"What would his worst fear be?"

At her question, I went still.

I'd known Blake for a long time, or at least, I'd known *of* him. But as far as what was he afraid of?

I had no idea.

"We'll have to play this one by ear," AB said.

"Ugh. Again?" I finished putting the suit on. AB wasn't lying; she'd taken the superhero suit I'd been given by Azure at the audition and modified, adding in some new features. There was a small wire in the hood that was clearly a communicator, and different parts of the suit now had thick pads sewn onto them around the armpits and the back of the knees.

It was an odor shield.

Great. First fat, and now apparently smelly.

"This isn't like chasing down Frank Whitey, Kallie. He has a criminal history and known predictable patterns," AB said.

"Okay, fine, that makes sense."

"Not to mention there's no tracker on your friend. Also, since that boy is still a technically a minor, we'll have to be much more discreet about this one. My contact on the force would enjoy earning another favor from me."

She always has to make this about herself, doesn't she? I smothered a groan and pulled up the hood. "Do you have the mask?"

"Here." AB gave me a new mask. "This one has a trail of camera lenses sewn in around the eyes, along with some LED liquid lights. I'll be able to see what you're seeing at all times, and the lights will protect you from other cameras and picture-taking devices."

I gritted my teeth but said nothing. AB *had* to have been planning this.

Was it possible she went so far as to give Blake the doughnut on purpose?

No. Surely, she wouldn't be that evil …

I looked at her again, as she continued explaining how she'd stitched up some more sensors in the gloves so I'd be able to scan things and send her full-blown 3D holograms renderings.

All the tech stuff was cool and shiny, but as I carefully learned how to use them, my stomach dropped. I would have to be careful when I went to go and save Blake.

All this Fatgirl stuff was just going to make the fans more fanatic. I was going to be playing into their hands. I would be helping Blake, but I would also be encouraging the fandom that their support meant more sightings of me.

And as much as I wanted to protect Blake and save him, and even flirt with him to give him a thrill, I did *not* want people to seriously cheer on Fatgirl.

I rubbed my forehead, exasperated. Why was I the only person who could see this superhero thing was clearly nonsense?

"Now, Kallie, tell me: Where is Mrs. Bakersfield's class?"

Before I could answer her, a scream cried out from down and around the hall, and it was closely followed by a loud *crash.*

Someone had thrown a desk against the wall, clearly.

I pushed my mask on tight, unhappy I was already nearly bloated up to the new normal Fatgirl figure, but still understanding that this was a necessary sacrifice if I was going to save my beloved Blake.

"I'll open a window when I get there so I can pass you the blood. Don't let anyone else see you."

"As if I want the government to know I'm out here," AB said with a huff. "I'm already on their blacklist. That's part of the reason I need you protected too."

"Okay, okay. Just do what I said. It should be fine." I groaned. "I guess I gotta go now."

After all my experience with being Fatgirl, I still never expected to be repulsed by Blake, literally ever.

But no, I supposed I just needed to have one more *worst thing ever* happen to make the day complete.

As I re-entered into Mrs. Bakersfield's classroom, the class was cowering back from the small, raging, ugly man-child formerly known as Blake Turner, who was having a full-blown tantrum.

Mrs. Bakersfield was sitting on the floor, shaking, with her knees up to her chin, and her eyes red. Some of the students close to her were trying to protect her, while others looked at Blake's shrinking, squealing form with terror.

"Blake was always such a nice boy," Mrs. Bakersfield muttered.

I cleared my throat, hoping to adjust my voice into something unrecognizable. "Hello—"

"Look! It's Fatgirl!"

Oh, goody. Here we go.

All at once, my fellow students—nearly all of whom I'd grown up with—began taking my picture with their phones like I was some famous celebrity. I put my hands over my face, suddenly thankful for all the planning AB had put into my new costume updates.

"Stop it!" Blake's weakling voice cried out in protest, as he threw another desk down onto the floor. "Pay attention to me!"

"What's happened to Blake? Are we all going to die?" One of Blake's friends, Matt Montgomery, looked at me, clearly terrified.

"It'll be okay," I said, carefully moving toward Blake.

As I closed in on him, another kid did, too.

And of course the kid in question was someone I did *not* want to see right then—or ever, really.

But there he was. Captain Super Sweaty Fat Kid himself, Zeus Evans.

He stepped up in front of Mrs. Bakersfield, protecting her from the raging child in front of them.

"You can go ahead and stop, Blake," he said.

I took the moment, as Zeus tried to take command of the situation, to study Blake. Looking at him, I felt sick in my stomach, and not just from the doughnuts this time.

I'd been face to face with a terrorist last week. Why was a man-baby with puberty that surprising to me?

Blake had transformed into a smaller version of himself, and as I watched, he was gradually shrinking in size. His well-defined muscles had shrunk down to slim sticks, and his eyes were bulging out of his face, while his cheeks were filling up with sweat and star constellations full of pimples.

I had to say, he reminded me of someone else, but I wasn't sure exactly who …

"I'll stop when I'm back to normal!"

"You're about to fall over," I said, stepping up behind him.

It didn't take me much to pick up Blake. It was actually almost like picking up a baby. He was still shrinking some as I held him, and I felt enough motherly compassion that I was determined not to squash him.

Baby Boy Blake Turner.

I had to stop myself from laughing at the thought of how that would be the perfect Alterant name for Blake. My website fans would love that. Especially if they liked Fatgirl. I mean, really.

I coughed, covering up my chuckles. As the others looked at me, I decided it was time to get to work.

"Um … right." I nodded toward the door. "Can you go ahead and go to another room?"

"What's happening to him?" Zeus asked.

"Can you just go, please?" I sighed. "I'd rather just get him fixed, and I need people to get out of here for me to do that."

I glanced toward the window, just in time to see AB's old-lady lily hand wave from the other side of the glass.

"You're a mean fat lady!" Baby Boy Blake whined at me, trying to fight me off him.

It didn't work, but Blake made it worse by starting screeching like a little baby. "Waaaahhhh!"

I told myself it was the doughnuts, of course, and it was the doughnuts that were making him extremely unlikable in that moment and nothing else.

However, he did get everyone else in the classroom to file out just fine, so there was some good that came out of that. Even Mrs. Bakersfield was relieved that someone else had taken charge of the situation.

"Waaaahhhh!"

Now I just had to stop myself from killing him.

"Waaaahhhh!"

I wondered if this was how every mother on an airplane felt, when her baby started crying uncontrollably.

Relief poured through me as the classroom door shut behind me, and I could hear some of the students heading down the hall to get the principal or someone else.

"Waaaahhhh!"

"Ugh, please stop!" I groaned. "I have enough to worry about!"

What would AB do if she were here in my position? At that thought, I scowled to myself; I couldn't believe I was already using her as an example to look up to, as though she really was my mentor or something awful like that!

Besides, nothing she would do was what I could do. She would merely tell me "Don't worry about it," and that would basically be it. I didn't think I could drug Blake or try to scare or hypnotize him into calming down.

Zeus came up beside me and reached out his hands. "I'll take him, if you want."

"Why are you still in here?" I frowned at him. "You should go with the others."

"I can help."

I frowned and shook my head. "I can handle this just fine, thank you—"

"Waaaahhhh!" Blake seemed eager to call me out on my bluff.

Quickly, I handed him to Zeus. "Okay, here."

To Zeus' credit, he didn't falter in the least, while I was able to move toward the window. "Hey, Blake. It'll be okay now. Fatgirl's here."

I rolled my eyes, trying not to gag. He was really using *that* as a way to calm Blake down? That was so *freaking* great, wasn't it?

I opened the window, and there was AB.

"It's about time," she muttered. "There's a police car that makes rounds here, Kallie. You're going to have to hurry and get me his blood."

"Right … how do I do that?" I glanced back at Blake. His form was so skinny and small now I felt like I wouldn't be able to get any blood from him without accidentally killing him.

"Just get it from his derrière." AB thrust the needle into my hand, and I nearly dropped it in surprise. "I just need a plunger-full."

"Uh … I can't believe this is not the worst thing I've had to do today." I pouted. "Can't you just come in and do it?"

"No. Your mask will protect *you* from the cameras in there, but not me," AB pointed out. "Think, Kallie!"

"Maybe your doughnuts are making me stupid," I said.

"No, chances are that's just your youth. Now, go get the blood and bring it back." AB glanced over her shoulder and then carefully ducked into the bushes. "I can't be here for long before someone notices me."

"It's not my fault your pantsuits don't double-up as camo." I wrinkled my nose and shook my head but hurried to do what she said. She was right about a lot of things, as inconvenient as it was for me, and AB was a weak point for my identity.

"Hold him." I pulled out the needle reluctantly. "I need some of his blood."

Zeus blushed and nodded. "Sure," he agreed, and I just gave him a strange look.

"I'm a big fan," he stammered, and I nearly slapped him.

I probably would've, if I didn't have to turn my attention back to Blake's baby-sized butt. I could berate Zeus for his stupidity later. In the meantime, Blake was nearly falling out of his pants, and I did not want to watch any needles go into any butt.

I carefully took aim, and then I took a deep breath and squeezed my eyes shut.

"Do you want me to do it?" Zeus asked. "There are some EMTs in my extended family. I can draw blood just fine."

I glanced back toward AB, but she was hiding again. I could see her, and that meant she wasn't able to disagree or give her approval or not.

I looked back at Zeus. "You're sure you can do it?"

"Sure can." He gave me a smile, and maybe it was because I was so much larger and much bigger than usual, but there was something about Zeus that just seemed … trustworthy.

So I handed him the needle and plunger, and I helped hold down Blake's body while also keeping his pants up.

Zeus was as good as his word. I watched as he carefully tickled Blake on his arm and his stomach, and Blake fights back as he started to laugh.

Once he was good and distracted, Zeus poked the needle through Blake's pants and drew out enough blood to fill the plunger.

Zeus gave me the needle and then went back to comforting the now-screaming man-child as I slid awkwardly back over to the window.

"Hey, you like Fatgirl, don't you?" Zeus kept talking to Blake, trying to get him to calm down. "You signed up for her website just a little while ago, didn't you? I saw the notice."

Huh? How did Zeus see any 'notice'?

A sickening thought hit me hard, and I nearly doubled over.

Surely … it can't be …

"Thanks, Fatgirl." AB smirked as she snatched the needle out of my hand reached into her purse, but I was more interested in the scene behind me, where Zeus and Baby Blake were getting along.

"Go lock that door," AB said, cutting through my concerns. "You don't want someone else coming into the classroom, do you?"

"How's the antidote coming?" I asked.

"It'll be ready soon," AB promised. "Just make sure our bases are covered. Check for other cameras. If I need to get the feed, I'll have to call in favors."

I sighed, but she was right about that. And I had to figure out if Zeus was who I feared he was …

So I walked around the room, trying to be nonchalant as I locked the classroom door. On the other side, some of my peers were still looking in at me, but I wasn't as worried about that.

Thankfully, it didn't seem like Zeus was worried about anything, either.

Why would he be? This would probably make him a small celebrity in the school, if Fatgirl was as popular as it seemed.

I watched him with Blake, just trying to talk to him about Fatgirl stuff right now.

"You'd better hope he doesn't crap himself if he's going to act like a baby so much," I said.

"He's not a baby," Zeus replied. "He's just a very weak, nerdy version of himself."

There were a bunch of chimes that emitted from Zeus' pocket. I saw him pull out his phone.

He gave me another flustered smile. "I've signed up the Fatgirl website," he explained. "The fandom's enjoying hearing that you're back in action already. Can I get a quote or something for them?"

"What? No!" I growled at him. "That website is not affiliated with me!"

"Oh, I know—I mean, it's just a fan website … "

Zeus blushed, and my earlier suspicions were uncomfortably growing.

Is it possible that Zeus is the one who was behind the new website?

"Waaaahhhh!" Blake screamed again, making both Zeus and me wince.

I was almost glad for the distraction.

"Okay, he sounds like a baby," Zeus conceded a moment later. "Hey, Blake, look here."

Blake was still significantly less tall and muscular, and he especially looked puny with Zeus was holding him like that.

Zeus wasn't flustered at all.

In fact, as I studied Zeus, he appeared almost happy he was stuck here, handling a baby version of Blake, who didn't get along with Zeus at all.

Oh …

I had a feeling that I knew what Blake's biggest fear was all of a sudden. Blake was afraid of being ugly and weak, having no social power or sports prowess—just like Zeus, only weaker. And uglier. And way uglier.

Zeus seemed to notice this, too, but he didn't say anything. He probably thought it was wonderful that Blake was finally more repulsive than he was.

AB waved at me from the window, and I hurried to block Zeus' view. "Here."

I hurried over. "That should do it, right?"

"Right. He'll need a couple hours to get the rest of the radioactivity through his system, but he'll be normal by tomorrow."

"Got it."

I took the new needle and waited for AB to duck down out of sight again. Then I walked over to Zeus and handed him the needle.

Without hesitation, he took it and injected Blake again.

Blake stopped screaming, but his face began twisting around, clearly uncomfortable.

"My, uh, partner says that he'll be fine tomorrow, if you can tell the other people at school." I swallowed hard. "And please let the others and Mrs. Bakersfield know that I hope they're okay."

"They are," Zeus said. "But I'll let them know."

"Thanks."

"You're welcome, Kallie—I mean, Fatgirl." He blanched. "Sorry. I mean, sorry. I know you're Kallie. I mean, I know you're *not* Kallie."

If I thought I'd felt sick from seeing Fatgirl's website before, and if I felt nauseous at the idea that it was maybe possibly possible Zeus was the one who'd started it, that was nothing compared to how I felt as Zeus stuffed his hands into his pockets and rambled on about how he'd figured out who I was, and how it actually wasn't anyone else's fault and this and that and so much and whatever, I stopped listening as the room started spinning and then went black.

"Ouch!"

I jolted awake—apparently, I'd fainted—as AB stuck me with a needle. I opened my eyes to see Zeus and AB both kneeling over me, still in the middle of Mrs. Bakersfield's classroom. I saw Zeus had managed to cover the door with some of the classroom posters that had been hanging around the room. Blake was passed out—something that I was pretty sure was AB's fault.

"What happened?" I murmured, but not loudly enough for them to notice.

"So that'll make her go back to normal?" Zeus asked.

"Not normal," AB said with a snort. "But her usual self."

Zeus was smothering a laugh as I shot upright and brought my fist up to his face.

"I'd think twice about laughing if I were you," I told him. "I'll kill you for this."

How bad was my life going to get? I made *one* stupid, overly emotional mistake by eating AB's doughnuts. One. Stupid. Meaningless. Mistake.

And now I was condemned to the highest elements of societal rejection and ridicule, and while that wasn't bad enough, *I was now forced to share that experience with two of the most insufferable people I had ever had the misfortune to meet.*

"So, this is a friend of yours, then? Well, any friend of yours is a friend of mine. Especially after your help back there. And not to mention, your work on Fatgirl's new website."

"Wha—?" I could barely move my lips.

So it is true.

AB gave Zeus an appreciative look. "Tell me what else you're good at doing with computers."

Zeus glanced at me, and then turned back to her. "Well, there's a lot I know how to do," he began, his face gradually getting more red. Except for his pimples, which were whiter than ever.

I was still in too much shock to do anything else as he talked about his family's cyber security company.

"I'd hate to have to call in a favor for ZZ's auction," AB said. "And possibly some camera work for the classroom."

I instantly realized where she was going with this and I stood up, preparing to fight.

"No." I slammed my fat foot down on the ground and crossing my arms across my ballooned-up chest. I knew I was throwing a tantrum, but this was too much. "We are absolutely *not* going to ask him to help us."

"Clearly, *you're* beyond help," AB retorted. "No, I'm going to ask him to help *me*."

"That's not any different!" I just gaped at her. "Why not just alter his memory, like you did with Frank Whitey?"

"So, you were the one who captured him." Zeus grinned. "I knew it!"

"Oh, no." I shook my head, trying to deny that any of this was in any way real. "This is not possible."

"We'll see about that." AB glanced over at him. "You there. I have a deal to strike with you. Are you up to hearing the details?"

Zeus looked at me again; I had a feeling he was eager to learn more, but he didn't want to make me upset. I could almost see the conversation going on his head.

"I don't want to make Kallie angry, but I want to have an excuse to bother her more, and an even better one than my Fatgirl website … but she's already upset, and clearly I'm going to bother her no matter what I do … so I might as well go with the old lady who's clearly a psychopath … but considering I'm a weirdo too, we might just bond over our desire to make Kallie's life even more awful, and so then I'll be safe from her jamming a laser into my head and leaving me with half a brain … "

Yes, that was clearly what he was thinking.

"I'd be happy to help if I can," he said, and I felt the blood drain down from my face again.

I shook my head, making me dizzy all over again. I tried to push back against my weakness, but I only fell to my knees. All I could do then was cry out with all my bitter anger.

"No!"

Fatgirl

THE NEW NORMAL

EPISODE 4

○ ○ ○ ○

C. S. Johnson

FATGIRL
THE NEW NORMAL

○ ○ ○ ○

Once upon a time, I had a normal life.

Back then, I would wake up and get ready for school. My mom would be up, maybe reading through magazines or doing her nails, or even sometimes cleaning the house if it was really messy. She never helped me with breakfast; Mom seemed to get that I wanted to be a model, and she remembered her own experiences growing up, so when I refused to eat breakfast, she didn't force me to change my mind. She didn't really encourage me in my modeling pursuits, either, which I thought was weird, until my best frenemy Amory told me that Mom probably didn't like how I was getting prettier while she only was getting older. Amory probably had a point, but then she followed it up with, "I imagine I would do the same, if I was worried about you getting prettier than me … just kidding, of course!" And then she laughed, and the rest of our group of friends joined in, so I painfully muffled out a chuckle or two and then changed the subject.

That's another story I'd like to forget, too—especially since that kind of thing still happened from time to time.

Thanks to his job, Dad was usually at work, but if he was home, he would sit with Mom at the table just off the kitchen. Mom didn't like sitting in the living room. She sometimes complained how small our house was. Dad would do his best to make her laugh, and he had about a fifty-fifty rate of success. I hated his jokes, especially the ones that were along the lines of "at least our house is so small, we don't have to worry about Kallie having a party here," but it made Mom smile, so I rarely bickered back. And it went by quickly; after that, they would often exchange silent glances that ranged to playful to bitter to strangely cryptic.

Still, they seemed happy, or at least happy enough, so I didn't think anything about it. I had other things to worry about—which camera filters made me look more angelic and authentic, where my homework was, what Amory and my other friends were up to this week. That sort of thing.

And then Mom left us, and Dad and I had to get used to a "new normal."

I hated that expression. *New normal.* It didn't allow for any possible correction, and it just assumed that this was the way things were going to be from now on. I felt as though I'd been pushed off a cliff I hadn't even seen, and now I was falling and flailing, and there was nothing left to do but wait for rock bottom.

But then it turned out I hit rock bottom and went crashing through it to something even worse.

"You owe me for this, Kate."

I was walking into the kitchen just as I heard my grandmother, Abuela-Blanca, talking on her phone—although hissing might've been a better term to describe the verbal venom barely contained inside her clenched jaws. I could feel the anger radiating from her small frame as I passed.

She took one look at me and then promptly turned away.

From that, I got the feeling AB was probably talking to one of her contacts. She had a few I knew of, despite all her secrecy; she'd talked to another "KP" on the phone before, when we'd been driving home from my complete failure of an audition for the Model Middle America show before. Was that the Kate she was talking to?

I decided I didn't really care, but I still listened in on her conversation as best I could as I took my newest jar of juice cleanse out of the refrigerator.

"You know you owe me. You wouldn't have anything if it wasn't for me. That's why you took my call. Don't be a fool." AB tapped her foot on the floor, clearly irritated. "But then I suppose that's a bit like asking a leopard to change its spots, isn't it?"

I snickered into my cup, trying to keep quiet. AB heard me anyway and headed back down the hall, toward the door to her basement room. I just sat there, reluctantly amused. There were days I would give anything in the world to have the old "new normal," instead of the one I had to face now, and AB was the worst kind of reminder of my plight.

But I had to give her props. She had a real skill when it came to insulting people, and as a high schooler, I could appreciate that.

AB was a former government employee, a scientist who'd worked with the NAH—the National Association of Healthcare—to apparently create bio-weapons and other strange projects, including her Project: SERUM, which was the reason I was known throughout the city as Fatgirl now.

I slumped into my chair. The old wood creaked even at my slender bottom, and I couldn't help but groan even more.

Not now. I don't need another *reminder of that mess.*

I winced again.

There was no escaping the truth.

A small *beep* chimed out from the tablet AB had left on the kitchen counter, and I read the notification.

Immediately, I groaned.

Fatgirl had made the news again.

My stomach rumbled and I thought briefly of the candy Dad had hidden in the back of the freezer. It was tempting, but then I remembered my mom, and I embraced the pain of my tummy rumblings.

Better to feel empty in the stomach than in the heart.

I did walk over to the sink and dump out my juice cleanse, however. Eating was what had gotten me into this mess anyway.

Thanks to AB's radioactive doughnuts, my own emotional turbulence, and accidentally stopping a terrorist, plus unintentionally acquiring a growing fanbase any modern-day influencer or activist would kill for, my life was anything but normal.

Now, when I woke up, my mother *still* wasn't home, and my more-than-odd grandmother was waltzing around my house as resident babysitter, secretly trying to figure out who it was who'd stolen her recipe and framed her for its theft.

And as petty as it might've been, I could only be happy I wasn't the only one who was suffering. I heard AB make her way back toward the kitchen, clearly eager to end her conversation, and I smiled.

Her pain was like a drug, one that made me into a more terrible person—but like a madman finally snipping the last thread of his sanity, I only felt intoxicating, abysmal pleasure.

"I'll be back in touch later, if for no other reason than to remind you that you could be rotting in prison now if it wasn't for me," AB scoffed into the phone. "You won't get rid of me so easily; I can assure you of that."

She cut off the line, and the frustration on her wrinkled face almost made me felt sorry for her.

Well, maybe I really did. I could see the unspoken sense of angry helplessness in her gaze—something I knew from experience and genetics she'd never admit to—and as I watched her clench her phone in her hand, I suddenly wondered if she was going to chuck it, like I'd done to my own phone only a week ago.

"If that lady needs a testimonial to your persistence, I'll give her one," I said, trying to add some levity to the situation. "I can't even get rid of you."

AB didn't take the bait. "You don't need to worry about it, Kallie."

"Good to know." As I sat back and rolled my eyes, I silently chided myself for hoping she would take me into her confidence.

"You shouldn't be listening in on my calls."

"You shouldn't be taking calls where I can hear them," I shot back. "Even Dad would agree with me. That's how he would hear about what I had going on."

"Why aren't you talking on your phone with your friends now, instead of worrying who I'm talking to?" AB retorted. "They didn't excommunicate you over the new phone I bought you, did they?"

"No." I dug my fingernails into my palms as I tried not to think about that. AB had "fixed" my old phone—the same one I'd thrown across the kitchen—but upon hearing me harass Dad for a new one, she "fixed" the situation by getting me a new phone herself.

It was a nice enough phone, even a tech-gen higher than the one I'd wanted, but AB had purposefully gotten me a neon blue phone case to go along with it. And I knew she did it to annoy me, since I'd told her before I wanted a pink phone even if it clashed with my coloring since it would keep Amory off my back about my color quotas. AB had made a big show of giving it to me in front of Dad, too, so I wasn't able to call her out on her trickery.

Not without sounding like an entitled brat, anyway.

"Speaking of getting rid of you, when are you going to LA?" I asked instead. "You need to find ZZ, don't you?"

Thanks to my considerable efforts as Fatgirl, AB and I had discovered that one of the people who had AB's radioactive doughnut recipe was Zina Morozova, the former daughter of a KGB agent who lived in LA. She would be auctioning off AB's recipe at a special gala soon.

AB sniffed. "Well, I wanted to go the other day but you weren't very eager to help, and then your little boy-toy went and ate my doughnuts."

"I don't want to help you anymore," I said. "And you promised. After Frank Whitey was returned to the city police, you said you'd get my mom back here. That was the deal you made, remember?"

"Of course I remember," AB scoffed. "But you're lucky I was able to help that Blake boy out. You don't want him to have any further complications due to my recipe, do you?"

"What?" My mouth dropped open in shock. "He's still in danger?"

"It's hard to imagine he would be, considering a relapse or re-exposure would only turn him back into a simpering little twit of a weak nerd, unable to carry the reputation and supposed glory he's managed to accumulate through the years." AB reached for her coffee cup. "I'm sure many people would step up to protect him."

"That's not fair!" I crossed my arms over my chest. "You gave him the anti-serum."

"Yes, but radioactivity is a treacherous science," AB said. "Perhaps you'd better go to LA with me, in case he eats some more of my doughnuts?"

"Does radioactivity make you insane?" I asked. I glanced back toward Dad's room, briefly wondering if he was home.

"He's not home," AB confirmed.

I ignored her remark, even if I heard it. "When was the last time you had a CAT scan?"

"Which movie did you take that retort from?" AB smirked. "It's *CT scan*, and the government still requires a psych exam, but it's not required unless it's tied to a legal matter."

"I'm still a minor, and your kind of manipulation can be considered abuse," I said.

"You're seventeen. That is the age of consent," AB said. She nodded toward the now-empty jar of juice cleanse. "And anyway, it's clear you've already made some more adult choices. Isn't that recommended for adults that are eighteen years or older?"

"You're threatening Blake's livelihood," I accused. "Not to mention the lacrosse team's sports record."

"Oh, yes, how important *that* is." AB snorted, clearly holding back a tidal wave of mocking laughter.

"Shut up," I grumbled. "You don't understand."

"No, *you* don't understand. My recipe is a matter of personal honor and national security, Kallie. This is dangerous, and if anything else happens, things are just going to get worse for me."

I paused for a moment, stricken with hope. If this situation really was as dangerous as she said, then she wasn't going to really let anything happen to Blake. She could try to manipulate me, but *she didn't want to make anything worse.*

"So how do I know if Blake has a relapse?" I asked, suddenly taking on the mask of the conscientious student. "What if he shrinks down into a mini-kid once like last time?"

"Call me," AB said. Her blue eyes darkened with suspicion. "And pray we don't need Fatgirl to calm him down again."

"I doubt I managed to calm him down the first time." I grimaced, thinking of how I didn't even want to stick him with a needle to get the blood sample AB needed to create the anti-serum. "But I'll watch out for him, and I guess I'll let you know if there's any trouble."

"Don't you dare think of lying about it to try to provoke me, Kallie."

The deadly seriousness of her voice made me swallow hard, but I stood my ground.

"Why would I want to cause trouble for *you*?" I asked, a little too sweetly. "It's not like you're threatening my friends or anything."

AB scowled. "I'll know if you're lying," she said. "I've been working with the Phi-ger to widen it's signal range. I'll know if there's a problem with Blake if the radioactivity levels in his blood increase. As long as he doesn't eat any more doughnuts, he should be fine."

Relief washed through me, but I didn't let her see it. It was clear I would have to be strong if I was going to work with AB at all—or, more accurately, if I was going to make sure I didn't have to work with her.

"Good. Then you'll be able to stop it before it gets too complicated. So Fatgirl can enjoy her retirement." I paused for a moment, before adding, "And my mom will be coming home soon, too, right?"

It was at this remark that AB looked away, turning her attention back over to her phone. "I'll see when we can get to LA," she said. "ZZ is there, too. We might as well have a personal reason to travel to LA if I'm going to confront one of the queens on the black market."

Before I could argue, she nodded toward the clock. "You'd better get going," she said. "You'll be late for school, and you can't threaten the livelihood of your school record."

I glared at her, but she was right. I hurried to grab my bag and pull on my shoes, and I was almost completely free of her when she called back to me.

"By the way, why don't you invite that nice boy over for tea sometimes?" AB asked. "I'd like to get to know him better."

"No! I don't want Blake within a ten-mile radius of you," I snapped.

AB chuckled. "He's already there, considering you live three blocks away from school."

"Shut up." I felt like screaming at her. "I'm still not bringing him home to meet the likes of you."

"Good. I'd hate for any extra radioactivity that might be in the air here to trigger him," AB said.

She probably knew how my heart dropped to realize Blake might never be able to come and meet Dad, if we ever started seriously dating.

Not while AB is here. I slowly let out my breath, trying to remain calm, even as that notion went against every instinct inside of me. *Get her out of here first, and then I'll be able to do it then.*

"Either way," AB said, "I wasn't talking about him. I was talking about the other boy. The one who came and helped us with Blake's Baby-Boy tantrum."

Zeus.

There was no way to explain how I didn't manage to scream up into the endless sky, venting a world's worth of frustration out into the cosmos. What do you know? Miracles do happen, and largely by stopping other things.

"I'm *not* going to worry about *him*," I insisted. "You're the one who just said that if this gets any worse, it'll be on you."

And then I ran away, somewhat desperately glad I was going to school where I could forget about AB entirely, if for only a few hours.

○ ○ ○ ○

"There you are, Kallie! We've been waiting for you for forever, practically."

Normally, Amory Franklin's cheerful tone would concern me. There were only a limited number of things that genuinely made her happy, and most of those things seemed to correlate to other people's miseries. But I was so miserable myself as I walked into school, I didn't see how it could get any worse.

"Hey, girls." I greeted my friends with a fake smile, hoping to at least convince them I was happy and normal, even if I knew I was not. "What's going on?"

"Did you see the news this morning?" Amory squealed, while my other friends huddled over her phone. June and Uli were whispering back and forth excitedly, while Lizzie was practically jumping up and down.

"Um … "

I thought of AB's tablet notifications, and the "Fatgirl" alert.

Do I want to hear this? I couldn't help but wonder.

"Model Middle America is going to do another episode in Cuttingham City!" Lizzie broke first, before she let out a loud, excited giggle.

"What?" Hope sparked inside of me again, as if I had been in a grave and was suddenly brought back to life. "Really?"

"Here," June said, stepping forward and showing me the news on Amory's phone. "Take a look."

I looked down to see the WACC Morning Show co-host, Gynnifer Stills. She was a popular news anchorwoman throughout Cuttingham City, looking impeccably perfect with her bright blonde hair brushed back and her makeup classy and respectable, even if it seemed a little uneven because of the TV studio's lighting. But, most importantly, Gynnifer was indeed talking about *Model Middle America.*

" … the executive producer of the show, Karen Bright, is hopeful that the show will air back in the city this week if there's enough interest, now that the FBI has cleared the use of the Amphitheatre after the notorious criminal mastermind, Frank Whitey, attempted to hold the building hostage nearly two weeks ago … "

The screen cut to a news briefing, where a familiar face caught my attention. It was Officer Max Powers, the man who'd originally helped me stand up after falling down and flattening Frank.

"The police will increase the security," he said. "We cannot let the terrorists win. We must continue on with our lives in quiet acts of bravery, and …"

As much as Officer Powers seemed like a nice man, and I was glad to see he was getting a bit of the limelight—truth be told, I was happy to give all of it to him—I quickly tuned him out, and then I hurriedly turned off the report.

I didn't want him to mention Fatgirl, but if he did, I did not want to hear it.

"See?" Amory held out her hand, and I gave her back her phone. "Isn't it great?"

"This is wonderful!" I could barely speak without shouting, and as the euphoria threatened to overtake me, I understood Lizzie's effervescence and joined in with her. Inside, I was overwhelmed, and I nearly wept with sublime happiness.

Dreams could come true, after all, if you were only willing or forced to suffer for them.

My friends agreed with my reaction, and we held hands and squirmed with excitement. Even though the bell was ringing with its last tardy warning, I felt nothing but joy.

There was a tap on my shoulder, and I whirled around like a ballerina, half-expecting Blake Turner to be there, ready to ask me to be his girlfriend at last.

"Uh, hi, Kallie."

The excitement inside of me came crashing to an abrupt halt.

There, in front of me, was none other than Zeus Evans, the boy who ran Fatgirl's popular fansite and the only other person on the planet who knew my secret superhero identity.

Not to mention he was tall, ugly, and fat, like some kind of toasted Marshmallow Man with bad acne and glasses.

At least he seemed to know he'd made a mistake in saying anything at all to me.

That didn't stop him from trying again, though; in some ways, I might've thought it was charming that he was terrified of my friends, seeing as how he was head and shoulders taller than all of us, and thicker than two of us tied together. But in other ways, I was probably just as terrified of my friends, too—and I was one of them.

Zeus cleared his throat. "I was wondering if I could talk with you?"

"Aw, this is so sweet." Amory laughed. "You're not going to tell her you have a crush on her, are you?"

Zeus blushed, looking flustered, and my other friends all began to chuckle, too. All of this happened while I just stood there, wide-eyed and choking on my tongue.

What could I say? I didn't even know if I literally *could* say anything. My mouth wasn't moving, and the rest of my body wasn't willing to cooperate, either.

"I had a question about Mr. Embers' class," Zeus finally said. "I was just wondering if you could help me?"

Well, he was hard on the eyes, but at least he was quick on the recovery.

"Uh, not right now," I said, finally managing to find my voice again. "And I'm sure Mr. Embers would be happy to talk—"

"I'd rather have you. I mean—"

Ugh, his face was so annoying. His glasses were thick, but I could see his eyes so big and lost as he looked at me.

Zeus blushed again, before stammering on, trying to explain it was a special project he had on the side, and he needed my help.

Clearly, he was talking about his website. AB's "Fatgirl" notification popped into my mind again. Maybe someone needed my help with something? Or people were trying to call me to a crime scene?

I didn't want to think about that.

"You know … Person … you really should have more respect for the beautiful people." June put her hands on her hips as she stepped between Zeus and me. "Perhaps you should leave now, before any of us scream. Right, Kallie?"

"Um—"

"See? Leave." Amory linked arms with June, and Zeus quietly nodded and turned away.

"Well, thank goodness that's over," Amory said. "You really need to be better about standing up for yourself, Kallie. It's a good thing we were here to help you."

"Women who are pretty and popular like us have a right not to allow men to treat them any way they don't want to be, and encouraging creepy behavior like that would be wrong," June added.

"I don't get it. He was only saying hi and asking for help," Lizzie said. "What's so bad about that?"

"Well, I thought he was Blake, for one," I said, unable to hide my glumness.

"Well, Blake's still out from that whole Fatgirl debacle," June said, making me flinch. "And anyway, this is much worse than that. This is a case of verbal rape, pretty much."

"What?" Lizzie looked confused, and frankly, I didn't blame her. I was actually glad she said something, so I didn't have to look dumb in asking the questions.

"Lizzie, don't be daft," June said. This is how people manipulate others. They ask for help, so if you say no, you're the bad guy, and if you do help, you're stuck spending your time with them. It's a classic tactic."

Lizzie and I exchanged a questioning look, but Uli reached over and patted my arm in sisterly comfort. "Too bad it's an issue in real life. On social media, you could so easily block him, Kallie."

"You should report him," Amory said.

"Maybe." I cleared my throat as I caught sight of Amory's clearly displeased look. "But only if he tries it again. I suppose I can be gracious this one time and allow him this once."

It was a compromise, a concession, and it worked. Amory and June were both appeased, and I felt pretty clever for winning a game that was supposed to be impossible.

As we headed for our classrooms, I turned back to see Zeus glancing back, looking over his shoulder. His expression reminded me of dog leaving with his tail between his legs, and I felt really bad.

I hope he doesn't tell anyone about my identity in retaliation for this.

At that pulse-pounding thought, I reluctantly slowed to a stop.

"What is it, Kallie?" Uli asked.

"I forgot a book from my locker. I'll be right back," I lied.

"Don't be late for homeroom," Amory reminded me. "We'll have to have a prep session at my house before the Model Middle America auditions reopen, and I'd hate to think you'd miss it if you're in detention for being late."

"I won't," I promised, before giving them a slight wave.

The instant my friends were distracted, I turned around and sprinted for Zeus. He was standing at his locker with another girl, one of the other girls from Mr. Embers class.

"I heard you ask Kallie for some help," she was saying. "I thought I'd offer to see if I could help you instead. I know she's pretty busy."

Who is this? I came up beside them just as Zeus was starting to answer her.

"Oh, please don't worry about it," he said. "I can figure it out, I guess. I just thought I'd … ask … "

He looked over to see me and stopped talking. His face flushed red again, as if he'd been caught red-handed in a crime.

Well, I guess if June was right in her way of thinking, it was a crime for him to talk about me behind my back.

"Oh, hi, Kallie." The girl standing next to him looked at me. Her eyes were a bland sort of blue, and her hair was a dusky blonde. She wasn't the sort of person who seemed to want to cause trouble, and for the moment, I could appreciate that.

"Oh, hi." I narrowed my eyes at her, trying to remember her name.

It was never really an important thing I thought I'd have to recall, so it took me a lot longer than I wanted.

"I'm Gloria," she said, just as I remembered it myself.

"Oh. Right." I nodded.

A small, awkward silence fell between the three of us. Gloria was clearly an average girl. I didn't know how smart she was, or if she was a nerd or not. She wasn't thin enough to be considered attractive, but she wasn't fat, either. I could see she was kind and considerate, like most blank slate people who had little to no definite personality traits. I realized I'd seen her before, the day of my fart attack in Mr. Embers' class—the day I became aware of Zeus at all, thanks to his kindness when he took the blame for my surprise TNT-sized tooting.

Come to think of it, Zeus and Gloria would probably be good friends, I realized.

Gloria gave us both a small wave and took a careful step back. "Well, see you guys in class."

Well, I guess Gloria was smart. She clearly knew no one else had anything to say to her.

"She's nice," I said to Zeus, as she walked away.

"Yeah, she is." Zeus looked away from me. "I guess your friends are gone?"

"For now." I almost smiled, seeing the relief on his face, and realizing that was close to how I felt, too. But then I corrected myself immediately.

Zeus and I weren't friends. I was here to make sure he didn't open his fat pie hole about Fatgirl the moment my actual friends were mean to him.

"Look, I'm sorry about Amory and them," I said. "They're … protective of me."

"I've noticed." Zeus put his hands in his pockets. "And I can understand how you would be a little jittery around me."

"You are?"

"Yeah. I know you're still kind of upset about the whole Blake thing. Although I swear it wasn't my fault he ended up like that."

I bit my lip. "I know that."

"That's good." Zeus let out a sigh of relief. "I thought you would've blamed me for the whole Baby Blake thing, since you knew Blake and I don't get along."

Zeus had told me once in passing how Blake was a bit of a bully to him, and after watching my friends be somewhat harsh to him, too, I guess I could understand. And thinking about how Blake had transformed into a white, baby-sized, weakling version of Zeus after eating AB's doughnuts—the same doughnuts that triggered transformations based on a person's biggest fears—I could really understand that there was a chasm between Zeus and me that wouldn't be so easily bridged. It'd be like trying to build an elevator to the moon, while the first floor was at the bottom of the Grand Canyon.

"I did hear he's doing okay, just resting at home, and he'll be back to school soon," Zeus added. "So that's good news."

I nodded in agreement. Blake had another lacrosse game in a few days, and he had to be back to school by then if he wanted to play in it.

"No, it wasn't your fault," I said. "But I can tell you what will be your fault. If anyone finds out about … Fatgirl … *that* will be your fault."

"I already told you, I wouldn't tell," Zeus said. "I'd like to try to help. That's actually why I wanted to talk to you. Someone's reached out through the website."

"Oh, come on. No one would do that," I said. "Not seriously, anyway."

"It looks pretty legit," Zeus said. "It's from a lady who says her fiancé has been acting strange. He's having panic attacks, seeing his dead wife's ghost, and as of this morning, he won't leave his house. She's worried he'll have a heart attack next."

"Unless the guy murdered his wife, that sounds more like a gas leak than a Fatgirl thing," I said with a huff. "Besides, that's not how these things work."

I already didn't want to be here, having any conversation at all with Zeus, but I especially didn't want to tell him about AB's radioactive doughnuts, her quest for a thief, and her mission to restore her government-given honor.

Zeus cleared his throat quietly. "I know it's not a bat signal in the sky, but people do want your help from time to time."

"Stop it." I rolled my eyes. "Who would really want my help? All I do is sit on bad guys."

"You give people hope," Zeus said. "And this lady is begging for you to come and see. She's a public figure, Kallie. Her email checks out. And I know her, too. Sort of. My dad does, anyway."

"What? What are you talking about?"

Before I could get an answer, the bell rang, and at that, I'd decided I'd had enough.

I was late for homeroom, I was likely going to get a detention, Zeus was clearly using this Fatgirl thing to manipulate me into spending time with him and giving perks to his friends and family, and if I didn't, he was going to find a way to emotionally blackmail me for the rest of my life until I gave in and just married him.

Or he died.

"Never mind. That's enough," I said. "Look, I'm very sorry your 'friend' has this 'problem,' but this is not something that I do. The whole Fatgirl thing was an accident, and I'm not going to talk to you about this again. And if you ever speak of this to anyone at all, I will literally kill you. I will eat another round of radioactive doughnuts, sit on your face, and suffocate you, and then I will laugh at your funeral."

I jabbed my finger into his hoodie, poking him in the chest. "Do you understand?"

"Kallie—"

"No," I snapped. "Yes or no, do you understand?"

"Yes." Zeus sighed. "I understand."

There was a note of glumness in his voice that echoed my own earlier gloominess, but I didn't let it stop me. I understood how awful

I was being, but I had to put my foot down when it came to standing up for myself, and I couldn't just magically be Zeus' friend and go out superhero-ing whenever he felt like giving his friends a photo-op. I was basically already doing that for AB, only instead of love she was getting her version of justice, and she at least had the decency to bribe me with getting my mother to come home.

What good could Zeus offer me?

He probably thinks he can be my "friend," too, just like one of those terrible, extra-cheesy after-school specials where the popular girl falls in love with the unpopular guy because he "truly gets her."

I rubbed my temples, trying to squeeze that image out of my head. "Ugh."

"You should know, I really won't tell anyone your secret," Zeus said. "I just wanted to help, really."

"How is forcing me into some superhero role with a website helping anyone?" I asked, exasperated. Before he could answer me, I shook my head, trying to clear myself of my stress. The last thing I needed now was Amory teasing me about getting stress lines. I cringed at the thought.

"Are you okay?" Zeus asked.

"No. But you know, this isn't helping at all. We're done here. I'll see you later in Mr. Embers' class, but *please*, for the love of God, don't talk to me."

I didn't wait for confirmation this time. Instead, I sauntered off to class. Hopefully, I could explain to my homeroom teacher I was late because of "female troubles," and only get a warning this time.

By the time I made it down the hall, I had my speech prepared, and fake tears on standby. Really, that was the easiest part—all I had to do was think of Zeus publishing a blog on how I, Kallie Grande-White, was really Fatgirl, and my eyes would be awash with teardrops ready to spill out and flood the world.

A few slipped out anyway as I finally made it to class.

○ ○ ○ ○

It really was a shame that Blake wasn't at school that day. I usually used him as a way to distract myself from my worries or boredom after I was finished up with my school work, and between Abuela-Blanca's lies and broken promises and Zeus' attempt to be all buddy-buddy and friendy-friendy while I was hanging with my actual friends, I could've used something nice to think about.

The only thing I really had was the hope of a new *Model Middle America* audition.

But after thinking about it, I realized how utterly hopeless even that hope was.

What if Azure was there, looking for "Arlanda," the name he'd thankfully given me instead of my actual name because I "looked like an Arlanda or something" apparently? He'd been the one who'd given me an array of clothes that included that hot pink mess from before, the one that my Fatgirl costume originated from—what if he remembered that monstrosity when he saw my face and made the connection? And there was the matter of the stage manager and the other girls who'd seen me before, too. What if in going there, I triggered a memory and someone else was able to find out I was Fatgirl?

I couldn't bear for any of that to happen. Even thinking about it made me feel paranoid. All day, Fatgirl's massive shadow loomed over me.

It didn't help I seemed to run into Zeus everywhere, either.

It was seriously like some kind of horror show, where I would run into him, lock eyes with him, and I'd be forced to remember how insistent he was that I should help his so-called "friend" with her fiancé and his agoraphobia.

I'd just be walking down the hall with my friends, and he was there.

I'd be walking into class and there he was.

I was finished up with gym and he'd be there—sweatier than usual—as if he was waiting for me by the exit.

Who does that, other than someone in a horror film?

By the time Mr. Embers' class started, I could barely concentrate, worried Zeus would say something to me. He sat behind me, and it was all I could do not to turn around and stare daggers into his skull like I was sure he was doing to me, even if I didn't catch him in the act. My anxiety further increased as I saw Gloria walk by, and I remembered our earlier greeting.

Why are these unpopular, irritating people making me so upset?

I didn't scream, but I was close to it throughout the entirety of my day.

My anxiety got so bad, I even cancelled on meeting up with Amory and the others after school. They were planning on going to June's house, to coordinate outfits for the new *Model Middle America* audition. I knew I wasn't likely going to go to the audition anyway, so what was the point of pretending to prepare for it? I would only suffer from my brain screaming all my fears at me, every second of every moment my friends talked about it, and so I feigned a headache, and headed home.

And when I got there, I vowed, I would make AB agree to use her memory device thing on Zeus. She'd used it before to protect my identity, right? Well, this time, it was even more warranted, despite my previous vows not to worry about it.

After all, Frank Whitey was a dangerous criminal, but he didn't know me personally, and he had nothing against me. And he didn't really even find out who I was for sure. Still, he was clearly a man who knew how to control himself and manage his resources, which included his secrets and favors. He'd almost killed me several times, and it was only because of my own unpredictable and somewhat mismanaged skill set I'd managed to finally sit on him. With AB's Agent Iris and her other tools, we'd managed to render him helpless long enough to alter his memory and get him back into police custody.

Zeus, on the other hand, was another story. He knew me personally. He'd somehow found out my real identity—something I would have to discover, just to make sure there were no more loose ends—and he apparently had a crush on me. Even if I couldn't blame him for that, he was easily flustered by my presence, with very little provocation. He was also in one of my central worlds as a fellow student in my high school. We were forced into close proximity several times a day, and enough so that I was going crazy just seeing him.

Yes. Clearly something has to be done about him—even if it meant making another deal with AB.

I couldn't trust Zeus any more than I could trust AB, and that was almost a non-entity in itself.

○ ○ ○ ○

"Okay, AB, you win. Apparently, I need your help."

I walked into the house, a defeated woman. I was ready to ask for help. I wasn't as prepared to pay for the anticipated help, but I couldn't do nothing when it came to Zeus. "I need you to use your memory swiper on that boy who's got a crush on me."

There was a sudden *crash* in the kitchen, as though someone had dropped a cup into the sink.

"Why, Kallie, you're so imaginative," AB called out to me with a hearty chuckle. "Memory swiper? How quaint."

"What're you talking about?" I frowned. "I know you—"

It was then that AB came out of the kitchen, making me look twice.

She was wearing a frilly apron and carrying an empty serving tray. She had all the hallmarks of a homemaker mother, right down to the bared teeth and the glaring eyes.

"Your father's home," she hissed at me. "And he's depressed. Whatever your problem is, we'll talk later."

"Dad's home?" I put my backpack down on the floor by the door. "Are you sure?"

Dad was a truck driver, for reasons I couldn't fathom, and he was often on the road throughout the week, traveling down south to Alabama or Mississippi, and sometimes even Florida. He told me once he liked driving, seeing how different people lived and the types of cities and towns he passed through, and I still couldn't fathom why he never wanted to be promoted to a steady desk job. He was smart enough, and definitely likable enough.

"You shouldn't bother him right now," AB told me, her voice still sharp.

"He's my dad," I snapped back.

"And he's my son."

"Good to know." I pushed past AB, even as she moved to stop me, only to walk into the kitchen and come to a quick stop.

Immediately, I had to wonder if perhaps she'd tried to stop me for my own sake, not my dad's.

My dad was definitely home. He was sitting at the kitchen table, along with the open bottle of scotch I'd seen him drink the night he told me Mom left. His eyes were glazed over and he seemed much more disheveled than he should've been.

"Dad?" I hesitated as I approached him. "Are you okay?"

"Oh. Kallie." He shook his head. "I'm fine. You shouldn't be here, though. Why aren't you at your friends' house today? Or isn't there a game at the school? You usually never come home after school."

"I come home sometimes," I argued, trying not to feel defensive. Dad was right about my habits, but this was not the right time to bring them up.

Not when he was bottoming out.

"What happened?" I asked. "Did you get fired today?"

"I wish." He forced out a laugh. "No. I heard from your mother today."

"Oh. You did?" I sat down next to him at the table. In a show of support, I wound my arm through his and leaned against his shoulder.

I sat there, holding him, for a long moment. I was shocked to think that I'd forgotten how much I loved my father. I could feel the warmth of his skin through his shirt and smell the last of the aftershave my mom used to buy for him. It was easy enough for me to know he wore it for her.

His black hair was starting to speckle over into silver, but he was still my strong warrior dad. His arms were toned from helping businesses unload the trucks he drove, and he was still very fit for his age. I almost never saw him anymore, whether by his choice or his schedule, and I'd gotten used to it.

Footsteps shuffled behind me, and AB appeared in the kitchen doorway.

"Well, tell us. How is Kate?" AB asked, making me jump. "Why did she call?"

Kate.

From the look on AB's face, I didn't have to ask; she'd been talking to my mother on the phone earlier.

"She called today and threatened to send the divorce papers if I try to contact her again," Dad said. "I don't understand it. I haven't talked to her in months."

Glancing over at AB, who looked uncharacteristically guilty, I realized what happened. She'd called my mom this morning, and my mom, even though she apparently owed my grandmother a favor, was striking back to delay her payment by using my dad and me as leverage.

AB sniffed delicately. "That's terrible, Johnny. But you shouldn't drink yourself into a stupor. Why don't you go upstairs and take a nap? I'll see to the house."

I narrowed my eyes at her. Comments like that were why women could never be taken seriously.

"Thanks. I will." Dad patted my hand affectionately. "I'm sorry you saw me like this, Kallie. I'll make it up to you."

It was hard to watch him as walked—stumbled—toward the door, before he turned around.

"Come to think of it, I can do that now," he said. He reached into his pocket and took out a colorful envelope, one stamped with a logo on it I immediately recognized.

"Here," he said. "My boss gave these to me before I left work. Apparently, the *Model Middle America* showrunners are going to do another episode this week. Sounds like something you'd like, right?"

I nodded, but I took the envelope without a shred of real excitement. I didn't even want to think about the show.

Did anything matter anymore, in this *new normal*?

I was not able to shake off the shackles of my heroic transgressions, Zeus was a problem, and AB was nothing but an irritation. The more I tried to escape my problems, the more I seemed to find more.

"I'll help you up to bed, Johnny," AB said, putting her arm around my dad's shoulder. She glanced back at me, but that time, I looked away.

○ ○ ○ ○

Despite how it might've felt, it wasn't long before AB came back downstairs. I was still sitting there, holding the tickets Dad had given me, when AB walked into the room and started cleaning the empty teacups stacked up in the sink. For a few moments, both of us said nothing.

And then I ruined the quiet peace we had by daring to ask the question I most desperately wanted to know.

"Why did you call my mom?" I asked.

For a long moment, she pretended to ignore me, turning up the water pressure.

"I heard you earlier," I said, this time more loudly.

"I'd rather not talk about it." AB turned off the water and began drying a cup before she carelessly slammed it down onto the counter. "Needless to say, neither of us enjoyed it."

"She was surprised, then?"

"Of course." She pursed her lips together tightly, as if she was forcibly sucking on a lemon.

I looked down at the floor. "I'm sorry."

"Oh, darling, do not ever apologize for her. That is not your job, to ask for her forgiveness, especially for her own transgressions." Her voice was so soft and sharp, her words were like a whip crashing into my heart. I almost teared up. AB was, in her own way, protecting me, and I hadn't felt that kind of womanly kinship in a long time.

And then she added, "You have enough to apologize for when it comes to yourself."

I rolled my eyes. "Good to know."

Another moment passed before she sighed. "As terrible as it sounds, I wish I could say that racism was the reason for the problems between your mother and me. It's easier to condemn such potent shallowness and move on than it is to fix years of distrust, betrayal, and disappointment—assuming that it's possible at all to do so, of course."

AB finished washing the dishes as I fell back into silence. After seeing my dad suffer, and knowing my own suffering as I did, I didn't like thinking AB had a point about my mother.

I didn't like thinking that maybe AB had a point about me, too. I'd been okay with thinking she was a psychopath and a liar, and yes, maybe she was those things, but she was keeping her promises to me so far. She'd tried to get Mom to contact me, hadn't she?

And that's when I realized another truth.

Mom probably called Dad to get AB off her back. My eyes snapped up to meet my grandmother's, and she looked away, doubtlessly guilty.

"I didn't mean to upset you or Johnny," AB muttered. "But the truth is, I will have to find another way to fulfill my promise to you, Kallie. I'll need a little more time yet, it seems."

"Whatever." I stood up from the table with a huff.

I was nearly out of the kitchen when a little chirp sounded out from AB's apron pocket. A second later, I saw her pluck a phone out of her pocket—a very familiar looking phone.

"Hey!" I stomped my foot. "That's mine."

"No, it's not. You have your phone. This one is mine."

I reached down and felt my phone in my back pocket, hoping to prove her wrong.

But here it was.

Ugh, I hated she was right. "Then why did you have to get a phone that looks just like mine?"

"I was reliably told this model was all the rage in fashion." She gave me a small, tight smirk, and I wanted to slap her for making fun of me.

"That's not funny."

"That's because you're not the one telling the joke."

I crossed my arms. "That's not funny, either."

"Well, it's worse than I thought. You don't have a sense of humor at all, apparently."

"Don't try to distract me," I said. "Why do you have a phone like mine? You already have a phone."

"I actually have several, for several different reasons," she said. "Not that you need to know that. But that might be something to keep in mind."

"Why do you have to have one just like mine?" I nodded to the blue phone in her hands. "Is it another way to get Dad to think we're getting along?"

"If you must know, this is my Fatgirl phone," AB said, her smirk growing more crooked as she looked at me. "Maybe I'll even get a special ring tone for it when it alerts me. Every hero needs a theme song, right?"

"You've got to be joking," I muttered, burning with anger. At that moment, it was a little fun to imagine myself as Fatgirl, squatting down on her with my big, flabby butt, crushing her Phi-ger and her trademark lab-in-a-bag as she tried to worm her way out from underneath me.

But in the next moment, AB frowned and pursed her lips together again. She was reading her text message.

"Hmmm. Excuse me, Kallie." She took off her apron and folded it, and then headed off toward her basement room.

"What is it?" I asked, still upset but also curious now. I brightened, suddenly hopeful. "Is it Mom?"

"Why would your mother be texting me on my Fatgirl phone?"

I gritted my teeth. "This is going to get old. Every kind of humor comes with an expiration date, even yours."

"Let's hope my expiration date comes first then, shall we?"

"Oh *we* already do," I muttered, making sure to keep my comments quiet enough she wouldn't hear. I didn't need her to give me another comeback.

Perhaps despite my better judgement, I followed her into the basement where she'd taken up residence only a couple of weeks ago—or was it even less than that? It was hard to say.

It wasn't the first time I'd been in her room, but the experience was still just as jarring as it had been before.

All the grandma clichés had been swiped from sight. There was no rocking chair or knitting basket, there was no collection of teacups or immaculately dusted furniture. Instead, AB's room looked like a small research lab—which, all things considered, was probably the most accurate label for it.

"Why are you still bothering me?" AB asked. She began typing on one of her many keyboards. She nodded toward the tickets Dad had given me, the ones I was still holding onto. "Don't you have a show to prepare for?"

"I don't think I'm going to go," I admitted. The bitterness in my voice was thick enough even AB did a double-take.

"Why not?"

"Someone might recognize me."

"You vastly overestimate yourself," AB said with a dull laugh. "If you did go, I doubt anyone would take a second look at you."

"Fatgirl's made quite an impression on people," I reminded her. "Which brings me to my next point. I need you to meddle with that kid's mind, the one who helped us out with Blake."

"You mean Zeus?"

The corner of her mouth twitched, and I crossed my arms over my chest, preparing for battle. There was something about the way she looked that suggested she was enjoying herself, and I hated her even more for laughing at my expense.

"You know who he is," I said. "And I don't think we can trust him at all. It's better we take your memory scrambler and erase his memories of Fatgirl. Of me, too, if you can."

"I'm not going to do that."

"What?" I snapped. "Why not? I thought you had to hide me for your own sake."

"Yes, I do," AB agreed. "But I think we can trust Zeus for now. Unless you do something stupid."

"Me?" I gasped. "What are you talking about?"

"Kallie, he managed to figure out you were Fatgirl. I had my contact down at the police station erase all the video footage and damage it beyond repair. How does this Zeus boy know it's you?"

I didn't know the answer to that, and AB knew that.

"He's a minor, like you, so there's only so many records I can ruffle through," AB continued. "And he's Hispanic."

"That sounds racist," I objected.

"It's a fact, Kallie, and facts are just facts. His family is large—"

"I've noticed."

"—and Evans is a fairly common name in the Hispanic community around here," AB said. "Finding information on him is going to take time. And depending on his family, it might take even more to gain the upper hand. That ties into why swiping his memories or altering his brain will not be the best step in this case, too."

I blinked, realizing what AB was actually saying. "So you don't actually trust him?"

"Goodness, no," AB said. "But we need to pretend to, for a little while, at least, until we're in a better position to negotiate."

I looked away, studying the various computer monitors and different piles of folders around the room, wondering what kind of life AB had, that she'd think that way. "That sounds more than a little cynical. I mean, he's just a high schooler."

"You do the same thing with your so-called friends," AB reminded me. "It's not cynical so much as practical. And it helps in the boy's case that he genuinely seems to like you and he wants to help. Case in point. He sent me a text about the executive lady who's asking for Fatgirl's help."

"What?" This time, I nearly yelled. "He *texted* you?"

"It's not techno-rape, before you get started," AB said with another smirk, and I suddenly wondered if she was able to listen into my conversations with my friends. "I gave him my number when you were all passed out in the classroom after tending to your baby-boy crush."

My head started spinning, and I felt faint. AB was working with Zeus?

"What on earth did I do to deserve all this?" I whined, dropping to the floor in a fetal position. I ducked my head between my knees, feeling a rush of needed blood to my head.

"We live in a fallen world, Kallie," AB said gently, surprising me with her light tone. "And we share the world's pain collectively as well as individually. That's how we add to it, too. But if you are willing to be strong and learn, you can help others. And that will help yourself, too. And helping out this lady and her fiancé will be a good start for you."

"I don't wanna," I muttered. "It was one thing to help Blake. I at least know him, and I like him. These people are strangers. And how do you know if I can really help them? It's not like they've eaten some radioactive doughnuts themselves."

"I wouldn't be too sure of that," AB said.

At that, I looked up at her. "What do you mean?"

"I've amplified the Phi-ger's signal, with a little unauthorized help." AB was clearly proud of herself, so it must've meant she broke the law to do it. "And the lady's fiancé is indeed showing signs of Protactinium contamination."

I could've asked what, or where, or why, but I chose the better question. "How?"

"How indeed," AB murmured. "I wonder if there's been another buyer, or if ZZ's auctioned my recipe off earlier? Come on, Kallie. Suit up."

"I don't want to." I stood up and brushed myself off. "I don't want to become Fatgirl again, and I don't want to help Zeus with this, either."

"I think you'll actually like this, you know," AB said, using the knobs on her Phi-ger to change frequencies. The small device started to creak and gargle, and then it started to beep. "The client who emailed into the website is Karen Bright, one of the executive producers—"

"From *Model Middle America*? Oh my gosh, is it really her?" The words sneaked out of my mouth before I could stop them, but I was momentarily in awe.

Karen Bright used to be a big-name model, even more famous than my mom. She was getting older now, but she was dedicated to helping younger models get into the business. If anyone could launch me into a career as a model, it would be her.

"I've always wanted to meet her," I admitted. "She's famous."

"Yes," AB said, clearly amused by my enthusiasm. "Miss Bright is asking Fatgirl to investigate her fiancé."

"Investigate?" My apprehension increased as my enthusiasm immediately waned. "I don't know anything about that."

"I'll take charge there," AB said. She reached down and pulled a box out of desk drawer. It was a pink box, and I didn't have to ask to know it was full of her doughnuts. "But the Phi-ger doesn't lie, and Zeus is right. This looks legit."

"How do you know?" I hesitated for a moment, unwilling to sound like a paranoid conspiracy theorist who hung out on the dark edges of the internet all day. "What if it's a trick to get Fatgirl onto her show or something like that?"

"Her fiancé is Robert Cuttingham III," AB said, pulling up a profile on another one of her monitors. "He's the heir of the Cuttingham City's founder, and one of the richest men in the state. He's grifting on his family name, but he's doing a good job maintaining its good reputation. And the man's cleaner than a soap dish. This week has been the first time in years he's had to cancel his appearances. The press is being mum about the specifics, but he would have a good PR team at hand."

"Still, it seems a little too coincidental," I said. "I mean, why this week?"

"Their engagement was just announced last week, but with all the Fatgirl talk, I'm sure it was lost in the news pile," AB said. "It's a very whirlwind sort of romance for the both of them. She's never married, and his wife of forty-some years died last year. If he has some enemies—especially ones who have access to my recipe—this would be the perfect time to strike."

"I guess you think we're going to his house then?"

"Now you're getting it," AB said with a smile. She pushed her pink box of radioactive doughnuts toward me.

I bit my lip. "I don't want to do this."

"But what else can you do?" AB asked. "Are you really going to go to the *Model Middle America* show this week with your friends and forget all of the good you've done?"

"I'd like to." I thought about Zeus, how he knew who I was. He said I could trust him, but what did I really know? That's exactly the sort of thing someone who couldn't be trusted would say.

AB, for all her cynicism, was probably right—I couldn't trust him, but it was good to pretend to, until I could be certain he wouldn't get in my way. And God only knew how much I hated it when AB was right.

That meant it might be a good idea to look into this problem he wanted me to solve. I mean, the guy was texting my freaking grandma over this, so appeasing him might go a long way, right?

"Well?" AB asked. "Are we going or not?"

"Okay." I sighed. "It's not like I have anything else to do otherwise."

AB grinned. "That's my darling girl," she said, and for all I hated her, I couldn't help but feel a little warmth stir inside my heart.

○ ○ ○ ○

Unlike my Fatgirl moniker, it was clear on sight that Cuttingham Cottage was a misnomer.

The prestigious mansion was perfect, like something Disneyland would envy. It had all the right touches, from the gothic arches to the iron fencing, and the meticulously organized garden. As I stood outside its fancy gates, I knew it was easily a home that would've been more fitting in Beverly Hills, California than Cuttingham City, Arkansas.

"I've got to say, if I were as rich as that guy, and I had that house, I might not want to leave it either," I said.

"He barely stays here," AB said. "Cuttingham has other houses around the world, but he wanted to be here for *the Model Middle America* show. This is the first time that this city's been featured for something so big."

"You've been here as long as the *Model Middle America* people have," I said. "You can probably tell why."

"Cuttingham City is a lovely, older city, which has a lot of traditional values clashing with modern problems," AB said. "It's not for those who seek stranger thrills."

I wrinkled my nose, letting out a dismissive snort. "You've got that right."

"Well, let's go," AB said. "You ready?"

"Yep." I patted down my large, balloon-esque stomach with my now-engorged palms. The pink suit I was wearing had a nice smoothness to it, so I didn't have to feel the hardened muscles of my belly beneath it. For all the "fat" I had, it was backed by a lot of sinew and power. While I didn't like being Fatgirl for a number of reasons, it was the only way I would ever be able to defeat a professional wrestler in the ring. Unless I'd had the game rigged beforehand, of course.

But that was another scenario I didn't think would ever be possible.

Of course, I didn't think this kind of situation would ever happen, either.

I was getting to meet Karen Bright, executive producer and former model extraordinaire, and instead of the well-groomed, lithe, and well-dressed model-to-be I'd imagined myself to be in such circumstances, I was the large and in charge superhero with literally zero overall fashion sense.

AB locked her car, and together, we made our way to the front of Cuttingham Cottage.

"How do I explain you?" I asked, realizing AB was still with me.

"You won't," she said. "I'll be at the side of the mansion, just like I was before."

"You really need to get a mask or something," I told her. "I don't like doing this by myself."

"What can I say? I can't coddle you with this. Growing up is painful." She handed me a small bag. "Here. Get his blood for me so I can make the cure. And see if you can figure out how he was poisoned."

"How do I do that?"

"Ask questions. He'll need to have ingested it in a food form," AB said. "The stomach acid helps ignite the radioactivity to its deadly forms, and then the blood carries it to all the recesses of the body. So see if he's gotten any packages lately, or if he's been invited to unusual dinners."

"Would it be doughnuts?" I asked, suddenly curious. "Or could it be any food?"

"Doughnuts are the best way to deliver it," AB said, clearly only begrudgingly sharing her secrets with me. "But it's possible they might've tried other similar foods as well. After all, it's hard to say what rich people will eat these days."

Recalling some of the latest trends I'd seen on social media, I knew AB was once more right. Before I could ask her any other questions, she disappeared behind some large hedges, and I was all alone.

I really didn't want to do this by myself. Briefly, I thought of Zeus, and decided whenever I got a free moment, I would stuff some of AB's freaking doughnuts down his throat. If he wanted me to suffer for the sake of others, the least he could do was join me.

The press could call him Lard Boy, I thought, and it was that small amount of amusement that allowed me to ring the doorbell without throwing up my own half-ingested radioactive doughnuts.

The door opened, and there was Karen Bright. She was clearly stressed: there were deep lines on her forehead and around her lips, and her lips were chapped, as if she'd been chewing on them. And for all the model physique made her slim, she needed to eat more if she wasn't going to look like a walking corpse.

She seemed much more pretty when she realized it was me at the door.

"Oh, Fatgirl, this is wonderful," she gushed, hurrying to shake my hand and give me the model air-kisses on my chubby cheeks. "I was so excited to hear you were coming."

I cleared my throat, trying to make myself sound more adult. "The pleasure is all mine, ma'am."

"Oh, no need to 'ma'am,' me," she said with a welcoming laugh. "Please, call me Karen."

"Okay. Call me—er, Fatgirl." I blushed at my near-mistake. There were no informalities with these things, I mentally scolded myself.

"I must thank you for coming again," Karen said, as she turned and walked back into the house. She gestured for me to follow, though all things considered, she was probably used to having people follow her anyway. "I know that modeling is probably not 'on-brand' for you, and then there is the matter of how I'm not sure you were the right party to contact over Robert's health, but I just felt so much better after doing so, I knew it had to be right."

"Um, well, we checked into things, and it does seem like there is a complication," I said, trying not to mumble. How would I explain radioactive doughnuts to someone like Karen, especially without sounding like a lunatic who'd gone crazy from watched too many baking shows? "Can I check your kitchen?"

"Oh, you don't want to see Robert first?"

Karen's large, pretty eyes were welled up with tears, but I knew I had to stand my ground. I had to get Robert's blood for AB to make an anti-serum, and that meant I would have to find a place to hand off the blood, and that meant I had to learn the layout of the house …

This never ends, does it?

Ugh. I almost wished I had Zeus with me, just so I didn't have to draw the blood myself. I felt the small bag AB had handed me before she went into hiding. There was definitely a plunger in there, and I would have to get some of his blood myself.

Maybe I should get a waiver signed for this first? I was hardly a doctor.

"I'd like to see him, but first I want to check a few things," I said vaguely. "I mean, I have a routine to follow here. Sort of."

Karen nodded glumly. "Robert and I were so happy when we met two weeks ago," she said, making me clamp down on my mouth before I could say something inappropriate.

Inside, my mind was reeling. *Two weeks? Fourteen days? And that's all it took to fall in love? Really? This guy has to be a serial killer. Or she's a gold digger.*

But as much as I thought that, Karen didn't *seem* like a gold digger. I knew from all the magazine I'd read she had her own legacy, and AB had just said Robert was cleaner than a soap dish.

Was it really so weird that they would fall in love?

Yes. I looked down at my Fatgirl suit and sighed. *But I suppose there are stranger things that happen.*

"He was just this lovely widower," Karen mused. "I just fell in love so fast, and we were so happy to be together. This is heartbreaking."

We walked into the kitchen, and I inwardly groaned at the sight before me. The room could fit my house inside of it. The walls were lined with cabinets and small wine collections, and I didn't know where to start, only that I had to.

"Tell me more about your engagement," I said, trying to distract Karen some more. "Did you have anyone who was worried about it?"

"Worried?"

"Well, from the sound of it, you've only known each other for two weeks," I said. "Maybe someone might've been upset at the short time you've known each other?"

Karen laughed, even though her eyes were still full of tears. "I've been working my whole life, and I've had romance after romance," she said. "Robert's only ever been with his first wife, Susan. She died a year ago, but he still talks of her in such a fond way."

"So he's seeing her ghost," I said, looking through another set of cabinets. "Maybe out of guilt?"

"You don't believe him." Karen sighed. "I know this sound strange, that we would fall in love and want to get married after two weeks. His therapist says this ghost matter is all in his head, and it's not real. But I had a feeling, and I wanted to see if you could help him."

"That's why I'm here," I said. "But are you sure there wasn't anyone at all who objected to your engagement?"

Karen went quiet for a few moments, and I used the time to search through the kitchen. Robert clearly had a staff who kept his house immaculately clean, and I steeled myself as I faced the trash can.

There were large amounts of bleach that were clearly used in the cleaning process, but there was something I recognized when I opened the container.

It was a familiar smell, and in this case, a damning one as well.

Darling Donuts.

I pulled out the familiar package with the old Darla Donut mascot on the front—the one that my own mother had modeled for, back when she first met my dad—and almost cried.

It was clear that Karen knew about pain, but I doubted she knew about loss like I did.

I swallowed hard and turned back to Karen. I was about to ask her who sent the doughnuts when the doorbell rang.

"I've got to get that," Karen said. "Normally, Robert's house is very well staffed, but I felt it was better they weren't around to see this go down."

"For which I am grateful," I muttered under my breath. I took the Darling Donut box out of the trash before I followed her.

"Are you expecting other guests?" I asked, suddenly remembering how coincidental all the timing seemed.

"No, but I'm sure Robert has some appointments I wasn't able to cancel," Karen said, reaching for the door.

I was half-expecting AB to be on the other side of it, figuring that she would find a way to make me feel uncomfortable if she could.

And it turned out, I was half-right.

The door opened, and there was Zeus.

My gut rumbled, my inner regret multiplying inside of me as I looked at him. He was wearing a collared shirt and khaki pants, and he had a large windbreaker on, one that had the name "Jack" embroidered on the side along with a company logo. He also wore a hat which only did him one favor; it sort of tamed his curly black hair.

"Hello there," Karen said. "Can I help you, sir?"

Zeus tugged down on his hat, pointing to the logo that matched the one on his jacket. The name Cyber Knight Security encircled a shield with a lightning sword crossed over it.

What is he doing here?

"I'm here to speak with Mr. Cuttingham's … administrative household assistant … regarding the cyber security of your household and install the updates to his current system."

"Oh. Well, Robert's dismissed the staff for today," Karen said, clearly uneasy. She looked back at me, but I didn't know why I would help her with this.

Zeus took a step forward. "It's just a small update, Madame, and if you can show me the cable box, I'll be happy to take care of it and be on my way. I can assure you, I've already been paid for my trouble."

Paid by Abuela-Blanca, I'll bet.

"It's okay with me if he works," I said, trying to smooth over Karen's uncertainty.

"Well, okay then," Karen said, clearly relieved she didn't have to make the final justification.

I thought it was strange for a woman who was used to wielding so much power in her career industry to be at a loss when it came to the household, but I supposed it wasn't personal when she had to make decisions for business reasons. If she really loved Robert—and she seemed to—she didn't want to upset him or overstep herself when it came to his personal life.

"Thanks," Zeus said. He tipped his hat to Karen again, and then the two of us followed her as she headed toward the garage, where the circuit breaker and cable box were located.

"I apologize for the trouble to day, Mr. … ?"

"Evans," Zeus said. "But please, call me Jack." He pointed to the name tag on his chest and smiled brightly. "And please, don't worry about your schedule. I can assure you, Cyber Knight Security caters to all our clients' needs, and Mr. Cuttingham has always been very welcoming and generous to us."

"You're the ones who have done the security for the show, too, aren't you?"

Zeus blinked, and then blushed as he looked at me. "Show?" he repeated carefully, but I already knew what Karen meant.

Well, that answers that question for AB.

Zeus had a connection with the security team who'd been the ones hired to monitor the Model Middle America set. He knew enough to see the footage, and since he was clearly smitten with me, he must've recognized me in all my forms, super-huge Bubble Gum Girl figure included.

"I thought I recognized the logo," Karen said. "Yes, your company has a stellar reputation among my crew."

"Thank you." Zeus ducked his gaze away from mine, as Karen introduced me.

"This is, of course, Fatgirl," Karen said.

It irritated how proud she was to show me off.

"Nice to meet you," Zeus muttered, giving me a quick nod.

"Yes, you, too," I murmured back. Before I could make it clear to Zeus we absolutely *would* be discussing this whole turn of events later, Karen began chatting again.

We both nodded along with her comments, which were generally about the weather and other non-specific things, such as how she would want to redo the house when she and Robert got married.

"What are you doing here?" I grumbled to Zeus, keeping my voice as low as possible.

"Dr. White texted me, so I thought I'd come and meet you," Zeus said, and I honestly didn't like how long it took me to remember AB's real name wasn't actually "Abuela-Blanca." Zeus shrugged. "When she told me what was happening, I offered to help. She said you would like that."

"I don't need help."

"I know you can do your part. But I'm here to do mine, too." He pointed to his jacket logo. "I'll grab the footage for the house and we can analyze it to see who's been in and out in the past week."

"You can really do that?" I asked.

"My dad runs Cyber Knight Security," Zeus explained softly. "The lady wasn't lying about our reputation. That's how I—"

"Found out about me," I finished. "Great."

"You can trust me, Kallie." He gave me a small smile. "Just wait and see."

"That's the problem with that, though. I have to wait to see if trusting you is the right thing to do or not. I don't just know that I can."

"Well, I'm here now, too," he said. "So if you can't trust me, then you can call the cops on me for fraud and impersonating a tech support guy."

"That's true, I guess … "

I hated how well Zeus managed to endear himself to me. I was about to warn him not to slip up and ruin our cover when Karen's voice cut through my concentration again.

"—so perhaps you'd even be interested in being a guest judge on the show for this week's new round?"

"What did you say?" I blurted out the question before I could stop myself. I mean, I was practically admitting I wasn't paying attention to her. "You want me to be a guest judge for *Model Middle America*?"

"Of course," Karen said. "I need your help with Robert today, and I'd love to find a way to pay you for your troubles. Since we're having another show here, why not? You are a beloved celebrity for the town, even if we're not exactly something you might concern yourself with when it comes to … personal taste."

The way she looked me up and down made me turn purple.

If I had met her in any other way, this would not be the conversation we would be having, I thought bitterly.

"Well … thank you. I'll think about it," I lied. I didn't even want to go to the show as a spectator, let alone as a judge. But there was no doubt, we had to take care of the doughnut business first. "Let's see if I can help Mr. Cuttingham before we worry about the show."

"Excellent."

"Susan?" A man's voice called throughout the house, and it didn't take a stretch of the imagination to know it was Robert.

"Oh, dear," Karen murmured. "He must be moving around the different rooms. He tried to do this earlier but I was able to get the doctor to give him some sleep aids."

Karen hurriedly gave Zeus some general directions to the garage, and then pulled me down one last hallway.

"Here we are," she said. The apprehension in her voice was palpable, and I found out why as she opened the door.

The room was bleak, barely lit by the sunlight sneaking through the thick curtains, I was glad Zeus was gone. I didn't want him to see me look scared, which I was. Nothing about this mission gave me any comfort, especially when I heard the older man call out in confusion.

"Susan? Susan, why are you here?"

Beside me, Karen sighed. "You can imagine how these last two days have been hard on us. The doctors all said nothing was physically wrong with him."

"They're certain of that?" I asked, before I remembered AB's Phi-ger had picked up his radioactive traces. "I mean, there's nothing more that I should know before I try to help him?"

"That's all I can tell you." She shrugged.

I handed her the doughnut box I'd taken out of the garbage, trying not to think about how dirty and germ-ridden it probably was. "Can you tell me who sent these?" I asked.

"They were a gift for Robert," Karen said.

"Susan. Susan, why are you doing this to me?"

From inside the room, a shadow stirred across the floor.

"Mr. .Cuttingham?" I asked. My spine tingled in fear as I looked into the room again.

Karen sighed.

"This is actually from my ex," she said. "His name is Trevor. Trevor Darlington."

I looked down at the doughnut box in her hands again. "Darlington?"

"Oh, yeah. He's the brother of the guy who owns Darling Donuts. You know the Darla Donut people?" Karen nodded toward the box. "He was always good about sending me these when we were dating. We broke up amicably, and when he sent these to us, I was pretty sure it was a sign of goodwill. Why do you ask?"

"Um … just checking," I said. "What are some other gifts you've received since your engagement's announcement?"

"Susan … Susan … no, Susan, don't hurt me," Robert moaned as he moved in the shadows.

From what I could make out, Robert was a good-looking man, especially one who had to be at least seventy years old. His white hair was bright, but clearly mussed up. He had a matching white beard starting to pop up on his sagging chin; there were spots on his collar, and his tie was undone and hanging limp and skewed around his neck.

Where is that bag AB gave me?

I felt around my stomach rolls, looking for my belt. I'd tucked her small kit there, to keep it safe while I talked with Karen.

"Susan, don't be angry … you know I love you." Robert's misty-eyed horror gleamed in his eyes, as he suddenly popped up, right in my face.

His hands grabbed hold of my arms, and he stared at me.

"Susan, what's wrong? You're not well," Robert said, as he looked at me.

"I'm not Susan," I said, and Karen began to sob.

"You see?" she cried. "He's sick."

"Allow me to take care of him," I said. "Excuse us for a few moments, please."

I pushed Robert into the room, careful not to make him fall over. He was an old man, and while I was certain there were very few people who knew my real identity, I didn't want to wake up to a court summons for breaking his hip while trying to fix him. Before

Karen could calm down enough to object, I shut the door and turned the lock as quickly and quietly as possible.

"What's wrong with you?" Robert asked.

"Nothing, um … honey.," I tell him, trying to disguise my voice. I didn't know what Susan sounded like, but I hoped I was close enough. Just for fun—because there was literally no fun I could possibly ever really have on these sorts of missions—I layered up my Southern accent, trying to sound like the belle of the ball. "I just need to you an insulin shot, sugar."

"No," Robert said. "I know you're upset about Karen, but you were supposed to be dead."

"Oh, Robert, it's okay," I continued, trying not to gag at myself.

Thank God I'd closed that door, or I would've died from hyper-embarrassment by now.

Robert whimpered and stepped back from me. "Trevor told me he'd seen your ghost," he said. "I didn't believe him, even when he admitted he still loved Karen."

Really … really? This is what you're afraid of most? That your first wife will return from the grave to haunt you if you find happiness with someone else?

I shook my head. Robert was clearly old. He didn't seem to know how things like this worked nowadays.

As I grappled with him, trying to hold him down long enough to get the blood sample, I wondered if Karen knew how lucky she was. For all I admired Blake and crushed on him, I didn't think we would ever get married.

Not if I was serious about my modeling career. But Blake was a cool guy, and a good-looking one, and he gave me the feeling that I was important when he talked to me. Surely if there was any real foundation for everlasting love, it started with that.

"Ouch!" I yelped as Robert gripped my wrist in a surprisingly hard grip.

"You're not Susan at all, are you?" he growled, suddenly angry. "You're a demon, aren't you? Did Trevor send you since I took Karen away from him?"

"Mr. Cuttingham—"

I pulled my fattened wrist out of his reach, but not before I managed to make him lose his balance. Before he could crash to the floor, I lunged out my legs, catching him on my lap. The old man's eyes boggled out in fear and I almost laughed at the sight, before using the momentum from my fall to roll him underneath me.

So once more, Fatgirl managed to save the day—by sitting on someone.

Someone who was as fragile as a china-faced doll and whined like a baby.

"Let me go," he whimpered. "I promise I won't marry her, Susan. If that's what you want. Please, just forgive me. Please, love me. I love you, and I just thought you were gone forever."

As he rambled on about Susan, and how much he loved and missed her, I couldn't stop but feel terrible for him. In some ways, he reminded me of my dad. He was a broken man who'd lost the love of his life, and he didn't know how to cope. Even if he had found happiness with Karen, he was still consumed with the pain of being away from his wife.

"I'll stay here, with just you," he said. "We can be alone here. Together. Forever. If that's what you want. Karen's a nice girl. I thought you would like her. But I don't have to marry her."

"That's not what Susan would want," I said, although I had to admit I didn't know what Susan would actually say if she was in my position.

Instead of playing the therapist, I focused back on my job.

I pulled out the plunger and squirmed.

AB had suggested I work on my science skillset, since I'd been clueless with Blake the other day. I didn't want to admit I'd probably be back at all the Fatgirl business, so I didn't take her seriously.

"Hold still," I said, before centering my weight on his upper thigh. That seemed like a safe spot for me to insert a needle, right?

I whispered a silent prayer in fervent desperation, as I hurriedly stabbed him with the needle.

At his scream, I figured I'd gone too deeply, but it was too late.

He would have to send me the court summons, I thought to myself, before condemning them to hell. This was part of saving his life. Surely there would be some kind of "radioactivity" clause in the law for this sort of thing.

I finished getting the blood sample and then headed over to the windows, grateful Robert was still stricken and largely unwilling to move for the moment.

Carefully, I pulled back the thick curtains and pushed open a large window.

AB was nowhere in sight.

"AB?" I hissed, looking in both directions. Where could she be?

As if she heard me, the door to the side of me opened up a second later. The light hid the figure's features, and I paused for a moment.

"Karen?" I asked. I fervently prayed I wouldn't have to explain this to her.

"Zeus let me in through the garage," she said, holding out her hand.

"Ugh, really? And you couldn't come here any faster?" I pointed down to Robert, whose leg was still bleeding from my puncture wound. "I'm not a doctor, you know."

"I've noticed. You need to look for a blood vessel before you poke someone." AB sighed. "Give me what you've got, and then I'll bandage him up."

She moved to do just that, and once more, I was taken in at how easily she seemed to be in control of the situation.

"Hey … out of morbid and misplaced curiosity, what would happen to you if you ate one of your doughnuts?" I asked.

AB sneered at me. "That's not for you to worry about now. Morbid and misplaced curiosity have their places, as do unanswered questions."

As we waited for the anti-serum cure to be reverse-engineered, I decided AB's biggest fear was that she would lose her voice, and possibly her face would go limp, and she'd be unable to bother me anymore.

"This might take a few more moments than usual," AB whispered, as she looked down at her portable lab. "How long has he been dosed with the Protactinium?"

"Possibly a week," I said. "Karen told me she'd gotten some Darling Donuts from her ex as a gift. The guy who gave them is the owner's brother."

"Hmmm." AB nodded. "I'll make note of that. If it's been over two days since his infection, he'll likely need another dose of the anti-serum before he goes back to complete normal."

"I guess that explains my life," I muttered.

My life would never go back to normal at this point, I thought.

And then another, more potentially horrifying thought hit me. "I'm not going to run into any weird side effects from multiple exposure to your doughnuts, will I?"

"Honestly … we'll have to see. But it's nothing I can't take care of, Kallie. You just have to trust me on that."

"Susan … " Robert was slowly reemerging from his fetal position on the floor. "Susan, where are you?"

"Here." AB thrust another plunger in my hand, this one with the anti-serum in it. "See if you can put this on in his arm. Better to get it to the heart faster, if we can."

"Can't you do it?" I asked. "I don't like this."

"Trust me—and trust yourself, too," AB said quietly. "You've come a long way, Kallie. Kicking and screaming like a toddler the entire time, but you're still making progress. Don't give up because it's hard."

"It's not hard to stab an old guy in the arm," I said, before grabbing Robert and holding him down again. "It's gross."

"I love you, Susan," Robert wheezed out, and I paused in my movements.

He really did love his wife. I could see for all the frightened horror in his eyes, he was only really horrified at the thought of losing his beloved again.

I hated knowing I was the one who saved him from something he was both afraid of and afraid to lose.

○ ○ ○ ○

I managed to shuffle AB back out the side door to Robert's room—which was apparently his den, now that I could see much more clearly when he allowed me to draw back more than one curtain—and side-step all the gracious and profuse thanks from Karen, as Robert returned to her in his normal self.

"Oh, Robert." Karen carefully and gracefully flung herself into his arms. He didn't seem to understand what was happening, only that Susan was gone again, but he had Karen back.

"She's gone," he whispered.

"She's not gone," Karen insisted. "She's still with you, and I'll respect that. How can I not? I wouldn't want to let you go, either, darling."

Robert finally tightened his grip around Karen, and I nearly barfed at the affection they clearly had for each other.

"I'm awfully sorry if I've caused you any pain," he said. "Susan was the love of my life. But now that I have you, I feel as though I have another life yet to live."

While all of this was happening, I stood there, focusing on the idea of tracking down Trevor, seeing if he had the recipe AB was looking for, and ending my so-called career as Fatgirl.

I did not want to watch this old-people-love cheese-fest, and when it got too much with all their smooches and declarations of undying love, I finally decided to make a break for it.

And then they caught me.

"Fatgirl, thank you," Karen pulled me into their shared hug, and I felt like a butterfly stuck between two spider's webs as she explained to Robert what had happened, and I tried to explain why his leg was bleeding and why his arm was hurt.

I left out the part about the radioactive doughnuts, but they seemed content, especially since Robert was back to his normal self.

Ha. I felt a pang of envy.

"Okay then, I'll just go," I whispered as they once more stared into each other's eyes. "Thanks, bye."

"Hey, Fatgirl," Karen called back. "I'll email you some tickets for this week's *Model Middle America* show, okay? Ooh, you know what, you should come as a judge!"

"That's really just too kind of you," I said, shaking my head, "but I fear my schedule is a bit unpredictable, so—"

"No, you have to! Let me know what you'd like, and we'll get it done, okay? Once you're ready, we can start promoting it! Think of the wide range of media that would bring us!"

I could think of a lot of wide things—including my bum, which I wanted to be small and cute again.

"Uh, well, the thing is—" I stumbled over a half-baked reply, before I decided to just shut the door to the room. Quickly, I muffled out a goodbye, and hurried away.

I'd saved the day, and now I needed to save my sanity.

So of course that was when I bumped into Zeus.

"I was just coming to see how you were doing," he said. "Everything all right now?"

I nodded. "They're fine, but I want to get back to normal."

Zeus laughed, and I pushed into him with my full weight.

"Stop laughing at me," I said. "You wouldn't feel this way if you were in my shoes."

"No, it's not that." Zeus gave me one of his kind smiles. "You've never been normal, Kallie. I don't think you'd ever have to worry about that. You're just a different kind of extraordinary now."

I didn't say anything to that.

Zeus pulled out a small device from his pocket; it was an external hard drive of sorts. "The best part is, I've managed to get the footage from the security cameras here, so you and Dr. White are safe. No one will be able to know you were here."

"And you, too?"

"I'm sure they'll figure out someone was here, but my dad'll be able to say it was some random impersonator if there's trouble."

"That is pretty cool of him. My dad would go bananas." I narrowed my eyes at him. "Does this mean you know you're safe, but now you have even more evidence against me?"

"Against you?"

"You know. As Fatgirl." I reached out my hand for the device. "Perhaps you'd give me that—any other footage you might've recorded of me as proof I can trust you?"

"Sure."

I didn't know what shocked me more, that Zeus handed me the hard drive or that he did it without the slightest hesitation. It was enough for me to stop in my tracks and stare down at it, momentarily wondering at it, before I looked back up at him.

"What is it?" He shuffled his feet, somewhat nervous again.

"We really can't be friends, you know," I said.

"We can't?"

His face was so crestfallen, and I felt a fresh, self-inflicted stab inside my heart, as I realized I didn't like hurting his feelings.

"I don't think it's a good idea," I finally managed. "I mean, what if someone else finds out about the Fatgirl Fandom and your website? They might be able to connect the dots, and … "

And I don't want to live in a world where anyone would ever call me fat, let alone "Fatgirl."

Zeus seemed to understand that a friendship with me would be risky, even if he didn't know the exact reasons why I felt it would be so difficult. He nodded.

"I understand your concerns," he said. "But you should know, I really will keep your secret. And you don't owe me anything for it, either. I'm just glad that you were able to help Karen today, just like you helped Blake."

I carefully resumed my steps, walking to where I could catch up to Zeus. I didn't let myself hug him or touch him, but I did stand next to him.

"Thank you," I said. "I'm sorry if I made you feel bad earlier. You know, at school. And I am glad you can keep your promise to me. That does mean a lot."

"Does this mean you think we could be secret friends?" Zeus asked, giving me a teasing smile.

I recognized he was trying to be friendly, so I stopped myself from hitting him and sticking my nose up in the air at him. "I'll think about it, but you shouldn't hold your breath."

We walked outside, and together we headed to where AB had parked.

She was already standing there, leaning against the side of the car. She clearly looked amused by something, and it didn't take me long to find out what it was that had her so tickled.

"So, you *are* going back to the *Model Middle America* show. And as a judge? Talk about good luck, huh, Kallie?"

"Just give me my anti-serum," I snapped. "I don't want to be Fatgirl any longer than I have to."

"Here you go. A dose of anti-F serum for you," AB said.

"Anti-F?"

"Anti-Fatgirl."

I stuck my tongue out at her, but I lived to regret it. She stuck me with the needle, and I nearly howled at the sudden prick.

"Are you okay?"

I groaned. I'd forgotten Zeus was there at all, and I nearly told him so.

But when I saw him look at me, so kind and concerned, I decided it wasn't the best move to irritate him.

Instead, I leaned back into AB's Imperial seats and let out a long sigh. "I will be," I tell him, keeping my voice heroic and sacrificial. "But it'll just take some time—and I'll need you to send Karen an email telling her why I'll be too busy this week to attend her show."

Zeus gave me a small smile. "I still think I'm the one who's better when it comes to diplomacy."

"Excuse me? I was perfectly fine in there," I objected. "That's why she wanted me to go on her show in the first place. I was helpful and smart and memorable, even if I look like a beached whale modeling spandex."

"Oh, darling, calm down," AB murmured, as she turned on the car. "There's no sense in arguing. You'll forget all about this by the time we get back to the house."

As she hit the gas pedal, I silently agreed with her, especially as she sped off, forcing Zeus and me to grip onto our armrests for dear life.

Yes, I thought. *Welcome to normal.*

Fatgirl

GOES TO THE FUGLY PRIDE PARADE

A BONUS EPISODE

○ ○ ○ ○

C. S. Johnson

FATGIRL GOES TO THE FUGLY PRIDE PARADE

○ ○ ○ ○

My last name is "White," and I absolutely hate it. It's seriously the whitest last name a person can have, and it's even worse for a half-Hispanic, half-white girl like me.

Ugh.

But as terrifying as it is—and it is terrifying, causing me a sense of distress so acute even my high school peers with the last names of "Nicewanger," "Bangs," and "Cox" would never understand—it's not the worst name I am known as, and the pain of this freshly cut wound ripped through me all over again as my phone began to chime.

"Fatgirl, Fatgirl, Calling Fatgirl … "

My ringtone, blaring out my superhero name, might as well have been a national breaking news headline. I could only be thankful literally no one would believe me if I told them the truth.

"What in the world is *that*?" I muttered. My fists clenched furiously, and I grew even more upset as I felt several of my nails chip at the sudden pressure.

I nearly began to cry. My high school's lacrosse team was playing a home game, I'd been so careful about selecting my outfit for my evening appearance—the tight jeans that hugged my slim legs, the high heels that added two inches to my height, and the long shirt with the square neckline that, with my long hair tied up in a bun, highlighted the elegance of my neck.

I was Kallie Grande-White, after all, and I was a true beauty among the people.

"Fatgirl, Calling Fatgirl … Hey Fatty, Pick Up Your Phone!"

I didn't need a surprise new ringtone, and I definitely didn't need any imperfection in my appearance.

Unfortunately, I was also the unlikely superhero of Cuttingham City known as Fatgirl, and Fatgirl was apparently needed.

This is not the time for this.

Not when school had just been let out for the week. I wanted nothing more than to go flirt with the varsity lacrosse team before the game—especially since I knew Blake Turner, as the star midfielder, would be there.

"Kallie, are you coming?" Behind me, all of my important friends, including Amory Franklin, were waiting.

I hurriedly grabbed my phone, shutting off the ringer as I tried to think of something to tell Amory. I didn't like disappointing her; I knew she would use it against me in the future, and there was no telling how ugly it would get after last time.

Another reason I am going to kill Abuela-Blanca.

My dad's mom, Dr. Margaret White, whom I often referred to as "AB," had already proven herself too much trouble for her own good. She was the reason I was Fatgirl at all, and the reason I had to stay Fatgirl while she figured out how to reclaim her job.

As a top scientist in her field, AB had spent the last decade working on Project: SERUM, a formula that, when consumed or injected into the bloodstream, was a superhero drug that enhanced the senses and strengths of its host. Despite being funded and secured by the government and a number of lobbyists, the recipe had been stolen, and she'd been the one sent to recover it, as she was the one who had been held responsible.

There was literally no one who could be that dumb, the PhDs in nuclear physics and nanotechnology aside.

How did someone lose a top-secret government project, anyway?

And how did no one have literally no idea who had it, even after several weeks of Fatgirl saving other Alterants—the serum-infected people—from their radioactive metamorphoses?

"Well, Kallie?" As Amory spoke, I could hear the last ounce of her patience die.

"Go on without me," I said through gritted teeth. "My, er, grandmother needs me."

Amory cocked a perfectly shaped eyebrow at me. "Your grandmother? Are you sure it's not something else?"

Amory and I were best friends and the ringleaders of our clique, but we both wanted a lot of the same things—and after I'd tricked her into missing the big audition for *Model Middle America* last month, perhaps she was right to suspect me of lying.

Me going around as Fatgirl really didn't help, either, but at least Amory didn't know about that. I'd never hear the end of it if she did.

But if she knew, I supposed it would give me an excuse to sit on her face till it went flat.

Quickly discarding that mental picture and soul-wrenching temptation, I shrugged my shoulders. "She's got a knack for poor timing. Sorry."

Amory and all the others behind her—Lizzie Myers, Uli Winters, and June Hideko—smiled brightly and waved goodbye to me.

The moment their backs were turned, they were all happily laughing—probably at me.

A growl rumbled in my throat, but it was quickly replaced by a thick lump; tears started welling up in my eyes as I ducked my head and ran down the hall, searching for an empty classroom.

"Why does this have to happen to me?" I moaned. "My life sucks."

I was supposed to be famous, like my mom. I was supposed to be a model, one of the grand beauties casually jet-setting around the world, getting romanced by big brands and serenaded by renowned companies, swimming in tons of free stuff. There were supposed to be lights, champagne—it's not illegal for seventeen-year-olds to drink in some countries, unlike unfun, fascist America—and clothes made of the finest materials and newest designs. My face was supposed to be plastered all over social media ads.

I had no doubt that was exactly the kind of life my mother, Katalina de la Carte Grande, was living now. After all, it'd been a year since she'd moved out of our house, and I supposed I couldn't blame her for leaving my dad and me.

Who really wants to live in Arkansas?

I certainly didn't want to, and I shouldn't have had to. I was beautiful, just like my mom, with a perfectly symmetrical face, and the same long, black-brown hair. My nose was pointed straight, with just a little bump on the end that tilted upward. My eyes, perpetually framed with eyeliner, were large and expressive, and if modeling ever turned out to be too boring, I was planning on working as an actor.

"Fatgirl, Fatgirl, Fatgirl, Calling Fatgirl … Hey Fatty, Pick Up Your Phone!"

My phone rang again, and I gave up. I threw myself into the nearest darkened classroom and slammed the door shut behind me.

"Jesus!" I let out a frustrated cry, punching a nearby wall. Without my Fatgirl powers, it hurt like the devil. "Jesus, Jesus, Jesus!"

I was not expecting Jesus to answer me.

"It's pronounced '*hey-Zeus*,' remember?"

I almost screamed as I looked up. Sitting there, in the back of the empty classroom, was none other than Jesus "Zeus" Evans, one of the various resident dork-face fatties of Cuttingham City High School.

"Ugh!" I glared at him. "It has to be you in here, huh?"

He gave me a wonky smile in return, as if he was trying to flirt, and my frustration instantly transformed into disgust.

"I told you before to call me 'Zeus,' like everyone else does," he said. "Although I suppose it's something different if you're actually praying."

I felt the faintest blush of crimson on my cheeks, and I tried to pull myself together, straightening my shoulders. I shoved my phone into my purse, wincing as another one of my cheap fake nails broke off. "I wasn't praying."

I'd stopped praying after my mom left. I couldn't blame her for leaving, but I certainly felt that blaming God was fair game.

"Sure sounds like you are."

Before I could screech out a reply, his creepy smile softened into an expression of genuine concern.

"Don't forget," he said. "I'm here to help if you need it."

I hated I was getting pity from a nerd, and especially that nerd in particular.

Zeus was new to our school this year. We were both in a lot of the same Advanced classes. He was much larger than me, and most of the other kids as well; it didn't help that he wore these huge sweatshirts with the hoodies and baggy pants; because of his curly black hair, he was sometimes called "Bigboy Baggypants," after some fantasy book hobbit-nerd thing. He always wore a stuffed backpack, and his fraying shoes had to be at least ten years old.

I only really put up with Zeus because he was the geek who ran the Fatgirl Fan Club website, and it was thanks to his work with computers—all the numbers and typing and stuff—that I knew where I was needed more often than not, especially if AB couldn't get a hold of me.

Zeus also knew I was Fatgirl, which didn't seem so odd to me since I knew he was in love with me.

Thankfully, he was content to keep my identity a secret.

At that reminder, I decided it was time to change the subject.

"What are you doing here?" I asked.

"Mr. Embers had some bugs."

"Bugs?" I blinked.

"Yeah, a couple of students ended up downloading spyware. So I'm removing it for him," Zeus said. He waved his hand toward several computers surrounding him.

I'd walked into a computer lab, not a classroom. Not that I'd noticed until just that moment.

"Good to know you're good at getting bugs out, I guess," I scoffed. "One of the good geeks, right?"

"I prefer 'nerd,' but you're right." He laughed, probably just to irritate me more. "I heard Blake Turner and his friends did it."

I could feel my nostrils flare with recharged fury at the mention of my long-time crush. "Blake wouldn't do something like that."

"*Sure* he wouldn't. Just like he wouldn't send the freshmen out on several 'harmless' hazing pranks targeting the new kids in town."

Zeus and I stared daggers at each other, and just a little part of me was happy I'd ticked him off. Blake Turner was a sore point for Zeus, who'd been the target of some of his alleged pranking. To me, Blake had always been the sweet boy who brought me Valentines when no one else in elementary school bothered, and I refused to believe he'd grown up into anything less than a prince, especially since Blake was still so nice to me.

When Zeus sighed and looked away a moment later, I knew I was the silent winner between us. I knew Zeus knew it, too, when he wiped his perpetually sweaty palms on his pants.

"But I guess computer bugs are nothing compared to your current dilemma, whatever it is?" Zeus pushed his thick glasses further up on his oily nose.

I tried not to wince; I hid my discomfort by swiping out my phone. "AB just changed my phone so when she calls it says 'Fatgirl' for its ringtone."

"She does tend to be concerned when you don't pick up," Zeus replied neutrally.

At his tone, I knew who helped AB do her dirty work.

"You know, I have a right to privacy," I said.

"Maybe you do as Kallie Grande-White, the next would-be Model of Middle America." Zeus stood up as he powered down the computer he'd been working on. "But Fatgirl doesn't have the same rights as you, since she's a public persona and there's not really an off-duty for stuff that tends to involve your … unique set of skills."

"Sitting on people until my Abuela-Blanca can reverse-engineer an anti-villain serum is hardly a 'unique set of skills.'" I crossed my arms, still frustrated.

"You don't sit on all of them. Just, well … okay, most of them. But some of them do put up quite a fight." Zeus reached out his hand to pat me on the back, and then probably thought better of it.

And I was glad he didn't try to comfort me. Ever since last month, since I first became Fatgirl during the live superhero edition episode of *Model Middle America: The Race to Find the Next Top Heartland Teen Heartthrob Model*, there was no comforting me.

The whole experience is still a monstrous blur in my memory. I'd wanted so badly to be a model like my mother, I'd starved myself for the part. And when I'd shown up at home, finding no one able to take me to Cunningham City Amphitheatre, I'd been unable to resist the stack of powdered doughnuts on the counter.

Little did I know until later, the doughnuts were baked with a test version of AB's serum, one that would make me eventually bloat out from my regular size zero into the plus-plus-size superhero currently known as Fatgirl.

My face scrunched up as I remembered how I'd been late getting to the audition, feeling overly nauseated besides. Once I'd been escorted to the contestants' section, no one noticed me as I shuffled through the room, following the other girls into the changing room stalls. I'd grabbed at any outfit I could find. I had just put my mask on when my transformation began. The spandex of the magenta outfit clung to my body, and I began to cry. I'd locked myself in the changing stall, unable to do anything.

Thank God, really, that the gunman decided he'd wanted to hold the audience hostage, or someone might have spotted me. When I heard the gunfire, I'd burst out of my fitting room, looking for an escape. I'd barreled right into the gunman and ended up crushing him with my growing body weight. I'd hurried away, knocking over plenty of others, as the police started to question me.

According to the reports, no one knew who I was, and, when AB found me and told me the truth, the legend of Fatgirl officially began.

My life sure sucked.

"Hey Zeus, Hey Zeus, Hey Zeus, we need Fatgirl … Hey Jesus, Pick Up Your Phone!"

"Ugh, you've got to be kidding me. Why does AB have your phone number?" I glared at Zeus as his phone continued to ring.

"She asked me to help find the people who had her serum," Zeus reminded me. "Especially since you don't answer your phone all the time."

"Don't pick it up," I said, as he took out his phone. "I order you *not* to answer your phone."

He arched his brow and answered the call anyway.

Immediately, I could hear my grandmother's voice on the other line.

"Hey Zeus, we've got a problem."

I groaned as I flung my head into my hands.

Abuela-Blanca *was* a problem, period. I could hear her perfectly enunciated words, urgent but still polite, blaring over the phone as she informed Zeus about how she'd found signs of problems in the heart of Cuttingham City.

"I'll see if I can do anything … Sure, no problem, Dr. White," Zeus replied calmly, and just as I lunged for his phone, he said goodbye and hung up.

"Don't ask me to help today," I said. "Please. *Please*. Please? I don't wanna go."

"Don't you even want to know what's happening? There are people in danger."

I bit back a string of cusses, strong enough to make the devil blush and a country music star go urban pop.

"AB says her Phi-ger's picking up some major readings in midtown at the parade."

"Phi-ger?"

"You know. Her Geiger, for the radiation, for the F-rays or whatever."

"Oh, yeah, I remember. Great." I rolled my eyes, before I stopped, mid-mockery. "Wait, what was that about a parade?"

"The Fat and Ugly Pride Parade is today."

"Eww, gross. Now I especially don't want to go," I said.

"Come on, Kallie—"

"No, if there's trouble, it'll be fine. The fat people there could use the exercise, right? I'll be doing them a favor by staying at home."

"They're still people," Zeus said. There was a faint tinge to his own cheeks, and I realized I was probably hurting his feelings, too. He wasn't exactly thin himself, with his hot-dog sized fingers and his jellyroll belly. "Anyway, Dr. White said whoever it was that took her serum will probably try to modify it. The parade would be a good place to look for test subjects and get attention from the media."

I jutted out my chin. "Well, they would still make horrible superhumans, especially if the serum just amplifies their biggest fears and insecurities."

"That's how Dr. White said it worked." Zeus grinned. "And since your transform into Fatgirl, I'd say it's a good hypothesis. Although your biggest fears were too taken literally at the time, if you ask me."

I felt like punching him, but before I did, a memory stirred inside my mind.

"Wait, this is the Fugly Pride Parade?" I asked. "Or is that a different thing?"

Zeus shrugged. "It's sometimes called Fugly Pride, yeah."

"Oh. My. God." I shook my head. "It's them! It's the thing."

"The thing?"

I began to pace about the room. "The people who run this thing, they had some lady invite me to go and speak, don't you remember?"

"That'll give you a good excuse to go."

"No! Now I *really* can't go." I grabbed his arms and shook him. "If I go now, they'll make me their hero! They wanted me to make some kind of MLK-I-have-a-dream-about-tacos speech!"

Zeus wasn't affected by my pushiness. "Kallie, you already are their hero, and others', too."

"But there's literally nothing special about being fat or ugly." I ran my hands through my hair again. "Don't they know there's an increase of health risks for obese people? That ugly people have soul-crippling self-esteem issues, usually for life, because therapy is also a society no-no? That being proud about that kind of thing is ridiculous and insults the rest of us who are fortunate enough not to feel like the world's conspired against us?"

Zeus started laughing.

"What is it? I know I'm right! Some stigmas are good for society."

"Society is one thing. People are another."

I paused in my arguments; I did not like how smug he sounded. It was as if he wasn't commiserating with me at all.

"It's not my fault that statistically speaking, fat-shamming works, Zeus." I eyed him critically. "Except on you, apparently."

He took the insult in stride. "What else would you expect from Fatgirl's biggest fan?"

"I would not expect him to literally be the *biggest* fan." I stuck my tongue out at him. "Well, I guess that gives you a good excuse to go to this thing."

"As long as you go, I'll go with you." Zeus put his hands in his pockets. "Come on, Kallie. Dr. White needs you. She said there's enough radiation that some Alterants are bound to show up."

"You mean there are more than one this time?" I gaped at him, traumatized.

"I don't know," he said. "But that's part of our mission, right? Find the Alterants, get them back to normal, and then see if we can find the serum supply line."

"Come on, Zeus, I don't want to be Fatgirl," I moaned.

"And I'm sure the other people who get injected with that serum stuff don't want to turn into their own worst selves, either."

"So why should I do it?"

"Because even at what you believe is your worst, I know you're still capable of doing so much good."

"You don't know that."

"Sure I do. You turned into a superhero, remember? The others didn't."

"That's just because of starvation and a metabolism thing," I said, but I hated how good Zeus was getting at manipulating me.

"I don't think that." He took off his thick glasses and used his sleeve to wipe them clean. In that moment, I got a small peek at the clarity of his blue, moonbeam eyes.

It really was a shame he didn't wear contacts, I thought.

Zeus could've been such a cute boy if he tried a little harder to take care of his pimples, take care of his sweaty palms, and lose some weight.

"You know," I said, "when hot guys hit on girls like me, we welcome it. When guys like you hit on girls like me, we file restraining orders."

"Great. We can pick one up at the city courthouse on our way to the parade. Dr. White said she'll be close by as she monitors it."

As he moved, steering me toward the school exit, I sighed in defeat. "I hate you."

"I know." He grinned at me again. "But the city needs you, and if you must suffer, so should I."

"That is literally my only comfort in all of this."

It wasn't hard to spot Abuela-Blanca once Zeus and I made it to the Fugly Parade; she was an old-looking patrician lady, dressed in white, metaphorically clutching her pearls while the colorful pagan worshippers peacockishly flocked around her.

I felt slightly sick as I waved to her from the other side of the street.

"There you are," AB said, making the sign of the cross over herself before she embraced me. "Oh, thank the good Lord."

I was never much of a huggy-touchy person, even with my family. I was glad when she quickly let go.

"I don't know if you mean God or the devil when you say it like that," I muttered as she began to rifle in her expensive, overly-immaculate purse. I groaned when she pulled out a perfect-looking powdered doughnut and held it out to me.

"There you go, darling."

In that moment, I hated AB for sure. She had come to live with us for only a few weeks, but she should've learned in that amount of time that my mom's first modeling job was for Darling Donuts. She'd been their poster girl long before other companies began to call her. Every year since they'd hired her, the owners of the Darling Company had sent her a fresh batch of organic white-powdered jelly donuts.

Dad had told me before that he considered Darling Donuts lucky, since he'd first met Mom at the press conference when they were announcing their factory's move to Cuttingham City.

"Well?" Abuela-Blanca looked at me expectantly. "Let's go, Kallie."

"Do I have to?" I asked.

"Come on, you said you'd help me," she said.

"There aren't any supervillain-monster-Alterants around," I objected.

"It's better to be prepared, and you know it's better to eat the doughnuts ahead of time."

"Fine." I swiped the doughnut out of her hand and took a glorious, resplendent first bite of the intoxicating deliciousness. I kept my scowl firmly on my face as I ate it, even though I knew even in heaven I wouldn't find any such sweetness.

If I made it to heaven at this point.

As I stuffed the last of the doughnut into my mouth, trying not to let out a sigh of pleasure and slit my wrists in self-hatred, Zeus took out his phone.

"Send me the Phi-ger readings," he said to AB. "I can track the findings on my phone one way, while you and Kallie can go the other."

"I'm honestly horrified at the thought of moving at all," AB admitted.

"Ugh, AB, stop acting so white," I grumbled. "You're embarrassing me."

"Darling, I am a doctor," AB said. "I have plenty of overweight colleagues, and I also happen to know why it's dangerous to be overweight. The fact that I'm white means nothing in this case; I am more concerned that people here have failed to dress. It is *not* what I would call hygienic."

As much as I wish I could've disagreed—I would've loved sticking it to her too-high-in-the-air nose and her jutting, judgmental chin—I hated how I agreed with her.

I hated how I agreed with her even more as several overweight men and women only covered in "FU" stickers walked by us.

I slid back away from them, but to no avail.

"Watch it," one of the ladies snapped. "I skipped work and paid good money for these stickers."

"Sorry," I muttered, unimpressed.

"Hey, it's not every day you get to see the great Sorra March," she snapped. As she hurried after her naked sticker posse, I heard her whisper, "Not that a skinny white girl like you would know anything about that."

"I am *not* white, you filthy fink-harlot," I shouted back.

"Kallie Grande-White." AB shot a frown over at me as she chastised me, probably secretly to remind me my last name was "White," even if my skin was not. "Would you watch your language, please?"

"I literally can't watch words, you know," I shot back.

"Oh, never mind. What are they teaching you in school these days?" AB pursed her lips as she handed me one of her satchels. "Here. Do something productive. Go change into your suit."

"Do I have to?" I whined.

"Yes, since you'll start transforming soon. If you want to keep those size-double-zero jeans intact, you'll need to get out of them, pronto."

"Can't I wait a little longer?" I asked. "I don't want people to see Fatgirl walking around here."

"Darling, haven't you been paying attention?"

I'd been walking with my eyes mostly averted, so I was shocked when I looked up and saw there were hundreds, if not thousands, of Fatgirl posters popping up through the crowd while I could see several others wearing the t-shirts from Zeus' website.

There was another face as well, of a plump lady with determined, fiery eyes and a picnic-patterned cape on. Her hair was chopped short and waved over, and several of the photos colored it in different patterns.

"Who's that on the posters?" I asked.

"That's Fatgirl, you narcissist," Zeus teased.

"No, the other ones," I grumbled.

Zeus smiled at my irritation before pointing to the nearest picture of her. "That's Sorra March, one of the city's leaders of the Fugly Pride Parade committee. She used to be a housewife who was known for her baking. When her husband left her she opened the Divorced Pleasures Bakery on South Main Street and sold her sweets. She's been mostly successful."

"Mostly?"

"She has a reputation that some people don't agree with," Zeus replied uneasily.

"'Some people?'" I cocked my eyebrow.

"Um, mostly men."

"Well, that makes sense." My nose wrinkled up in disgusted sympathy. "If she was that fat before, I can see why her husband left her."

"She reportedly got fat after he left, since she'd spend all her time baking."

"Stop trying to guilt me for just saying what everyone is thinking."

"It's better to stop you from thinking wrongly."

"At least I'm thinking at all." I glared at him. "You know, in movies, it's the bad guy who gets all the best lines. You're pushing it."

"If I ever end up as your enemy, you'll only have yourself to blame," Zeus said.

"Kallie, go." AB pushed me away. "I'm getting larger readings near the front of the parade. Head up there and watch your phone. Zeus and I will call if something happens on the side streets."

"Fine." I grabbed the bag from her and hurried off.

Even though I was already starting to bloat up into Fatgirl's muscled mass, I felt a weight lift off my shoulders as I left them behind.

As I ricocheted my way between the parade-goers, I silently vowed I would take an extra-long shower when I got home. As my body began to get bigger, getting thicker and adding inches every moment, I realized it was actually a good thing AB had told me to change; I didn't care as much if my Fatgirl super suit got smelly, especially since AB was in charge of the suit. Watching her learn how to do laundry properly after designing a superhero outfit like Fatgirl's was one of my greatest joys since our whole situation began.

The suit design itself had gone through a few different transformations since I'd picked up its original predecessor at Model Middle America. It was a full-length bodysuit, almost like a wetsuit. I could weep, thinking of how I went from a size 00 to a 22 within the span of two minutes when I transformed into Fatgirl. The hot pink coloring had darkened some with AB's modifications, but it was still bright enough I felt like I should charge onlookers a freak-show fee. I had a tight hood that came over my hair and my head. The boots were black and made of a flexible kind of material, but still sturdy. Between AB and Zeus, they had plenty of plans for my outfit and weapons in the future. I had a mask on, and I felt so much better when I wore it. I was not recognizable at all, and I would die if anyone, especially anyone important, saw me like this.

At first, I'd been worried I'd be recognized as Fatgirl, but thanks to my semi-viral social media videos, there were plenty of other psychotic people who were dressed up as me, and even some who tried to get gigs as impersonators. As I bobbed-and-weaved through the crowds, I wondered if I could sue any of them.

Model Middle America almost tried to do that with me. I'd been getting ready for my initial audition, which required me to wear a "superhero" costume from some "new, upcoming designers," which is how I'd gotten stuck with the hot pink spandex one-piece with a black hood and a mask. At the audition, my hair had been done up in pigtails, so as bad as "Fatgirl" was, I supposed I could have just as easily gotten stuck with "Pink Elephant Lady," or "Super Pig," or "Balloon Girl."

"Balloon Girl" would've been better.

Whoever was writing the newspaper reports for Cuttingham City should've been fired for "Fatgirl."

"—we are the noise makers, the eaters of dreams!"

I cringed as I made my way to the front of the parade, working on keeping my head down as I finished bloating out to Fatgirl's full size. The boots on my feet tightened painfully, and I suddenly wondered if my Fatgirl transformation was going to get worse the more I did it.

That thought stopped me in my tracks.

Weren't the swelling crackles of stretch marks on my shoulders, knees, and all over my back bad enough? If AB didn't have a specific cream (chitin-based, who would've guessed?) to remove them, I would've quit even sooner. Then there was the thickened trunk of my neck, the inflated mass of my cannon-sized limbs, the near-misses of people figuring out who I really was and exposing AB's top-secret mission to the public.

There was also some concern about being so frequently exposed to radiation—Abuela-Blanca said there was a teeny-tiny risk of something like that, and I was more offended by her words than ever.

But that was also the moment when I blinked and, as if my ears had been flushed open, I began to hear the speaker's words again.

"—I want you to know that everything I do, I do it for you. The downtrodden, the overlooked, the overweight."

I finally saw the real Sorra March. She was shaking with passion and power as she stood, banging her meaty fists across the fiberglass podium.

Before the whole parade she was talking about herself. And her weight problems. And how she was somehow noble for being fat, feeling fat, and organizing a parade of all these fat and ugly people.

Literally, every other word out of her mouth was "fat."

Well, not literally … well, actually yes; it wasn't my fat-foggy mind transforming my observation skills into mush. Sorra was literally only saying fat.

"Fat … fat … faaaaat."

"Oh, no." I shook my head and pulled out my phone. Between the last of my fake nails and my engorged fingers, I couldn't dial AB. "Call Abuela-Blanca," I whispered into the phone.

I was distressed when "Call for a bowl of blan co" came up on the small screen.

"I'm sorry, I didn't understand."

"Great." I shoved the phone down into the recesses of my excessive chest and hurried forward as the parade goers, all shocked at Sorra's slurring words, began to whisper in furious waves.

Sorra's body began to metastasize. Her neck began to disappear between her body and her face as roll after roll of body fat began to unfold, and despite being the original Fatgirl, it was hard to watch her swell up in size. Her clothes stretched painfully across her body, and I found a reason to be grateful for those "FU" stickers as her legs, growing outward at an astonishing rate, sucked into her body.

Some of the security guards approached her while she continued to morph into a massive human ball. Sorra was suddenly this gigantic, overly fleshy wrecking ball of a person.

She continued to grow as I began to inch closer to her. I saw her eyes roll back into her head, and she fell to the stage floor as her body began to weigh too much. She was unable to stand under her own weight.

I breathed out a sigh of relief. *At least she isn't going anywhere for a while.*

The stage underneath her feet cracked and then snapped, and I knew I'd been too hopeful.

Her body slid down the wooden stage slabs, and she bowled into the crowds.

I lunged forward and shoved my foot deep into the cement of the road. There was some pain, but I held back my body's protests as I prepared to slow Sorra's body roll.

"Arrrgh!" I groaned loudly as she flew into me. For all my bracing, I still felt the pushback. I would need a new pair of superhero boots when this was over, I thought with a grimace.

Sweat beaded on my forehead as Sorra's increasing mass finally stopped rolling. I let out a shaky sigh of relief, just in time to hear the cheers behind me.

"Hey everyone, it's Fatgirl! The real Fatgirl!" Cheers erupted behind me, and I saw several attempts to start the wave, and some others, probably from Alabama, call out for a "Roll Tide."

Through all of this, I somehow managed to hear AB's voice.

"Get me a sample of her blood," AB said. "I'll be able to get the toxin-reversal antidote then."

"Okay, sure," I grumbled, panting hard as I looked around.

What am I going to do?

If I moved, Sorra's ball-body would, too. I couldn't move my feet, my hands were fat-filled, and I was absolutely *not* going to bite her to get her to bleed.

"Fatgirl, I'm here!"

I'd never been so happy to see Zeus. He'd pulled up his hood over his head, and thanks to an ugly hat he'd probably swiped from one of the parade goers, all other facial features were hidden.

"Great," I said, breathing deep as my feet were pressed further into the street. "Get her blood to AB. Hurry."

I didn't want to watch as Zeus pulled out a pencil and began stabbing her. The little I was forced to watch because of positioning, and my perspective made me want to toss my own cookies a few times.

"She's getting too heavy," I warned him.

"I've almost got enough."

"We need at least ten ounces, right?"

"Ten *milliliters.*"

"Oh, shut up. This science stuff is hard," I shouted. My fingers tensed as Sorra's body rumbled, and I realized she was getting bigger. "But you've got to get out of her way, fast!"

"Faaaaat!" Sorra roared again. This time, her cry was accompanied by the sound of rushing water. I looked to see her eyes leak with tears the size of a pipeline.

The salty spring raced down her skin, threatening my grip even more.

Zeus needs me to save him.

I grimaced all over again. *And all the other people, too, that's right.*

As my hands began to get wet, I felt my grip slip. Hurriedly, I glanced over my shoulder; my neck cracked in objection, but I ignored it. When I saw there was a large area between the other people and Sorra's huge mass, I nodded to myself.

Enough was enough.

"Run, Zeus," I yelled, as I gave Sorra one last push off to the right.

I grabbed Zeus, driving him off to the left as Sorra headed in the other direction.

"I got it," Zeus told me, showing me his palm.

"That's so awful." I scowled. "Put it away."

"I'll go give it to AB. You'll need to do something about her," Zeus said, nodding toward Sorra.

"Faaaaat, Faaaat, Faaaat." Sorra was unhappy as she bounced into some cable lines. Several of the parade attendants were screaming, while some were pointing and shouting, "It's Fatzilla!" while taking selfies.

I sighed. "Okay, I'm on it."

I knew Sorra wouldn't be able to come to a full stop for long.

As if on cue, the cable lines snapped in quick succession, and Sorra continued to roll down Midtown's main street. Her body pressed into cars, cracking windows and overturning motorcycles.

I hurried after her, trying to stop her from rolling again.

"Move away!" I waved away the onlookers, cursing every last one of their cankles as they scuttled out of the street.

I finally made it to where I was in front of Sorra again, and I poised myself for another impact.

"Ooofff," I gasped as she came careening into me. This time, she'd picked up enough momentum that I was nearly bowled over myself. I managed to make her move off to the other side of the street, just barely avoiding getting flattened by her.

There would be no sitting on this one, that was for sure.

It was like playing some kind of weird, fat-person pong on the streets of Cuttingham City. All I could do, I realized as I raced to stop her again, was keep her from rolling over the people and hope she'd find something to run into that would manage to stop her. Over and over again, I tried to roll her into a position where we could get her to stop.

Zeus called out to me. "Hey, Fatgirl!"

"What is it, Lard Boy?" I yelled back, angry he was distracting me right now. I was like a child with a video game, intent on winning, and Zeus should've had more respect for my circumstances.

"Make a hole in the ground," Zeus said. "It'll trap her. Like pinball!"

"Oh. Good idea." I didn't say it loudly, but I nodded.

I waited until she hit a highway ramp, and then I made my move.

Jumping high, I thrust all my weight into my legs as I flew into the ground. Five times I did this, making a small oval-sort-of-circle on the street.

"Looks good!" Zeus cheered me on from the sidelines.

My feet were sore, and if I'd been my normal self I'd have snapped in two or three by then. All I had to do was get her into the street circle now.

"Kallie."

From behind me, AB appeared. She'd donned her lab coat and even a mask for good measure, and I was unusually grateful to see her at that point in time.

"Do you have the antidote?" I asked.

"I'm working on it. A few more moments in my portable lab and we'll have it."

"Great. I'll see if I can get her to stay still."

"Yes, that Zeus friend of yours is a good addition to our team. I thought he might be."

"Yeah, yeah."

I hurried off, not wanting to end up arguing over Zeus' apparent charms with my mad scientist grandmother. And it wasn't like I didn't have work to do.

A few shoves later, I cheered and wiped the sweat off my forehead.

"Last time," I muttered, as Sorra's body came rolling my way once more. I stood in front of my circle, ready to catch her and ease her into her final goal.

"Umphf." Sorra's body fell into my hands, and this time, I felt like I'd just had a workout. Carefully, and achingly, bone-shakingly slowly, I led her into the center of the dented cement.

Behind me, I could hear a helicopter fluttering around, as the crowd bellowed with cheers for me, and I took a moment to wave and relax.

I could see the headlines already: "Gargantuan Drama at the Fat and Ugly Pride Parade" or "Fugly Parade Follies."

I wasn't expecting the loud roar behind me.

"Faaaaaaaaaat!"

"She's too big," I realized. "Is the antidote ready yet?"

"Not yet. Close though!"

"Close isn't good enough." I watched as the cement broke further down, and I suddenly and sincerely hoped there was no metro train station underneath the street.

"Can you make her throw up?" AB asked. "I know it's gross, but it might help get some of the extra radiation out of her."

"Eww, that's nasty." I nearly gagged at the thought. "At her size, she might barf up enough to drown someone."

"It was just a suggestion."

"Give me one that doesn't involve me shoving a telephone pole down her throat, please."

I had to move as Sorra glommed onto the broken cement of my dotted circle and began to bulge out even more.

"Faaaaaat!" Sorra's battle cry was getting older and uglier by the moment.

AB appeared behind me. "Remember what I told you about the serum. Maybe you can talk her down. You're supposed to be one of her heroes, right?"

"Her biggest fear is that she's fat. Would that really work, if I talked to her?" I was skeptical. "She's just been bragging about that for the last hour, hasn't she?"

"It's not that," Zeus said as he came up to us. "It's that she's afraid that's *all* she is."

"Well, she should've thought about that before she made up a whole parade for it," I said.

"People don't think about what they're really afraid of." Zeus looked over at me intently. "You can sympathize with that. You were afraid of being too fat of a superhero while you were in that modeling audition, right?"

I sighed. "That seems very specific. This is more like a complex for her."

"Maybe that's part of the reason you're Fatgirl and she's just … Super Fattie?" Zeus asked.

AB nodded. "I've been hearing 'Sorra Loser' on the news reports."

"They've already got news reports for this?" I shook my head, appalled.

"The press is always under pressure," Zeus said, and I just groaned.

The sound was drowned out, as a distinct beeping noise from AB's coat went off.

"Either way, here's the cure," AB said, handing me a large medical plunger. "See if you can get it close to her heart. It'll work faster once it's in the bloodstream."

"I thought you said it was better to digest it."

"To start the change. To change back, the bloodstream is better."

"All right." I gripped the plunger carefully, before I started to climb up into the folds of Sorra's various flab lines.

"Sorra!" I felt weird saying her name. It seemed rude, after all. But even though I'd only just heard of her, I was climbing on her exponentially growing body while intending to stab her with a needle and inject government-rejected substances into her, calling her "Miss March" didn't seem right, either."

Sorra, for her part, didn't seem to mind. As she waddled about in the street hole, she turned her eyes to look at me.

"It's me," I said. "You know, um, Fatgirl. Here to save you and all that good stuff."

At my voice, she seemed to quiet down, and I swore her heart even stopped beating quite so fast. Of course, as far as I knew, it could've been beating even faster and I was just feeling its rhythm like a flatline.

"You wanted me to come and talk at the parade today," I went on, not sure of what else to say. "And I guess you managed to get your wish, right?"

There was an unmoving howl from inside of her as I climbed up the two stories of her flappy flesh and came closer to her heart.

I didn't even want to look at where I was. The folds of her skin were ballooning out; her clothes were missing in large gaps, though the X-rated areas were all covered with extra rolls of fleshy fat.

"You know," I said. "I'm not really happy being fat. I don't like it. I wanted to be a model, you know? Skinny and happy and famous."

Sorra didn't seem to like that. She began to move again, and I quickly shook my head.

"Wait, wait, wait," I shouted. "It's not like that."

She stopped, and I took my chances.

"It's like this," I said, as I took the needle full of her blood-specific cure and thrust it deep inside the skin flabs, before pressing down on the plunger.

Sorra's body began to shake more violently, but my heroic deed was done.

I rolled down the slope of her body as she began to shrink. Once I was back on the ground, I backed up, watching until I could recognize Sorra March's regular face among the massive amounts of flesh. I was grateful a medical team arrived on the scene and basically took over while reporters began to circle like vultures leering down at a roadkill buffet.

"Miss … Miss, um, Fatgirl?"

I turned around, ready to fight off a request for an interview, only to see an EMT was behind me. "What?"

"She's requesting to see you."

"Oh."

I grimaced, but nodded, and then walked over to the small divot I'd made in Midtown Main Street. The cement buckled under my weight, but it didn't break.

I forgot all that as I saw Sorra lying in the middle of everything, of all the destruction we'd caused together. I hoped I would be able to get a good lawyer for collateral damage.

"Fatgirl."

"Yep, that's me," I grumbled. "You're welcome."

"I … I … " Sorra was wide-eyed and stupefied as she looked from me to her sagging skin.

"Don't worry about the stretch marks," AB said. "I'll send you some special cream in the mail for those. And if you're lucky, it'll only take a few days for the skin to reform itself properly. Otherwise you might want to schedule an appointment with a plastic surgeon."

For a second, I thought Sorra would argue with AB, telling her that she didn't have to care about how she looked or anything like that. But the moment passed, and I was pleased when she relented.

"Okay," she muttered.

"Good. Now, I'll go and see if I can ward off the press some. Excuse me."

I watched her leave and sighed. I didn't like being alone to take care of the victim. "Well, Sorra … Miss March … are you feeling better?"

I wasn't exactly surprised when she began to weep.

"I shouldn't have tried those new doughnuts today," she whispered, still profusely crying. "My stomach's been aching since even before … everything that happened."

I thought about making a rude comment about how "everything that happened" was the best possible way for a PR firm to spin it, but I was more interested in the doughnuts.

"What kind of doughnuts?" I asked.

"Oh, the Darling Company ones," she said. "They want me to endorse their new products. When Richard came by with their newest flavor, I couldn't resist."

"New flavor?" I felt like I was turning into a parrot lately.

"Fatgirl Fudge." Sorra blushed as she looked up at me. "Richard's been wanting to put more fudge into the market. I wasn't supposed to talk to you about it; I know you didn't want anyone else to know about your collaboration with them yet."

Collaboration? What collaboration? There is no collaboration!

I felt like slapping her again. Doughnuts were how I'd gotten into this superhero mess. I wasn't looking for brand expansion.

I glanced down at my thunderstorm-level thighs.

If anything, I wanted brand shrinkage at this point, I thought with an indignant huff.

"You're not mad at me, are you?" Sorra asked.

Even though she'd been a searing mess just moments earlier in her super-fattie mode, she'd never looked so pathetic as she looked up at me with that hopeful, fearful look.

"No," I said.

She relaxed at once, and then I saw her eyes bug out. "Oh, I know! Come and join the parade. We were hoping you'd come today. We really wanted you to speak for us. You're so great. You really show society what fat people can do. You can inspire so many fat people. And the ugly ones, too, of course."

As she rambled on about how I could talk about how showers weren't big enough to fit me and how I could talk about my issues with shaving body hair and how it was 'empowering' to be fat and proud, I just stared at her.

After AB's solution had worked, it was clear Sorra hadn't seen that maybe a change was needed in herself, rather than societal norms.

"You know, Sorra," I said, interrupting her. "One of my friends told me that society is one thing, and people are another. And he was right. But to society, to everyone here, I *am* Fatgirl. But I'm not *just* Fatgirl. There's more to me than how much I weigh, even if that's how I mostly deal with the Alterants."

"What? What are you saying?" Sorra frowned, and I wondered how someone smart enough to rally a ton of fat people together in an unknown city like Cuttingham could be so dumb.

"I'm saying that I actually, literally can't celebrate Fugly Pride with you. I'm sorry if that hurts your feelings. But if I really get to be true to myself, I have to be honest with myself first. And I'm not here to stand for the same fat and ugly person values as you."

I reached out and hurriedly shook her hand, briefly shocked at how soft and frail it seemed now that she'd been completely neutralized. "Excuse me."

"Oh, great! You're just one of those self-hating fugly people," she snapped. "Admit it. You're just one of those people who'd love to see all of us die … "

I didn't bother to point out if I was, I wouldn't have bothered saving her, and I would've laughed as she herself had bowled over all the other parade goers in her rolling wake.

Thankfully, she didn't try to chase me as I left, and for that, I could only thank God for his kindness in this matter—and this time I was certain it was God, because she'd had the very devil acting up inside of her not even an hour prior.

I wasn't really thinking very clearly as I made my way through the crowds. I was surprised when AB found me anyway.

"There you are," she said as she approached me. "I've got your shot now that the Phi-ger's gone back down. Hold still."

Before I could stop her, she grabbed my neck and thrust a small plunger full of anti-F-radiation mix. I yelped and tried to back away, but for a thin lady, AB was pretty strong. She forced me to stay still while she pulled out the needle and slapped a bandaid over the bleeding point.

"You're just going to make it worse if you move," AB said.

"You're going to poke me full of holes," I retorted. "What am I going to tell the model agencies who'll have to airbrush over my pockmarks?"

"Hopefully it won't come to that. Modeling ruined your mother's life."

"Abuela-Blanca, I swear—"

"Oh, darling, stop." AB interrupted me smoothly as she gave me a pat on the cheek and then tucked some of my loosened hair behind my ear. "We'll just tell them you're at risk for Diabetes. Insulin shots and all that."

"You're a doctor and you're not worried about medical fraud?"

"I'm a nuclear nanotechnologist, not an MD."

"Ugh!" I threw up my hands and gritted my teeth. "You make things so hard sometimes."

"Come on, Kallie," Zeus said. "We won for today, didn't we? Let's not fight now."

"Zeus is right," AB said, checking her Phi-ger. "You should go and do something fun. It looks like we're clear for now. I've got to get to my lab and have Pham look this over."

"Pham?"

"My lab partner. Dr. Pham. He's one of the best." She gave me a polite nod, pocketed her gear, and then headed off.

She almost seemed like a lady cowgirl, clutching her purse and walking off into the empty horizon.

It took a considerable amount of my willpower not to throw something at her.

"Hey, Kallie. Let's go," Zeus said. "We're going to be late."

"Late for what?" I asked him.

"The game. You wanted to see it, right? I'll take you, so you won't be lonely while you shrink back down into your regular self."

I didn't even remember which game he was talking about, but I said nothing as I mindlessly followed him. The last thing I said to him before we left was, "Thanks, I think," as he tugged off his large hoodie and handed it to me.

We didn't talk again until we were out of midtown, but when he reached for my hand, I took it in mine and clung to him.

It wasn't long before I was back at the school with Zeus. The lacrosse game was off to a good start, but I don't think Zeus and I were really paying attention. I was still wearing his hoodie so people wouldn't have to see a shrinking Fatgirl on display. That didn't stop me from worrying that someone would recognize me.

Zeus was more concerned with food. I'd barely shook my head when he asked if I wanted anything to eat.

I looked down at my hands as I sat at the top of the stadium bleachers. My fingers were still bloated from the Fatgirl transformation, but I was more than relieved to be getting back to my regular self.

I didn't think that would be much of an issue anyway; after the news got out that "Fatgirl had been spotted at the Fat and Ugly Pride Parade," courtesy of the clickbait news, nearly everyone from school had headed out to go catch a glimpse of their favorite overweight superhero. The stands were almost completely empty as we sat down and the visiting team came out onto the field.

Zeus came up to me, holding a hot dog with ketchup and mustard from the concession stand. As I watched him eat, slightly less disgusted than before, I thought about how he could've told everyone on the Fatgirl social media pages I'd already left the parade.

And that wasn't the only thing that was weird about him, I realized.

"Hey Zeus, I have a question for you," I said.

"What is it?"

"Doesn't it bother you that people think you've got some kind of Fatgirl fixation? That you're a weirdo who's obsessed with a colorful beached whale in superhero spandex?" I glanced around the stadium, watching as the lacrosse team came charging out from the sidelines. I spotted Blake Turner as he took his position on the field, moving around like a dancer as he stretched.

"Fatgirl is not a beached whale," Zeus said with a laugh.

"But you know what I mean, right?" I sighed. "It would bother me if someone thought I was singularly focused on some kind of odd fetish."

"I'm not bothered by it at all, Kallie." Zeus put his hand down next to mine. Instinctively, I knew he wanted to hold my hand, just as much as I knew his palms were still clammy. I was glad he didn't, but I was also a little disappointed he didn't.

"Why not?" I asked.

"Because I know something the rest of them don't."

"Just because you know I'm Fatgirl doesn't mean—"

"That's not it," he said. "Well, it is, and it isn't. I love you for you, and that includes Fatgirl. It's nice to have an excuse to hang out with you, even if it means other people think I'm weird in the meantime."

I was glad I was wearing Zeus's larger hoodie, as protection from both the chillier April temperatures and my dwindling fat-form. Zeus wasn't able to see my face as I blushed.

I'd referred to him as my friend while I'd talked with Sorra, and I didn't really mean it until that moment. Zeus *was* a good friend, and it was actually really nice that for all my whiny self-centeredness, he still believed I was a good person.

Very carefully, I gave him a companionable pat on the arm.

"Well, I guess if it wasn't for me, you wouldn't come to the lacrosse game and see Blake Turner play," I joked.

Zeus's smile disappeared, and I clenched my fists again as I realized I'd messed up; I shouldn't have said that.

"I'm going to get a soft pretzel and another soda," Zeus said a moment later. "Be back in a moment. Want anything?"

I shook my head. "No, I'm good."

He stopped and glanced back at me, a wry look on his face. "No, you're not, but I like you anyway."

As he left me behind, I looked down, still angry with myself for being careless with his feelings.

I stared at my hands, finally shrunken down to their regular, delicate size. It was still strange to think that I was more than just how I looked. I mean, I still wanted to be a model like my mom. But there was something beyond "Fatgirl" just as much as there was something beyond "Kallie," and even beyond "Kallie Grande-White." It was hard for me to explain it, exactly, even though I knew I didn't need a parade to know its truth.

There was a greater destiny out there for me.

Even if I hoped it wasn't a "bigger" one.

I'll figure it out later. I smiled as I snuggled into the large sleeves of Zeus's sweatshirt. I had plenty to worry about, but right now, the game was about to begin, and I didn't want to miss it.

Fatgirl

FAKE NEWS

EPISODE 5

○ ○ ○ ○

C. S. Johnson

FATGIRL
FAKE NEWS

○ ○ ○ ○

Everyone wants an extraordinary life, but no one wants to pay the price that comes along with it.

Especially when that price involves as much pain, humiliation, and radioactivity as I'd had to deal with in recent weeks.

Not to mention the other fun things that go along with it, including—

"OMG, can you believe it?"

I stopped in my tracks. From the cringy, blood curdling edge in her voice, I already knew my socially-labeled best friend, Amory Franklin, was more than likely laughing at the latest Fatgirl update.

And that meant she was technically laughing at me.

And I technically hated that.

I mean, me, Kallie Grande-White, the real-life Fatgirl? No way, right? After all, I was the daughter of a model, and I was quite a popular figure—no pun intended—at Cuttingham City High School.

No one would really, actually, truly believe that I was secretly parading around the city as Fatgirl, the city's accidental superhero who'd stopped a terrorist and now some other Alterants, too.

I can't do this.

I felt paralyzed as I stood in my school's already-crowded hallways, watching Amory and my other friends laugh and talk with each other.

Honestly, I think I would've killed myself if anyone found out the truth about Fatgirl—especially Amory or any of my other friends. Given that my semi-sociopathic grandmother and the most awkward fat geek kid in school new my secret, I should have already died from embarrassment.

"Kallie, hi!" My bespectacled friend, Lizzie Meyers, called out and waved at me, and I had to swallow hard and move forward.

I really can't do this …

The dread inside of me kept threatening to overwhelm me, even as I squared my shoulders, put on a fake, bland smile reminiscent of the ignorant masses, and curled a lock of hair around my finger, pretending I had no other care in the world other than how happy I was.

"Hey, girls—I mean, *hola, chicas*," I replied cheerfully, before scooching between Amory and Uli, the hot German of our group. "What's going on?"

"Amory's just told us the news. It doesn't look like we're going to be participating in the new Model Middle America round on Friday," Uli said.

"Oh? We're not?" I hastily included myself in that group, even though I'd already more or less decided I wouldn't risk showing up at the Amphitheatre again, having made my stunning and brave Fatgirl debut there just a couple of weeks ago.

Amory grinned like a jackal. "Model Middle America's producer, Karen Bright, just announced this morning on the WACC Wacky Morning Show that they've decided to open it up to plus-sized models only."

I'd been expecting something silly, or even somewhat normal regarding the news about Fatgirl—like exposing some of the fake social media accounts, or maybe even some imposters running around downtown Cuttingham City. But I was not expecting something that grated on my nerves like a mutant sandpaper monster.

"Plus … sized … models?" I barely choked out the words.

"It seems Ms. Bright thought it would be better to do something more 'on-brand' for the guest judge, who is rumored to be Fatgirl." My other close-clique friend, June Hideko, wrinkled her flat little nose in displeasure. "I guess that means we don't qualify."

"Not unless we want to engorge ourselves with some sausage and gravy biscuits this week," Amory said with a giggle. "Can you imagine?"

In a stunning move of mutiny, my stomach growled hungrily at the prospect.

Thankfully, no one heard it as a wonderful, familiar voice came up behind me, as if to save me from all my darkness and despair.

"You're getting some sausage with biscuits and gravy? Count me in, too, Amory."

The sound of Blake Turner's voice was like hope gas, and my heart was an old, leaky engine beyond empty and coming up on my two-time life expiration date. My heart almost exploded with gratitude as he gave me—and all the others, too, I suppose—a nod in greeting.

"Hello, Blake!" I swallowed a squeal as his glorious, shining, sky-blue eyes met mine. "How are you feeling?"

"Oh, hey, Kallie," Blake said. "I'm doing well. My mom was all freaky and took me to a bunch of doctors because of last week, but there wasn't anything they found after the 'incident.'"

"Well, I can't tell you how glad I am you're back." I gripped my bookbag tightly in my hands, hiding the stress of that admission.

If I thought the truth about Fatgirl's real identity was difficult to deal with, it was nothing compared to the truth about Blake's "incident." He'd eaten one of my Abuela-Blanca's radioactive doughnuts when she'd come to find me for Pi Day last week at school.

Once he ate it—Blake had no way of knowing—he was destined to become Baby Boy Blake, which was my term for his whiny, weak, deflated-youngish-looking boy Alterant self.

The special brand of radioactivity made the consumer transform into their biggest fears—which made my metamorphosis into Fatgirl all the more insulting—and it turned out there was nothing Blake feared more than being weak and helpless, and looking like a nerd.

I'd been hesitant to become Fatgirl before Blake's incident, but I knew I was in love with him enough to save him, even if it meant transforming into my most grotesque and secretive form.

"Thanks, Kallie. I'm not wild about all that make up work. But if you ladies are working on a feast-fest, I'll gladly make room for it at my party."

"Party?" Amory arched a perfectly tweezed eyebrow with interest.

"Oh, yeah, I need to make up my Pi Day assignment for Ms. Bakersfield's class, and I've decided to do jumbo-sized pies. So, to eat it all, I'm thinking I'll have a lacrosse team party this Friday."

"This … Friday?" I didn't really want to know if it was because of—

"Yeah, Fatgirl's going to be the guest judge this week for that model show you like, right?"

My heart literally seemed to stop, right then and there.

"Everyone'll come over, and my parents have a huge TV screen and also a projector if we want to go out into my yard. Then we can turn on the show, and we'll watch it together."

"Watch it together? Don't you mean we can all laugh at it together?" Amory asked, unable to stop herself from smirking.

To his credit, Blake looked genuinely confused. "Laugh at what?"

"I mean, it's Fatgirl," Amory explained. "It's funny more than anything."

"Why?" Blake's confused look only deepened, and my heart gave a tentative beat again. "She saved my life, after all. And she's pretty cool. She's finally put Cuttingham City on the map."

"Yeah, for obesity awareness," Amory murmured, but Blake didn't appear to hear her as he praised Fatgirl's heroics.

It wasn't the first time that Blake was probably the only reason I had for staying alive, but this time, he was also the reason I didn't break down and start bawling.

"Fatgirl's a nice superhero. I'm happy she's on our side. She's been doing some good work with other people, too, so far as I've heard. I think it'd be awesome to meet her."

I had to blink away the tears bubbling up in my eyes.

"Geez, Blake, why don't you just see if you can send out one of those 'date me' video requests?" Amory asked.

At that, Blake shut his mouth, and rather abruptly, too.

"Well, he's got the party to worry about first." I stepped forward and slid my arm through Blake's in a show of support as much as it subtly encouraged him to follow my lead. "I mean, Friday's almost here."

Amory snorted. "We have two days, Kallie."

"Well, parties take time to plan."

"As long as his plus-sized pies are ready, sounds to me like Blake's got it covered," Amory said. "And it's even on brand for the show, so kudos, Blake."

"Thank you," Blake said, blushing.

"There are still other things to plan," I insisted, fervently hoping we could get off topics like "Fatgirl" and "plus-sized" things.

"I'm sure it's nothing that can't be settled," Amory argued. "It should be pretty easy to plan a party."

"Well, it's not like you would know that. We've never really had a party at your house before, so …"

The words were out of my mouth before I could stop myself, and as Amory's eyes burned with first surprise, and then anger, I knew I really should've stopped myself.

For all intents and purposes, Amory was the leader of our group, but as much as she considered herself the leader, and the rest of us just let her think that, too, we usually met at June's house or even Lizzie's house for parties during the school year. Uli's parents had a pool for the summer, and the girls were supportive of me not having parties since Mom took off for LA last year. But while we would go to Amory's house after school for a few hours on occasion, she usually always managed to run us out before her mom came home from work.

"Hrumph." Amory grabbed her bag as the bell for homeroom rang, and we had to get to class. "I'll look for the address, Blake. Text me, 'kay?"

"Sure." He grinned and waved as she walked away, and I just stood there, torn between relief, elation, and anxiety.

Amory would get her revenge later, I was sure.

But this was my chance to talk to Blake alone, and I quickly seized it.

"So, Blake, do you really like Fatgirl?" My arm was still looped through his, and to show him I wasn't going anywhere, I twirled the loose curl of my hair around my fingers again and looked up at him as though he'd hung the moon.

"Enough to go out on date with her, you mean?" Blake asked.

"Date her?" I repeated, a little surprised.

I wasn't trying to ask that, but now that I was standing here with Blake, hanging on his arm, and still in my usual, wonderfully attractive form, it would be a great time to see if I could get him to ask me out.

Blake shrugged. "Well, I'm not really available to date anyone until the lacrosse season's over—"

"You're not going to date anyone till the season is over?" My fingers tingled, already numb with disappointment and shock.

"—and I don't know if I'd 'date her,' you know? I mean, she's got to be kinda busy, and, well, there's someone else I kinda had in mind to date—"

My heart lit up with daring hope once more. "You do?"

"—but if nothing else, she should come to the school," Blake barreled on. "I mean, I'd love for Fatgirl to come and see me play."

"You would?" A new voice asked from behind us.

Blake and I turned to see the blonde lady with a microphone who'd suddenly appeared behind us. She was perky and wearing a classy suit, along with a smile that seemed like it was forced.

The lady leaned forward, forcing me back away from Blake. "Well, let's see if we can arrange that, why don't we?"

"Who're you?" Blake stepped back, letting my arm drop out of his. He was clearly confused, so I didn't take it too harshly that he'd pulled away from me. "Are you Fatgirl's agent or something?"

"You're Blake Turner, aren't you?" The lady pressed onward, ignoring his questions as she began pestering Blake with her own.

I frowned. I was about to demand the lady tell us just who on earth she thought she was—and why we should take her offer to find Fatgirl for Blake seriously—when I finally recognized her.

It was Gynnifer Stills, the local news anchorwoman from the WACC Morning Show.

Oh, no. I sucked in my breath, terrified. *This is not good.*

I pulled out my phone and hurriedly texted Abuela-Blanca as Gynnifer peppered Blake with praise about his lacrosse prowess while sneaking in questions about his transformation experience and meeting Fatgirl. Each passing second was scorching hell as I waited for AB to reply to me.

Come on, AB. Respond!

I mean, *I* couldn't handle this. I didn't know what to do. It was clear Blake was content to talk about himself; this was the perfect chance for him to gain some good media.

This was a situation that my former-government worker, half-sociopathic, honorably unethical, somewhat racist grandmother could handle much better than I could.

"Blake, it's almost time for class," I finally said, butting in as best as I could. "Coach doesn't like it when you're tardy."

"I think your coach would make an exception after the horrendous ordeal you've gone through, Blake," Gynnifer cut in smoothly.

"I'm sure that the media doesn't want to encourage students to miss out on their academics," I retorted. "Perhaps Blake can talk to you some other time?"

"Oh, I'm counting on it," Gynnifer agreed. "I'm actually hoping you can come on the news with me today at noon."

"Well, I have practice today, so I can't really miss any more school," Blake said. "I've already been out for a few days because of the whole … *incident* … thing."

Almost as if she was sensing his weakness, Gynnifer quickly swooped in. "My team and I would be happy to come and watch you practice and then interview you afterward. I can air the segment on my morning show."

As Blake beamed with pride and pleasure, I felt my soul start to collapse into itself like a dying star—it was appropriate, I guess, for me to think of a comparison that involved a lot of gas.

"Aunt Gynnifer!"

I whirled around to see Gloria—a plain-ish looking girl from a couple of my classes I never really paid much attention to before—as she came up to Gynnifer and reached for a hug.

Gynnifer took a small step back. "Sorry, Gloria," she said, and I was surprised to see she looked genuinely sad. "I've got all the hair and makeup on."

"Oh, right." Gloria gave me a friendly smile before turning back to Gynnifer, who must have actually been her aunt. "Are you here for work?"

"She's here to talk to me, actually," Blake said, his puffed-up chest making me cringe.

Yeah, she was here to talk to you, so you could talk about Fatgirl.

"My boss said he'd love to do a segment on all of Fatgirl's biggest fans, and the people she's saved," Gynnifer explained. "Especially after this morning's ratings with Karen Bright on the show. They were through the roof, and that's only the beginning. We're going to have Robert Cuttingham III on our show, too. The station's hungry for any stories about Fatgirl we can get!" Gynnifer's eyes sparkled, as she stared off into the distance. "Can you imagine the promotions I'll be up for if I discover who Fatgirl really is?"

"I'd love to know myself," Blake agreed. "She could come to the school and watch me play."

I can't do this anymore.

I always tried to make it to Blake's games, and over the last few weeks, I'd only missed a few, even with all the Fatgirl mess that had been going on.

I was near fainting with the steep levels of stupidity around me as the bell rang again.

Gloria looked shocked, Blake didn't hear it, and I felt unnaturally high levels of relief; I'd never thought I'd look forward to class so much as I did in that moment.

But before I could get Blake to head off to class and leave Gloria along with her aunt, Zeus Evans appeared in the hallway.

His eyes fell on me, and I could see them brighten.

He'd been looking for me, I guess.

I sincerely hoped to high heaven AB hadn't texted him and told him to go and help me, but I also knew that it was almost too much to ask for.

That was when Gloria pointed to Zeus. "If you want another story, Auntie, you should talk to Zeus. He helped Fatgirl save Blake when he'd been causing all the trouble in Mrs. Bakersfield's class."

At once, Blake balked. "What? No way. That loser is part of the reason I felt as bad as I did and needed Fatgirl's help at all."

"Really?" Gynnifer's eyes went sharp as she looked over at Zeus; I quickly signaled to him to stop where he was; as bad as things were, I didn't need him to make our situation worse. "Is he a rival for Fatgirl's affections?"

"What?" I was quickly losing my temper and my patience with this lady. "What are you talking about? Blake doesn't want to date Fatgirl."

Blake coughed. "Well, she's a powerful woman, and I'm not scared to date her or anything. I mean, people shouldn't be making fun of her for sure, and she's definitely a role model for future generations—"

I "accidentally" stepped on Blake's foot as he hurried to offer his addendum to my assertation. Gynnifer didn't likely hear him anyway; she was already running after Zeus, who'd wisely decided to back away.

"Oh, great. She was supposed to interview me," Blake said. "Figures that geek would ruin things for me."

"I think he prefers nerd," I muttered.

Blake just sighed. "Doesn't help, Kallie."

I felt bad seeing the look on his face; I hadn't meant to hurt Blake's feelings.

"I'm sure my aunt will find you again," Gloria told him.

I nearly snorted. It was clear Gynnifer was only here because she was after a story, and that meant scandal. And what bigger scandal could there be where Fatgirl was concerned?

"Come on," I said. "Let's get to class. Our teachers won't likely believe us that we were talking to someone as famous as your aunt, Gloria."

"I'll talk to them," Gloria said with a kind and generous smile. "Don't worry."

Yes, yes, don't worry about that. Clearly, there were other things I needed to worry about instead.

I pulled out my phone again, angry to see the screen was still blank.

What in the world is AB doing?

"All right, AB." I stormed into my house after school having spent the whole day simmering as I waited for her response—which never came—and now I was ready for blood.

I thundered into the kitchen, expecting to find her giving me that "oh-you-need-something" look while she sipped on her tea and the world went to hell in a handbasket outside.

When I didn't see her, I frowned and then called down to her room. "What was the point of you buying me a phone if you're not going to answer me when I need it?"

There was no response.

Typical.

But as I walked through the house, I realized how silent it was.

"AB?" I called again.

I glanced outside—AB's Imperial was missing. Usually the bright white, ancient car screamed for attention; it was strange I'd missed its absence.

"Figures," I murmured. AB *would* disappear on me, right when we have a crisis coming as bad as this one appeared to be.

I started to text her again when the Imperial approached the house and slowed to a stop in front of the driveway.

I didn't even wait for AB to get out of the car.

"There you are!" I shouted. "Where have you been? We've got a major problem."

"Oh, Lord, don't tell me you've gotten into more trouble," AB said as she pulled off her sunglasses. "You're not supposed to go in my room without me in there. You've already got into my doughnuts. Why can't you leave my property alone?"

"What are you talking about?" I snapped. "I'm talking about how Gynnifer Stills is showing up at my school asking all sorts of questions about Fatgirl."

"Hmmm." Abuela-Blanca arched her brow at me, still suspicious. "You haven't been in my room? And you haven't eaten anything I've cooked."

"Never. Other than the doughnuts." I scowled at her. "Oh, I don't care about that. I just got home. Tell me why you haven't been answering my text messages."

"I saw your first one, and I sent Zeus to rescue you," AB said, confirming my suspicions. "He didn't text me back, so I assumed things were fine."

"But I kept texting you!"

"Hmmm." AB looked back toward the city and sighed. "I suppose I was in a few sketchy areas earlier. Perhaps the signal is still relatively poor here in Cuttingham City."

"Seriously?" I groaned. "Bad cell phone reception today is just a hoax, and you and I and everyone else who's seen a cell phone company commercial knows it."

"I think you'd be surprised," AB said with a creepy, knowing smile. "Sometimes it's an intentional one, which is why the government enjoys the little lapses in service from time to time."

I narrowed my eyes at her as she pulled off her driving scarf.

"Okay, fine," I said. "We won't argue about how you're not helping me enough. Instead, we'll discuss how Gynnifer Stills showed up at my school, bragging about how the news station wants to have a Fatgirl extravaganza this week."

"You know, Kallie, you're really going to have to get used to the drama that comes with this superhero business."

"It's not superhero business." I crossed my arms over my chest. "It's supposed to be 'you getting your job back and bringing my mom home' business, and I can't do it."

"Why ever not?"

"What do you mean, 'why not?'" My fingers dug into my skin, forcing me to stay still and not scream or slam myself into the floor in pure outrage. "I can't do this stuff, AB, and you know it."

"Can't you?"

"Come on, *no*. Gynnifer's hosting Karen Bright, Robert Cuttingham, and now Blake Turner this week on the news. I don't know how to get the media off my back, and not even those people were able to say no."

Though they probably didn't want to, I thought grimly.

"Darling, you just need to cancel your appearances." AB pulled out her phone and scrolled down her notes. "According to her show, you're supposed to be a guest judge at that model show this week. You did talk about it while we were at the Cuttingham mansion."

I crossed my arms. "Well, I didn't agree to it."

"That producer lady seems to think you did."

"She was all lovey-dovey with her fiancé after he saw the ghost of his dead wife while I said no," I hissed. "And you would never agree to it either, so I don't know why you would think I did."

AB shrugged. "Actually, I don't mind if you do. It's good distraction for us. But you'll have to let me know about needing doughnuts. I'm going to have to get some more ingredients soon."

"Come on, AB," I whined. "I can't do that."

"It seems to me that there's a lot of things you don't believe you're capable of doing," AB said.

"Well, I'm not. The only reason we're doing this crap at all is because of you. So now I need your help."

AB smirked. "Are you sure? That lady's even arranged for you to judge the 'plus-sized' models."

"Plus-sized models are just average people. Fatgirl's fatter than all of them put together."

"She said it was more 'on-brand' for you."

"Ugh! I'm starting to get the feeling she just says hip lingo like 'on-brand' to make it sound like she knows what she's talking about. Honestly, if she knew me at all, she'd've never made the offer. And she should've never said I would be a guest judge. Honestly, that's such a stupid thing to say on live TV."

"You could call up this Gynnifer Stills lady yourself and set the record straight," AB said. "She'll get her interview, and she'll back off your so-called friends at school."

"I'll get Zeus to email her and Karen Bright later," I said.

"Just do it yourself, Kallie."

"How?" I asked. "He's at least got a website and an email I could use, and all the connected social media accounts."

"You could at least write it out for him."

"He's the one who wanted the site, remember? Besides, aren't you concerned at all about this?"

"I can only be so concerned about so many things at one time," AB replied smoothly. "I'm afraid something much more serious is happening."

What could possibly be more serious than a power-hungry, over-ambitious news anchorwoman determined to find out my secret identity?

I groaned. "I don't want to know, do I?"

AB led me into the house. "Remember what I said. You're going to have to get used to problems, Kallie. You'll get paid more for handling more difficult problems. The people who can't handle problems are the ones who feel the most entitled to a life without them."

Grumbling, I followed AB down the stairs into her bedroom-turned-lab.

The instant I stepped inside AB's room, the *tickety-clickety* sound of her Phi-ger beeped out softly. I didn't like how it sounded, either, and I could tell as AB looked down at it, she wasn't happy, either.

"This is what's got me worried," AB said, pulling up another screen. "I've been able to home in my Protactinium's radioactive signature. I've been able to keep watch on it as it metabolizes through the different people who ingested it. But there's a soft radioactive trail popping up around the city."

"You said before that Frank had some residue on him from me sitting on him that first time." At the thought of the terrorist I'd ended up capturing for the police—twice—I allowed myself to smile with a small sense of pride.

"Yes, and thank the good Lord for that," AB murmured. "It's easier to keep tabs on Frank while he's in secure custody. And it was nice since there was no signal after he was transferred to a black site high-security system. Some free information that my contact on the force doesn't need to know he'd inadvertently given me."

"Your contact on the force?" I paused for a moment. "Is it Officer Powers?"

Officer Powers was the man who'd helped me at my Model Middle America debut when I'd first become Fatgirl. He was a nice man with a gentle smile and an impressionable face, and if he was AB's contact, I wouldn't have been upset about it. I would've felt better, knowing we were helping him. Even if that meant he would be stuck helping us from time to time, too.

"You don't need to worry about it, Kallie." AB pointed back at the scanner. "This is what we need to worry about right now."

I looked back at the little trails of lines that crossed the screen. "Is it really so hard to believe that the radioactive signature would spread?"

"It doesn't spread like this," AB said. "Plasma is the best way to maintain it; part of the reason jelly doughnuts are the best way to have it ingested."

"Shut up." I rolled my eyes.

"Something is happening." AB traced the lines across the screen. "Look at these lines. They're definitive, working through streets. Someone else has it now, and they're sending out the recipe to different people."

I looked at the scanner screen she was showing me. There were thicker lines throughout the streets, almost like …

"Post office workers?" I asked. "Delivery guys?"

"Yes," AB said. "Someone has my recipe, and they're moving it. Possibly to other people."

"Well, we did find out that Karen's fiancé had it from one of her friends," I reminded her. "Well, he'd been sent it through the mail … so maybe it wasn't him?"

"I'll have to keep looking into it," AB said. "The problem with Trevor Darlington is that he's almost never around Cuttingham City."

"Dad's worked for the Darlingtons," I said. "They're the ones who own the Darla Donut lady logo. Do you think it's really Trevor Darlington who's behind everything?"

"I don't know." AB frowned. "But the Darla Donut factory would have the resources for distribution as well as creation of my doughnuts."

"You made them in our oven upstairs," I reminded her. "Anyone living in a suburbs would have *that* available to them."

"They wouldn't, unless they had the actual radioactive elements," AB said. She sighed. "Either way, I've got to find ZZ."

ZZ, the former KGB agent, whose real name was Zina Morozova, was apparently going to auction off AB's recipe at some point in the near future, at some kind of special gala. Once AB got the recipe from ZZ, she would find the person who'd been responsible for framing her for its theft from her former government job archives.

"Have you heard anything about her lately?"

"Not much that would help at the moment," AB admitted. "ZZ was last seen in Las Vegas. Your mom was there, too. Both of them were doing an event with the Rockettes and some other modeling 'charity' event."

"What's that supposed to mean?" I asked.

"Money laundering, most likely," AB admitted. "In Las Vegas, it's possible it could be a politician or a cartel leader, or even both of them, if the news is offering any indication."

"What?" My eyes widened in horror at the thought. "What does money laundering have to with my mom?"

"Nothing official, so far as I've seen."

"You mean Mom might be involved with criminals?"

"Oh, Kallie, trust me, you don't need to worry about it." AB shrugged. "Though of course, there's not really 'news,' about it. Those stories don't get pushed. A lot of people in powerful places don't want the word to get out.

"And let's be honest; more people are concerned about celebrities, politicians, and money markets than crimes. Local crimes are the hardest for people to listen to. Life gets a lot more terrifying if you know your neighbors' criminal records."

"Our neighbors are criminals?" I put my head in my hands. *This just keeps getting worse.*

"Oh, I've checked them out, and they're harmless enough. A few DUIs aren't going to make me nervous. In fact, it gives me insight into weakness, and I enjoy knowing other peoples' weaknesses."

I wrinkled my nose. "You don't have to tell me that. I already know you like finding other people's fears and weaknesses with your Project: SERUM."

AB let out a small cackle. "Yes, that's true. Fear is a great weakness."

I went quiet as AB went back to her typing; I didn't always know if she told me things to freak me out or because she was genuinely being honest, and most of the time I didn't want to know.

Then other times she would joke about plausible deniability, and that didn't make me feel any better.

"ZZ will still be hosting her gala soon," AB said, reverting my attention back to the more important matter. "We'll get to her eventually. But this is much more troubling right now."

"Well, look at the bright side. It's not that many lines."

And in truth, there weren't that many red lines of Phi-ger concentrations; Cuttingham City wasn't the largest city in Arkansas, but it was fairly big; there were a few streaks toward the Cuttingham Mansion, and there were some down by the school, and in the inner city regions around where I'd been before.

"We'll still have to take note of any patterns that come up," AB said. "And of course, we'll have to watch for any signs of movement on it. That'll show us if an Alterant is active or not."

"Well, that's … helpful." I slumped over, gloomy over the prospect that Fatgirl might have to go in and save someone else from their stupid fears.

"Speaking of," AB said, "since Johnny won't be home for a while, I have an assignment for you."

Of all the days for my dad to be working late, it had to be that day. Everything was going from bad to worse, and I didn't think I could take any more trouble.

"I don't wanna go and do Fatgirl work," I whined. "This is bad enough. And then there's still my issues to work through."

"Six therapists on government budget wouldn't be able to work through all your issues the way I can," AB said. "Grab my purse over there and then follow me. We're going to have a girl's night."

"We are?" I didn't know how I felt about that. I wouldn't mind getting a manicure or pedicure, or even possibly getting my hair done—then there was shopping to consider, too. "Well … what about Gynnifer Stills and Blake and the media stuff?"

"I already texted Zeus to run interference. If you're not going to do it yourself, you should make sure he gets you out of that judging gig, especially if it's coming up soon." AB sighed. "But as I said, we have other things to worry about. And this girl's night is a great opportunity to do something to help you gain confidence and maybe even relax some."

It was true that Amory and the others hadn't been around as much lately; I wasn't up for being around them since Amory invariably brought up Fatgirl, and I didn't want to do or say anything that would give away my real identity on the matter.

In addition to that, I could use a break from thinking about all the Alterants and Mom and ZZ and Zeus and all the others, too. At least for a few hours.

God only knew I couldn't keep Fatgirl from returning before too long, especially with Gynnifer Stills interviewing Blake tomorrow and the whole Model Middle America show happening the day after that.

Maybe a girl's night wouldn't be a bad idea. Even if it was with AB.

"Okay," I agreed. I grabbed her purse, ignoring how heavy it was, and then followed her out the door. "Let's go have some fun."

I should've known AB's definition of "fun" was vastly different from mine. As I watched her shoot off a stream of bullets into a paper target, I dug my fingers into my arms and tried not to scream.

Not that anyone would hear me, let alone AB. She turned back to me, her smile wide between the two huge, padded earmuffs. I was wearing a matching set, and I felt even more miserable because it was ugly and mussing up my hair.

AB pulled out her gun's empty magazine. "Okay, now it's your turn," she called, her voice muffled but still sharp through my earmuffs.

"No." I gulped hard as she put the gun in my hand. "I can't do this."

"What are you afraid of?" She rolled her eyes, clearly annoyed. "If you're going to work with me, you should know how to shoot. You're not going to always be Fatgirl, so sitting on people won't always work."

"Why don't you yell louder, so other people will hear you talk about how I'm Fatgirl?" I took the gun from her reluctantly. She'd better hope if I learned to shoot, I'd never have to use it on her one day. "Believe it or not, superhero or not, I don't actually want to kill other people."

"It's not about killing others. Primarily, anyway," AB said. "A gun is a deterrent against violence in the right hands, Kallie. You need to be able to take care of yourself, and possibly others."

I didn't want to tell her how I'd tried using a gun before, back when I'd been chasing Frank Whitey through the sewers. It had been loud—so very loud, much louder than in the movies—and so much harder, both physically and psychologically, than I'd ever expected.

"Remember the fundamentals," AB reminded me. "Treat all guns as if they're loaded. Don't aim at something you don't want to kill. Aim carefully, take note of your biases, hold the gun steady, and shoot straight."

Mimicking her movements, my fingers slowly tightened around the trigger—until I had to just jerk it back and shoot.

Bang!

A small yelp escaped from me as I took a quick step back, barely avoiding the bullet shell.

"Not bad." AB studied the target, ignoring my state of mind-shattering anxiety. "You'll need to build up your strength if you want to keep your hands steadier. And you tend to lean to the left. Is that your dominant eye?"

"I don't know," I said, trying not to grumble. "What does that have to do with anything?"

"It's a bias," she said. "You'll need to know for your aim, if you want it to be straight. If you know you go left, you'll have to compensate. Just don't overcompensate."

"I don't think I can do this," I said again.

"Stop that, Kallie," AB snapped. At the more hostile tone, I blinked in shock, and then she sighed. "Look. There's no reason you can't learn this. No one is born knowing how to do something perfectly. When you're good at something, it looks easy. But nothing's really easy, especially if it's worth learning."

"I don't know if learning how to shoot a gun is worth learning," I argued.

"Well, I'll teach you now, and then we can determine how useful it is later on."

"That's convenient for you."

"It is." She gave me a smirk. "But you should know it wasn't easy for me to learn, either. My father taught me how to shoot. He was a hunter, so I learned on rifles."

I had to admit, AB was right about that. Rifles looked a lot heavier than the revolver I was using.

AB loaded another magazine into my gun. "Over the years, I've grown to appreciate handguns. Easier to conceal, more rounds, less expensive ammo."

"I get it," I muttered. "Psycho."

"A psycho, as you say, will shoot indiscriminately and feel no remorse for it," AB corrected me. She handed me the gun again, pressing into in my palms. "Even those who shoot to protect others feel remorse, though some of it might be manageable in the end."

"I wish we could live in a world without guns." I put it down on the small counter, looking down the long lane where the target we were using hung. "They're so loud and violent. This honestly makes me even more scared—I don't know why you brought me here."

AB sighed. "I wish we could, too," she admitted quietly. "It would be nice to live without guns and lies. But given the fallen nature of humanity, if we didn't have guns, we'd have something else, and probably something worse—really, we do have much worse. And much as I like to believe they can be used solely for defense, I know that's not true."

She picked up my gun and held it out to me carefully. "But I like them because they are much like the truth. Guns can be used for the good, the bad, and the frivolous. Some people use it as a tool to get what they want, and others use it as a fashion statement or a political slogan. Part of growing up—and becoming more responsible—is acknowledging the difference between the good and the bad, the fake and the true, and preferring the good and the true to the bad and fake."

"That's a bit of a stretch." I rolled my eyes.

"It is not. You'll still want someone on your side who can handle the truth, especially under pressure." AB grinned down as she pulled out a matching set of Berettas. "Just like guns."

"I guess I'll agree with that, but I don't think you're really seeing things from my perspective."

"Well, it's hard to go back to being innocent without feeling ignorant. And then, are you able to see things from my point of view?"

"I'm here shooting stuff, aren't I?" I gave her a bitter look before I positioned my feet and fired off a few more bullets, still squirming as the bullets were ejected out of the barrel. I tried getting used to the heat of the gun and letting the empty casing flip out of the top of the barrel.

"You only ever feel grown up after, never during," AB said. "You'll feel better when we're done here, even if you hate it now."

I narrowed my eyes at her, likely because I knew she was right. That was how I'd felt after capturing Frank Whitey, after all, wasn't it?

After a few more rounds, AB smiled at me. "Good work. You'll still need to practice, but you've got the basics done. And that'll help."

"I don't actually see how this will help us with your doughnut business. Especially if I don't want to use a gun."

I didn't want to admit it, but after all of this, I preferred the thought of sitting on the villains I chased.

"Maybe you'll grow to like it better, as I have," AB said. "Guns are a good indicator of character, among other things. Find me a person who suddenly has the power that a gun offers, and you can tell what kind of person they are by how they use it."

"I don't want to give anyone a gun to see how they would use it."

"Ah, but I gave *you* one," AB said with a laugh, and I gritted my teeth at her snark.

"Let me tell you something true, Kallie. I get some amusement out of this whole Fatgirl situation, because I am, as you've noticed, not a nice person."

I pulled back from her. "Yeah, I've noticed that," I said, rolling my eyes.

"But neither are you," AB continued, making me scowl. I was ready to give her a nasty retort when she took my hand in hers and patted it affectionately.

"However," she said, "there is one thing we have in common that makes me certain this is the right choice going forward. There are a lot of things that I've been able to find out and do since the Model Middle America fiasco, but I've seen you with the power to take a life and to help others, and you've risen to the occasion. Yes, sometimes kicking and screaming the whole way through—even as you're doing now." AB gave me another smile. "But you still want to help others, don't you? Even if it's me. And even if you have to pay a price for it. That's something *good*, and I can work with good."

I swallowed hard. I hadn't been expecting AB to say anything like *that.* It was almost too nice for her to say such a thing, and I had to shake it off.

"Well, come on, then," I said, reaching for the box of ammo we'd bought earlier. "Let's do another round."

I thought about what AB said well into next day, and some perverse part of me—the part of me that shared the same DNA as AB, probably—was amused by the question of what my friends would do with a gun. I didn't think they would do anything bad, but I could see Amory complaining about how it would break her nails. June was a bit of a pragmatist, and I could see her learning how to use it in a resigned sort of way. Uli and Lizzie wouldn't even touch it, probably too afraid they would set it off by mistake.

So as much as I hated to admit it, I did feel better about taking AB's lessons to heart. And it did help she'd complimented me enough I didn't feel completely helpless at the thought of using one.

AB was also right about Fatgirl: one day, I would stop sitting on people.

Then I spotted Blake talking to Gynnifer Stills after school. After watching them for a few moments, I decided I wouldn't mind sitting on her, if only to get her to shut up about Fatgirl.

I was getting more and more irritated watching Gynnifer interview Blake, and I barely noticed when Gloria walked up beside me.

"My aunt is pretty passionate about her job," Gloria said. "Dad says it's all she cares about."

"I can see that," I said, forcefully keeping my tone neutral. "Blake doesn't seem to mind."

"I would, I think," Gloria said, surprising me.

"What do you mean?"

"She's really only interested in interviewing him so she can possibly get a shot at interviewing Fatgirl. I know Blake thinks it's a good time for college scouts to notice him, but I doubt anyone is paying attention to him for that."

"I don't know why she'd think Fatgirl would be here, of all places," I said.

Gloria nodded. "No one really knows why she was here in the first place, the other day when Blake started to get all weird. Auntie's probably hoping for a second sighting. I wouldn't be surprised if that's why she's asking Blake what happened."

I nodded slowly, and my pity for Blake shrunk as my contempt for Gynnifer grew. "What do you think your aunt'll do if she doesn't get her interview?"

Gloria adjusted her backpack over her shoulder. "She'll probably just bombard her at the Model Middle America show."

"Well, Fatgirl's not coming to that," I said. "Too bad your aunt will be disappointed."

"Karen Bright herself has said Fatgirl was coming, though." Gloria frowned, and then looked over at me. "How do you know she's not? Did you hear something?"

Stupid, stupid, stupid.

"Oh, well, I mean, it didn't say anything on Fatgirl's fan website about her being there," I hurriedly said, trying to cover my tracks.

I'd have to get Zeus to fix that, I thought, looking around for any sign of him. I'd seen him in Mr. Embers' class, but he seemed tired, and I wasn't able to get his attention without making a spectacle.

And frankly, considering how we'd met when I'd farted horrifically loudly in computer class before, I didn't really want to make a habit of calling unwanted attention to myself.

"I'm sure Auntie will find another way to get her interview, even if Fatgirl doesn't come to the show tomorrow," Gloria said. "Either way, I've heard ticket sales are up, and interest is an all-time high. Will you be going to the show, Kallie?"

"Huh?" I wasn't really listening to Gloria talk as I watched Gynnifer hand Blake a familiar-looking pair of tickets.

It hadn't been that long ago that my own father had given me some tickets to go see the next Model Middle America show. I'd burned them, more or less because I didn't want to go back to relive the horrors of Fatgirl's origins.

"Auntie told me she could get me some tickets," Gloria continued, but it was then I completely lost track of the conversation, as Zeus walked into the gym.

His eyes lit up when he saw me, and he started to wave, but stopped suddenly, as if he remembered we were only really "secret friends," rather than open ones.

Zeus might have been looking for me, but it was Gynnifer who found him.

She'd chased after him before, and Blake objected just as strongly this time. "You don't need to talk to him." Blake was pouting as he reached for her arm. "He's the reason I turned into a weakling and had my traumatic breakdown."

If that was meant to deter her, it couldn't have backfired more.

I could hear Blake asking Gynnifer if she wanted to see him play when she turned away and made a beeline for Zeus, with Blake following her at her heels—which were actually nice heels, if I did say so myself. But then, I would say that about designer heels.

The glitter of glamour faded, however, when I saw Zeus' face. He was a deer caught in the headlights of an eighteen-wheeler racing down a mountain, and I wasn't sure if I could save him.

"Excuse me, Gloria," I murmured, hurrying to run interference.

"He's no one important," Blake said. "He's one of those computer nerds, that's all."

"But you said Fatgirl was talking to him?" Gynnifer looked at him, wrinkling her nose. "Why would he be talking to her? Are you friends with her?"

"No," I said, interrupting quickly. Zeus and I exchanged a quick look, and Blake was even looking a little exasperated as I faced down Gynnifer Stills. "I mean, Fatgirl is just a local celebrity—"

"Do you know who she is?" Gynnifer asked Zeus. "How are you connected to the Cuttinghams?"

"Who's that?" Blake asked.

"I can't say who Fatgirl is," Zeus said, stepping in front of me. "I … um, I just run her fan website, that's all."

I felt myself turn numb as Zeus admitted he was the webmaster for Fatgirl's fansite; I barely heard Blake's huff of disgust, although I definitely heard Gynnifer's squeal of delight.

My fingers curled into fists, and I could almost picture the saliva practically drooling out of Gynnifer's mouth as she began shooting Zeus with more questions.

"Sorry, if you'll excuse me, Ma'am," Zeus said, clearly floundering. "Um, Mr. Embers asked me to get Kallie. He has a special project for us to take care of."

"Hey, Kallie was going to watch me practice today," Blake objected. "She was going to bring her other friends, too."

It was so unfair.

Blake wanted me to watch his practice, and I wanted to watch his practice, too.

And there I was, stuck hauling Zeus out of there before Gynnifer Stills managed to pry anything else out of him.

"I'll be back in a flash," I lied to Blake, and then I hid my face from him so he couldn't see how embarrassed I truly was.

The moment I was free, I texted AB again.

This was getting out of hand, and I needed reliable help.

That realization infuriated me.

"Well," I said, the instant we were out of Gynnifer and Blake's sight, "it's a good thing you didn't have a gun back there."

"What?" Zeus looked even more startled, and I only sighed.

"Never mind," I said. "But what was all of that? Why did you tell her that you're the owner of the Fatgirl site?"

"I thought it was better than anything else I could tell her," Zeus replied. "If I told that lady we weren't friends—"

"Which we're officially not!"

"—then she would've just kept going. She did that yesterday." Zeus scratched his head nervously. "I thought this would give her a new angle to chase."

"Yes, and it's one that leads right to me," I snapped. "What in the world were you thinking?"

"I'm sorry," he said. "I guess I'm just tired today."

"That's not good enough."

Zeus sighed, and for a moment, I thought of how weary he'd seemed earlier in Mr. Embers' class.

My head fell forward into my hands. "Jesus."

"Ha." He gave me a half-hearted smile. "It's hey-Zeus."

I almost hit him. I didn't need levity at that moment; if anything, I needed security.

"Okay, enough. You have to help me fix this," I said. "First, go and email Karen Bright and tell her Fatgirl is busy, and she won't be able to come to be a guest judge tomorrow night. Can you do that?"

"Yes. Yes, I can do that."

"Okay. Let's start with that." I glanced back down at my phone. "I'm going to go home and talk to AB. She's not answering her phone again, and if I have to get her to wipe your memory, I want your word you'll let me do it."

"But—"

"No 'buts,' Zeus. You've almost blown my cover, and you're getting careless." I shook my head. "There's nothing more important right now than this. Please take care of it."

"I'm sorry about this. Things just … got away from me." He bowed his head apologetically. "I will take care of all this mess, Kallie. Please give me another chance."

"Just go," I said. His tiredness was catching, and I just wanted the stress to go away. "I can't do this right now."

"There. You can relax, Kallie." AB turned the sound off her computer screen and looked back at me. "That boy you like doesn't seem to remember the doughnuts, and he really only talks about himself."

As I watched the WACC Morning Show credits, I let out a long, slow breath; every nerve inside of me had been screaming in silent pain as I'd watched Blake's interview with Gynnifer that morning. I hadn't been able to go to school, I'd been so sick with worry something would've aired that would've damned me to social outcast mode for the rest of my life.

"Feel better?" AB asked. "I told you that you didn't need to worry about him. Blake doesn't remember the doughnuts, and he's focused more on himself and what he wants than anything Fatgirl related."

"He said he'd be willing to take her out on a date in the interview." I leaned forward, still breathing slowly. "Isn't that something to worry about?"

"No. Before you get too many crazy ideas, he said he'd take her out on a date, not that he wanted to date her. Semantics, Kallie. He's in it for himself, and that's it. Telling him about your identity will not win him over before prom."

"I wasn't going to tell him," I snapped. "I'd die of embarrassment. But at least he said it wasn't a good idea to make fun of her. Maybe that will get Amory to stop laughing at the Fatgirl news."

"That's the hyper-uptight one?" AB snorted. "Fat chance."

I *almost* giggled, but then I thought of something else. "Why do you think Gynnifer didn't air the part where Zeus talked about owning the Fatgirl website?"

"It could be a number of things. She could be using that as bait for another special segment, like she's been doing all week since Karen and Robert's appearances."

"So … we don't have to worry about him?"

"That Blake boy? No." AB snorted. "He's too vapid to realize there would be a connection between the doughnut he stole from me and your appearance, and he wouldn't know about Robert's issues with the doughnuts, either."

"We only know there's a connection because we investigated the Cuttingham mansion," I said.

"And it's a very loose connection at that," AB said. "I did a little research last night, and Trevor Darlington, Karen's former boyfriend who sent the doughnuts, has checked into a special rehab clinic."

"Then, he did it?" I frowned. "He poisoned the Cuttingham doughnuts and then had a breakdown?"

AB pursed her lips. "It seems that way, but that might be something to keep in mind. I've been studying the trails of my Protactinium. Darling Donuts has a specific delivery route from their factory outside the city."

"Darling Donuts is the owner of that Darla Donut logo lady Mom used to model for . . ." I glanced back toward the stairs, up to where my dad's room was. "Do you think Dad could be working for the company that's got your recipe?"

AB sighed. "I'll keep tracking it, and hopefully that will lead us to something soon."

I heard her phone beep as a new text message arrived, and I sat back on the stool in AB's room, continuing to watch the monitor while she answered it.

"Zeus is asking about you," AB said. "Should I tell him you've had a nervous breakdown and checked into a special rehab?"

"At least I didn't poison anyone," I said. "You know, other than myself."

AB came up beside me. "You might just want to give the poor guy your own cell phone number, you know. I think you can trust him."

"No, we can't." I shook my head furiously. "That's why I couldn't even get out of bed this morning, barely. He messed up."

"He said to tell you that he'd emailed Karen, and it was all taken care of. He said his dad's company is working on the Model Middle America show again tonight, too, so he'll make sure there's no issues there."

"Fine. Good to know." I shifted uncomfortably. "He should do his best to make up for all the stress he's caused me, even if he has to suffer for it."

"Well, now you know how I feel dealing with you, don't you?" AB asked.

I scowled at her before I headed out of her room.

I didn't need this kind of negativity in my life; I already had plenty.

The rest of the day was more manageable, especially now that I knew Blake hadn't blown my cover, and Zeus wasn't on Gynnifer's show, even if she would probably come a-hunting again sooner or later. Perhaps by then we could think of a better cover story.

Or fake Zeus' death, or maybe AB could get one of her contacts to take care of Gynnifer.

I probably would've thought of a whole long list of ideas if I wasn't distracted by other texts from Uli and Lizzie about Blake's interview. I was especially delighted and horrified when Lizzie told me Amory was curious who it was Blake actually wanted to date—apparently, I'd missed that part of the interview, since I was so worried about hearing "doughnut" or "Fatgirl" or "Kallie Grande-White is Fatgirl" during the interview, even though I logically knew I had nothing to worry about there. Probably.

AB was more than a little right about Blake. He was happy to talk about himself, and I was never more grateful for that while I had a clue-hungry trend-hound on Fatgirl's tail.

It wasn't until AB called me down to her lab again that I started to feel like my worry-free hours were over.

And the *clickety-tick* of the Phi-ger was the first sign the end of my free time had come.

"Oh, no!" I moaned.

"Yes," AB said. "Look at the monitor. It's centralizing down in the news station."

"And it's turning red," I muttered. "Great. Someone ate some more radioactive doughnuts, huh?"

"Speaking of …"

She pushed a small box of Darla Donut-like doughnuts toward me, and I felt the reluctant call to superhero work.

I imagined it was similar to getting called into the hospital to receive an enema.

"No, no, no, no," I groaned. "No-ooh-ooh."

"Come on, Kallie." AB smirked. "Look at the bright side, right? You get to actually eat something that will stay down this time."

"It might stay down in my stomach, but my stomach gas is only going to go up." I took an unwilling bite out of the first doughnut and nearly wept at how warm and fluffy and gooey it was.

Freaking doughnuts.

As AB and I shuffled into the car—me wearing my God-awful, uber-pink and navy superhero suit under a large, floor-length jacket that used to be my dad's—I heard her phone beep again.

She was hurriedly texting a reply as she sped up toward the Interstate.

"You're not supposed to text and drive," I yelled as I started to bloat up into my Fatgirl form.

"You only get a ticket if you're caught," AB said.

"You don't get a ticket if you die," I shouted back, my belly aching from a combination of bad driving and the radioactive chemicals coursing through my blood.

"We won't die." AB glanced back at me. "I've got you in the backseat.

"Just pay attention to the road!"

It was a long ride to the news station, and it was made even longer as AB held up her phone.

"Why don't you just give Zeus your phone number, like I suggested before?" AB asked. "He's a good kid, Kallie."

"Why do you think we can trust him?" I asked.

"Why else? Because I know his weaknesses now," AB said. "He's quite forthcoming about it, really."

"Ugh." I pulled out my own phone. "I'd rather not. He confessed to Gynnifer Stills he was the owner of the website. What if she starts an investigation to see if he knows who Fatgirl is?"

"Look, Kallie, I need your help to keep the Protactinium out of the government's hands even more that it already appears to be," AB said. "I appreciate you as a distraction as much as an assistant, and Zeus is eager to help us. I think you should talk to him some more about things, and you'll see I'm right about that."

"I wouldn't trust him with a gun," I snapped, hoping the absurdity of the statement would keep her from bothering me anymore.

It did not.

"Well, I wouldn't either," AB said. "But I think I can trust him when it comes to you, Kallie, if nothing else."

"What if you're wrong?"

I expected AB to brush that idea off. I was even sure she would tell me to stop thinking so outlandishly, and it was time to focus on the mission. So I was surprised when she fell silent for several long moments, before she gave me an answer.

"I'd have to call in some more favors," she finally said. "But I'd make it work out okay. That's what I've been taught to do, Kallie. I can't do anything else."

"Well, it must be nice to be unable to fail," I huffed. "Zeus doesn't have that ability."

"You should still give him your number." AB sighed. "If for no other reason than it might save me some time when it comes to dealing with the two of you."

"I still don't want to give him my phone number," I said. "It would be a concession, and I'm tired of making concessions."

Frankly, I was tired about a lot of things.

"Oh, darling." AB shook her head, sadly and sagely. "That's part of life, I'm afraid."

○ ○ ○ ○

As we pulled into the station's parking lot, I couldn't help but cringe when I noticed that we were only a block away from the Cuttingham City Amphitheatre, where the Model Middle America crew members were no doubt getting ready to go live for the night.

"I can't believe I'm here."

"Stop blubbering," AB said. She pulled on her own mask, one that matched mine in color and shape, and I felt almost as though I had a kindred spirit beside me.

Kind of like the Ghost of Fatgirl Future, or something, maybe? Something terrifying and awful, but still so strangely recognizable that it's almost comforting?

"So what's the plan?" I asked AB.

"You're going to go into the station and tell them you're there for your interview with that Gynnifer lady, and then see if you can find the source of the radioactivity."

"Ugh." I rolled my eyes. "Fine. Just make sure you're out of sight so no one connects you to me."

AB laughed gaily. "Believe me, you're not the one who's more appalled by the prospect."

"Shut up."

I took off my dad's coat and slipped—or more accurately, fell—out of the Imperial, and headed toward the building.

Only to veer off to the side as the doors burst open, and Gynnifer Stills, followed by several men and women wearing large earphones, came running out.

"This isn't happening to me," she screamed, as she hurried off toward the Amphitheatre. I couldn't help but notice that her once-shiny heels were getting grimy.

None of them noticed me, and I took that as a good sign.

I walked around to where I'd left AB, only to find there wasn't anyone there anymore.

This is what I get for telling her to park somewhere where no one will notice her.

It wasn't possible to call her, either; my phone still made it hard for my fattened fingers to text, and I'd rather shout for her and scream while running around the nearby parking area than actually call her.

There was a little scratchy noise beside my ear inside my hood.

"Kallie, can you hear me?"

"AB?" I looked around, turning around all around me, trying to find her.

"I'm on a secure line through the radio," AB said. "I'm heading over to the Amphitheatre. Zeus texted me that Gynnifer's had a bit of a breakdown."

"Apparently it's a good week for it," I said, thinking of Trevor Darlington and of my own neediness. "Let me guess. She's our radioactive target."

"Yes. Come over to the Amphitheatre and we'll get her."

"Is she … dangerous?" I asked. "I mean, she's not seeing any ghosts or … losing her voice or something?"

Having just seen her, I didn't think that was it, but it was still good to get confirmation she wasn't dangerous.

"Zeus says she apparently barged in on the nightly news program yelling about how she'd lost her chance at real happiness, and she had nothing else now that Fatgirl had ruined her career."

"Great." I shook my head. "I can't tell if she's actually radioactive or just having a bad day."

"Well, the radioactive signals don't lie, fortunately," AB said. "It's her, all right. She probably has a large fear of losing control on air. Or maybe telling the truth on air? She's also accused her fellow newscasters of lying through their teeth about the nightly news, so you know it'll make the media rounds tomorrow."

"Probably on the other city channels."

AB laughed, and I felt a little better.

"Well, at least it's nice to know I'm not going to have the worst day today," I said. "There's no firing me from Fatgirl."

"No, but there is still such a thing as bad press, and there's no need to give them more of an excuse after Gynnifer's performance. Get over here, ASAP."

"You got it, AB." I sighed. "Tell Zeus to keep track of Gynnifer until I get there."

"He's waiting for you."

○ ○ ○ ○

AB was right; Zeus was waiting for me at the side door, near the one I'd sneaked in before, back when I was first trying out for *Model Middle America.*

I swallowed the lump in my throat and hurried to where he was waving.

"Come on, Kal—I mean, Fatgirl," he said.

"Can you please just shut up?" I hissed, as he held the door open for me. "This is already more than your fault that we're here."

"You're the one who cancelled on this show," Zeus reminded me. "And you're here anyway, right? So, you're going to have to be careful."

"Where's AB?" I asked.

"Here I am." AB popped out of a nearby door and pulled us inside the room.

"Does my father know you're in here?" Zeus asked nervously. "I'd rather not involve him in this. And I don't want him to get mad."

While AB assured Zeus his father was none the wiser to her presence, I noticed nearly an entire wall was plastered with screens showing us the camera feeds from around the stage and backstage areas.

"Look." I pointed up to one of them, where Gynnifer was being held back from the stage area by a familiar-looking face.

Azure.

He'd been my stylist when I'd managed to make it backstage before. I could tell he was struggling to hold Gynnifer back as others came around to help him.

"It seems like this should be pretty easy, given security here," I said.

"The crew workers are eager to get her out," Zeus agreed. He walked over to another computer and pulled up a video link. "This is her performance earlier."

"I see it's already making rounds on social media," AB said. "Is she out of a job yet?"

"Well …"

Zeus and AB talked quietly while I watched as the WACC evening hour show began, and then Gynnifer lunged herself in front of the camera.

"They lied to me," she hollered. "I've been betrayed! All my life I was told I would be number one if I just worked harder and looked better than everyone else, I would be happy!"

"Gyn? Gyn, what're you doing here?" Another voice cut in, and the news anchors behind her didn't seem to know what to do.

I watched as she turned to them. "Do you know how much I've lied while I was working here? Did you know we had a segment on how to make a delicious, three-course meal, *including dessert*, from just kale and kippers? Why do people believe us when we say such obviously silly things all the time?"

"Gyn, get off the stage!"

A stage manager rushed up, ready to pull her off camera. He made the cut signal, but Gyn stopped him.

"Stop, Greg!" she hollered. "You shouldn't try to keep a depressed woman like me even further down than you've already have. I want answers for my lack of happiness."

I watched until the end of the clip, where finally the rainbow-colored "Technical Difficulties" sign came up and the loud *beep* signaled its end.

"Well, that was painful to watch." I cringed. "She sounds like she's drunk."

"That's probably how the media will swing it," AB said. "And we can only hope so. I'd hate to think someone would actually investigate her radioactivity. That would send a few red flags up to DC."

"DC?" I asked. Recalling her other contacts, KP and ZZ, I wondered if there was a new one. "Another colleague of yours?"

"No, darling. Washington, DC. The seat of the government. Perhaps even the president himself."

"Oh, I'm sure he has better things to worry about than radioactive doughnuts," I said. "Just like we do."

"True. We still have to get this mad woman her antidote," AB said.

"Why?"

AB frowned at me. "What do you mean, 'why,' Kallie?"

"I mean, what's the worst that could happen? The chemical gets broken down and can be pulled from the body, can't it?" I wasn't trying to be stubborn or contrary, but all of a sudden, it did strike me as very odd that we had to do anything for Gynnifer. She was normal enough; it wasn't like she'd transmorphed into a baby weakling like Blake or blown up to the size of a small air balloon.

AB glanced behind me, and she seemed to figure out what I was worried about. "Are you really worried about someone like Azure remembering you before you became Fatgirl? I doubt anyone would make the connection."

"Oh, I'm sure someone did," I said, glaring at Zeus, who looked away quickly.

"If you need me to get some of her blood, I can probably do it," he offered. "There's no reason Fatgirl should have to be bothered with this, right?"

"No," AB said. "Look, the radioactivity can cause a lot of problems, okay? Some of it's unexplained. That's part of the reason you're such an interesting case, Kallie. I barely have to alter the original recipe for you to maintain your transformation."

"What are you talking about?"

"I'm saying that I've had to adjust things a little, but you're an outlier in itself anyway, since you can keep your sound mind while you transform." AB nodded back over to Gynnifer's screaming performance; without the sound, it almost looked like a reunion cover band of old, with people screaming and throwing fits in a dancing sort of way.

"If you don't get her, she'll further lose her mind and wreak havoc on this whole place."

I watched as the camera screens gradually changed, and—no kidding—I could see Amory, Uli, June, and Lizzie all there, in the rows near the front of the auditorium.

The door to the security room snapped open, and a man I could only assume was Zeus' father—or uncle, maybe; I mean, he had a big family—came inside.

"*Jesus*, what's going on in here?"

The name on his Cyber Knight Security uniform said "Jose," but I didn't have a chance to say anything as Zeus hurried forward.

"Hi, Dad. I was just working on the feeds in here, and Fatgirl here came in and asked if she could take a look, so I—"

"No." The man's eyes narrowed into dark slits as he stared at me. "No one but family is allowed back here."

Zeus pointed at the screen with Gynnifer and the others. "But Dad, she needed our help—"

"And now she can leave," Jose snapped. "And everyone else, too. You know the rules, son."

Zeus glanced over at me nervously.

"Well, I think we're done here," I said, nodding to Zeus. "Thank you for your help."

Jose crossed his arms. "You're not welcome. This is my company's assigned area. You could get us fired and lose our clients."

"We wouldn't do that," I objected.

"We're leaving," AB assured Jose as she took me by the arm. I saw her grip tightly onto her purse, and I really hoped there was no gun in that one.

When I asked her about it, she assured me she'd left the heavy heat at home.

"I've got a Tazor instead," she said. "I'll keep it on hand if Gynnifer needs it. Just get her blood and I'll quick about the antidote."

"Can't we just call Officer Powers and get him to get you some of her blood for this?" I asked.

AB grinned. "Come on, just go, Fatgirl. Your fans await."

As we neared the auditorium entrance, AB slipped into a small alcove.

"What're you doing?" I asked.

"I'll be here," she said, slipping into shadows. "Go and get Gynnifer, bring her here, sit on her, and I'll do the rest."

I scowled, but I didn't like the feeling of my now-flabby skin wrinkling on my cheeks.

After that, I hurried away to find Gynnifer—well, not hurried, exactly, but I did walk toward the backstage area.

I got to the door to the dressing room area, and from where I was, I could see Azure still held Gynnifer down in a chair, and there were a few other hairstylists, designers, and workers standing around, trying to look useful or helpful while really being neither.

Especially for me. *If only I could draw some blood without walking out and having to face all that scrutiny.*

"Is there a way to get her over here?" I wondered aloud. "Probably not without making a scene … "

I mulled over this for a long moment before I noticed the footsteps approaching me from behind.

"Fatgirl? Is that you?"

I nearly groaned at the sound of Gloria's voice. I'd been so afraid of scrutiny in front of me that I'd failed to see it coming from behind.

"Um … hello," Gloria continued carefully. "Are you here about my aunt?"

I cleared my throat and did my best to sound not like my usual self. "Unfortunately, yes. She's been … infected … by the same … thing … as the other Alternants around Cuttingham City have been, and she needs to get the cure."

Gloria, to her credit, didn't even blink at any of this. "How can I help you?"

"Well, actually …" Perhaps this was a stroke of luck. I pointed over to a nearby dressing room, just a little ways down from where AB was hiding in her alcove. "Can you bring her to that dressing room over there for me?"

Once more, Gloria didn't seem to question me. "Sure," she said. "I think I can."

So, I kind of just stood there, watching through the doors as Gloria went up to Gynnifer and her would-be captors, and managed to get them to all work together to move her back toward the empty room.

I scooched back down the hall, not wanting to add to the scene Gynnifer was making.

"Oh, Gloria, my sweet Gloria," she howled. "I'm also so sad I can't get to spend a lot of time with you. I was so happy when you were born, and now you're just so old … and so am I! But you have such a bright future—please don't squander it the way I did with work!"

"Auntie, it'll be all right," Gloria promised. She turned to the others. "Thank you for helping me. I've called a … doctor, I guess, and she should be here shortly."

I snorted, but Azure gave a loud huff.

"You'd better take this time to get your aunt to promise you things in writing," he said. "No better time to crack down on a family member who's never around and always working."

Gloria cocked her head to the side a little as she looked at him. "I guess you speak from experience?"

"Honey, you don't want to know," Azure assured her. "Now, get your empty words and meaningless promises so you can feel better for the next two or three Christmases when she's unavailable to take your calls."

Ouch. I had to wonder what side of that deal Azure had been on. From the guilt I saw on his perfectly smooth face, I had to wonder if it was maybe both.

Just as the others left, I heard Zeus call out for me. Properly, this time.

"Fatgirl," he said, and I turned to face him.

"Hey, Zeus," I said, giving him a quick smile at our inside joke before I noticed he seemed worried. "What is it?"

"My dad told me to go home, so I thought I'd come around and help," he said. "Even though that might make it hard for me to get AB her tapes later."

"We'll let her worry about that," I said. "I'm just glad you're okay, really. I didn't like getting you into trouble with your dad."

"It's all right," Zeus said. "He'll get over it. He's stressed out since this is one of our bigger contractors. He's usually very nice."

"I guess with any Model Middle America show, your dad and his company would be pretty busy." I jerked my thumb in the direction of Gynnifer's dressing room prison cell. "This sort of thing doesn't help at all, either."

"Yeah, there is that." Zeus looked away.

"What it is?" I asked, suddenly sad and curious at his expression.

"I had to help him a few times this week."

I frowned. "So? You're new around here; I mean, you've been here for only a couple of months. What else do you have to do besides school?"

Zeus sighed. "That's true."

I had a feeling there was something more he wasn't telling me.

But when I heard Gynnifer's screaming cries from the dressing room, I knew it was time to move.

"AB?" I touched the area on my mask where I'd heard her before, and she answered at once. "Come down to the dressing room in the west hallway. You'll see Zeus standing guard."

I looked at him pointedly, and he saluted me in silent reply.

It was good enough, and so I went inside.

Gynnifer might've spent the last several moments on the set of *Model Middle America* whining about her life choices, but now she was robbing me of nearly all of mine.

"Auntie, hold still," Gloria said, as I approached her with my request for a blood sample.

"I'm scared of needles," Gynnifer moaned.

"I thought you weren't scared of anything," Gloria said. From the sound of her tone, she seemed like she was almost teasing her aunt.

"I lied," Gynnifer admitted. "You don't know how hard it is to be me. I have to lie to myself every day, saying things that just begin to sound ridiculous the more I say them."

"Like what?" I asked, unable to stop myself as I stuck her with the needle.

"Like I should be gluten free in all my foods, even though I'd never had a problem with it," she said. "And how I don't need a man, but I really secretly want one when I break something around the house or there's a really bad thunderstorm. Like I should be the best of the best of the best, but I'm tired and I need to rest, but the best don't rest. There are all these things that people tell you, and you have to believe them, even though you don't." Gynnifer looked over at me with weary eyes. "You were supposed to make my career, you know."

"I think you did that by yourself," I told her. "You don't need me to make your career, or even make your career successful."

She seemed shocked by this—this idea that I, someone who is not herself, would find her career successful.

Gynnifer had been lying a lot, apparently; it was so bad she couldn't even tell the truth to herself, not without fearing it and running away and hiding it.

As AB handed me the cure and injected it into her, I felt relieved to know I could actually do this mostly by myself, and while I hated the thought of people finding out I was Fatgirl, I did like helping people.

AB had been right about me. I smiled at the thought.

Now if I could just trust her about other things, I thought, thinking of her promise to get my mother home and how much she seemed to be pushing Zeus on me.

"Well, this has to be the easiest job I've ever done," I said as I turned to face Gloria. "Thank you for your help."

Gloria looked pleased, and I was even more pleased when she didn't ask me for my autograph or picture or any sort of permission to post something on social media—really, all the things my other friends would've done, probably. Myself, included.

I'd thought before that Zeus and Gloria would get along, and as we stood there, with Gloria thanking me for all my help, and then tending to her aunt, I knew I was right. Zeus never asked me for my autograph or even anything for his website. And he was supposed to be Fatgirl's number one fan and all that.

"Oh, thank heavens. There you are, Fatgirl; I'm so glad to see you. I can't believe you're actually here!"

Until that moment, I didn't know it was possible to hear yourself cringe.

I can't believe this is happening.

I'd managed to get Gynnifer fixed and back to semi-normal, but at the sound of Karen Bright's chipper voice, I knew I still had some work to do tonight.

"Hi, Karen," I said. "How are you tonight?"

It wasn't much later that AB drove me and Zeus home, chatting in a lively voice as she swerved throughout the city streets. She was excited Zeus was able to fit into the car with me, especially since Gynnifer had started to return to her normal self before we left. We were there long enough for her to ask us to schedule an interview with her.

We declined. Immediately, if not sooner.

But it was a nice move of Zeus' to suggest to Karen that Gynnifer be the guest judge in my place, since Gynnifer was the lead investigator when it came to everything Fatgirl. It helped that explaining I was searching for others who were being experimented on, and I couldn't just stop the search to judge a reality modeling show.

Both Karen and Gynnifer seemed agreeable to this, but I could see their similar clenching jaws, which was enough of a show that *I* was fully entertained.

Stress was always funnier when it happened to someone else.

"It's so nice of you to join us on the way home," AB said to Zeus. "I've been wanting to talk more about your expertise in a few different areas."

"Oh, I'm not that interesting," Zeus insisted.

"He's really not, AB," I said. "This all happened because of him."

"Really? And here I thought it was Gynnifer's own insatiable ambition that caused all of this."

Zeus shifted in his seat. "Well, from what she admitted while she was on air, she's actually pretty unhappy."

"Serves her right," I muttered under my breath.

"I'm sure she'll be fine," AB said. "Some people are able to live with unhappiness better than others, right Kallie?"

"Just like those who live with stress and problems, right?" I shot back.

"Of course, darling." AB smirked at me in the rearview mirror. She turned her attention to Zeus. "So, young man, may I drop you off at home?"

"I'd rather you just let me walk home," Zeus said.

"That's perfect. You can come to our house and we can discuss a few things."

"What? No. I mean, he's got to get home.," I said, giving him a hard look. "I mean, don't you?"

Thankfully, Zeus nodded. "My mom will be wondering where I am. Especially since my dad probably knows I'm not at the Amphitheatre anymore."

"See, AB? He's got to get home."

AB glared at me, but she said nothing else for the rest of the drive.

By the time we arrived back at my house, I was mostly back to normal. I could feel the upgrades to the new suit I had kick in; the material started to retract so I could walk normally, and not look too odd.

AB pulled next to the driveway and stepped out. "Kallie, why don't you say goodnight to Zeus? I've got some notes to make for this mission."

I didn't like the hint-hint, wink-wink sort of look she gave me. I wanted to scream at her that this *was not a date, and it never would be.*

"Your *abuela* is pretty gutsy," Zeus said as AB ducked inside the house. "I'm glad she's on your side."

"That's true," I said. "I can't imagine this would be better if she was working against me all the time. Even though it seems like it."

"I'm sorry." Zeus got out of the car. "I know what it's like to feel alone. It's awful."

I followed him out of the car, tightening my death grip on my dad's trench coat. It was dark out, but I still didn't want to run the risk of someone seeing me. But I was more than a little peeved, and I was going to get answers. If Zeus knew what it was like to be my situation—sort of, anyway—why had he been so careless before?

"This … just got out of hand this time," Zeus said. "I'm very sorry, Kallie. I won't let it happen again."

"Well, that doesn't sound promising," I huffed. I crossed my arms. "And now people know you're the one behind the Fatgirl fansite. Can we just agree that you should shut down your site and let AB fiddle with your memory?"

"I hope I haven't disappointed you so much you would let your grandmother near my head with her gadgets." Zeus gestured toward the Imperial. Especially since I know how she drives now."

I had to bite back a laugh. "Well, it's pretty close. I'm sure if today had devolved into a further mess, I would've made sure your life would be over."

"Some days that doesn't sound so bad."

I frowned at him. "What's that supposed to mean? You know I'm just joking."

"Do I?" Zeus shook his head. "Never mind."

That feeling I'd felt earlier that he'd been keeping something from me came rushing back, this time much more powerful than before.

"That's enough," I said. "Tell me. What's wrong with you these past couple days?"

"Well …" He hesitated for a long moment, but he nodded a moment later. "I was working with my dad on a few jobs this week."

"So? I've seen you work with his company stuff before. Are you worried about breaking the law?"

"No, I just … some of them were pretty high-stress jobs—you know, clients unhappy, all that." He looked away. "I came home exhausted, and then there's always more to do once I get home."

"Well … that sucks," I said, more sympathetic. I'd had my own issues with stress this week for sure. "You need to tell your dad to get more workers if you're doing more work for him than you should. What if your grades suffer? Colleges won't be happy."

"I don't really have to worry about that right now."

"Really?" I blinked in surprised. "Even Blake is concerned about college."

"Yeah, well … my father's family has a job for me when I'm done with school in another year. And well, there's some other things that we …" Zeus let out a long sigh.

"You don't want to do that, do you?" I asked.

"Pretty obvious, huh?" Zeus chuckled nervously. "The cyber security work is cool for now. But there's more to it."

"More?"

"We've been doing some extra jobs lately to help my mom," Zeus admitted quietly. "She's … well, she's dying."

Out of all the things Zeus could've told me, that was not the one I was expecting to hear.

Thinking of leaving? Tired of being poor? My own mother's various possible excuses were the first ones I'd thought of, and the moment he said it, everything else faded away, and I found there was nothing I could say.

"She was diagnosed with terminal ovarian cancer at the end of last year," he continued. "We moved here because the tech needs of Cuttingham City meant more income for my dad, and some of our extended family is here to help support us."

"Oh." I looked away, utterly ashamed, and then looked back at him, my hands held out apologetically. "I'm sorry."

"It's okay." Zeus gave me a bitter smile. "She's made peace with her upcoming death, though we are trying all the treatments and alternatives we can. There are good days and bad days. So it's actually been kind of fun hanging out with you and chasing Fatgirl around while she's sick. It gives me something else to do, besides help my dad."

"Are you sure … there's nothing they can do?" I asked. "I mean, miracles can still happen."

"Well, I believe in miracles, too, but I've also noticed miracles don't tend to happen the way we wish they would." Zeus shrugged and then scratched his head nervously. "So for now, I love my mom, and that's all I can do. She's great. You would like her, I think."

"Of course I would," I assured him. "I'd love to go visit her."

"Really?" Zeus brightened for a second, before he blushed. "You don't have to do that."

"No, I want to," I said. "I mean, good mothers are hard to come by, aren't they? I should at least go and thank her for sticking by you and your dad. My own mother couldn't do that."

"Maybe there's more to your mother's story than you realize," Zeus said. He hesitated long enough for me to frown at him; he wasn't the kind of person who would give false hope to someone, so it was weird to hear him say anything.

But then, this was a weird situation, not even including the radioactive doughnuts.

He cleared his throat. "I mean, Dad didn't tell me anything about Mom until they were told it was terminal. They say she's got about six months to live, and that's with everything we have now."

It was probably not very kind of me to wonder if Zeus had a point about my mother, when we were actually supposed to be more concerned about his.

"Do you think it's possible my mom is involved with AB's stuff?" I asked. "I mean … I know it's very unlikely and all, but I once heard AB tell my mom that if it weren't for her, Mom would be in jail still. And the lady she's trying to reach, Zina Morozova, was in LA the same time as my mom was last week."

"I don't know," Zeus admitted. "If you want, I can check into it. I've got some mad computer skills, remember?"

I gave him a cheeky smile. "You don't have to do that."

When he huffed out a laugh, I was glad he seemed a little more comfortable. I hadn't known him long, but I knew Zeus would like having a problem he could solve. It wasn't as though he could become an oncologist in the next six months and find a way to fix up his own mother; but helping me find a way back to mine seemed like something that he wanted to help with, and honestly, between him and AB working on her, it gave me hope that it was something that would just have to happen after all.

"Hey." I swallowed hard as I stood there, looking up at him. "You know, if we're going to be friends, we should be able to trust each other with stuff like this, you know?"

"You mean, like real friends?" he asked, arching his brow enough that I just had to roll my eyes; I never wanted to apologize for anything, and now was not the time to remind myself I should.

"Real enough friends," I assured him. "But anyway, my bigger point is that there's plenty of fake news and false stories out there, especially with people like Gynnifer going around blaring them out nonstop."

"To be fair, I'm sure she has her reasons for it," Zeus said.

"I wanted to make sure that this stuff doesn't happen between us, okay?"

"Okay." Zeus held out his hand, and despite the sheen of sweat on them, I took it and shook it, and I managed not to wince back in disgust.

When we separated, I moved my hands behind my back and wiped it off on the coat.

"Well … thanks for all your help," I said, glancing back at the house. I didn't have to see her to know AB was watching, and I didn't have to guess she was hoping I would invite Zeus inside, too. "I'd better get going. I've had a long day."

"No kidding." Zeus and I laughed, before I walked down my driveway.

I was just about to go inside when Zeus called out to me again. "Kallie?"

I turned around and bit back a sigh. "What is it?"

"You should know I'm in love with you," Zeus said.

My mouth dropped open, and I hurried to compose myself. "Well, um …"

He just said it, like it was nothing special. He could've just as easily been informing me of the time or telling me it was going to rain tomorrow.

I didn't know how to tell him I didn't think I could do this, either, but he interrupted me before I got started.

"It's okay; I know you don't feel the same way about me." He gave me a small smile as he stuffed his hands into his jacket pockets. "I just thought I'd tell you, since it's the truth."

It was hard to know exactly what was running through my mind at that particular moment. Zeus was a nice kid, and yes, he was very friendly, and it seemed like I could trust him, and it was frankly very obvious he liked me anyway—and as social awkward as he appeared to be, it was even reasonable to assume he would think that was the same thing as being in love.

I felt like I should've said something, but I didn't know what to say. I mean, there was literally nothing I could say that would make any sort of improvement of the silence that echoed between us, and I was eternally grateful when he shuffled his feet.

Good thing that he didn't have a gun.

That. That was the clearest thought I could manage, because he basically shot me anyway. It certainty left me just as breathless as I imagined, anyway.

"Well, I'm going to go now," he said. "But I'll see you soon."

"Yeah. I'll see you soon," I agreed, barely able to choke out the words as I opened the front door and nonchalantly hurried inside.

AB was sitting at the table, sipping from her teacup.

"Are you okay, Kallie?" she called, and I could tell from her tone she knew everything.

"I'm fine." My words came out stilted, and my mouth felt like it was full of cotton.

AB seemed to know that, too. "Good to know," she said. Her voice was soft but still snarky, with only the slightest hint of caring.

Still, I walked into the kitchen, where she was sitting at the table. "Is Dad home?"

"He'll be in late today; it's probably for the best," AB replied. "Do you want some tea?"

"That's not going to help me get to sleep," I said. "Not sure why you're drinking it. Those notes can't be that demanding."

"Who said that was what I was drinking?" AB grinned. "I got some gin out of the liquor cabinet."

"Gin?"

"You're too young for it, and as a point of fact, I don't recommend drinking at all. Put it off as long as you can," AB said. "Those who start young have a harder time dealing with the uglier truths in this world, and alcohol does rather tend to make men's hearts weak."

"What about a woman's heart?" I asked, unable to stop myself.

AB smiled humorlessly. "That's assuming the woman in question had a heart in the first place."

It was nice to be able to laugh. It caught me by surprise, but the moment I released it, the more I felt like crying.

"It's been a long day," AB said, reiterating what I'd told Zeus earlier. She stood up and patted my shoulder. "Go to bed, darling. I'll keep watch over the Phi-ger and let you know if there's any other trouble."

I only nodded; usually, I would've snapped at her, reminding her that this was all her fault, and that I shouldn't have to be dealing with any of this, but I almost would've welcomed a doughnut-worthy distraction.

She wasn't the typical grandmother, I guess. But at that moment, I was glad AB didn't press me for details or pass me a pint of gin, either. She was letting me figure out what I needed, and how to communicate that to others, and as painful as that was to learn, that was part of growing up.

"Good night, darling."

"Good night, Abuela." I reached out and gave her a hug—the first time I could ever remember doing so intentionally.

She seemed as surprised as I did, and I felt her hesitate as she gave me an awkward pat on the back. When I pulled away, I could almost feel her relief—and maybe a little bit of happiness, too.

"Well, now, go and get your rest," she said. "Tomorrow is another day, after all, and we can work then. You might be able to sit on people or fire a gun but those aren't the only skills you'll need."

I heaved a reluctant sigh but stood firm. "Okay. I think I can do that."

Fatgirl

FAT CHANCE

EPISODE 6

○ ○ ○ ○

C. S. Johnson

FATGIRL
FAT CHANCE

○ ○ ○ ○

"I can't believe I agreed to this," I muttered.

"Come on, Kallie. You could use a distraction after everything that happened last week."

At the sound of my grandmother's voice chiming over my earpiece, I instinctively gritted my teeth. Before I could remind Abuela-Blanca I was in my current situation because she'd lost her job, she added, "You were the one who suggested we check the TV station for clues since it's been a few days and we haven't had any new Phi-ger activity."

"I was being sarcastic," I insisted. "That's what teenagers *do*."

"Well, Fatgirl saves the day. Get to work."

Ugh. I was going to ground my teeth into gums. "I'm not technically Fatgirl right now."

If there was any bright side to anything, it was literally only that. I might've been sneaking around the WACC TV station down in Cuttingham City, but I was not wearing pink and navy spandex, nor was I bloated up to roughly the size of a sumo wrestler.

For once.

"You're still on a Fatgirl mission," AB said. "Should I call you 'Spygirl,' when you're like this?"

"If I'm supposed to work on those so-called 'essential skills' you wanted me to learn, how about you stop talking to me?" I finally asked, glancing around nervously. I was in a long, bland hallway, one that only boasted of color from its cheaply framed posters. Thankfully, it was empty, but I couldn't discount that there was a camera somewhere. "People are going to hear me and think I'm some psycho, talking to myself."

"But think of all the fame and attention you could bring with a modeling career for the mentally ill."

That did it.

I flicked the mute button on the ear piece I had hidden behind my ear. I carefully went over my plethora of memorized cover-up stories for why I was sneaking through the station, careful to keep a confused and lost look on my face.

I'm an activist investigating your hiring practices and seeing if you discriminate against Hispanics. You wouldn't stop a Hispanic girl like me from asking such important questions, would you? Or are you racist?

I'm here to ask about an internship opportunity.

I'm looking for Gynnifer Stills to see if I can interview her for a school project.

Inwardly, I shuddered. My white lies were growing darker every day, and for all its usefulness, I was beginning to hate using my half-Hispanic heritage as a "Get out of Jail Free" card.

Stick to the last two stories.

They were more forgettable.

I turned down another hall and tried a new door. The doorknob opened easily and I bit back a triumphant cheer. Carefully, I peeked into the room and glanced through, making sure the room was empty before I stepped inside.

"Clear," I whispered. I'd muted AB, but even if I wasn't listening to her, I figured she would want to know what I was doing.

Spying was actually a little fun. For some reason, it made me think of *The Art of War*, the book my mother had kept on her nightstand. After she'd abandoned me and I was left to navigate the rest of my tenth-grade year without her, I'd actually found Sun Tzu helpful in way I'm sure he hadn't meant for teenagers. It certainly helped with my social battles, and now it made me feel better here, too.

"Let your plans be dark and impenetrable as night, and when you move, fall like a thunderbolt."

Remembering that advice—and trying not to laugh, remembering how I'd used it over the summer to one-up Amory on her trip to Dauphin Island by organizing an "impromptu" swim party for the rest of our friends—I skirted around the room, looking for clues. It was a cheap lounge area of sorts and just as ugly as the rest of the station. I sifted through a pile of papers on a countertop, scanning them carefully, looking for anything that might be important.

"It would be helpful if I knew what was important," I said, re-stacking the papers. Nothing serious there, other than updated scheduling and programming changes. There was a request from Gynnifer the scheduling department to allow her to work as a debate moderator this week, but it was stamped with a large, red "Denied" stamp.

The earpiece crackled back to life. "You're looking for the donut box Gynnifer received," AB said. "Zeus helped us confirm there was a Darling Donut delivery there a few hours before she became an Alterant."

I bit down on my lip, trying not to say anything. I didn't want to really think about Zeus at the moment. It had been a busy week since Gynnifer's transformation and the whole Model Middle America guest judge fiasco went down, but whenever I saw Zeus, all I could think of was how he just stood there in front of my house and confessed he was in love with me.

It was terribly uncomfortable, but at least he seemed to sense I wanted some distance between us. He usually ducked away when we came close to crossing paths, and if I caught him looking my way, he looked down, properly ashamed of himself.

Sure, I was glad he was my friend—and that he seemed trustworthy enough when it came to dealing with the Fatgirl business—but I didn't want to think about anything more.

Anyway, if I wasn't doing "Spygirl" business now, I'd probably be thinking of Blake Turner instead.

"Kallie?" AB's voice cut through my inattention fast.

"What is it?" I asked.

"Check the trash. Trash is good for clues."

I groaned, but I headed toward the trash can on the other side of the room and opened up the lid. I pinched my nose shut at the overwhelming pungency. "It would've been nice for you to suggest this several rooms ago."

"This is the break room, right?" AB asked. "You'll find a bigger selection of trash in a break room, because multiple departments use it."

"I don't know if this'll be helpful at all," I said, pinching a moldy wrapper between my thumb and forefinger. It was still full of some kind of hummus … or bean dip? It was hard to say.

I turned away to gag just as the door opened again.

"Crap," I muttered before diving behind the trash and crushing myself into a shadowy corner.

My blood hummed through my body, but I kept silent; I let out a silent praise that I didn't have to climb into the trash; thankfully, it was large enough I could just duck behind it.

And thank God I was not in my Fatgirl form, or this would've never worked.

"—you'll have to excuse my boss for this, but he's just really eager to see your star shine even brighter, and he's sent me here to make sure that happens," a woman was saying.

"Oh, I fully intend to do just that myself," Gynnifer Stills trilled happily. Her voice alone was enough I buried more deeply into my fetal position. She was just so unaware of how cringy she was sometimes.

Perhaps if she catches me, I can claim to be her stalker.

From the conversation she was having with the other woman, I was pretty sure Gynnifer would be ecstatic to hear the news she had a stalker-fan.

"—just wants to help you, and he can—once he's elected. He just wants you to tell him all the information you have on Fatgirl and how to find her."

Some part of me wants to vomit. Fatgirl had a would-be stalker of her own, by the sound of it—and that was literally the last thing I wanted.

Isn't Zeus bad enough? God, what are you thinking right now? I clenched my fists and shove them into either side of my head, doing my best not to make any noise at all.

"I've already told you what I know about Fatgirl," Gynnifer said. "I've donated the maximum amount to his campaign, and I'll be voting for him in the election. But I can't show too much favor to him on the news. My bosses frown on that sort of bias, even though they're the first ones to talk about their choice politicians when they get the chance."

Instantly, I regretted everything I'd ever done for her. AB and I had saved this woman from a mental whirlwind of reliving all her worst mistakes and screaming them out on-air. Not to mention, it was thanks to me that Karen Bright, the worldwide famous model producing the Model Middle America show, gave Gynnifer a guest judge position on her show!

I'd managed to do so much for her, and this is how Gynnifer was repaying me?

I could already hear AB chiding me. "People are generally not good investments, Kallie," or something like that.

"Perhaps we can sweeten the pot?" The woman pulled out her phone. "Mr. Weber is waiting to talk with you directly."

"He is?"

I peeked over the top of the trash can. Gynnifer eyed the other woman's phone with interest. She took it less than a second later.

"Hello, Mr. Weber," Gynnifer gushed. "It's wonderful to finally get a chance to talk to you."

My legs started to go numb while she chatted with him, and as each second passed, I hated her more.

Gynnifer continued to talk, and the other woman opened the fridge. I nearly gasped when I caught sight of a familiar pink doughnut box. I didn't have to see the top of the carton to know it was topped with Darla Donut's face. It was the face of my own mother, dolled up to make her look just like the loving mother and housewife she'd never really been.

Darling Donuts.

I watched as the campaign woman put it back in as she pulled out a bottle of water. Quietly, I sighed with relief.

Last thing I needed was for another accidental Alterant to show up now. I wasn't prepared to fight her as my usual self, and while AB was just around the corner using her Imperial as a mobile base, I didn't know if I would be able to eat my own doughnut, transform into Fatgirl, and still contain the situation before a bunch of news cameras caught the action.

"If you can guarantee me that spot as a debate moderator, I'll take it," Gynnifer said into the phone.

The other lady smiled brightly as she took the phone back from Gynnifer.

She nodded and muttered into the phone a little before she shut it and held out her hand to Gynnifer. "Deal."

Debate moderator? I frowned. Was she talking about the paper I'd seen?

"Look, I'm not sure of the kid's first name who runs the Fatgirl website," Gynnifer said a moment later. "It's something like Ethan, I think. But the last name is Evans. His father works in IT, and I've seen him around the Model Middle America set. The boy's a big fan of Fatgirl—literally big, too. He's a bit of a porker."

I scowled to myself. Gynnifer was really an inconsiderate moron at times.

"I'll bet if you get a hold of *him*, he'll be able to tell you how to get ahold of *her*. He's in one of my niece's classes at Cuttingham City High."

I had to stuff my fist in my mouth to keep myself from standing up and yelling at her.

The other woman took the phone back and shut it off. "Thank you, Ms. Stills," she said. "Mr. Weber can't publicly thank you for your service, but Fatgirl's target demographic is key in winning this election, and he's very eager to get it. The help you've given us is invaluable."

"You're welcome," Gynnifer replied, opening the door back up, and gesturing for the other woman to go through. "Once he's won, I'll be happy to have him come on my show for an exclusive interview."

"We'll have to see. First interview is fine, but exclusive might be hard to swing … "

I waited until I was sure they were down the hall before I stood up.

"Well, this sucks," I muttered, wiggling my legs out of their sleepy state.

"What is it?" AB asked. "You're not talking about Gynnifer talking what is essentially an illegal bribe, are you?"

"You mean about how she told that lady about Zeus?" I groaned. "What else would I be talking about?"

"That's why I asked." I could almost see AB smirking on the other side of the communication link. "You don't need to worry about it, Kallie."

"Good to know," I muttered darkly. By now, I'd realized AB was usually right when she said stuff like that, though I was smart enough to know she'd be wrong someday. And any day that I had to worry about someone going after Zeus to get to me, I had to worry, period.

"I meant you don't need to worry about it, because I recorded it." AB punched in a few buttons. "I'll save it for now. You never know when you need a good piece of blackmail."

"Gosh, stop being racist. Say 'extortion.'"

AB scoffed. "Goodness, darling, no need to get your feathers ruffled over a colloquialism. Or is that species-ist of me to say?"

I ignored her. "Speaking of darling, I saw a Darling Donut box in the fridge. I'm going to bring it to you, okay?"

"Tired already?"

"I've been here for an hour," I whined. "Isn't the smallest amount of progress good enough for you?"

AB sighed. "Fine. I don't want your complaining to get out of control."

"Thank you," I snapped under my breath, before grabbing the doughnut box and practically skipping as I headed out the door.

I was nearly out the station's back door when I heard someone call my name.

"Kallie? Is that you?"

God in Heaven, why?

"Hi, Gloria," I said, doing my best to put on a genuine smile.

Gloria was a very nice sort of girl, the kind who didn't cause trouble or incite any sort of real excitement, either. If there was a prize for "average," Gloria would have won it.

But I didn't want her to see me here. Not when I was investigating Fatgirl stuff.

"What're you doing here?" she asked, struggling to hide a yawn.

"What am I doing here?" I didn't hesitate to turn the question back onto her. "What are you doing here?"

"I was supposed to hang out with my aunt today, but she's been busy for the last couple of hours at a few meetings that suddenly came up."

"Oh. I'm sorry."

"It's okay," Gloria said. There was a tired sadness to her voice, and if I didn't have to worry about other things—like my secret identity and Alterants and possible election fraud—I would've offered to take her home.

"At least she invited you, though, right?" I attempted to comfort her instead, but it was likely causing more suspicion instead of less. "That was nice."

"I guess so." Gloria shrugged, and then she glanced at me. "Did someone invite you here, too?"

"Well, um … no, I'm … just here for a project," I said, trying to remember my cover stories. I didn't think she would buy the one about the job, and she definitely wouldn't believe the one about school, and she was white, so she probably didn't care if I mention the racism one.

What else can I say? Think, Kallie! Think!

Thank God, inspiration struck.

"Actually," I said, doing my best to hide the Darling Donut box underneath my arm, "I've been looking for you. And thank goodness I've found you. I was just about to go home and give up."

"Me?" Gloria's eyes widened. "Why are you looking for me?"

"Well, you may not know it, but Zeus Evans has a crush on you," I lied. "I'm here to kind of warn you about it."

"Oh? He does?" Gloria asked. She seemed like she believed me, but I still couldn't be a hundred percent sure. She eyed me suspiciously. "This isn't some joke or something that Amory put you up to?"

"I wish," I muttered. "I mean, no. Zeus told me so himself. And I wanted to see if you liked him, too."

"You're friends with him?"

"Um … " I cleared my throat and coughed. "Well, we're working together on a school project. And he's helping me with some of Mr. Embers' classwork. So he told me then. And I thought I'd tell you."

Gloria laughed. "I'm not sure I believe you."

"Why not?" I asked, suddenly offended. I was a good liar, even if it was bad to be a good liar. My white lies were nearly legendary! "You can ask him when we're at school tomorrow. Of course, he'll likely be terribly embarrassed, and you'll hurt his feelings."

"It's cool, Kallie, relax," Gloria said. "If that's really why you're here, that's fine. But I think you wasted your time. I mean, Zeus likes *you*. It's pretty clear to me he does, anyway."

"Well, he's using me as a cover, then." I put my free hand on my hip, taking a dominant stance. "Because he told me he wanted to ask you out, and he wasn't sure you would say yes. He actually *wanted* me to come here and see how you would react. This was part of the payment agreement we arranged, since he's tutoring me in computer stuff."

I was really good at lying, and getting better by the second, apparently.

"Really?" Gloria blinked. "I'm really not sure he was telling you the truth, Kallie. But Zeus seems nice enough. If he wants to go out on a date, you can tell him I'd be happy to meet him after school one day."

Really? I was not expecting that. *Ugh … ugh … okay.*

"Great, you should do that," I said. "I'll tell him to go for it when I see him tomorrow."

"Okay." Gloria glanced back at the door. "Is that all you came here to do?"

"Yes, you bet," I said.

"Seems a little late to be out, doing that sort of errand," Gloria said.

"Well, I just figured I'd come down and talk to you myself, so you could see in person I was telling you the truth. And now, since we have talked, and you're comfortable with Zeus asking you out, I'm going to go home. I need my beauty rest, after all."

Before Gloria could say anything else, I nearly ran out of there.

I slid into AB's car and told her to hit the gas.

I'd been at the station for more than two hours. It was nearly midnight and would be well past it by the time I got home—well, maybe not, given AB's speeding tendencies.

But hopefully, I thought, I would get home in time to get a decent night's sleep.

"Oh, Kallie! I absolutely love your make-up today!"

I had to stifle a yawn as Lizzie Myers, my white-girl friend, oozed praise and awe for my mascara-heavy, black-lined eyes today. She didn't comment on all the concealer and light-shadowing.

I'm sure that plenty of people, including my best frenemy, Amory Franklin, would think I was going goth. When AB said I should call it the "Donut-Eyed" look since it looked like I had fallen into a box of powdered doughnut holes. I'd promptly flipped her off and left, but the instant I got to school, I couldn't help but think she was probably right.

Still, I was popular, you know? So I had to pretend it was *avant garde, stunning and brave,* and *neveux-niche*—all the fancy French and flashy words which would guarantee immediate acceptance and promotion among the simpletons.

So Lizzie's praise was no surprise.

"Oh, thank—uh, *gracias*, Lizzie." I blinked a few times in a flirtatious manner. "I was just inspired this morning."

"By what? A cat?"

Despite my desire to cringe, I only widened my smile at Amory's disapproval.

"Why, yes," I lied. "I happen to *love* cats, and today I wanted to have kitty-cat eyes." I modeled my best cat-face look, and my other friends, June and Uli, both nodded in tepid approval.

Amory still wasn't convinced.

"That's not all," I added quickly. "The make-up I'm wearing has never been tested on animals, so this is a great way to show our support for the movement. I mean, no one would object to keeping animals safe from chemical testing, would they?"

That seemed to soften Amory a little. Literally no one would ever object to that, unless they were some kind of monster.

But it also helped me that Amory did like animals. When we were younger, she'd been known to rescue injured birds and find stray cats a good home. We might've grown up a little since then, but we were still somewhat the same, too. Weren't we?

Amory slowly nodded, and I felt a little guilty. I didn't actually know if the make-up I was wearing tested on animals or not.

"Using your clout for good, I see." Amory finally gave me a big smile in return. "I can see the beauty of that. Good idea, Kallie."

She probably wasn't very happy with me, but the other girls were happy to pull out their eyeshadow kits and start giving themselves a form of "kitty-eyes," so Amory soon followed suit. After I suggested she use some golden glitter to get the look of a lioness, and she actually agreed, I knew we were on good terms again.

As the bell rang for class, I breathed out in relief.

One problem down.

Sure, the Darling Donut box I'd snagged from the WACC TV station's break room wasn't radioactive in the least, and I didn't relish the idea of wearing six coats of eyeshadow, especially right as summer heat would start rolling in. I didn't have much of a choice if I was going to hide the huge black bags under my eyes. But I'd managed to bluff and lie my way out of any other negative repercussions.

Maybe I am getting better at this spy stuff.

I felt a little taller as I walked into Mr. Embers' class, until I caught Zeus' eye, and the guilt came rushing back. If I was getting better at this "stuff," it was because I had people I could count on to help me. Recalling someone was looking for Fatgirl, and Gynnifer had allowed her fat, over-lipsticked mouth to point him in Zeus' direction. Then, I'd further thrown him into trouble with Gloria. My guilt twisted into shame.

Class went on forever, and I didn't know what was worse; smiling and nodding until Uli, who was sitting next to me, finished her work and left me alone, or waiting until everyone else left the room, so Zeus and I could talk.

I almost had to wonder if he'd talked to Gloria earlier, too, because the first thing he said when we were alone was, "We need to talk."

"No kidding," I muttered. "You're in trouble again."

"I am? I haven't done anything in the last week," Zeus said. His blue eyes, such a mismatch with the rest of his own Hispanic heritage, were wary and hurt as he looked at me.

Talk about a gentle giant, I thought. Zeus had to be at least a head taller than me, and I felt like I could just push him down and walk all over him. And I probably would, in all honesty, if I needed to.

But I wouldn't do it in these shoes.

I had my two-inch heels on, and it was hard enough to walk on flat ground. I couldn't imagine trying to walk all over Zeus' flabby belly or chunky arms.

"I'm sorry," Zeus said, shaking me out of my runaway train of thought.

"No, you're not in trouble with me," I quickly assured him. "Sorry. I mean to say that, after a lot of strange decisions, I overheard that someone is looking for Fatgirl, and Gynnifer Stills managed to give out your family's name."

"Oh." He looked a little relieved, and then he grimaced. "Oh. Great."

"You're telling me." I crossed my arms. "I told you that website was a bad idea."

"It probably *is* a bad idea, but it's also a wall they'll run into," Zeus said. "So I can protect you this way."

My guilt twisted another knot into my stomach, as though it was trying to make a noose. It let out a bitter *roar*, and even Zeus gave me a surprised look.

"Shut up, don't say anything." I blushed as I scowled at Zeus. "I'm getting tired of my gut trying to humiliate me."

"It might stop if you didn't starve yourself." Zeus pulled out a snack bar from his backpack and gave me a teasing smile as he held it out to me. I wanted to smack him. The smile was one of those all-knowing smirks, but without the pride behind it, and that made it worse.

I took the bar and gave him a haughty look in return. "I'm only eating this because I'm saving you the calories, okay? You're welcome."

"Thank you." Zeus laughed. He probably realized I was grateful, even if I hated being grateful to him. "Don't choke on it."

At his general good-naturedness, it was really hard not to laugh along with him, and I almost forgot why we were even meeting in the first place when Zeus turned serious.

"I had someone reach out to me yesterday," he said. "It was on my cell phone, and I don't give that number out at all. It was a representative for James Walter. He said he wanted to speak with me about Fatgirl."

Zeus looked down at his feet.

"What else?" I asked.

"He said he'd be able to help my mom some," he admitted. "I guess he found out all about me and my family, and he's trying to bribe me."

"Wow. That's low." I stopped eating the snack bar, suddenly too disgusted to eat.

Zeus had told me just the week before his mother had terminal ovarian cancer. She had six months or less to live, by what the doctors told her, and nothing was helping.

"What did you say about that?" I asked, suddenly nervous. Zeus' loyalty to me was nothing compared to the love he felt for his mother. I wouldn't hesitate to throw him under the bus if our situation was reversed.

And I was certain about that, too, given how I'd already done that, and for much less.

"I told him I'd need it in writing first," Zeus replied with a small smile. "The guy I was talking to said the politician guy wasn't willing to work with paper. He didn't want a trail."

"You're sure it was a guy?" I frowned. "There was a lady with Gynnifer, talking to another guy over the phone. Same person, you think?"

"Maybe it's his rival, John Weber." Zeus sat down again and logged onto his computer, pulling up the information. "Both of them are running for mayor of Cuttingham City. There's a political debate being held at City Hall on Thursday."

"Gynnifer wanted to be a moderator." I . "So that means both James Walter and John Weber—"

"You mean, 'James Weber and John Walter,'" Zeus cut in.

"Whatever. Both of them would be able to arrange that, I imagine. Or their supporters would. I guess they will, if they want Fatgirl's endorsement for their campaign." The absurdity of it all just hit me, like a ton of bricks thrown through a glass window. "But *why*?"

"It seems they're both polling in the forties," Zeus said, showing me a graph of some kind. "Given the third-party voters—and those who aren't likely to vote at all—that's pretty high. But both of them have their downsides, too. Weber's been in politics for years and there are a number of allegations against him for bribery and fraud. And Walter's not much better. He's an entrepreneur who has a police record from growing up in the streets, and accusers say his company took government funds and used them unethically."

"Illegally, you mean?"

"Not necessarily." Zeus pushed the bridge of his glasses back up his nose, which was glossing over with sweat. "He used the funding to buy a bunch of smaller companies, and then he laid off the employers, let the individual businesses go, and wrote it off as a loss. So he used government money to get a break on his taxes."

"You can do that? That sounds pretty awful."

"There are some hoops to jump through and some loopholes to skirt, but basically, yeah."

"I'm surprised he's polling so high, then."

"Walter's made a lot of noises about social issues on social media," Zeus said. "The kind that gets on trending lists and all that. So he's popular, even if he's not considered the best fit for the job."

"And the other guy?"

"Weber's a career politician, so he knows the system," Zeus said. "If he wins, he'll probably get a lot of those allegations to go away."

"Well, *this* whole thing certainly is depressing. Fatgirl's going to vote third-party at this rate," I muttered, sitting down beside Zeus and putting my head in my hands. "But I will find a way to keep you out of it, okay? And your mom, too."

"Thank you." Zeus brushed his sleeve over his face, getting rid of some of his sweaty sheen. "I'll feel better knowing you're on the job.'

"I wonder if I can get AB to help? Although … Ugh, she'll probably use this to make me do something for her."

"This is going to be a hard one," Zeus added. "We don't know what kind of money or connections either of them have. This could be bad for you."

"This could be bad for *you*," I corrected him, before turning back to the computer screen as my face flushed over.

I hadn't meant to sound so adamant. I brushed my hair back from my face to give myself another moment to recover.

Dealing with these two power-hungry politicians wasn't going to fun, and I'd have to be careful; I had keep my own identity a secret, but I needed to protect Zeus, too.

A new thought struck me as I sat there. Maybe Zeus could post a notice to my website, saying I wouldn't be endorsing candidates or movements?

But I thought of how happy Amory had looked when I'd mentioned the make-up movement that was free from animal testing. A public announcement like that might keep me from harm, but it might keep me from doing good, too.

Those sort of announcements were tricky to handle. Plenty of celebrities and other people had been punished for speaking out on issues or seeming to speak out just for the social brownie points.

I was still vacillating about whether or not to ask him to post about not endorsing people when Zeus tapped on my shoulder.

"Oh, if you need something to cheer you up, I wanted to tell you that I talked with Gloria earlier today." Zeus pulled out his phone and showed me her contact information. "She said you talked with her, and she's okay with me asking her out on a date."

"Oh, yeah. There was some other stuff I wanted to talk to you about."

I quickly explained what had happened at the WACC station, telling Zeus all about my sneaky eavesdropping, my cunning bravery, my daring escape, and my plausible lies. He seemed to understand and even laughed as I explained the doughnut-eyes fad that was already taking over the school.

"So you're not mad at me?" I asked, finishing up my grand storytelling performance with a pretty pout and wide, sad kitty-eyes—which were actually perfect for me to use during an apology.

"No, I'm not mad," Zeus said. "Gloria and I are going to hang out next week."

"You are?"

I absolutely *hated* how my voice squeaked. I was too surprised, too taken aback, and too completely irritated to hide my reaction entirely.

Zeus was clearly holding back another laugh as he nodded. "Yeah, it was nice of you to try to get us together. We do have a lot of the same classes and interests."

"Oh." I cleared my throat. "Oh, good, then. Thanks. I didn't mean to force you to do something else for me, but I appreciate how well you're taking it. And I'm not jealous or anything."

I was good at lies, but even I knew when I was lying to myself. My stomach twisted angrily at me.

"No problem." Zeus' eyes gleamed in amusement. "I'm here to help, and I'm happy to do so if I can."

Since Blake was traveling for his lacrosse games that week, I didn't have anything else to do after school. Before I could decide I was comfortable with talking with Zeus, I waved goodbye to him, chucked the last half of his snack bar into the trash, and chatted with my friends before I made enough excuses to go home without any issue.

Surprisingly, I was glad for the escape, and I didn't know why until I saw Zeus waving hi to Gloria as I left him behind.

I gritted my teeth at the thought. I was actually pretty angry over Zeus' overly "helpful" response to me telling him he had to date Gloria Stills as a cover for me.

Ugh, it's like he planned it, just to irritate me.

It didn't matter that I'd been the one who'd randomly run into her and that I'd had no idea I would see her. Zeus seemed all too happy about this.

Clearly, it was all his fault, too.

It was tempting to ask Abuela-Blanca if we could still use her Memory Swiper device on him.

The notion proved to be too tempting, and I couldn't resist making my case as I arrived home and found AB alone in the kitchen.

"Not this again." AB rolled her dark blue eyes. "You really just need to trust him, Kallie. Accept it."

"This is from someone who was betrayed and forced out of her supposedly great job?" I crossed my arms, ready to support my position. "I'd think you would empathize with me more here."

"There are some people you can trust," AB said over the rim of her teacup.

"And then there are some people that you can use your Memory Swiper on and never have to worry about trusting." I twisted the cap off a water bottle and took a sip, all while staring at her.

AB bristled. "Well, you can trust me."

"If I can trust you, I don't need Zeus," I shot back.

"*Trust* me, Kallie. You'll need him. Who else is going to be eager to hear all your troubles when your mother comes back, and I am gone?"

AB caught me off guard at the mention of my mother, and some part of me suddenly wondered if she'd done that on purpose.

I gripped the bottle hard enough that several drops of water spilled out. "Have you heard anything about Mom?"

I tried not to think about how I would feel once AB left. Probably some mix of relief and more relief, but I was more concerned with my mother, anyway.

"I've got a lead on her schedule." AB smirked. "And ZZ's, too. We'll be taking a trip shortly, you and I, and I think you'll enjoy it."

I was just about to ask why I would going when she added, "I'll need some help from Zeus, too."

"What?" I nearly choked on my water. "Why does he have to come? And why do I have to come? I thought you were going to handle ZZ on your own."

"We're a team, aren't we?" AB's eyes narrowed at me, as though she was daring me to contradict her. "Hopefully, we won't have to bring him, but I think I'll need him to manage a couple of things."

AB stood up. "Which reminds me. I won't be able to go Mind-Sweeping with you and Zeus right now anyway, since I've got to pack."

My eyes widened. "You're leaving?"

"Don't get so excited. I'm going to go meet one of my contacts. On Friday, my contact, KP, has an unscheduled, eight-hour drop off at the airport in Little Rock that he's going to find out about mid-flight, on his way to his conference in New Orleans."

"Who's KP?" I didn't recognize the name, but I was beginning to wonder if AB's contacts were all secretly arranged like the *Men in Black*, where they only had an initial or two to cover their identities. It was getting close to alphabet soup.

"I'll tell you about him later. That's all you need to know for now." AB grinned mischievously. "That's enough time for me to interrupt him and see about why he hasn't been answering my calls lately."

A shiver went down my spine. I didn't want to think of who—or what—AB knew that she could get a whole plane grounded mid-flight.

As she brushed past me, I remembered the other Zeus-related concern I had to deal with—I would worry about swiping his memory another time.

"Hey, AB. Will you be back by Thursday?" I asked. "The political debate for Cuttingham City's new mayor is scheduled for seven."

"Are you really that interested in politics?" AB was already walking down the stairs to her basement bedroom-turned-science-lab. "I'd advise against it. The political arena is a hotbed for misery and immorality. I'd honestly rather you be a model, and after dealing with your mother, *that* is saying something."

"What does that mean?" I stomped my foot, suddenly more angry than ever. Even Zeus' blasé surrender to a date with Gloria was only a spark compared to my frustration now.

AB's footsteps stopped on the stairs. She let out a small sigh. "I don't think you need to worry about it."

"That's bull!" I stood up so fast I knocked my water bottle onto the floor. Water spilled everywhere, but I left it and hurried after AB. "She's my mother, for goodness' sake."

"Yes, and there are some things about your parents that you'll never understand, and it's better that way."

I followed her into her room, shut the door, and crossed my arms over my chest, blocking the way out. "Does that mean Dad knows about your job issues?"

"He understands what I want him to." AB's nose wrinkled. "But that's neither here nor there." She began throwing things into her large handbag.

I glared at her, and after a very long, very quiet moment passed, finally, *finally*, she seemed to have had enough.

"Fine," AB snapped. "I'll tell you the basics, and that's it. Don't ask for more. Deal?"

"Fine." I mimicked her tone, and her scowl deepened, but I had enough anger for the two of us, after Zeus and the two politicians picking on him, and dealing with Zeus' surprising agreeableness when it came to dating Gloria.

AB rolled her eyes. "Well, when your father first met Kate—yes, her *real* name, Kallie—she was just starting to rise up in the modeling world. Her work as Darla Donut did not go unnoticed. She signed with an agency and began traveling the world, and—you have to understand—it's very easy to control models."

"Modeling is all about control," I agreed, thinking of all the dietary restrictions and the limited exercise routines I'd undergone in the last few years.

"All it takes is an ugly scar across the face, and you're done," AB continued. "Plastic surgery is available, true, but's still limited. So when the agency your mother signed on with began using their models to smuggle 'valuable assets' to different countries—I told you not to ask me, Kallie." She pointed her finger at me when my mouth opened up to ask what she meant by that.

After my mouth closed, she continued. "I don't think your mother knew about the deals that were going on behind the scenes right away. But she eventually discovered it—and then she wanted out."

"She stopped working as a model shortly before she married Dad," I remembered, having looked through my mother's pictures countless times.

"Believe me, that was the *only* reason I helped her," AB said. "Johnny wasn't any wiser to the situation. But Kate eventually hated me for what I'd done for her. Basically, I made her give up a career she loved so she would be safe."

"That's the reason Mom hates you?"

It was more than what I'd been expecting. If AB was telling the truth—and I didn't think she was lying, even though she'd admitted she wasn't telling the whole story—she was the reason my mom was safe, as well as the reason I had grown up with my parents.

AB arched her brow at me. "Come on, Kallie. You didn't think I was *really* a racist, did you?"

My tongue felt thick as I tried to explain myself. "Well, you are white—"

"Yes, and collectively judging white people by their skin color is hardly racist at all." AB grabbed her bags and slung one of her large purses over her shoulder. "But in regard to Kate, that's all I'm telling you for now. Maybe one day I'll tell you more of the specifics, but right now, if we're going to catch our doughnut maker, I've got a terrorism threat boon to cash in."

Speechless, I followed her out of the house, trying to think of something else to say. It wasn't until she was pulling her pristine white Imperial out of the driveway that I stopped her.

"Wait!" I knocked on her window. "What about the debate issues? And the politicians who are looking for Fatgirl, and using Zeus to get to me?"

"What? What on earth are you talking about?"

I started to tell her about the fight between the politicians and how they were using Zeus to get me to when she waved the matter aside.

"Oh, is that the issue?" AB put on a pair of sunglasses and arched her eyebrows. "Well, Spygirl, I guess you're going to have to work on a few of your next lessons on your own. Think you can handle it?"

"I can work … on these things … on my own?" Saying the words felt like I was speaking new, foreign language.

"You'll have to. I need to see KP this week, Kallie. If I'm going to nail down the details for ZZ's auction and gala, I've got to move."

I couldn't argue with her there. ZZ was the one who would likely know the person that sold AB out from her government job. This was personal for AB, and I wanted to help her. But I was still kind of afraid of not having her backup.

"What about Fatgirl?" I asked, still hesitant.

"I've got you covered already." She gestured back toward the house. "There's a couple of doughnuts I have saved in my lab freezer downstairs. You'll have to let them thaw in the fridge if you need to transform. And don't forget, you're going to have to get Zeus to stick you with the Anti-F agent if you don't want to do it yourself. So you might want to wait until next week to scramble his brains around, darling."

I cringed, but it was the truth. "Point taken, Abuela."

"I don't want you to blame him if things go wrong." AB pointed at me, poking me in the chest. "In fact, consider it a test. If you pass, *I'll* owe *you* one. Another one, I suppose, if we're going to get Kate to come back home. I'll be back in a couple of days otherwise."

I didn't say anything else as she rolled up her window, waved goodbye, and sped off.

As much as AB infuriated me at times, I envied her. She always had a plan, she always seemed to know what to do, and she didn't have to lie to everyone all the time to get what she wanted. Plus the Imperial was starting to grow on me.

I wrinkled my nose at the thought. I might've envied her for her freedom, but not for her driving skills.

But she was giving me a chance to prove myself, and I didn't want to disappoint her any more than I wanted to let Zeus down.

So that meant I needed to do some research.

"All right," I murmured. "Time to find out just who John Williams and James Wilmore are … or John Weber or James Patterson or … what were their names again?"

I wouldn't liken AB and me to the idea of "good cop, bad cop," or even "fat cop, fit cop," although that last one might have legitimately worked. But she was the researcher of the group, and I usually depended on her to get the "science-y" and "planning" parts of our projects together.

She was the one who knew who Frank Whitey was, and ZZ. She had contacts. I was more there to run media interference—thankfully, besides stuff like my "Kitty Eyes" campaign, I'd managed to convince Zeus to forgo any social media sites for Fatgirl—and provide a wide range of distractions for the police, media, fangirls, fanguys, and the general public when needed.

So taking on her role was not an appealing prospect for me, even if I got to use her Phi-ger, check on a frozen supply of donuts, and check through her scary lab equipment to make sure she had enough of the antidote and other supplies ready to go.

Even with creepy-looking science experiments, I was much happier at home, for once. The political arena was *not* one I wanted to wade into. Convincing other girls to wear eyeshadow the size of sunglasses was one thing; using my social clout to sway a city-wide election was another, and I would've rather gone swimming in a pool of dog drool.

In the end, I decided the best thing I could do was just get to the station the night of the debate and talk with the politicians themselves, in a room full of cameras, and get them to agree to lay off Zeus and his family.

It couldn't be *that* hard, right?

○ ○ ○ ○

AB had made it clear that I shouldn't use Zeus as a scapegoat for my failures, but that didn't mean I couldn't use him for plan feedback. I watched him carefully as I explained my idea.

"So, what do you think?" I asked as I finished presenting my plan.

"Hmmm." Zeus took his precious time thinking through all the details, probably just to irritate me some more. After everything I'd prepared, I might just strangle him if he made anything the least bit difficult. He should be thanking God on his knees I was even talking to him after all the times I'd asked AB to swipe his memory, even if I needed his help for this to work.

I crossed my arms, forcing myself not to dig my nails into my flawless skin any further as I waited. "Well?"

Thankfully, and strangely disappointingly, Zeus took everything in stride. "Okay. And I think I can help."

Maybe I was still a little steamed about the whole *Oh, I don't mind dating Gloria for you* thing—I didn't even really know *why* I was upset with him about it. I wasn't jealous or anything. *That* would've been crazy—but I was amused.

"Oh?" I arched a perfectly-plucked eyebrow. "You really think that's a good idea?"

"Yeah. I should be able to get in with my dad's Knight Security cover."

I lost all amusement at the mention of the company run by Zeus' father. I'd only seen his dad a few times, but he'd been upset with Fatgirl for barging into his space at a previous Model Middle America show. "Yes, and your dad will love that. Why not just tell him I'm Fatgirl, too?"

"If you don't like that idea, maybe I can ask Gloria to get me in," Zeus said.

"Please, you don't have to bother her," I muttered. "I don't even see why you need to be there."

"Liar. We both know I'm better with the tech side of thing then you," Zeus reminded me. "Without AB in town, you'll still need some backup with the Phi-ger and the centrifuge for your antidote needs."

"Hey!" My anger flared at his unmitigated gall to call me out on my bluff. "We're not going to stop an Alterant, remember? I won't need any help on that front. This is just Fatgirl showing up to warn off politicians."

"You'll need it to get back to your skinny-thin self," Zeus pointed out. "It's not like you can call into the studio. You'll have to be there in person. How else will you get away?"

"That's true … " I gripped my hands into my arms, finally letting my nails sink into my skin. The pain helped me focus on the problem, not on the fact that AB had allowed me to have access to her radioactive chemicals but not her precious Imperial. "I guess I could take the bus. But I don't really want to use public transportation."

At that, I shivered in disgust. That would be awful.

I never thought I would miss AB so much.

"Great," Zeus said. "I'll drive us there in my mom's car."

"Keep your voice down," I hissed, suddenly very aware we were in an empty classroom. The words seemed to echo more than loudly in my ears, and I was eager to get away.

I cleared my throat as I headed for the door. "All right, then, person who's name I've forgotten, thanks for finishing up that project with me."

My voice was raised slightly, just to make sure if any of my friends came looking for me, they would know I wasn't here for any voluntary reason.

Zeus bit back a sigh, but he played along. "You're welcome, Kallie."

He didn't miss a beat. He even walked down the hall in the opposite direction, even though our lockers were both the other way.

I felt bad as I watched him leave. Perhaps it wouldn't be *complete* social suicide if I let people know I was working with him on a project and I was being nice to him. Niceness to nerds could only be a good thing for my public image, right?

I almost laughed. Zeus had told me before he liked being called a nerd. Or at least, he preferred it to "geek," which I still had yet to figure how that was really that different from nerd, but oh, well.

Taking a deep breath, I turned on my heel and headed to catch up with him.

"Hey, Zeus!"

I called out to him, but with the hallways full of kids now that school was over, he didn't hear me. And thankfully, I don't think anyone else really heard me, either.

I caught sight of his backpack and his usual ugly hoodie and smiled. I was about to call out again when I noticed he was talking to Gloria Stills.

The smile fell off of my face, and I stopped short. Quickly, I pressed myself against the lockers and pulled out my phone. I could pretend the rest of the world didn't exist when I was on my phone, and I was happy to do just that while I watched Zeus and Gloria out of the corner of my eye, growing more irritated by the moment as I waited for Zeus to notice me again.

I had a right to be upset, too. Gloria wasn't really that pretty. She wore a magenta-colored T-shirt, which did nothing for her complexion. Her jeans were average, just like the rest of her, but she should've worn a belt to bring out the shape of her hips. Her sneakers were a little worn, and her hair was a largely straight, dark blonde color. Her aunt might've been a pain, but Gynnifer Stills certainly had better fashion sense.

Gloria was nice enough, polite, and seemed to have sense of humor. I didn't know her that well. But for some reason I really didn't like her very much, and I was liking her less by the moment.

I watched as she giggled and nodded, and Zeus nodded in reply and pulled out his phone, probably to get her address.

At that, I gave up walked away.

I would have to punish Zeus for ignoring me later, I decided.

"Hey, Kallie!" Blake Turner called, and I cheered up at once.

Blake Turner was a daydream incarnate, with his bright blond perfect hair and his perfect face, and his perfect smile. I could stare at him all day.

And then I turned around and saw him … wearing "Kitty-Eyes."

"Oh, hi. Blake." I couldn't decide between gagging and laughing at how absolutely insane he looked, but even in my indecisiveness, I managed to cover it up with a cough. "Sorry. Um, what's up?"

"Do you like it?" Blake pointed to the doughnut-sized black powder spots around his eyes. To his credit, I saw under a closer inspection that it was sports paint instead of eyeshadow, but instead of the "tough-guy" lines under his eyes, he had two huge black eyes, like some kind of skeleton cosplayer.

"Oh, it'll be great for your next game," I squeaked, desperate to wipe away the last of my disgusted, internal vomit-laughter.

"Do you think Amory will like it, too?" he asked. "I know she's so excited that it's for some animal support charity."

"Well, Amory does love her animals." I pulled out my phone and held it up. "Maybe I can take a picture and send it to her?"

Blake shut up long enough for me to take a few pictures—and send Amory the "best" ones—and I managed to regain my composure. For all I hated the thought of dealing with Zeus' politicians, I was sure sounding like one.

"I heard you were the inspiration behind Amory's new look," Blake said. "So I wanted your opinion on my attempt."

"Maybe you can get the rest of the guys on the lacrosse team to match it," I said, thinking of how strange and surprising that would be. "It might throw your opponents for a loop."

"Great idea!" Blake nodded and walked with me toward the exit. "The Eagleston Eagles are pretty hard to beat."

"Oh? But you can do it, no problem, I'm sure," I murmured. "You're the best."

"Thanks, Kallie." Blake didn't seem to notice my disinterest as we walked, and he kept happily chatting about the team's season starting to coming to a close and how semi-finals or something were happening. I honestly didn't really know anything much about sports, and I didn't really care much, either. Sure, boy sports were good because the boys played rough and looked hot doing it, and girl sports were good because we looked tough and pretty—except for the ugly people, that is. That was about the extent I cared. Somehow, listening to Blake talk about it wasn't really exciting anymore.

In fact, even though it took me a few moments to notice, and I didn't know exactly why, I was suddenly very eager to get home. Even though I was walking around with Blake Turner, lacrosse player, semi-famous sweetheart, hashtag-dating-goals material!

This has to be Zeus' fault.

If he'd just *not* talked to Gloria and left me with Blake and his near-black-out eyes, I wouldn't have been so excited to escape just now.

"Well, thanks for talking with me," Blake said. "I was really worried about that, you know, and I'm just glad you're on my side about it."

"Oh, anytime," I said, without any real idea what he was talking about. "I'm sure it'll work out great."

"I hope so." He pointed to his face. "Are you and the other girls coming to watch us practice today?"

"Well, I wouldn't want to use all the luck we bring you for just a practice." I gave him a quick, flirty toss of my hair over my shoulder and a wink. "But if you ask us tomorrow, I'm sure we'll be more inclined to see you play the game."

"Awesome."

"Besides," I said, "I have to watch the debate tonight. Part of a homework assignment, you know?"

"Oh, yeah. I think I'll just catch the highlights from the internet later and do my summary that way." Blake shrugged.

For a moment, I was weak. I liked having someone to talk to that wasn't part of my Fatgirl life, even if it was Blake Turner and his self-obsessed sports-manic self, with face paint blacking out his eyes like it was Goths Gone Wild Week.

"I'm actually thinking of going," I admitted. "See if I can get brownie points, you know?"

"Sounds boring," Blake said. "But if you do get some brownies, please bring them in, too. I haven't forgotten how good your grandmother's doughnuts were, even if I don't remember much else from that day."

"Oh?" The word squeaked out unexpectedly, but Blake didn't seem to notice that, either.

"Yeah, that was the day Fatgirl saved me." Blake grinned. "She's so cool. I signed up for that website, too, you know, and it's pretty nice, too. I've been keeping up with the posts—"

Hearing each word come out of his beautiful mouth was a pernicious, verbal poison.

I hurriedly picked up my phone and pushed the ringer button. It let out a quick tune, and I pretended to answer it.

"Oh, hi—*hola, padre*. You need me at *la casa?* Oh, well, I'll be there ASAP. Love you, bye!" I snapped my fingers together. "Oh, sorry, Blake. I gotta run. My dad needs me at home."

"I thought you said he needed you at *la casa*," Blake said, but I hurried off.

Well, it's best to leave people wanting more, right?

And let's face it—I was pretty good at that, both as myself and as Fatgirl.

"Ugh."

I was more than grateful for my escape from school. Walking into my home felt like walking through a waterfall of pure relief.

Until, of course, the door shut behind me, and I realized Dad was working late and AB wasn't back from her field trip with a side of fake terrorism yet.

And of course, Mom wasn't home, either.

Thinking of that, I went up to my room and reached under my bed. There, stuffed behind some of my older shoes, was my mother's old copy of *The Art of War*.

I picked it up and thumbed my way through it, thinking of Mom. I wondered what had drawn her to the book in the first place. I mean, I liked the advice, even from a high schooler's perspective—and now a so-called superhero's, too—but Sun Tzu didn't seem to know much about women. He said to "know thyself," and by knowing yourself you would know who your enemy was. I'd thought I'd known my enemy—Amory and I were opposing sources for social power, my parents and I were at odds with each other sometimes, and now I had to deal with Alterants.

I bit my lip. Was that what Sun Tzu meant? That I was, at heart, my own enemy?

Well, that would explain all my loneliness. I glanced around my empty room, in my empty house, feeling empty inside.

Too bad Sun Tzu didn't say anything about how to change yourself, especially for the better.

And change seemed difficult.

I didn't even think I'd needed to changed when the whole Fatgirl thing had started. But perhaps it was good I had the radioactive help?

A car honked from outside.

Even though I'd been mad at him earlier, I was excited to see Zeus pull up in my driveway.

He said he'd come in his mom's car, and I had to admit, the car definitely had the mom-car look. It was older, with a larger frame and four doors. The dull gray had a few, well-worn dents, and there was a bright pink decal on the side, with Hawaiian flowers and stars.

Anyone who knew us that drove past would probably assume my dad was dating again.

Shuddering at the thought, I hurried to go let Zeus in.

"Why are you so early?" I blurted out when I opened the door.

I guess I was still a little angry with him.

"I was hoping I could make sure I had AB's lab stuff down, so we wouldn't run into issues later," he said.

Something about how he said that made me arch my brow. "Really?"

He scratched his head nervously. "Well, if you must know, I had a bit of an argument with my dad, too. He's not happy I'll be going to the debate tonight."

"Is your mom okay?" I asked, softening a little.

"She's all right today," Zeus said. He cleared his throat, and I had a feeling it wasn't me he was lying to, so much as himself. "My dad is pushing me to help with the business stuff more, though."

"Why?" I asked. "Money issues? Your mom's medical expenses?"

Zeus flushed, making his white pimples pop out of face even more noticeably. "Not necessarily—"

"You're only seventeen." I finally moved out of the doorway, so Zeus could step inside. I shut the door behind him. "What does he expect you to do? Drop out of school to help him?"

"I could." Zeus shrugged. "My mom is hoping she'll be able to live to see me graduate. And then I'll go work more with my dad. If she doesn't … make it to next May, then …"

His voice trailed off again, and I decided to distract him with Fatgirl nonsense so he wouldn't make me more sad, too.

"Well, I'm glad we've got Gloria as your cover then," I said. "So you won't be alone."

"I won't be alone. I'll be with you."

"Well … " I didn't know what to say to that.

Instead, I shoved him down the hall and led him into AB's room. It amused me to watch Zeus' expression change from somber to stunned when I unlocked the door and ushered him inside her lab-turned-bedroom.

"Your *abuela* is my hero," Zeus murmured as he walked around the room, gazing at all the tools and screens and such. "After you, of course."

"Come on. I'm no hero. And if I am, it's only because I have help." I clamped down on my teeth, trying not to blush. "Which, speaking of, I need for tonight. So let's get to work."

Zeus was pretty smart, and it didn't take him long to master the Phi-ger and figure out the portable lab equipment stuff. I was grateful when he assured me he wouldn't poke me with the needle quite so hard as AB did.

And then it happened.

Beep!

Just as I was ready to forget about all the Gloria stuff from earlier, the Phi-ger started beeping—much more rapidly and much more loudly.

Zeus and I exchanged a knowing glance. He was resolved, and I was nervous.

"I didn't touch anything," he explained, and then he sauntered over to one of the computer screens. "Can you log me in? I'll see if I can get a lead on the location."

I did, hoping this wouldn't mess up our plans for the night.

Please, dear God in Heaven, please don't let this be a nightmare.

It seemed that God was willing to humor me—perhaps too much.

Zeus pointed to the screen. "Here it is."

He was pointing at the TV station.

"Oh, goodness." I rubbed my forehead. "What are the chances Gloria would be willing to meet you there early?"

Zeus gave me an apologetic look. "I'll give her a call. You'd better get your doughnuts ready."

"They're ready." I pulled out one of AB's pre-prepared radioactive snacks and slumped over. "Even if I'm not."

"Why are you so interested in the debate tonight?" Gloria's voice sounded unassuming as she sat next to Zeus in the passenger seat of his car, though it was hard for me to tell for sure. Her voice was muffled from where I was—the trunk.

Zeus and I had decided it was best if I didn't show up, too. As much as Gloria had helped both me and Fatgirl in the past, I didn't want to drag her into this any more than I had to. It wasn't like she needed to know my secret superhero escapades, anyway.

But because of that, I was stuck in the trunk of Zeus' mom-car, trying not to vomit as he drove over bumps and potholes on his way to the station.

"I mean, I know it's a close race, but we're not even able to vote yet," Gloria continued.

"Oh, well, I've been working on helping the different sports coaches with their training videos lately. I'm hoping to get some more experience with camera work," Zeus said.

I bit down on my tongue; for all I hated Zeus some days, he was a good liar, though I didn't really know if that was really a good thing.

At least he was lying for me.

And at least he seemed to be enjoying himself.

I knew how it felt to have someone coerce you into doing something against your wishes—that was how I'd been more or less forced into this Fatgirl gig in the first place, wasn't it? I hadn't wanted to be Fatgirl, But AB would get Mom to come home, and she'd be able to exonerate her record and resurrect her government career.

"Oh, that's cool," Gloria replied. "Auntie wants me to see about getting an internship at the station over the summer. It's her way of being around me but not paying attention to me. I was actually glad when you suggested coming with me tonight."

"I'm glad I can keep you company, and you didn't mind heading over there early."

Zeus and Gloria were very nice together, I thought bitterly. He was caught up in my web of lies, and she was nice enough to go along and help us out. I knew Zeus was supposedly in love with me, but I had to admit, I didn't have any idea of how Gloria felt.

"Is Kallie coming, too?" Gloria asked.

"Kallie?" Zeus asked, probably too innocently.

Gloria laughed. "You're not trying to get some more video skills to see if you can do the prom video for next year for her or something, are you?"

"No." Zeus paused, and I held my breath. "No, this didn't have anything to do with that. She's not really impressed with my videography skills, anyway. But of course, when I film the lacrosse team, I don't keep the focus on Blake Turner, so there's that."

Gloria laughed again. She was starting to get on my nerves.

"I saw he had joined the 'Kitty-eyes' craze Kallie started," Gloria said. "But then, if Amory Franklin told Blake to go jump off a bridge, he'd build a bridge himself just to make her happy."

"Yeah, I heard he liked her," Zeus agreed. "I even heard he was planning on asking her to the Spring Fling next month."

My mouth dropped open. "What—?"

Zeus slammed on the brakes, covering my yelp of surprise.

"Whoops!" he said. "Squirrel came out of nowhere. Sorry about that. You okay?"

"I didn't see anything," Gloria said. "But I'm okay."

I clamped my hand over my mouth for the rest of the ride.

Had Zeus had actually meant that Blake liked *me* instead of Amory?

Thankfully, we arrived at the station a few moments later, and I didn't have to worry long. Really, I *would* worry about it—because if Blake didn't like me, why would I want to keep on living?—but for now, I had to settle the matter with Zeus and the politicians, and I had to stop whoever the Alterant was from going on some kind of monster-empowered rampage or pseudo-therapy session before the debate started.

The *last* thing I needed was for either James or John to use an Alternant to push some kind of agenda against me. I'd had enough social media and mainstream news fame for two lifetimes.

As Zeus finished parking, I could just imagine the headlines:

Monster Lives Matter.

Believe All Monsters.

Fatgirl is intolerant to Differently-Powered Peoples.

Monster Bigots: Why do we assume Superheroes are "Good"?

Politicians could so easily do that, too. I cringed. Two months ago, a celebrity choked on a hot dog. Some journalist wrote an editorial on how hot dogs were a symbol of the toxic patriarchal privilege. Said celebrity had to apologize for intentionally eating it and *accidentally* choking on it, and then had to universally denounce hot dogs. Fans everywhere called on the hot dog company to apologize, and their stock probably took a good hit until the next day when another celebrity, a white guy, was caught eating tacos, and the news cycle shifted to white toxicity and cultural rape.

Whatever that meant.

Zeus and Gloria left, and I waited several minutes before getting out of the trunk, using the time to start eating my doughnut, and then quickly headed inside.

It was time for full-super-sized, superhero me to make her surprise appearance.

Maybe it was only because I knew both of them were trying to use Zeus to get to me, one by bribing him and the other by enlisting the likes of Gynnifer Stills to help track me down, but the first time I saw John Weber and James Walter, I automatically disliked both of them.

From backstage where I was hiding, John—I was pretty sure it was John—smiled like a robot as he ordered his assistant under his breath. I heard him tell her to go inform the racists running the teleprompter that he was a "person of multiple colors," not just black. Gynnifer, wearing her classy suit, approached him warmly, smiling just as broadly as he side-hugged her. When she only shook hands with James, keeping a cool reserve, I knew for certain that John was the one who'd helped get her the moderator gig.

James was just as bad. He looked like a human cloned with Great White Shark DNA. Even his suit seemed sharp and white, but I heard his assistant tell him he could claim that he was a "native American," since he was born in the USA, and no one needed to know "native" wouldn't be capitalized.

To his credit, James shook his head.

"No one cares about color unless it's green. I'll play up my business experience." He paused as he straightened his elegant, crispy-purple tie. "But keep that line for later. We can feed that to one of our side's journalist if we need to talk about race later."

I straightened my headset a little, adjusting it. "Zeus? Can you hear me?" I whisper into the headset, careful not to draw attention to myself. I'm hiding behind props from other TV shows.

"Yes." There was a small crackle from the other line as Zeus cleared his throat loudly to cover up his reply.

"They're getting ready to start the debate," I said. "I haven't found the Alterant yet. Can you get a lock on it for me?"

"Not now," he said through gritted teeth. "Gynnifer's coming our way."

Just as he said that, Gynnifer's voice came through the radio.

"Oh, Gloria! You're here!"

I groaned. "All right. I'll look around some more. But I'm going to have to wait till someone appears or the debate starts. I'm not going to go unnoticed."

"Uh-huh," Zeus replied, then asked Gloria about the politicians.

I started searching for Darla Donut bags or boxes. AB had told me before that the jelly in the doughnut recipe helped keep the radioactivity potent longer, allowing for easy transport and digestion. I'd found the doughnut boxes before where Darling Donuts had been implicated—Karen Bright's fiancé, Robert Cuttingham III, had one delivered to his house in "celebration" of their wedding announcement, and Gynnifer had one sent to her office.

It wasn't hard to see that the next victim would be chosen as someone important, and a politician seemed like a natural selection to make.

Gynnifer would love that, I thought with a grimace.

She was probably excited to be able to get on the moderator panel tonight if only to push back against some of the "Femi-monster" memes the Internet came up with from her Alterant "I'm going to die alone with a bunch of cats" speech last week.

Karen and Robert were probably glad for the political debates this week, too, so they didn't have to worry about doing another show here. They would be moving to a new city in the Heartland soon.

A prickly feeling behind my enlarged nose swelled up, making my eyes burn with unshed tears.

And I wasn't going to be one of their winners.

If anything, I'm more of a loser than ever, thanks to that show.

I pushed that thought aside as a loud round of clapping ensued, reminding me I was on a mission. I had to take care of the politicians, but I also had to find the source of Protactinium that was setting off AB's Phi-ger.

Carefully, I made my way throughout the studio, trying not to call attention to myself. Even in full Fatgirl mode, I could still sneak around—well, everyone at the studio was pretty busy, catering to guests and trying to leech drama out of every shot. It was as the studio audience quieted down for the first questions that I paused and ducked, taking a short break in my search.

"Thank you for that question," I heard James say. I looked up to see a screen, and there he was, happily straightening his tie again. "And I am happy to speak on racial distinctions and financial disparity. But I also think we get along best when we live in a color-blind world."

"That's easy for you to say!" John interrupted with a sneer. "You are *legally* colorblind. How can you claim to be able to represent people, when you can't even see them as they see themselves?"

Gynnifer grinned, clearly not biased at all. "Mr. Weber brings up a good point, Mr. Walter. How can you represent your constituents with your condition?"

"The same was FDR did, even though he was crippled," James shot back, clearly annoyed he'd been interrupted. "But money—"

"Don't you mean, 'differently-abled,' James?" John shook his head at him. "'Crippled' is such an old, derogatory word to use."

"Are you being ageist now?" James shot back. "And what's wrong with 'old' words? People know what I mean."

"Do they? Or are you just coming from a privileged background?"

"I grew up poor, with a single mother! She didn't make enough money to support me and my family, so I learned how to work for myself. I'd hardly call that 'privileged.'"

"So you're saying you hate women then? That's just awful. I love women so much and have enormous respect for them, even women like your multiple ex-wives. Do you really think that women are better off working simple jobs that don't pay enough to support their own families?"

"You're using my failed marriages and my own mother against me? Well, I guess I'm not surprised, given how you hate families."

"I hate families? Your purposed policies encourage sexual promiscuity and abortion on demand." James huffed angrily. "A child is a natural result of sexual activity, and it's a slippery slope from dismembering children in the womb to dismembering them while they're alive."

"I am vehemently against child dismemberment," John shot back. "And animal dismemberment, too. A vote for me is a vote to strengthen animal rights."

"You're just using this to lengthen prison time for people of color, because they can't afford the bail and they are more likely to victims.'"

"How dare you imply people of color hate animals!"

"Might I remind you I'm a person of *multiple* colors? My people deserve reparations for your statements alone tonight!"

"Reparations is an outdated idea, and should be a charitable endeavor, not mandated from the government."

"Justice shouldn't have a price tag attached to it. The bail money can go toward funding them!"

"Any form of reparations *is* a price tag!"

"Racist!"

"Bigot!"

At some point, a popcorn vendor showed up. I'd be willing to bet if there was going to be any winner at the debate that night, it would be him.

The two men, so cultured and mature-looking on the outside, were practically frothing at the mouth and spewing spit like liquid hatred as they traded half-insane positions and fully-disgusting insults to each other.

A stark realization hit me.

"Zeus?" I clicked on the headset. "Zeus, I think we've got a problem. These two are obviously infected with the doughnuts. I'm moving in to stop them. Get the lab ready."

"Are you sure, Kallie? I'm working on honing the signal to get to the source—"

"Haven't you heard them? Just do it!" I snapped, before I bounded out of my hiding spot and careened onto the stage. Some stage crew workers tried to stop me, but no one could pin me down.

Believe me, that was *my* job.

My sudden and voluptuous appearance was probably right in line with what the audience and the moderators were expecting. The whole show had devolved into some kind of fake reality show. James was waving his arm in the air, and John was banging his fists against the podium.

And then everyone went silent as they saw me.

"Um, good evening," I said.

"Psst! Fatgirl." Gynnifer waved at me. "Step over about two feet to your left. There's a mic hanging down there."

"Oh, right. Sorry." I scooted over to the right, and then to the left when I heard the giggles from the crowd. I was relieved to see there was a mic hanging down in front of me after that adjustment.

I glanced back to where Zeus and Gloria were supposed to be sitting. I only saw her, and I knew Zeus had to be nearby, getting the antidote mixtures ready. I just needed blood samples from the victims.

"I'm sorry to interrupt, everyone," I said. "But these two"—I pointed at John and James—"are clearly Alterants under the influence of a radioactive drug."

A lady standing off to the side at another podium said, "I prefer mind-altering drugs myself, which is why I'd like them legalized."

Some of the audience laughed nervously.

That was when I realized she was a third-party candidate.

"Ugh … " I rubbed my forehead. I didn't know what to think about that, other than *how can you all be this cringe-worthy?* But I didn't think saying that would help at all.

"Kallie." Zeus' voice was low inside my ear.

"What is it?" I whispered back, turning around to face the two main politicians, who were both staring me with their robot smiles again.

"Oh, Fatgirl," James said. "I'm very pleased to meet you."

"Stay where you are!" I said, holding out my hand to stop them. I should've known they would've thought themselves above my orders.

John stepped forward, holding out his hand. "I'm so grateful you chose to appear tonight. Gynnifer speaks very highly of you, Fatgirl."

"Not just the media," James added, hurrying up after John. "But the people, too—the people who are voting for me, at least."

Seeing their advance, I slid forward, slide tackling them. Both James and John fell over, and the audience gasped behind me. To finish it off, I sat down on both of their backs.

"Just hold still," I said, reaching for my blood sample bottles.

"Kallie, stop," Zeus said. "I've been able to search the green rooms. There are two boxes here full of Darla Donuts, but they're all here."

"No one's eaten any radioactive doughnuts?" I whispered back, suddenly feeling very foolish. I looked down at the two men, who were squirming beneath me.

"I know as a man I deserve this and I am not afraid of submitting to a woman, but can you please consider getting off me?" John asked.

"This could be considered sexual harassment, you know," James grumbled.

I put my hand up to my ear. "What do you mean, all the doughnuts are there?"

"All of them," Zeus said. "I've followed the signal to these two Darla Donut boxes. And they are all still full. Twenty-four doughnuts total."

"How could these guys be like this, though?" I asked. "They were fighting like mad here."

Gynnifer finally came over. "Um, Fatgirl, is there a problem here?"

"Yes, but not the one I thought," I said sheepishly. "Sorry."

I stood up and helped the two men up, offering them a quick apology.

"I'd be happy to accept your apology," John said. Without the mic, his voice was very deep and soothing. "I'd be even happier to accept your endorsement for my campaign."

"Don't threaten her for her support," James argued. "She should be free to pick the man for the job."

"Or the woman?" I asked.

James looked skeptical, but nodded. "Or woman," he agreed. "Or even a dog, if you wanted."

"I think I'd prefer the dog," I muttered. But then I remembered Zeus, and seeing the audience behind me, I decided it was time to activate Kallie's superhero power and charm the masses into going along with me. "Actually, I haven't decided who to give my support to. I have a question I'd like to ask before I determine who I would vote for."

I glanced over at Gynnifer. "May I?"

She nodded profusely at once, enough I could see the new layer of bleach she'd used for her hair roots since the last time we'd met. "Of course, Fatgirl, go ahead."

I took the mic from a stage crew member, and then turned back to the audience. "I'm sorry for the trouble tonight. I thought these guys were turning into Alterants from all the things they were doing and saying."

The audience laughed, and some even cheered.

"So, I know you are all fans of mine," I said, and the cheers echoed more loudly as another round of applause broke out.

"We love you, Fatgirl!" a man called out, followed by some whistles.

"Okay, okay, that's good," I said. "Now, I have a question for all the candidates, and then I will give my answer. My first question is this: Would you lie to get someone to vote for you?"

"I wouldn't need to," James said. "My policies speak for themselves on their superiority."

"So … no, then?" I stared at him.

"Of course not," he said, but he tugged at his tie again.

"Me, neither," John assured the audience.

"Okay, then."

"What about me?" The lady from the third party spoke up.

"You wouldn't lie, right?" I asked, trying to appease her.

"No. Unless I did it by mistake."

Cringe again.

Still, I smiled brightly. Even when I was the size of a small hot air balloon, my smile still held up. "Okay then. I've decided who I will endorse."

The two men—and the lady from the third party—awaited my question eagerly. James leaned forward over his podium, and John seemed to be holding his breath.

"I will endorse the person whose campaign *didn't* try to find me by offering a bribe to the kid who runs my fandom website by offering to help pay his mother's medical bills. The one whose campaign *didn't* get a certain moderator on the panel in exchange for information regarding the owner of a server." I glared over at Gynnifer Stills, who seemed shell-shocked by my statement. "Since you've both—well, all of you, mostly—have said you wouldn't lie to get votes, tell me: Which one of you will I be voting for?"

I didn't mention that I was only seventeen, and therefore, I wouldn't be able to vote at all. But judging by what I'd seen of the candidates, I wouldn't have bothered, anyway.

I was about do a mic-drop when John leaned over past his own podium mic, muffling his voice some. "I would like to state for the record that I would never offer to pay for medical bills, unless of course you mean getting universal healthcare—"

"Stop!" I interrupted him quickly, not wanting to give him any sympathetic leeway. "I have proof you got Gynnifer on the debate panel in exchange for information on her niece and the guy who runs my website. Recorded proof. Do you want to repeat that for the audience to hear?"

That was also a bit of a lie. AB had it, but I figured it wouldn't be hard to get it if I needed it. And if there was any time to lay down the law and protect Zeus, it was now.

In fact … maybe there was something else I could do for him.

"Ladies and gentlemen, and people of all backgrounds and … present grounds," I said, sweeping my hand across the stage. "Both of these men have tried to find out my identity by going through the minor—yes, *minor*—who runs the Fatgirl Fandom website. I want to personally announce to people here to tonight that I *do not know this kid, and he does not know me, and there is nothing he can tell you about me.* So, please leave him alone. And, if someone could do me an extra favor . . . "

I waited until I had plenty of catcalls before I continued. Even John and James were looking like they wanted to hear if there was a way to make up for their mistakes.

"I'd like it if someone could set up a crowdfunding account for the kid," I said. "For his mother's medical bills. I can't say what is going on exactly, but if a politician's going to come and offer to pay them, they must be pretty bad."

"I will donate," James agreed. "I will set it up and see to it that he will receive the benefits of my charity—not some forced government wealth redistribution program."

"I will donate, too," John added. "Since government laws allow me to spend my extra campaign donations on non-profits."

"Good." I nodded. "Now, if you'll excuse me, I'd like to leave."

"Wait, Fatgirl," Gynnifer said, standing up. "So this means that you don't reciprocate the feelings that the Evans kid who runs your fandom site has for you?"

"Um, no," I said, feeling slightly guilty. "I don't know him at all."

I was really glad I'd gotten the politicians to agree they would never lie for votes, because I certainly wouldn't pass that test.

"Does this mean you're gay?" Gynnifer asked.

I did a double-take. "What?"

"I'm so sorry. I meant, are you a lesbian?"

"Oh, stop," James said. "This has nothing to do with being gay or lesbian. Fatgirl is a lovely woman, and not all lesbians are fat women, Gynnifer. Why are you so anti-bisexual in your reporting?"

I was too horrified for words.

"Hey, she might not even be sexual at all," John said. "Asexuals are real, too, *and* they are severely underrepresented in the media."

"Fatgirl is strong, independent woman," James argued. "I mean, if she identifies as a woman. But I also agree she doesn't need a man. Still, if she wants a man, who are we to argue? She might want more than one!"

"I'm leaving," I shouted. "This is ridiculous."

"Stop victimizing her," John said. "All women need help and protection, and you're clearly making her uncomfortable with your words. Words are violence and cause great harm, especially to women."

"Words aren't violence," I objected. "But assuming I'm a lesbian is illogical."

"Oh, so now you're the homophobic one?" Gynnifer asked me with a surprise look on her face. "I would've thought you would be more inclusive, given your own identity, Fatgirl."

"What? No." I looked around. "How did this political debate turn into discussion on my personal issues?"

John looked triumphant. "See? She's saying sexual orientations and preferences are issues. She's clearly an asexual!"

"Kallie, just leave," Zeus said over the radio. "This is politics. It's only going to get worse if you stay."

There was a confused round of applause, with several people calling me "stunning" and "brave," as I hurried away, using my impressive girth to bowl away any other reporters or stage crew members as I headed out of the station.

○ ○ ○ ○

"Well, I guess I'm not ready for the political arena."

I squirmed as Zeus pushed down the plunger of a needle, giving me the antidote that would transform me back to normal. We were out of sight from the station, but still close enough he could check for Gloria and run to meet her at the car if he wanted. He'd managed to slip away for a bit, telling her he'd needed a restroom run, but it was nice to see a friendly face after all of that.

"Stick to dealing with Amory and your other friends." Zeus chuckled. "No one is wonder about your dating preferences when you're wearing kitty-eyes."

"I thought when I finished high school that would be the end of it. I never thought it might be *better* than what's out there once we've graduated." I shivered at the thought of all that cringe and stupid.

"So you'll be voting for the third-party candidate lady?" Zeus asked. "To get some of those mind-altering drugs once they're legal?"

I laughed. "I already have that with AB."

Zeus joined in with my laughter, and for a moment, it was just nice to relax.

"Thank you for what you did for my mom, by the way." Zeus handed me my usual trench coat, the one I could wear while I was shrinking down from my elephant-size. "I don't know if my dad will be pleased or not, but I am."

I didn't understand why his dad would be upset to get the money, but I decided not to worry about it for now.

"You're welcome." I smiled up at him, meeting his gaze. I wanted to tell him I was grateful for all his help, too. I had a lot to thank him for—whether it was collecting the Darling Donut boxes, with my mom's Darla Donut logo on it, or getting my Anti-F antidote, or manipulating a mutual acquaintance of ours into sneaking us into a TV station.

Or even for not buying into the kitty-eyes fad I'd accidentally, intentionally, started at school.

Zeus would look terrible with kitty-eyes.

A giggle slipped free as I thought about that, and Zeus frowned.

"What is it?" he asked.

"Nothing," I said. "I just … okay, I was thinking about what you would look like with those black-cat-eyes. I saw Blake tried wearing them earlier and it seriously looked like he'd gone super-goth."

Zeus and I shared another laugh, and when we stopped, I realized I was actually having fun. I thought about hugging him as the silence between us dragged on, and we just stared at each other.

Why would it be so weird if I did?

Zeus just seemed to be fine with letting me decide about that. But before I could say something, Gloria's voice cut through the silence.

"Zeus?"

We both turned to see Gloria was approaching the car, and I bit back a disappointed groan.

"I guess we'd better go," Zeus said. "I don't want to keep Gloria waiting for too long. She'd mentioned we might stop off for some food somewhere. I know I don't have to worry about buying any for you, but do you want to pretend to 'meet' us there?"

"Um, you know what?" I said, suddenly feeling awkward. "Why don't you just go ahead without me? It's going to be too hard trying to sneak me into the trunk anyway."

"You sure?"

I was a little disappointed he didn't press me.

"It's fine," I assured him. "I can catch the bus home."

Zeus looked uncertain, but when Gloria called for him again, he nodded. "All right. I'll see you tomorrow in school, Kallie. I can give you the doughnuts then."

"Maybe. We'll have to work off a drop-off," I said, trying to smile again. It was harder this time.

I didn't really want to say goodbye. I would just be lonely again. But I also didn't want to cause Zeus anymore trouble.

"Here," he said, handing me a small slip of white paper.

"What it is?" I asked.

"This is the order receipt," Zeus explained. "It was in one of the boxes. Both were marked with '1/2' and '2/2' when I saw them, and it looks like they were both ordered under the name 'Ima Donor,' so we at least know it was from the same person."

"And that person would have access to a Darling Donut bakery," I mused, remembering how AB told me how to make the radioactive doughnuts.

"Well, it's a lead." Zeus cracked his knuckles. "I might be able to hack into the security cameras and check out the delivery itself."

I hated to admit it, but it was a good plan. And I didn't doubt for a moment that Zeus could handle the hacking. AB seemed to like the thought of using him, and besides the upsides of being a minor and not having a record, he was actually good at the jobs AB gave him.

Unlike me.

I grimaced at the thought of all my forays as Fatgirl and my attempts at playing the somewhat-better Spygirl.

Perhaps for all the trouble I had with Zeus on a personal level, it was for the best that I just let him keep his memory—for now.

Maybe when this was all over, I could get AB to swipe mine instead, and I could let Mom take care of me like I was some kind of comatose patient when she got back.

I waved goodbye and watched as Zeus hurried to meet up with Gloria. I was glad Gloria seemed to be okay with his absence. I had to wonder if she knew more than she let on, but I didn't want to question her too closely, especially right then. Still, I wasn't too worried; AB did have her Memory Swiper if we needed it for Gloria.

Zeus and Gloria drove off, and I sighed and headed toward the bus station.

I didn't really have a right to ruin Zeus' life, but I had managed to complicate my own.

Public transportation was a new low for me.

Just as I pulled out my phone to check for a bus stop, a familiar white Imperial pulled up in front of me. The window rolled down. I grinned.

"Long night?" AB asked.

I nodded, almost ready to cry with gratitude that she was here, and not just because I didn't want to ride the bus home.

"Well, get in, darling," she said. "You can fill me in on the latest developments on the way home."

"Sounds good," I agreed, hopping into the red- colored backseat.

"If you think that sounds good, wait until you hear my news," AB said.

For the first time, I saw her eyes were lit up with excitement. "What is it?"

"I've found your mother. And ZZ, too." She grinned at me in the rearview mirror. "We're going to take a vacation to Fort Lauderdale soon, Kallie."

I settled into the car seat cushions, thinking about the last day without AB and all the night's debacle.

"Sounds great. I could use a vacation."

Fatgirl

SPRING FLING

EPISODE 7

○ ○ ○ ○

C. S. Johnson

"Florida Man" has nothing on "Florida Grandma" …

FATGIRL SPRING FLING

○ ○ ○ ○

I looked out the window of Fort Lauderdale's cheapest hotel and crossed my arms over my chest. I dug my nails into my skin as I did my very best not to scream in angry resignation.

I could hear my mother's voice inside my head already: *"Yelling will only cause stress and wrinkles, Kallie."*

For once, I rolled my eyes at her advice. Given my current situation, surely Mom would allow me an exception, if only this once.

Nothing I did seemed to ever go according to plan, and I was furious at the world for its belligerence and indifference—and then there were all the stupid people in my life who seemed so keen on ruining it.

At that thought, I glanced over at my grandmother, who I semi-lovingly called Abuela-Blanca. I narrowed my eyes as she diligently unpacked her large suitcase. AB was apparently oblivious to the third-world conditions of our room—the pasty-looking walls, the cheap sheets on the beds, the less-than-stellar color scheme …

Ugh. I shuddered at the reminder of my immediate vicinity. Even though I wanted to be a model, it was good I wasn't inclined toward bulimia; I would've barfed several times by now otherwise.

"Kallie, are you okay?" AB pulled out some silk blouses and *another* Coco Chanel pantsuit—AB must've had the world's largest collected depot of the classy-old-lady-suits—and I wondered all over again how my life managed to be this terrible.

"Oh, don't worry about me. I'm just watching for cops." I clenched my jaw, being careful not to grind down my teeth; I didn't need wrinkles, and I didn't need tooth decay, either. But I was still very angry and upset and it was hard not to do *something* destructive, even if it was self-destructive. "From the way you were acting down there, the receptionist guy probably thinks you're here to sell me at some auction."

"Please. He's more likely to think you're engaging in elder abuse." AB chuckled as she pulled out an unusually large-looking gun. "I'm just the sweet, old granny who doesn't realize she's footing the Spring Break bill for her wild granddaughter."

I scowled. "Not after that story you gave him about being mugged."

"Well, why would I lie, darling?" AB gave me a saccharine smile. "He didn't seem the least little bit suspicious."

"After you pulled cash out of your shoes to pay for our room, he was too disgusted to be suspicious." I frowned at the reminder. "Ugh, I still can't believe that happened. So gross."

"He still took it."

I gagged. "Yeah, and he probably took a bath in hand sanitizer afterward, too!"

"So what if he did? No one's going to call the police over that, and paying in cash allows us some anonymity." AB gave me a pointed look. "But he might call if there's a bunch of shouting going on. And the walls are thin, Kallie, so lower your voice. I prefer silence, if you'll indulge me while I get ready."

I wrinkled my nose disdainfully. "If the walls are that thin, I guess I'll have to wait until we're outside to eat my doughnuts."

"There's my smart girl."

I glared at AB again, before turning back to face the window.

While the hotel left much to be desired in terms of quality, Florida at least had some great views. From our room on the sixth floor, I could see the clear blue of the sky as it met with the blur of the ocean. Palm trees and beaches were scattered along the horizon between us, and buildings, high-rises, and even a few cruise ships spotted the waterfront, pretty as a postcard. Along the street below us, a variety of people—young and fun, old and spry—all walked around in crop tops, sandals, and swimming gear, no doubt yelling, cheering, and singing with unbridled, unburdened, early Spring Break joy.

A joy I will never know myself . . .

I tapped my temples and forehead in a rhythmic pattern, trying to calm myself down a little.

Clearly, I was going to be scarred enough as it was when our business here was done, but at least AB dressed her age; I did *not* want to see my grandmother walking around in a string bikini on top of everything else.

Be grateful for small mercies, I guess.

I had other reasons to be grateful, too, despite all the terrible things I faced here in Florida.

"Kallie?" AB's voice had a softer, more seeking tone to it this time, and I knew she was actually worried. "Are you sure you're alright?"

"I'm fine." It was hard to swallow the lie as I said the words, but I did it. It had been a while since I'd felt like someone really cared about me, and for all she was the source of my problems, I was oddly humbled by AB's concern. "Besides, there's nothing you can do about anything. So don't bother me about it."

"Kallie." AB paused for a moment. "Are you more upset about missing the Spring Fling than you've admitted to me?"

"What? *No.*"

I was probably a little too emphatic with my "no," since AB suddenly looked unbearably smug.

"I thought you said you were glad to have an excuse not to go," she continued. "Especially since all the issues you had with Blake Turner and—"

"Stop. I don't care about him anymore."

"That's not the Kallie I know," AB said a little more softly. "You don't give up so easily on the things you want."

"I'm a teenager, and a woman." I scoffed. "I don't know what I want, and I'm allowed to change my mind."

AB looked amused. "Well, you certainly know how to make me laugh."

"Go ahead and laugh then. But I don't want to talk about Blake."

AB paused, almost delicately. "You're not more upset about Zeus, are you?"

"*No.*" I tightened my grip on my arms. "I don't want to talk anymore, AB. I'd rather go over our Fatgirl business for once, and you should take advantage of my mood."

"Well, I won't argue with that. Let's get ready to go, and then we'll go over the plan."

"Fine." I smothered a groan as AB went back to getting her guns ready.

It was bad enough we were here, but it was worse that AB was right: I was upset about the Spring Fling.

The whole thing had been a disaster ever since my conversation with Blake.

When AB initially told me we were going to Fort Lauderdale the same weekend Cuttingham City High was holding its one-time annual dance, I'd been fully prepared to blow her off.

Ever since I started high school, I'd dreamed of getting to go to a fancy dance and party with my friends while hanging onto the arm of a handsome, talented, hopelessly in-love-with-me man who would bring me a lovely corsage, buy me a grand dinner, and maybe rent me a limo for the night. Such an experience was practically a rite of passage for a beautiful teenage girl like me, and I could almost taste my dream coming true as I watched Blake Turner walk down the hall yesterday afternoon.

I cringed as the memory overtook me.

Even in my dimly-lit, public-school hallway, Blake Turner never failed to look perfect. His blond hair was so perfectly perfect, and his greenish-gray eyes were so expressive and lovely; it was like looking into a reflection pool that was filled to the brim with perfect happiness.

He was walking down the hall toward me when he met my gaze and waved.

Instantly, my heart wanted to sprout wings and fly away. My stomach did cartwheels, and I was breathless as I waved back.

"Hey, Kallie," he called. "Can I ask you something about the dance tomorrow?"

I barely refrained from giggling nervously. I had to scrunch my toes up inside my heels; the pain in my feet kept me focused and poised as he stood before me.

This is it. This … is … it!

I felt certain my dream was never so close to becoming true. My pulse was racing, my head was spinning, and my breath was caught in my throat.

"Hi, Blake." I batted my eyes at him flirtatiously as I nearly whimpered out his name. "What was that about the Spring Fling?"

Thankfully, he didn't seem to notice how utterly awkward I was; or at least, he didn't hold it against me.

Instead, he smiled that charmingly crooked smile of his and leaned against the lockers behind us. "Hey, are you and Amory and the other girls planning on going at all?"

My heart was pounding in between my ears as I just stared up at him, basking in his perfection. I desperately wished I could find a way to stop time and just stare at him like this forever.

"Kallie?" Blake gave me another look. Playfully, he tapped me on the head. "Hello? Anyone in there?"

"Oh, um … sorry, I was just trying to remember what Amory said," I hurriedly explained. "So, I'm certain we were going to go—"

"—but we were *absolutely* not going to go with any dates."

Amory smoothly interrupted me as she came up beside me.

At once, my mouth dropped open, and I nearly choked. I could only watch in stunned silence as my supposed best friend came up to me and put her arm around my shoulder. The move was supposed to appear friendly and protective, but it only felt deceptive.

Meanwhile, I couldn't even sputter out a reply.

Of all the times my best frenemy turned out to be more enemy than friend, this time was the absolute worst.

The absolute worst times a gazillion.

"Kallie and I and the 'other girls'—who all have names, as you should know, Blake—are just too popular to decide who's worthy enough to escort us. So, I've decided we're just going as a group."

"Group?" I finally managed to gasp out a response.

"Yes, Kallie. Come on, you don't want all the lacrosse team fighting over who gets to date us, do you? They'll just end up super jealous of each other, get into terrible fights, and they won't be able to pull together as a team. And we wouldn't want that." Amory gave my shoulder a constricting squeeze. "We have to think of the greater good."

"So … none of you are going with dates?" Blake asked, and I could only look at him helplessly as Amory nodded.

"That's right. Sorry, Blakey-boy," she said with a teasing giggle. "Perhaps you'll have to try harder to convince us you're worthy."

No! He is worthy! He is worthy!

"Oh." Blake looked slightly dejected, but then he shrugged. "I'll make a note of that, Amory. There's always next year, right?"

"You can try," Amory said, her voice sweet and coy as she began pulling me away. "But Kallie has such high standards—"

No, no, I don't. I swear. They're not high if they're Blake Turner! Why can't I say something? Why can't I object?

"—and you know I'm probably right about the team all being jealous of each other," Amory said. "And if you and Damien and Declan start a war over who gets to go with us, you'll lose the championship."

"Hmm." Blake nodded blandly. "You may be right."

Some part of me wanted to shake Blake hard for the consideration he was obviously giving to her theory.

"But there's still a little time," Blake said, a little more hopefully. "Maybe I can get you to change your mind?"

Yes! Yes! Yes, you can!

I wanted to scream, but I could barely breathe. I was still too shocked to say anything coherent.

"Maybe you and the boys could just go as a group as well," Amory said, batting her eyes at him in a pathetically desperate attempt to get her way. "That way we can all take turns dancing with each other, and no one will feel left out."

"Oh, that might work," Blake agreed. His hesitant smile widened with confidence. "Can I have your first dance if I get them to agree with me, Amory?"

"Hey, Turner, you coming or not?" Damien, the lacrosse team's giant hulk of a forward right, suddenly tapped Blake on the shoulder. "The guys are headed out. It's leg day—no skipping!"

"Oh, right," Blake murmured. "Well, see you around, Amory. And you, too, Kallie."

As he headed off, I pulled away from Amory, trying to follow him. The hallway was too clogged with the crowd for me to get very far. "Wait, Blake—"

"Stop, Kallie," Amory hissed, grabbing my arm. "Be cool, would you?"

"No," I snapped.

"Excuse me?"

It was suddenly easy to remember that I'd sat on a terrorist, helped capture a wanted criminal, defeated multiple Alternants, thwarted a secretly depressed journalist, and upstaged two political hacks; I didn't need to be afraid of Amory.

So I crossed my arms.

"I wanted to go with Blake," I said. "He's the most popular kid in school. Why shouldn't I be able to date him?"

At first, Amory looked shocked, and then her expression soured. "Didn't I explain this already? This isn't about you, Kallie. It's about something greater."

"There's nothing greater about going as a group date to the Spring Fling," I argued, unsure of why my voice was suddenly so loud. "Not when I could have Blake Turner as my date."

"Please, Kallie, stop embarrassing yourself." Amory put her foot down. "I'm doing this for you."

"No, you're not! This isn't helping me at all. Are you insane?"

Amory's eyes narrowed. "Am *I* insane? What about you, Kallie? You look like a fool, gushing over some silly-boy crush. Sure, Blake's good-looking, and yeah, he's a pretty nice guy. But dating him isn't worth the cost of losing your dignity. You should be thanking me for all that I've done to help keep you presentable in recent weeks. Honestly, I'm beginning to think you're not even grateful to be my friend."

She said this with more of a warning in her voice, and I knew she was getting close to writing me off.

Then a startling thought hit me: Amory was probably still upset with me about the whole *Model Middle America* incident, where I'd purposely caused her and the other girls to be too late to audition. She'd probably been waiting for weeks to get a perfect opportunity for revenge, and I'd foolishly just given it to her.

That's it—that has to be it. There's no other reason for her to be this cruel to me.

"If I was really your friend, I wouldn't have to explain to you how much you've hurt me," I said slowly. "You know what? I don't think I'll be going to the dance at all. My grandmother—er, my Abuela—said she's going to take me to Florida and we're going to hang out on the beach, and right now that's more appealing than wasting another moment with a selfish jerk like you."

"Kallie!" Amory's mouth dropped open.

"Please, give the other girls my regrets," I added, before I turned on my skinny heels much more gracefully than I felt, and then I stormed off down the hall.

Discreetly, I looked for an empty classroom, eager to cry before I got home and had to ward off AB; she was always a pain to deal with, but it was worse when I was unhappy. She could probably smell my tears from her basement headquarters.

I was just wondering if Mr. Embers was in his computer lab when I caught sight of Zeus. I almost waved, before I saw he was with Gloria.

They seemed to be talking nicely with each other. She was smiling and nodding, and he seemed more talkative than usual. I was about to walk up and signal to him to come and talk with me—so I could complain about Amory and Blake if nothing else—when Zeus mentioned the Spring Fling.

"So, you really don't mind going to the Spring Fling with me?" he asked.

At his words, some part of me felt like I'd been hit with a bulldozer; the air in my lungs rushed out, and I felt dizzy again, and not the good kind of dizzy I felt when I looked at Blake.

It got worse when Gloria nodded. "Sure, it's no problem. I think it'll be fun."

"Thanks. I appreciate it." Zeus smiled down at her.

I frowned.

What did Zeus think he was doing? He wasn't a good match for Gloria. She was a head shorter than he was—of course, so was I, but still—she just didn't look good next to him. Her dark blonde hair was straight and average, and she easily needed to lose ten pounds to look better. She was just so plain, too; there wasn't anything even outright ugly about her. She just didn't look good.

But then, I reminded myself, Zeus didn't look that good next to anyone else, either. His skin was oily with pimples, and his eyes were hidden by overly large, thick-framed glasses. And he was fat, too, even if he wore raggedy clothes to cover it up.

"Hey, Kallie." Gloria waved at me, as she finally noticed me.

I held back a flinch as I tepidly returned the gesture. "Hi. What's going on?"

"Nothing much," Zeus said, suddenly looking from me to Gloria with concern.

I arched my brow. "Really? Well, that sounds boring. Excuse me for now, I've … got to get home to AB. But I wanted to see Mr. Embers first. I … left my notebook in his class, and I—augh!"

I stumbled over my words as much as my heels, and I was beyond humiliated when I fell forward, crashing into Zeus.

He caught me and held me firm against his sweatshirt until I could steady myself.

"Excuse me." I could feel the steam rising out of my ears as my face burned. Angrily, I pushed away from him, and then hurried off.

"Kallie, are you okay?" Zeus yelled after me as I fled.

I didn't answer him.

I didn't want to answer him.

"Mr. Embers' class is the other way," he called, and I realized I was being more than dumb.

But I didn't care.

It was too late to care.

First, I'd lost Blake, and my dreams.

Then Amory betrayed me, and our friendship.

And finally, Zeus had forgotten about me, and settled for Gloria.

It was bad enough my own mother had left me and my dad, but all of this was worse.

Mom had left us for a modeling career I would kill for, but Blake? He didn't have the balls to stand up to the likes of Amory.

Amory herself didn't seem to care at all that my dreams were hanging on by a thread. She went ahead and made that thread into a noose and hung me on it without reserve.

And then Zeus ... well, he wasn't really doing anything wrong, but he was still choosing a dumpy average girl over me, and as much as I told myself it was a relief he'd found someone to glom onto besides me, his choice still unbelievably, unexplainably hurt me.

I ran into the nearest girls' restroom and stayed there, crying silently as I waited until I was certain everyone was gone. I finally limped home, only to find Dad working overtime and AB waving plane tickets in my face.

After all that, I *had* to look forward to going off to Fort Lauderdale, even if it meant infiltrating a former KGB agent's retirement party while I was there.

I had literally nothing else.

I pushed my forehead into my hands, desperately wishing I could forget everything that had happened, instead of forcing myself to relive it every time I had a spare moment.

Not that I even had that.

It was the middle of the afternoon, and AB and I were standing outside our hotel. I was wearing a tourist jacket, hiding my Fatgirl suit, which also housed an ice-cold pair of radioactive doughnuts; I couldn't hate them, even if it was uncomfortable; I liked the chilliness they offered, especially standing there in the full heat of the Florida sunshine. And it didn't hurt to see I'd look good with some implants if I ever needed to get them for my modeling career.

"Stand up straight, Kallie," AB murmured as she tugged down her silk shirt.

Standing there, it was easy to see I contrasted nicely with AB in her classy pantsuit skirt and her pinned back, old-lady white hair. In addition to her huge purse, she was holding a pair of evening cruise tickets that was supposedly going to be our alibi for the night.

Our masquerade had begun.

"It's only a matter of hours now, until I find out who betrayed me." AB was gushing with excitement as she hailed down a cab and one came to a slow stop in front of us.

"Okay," I murmured as we climbed inside the hot, sweaty car. "And once you've got your answers, we'll get Mom to come home, right?"

"Of course," AB agreed.

She sounded too happy and upbeat for me to believe her. And I was starting to wonder if I even wanted Mom to come home. She seemed pretty content to leave us in the first place, and she'd threatened my dad with divorce papers if we bothered her again.

Maybe Mom was just as bad as all the others, I thought bitterly. Maybe I was bad enough I deserved to have my mom run out on me. And while I'd die defending my dad's honor, I knew there were some problems in marriage that couldn't be solved—some that couldn't even be spoken. Maybe she was justified in leaving him, too.

I wallowed in my miseries as AB gave the directions to one of the nearby ports, and the driver asked if we were going on the Party Time Cruise Line.

"That's the one." AB nodded. "I got a good deal on it."

She continued to make jovial, but largely forgettable, conversation with the man as we headed to the port drop-off area. She asked questions, some of them stupid, some of them esoteric, and she made cranky old ladies comments in between.

Even I managed to smile more than once at her performance.

I didn't want to think I got my sense of humor from AB at all, but it was at least nice to see she could be less than completely embarrassing.

At the end of our ride, AB paid with cash, and I was just thankful she'd pulled it out of her shoe before we'd left the hotel, so he wasn't repulsed by it.

"Enjoy your trip, ladies," the driver said, giving me a charming grin and a quick nod of his cap. I smiled and waved back. "Don't forget to take some pictures."

As he pulled away, I decided to do just that.

AB was looking through her purse as I pulled out my phone.

It was the perfect time to take some pictures. I posed facing the sunlight got a few selfies with the palm trees and large cruise ships behind me.

The pictures were really nice ones, too, which cheered me up considerably; I could post them to my social media profiles and maybe Amory would even feel a little jealous, at least.

She might've organized the Spring Fling group date, but I was far away and out of her reach. I'd disobeyed her command, and insulted her, too. But she couldn't scare me with that many miles between us.

I bit back a sigh.

I didn't know what I would do when I got back home. I could blame my angry outburst on PMS and tell her there was no way I could get out of a family trip to Fort Lauderdale, and maybe we'd be best frenemies again.

Or maybe I'd ignore her, lose all my friends, and start over with nothing.

I couldn't say if it would really be that different. At least I wouldn't have to lie about being Fatgirl to anyone—no one would bother me at all, and I'd just be some has-been loser-turned-outcast. And at least I would still be pretty enough people would just assume Amory cut me off from the group because I was too much competition for her.

Beside me, AB groaned. "Really, Kallie? You brought your phone?"

"Of course," I said. "Dad will want to be able to call me at some point."

"Fine," she grumbled. "But give it to me when you're done. I'll have to make sure the signal isn't tracking us."

"You're not going to destroy it, are you?" I hurriedly posted my pictures with my favorite keywords and symbols. "I'll still need it."

"You won't need it, but I'll make sure it's not ruined." AB began walking down the street, heading away from the cruise ship ports as I ruefully handed her my phone. She began typing on it with a speed and confidence that belied her age; before I could ask her what she was doing, she handed it back to me. "Now, let's focus. From the limited information Frank was able to give me, ZZ's going to hold her auction tonight in the warehouse down at 22nd Street and

Beachfront Boulevard. We have twenty minutes before the guests start arriving. We'll sneak in separately, and then I'll give you the signal and you'll create a distraction. That's when I'll get a hold of ZZ."

"That sounds a lot easier than it will be," I murmured.

"You're right." AB handed me my earpiece. "You've got your Fatgirl suit on, right?"

"Yes." I nearly spat out the word.

"Good. Be ready. ZZ didn't get where she is today by being careless. She'll have security around. I've added a radio wave disruptor to your mask that will short-circuit their signals. You'll be able to slip through posing as a waitress while—"

"Wait a minute. I'm going to be a *waitress*?" I scowled.

"You can handle it," AB assured me. "Just look dumb and apologetic at every chance you get. You're pretty enough you don't have to be smart. It'll be clear you got hired from your looks."

"Gee, thanks."

"Take it as a compliment."

"Take it as I'm so beautiful that people will excuse me for being dumb?"

"No." AB grinned. "Take it to mean that you'll have the upper hand in most situations you encounter. It's a great thing to be underestimated."

I didn't say anything to that; I usually did that with others at school already. But it was nice AB thought I could do something with it, I supposed.

"What time is the KGB Queen's Retirement Party going to start?" I gave AB a small smirk. "The reception guy was quick to tell you that they have a three-thirty early bird special."

"Ha." AB looked amused. "In Soviet Russia, Early Birds are bombs."

"Excuse me?" My mouth dropped open and I stopped in my tracks. "What?"

There are going to be bombs here?

I began to feel like I was walking around in a dream.

Why did I think this was going to be fun? Or easy? Or even preferable to the worst sort of humiliation that came from ditching my friends, losing my dignity, and failing to get my dream date?

What would it cost, I wondered, to have this only be some kind of nightmare, where I could wake up, and find my mom back at home, tending to me as I slept in some kind of coma?

"I'm joking, Kallie," AB muttered, breaking into my cycle of self-despair-care. I was just about to relax a little when she said, "Obviously they don't use the English names."

"Ugh." I put my hands over my head, putting my head on my chest, full of pure hopelessness. "Why did I think I could do this?"

"Because you can, of course."

"That's easy for you to say."

"Yes, it is," AB agreed in a crisp but patient voice. "Because it's true."

I didn't look up at her as I silently wished for a random meteor to suddenly strike her dead. When it didn't come, I could only imagine it was in my best interest to keep her alive until we got back to Arkansas.

AB put her hand on my shoulder. "Please, Kallie, get it together. Part of growing up is being able to emotionally distance yourself from pressure."

"But what if I fail?" I barely spoke the words, but she still heard me.

"So what if you do?" AB shrugged. "I'll be there with you, and we're clever enough that we'll find a way around any mishaps."

Some part of me—probably the adult part of me that AB was appealing to—really appreciated how she was giving me wisdom and encouragement. But the teenager in me still didn't want to admit she was right, either.

"None of my other plans have worked out," I muttered.

"That can be a good thing, you know. And don't forget." AB patted my hair kindly, making me think of Mom of all people. "Once we're done tonight, you'll get your mother back. That's what you wanted, and I aim to deliver. And after tonight, I'll know who it was who stole my recipe and got me fired, too. To get what you want in life, you need to make sacrifices."

I peeked up at her through my hands. AB was right about plenty, even if I hated her for it, and she was right about that most of all: We'd agreed to help each other out, and we were both due to get exactly what we'd wanted and worked for.

I dropped my hands from my face and rubbed my eyes. "I still don't like this."

"Do you think I like hunting down someone who betrayed me?" AB wrinkled her nose distastefully. "It has to be someone in my own lab—someone I've known for years. And someone who is connected to ZZ and whoever it is who is creating Alternants in Cuttingham City."

"Haven't you figured all that out yet?" I raised my head up, suddenly curious. "I thought spies and government workers were able to use all their tech and everything else to find out all the answers."

"It may surprise you to know, but innovation doesn't stop just because it can." AB gave me a half-hearted smile. "What was secure in one generation is vulnerable in the next. As security evolves, so does the world, and that means villains can become heroes as much as heroes become villains. But we still rely on people to be our best and most meaningful sources. That is why I am hoping ZZ will cooperate."

"What do you mean?"

AB loaded a new clip into her gun, and then she tucked it into the back of her skirt as we started forward. "What I mean is that ZZ is a former KGB agent. The Soviets have been out of service for decades now—or at least, so they say. It's more likely they've been rebranded as heroes of some sort, courtesy of the Russian Federation and its oligarchs. But ZZ was one of their youngest inductees, and she's rumored to have a perfect memory. One of the reasons she's so dangerous is because she doesn't rely on tech as her backup."

"Well, if she has a perfect memory, she'll be able to tell you who gave her your recipe," I said.

"Yes. And I have Agent Iris in here to help me, along with my memory scrambler, as you so charmingly call it." AB patted her purse. "You distract the others, I'll question her, and then you'll need to escape once I'm done. We'll meet up here at the port when we're done and head back to the hotel once the evening cruise gets to port again."

"Sounds easy enough," I murmured.

"Yes." AB nodded grimly. "Easier said than done, for sure. Now, let's get going. It's only a few blocks away. Try to make sure you don't draw any unnecessary attention to yourself."

I hesitated for only the briefest of moments, before I turned my earpiece on and walked into the looming shadows ahead.

Up ahead, I spotted the building where ZZ was holding her gala. It looked like any kind of normal convention center; I wasn't surprised to see it was a casino.

Old people love to gamble …

There were lights shining brightly and music blaring loudly, and if I didn't know any better, it could've almost been a Hollywood premiere. Several people—all dressed in evening wear, military uniforms, and formal tuxedos—were heading inside, whispering in eager, hushed voices.

"Let's go around the side. There will be a service entrance for you, and I'll be able to sneak in my own way," AB murmured, shuffling me off toward the side. She was used to issuing commands, and as we made a nonchalant, roundabout way toward the other side, I was able to calm down a little.

This was very similar, actually, to what had happened the night of my *Model Middle America* audition. I'd managed to come late enough to be early for the show, and I'd slipped in easily enough thanks to my shameless lies and bravado.

"Alright, Spygirl," AB whispered. "Keep your eyes alert and your ears open. Mic working?"

I gently touched the earpiece I wore and nodded. "Yes."

"Good to know." AB gave me a small wink, and I finally felt a genuine smile form on my face.

My plans might had gone wrong plenty in the past, but AB had it together much more than I did. Her plans had to work out better than mine.

I was content with this logic, and I was even starting to get excited about infiltrating the gala.

But then it happened.

I saw a familiar figure walking into the building where ZZ's Gala was starting. It was a woman.

She was tall, beautiful, and wearing a red dress that enhanced her beauty along with every feature. Even in the Florida heat, she wore a sleek, fur wrap around her arms, and a string of pearls gleamed at her throat. I took in her black hair and red lips and big eyes, and my eyes suddenly watered.

Mom.

AB didn't seem to notice I stopped in my tracks. She was fiddling with something in her purse, and just like before with Blake and Amory, I couldn't find the right words to say.

Clank!

Something small fell down to the ground beside AB, who looked up.

At once, she scowled. "If I'd known you were going to be here, Eugene, I would've put on my Sunday best."

"I always appreciate how much you wish to impress me, Madame."

The voice was calm, distinctly Welsh, and full of good-natured humor.

My gaze flickered up toward a window, where I was surprised to see a friendly-looking old man smirk down at AB. From the window, I could see he was wearing a formal tux of his own, and he held a scope in his hand. A large, black, scary-looking rifle stood just behind him.

I swallowed hard, but AB only smirked.

"Not impress you, Agent Grey," she said drily. "Rather because I'd have more holsters."

I looked back over where I'd seen Mom, only to see she was gone. She'd disappeared inside.

There was a quick whirring noise, and I glanced back to see the old man from the window was suddenly on the ground beside us.

How did he do that? I gaped in astonishment, not in the least because he seemed to be at least sixty, and I couldn't imagine how he'd jumped down without breaking a hip.

"I assume you're here to congratulate ZZ on her retirement, too?" he asked.

I was surprised to see AB stiffen. "Something like that. Of course, I imagine your version of congratulations is much different than my own. I was never one of her former lovers, after all."

"I've always found the American conflation of lovers and sexual partners to be rather unkind," he replied, holding out his hand as he gave AB a cordial bow.

"You might want to watch your language," AB muttered, nodding toward me. "We have a minor in our audience. She doesn't need to hear of your indiscretions."

"Alleged indiscretions," Agent Grey corrected, before he turned and nodded to me. "Pleasure to meet you. Agent Eugene Grey, at your service. I'm with a division of Interpol."

"I'm … um, just here for Spring Break," I said, catching AB's warning glance. "But if it makes you feel better, I've heard way worse things at school."

"I see." He looked back at AB. "This is Kate's daughter, then?"

"Do you know my mom?" I asked, as AB sighed and Agent Grey grinned.

"Of course. She's a world-famous model, and one of ZZ's oldest friends. Oh, but perhaps I shouldn't say old like that? I know how models are so particular about their age." He laughed, and then he shrugged. "But then, ZZ doesn't have many friends, and the ones she does have tend to die young."

My heart constricted, suddenly filled with dread. "What do you—"

"Eugene, stop scaring her," AB interjected. "Anyway, she might be Kate's daughter, but I prefer to think of her as my granddaughter." Her lips were pursed in irritation, almost as if it hurt to praise me in such high terms. "Now, stop distracting us. Are you going to interrupt my plans for the evening or not, Agent Grey?"

The use of his business name seemed to get his attention, but he brushed away AB's annoyance with a smile. "Not any more than you'd planned to ruin ZZ's, from what I know of you, Madame Margaret."

In the soft reflection of the street lights, I swore I saw his eyes light up with flirtatious delight.

I gave him a curious second glance. His hair was gray, as were his eyes. His face was wrinkled with age but it still held a surprisingly youthful charm, and as I watched AB fumble for a response, I almost laughed.

It's not possible she likes him, is it?

Her face hardened a second later, and I saw the truth.

She did like him—but she also had problems with him.

"Kallie." She nearly barked out my name. "Get in there and wait for my signal. Agent Grey and I have things to discuss, apparently."

I looked back and forth between them, and then I nodded. I was newer to the whole Spygirl life, but I didn't have to be a newbie to know AB was right, and it was best for me to leave.

And I'll be able to catch up with Mom.

I didn't mention that to AB as I slipped away. I figured she had enough problems of her own for the moment.

I managed to sneak up to the door my mom had walked through without issue. There were a few other women who were also making their way to the door, so I slowed down and let them catch up with me.

"You new here?" A young blonde woman, just a few years older than me, touched my shoulder.

"Um, yeah. First time," I said, trying to sound normal. "I'm a bit nervous."

"You seem pretty young," she replied, giving me a critical look. A second later, she shrugged. "But I guess I was, too, when I started. Who's your referral?"

"Um … " I stared at her blankly, before sputtering out, "Kate. I mean, Katalina de la Rosa-Grande."

"Irina, stop fooling around with the new girl," one of the other women said as she passed us and walked inside. "If she's here with Kate, just take her over."

No.

"Oh, um … I thought I was supposed to be a waitress," I explained, feeling genuinely dumb as I looked at the other models around me. "I was, um, looking for a good paying job."

"Well, you're in the right place," Irina said. Her voice was hard and sympathetic. "But it's not really a waitressing job. It's more of a personal shopping assistant. Have you ever done that before?"

"Well, I've done plenty of my own shopping," I said, and Irina smiled.

"I think you can handle it, then. Come on. I'll get you to Kate. Mandy's right." She nodded to the other lady who'd marched past us earlier. "Zina doesn't like it if we're late. She wants us to start serving the guests the drinks as they arrive. We've got to get them liquored up if we want to secure their bids."

"Right. Thank you for all your help." I was more grateful than I should've been, considering I still had no idea what I was doing.

"Just don't mention it." Irina gave me another critical look. "Since you're new, you'd better prove you're worth it. I guess if Kate's your referral, you should be okay."

"Oh, yes. Kate is wonderful," I agreed. "She's so nice and thoughtful and—"

"You must know her much better than I do," Irina snorted. "She's quite ruthless."

"She is?"

"Oh, yeah. She's one of Zina's regular confidantes." Irina then narrowed her eyes at me. "I don't mean anything personal in saying so, of course."

"Of course." I was eager to assure her I wanted to be friendly, but I saw a flicker of hesitation in her gaze before she turned away.

My fledgling hope died, remembering the rules of social politics.

I grew increasingly uncomfortable as Irina went silent and led me through the back halls of the casino. The world was just like high school in that it was a matter of pecking order and dominance, a question of strength and weakness, an ongoing, ever-changing battleground for control and security.

When Irina asked a few other young women where Kate was, they couldn't answer her.

"Maybe she's up in Zina's tower," one of them said, and Irina nodded and sighed.

"We'd better hurry," she said to me. "Follow me."

"Okay." It was then I brushed some of my hair away from my face and hit the earpiece I was wearing. Instantly, I could hear AB arguing with that Agent Grey guy.

"So you're just going to follow me around now? I need to talk to ZZ." AB was snippy and angry, and I could hear the frustration in her voice. "I can't have you on my tail the whole time."

"I happen to know you enjoy having me on your … tail," Grey replied smoothly, nearly making me gag at his double-entendre. "I remember all the times we—"

Irina stopped in front of me. "What's wrong?" she asked. "You look sick."

Quickly, I turned off the reception. The thought of my grandmother hooking up with Agent Gray was somehow worse than the image of her in a string bikini.

"Hello?" Irina put her hands on her hips, getting frustrated with me. "Come on … what's your name, anyway?"

"Um … Arlanda." I sputtered out the stage name Azure had so carelessly given to me at the Model Middle America audition. "I think I'm going to be sick. Excuse me."

I ducked around her and scampered as quickly as I could.

"The bathroom's the other way," Irina called after me, sounding much more frustrated.

I'm sorry.

She'd been so nice and helpful to me, I hated how I was disappointing her.

As I hurried away, I slowly shed my jacket; AB had taught me how to disappear into crowds, and I meant to at least report back to her that I'd learned that. I grabbed a wide-brimmed hat from off a chair and pulled down a lace wrap I found on a clothing rack, making sure my Fatgirl suit was still hidden under my other clothes as I pulled up its hood.

My mask was supposed to keep cameras from reading me, but I knew I wouldn't be able to put that on without someone being suspicious.

Just then, my phone rang.

"Ugh, you've got to be kidding me," I grumbled, pulling out my phone.

I was about to ignore the call when I saw it was from Zeus.

Why on earth would he be calling me?

Judging by the time, he should be in the middle of the second or third dance at the Spring Fling, hanging out with Gloria, trying not to break her foot when he stepped on it.

Stop being mean to him, Kallie. Some part of myself was upset I was being so mean to him. I didn't know if Zeus was a good dancer or not, and even if he wasn't, it wasn't likely Gloria's foot would break even if he did step on it.

Against my better judgement, I answered it.

"What?"

"No need to sound so angry," Zeus said. "I'm calling to get a lock on your location."

"What?" I felt dumbfounded, gobsmacked, and bewildered. "Why?"

"AB told me to."

I gripped my phone tightly. "I thought you were at the Spring Fling."

"Oh, I am."

"Did you tell Gloria about me being Fatgirl?" I hissed, suddenly ready to bring the full wrath of hell against him if he even suggested I was right.

"No, of course not," he said. "Do you want me to tell her?"

"No!"

"Okay, I thought so." Zeus was smiling by the sound of it, and I would've given just about anything to reach through the phone and strangle him. "You know I wouldn't do that."

"What are you doing then, and why aren't you with Gloria?"

"Gloria is checking in with her other friends here while I excused myself for a bit," Zeus said. "I told her I wanted to check in with my mom."

"Oh."

We were silent for a long moment. Zeus' mom was in the terminal stage of her cancer, and as much as I was glad he was calling and … and doing whatever it was AB asked him to do, I didn't like that he'd lied using his mom as his cover.

"She's asleep," Zeus added. "So no updates from her."

"Oh. I'm sorry."

"It's okay."

We went quiet again, and when I felt enough time had passed proving I wasn't completely selfish, I spoke again.

"Why are you calling me?"

"AB wanted to make sure I could track you, so I'll be able to locate any cameras on you and delete the footage later," he explained. "It's better if I'm further away for this sort of job. It's harder for other lurkers to get a signal on me."

"I'll take your word for it." I turned another corner, only to run right into another clothing rack.

I was about to scream in frustration when I suddenly heard my mother's voice.

"—make sure to assign Mandy to the new congressmen's oldest son," she was saying. "He's got a weakness for a domineering woman, and his dad's already had to get him out of a few tight spots."

I hung up on Zeus and peeked through the hanging dresses to see my mother talking with another woman—one who unironically reminded me of Bernadette or Berenice or whatever her name really was from Model Middle America. She carried a tablet and was making notes. "Yes, ma'am. And what about the new girl?"

"New girl?" Mom blinked in surprise.

"Yes. Irina told me that Arlanda was here."

"Who? We don't have any new girls working tonight."

"Irina said she came in by your referral."

Mom was silent for a moment. "Where is she?"

"I'm not sure. She ran off and got lost."

Mom let out a soft curse, and I recognized her tone at once. She was more than angry, but she was doing her best to hide it. "I see. Let me give Zina a quick call and let her know. I must've forgotten about introducing her to Arlanda."

"There is a lot going on," Would-Be-Bernadette agreed.

"Never mind that. Go and get the rest of the girls out there. Zina wants her quota."

The assistant skirted off, and I was left alone there, watching as my mom reached between her legs, pulled out a small cell phone, and dialed a number.

I pushed the button on my earpiece. "AB? Mom's here."

Over the line, I could hear AB's phone ringing.

"Did she see you, Kallie?" AB asked. "Does she know you're there?"

"No. I'm close by, but she hasn't seen me."

"Okay. I'm going to keep her on the line. Get away from her, and get ready to cause a diversion. Make sure she doesn't see you, and don't say anything to her. Do you understand me?"

"Yes."

I understood her just fine.

But I disobeyed her just fine, too.

Instead of following her orders, I squashed myself behind the clothes rack as much as I could as AB finally answered her phone.

"Hello, Kate. It's nice to hear from you. I didn't think you'd call me again after our last chat."

Even from where I was, I could see Mom grip her phone. Apparently, she would've given anything for the ability to reach through the phone and strangle people, too.

"That is not funny, Margaret," Kate hissed. "What are you doing here?"

"Whatever could you mean?"

"You know what I mean. I hear from you for the first time in years, and not even a month later, my career plans are suddenly ruined?" My mom's jaw tightened. "I know you're here with one of your lackies or blackmail victims."

I didn't like to think of myself as AB's lacky, and if we were going to be technical about it, I was more of a guilt-trip victim than a blackmailed one. But either way, I stood there, still as a statue, forcing myself to breathe as quietly as possible. My eyes watered with tears.

"Am I really there, Kate? Or are you just hoping I am?" AB was taunting her now, and I couldn't believe I was hoping she'd win this argument. "Either way, I'm sorry to hear you're upset. But I should remind you that your 'career plans' include various crimes against humanity."

"Stop playing this game. You know where I am, and you know that I'm here for Kallie's own good," Mom said. "I've already warned you away once. I know you'd do anything for Johnny, and if you don't want me to break his fragile little heart, and Kallie's, too, you'd better get out of here."

"Where's 'here,' Kate?" AB asked.

At that point, I knew I should've been running away.

Hearing Mom echo Amory's words was like a slap in the face.

My tears began to slip free.

"This is the last time I'm telling you," Mom said. "Get your contact out of here, or you'll be sorry."

She slapped the phone shut.

I thought about stepping out my hiding spot and confronting her.

But what could I say?

I'd only ever wanted to be a model like my mother. She was gorgeous, and to me, she'd always been a kind and loving mother. She'd been bored by our life in Cuttingham City, and she did seem a little aloof and lonely at times. Still, my dad adored her, and I looked up to her.

But did I really even know her?

Watching her at that moment, I couldn't say for sure, and my entire life's foundation was shaken all over again.

"What is it, Kate?"

A silky smooth voice with a slight Russian accent called out to my mother. I peeked out of my hiding place again, and I saw a woman heading down toward the hall.

My eyes widened in shock.

ZZ.

It had to be her. She was a platinum blond model in an extremely expensive, extremely gorgeous gown. Her hair was pulled up in a French knot, while diamonds glittered all over her ears and throat. She was clearly older than she seemed at first glance, but she was still only a few years younger than my mother at most.

"Zina," Mom said, straightening up as she saw her. "We're ready to begin the auction. The girls are in place."

"Perfect."

I didn't even dare to breathe as ZZ looped her arm in my mom's and began to walk down the hall with her. "It has taken us a long time to get here, but at last our night has come."

"Your night," Mom corrected her with a friendly smile. "You deserve tonight, Zina. It's your time to shine."

At first, ZZ seemed a little surprised, but then she smiled brightly.

"Of course," she said. "Why else would I wear all these diamonds?"

I felt sick in my stomach as they laughed together, almost like they were best friends or something.

Once they were gone, I pulled out one of the doughnuts I'd tucked away for safe keeping.

As if she was reading my mind, the earpiece crackled, and AB gave me the signal.

"Okay, Kallie. I'll need that distraction now."

"I think I need it more than you," I whispered back, before taking a bite of the radioactive doughnut.

Not for the first time, the tasty treat was wet with my salty tears.

I've come a long way.

I'd gone from sitting on a terrorist to stop a mass shooting to breaking into a terrorist's retirement party.

That's all I could think of as I stared at the scene around me. It was all I could do to keep my mouth from hanging open as I began barging through the small crowd of models.

Transforming into Fatgirl was never fun, and surrounded by beautiful, thin, and extravagantly dressed women made me feel especially young, awkward, and ugly.

My navy and pink bubble-gum ball of a suit didn't help, and I was more grateful than ever to be wearing a mask.

"Augh!"

"It's a monster!"

"Run!"

Various models scrambled to get out of my way. I did my best to stop them without hurting them. I pulled at some of their dresses, slammed down on some of their stilettos, and messed up their hair as I bumped into them. Several of them went flying into the walls as I collided with them.

"AB," I whispered, starting to pant as I cat-slapped a few more women in my way. "What's going on here, anyway? Why are all these models and my mom here?"

"They're here to help with the bidding," AB explained quietly, telling me exactly nothing new. "Keep going. ZZ's set off the silent alarm."

"I didn't hear anything."

"That's the point," AB reminded me. "Head for the main exhibition hall. It's down the hall, take a right, and then head up until you see the sign."

I didn't see much of a choice. "Okay. But how are we going to get Mom to leave with us?"

AB was silent for a long moment, and I didn't like that at all.

Finally, she sighed. "I don't know."

"Is she actually ZZ's business partner?" I asked. "They seemed real friendly."

"We'll talk about it later, Kallie. For now, just do what—"

Her voice broke off as the gunfire started.

"Oh my goodness," I nearly squawked, shaken by the loud sounds. I hurried to duck into a doorway and hide, but I couldn't see where the shooting was coming from.

Please God, don't let me die like this …

I silently prayed for deliverance as the gunshots whipped through the air all around me.

"Ouch!" I felt several spots of stinging pain all over my body as I turned and ran toward the exhibition hall.

"Kallie? Kallie!"

AB's voice broke through my concentration, but only because my eyes had filled up with tears again, this time due to the shock of being shot. I could just barely make out what AB was saying.

"—your suit's bulletproof, but it'll still hurt some," AB warned me. "You'll be black and blue for a bit after we get you back to normal."

I whimpered in reply, and then pounded through into the exhibition hall.

Several models I hadn't run over were already in place around the room. It looked like a casino of its own sorts. Some were standing at different displays, while others were gathered around round tables. There were a few guests already present, too, and quite a few of them were just as confused as I was as they looked back at me. The models carried drinks and giggled and flirted disingenuously, while others helped translate the pricing and item descriptions to the guests. In the far corner of the room, I saw Mandy cozying up to a young, fresh-face man; from Mom's comments earlier, he was the congressman's son who was already in a bunch of trouble, and would undoubtedly find more soon.

I hated how I couldn't help but feel sorry for the naïve, evil idiot, even if he was engaging in crimes against humanity. Remembering that, I still felt sorry that he was clearly outmatched, but I also hoped he'd go to jail where he couldn't hurt anyone with his stupidity anymore.

And he was only one such useful idiot. More were coming into the room.

"Kallie? Are you better?"

I shook my head, relieved that some of the pain from the bullets had disappeared.

Time to focus on the mission.

We were here to find out how ZZ had gotten AB's secret recipe.

She had other secrets and items to auction off, too—and there were plenty of them.

I saw a table full of various objects; there was one full of weapons, and other with jewels, and others with notes and displays. There was one with a kill count on it, and I didn't want to examine things too closely. The gala was almost like a museum, and as much as I hated it, I picked a table full of delicate-looking objects and hurried over.

The bullets paused as I prepared to overturn the table.

"What's going on?" a nearby model wailed, before several of ZZ's security Stasi officers burst into the room and started calling for me to stay where I was and surrender.

I didn't answer them; I was too frightened.

But then I dared myself to do it, and I did it.

I overturned the table.

Glass and ceramic and clay objects shattered on the ground, and gunfire resumed.

"You've got your distraction, AB," I whispered.

But AB wasn't paying attention to me.

"Hello, Zina," I could hear her say.

For a moment, I faltered, stricken by deadly curiosity; I barricaded myself up against the overturned table and let the gunfire ring all around me as I focused on listening in on AB's conversation.

"Margaret White. I've heard plenty about you," ZZ practically purred.

"You shouldn't believe all that you hear."

"I heard you're a brilliant woman in the fields of nuclear nano-tech," ZZ told her.

"Well, I guess you can believe that."

"You're quite an impressive role model for women your age."

"No need for flattery, Zina," AB replied. "We both know we're accomplished women in our respective fields."

"If I had known you wanted to come here, I would have sent an invite."

ZZ seemed to like AB, and I was getting frustrated as they continued to chat amicably with each other.

"Where would the fun be in that?" AB continued. "Besides, my present circumstances are precarious enough. I'm lucky I'm not on the no-fly list."

"Yet."

I could almost see ZZ smiling as she spoke.

The bullets were slowing as more people were trying to escape the room.

I saw a shadow move out of the corner of my eye.

Pain slashed through my arm, and I hollered as my Fatgirl suit ripped down my sleeve, and blood squirted out freely.

"Ow!" I shouted and grabbed my arm, but shifted away.

My feet managed to whip out, and my attacker fell down to the floor with me.

Mom.

It was my own mother. She lay on the floor beside me, a gleaming dagger between us, its blade lined with my blood.

I grabbed it as she did, and we both fought with each other, and I couldn't believe any of this was happening.

How did it come to this?

I always expected Mom and me to fight over things.

But not like this.

I looked into her eyes as we wrestled with the blade, and I almost faltered again.

My mother's red dress was wrinkled, her hair extensions were falling out, and her makeup was smudged.

Plus, she was working for an international criminal, so notorious she'd defected from her own country.

"Let go," Mom shouted.

I didn't.

She kicked her legs out at me, but I held firm.

"Why are you doing this?" I finally whispered. "How can this be for your daughter's own good?"

Mom was caught off guard.

She faltered this time, and I would've been genuinely proud of myself if I didn't want to know the answer so badly.

Before she could answer, or recover from her shock, another figure moved in behind her.

"No!" I shouted, but it was too late.

Agent Grey had reappeared, and he thrust his shotgun down onto my mother's head.

I could almost hear the *crack* of the impact of his weapon on her skull.

"Kallie," Agent Grey said. "Go. Get to Margaret. She'll need your backup with ZZ, especially in her tower."

"What did you do to my mother?" I gasped, looking down at Mom as she lay on the floor.

"I just knocked her out a bit, that's all," Agent Grey assured me. "She'll be fine. Now, I'll cover you here, get what I need, and you go save your grandmother."

I could only nod.

He was likely right; and as much as AB didn't necessarily like him, he'd saved me from my mom's attack.

I held up the dagger. It was a beautiful piece of weaponry, with a sharp edge lined with crystalline steel that glimmered with a violet hue.

"Careful with that," Agent Grey warned. "It's known for its sharpness as well as its beauty."

"What is it?"

"One of ZZ's collected artifacts from her various assignments. She'll likely be able to tell you more about it. But you really must go, Kallie."

I nodded and headed for the door, as Agent Grey pulled out another pair of guns from inside his tuxedo and began firing.

He was certainly a spry old man, I decided.

I held onto my arm as I headed out the room and down the hall. My suit was starting to spilt at the seams some more, and I hated seeing all the bulging fat lumps protruding at my elbows.

As I ran around, looking for ZZ's tower, my phone rang again. When I saw it was Zeus, I reluctantly picked it up again.

"Okay, I can't really talk right now, so this better be good," I said.

"AB's signal is down the hall to the right," Zeus told me. "She's texting me to let you know where to find her."

"Oh. Thanks."

"You're welcome. You know you can count on me to help you, Kallie."

"Yes," I murmured through gritted teeth.

I didn't know why AB always wanted me to trust Zeus—for now—so much, but it was hard to deny his usefulness.

Still, I was tempted to ask how Gloria was taking his absences at the dance, if only to remind him subtly that he needed to apologize to me still.

"Turn left up here, and go through the first door," Zeus instructed. "There's a staircase that'll lead up to ZZ's tower room where AB is waiting."

I turned left down into a new hallway, but there was no door in sight. The walls were full of individual tiles, almost like a bathroom floor, and I swallowed hard. "Are you sure?"

"Yes."

Crimes against humanity, blackmail, likely trafficking, personal security guards … why not a hidden staircase, too? I wondered.

I knocked on the wall, listening to see if I could hear a difference like they do in the movies. I didn't hear anything.

"Can you just push through it?" Zeus asked, and I shrugged, forgetting he couldn't see me.

"I don't think so," I said. "What if it opens up toward me? That won't get me anywhere."

That's when, using my good arm, I pulled out the dagger I still carried. I slid the blade down some of the tiles, hoping to find the lock.

"So, how's the dance?" I asked Zeus, trying to distract myself from how terrible I felt. "Tell me about it. Is Blake there?"

"Yes, and he's drooling over Amory as usual," Zeus said.

"Amory?" I repeated slowly, as my heart sank.

"Yes," Zeus said. "Honestly, it's good you're not here. You'd probably be upset."

I scowled. "You know, you don't have to lie like that," I said. "I know you're eager to make me suffer because you're ugly and I don't want to date you, but I can assure you, I'm already suffering enough right now."

"Kallie, I'm not lying," Zeus said, his voice sad and pathetic, just soft enough I felt sorry for calling him out.

I started to feel worse when I thought of how he and Gloria had mentioned Blake had a crush on Amory, and that he'd wanted to take her to the dance.

"I don't want to hear it," I snapped. "I don't want to—"

Just as I was about to go on another rant about how Blake was perfect and Zeus could shove it, the dagger's blade clicked against something hard, and then it sank into the wall up to its hilt.

If I wasn't so upset, I might've been happy.

My voice trailed off as I leveraged the blade into the wall, and the doorway cracked open. "Jesus."

"It's 'hey-Zeus,'" Zeus whispered quietly, and I immediately felt ashamed of myself like never before.

"I don't want to talk about it anymore," I murmured.

"I know." Zeus sighed. "But if it'll make you feel better, Amory keeps shooting him down. She's made it very clear she's not going to date him. She's even blaming him for losing you as her best friend."

I walked up the staircase, much more slowly than AB would've appreciated.

"I'm sorry I yelled at you," I whispered.

"It's okay. I know you're upset."

"It's not okay," I snapped. "Look … I've got to go save AB, according to Agent Grey. I'll call you later."

"No, Kallie," Zeus said. "Keep me on the line so I can keep helping you."

I arrived at ZZ's door. "Fine," I said, stuffing the phone down into my suit. "I can't talk though, okay? And don't talk loudly, either."

I didn't wait for him to reply.

And then I burst into the room.

"I'm here," I announced, both grandly and stupidly, as I made my entrance.

ZZ and AB were in the middle of the spacious office, engaged in a standoff, almost like the kind from the old western movies. Both of them were armed, their guns aimed at each other with ease. I almost wanted to laugh at the absurd horror of the scene; both ladies looked as cool and calm as ever, almost as if they were enjoying themselves. Several of ZZ's Stasi security guards were lying on the ground, motionless. Behind them, there was a window that spanned the whole wall; through it, the lights of Fort Lauderdale seemed to glow with energy and night life. I could see the evening cruise AB and I were supposedly on in the far distance, sitting out on the ocean's horizon.

"What is *that*?" ZZ finally asked, seemingly amused as she glanced at me.

"My partner," AB replied easily enough, and I felt a twang of pride as the odd smile on ZZ's face quickly disappeared.

"You have become quite eccentric in your old age," ZZ murmured.

"Assuming you make it to my age, perhaps you'll enjoy it as much as I have." AB grinned. "Right now, I'm rather hoping you'll be more docile and finally answer my questions."

"I do not owe you any answers," ZZ said.

I was bleeding and emotionally exhausted, and I was tired of waiting for the today's episode of "Guns, Grit, and Wit" to be over.

Without warning, I launched myself at ZZ. She fired her gun at me, but the bullet missed the mark as I tackled her and squashed her to the ground. I shuffled around as she fought against me, but I'd done this before: I sat on her much more easily than I had done with Frank Whitey, Sorra March, and other Alternants who'd needed a time-out.

"Got her," I said to AB, breathing hard.

"You lack finesse, but I appreciate your arrival," AB said.

"Agent Grey said to come and save you," I said.

"Hmm. I wasn't being a threat to ZZ herself," AB said. "I was rather hoping we could negotiate without bringing violence into it."

"Why do you have the gun out then?" I nearly shouted, as ZZ squirmed underneath me. Her diamonds were digging into my suit, making me even more uncomfortable.

"It's for one's defense as well as offense," AB retorted. "Goodness, have you forgotten all I've taught you about guns already?"

"No," I said, flushing over. "I'd just rather get this over with."

As if on a cue, the loud sirens began blaring out in the distance, and I could gradually hear them getting louder as we listened.

"Shoot," AB muttered. "Eugene probably called for backup."

"Why is that bad?" I asked.

ZZ finally managed to speak. "You will pay for this," she vowed.

"I'm not your real enemy," AB insisted. She glared at me. "I just want the name of the person who sold you my radioactive doughnut recipe. The one that calls for the isotope of Protactinium."

"It was not sold to me," ZZ said haughtily. "It was given to me as a gift for my … more intimate talents."

I nearly gagged. "Ugh, gross."

ZZ smirked. "When you are as alone in the world as I am, it is not that odd—or 'gross,' either. It is a practical reward for being patient with ugly, lonely, insecure, inadequate men."

"Don't make me do this the hard way," AB warned. "I apologize for the unnecessary violence, but if you can just give me the name, I will help you escape."

"Hey!" I objected. "Didn't you tell me that she's a former KGB agent?"

"We all have terrible things we've done in the past," AB said. "I'm not here to make her answer for those crimes—I'm just here to rectify the one against me."

"I do not cooperate with terrorists," ZZ said.

AB reached into her purse. At first, I thought she was going to get another doughnut out. But then she pulled out a small tube.

Agent Iris.

She opened it, put it under ZZ's nose, and after a moment, I felt all resistance fade.

"Just tell us a name," AB said.

"No," ZZ replied.

"Get the memory scrambler," I said, slowly moving off ZZ's body. She was unable to move, thanks to the drug in AB's Agent Iris potion. "I'll look around at what's here."

"I'd rather not force it out of her," AB said. "ZZ's capable of revenge."

"You're worried about that *now*?" I rolled my eyes.

"Good point."

As AB began to alternatively coax, plead, and threaten ZZ, I looked around for clues or items of interest. ZZ's Tower was an office of sorts, and there were plenty of papers and notes strewn about, all written down in Russian, so I couldn't read them, of course. I scooped up a handful anyway and stuffed them into my suit along with the dagger I'd grabbed from Mom.

"What happened to your arm?" AB asked me.

"We'll talk later," I said. "Just get your information and let's get out of here."

I winced as AB shoved the two electrodes into ZZ's temples.

"All right, Zina," AB said. "Tell me, where is my recipe?"

ZZ seemed to resist at first, just as Frank had. "I sold it."

"I thought you were going to auction it off tonight," I said. "Why did you sell it already?"

"You are new to crime, are you?"

AB shook her head at me. "Not now, Fatgirl," she said. "It's something easy to replicate. She can sell it off as much as she wants, even with the promise of it being the original copy."

I guessed I shouldn't have been surprised at the duplicity of a criminal who was trying to retire from the business without getting killed.

"Who did you sell it to?" I asked, making AB glare at me.

"One of my former lovers," ZZ said. Her voice was a reluctant monotone, as AB fiddled with the buttons on her memory scrambler. "Trevor Darlington."

AB and I exchanged a knowing look. We'd come across some evidence before he'd been involved with the Alternants in Cuttingham City; he'd sent a box of radioactive doughnuts to Karen Bright's fiancé, causing the poor old man to see the ghost of his dead wife.

"Why did you sell it to him?"

AB frowned. "So she could blackmail him, for one."

"What?" I glanced back at ZZ, surprised.

"The male ego is a fragile thing," ZZ said. "He was seeking a new venture out in the Heartland. No one takes that part of the country seriously. I knew he was depressed and desperate. As ... small of a man as he was, I did not want him to kill himself. And blackmail money is good money."

"You sold him something he could use to terrorize others."

ZZ laughed quietly. "Power over others is the one thing that makes us believe in ourselves. It is the one thing that allows us to be free."

I could hear someone on the stairs outside the room. I glanced over at AB nervously. The sirens were getting louder.

"Who gave you my recipe?" AB demanded.

The door to the room opened again, and Agent Grey waltzed in. "Margaret, you need to leave now."

He looked over at me. "You'd best leave, too."

"What's happened?" I asked.

"A S.W.A.T. Team has the building surrounded," he explained. "They're making their way up."

"Why did you call in a S.W.A.T. Team?" AB asked Agent Grey, who looked offended.

"I didn't call them in at all," he assured her. "But they're here, and I've already gotten my officers out."

ZZ flinched, and I was starting to realize the Agent Iris was wearing off. As AB argued with Agent Grey, I tried to get their attention.

"You've always caused me trouble," AB accused. "Ever since you were called in to 'consult' on some of my early work, you've always been eager to derail my progress."

"Progress is only useful if it's done the way we want," Agent Grey told her. "Interpol and other agencies around the globe would prefer you didn't accidentally cause an earth-shattering explosion."

"After all the regime changes you've assisted in, that's ironic."

"I'd gladly spark a regime change in whoever's in charge of your common sense, Madame."

And then it happened.

ZZ twitched again, and this time, she scooted away from AB's electrodes. They jerked around, and AB, caught by surprise, fell forward on her control panel.

I was too late.

ZZ cried out in pain, grabbing her head and struggling to get free. The more she struggled, the more she screamed in pain.

"Stop moving," AB hissed, struggling to get her back under control. "Fatgirl, help me!"

I jerked in surprise at hearing her call for help. I hurried to sit on ZZ—a little more gently this time—as AB worked to pack up her stuff.

"Great," she muttered. She turned around and glared at Agent Grey again. "You've cost me my witness."

"She should be fine," I said. "Just like Frank, right?"

AB didn't answer me.

"We've got to go," Agent Grey said, suddenly pulling on me and AB. She packed up her memory scrambler hastily as he pulled us toward the tower's large window. "There's something wrong—"

Smoke and fire suddenly exploded around us.

The building began to crumble and collapse, and I was screaming as Agent Grey placed a strange bracelet on my good, non-bloody wrist, and a moment later, we were falling.

But the bracelet caught me; a line flew out and hooked onto a railing on the opposite side of the street. Beside me, AB and Agent Grey were swinging as well, and I calmed down long enough to see AB looking up at Agent Grey—Eugene—with a sparkle of admiration in her eyes.

Much like he'd done earlier, we were on the street a second later, watching as the convention center casino burned.

Half the building was smashed in and on fire, and I began to cry all over again.

"Your mom is safe," Eugene told me quietly. "I made sure she got out."

I nodded in thanks, still unable to do anything but cry.

"What about ZZ, do you think?" AB asked, looking at the top of the building. The Tower window was blown out, but it was possible she was still alive.

"We'll find out," Eugene said. He put his arm around her. "Shouldn't take long, if you're up for a late-night meeting."

AB looked over at me. "I think I'll have to take a raincheck," she said. "Kallie deserves a bit of a real vacation after all her hard work."

"What about your answers?" I asked miserably.

AB shrugged, and then looked at Eugene. "Answers take time. While we're waiting, you need some self-care."

"But—"

"No buts," AB insisted, eying my bleeding arm and my soot-covered suit. "You're more important than my answers right now."

○ ○ ○ ○

I wasn't sure how I managed to get to sleep that night.

My dreams were full of fire and blood, and my mother was there, both comforting me and trying to kill me at the same time. I didn't sleep well.

But I, evidently, got some rest, since I managed to wake up the next morning; I didn't think AB even slept. She was waiting to get answers, and I wasn't sure she would get them.

But even though we'd had a rough night, or perhaps because of that, AB took me to a grand, expensive spa for a real girls' day.

We spent the day getting mani-pedis, facials, mud baths, and sitting in the sauna in between massages. It was almost like a real vacation, as she'd promised.

It helped that I felt much better, having been returned to my normal, non-Fatgirl self.

I also felt much better that AB paid with a credit card, so there was no more cash-out-of-the-shoe business.

Many of my black and blue marks from the bullets were still present, but they were like little freckles along my body. When my body shrunk down with the anti-F serum injection, the bruises shrunk, too, and AB assured me they would heal quickly. The large cut down my arm faired about the same; by the time I was back to being my regular size, it was only a few inches long. AB promised me she could take care of the scarring when we got back to Arkansas, and she would get me a new suit.

I almost waved her off; I wanted to keep the reminder of my mother's corruption. I didn't have the whole story, but even if she was doing this all for my "own good," I wasn't sure I wanted to know what justified her to violent alliance with an international criminal like ZZ.

For a long time at the spa, we were silent. It seemed like hours passed, and then she finally spoke up.

"I talked to Zeus," she said, speaking as though we'd been talking for hours. "He wanted me to know there was another tracker following us around."

"A tracker?"

"Yes. A ghost lurker," she said. "Or some other strange, internet term. Someone was watching us. I have a feeling it's not a coincidence the building had a sudden 'gas leak,' especially right as I was supposed to be finding out who gave ZZ my recipe."

I rolled my eyes at the news broadcast we'd seen on the events of the previous night. There were numerous reports of rumors, but nothing about ZZ or anything like that.

It was a report worthy of Gynnifer Stills, and that was not a compliment.

"We'll still have to find out who gave her the recipe," AB said slowly. "But if what Zeus said was true, if we can find Trevor Darlington, maybe we'll find some more answers."

"We should find him anyway," I said. "We have more proof that he's the one who tried to sabotage Karen Bright's relationship. And if he's using Darling Donuts to make the radioactive doughnuts, Dad could be in danger."

AB nodded. "I hadn't thought of that. You're right."

I beamed. "See? I make some good calls."

"Speaking of calls," AB said, "Eugene said that someone else called in the S.W.A.T. Team."

"So?"

She shrugged. "I have a hard time believing him."

"You like him, don't you?" I asked, suddenly feeling better.

"Eugene and I have known each other for a long time," AB said non-committedly. "I work in research. He works in law enforcement. Occasionally, our paths cross for the better. Most of the time, it doesn't." She wrinkled her nose, and I didn't want to ask her to explain. "I'll bet he had a field day with all the evidence ZZ had on her. Shame that she'll likely go unpunished. They might even let her free, depending on if they were able to find her or not."

"They weren't able to find her?" I repeated.

"So Eugene says." She scowled. "This is what I mean. I don't like working with someone who lies for their own benefit."

"So she might've gotten away?"

"Yes. There's no trail on her yet, either."

I was curious about something else, as I thought of AB and ZZ talking to each other in the Tower.

"You knew about ZZ's dealings beforehand, with the blackmail and the auction and everything," I said. "Why couldn't we have call the police ourselves? If there were traffickers and drugs and weapons all there, wouldn't the police—"

"Come on, Kallie. Don't be like this," AB said. "If the government wanted to clean up crime like that, it would've been taken care of by now. There's good money to be made in these deals—and blackmail, too, as you've seen from ZZ. As much as you don't like it, plenty of ill-advised activities go on, and we let them go on so there isn't an active war every other week. Or something worse."

"But—"

"You know what? Never mind." AB shook her head as I felt some amount of goodwill and hope die inside my heart. "You don't need to worry about it, Kallie."

I sank further down into my mud bath. "Good to know."

A few moments passed between us before I looked over at AB. She was sitting in her own mud-filled tub, her gaze lost in space. Usually it was a bland, critical-thinking look; but this time, there was a tiny sparkle in her eye. "Are you thinking about that Agent Grey guy again?"

"That," AB said deliberately, "is something you don't need to know."

I smirked. I had a lot of trouble in my own life to deal with when we got back to Cuttingham City; I had to find Zeus and apologize and thank him for his help in person, I had to make-up with Amory, I had to find a way to convince Blake I was the one he was better off dating, and I had to protect my dad while I struggled to make sense of what my mom was doing.

But for now, it was nice to see AB had her own personal issues, too.

Yes. That's definitely good to know.

Fatgirl

BLACK POWERS

EPISODE 8

○ ○ ○ ○

C. S. Johnson

It's "Good Cop, Bad Cop," Not Radioactive Alternant Cop …

FATGIRL
BLACK POWERS

○ ○ ○ ○

Glumly, I watched the numbers on my phone as they changed from 6:29 to 6:30. I'd been awake for three hours already, dreading the start of the new day and the new week. My alarm was just about to sound when I quickly and vehemently hit the snooze button.

I slammed my phone down on my nightstand before I smothered a moan into my pillow.

Not only had I lost precious beauty sleep, I would look like I had, too.

I could put on some Kitty-Eyes.

Violently, I shut that thought down, too. Amory would denounce me as a "fad-chaser," no matter that I'd started the fad in question.

It was just a simple fact of life: Now that the Spring Fling was over, trends had to switch.

If my life were normal, I would've made it my goal to show up to school with something even more outrageously outrageous. Maybe bring goth fashion into the forefront, or some heavy, Egyptian-style eyeliner; maybe even temporary face tattoos or something with glitter. No matter what I picked, I'd get people to follow me in my outrageousness before denouncing it roughly two weeks later.

If my life were normal …

I sighed into my pillow. Normal didn't mean I wouldn't run into problems.

At the school's last lacrosse game, Blake Turner and the rest of the Cuttingham Crusaders donned Kitty-Eyes to show support for "animal rights." It was the same fake reason I'd given to justify using the Kitty-Eyes look to cover my large, drooping eye-bags, so the whole team had looked like idiots, even if they were well-meaning idiots.

It really shouldn't have been so bad.

But then the team lost to the Eagleston Eagles—and by a large, humiliating degree, too.

No one really cared about animal rights after that.

Who really wants a bunch of losers defending their cause? I even saw a news report that discussed how one of Cuttingham City's pet shops cheered for our team initially, and then they distanced themselves afterwards on social media. I couldn't believe that even made the local news until I remembered Gynnifer Stills was still employed by WACC's TV station.

My friend June told me the Eagleston Eagles and their school were now wearing Kitty-Eyes to celebrate their win.

I pushed my face further into my pillow.

My cause had been co-opted and turned into something radically different from what it originally meant. When I told AB about it, she just stirred her tea with a spoon and said, "Well, now you know how Ben Franklin would feel about modern-day democracies."

I promptly replied that he was dead, and so he probably didn't care, and that was all I could handle of AB and her apathy toward my dilemma. Then, I turned around, marched upstairs, and went to bed.

Only to wake up at three and wind up staring at my ceiling as I tried not to think about my mother.

My phone's alarm buzzed again, and I slid my face off my pillow enough to glare at it. I reached over and slammed my finger down on the snooze button again.

I missed at first, and hit my nightstand instead; it jolted sharply and several of my books and other items dropped onto the floor with a graceless crash.

Groaning, I finally got out of bed.

Reaching down, I gathered up the fallen items. There were magazines, and I tried not to examine them too closely. More than one of the magazines held several pictures of my mom. Eagerly, I threw them in the trash.

I picked up Mom's old copy of *The Art of War*. I didn't know what to do with it; I didn't want to think of her while I read it, but I'd also learned a thing or two about being popular from it.

In the end, I stuck it back on my nightstand. If I wanted to lose everything that reminded me of my mom, I would have to scorch the earth and then kill myself.

I didn't want to do that; it would be worse than giving up.

Instead, I decided I would take what I'd been given and make my own way in the world.

Easier said than done.

Immediately after making my silent vow, I caught sight of the last item that had fallen to the floor.

It was the dagger I'd accidentally stolen from ZZ at her retirement gala—the same one my mom had used against me, the same one which I'd used to find the entrance to ZZ's tower, and the same one I'd accidentally stuffed into the spare radioactive doughnut I'd concealed under my Fatgirl suit.

I swallowed hard, and then reached out for it.

I didn't know any of its history, or how ZZ had managed to acquire it. Either way, I didn't really care. It had scratched me, made me bleed, and now things were personal.

So, now it personally belonged to me.

Still, I tucked it under the side of my mattress. I didn't need Dad to find it and wonder what kind of funny business I'd gotten myself into.

Although, I had to admit to myself, it would be interesting to see what he thought of AB being a "house grandma."

I dressed in a new outfit I hadn't worn, hoping that the new baby-doll dress would be enough to excuse me from a new make-up trend. I was happy with it; the dress was a bright lavender color, dotted with pansies and violets, and the little droopy-bubble sleeves managed to hide the scar I'd gotten from fighting with my mom in Fort Lauderdale.

After checking myself over and applying a double-layer of concealer under my eyes, I picked up my phone and headed for my door. I paused for a moment, and then grabbed a flower-patterned parasol from behind my door, feeling inspired.

Maybe this can help hide some of the shadows.

After that, I put on a smile, small as it was, and walked down to the kitchen.

AB was there, sipping from her teacup, reading over a stack of papers. It was almost as if she'd been a fixed point in our home for years instead of the last six weeks or so. I glanced around and saw a note from Dad on the refrigerator, telling me he'd be home late and he loved me.

Well, it was a nice gesture, anyway.

I turned back to AB.

"What are you working on?" I asked as I opened the fridge.

"Good morning, darling. I'm just looking through some of the papers you stole from ZZ's office." AB grimaced. "My Russian's a little rusty. What are you doing up so early?"

"Uh, I have school, remember? Duh."

"It's Spring Break this week."

My fingers clenched the side of the fridge door, and as gently, nicely, as cool and in control as possible, I shut it.

AB grinned from behind her teacup. "Spring Break comes after the Spring Fling, remember? Duh."

How does she know that? And how did I forget that?

"Well, I'll feel better about going back to bed at least," I finally muttered after I found my voice again. "And I guess that'll give me some time to properly figure out what to wear."

"I think you look lovely." AB's compliment had no hint of insincerity, and I completely had no idea whether she actually meant it or not.

But at least I had the week off. I could pretend I was still in Florida. I didn't have to see my friends, I didn't have to pretend everything was alright, and I didn't have to do much of anything, other than make sure I didn't eat and veg around all week. After all, I still had to maintain my figure.

For what?

I paused; I thought I wasn't going to be like my mom anymore.

But what was I going to do? Just give up on everything? All at once?

I shook my head. I still had to maintain my figure—for myself. I liked who I was. Or at least, I liked how I looked.

I opened the fridge again and pulled out some eggs.

"So, tell me, what's our next plan? Are we going to try to call Mom again? Go after Trevor Darlington?" I pulled out the milk and turned on the stove. A teasing grin curled onto my lips. "Set up a midnight rendezvous with Agent Grey?"

AB arched her brow at me but said nothing as she took another sip of her tea.

"Is there any gin in there?" I asked, suddenly curious.

"Not this time." AB smirked. "Despite what's in movies or TV shows, alcohol isn't recommended or required for jobs such as these."

"I see you've managed to switch the topic off Agent Grey." I cracked several eggs into a bowl. I took out half of the yolks and began to whisk it all together with the milk. "Does he bother you that much?"

"In truth, no." AB shrugged. "I'm just glad we were able to get out of the gala without me owing him another favor."

"Another?" I narrowed my eyes. "What kind of favor, anyway?"

To my surprise, AB turned away and coughed, almost as if to hide a blush. "Nothing you need to worry about, Kallie."

Immediately and perhaps instinctively, I agree with her. "Good to know."

"He did want me to tell you thanks again," AB said. "He was glad Interpol was able to get a hold of ZZ after all these years. Although I imagine she is pretty grateful for you, too."

"She is?" My eyes widened in surprise. "Why?"

"She's nice and safe now, in her own special prison," AB explained. "Being taken care of thanks to her new Sugar Daddy, Uncle Sam. Thanks to American taxpayers, she'll have 'free' healthcare and education for life, unless she works out a deal. I'm sure she will, too, thanks to her still-apparent sex appeal."

I gripped my spatula more tightly. "Shouldn't it be because of her information and secrets, instead?"

"Sex appeal and sexual experience are vastly different things, no matter what people say, but they have their mutual advantages," AB said. "She'll make it seem like she has more than she does, and then she'll still hold out. Although she's giving them a new reason to think she can't be so cooperative."

"What's that?"

"Agent Grey mentioned that ZZ's saying she can't remember things perfectly anymore, and that my memory swiper device caused several of her brain functions to be compromised." AB rolled her eyes. "Plenty of stupider, uglier, more ambitious people have used that excuse and gotten away with it. I don't see why ZZ won't, even if she's lying."

"She has to be lying." Angrily, I finished scrambling my eggs, trying not to think how that could've had happened with ZZ's brain while AB was questioning her.

"I honestly believe her. It's true that I didn't release her from the device properly," AB murmured in a low, disgruntled voice. "She's showing signs of severe anxiety."

"Oh, how sad," I murmured sarcastically. I didn't know whether or not to feel sorry for ZZ. She was a wanted criminal who was seeking her fortune through blackmail and other unsavory methods. From what AB had told me of her, she'd been trained from a young age to grow into a life of crime, but if I had to feel sorry for anyone, I decided I felt sorry for her teenage self.

It pained me that I could still see her with Mom, talking with her like they were best friends, back at the gala.

"Don't feel sorry for her, Kallie," AB said. "ZZ might've been groomed for a life of crime, but she still did a great deal of damage, and knowingly, too. Those of us who experience violence are called to break the cycle, not embrace it."

"How do you do that?" I crossed my arms. "I swear, you can read my mind some days. You need to stop that."

"Believe it or not, I was once your age. I know what it feels like to have sympathy for the devil. But I've learned at this point you can't expect the devil to do the same for you, and when he gets some semblance of justice, he deserves it." AB put her empty teacup down.

"But who are we to dole out justice?" I asked quietly. "And if it was our fault her memory's shot now—"

"Well, you're Fatgirl. And I'm the one who's good name has been tarnished by the loss of my recipe—and further implicated by her selling it to Trevor Darlington." AB smiled. "If you ask me, we're the perfect ones to give her some comeuppance. You're an overweight superhero, and I'm an old lady with nothing to lose. We're the last people she would've suspected of causing her trouble. Ironic, isn't it? We didn't even use the doughnuts for her."

"We still didn't get the name of the guy who gave it to her," I pointed out. "And with her memory all scrambled, she's not going to confess anything reliable now."

She held up the papers she'd been reading when I came into the room. "Thankfully, she had plenty of records. And you managed to grab some of them before we got out of there. This is good work, Kallie."

"You know it." I concentrated on getting my eggs out from the pan and onto my plate to hide my smile.

"Once I finish translating these, I'll be able to piece together something useful. Maybe I can leverage it for another favor from someone."

"Agent Grey?" I asked, teasing her again.

AB's lips pursed together. "I imagine not."

I grabbed some salt. "What about that other guy? The one you met at the airport after calling in a terrorist threat?"

"KP?" AB frowned. "Perhaps. Keith's a little peeved at me at the moment."

"What, you mean he can't take a joke about terrorists?" I pretended to be surprised. "Frankly, I think Agent Grey would be willing to owe you some favors."

"Kallie, I'd rather not talk about him."

"I've noticed," I replied, eating my eggs. "But I also overheard quite a bit of your conversations while we were in Florida. You might want to consider asking him out on a date or something."

"Eugene and I have a complicated past," AB muttered.

"Well, you both still have a shot at a simple future."

"It's not so simple, I'm afraid." AB wrinkled her nose. "He could be one of the people who sold my recipe to ZZ."

I didn't know what to say to that. "Does he really fit ZZ's description?" I asked. "She said your recipe was a practical payment for ugly, insecure, and lonely men. I don't know about lonely, but Agent Grey didn't seem ugly or insecure. He was pretty in-control of things while we had to get out of the gala."

"Hmm." AB shrugged as she stood up and refilled her tea. "That's something to think about, I guess. If nothing else, she did confirm it was a man she got it from. I suspected as much, but it's good to hear it for certain … "

Her voice trailed off, and I went back to finishing off my eggs.

Before I could go back to teasing her about Agent Grey—since it was clear she didn't mind pushing Zeus on me—my phone buzzed.

I saw the notification pop up and groaned.

"Can you and Zeus *both* read my mind?" I asked, glaring over at AB.

"We can't read your mind, Kallie, but we're not stupid, either."

I wisely decided to ignore that. "I was literally just thinking of him and he texted me asking if it's okay if he comes over. Says he needs me to help him with something today."

"Well, help him, then," AB said, shooing me away from the table as she gathered her things and wiped down the table. "I agree we'll need to check in on Trevor Darlington, and I'll need to finish examining these documents."

"Ugh." I put my face in my hands. "I don't want to do anything today. I still need to recover from this weekend."

"You'll be fine." AB patted my shoulder encouragingly. "And anyway, Zeus is doing me some favors. You can at least do something for him."

"What kind of favors are you getting from a high school boy?" I asked, narrowing my eyes in suspicion.

"Nothing like the ones I get from Eugene," AB assured me. "But you don't need to know about them, either."

I scowled at her and angrily snatched my parasol up. "Fine. But I'm only doing this so I don't have to be stuck here with you all day."

"Whatever gets you moving, darling."

○ ○ ○ ○

"Whatever gets you moving, darling," I muttered, angrily mimicking AB's voice as Zeus pulled up to my driveway a short while later.

His mom's car still had the embarrassing decal on it, and Zeus himself was still a bit of an embarrassment, too—although I did notice he'd tried to improve himself. I first saw that he wasn't wearing his usual oversized sweatshirt. Instead, he was wearing a button-down polo, and he'd combed down his shaggy-hair look.

He was actually sort of nice looking.

I didn't want to think that, though, and I consoled myself by remembering he was normally ugly, and just cleaning up didn't make him suddenly handsome.

He's no Blake Turner.

Zeus pulled up next to me and got out of the car.

"What's wrong?" I asked, watching as he practically scampered over to me.

"I'm getting the door for you," he said, before opening the passenger side of the car. "You're okay for hanging for a while, right?"

"I guess so. But I don't need you to do that." I rolled my eyes as he opened the door.

"It's a respectful thing to do."

"It's a patronizing thing to do."

He sighed. "Are you going to argue with me all day?"

"If I feel like it."

Zeus laughed. "I know Florida was bad, but I have to admit, I don't know how you've managed to become our city's great superhero. You're not really that mature, you know."

"Government contacts, radioactive doughnuts, and a psycho-grandma on a quest for revenge," I said, counting off my fingers all the reasons why I currently hated my life. "I'm just collateral damage when it comes down to it."

"Well, you're the muscle, too. And don't forget, you're using AB to get your mom back."

At that, I slid into the car without a word. I'd been angry, but at his remark, I just felt depressed.

I was glad I had an extra moment to myself before he got back into the driver's seat; it gave me a moment to compose myself and prepare my list of terms and conditions.

"Thanks for helping me out," Zeus said. He put the car back in drive and we started off.

"Let me stop you right there." I was the passenger, but I was going to be in control of this outing. "I just want to get this over with. Where are we going? And before you get some kind of idea that this is a date, let me just stop you right there. This is *not* a date."

"I never said it was," Zeus said, although I managed to make him blush. "I just asked if you could come over to my house for a while."

"There's a lot that that implies," I snapped, irritated he was trying to gaslight me into thinking this was just something harmless. "Tell me now, did AB put you up to this?"

"AB?"

"Yes. She knows the Florida trip was hard for me, and getting you to distract me with some kind of goofy afternoon adventure seems like something she would do."

Zeus stopped at a red light. He kept his eyes straight ahead, but I saw his hands grip the steering wheel more tightly. "No. My mom wanted me to invite you over, so I did."

The silence between us was sudden and palpable.

He looked down. "I'm sorry if I was too insistent about it—"

"No," I cut him off. "You weren't."

"She's doing okay, just so you know," Zeus said quietly. His voice was shaking a little as we started driving again. "But she wanted to meet you."

A lump formed in my throat, so I could only nod. Shame burned through me more than ever as I remembered I'd promised Zeus I would come and meet his mom since she was sick. I looked down at my outfit again. The bright colors and the flowery parasol seemed too bright and happy; it almost made me sick now.

"Thanks to that call for donations Fatgirl made at that political debate, we were able to get a lot of the equipment and nurses to come to our house instead of having to put her in a hospice," Zeus added.

"I don't actually have to be Fatgirl for this, do I?" I asked, suddenly feeling queasy.

"No. Oh, no, of course not." Zeus let out a half-laugh. "No. I told her we're just friends and you've been real fun to hang out with lately. So she's happy."

I couldn't imagine why. I was hardly the best company Zeus could've had. "Are you sure she's not confusing me with Gloria?"

"I'm sure."

I hated how he smiled when he said that, but I remained silent. I'd already been enough of a jerk. He was entitled to be one back to me.

And Zeus wasn't much of a jerk, really. I'd never seen him be mean to anyone, even Blake Turner when he was making fun of him.

We pulled up to Zeus' house, which was actually very nice and normal. I didn't know what I'd been expecting; maybe a slum sort of neighborhood, or perhaps something a little more Mexican? But I saw the house wasn't that different from my own; no one would've expected it holds such secrets and sadness.

Zeus helped me out of the car, and I let him. I gave him my hand and squeezed it, trying to comfort him and assure him I would be good while we were here, and that I was sorry his mom was dying and that I was also sorry for being a pretentious drama queen.

It was hard to convey that mix of feelings into what roughly amounted to a handshake, but I hoped I succeeded.

Zeus led me inside. "Mom? We're here."

A warm, weak voice called out to us. "Come to the sunporch, honey."

Zeus nodded to me, and gestured for me to follow him.

We headed back through the halls to an atrium. I could see the light reflecting off the windowed walls; there must've been a whole garden of vases, all full of flowers, all strewn abundantly about the room. Just before we entered, I grabbed Zeus by the arm. "Wait."

"What is it?" he asked, surprised and quiet. If he was afraid I was going to back out, I wouldn't have blamed him.

I did kind of want to leave.

But I didn't want to abandon him and leave him all by himself, either.

I took his hand and held it and curled my arm into his, and I leaned against him ever so slightly. My eyes met his; I understood that I was here in hopes of cheering up his mom, and I wanted him to know, without a doubt, I was determined to do just that.

"Okay," I whispered. "Ready."

He nodded.

Together, we walked into the room.

I'm not sure what I'd expected his mom to be like, so I was a little surprised to see a willowy looking woman. She was clearly very underweight, and the model part of me was conditioned to be jealous more than the grown-up part of me was instinctively sympathetic. Her hair was most likely gone, but I couldn't tell for sure, since her head was wrapped up with a pretty silk scarf. She wore a lovely lace-covered housedress under a soft-looking robe as she reclined on a small couch. I saw there was a medical bed in the room; the vases full of flowers had hidden it from my view, but as we came into the room, I saw there was other medical equipment, too.

When she saw us, her eyes lit up and her smile brightened her whole demeanor.

Zeus walked over to her and dropped my hand to hug her and give her a kiss on the cheek. "Hi, Mom."

"Hello there," Mrs. Evans replied. She turned to me. "I am excited to meet you at last, Kallie. Zeus has told me so much about you."

"Hopefully I'll live up to the hype," I replied, as Mrs. Evans extended her arms to me, too.

I didn't hesitate; I stepped right up into them. I fell into her hug deeply, thinking of my own mom, and I hugged her as delicately and ardently as I could.

When I pulled away, I reached for Zeus again. He took my hand and led me to sit down at an identical couch just off to the side of his mother's. I shifted closer to Zeus as we sat there.

"You have a lovely home, Mrs. Evans," I said, looking around.

"Thank you." She gestured toward my dress. "I love your dress; you look just like a princess in springtime wearing it."

"Thank you. I especially like it because it has pockets." I grinned as I pulled out my phone from one of its hidden folds. "I guess you like flowers. Did Mr. Evans rob a flower shop for you?"

"Something like that," Zeus muttered disgruntledly.

Despite his sour expression, I assumed he was joking when Mrs. Evans only laughed.

"My husband knows I adore them," she explained. "With the medical funding we'd been given from Fatgirl's campaign, we were able to afford to get a lot of them."

Beside me, Zeus leaned against me a little more firmly.

If I'd tried to tell him of my sorrow and selfishness earlier when I'd held his hand, he was thanking me now with his touch.

"They do cheer me up after a long day. And it's comforting to see them when I wake up."

I nodded. "My dad's tried to keep our house garden alive for a while, but he'll have to get some professionals in to fix it up at this rate. My mom was the better gardener between the two of them, but …"

But I don't want to talk about my mom.

My voice trailed off, and Zeus jumped in to save me.

"Would you like me to get something for you to drink?" he asked. "I think we have some lemonade in the fridge."

"Oh, that would be lovely," Mrs. Evans said. "Get a tray out and put some cookies on it for Kallie, too, please."

"Do you need some help?" I asked.

Zeus smiled at me. "No, I'll be fine. Be right back."

He left me alone with his mother, who let out a weary sigh once Zeus was out of earshot. "He's such a good boy."

"Yes," I agreed warmly. "He is."

"Jose, my husband, wants him to work in the family business more, now that he's getting older. But I am glad he's going to school, and he's making friends like you. I was sorry to hear you were out of town for the Spring Fling."

"Oh, yeah, I was in Florida with my grandmother. But I'm glad he was still able to go and have fun."

"He assured me that you didn't mind that he took another one of your friends. She didn't have a date and wasn't sure she wanted to go alone, so I'm glad he was able to help her, too. Did you see the picture the school sent home?"

She reached over to the end table and picked up a small scrapbook. Inside was a picture of Zeus and Gloria at the Spring Fling, smiling underneath a small garland of fake flowers. Gloria had on a minimal amount of make-up and a nice, if generic dress, and Zeus had on a nice shirt, tie, and jacket. He did look pretty handsome, all things considered. The jacket made him look thinner, and standing next to Gloria made him look taller.

"It looks very nice," I said. "I'm sorry I missed it. Zeus and I would've had a lot of fun. Maybe next year, we'll be able to go together."

"I hope so." Her eyes twinkled. "I think it's very important to have those growing up experiences."

"Well, there's plenty of time to be old when you're actually old," I said, making her laugh a little.

"I can see why Zeus likes you so much," she said, making me feel utterly pathetic as I remembered she probably wasn't going to get much older.

I was torn between telling her she didn't know me that well and begging her to tell me what exactly it was that made her think I was such a good friend for her son.

"Can I ask how you two came to know each other?" Mrs. Evans asked, thankfully changing the subject.

"I told you, we met in Mr. Embers' class before, Mom." Zeus appeared in the doorway, carrying a small silver tray. On it, he balanced a pitcher of lemonade with several cups and a small plate of cookies. I noticed he was blushing a little as he set it down. He began to pour out the drinks.

"Let me hear Kallie's side," Mrs. Evans said. She looked back at me. "Zeus tells me these things, but I know it's only one side of the story. He's a little shyer than he'd like to admit, I think. Especially since you're his first real girlfriend."

My eyes opened in surprise and panic.

But before I could say anything, Zeus dropped the cup he was holding, sending it flying to the floor. "Mom! It's not like that. Kallie and I—"

I could already see the light in Mrs. Evans' eyes dimming as he struggled to explain we were just friends.

"Zeus, stop." Quickly, I stood up. "I think this has gone far enough."

Zeus looked crushed.

"I think your mom is smart enough to know we've been dating for a while now. Even if we weren't sure how she'd feel, I think we might as well admit the truth."

He went from looking crushed to looking confused, and at his stupefied look, I grinned and turned to his mom. "I hope you're not upset, Mrs. Evans."

The sparkle in her eye came back, stronger than ever. "Oh, of course not, Kallie. But Mr. Evans might be, so we'll keep it our little secret."

I felt ashamed at how relieved I felt.

"My dad's not eager for me to date anyone either," I said hurriedly. "But Zeus has always been so nice and friendly, and … "

I turned away from him, picking up the cup he'd dropped as I thought of all the time we had spent together because of my Fatgirl troubles—but even before then, he'd been the one to cover for my humiliating, world-ending fart in Mr. Embers' class, and not only had he recognized me as Fatgirl, he willingly stayed by my side and helped me and AB in our mission.

I looked back over at him. "And he's the only one who really knows the real me."

Zeus gave me a grateful look as I handed him the cup he'd dropped. "Thank you."

I knew he didn't mean giving me back the cup. "Of course, darling."

We sat down together and I began to tell Mrs. Evans about how we met; I largely told her the truth, even about my huge fart catastrophe, and just changed all my Fatgirl stuff to school assignments. Zeus seemed too shocked to lie, so I did all the lying for us, only prompting him to nod or verbally agree with me every so often.

It was only when his mom was starting to nod off that I realized we'd been there for nearly two hours. I nudged Zeus.

"If you don't mind, I think I should be heading back home, Mrs. Evans," I said politely. "My, er, grandmother and I had some things we needed to do today."

She nodded wearily. "I've had a lovely time today," she said. "Thank you for coming. You've been an absolute joy, Kallie. I'm glad Zeus has someone like you in his life."

I reached down to hug her again while Zeus cleaned up the lemonade and leftover cookies. She embraced me tightly. "Promise me you'll take care of him," she whispered. "He's my baby, and I know I can't be with him forever."

Tears burned in my eyes as I held her. After all the lying I'd done, it was hard to believe I could finally hesitate. I swallowed the lump in my throat and nodded into her shoulder. "I will. I promise."

After Zeus finished cleaning up, I excused myself while he said goodbye to her, claiming I needed to go to the restroom.

Once I was inside, I locked the door and turned on the fan. It was loud enough that I let myself cry quietly, upset at the world.

All of this would've turned out much differently, if Mrs. Evans wasn't dying … if my mom wasn't some human rights abuser … if my life wasn't in shambles …

It took some time, but I fixed my make-up before I left the room, determined to hide all my weakness and sadness.

Zeus escorted me out of the house. Neither of us said a word until he opened the car door for me.

"Thank you for that," Zeus said quietly.

"Yeah, well, you're welcome." I felt really glum about lying to his mom. I didn't lie about how Zeus was the only one who really knew me. And yet, he'd admitted he loved me anyway. And aside from the "school assignments," I didn't even lie about much else. Zeus was a nice guy who'd saved me from trouble, and other times joined me in getting into trouble.

Would it really be so hard to date Zeus? For real?

I already knew the answer: yes—and no.

I pulled out my parasol and opened it, trying to put on my best haughty face. "Just don't tell anyone at school, okay? Or I'll have no choice but to kill you."

"Oh, Kallie." Zeus choked out a small laugh as he reached out and wrapped me in a hug.

I wasn't prepared for that.

Zeus was taller and larger than me, but he was soft and warm. I felt as though I was being swallowed up by a sweaty, flower-smelling teddy bear. At first, I went still and dropped my parasol in surprise—but then I wrapped my arms around his neck and hugged him back.

I knew he was sad about his mom. Who wouldn't be?

Zeus had told me before they'd moved here to Cuttingham City because they had some of the best and most recent cancer treatments in the country. While I found that incredible in itself, especially since it was true, he'd only been here for a few months. He didn't have a lot of other friends—really none, if I thought about it.

That meant he only had me, as much as I might not have liked it all the time.

"I'm sorry," he whispered.

"No, it's okay." I brushed his hair off to the right side of his face. It looked nicer that way. "I understand. And I'll be here for you. Just like you're here for me."

I was about to tell him we would face his trouble together, even if it was an enemy Fatgirl couldn't sit on, when my eyes met his.

All over again, I was struck at how his eyes didn't seem to match up with the rest of him. They were a beautiful moonbeam blue, full of sadness and love and stars.

He wants to kiss me.

The second I realized it, I knew it was true. But I didn't retreat.

Instead, very, very slowly, I leaned in and closed my eyes.

"Fatgirl, Fatgirl, calling Fatgirl … "

I nearly jumped a mile high at my phone's ringtone.

Zeus barely moved, but I saw his cheeks were bright red as I scrambled to pick up my phone.

It was AB, of course.

"What is it?" I asked, trying not to sound as frustrated as I was. "We're just finishing up our visit with Zeus' mom."

"I'm going to need Fatgirl," AB said. "We have a situation."

In the background, I could hear the familiar beeping of the Phiger going off. Dread trickled through me, sending a chill down my spine.

"There's been another doughnut delivery," AB said. "And we've got to move quickly."

"Who is it?"

"Officer Max Powers."

I frowned. "Who?"

"He's the officer who helped you the night the Amphitheatre was nearly shot up. Tall man, deep voice, very gentle eyes? He helped us get Frank Whitey back into prison?"

I thought back to that night and sighed. "He was also your contact on the police force."

"Yes."

"So, someone is making this more personal to you."

"We can't be sure about that," AB replied smoothly. "But it sure seems like it, doesn't it? I'm on my way to get you and Zeus. We're going to need his help. I'm afraid the Protactinium is going to have a very negative effect on Officer Powers."

"Why?"

"I'll explain when I get there. But we need to hurry. Otherwise, this could get very, very ugly. Trust me."

"Well, you would know ugly," I muttered as she hung up on me.

I was about to explain there was a new Alterant we had to go deal with when AB's Imperial came racing around the block.

"Kallie." Zeus somehow blushed even more as he said my name. "Um … "

Oh, no. He wants to ask about what just happened.

Heat flared onto my cheeks as I shook my head. "Later. AB's here."

Zeus nodded, as understanding as always. "Okay."

It didn't take me long to be glad AB interrupted us, even if we had to put up with her horrendous driving.

I didn't know why I almost kissed Zeus.

Curiosity?

Sympathy?

My own loneliness?

Some detestable combination of all those?

I would worry about it later, I decided. Or even better—not at all.

It helped that AB was practically flying through the city highway lanes, and since I was still the normal-sized me, I was rolling around in the back seat at the sudden swerves and twists and turns and cut-offs.

Zeus was just as uncomfortable in the front; from where I was sitting, I could see his knuckles were white as they gripped his armrests.

"Thank you for coming," AB said to him, much more warmly than she would ever talk to me. "Max and I have a good history together, and if Kallie is right and more dangerous, personal connections of ours are being targeted, we need to be proactive."

"How long have you known him?" Zeus asked as AB zealously rounded another corner.

"I was working on a testing site in Atlanta with one of my other projects—"

"Wait, stop," I said, suddenly horrified. "You have other projects besides Project: SERUM?"

"Of course, Kallie," AB said, whirling the wheel around as she cut off another trucker. I was about to remind her that her only son, my father, was a trucker too, when she continued. "Before he became an officer, Max Powers was studying to be a psychologist. He met me as an intern for the NAH. That was also the year his brother was murdered."

"Murdered?" Zeus asked.

"His younger brother, Will, was coming to visit him from Chicago and got mugged on the MARTA system. From the reports, a cop was nearby and tried to shoot the mugger. He missed and hit Max's brother instead."

"That's terrible," I said.

"Yes." AB wrinkled her nose. "The mugger, a man named Larry Martin, is still in jail. The cop's been put into a witness protection system."

"Why?" I asked. "Wouldn't he be in jail, too?"

"It was ruled an accidental death in court. Incidents like these are heavily investigated to make sure there was no malfeasance." AB gripped her steering wheel before she slammed her foot on the gas again. "Bad cops, and possibly-bad cops, undermine the faith and goodwill of their community. The media had a field day with the story, of course; it lets their industry look good in comparison."

Ominously, AB's Phi-ger on the dashboard beeped in warning. We were getting closer.

"So, what happened to Officer Powers after that?" I asked. "Why did he become a cop?"

"I imagine because it was a way to make sense of his trauma. Too bad. He would've been a good analyst. Now he does street work here. Not much seems to have changed, personality-wise, but this is where the Protactinium comes in."

I swallowed the sudden lump of fear in my throat. "What's happened to him?"

"Let's just say you should be glad I have an extra bullet-proof suit ready for you," AB said, as she passed me back a brown paper bag and fabric spool of navy blue and bright pink. You'll need to keep your hood on, too."

"How can I help?" Zeus asked.

"I need you to keep watch on Kallie and Max's movements, same as you did while we were in Florida," AB said. She pointed down to her purse, which was at Zeus' feet. "I have a computer set up in there. Get it out and get started."

"Sure thing, Dr. White," Zeus agreed. He paused for a moment. "Hey … I was wondering, would I be able to ask you for a favor, too, one day?"

At his question, I frowned. What could Zeus possibly want from AB? As much as I'd seen her work in action, I didn't think AB would have access to the cure for his mom's cancer.

"Depends on the favor," AB said breezily enough. "We can talk it over later."

"Okay."

"Right now, I need you to focus on finding out if we're being watched over the web, and then if so, I need to know who it is. ZZ's information wasn't much, but it's enough for me to conclude the one who sold it to her knows I'm looking for it, and he's eager to distract me," AB said.

"Not to mention humiliate me," I grumbled, pulling on my suit with extreme care.

The fabric was tight and light, and if I didn't have to balloon up to the size of a small whale, I would've enjoyed wearing it. I opened the paper bag and sighed at the sight of a doughnut.

"I swear, if I ever get out of this Fatgirl mess, I'm never eating doughnuts again," I muttered. I ruefully took a bite, but it was the sweet taste of my childhood, and I couldn't completely hate it.

"We're headed to Maple Lane," AB said, as she blazed off the nearest highway exit, nearly sending the car into a spiral. "That's where Max was last seen."

"What does he look like?"

"That's the worst part," AB said. "He didn't have a noticeable transformation like some of our other Alterants. He's in his uniform, and he's holding up and threatening others. If we don't move, he'll be killed—and others will be, too."

"Be careful, Kallie," Zeus said. He was already typing on AB's mini-laptop. "I'm getting a lot of chatter about it, and none of it is good. Some people are already injured."

"He shot people?"

"No. But there was a stampede of people trying to get away from him." Zeus held up the computer to show me he'd hacked into some of the traffic feeds.

In the streets over, I could hear the ambulances.

"This isn't good," I whispered.

"No. It never is, really," AB agreed.

I could only hope I would be able to stop it before other people—and myself—got hurt.

AB dropped me off a block over from where Officer Powers was stuck in bad-cop mode. I was nice and fat and muscled up as I slid out of her car and rolled into the nearest alleyway. I felt better knowing Zeus was keeping watch out for us, too, and that he knew how to obscure the cameras and blur their feeds. After more than a few runs as Fatgirl under my belt, I was beginning to almost enjoy myself.

But at the gunshots in the distance, I literally slowed my roll a bit.

I clicked on the earpiece. "Are you sure about the bulletproofing on this suit?"

"It'll be fine," AB replied. "Just find a way to sit on him, and I'll be around to get the blood sample."

I groaned. "All right."

AB chuckled a little. "Oh, come on. It's not homework, Kallie. Cheer up."

"I'd rather be doing homework," I muttered back.

I came out of the shadows and there he was.

Officer Max Powers was in the same uniform he'd been wearing when I'd met him, all the way back when I'd first found my newly-Fatgirl-self sitting on Frank Whitey at my Model Middle America audition.

Everything about him was the same—except for his eyes.

Before, the kindness and patience I'd seen had been evident. Now, they were glowing red and leaking blood down his cheeks as he held his guns up, ready to fire.

"Where is Larry Martin?" he growled, while his radio barked out orders to stand down. Above us, I could hear the whirring of a helicopter, and around the corners, ambulance and police sirens blared out their warnings.

There were some people in the street, clearly too terrified to move.

"Look! It's Fatgirl!"

I tried not to grimace as someone yelled. I could almost feel the eyes, phones, and cameras as they all seemed to look at me at once.

I waited until Officer Powers looked my way before I stood tall.

"Officer Powers," I shouted as I tried to motion to the other onlookers to get moving out of there. "Stand down! You're a good cop and you have your orders."

Max's eyes burned as he looked at me. "What do you know of my pain? My injustice?"

My stomach churned; I felt a little sick at the sight of him like that.

Another small group of cops appeared with a megaphone. "Fatgirl, stand down. We're the police. This is our jurisdiction."

AB buzzed in my ear. "Ignore them."

"Please just tell me they're not going to arrest me."

"No guarantees, but once Max is back to normal, I'll get him to drop the charges."

"He's going to have enough issues of his own to deal with," I muttered. "Look, I'm going to get him out of here and bring him to you. Let's meet at the entrance of the sewage system where we went to get Frank Whitey."

"Sounds like a good plan."

I clenched my fists. "Let's see if it works."

My eyes narrowed under my mask as I burst forward; as Fatgirl, my legs seemed to stop me from falling more than they propelled me forward, but I managed to run pretty fast.

The other cops held up their guns, and for the first time, I saw that they were not their usual, normal *pew-pew* type guns.

They were Tasers.

"AB, can this suit stop—ouch!" I fell over and began to roll as two wires stabbed through my suit and sent a small round of electric shocks through my arm and down my body.

As I rolled, Max also started shooting at me. My fingers were shaking as I covered my face. I could barely move as the spectators finally began running away.

"Are you alright?" AB demanded.

I whimpered into the earpiece. My mouth could barely form words. "I can't move."

"It'll wear off in a moment," AB said. I was surprised to hear the concern in her voice. "Do your best to keep moving."

"How can I keep moving if I'm not able to move?" I grumbled.

"Push through it, Kallie."

"Easy for you to say." I gritted my teeth together and did my best to roll over, and surprisingly succeeded. My arm burned as I pulled out the electric bullets, but I managed to get free as the cops crowded around me.

"Get away from me," I yelled. "I'm just trying to help."

"We're here to do that."

"You can't," I shouted back. "Just get everyone else out of here, and I'll take care of it."

Before they could argue, I bowled one of them over, heading for Max as my strength gradually returned.

"Max." I came up to him as he reloaded his gun. At his piercing gaze, I held up my hands, trying to get him to calm down. "Stop this. Your brother wouldn't want you to do this."

"My brother is dead!" Max's bleeding eyes glistened over with tears as he held up his gun to my chest.

I moved out of the way as he squeezed the trigger, and less than a second later, I wished I hadn't. The policeman behind me—the one who'd tasered me—was suddenly lying on the ground while Max only laughed.

"No," I gasped, as tears came into my own eyes. The other cops rushed over to help their fallen comrade.

"Kallie, I thought you were going to get Max out of there," AB hissed.

"I'm working on it." Pushing back my tears, I lunged forward and tackled Max.

I could feel him struggle against me, but I couldn't feel bad about sitting on him. "I know where the man is who murdered your brother," I told him.

"You're one of them," Max spat back. "You're happy my brother died."

"No, I'm not," I objected.

"The cop didn't care about what he did."

"I don't know if he did or not, but I care," I replied. My eyes burned as I thought about Zeus losing his mom, and my own mother abandoning me. "I know what it's like to lose people. It's like losing part of myself, and I know it's so painful and there aren't any words for it. But I do know causing others pain doesn't make your pain go away."

Max went silent.

He still kept struggling to get out from under me, but I looked into his eyes carefully, and I could see some of the radioactive doughnut's effect had dimmed.

"Fatgirl's got him!" One of the other cops called out.

Max's eyes glowed again, and I shot an angry glare at the policeman who was ruining my plans. Reluctantly, I stood up and peeled Max's body off the ground and grabbed onto his arm tightly.

"Come with me," I ordered, running away again. I glanced back to see the two remaining cops behind me had pulled back out their Tasers, and I immediately positioned myself in front of Max as best as I could.

And when Max cried out and fell after he was tasered, I could only groan.

Dragging him around the nearest corner, I tapped my earpiece. "I got him, AB. Headed your way. Any chance you can help me?"

"I'm already at the rendezvous point," AB said. "Let me see if Zeus can do something."

"Where is he?" I asked in between panting breaths as I dragged Max behind me. "Come on, Max, push through the pain and move!"

AB didn't answer me for a few moments; I tried not to grumble too loudly as I made my way toward the sewer entrance.

There was a large riverbank that huddled around a small trickle of a creek, and on both sides were large holes that helped move excess rainwater out of the city. It was inside of them that I'd been able to get into the sewers, the watery underworld of my city.

I'd come here before, I remembered, because I'd been too fat to fit through the manhole covers.

This time, it felt more like I was there to dump a body off.

I was relieved when AB waved to me, already wearing a white pair of her lab gloves as she peeked out from around a large grate.

Max started fighting with me, but I slammed him down onto the ground and sat on him.

"Just come the rest of the way, would you?" I slumped down on Max's body, thankful for a chance to catch my breath.

AB came over, wagging her purse in irritation. "People will be able to see us out here, Kallie."

"Put your mask on, then." I glanced around. "And hurry up with the Anti-F antigen stuff."

"These things take time. And I left my mask in the car."

"Well, this sort of thing takes energy," I countered. "I'm wiped out after getting electrocuted. You're lucky I made it this far. Besides, I thought Zeus was in charge of wiping off the city traffic cameras."

"He's not going to be able to wipe away people's own eyes," AB muttered as she walked toward me. "Besides, he's getting a lead on our lurker. I don't want him to get distracted."

"Did we actually have one this time?" I asked.

"He said we did." AB nodded her head toward the far end of the block. "He's on the computer in the car still."

"So that's further proof that someone knows you're looking for the guy who sold ZZ your recipe." I gave her a smile. "Do you think that's good enough to get your job back? I mean, clearly you're not doing all of this."

"I'll need a confession," AB muttered, pulling out the syringe. "Here's the Anti-F formula."

Max twitched as I stuck him. "I'm getting better at this part," I said. "Maybe I can be a doctor now, huh?"

"Just like me?" AB asked, arching her brow at me as she smirked.

"No." I stuck my tongue out at her. "I'd be a better doctor than you, if anything."

"You'd make a good cop," Max muttered. His voice sounded scraggly, but more controlled. I scooted off him as he slowly sat up. "Unlike me."

I put my hand on his shoulder. "You're a good cop, Officer Powers."

"I wasn't today," he said glumly, wiping his hands down his face.

"You were under the influence," I explained. "You can't be blamed for that."

"Yes, I can." He shrugged. "I guess if you become a cop, you'll have to learn a thing or two about the law."

I sighed. "Everyone has their weaknesses and everyone makes mistakes."

"Some people's mistakes get others killed." He stood up and began to brush himself off. There was a lot of blood on the front of his uniform. "There's no taking that back."

"I'm sorry about your brother," I whispered.

"His death was the reason I became a cop, you know," Max said. "I wanted to show other people how being a good cop was done. Now that I've failed, there's only one thing a good cop can do at this point."

"What's that?" Dread crept into my voice. I could only hope he wouldn't turn me in as some kind of consolation prize for his department.

"You *have* been a good cop." AB came up beside him.

"I killed one of my brothers in arms today," Max said, shaking his head.

"Well, you just shot him," I said carefully. I looked over at AB. "That doesn't necessarily mean he's dead."

AB frowned at me, and then put her gloved hand on Max's arm. "We've worked together in the past a few times. I'll help you as best as I can, as a favor to you."

"Thank you, Margaret."

"It's Dr. White," she told him with a playful smirk. "You're still too young for me to date, anyway."

"Ew, gross," I moaned.

AB ignored me. "You might not have been a good cop today, Max, but you're still a good man. I don't even think I'll have to scramble up your memory this time."

Max finally gave her a small smile. "You might want to consider it anyway, given everything that happened today. It's better if you're able to protect yourself."

"I'm able to protect myself just fine," AB assured him. "I've got my own larger-than-life security detail here, if you haven't noticed."

"Please stop," I muttered. "That's not funny."

"I guess it's 'insecurity detail,' actually," AB said.

I only scowled at her and crossed my arms over my chest. After that, AB took charge, cleaning up her things.

And I was content to let her, really I was; I was tired, both physically and emotionally, and I wanted all of this to be over.

"So, Max, do you think you can do me a few favors *before* you submit your resignation?"

We were just putting Max into a special ambulance when Zeus came running up beside us. "I found the lurker's location," he said.

"Did you get a name?"

"Well, no," Zeus admitted. "But you'll recognize the location."

He pulled out the laptop and showed us the map. In the middle, there was a large building in the downtown area that was highlighted.

AB and I exchanged a look.

"That's the Darling Donuts factory," I said. "That's the one attached to the distribution center where Dad goes to work, and their main offices are there, too. Do you think that's enough proof that Trevor Darlington is the one behind all of these Alterants?"

"I've already checked on Trevor Darlington this morning," AB said. "He's still doing his rehab in the Fairview Mountain Center, just a few miles outside of the city."

"But you said before the Phi-ger was able to pick up trace elements of movement," I said. "And the factory is part of the delivery path. This has to be where they're made at least. That means he has to be doing something with it, even if he's just ordered someone else to do it."

"Yes, that's possible." AB looked back at Zeus. "What do you think?"

"The computer terminal being used is where the lurker's signal is coming from," he said. "That's all I know. It could be anyone using a computer there, or using a hacked computer there. Trevor could even be doing it himself from the rehab center if he's got a remote login capability."

"I see." AB frowned, and I could see she was thinking things over. She rubbed her temples. "Let me think of something. I'll need to research a few more things—and I'd like to see about making sure Johnny is safe, first."

"Sounds good to me," I said. "Let's get out of here. I want out of this suit."

"Yes, I'll add that to my list, too," AB said as she ran her hand over my arm, where I'd been hit with the electrocution rods. "Another new suit."

"What can I do to help?" Zeus asked, and I honestly about retched at his eagerness.

"You've done enough for now," AB said warmly. "I'll get your favor done as soon as this is over, too."

"Thank you."

"What is it?" I asked. "What do you need done?"

"Um, well, it's nothing for me, really," Zeus said. His cheeks were burning again, but this time, it was from shame, not embarrassment. "It's more for my dad, really, and his business."

AB didn't say anything as I looked over at her, and then back to Zeus. After that, I shrugged. Zeus was a good kid; his dad just must've had some trouble with his taxes or something.

"Come on," I said. "Let's go home. I'm hungry and I want to take a nap after all this excitement."

"I'll stop for some burgers on the way home," AB said. "I think we could all use some good food after today."

"Alright!" I cheered immediately at the prospect.

It wasn't much longer after that I was back to my normal-sized self, and I was lying on my bed in my room. I was alone now, and I'd done some good work with stopping Max. Even if I hadn't been able to stop all the bad things from happening, or stop his heart from hurting, I knew I'd done all I could do, and I wouldn't hesitate to make the same choices as I had all over again.

The cop Max had shot was in critical care at the hospital, but it looked like he would make it out of there alive.

Max himself had offered his resignation, but AB told me the police chief wanted to put him through a trial first. Thankfully, it would not be public, or at least, it would be a little smaller and less publicized. I imagined it was pretty hard to hide something like one of my appearances from the city news, so I could only hope it worked.

I also hoped they wouldn't call me in to be a witness. I would have to refuse.

I would refuse.

Or I would get AB to refuse for me.

Either way, I decided not to worry about it.

I had other things to worry about.

I glanced back over at my phone, where Zeus' latest text message was practically glaring at me.

"Thanks again for coming to see my mom. She was very happy to meet you."

At that, I curled up into a ball and tried not to think of Zeus and our almost-kiss.

Between the thought of getting called in as a court witness, preparing to confront AB's recipe-abuser, facing down a cop on a rampant, radioactive-doughnut fueled rage run, and kissing the boy I'd largely known as "Sweaty Fat Kid" for the first several weeks of our association, I knew which problem made me feel the most afraid—and it wasn't the one I would've guessed otherwise.

I almost wished Spring Break was over so I could go to school and ignore everything else.

"This is going to be a long week," I grumbled, before I turned over and pulled the cover over my head.

Fatgirl

AZURE SKIES

EPISODE 9

○ ○ ○ ○

C. S. Johnson

We'll have a gay, old time!

FATGIRL
AZURE SKIES

○ ○ ○ ○

"Are we there yet?"

Out of the corner of my eye, I could see AB's hands tighten around her steering wheel in irritation.

"Not yet," she replied through gritted teeth. "And if you ask me that question again, I swear to God I'll slow down and it'll take us longer to get there."

I smirked. "Oh, so I guess that means you'll only go ten miles over the speed limit, instead of fifty?"

"Do you want to drive?"

"Can I?" My eyes went wide, as AB caught my genuine interest.

Instantly, at the sight of her smug, pleased little sneer on her face, I regretted saying anything.

Which was likely her goal all along.

"Can you?" AB teased. "Maybe. Will you? No. Can you do it better than me? Doubtful."

"Were you a monster truck driver in another life?"

"I don't know. Should I try to drive onto the car in front of me and see what happens?" AB slammed down hard on the gas pedal, propelling us forward.

"No!" I bucked and thrust back into my seat. "Stop it, would you?"

AB started laughing—or maybe she was cackling. Either way, I gave her my most vicious scowl.

"This isn't funny!" I clawed at her armrests as she came within an inch of the car in front of us. It was only then she finally took her lead foot off the gas.

"It's not funny to *you*," AB remarked. "Humor is subjective."

"No, humor is *relative*," I said. "If I were doing this to you, you wouldn't think it's funny."

"I don't know about that; I have more of a sense of humor than you do. We'll have to find out when you finally get your license.

Anyway, subjective and relative are the same thing in the context of our conversation."

"Well, me asking if we're there yet is not irritating to me." I stuck my tongue out at her. "If humor is subjective and relative, so is irritation."

"Humor and irritation are not necessarily mutually exclusive."

"You're making me tired." I sighed. "All right, fine. You win this round of snarky humor exchanges. I give up. If for no other reason than I'll likely throw myself out of the car if we keep going."

"Well, wait till we're going home, then." AB nodded toward the looming building in front of us. "We're close enough the people at Fairview Mountain might think I'm checking you in as a new patient, rather than visiting my 'nephew.'"

I put my head in my hands, grateful I hadn't even tried to look glamorous today. Really, I looked beautiful anyway, but between my nerves and the heat from the growing Arkansas sunshine, my makeup would've only been wasted.

I'm already wasting my time doing this. No need to waste my makeup, too.

I crossed my arms and looked back out of the window, watching as the farmland and countryside of northern Arkansas passed by.

If this had been any other year, I would've been hanging out at Uli's house, or Lizzy's, or June's, or even Amory's, probably planning on how to get Blake Turner to ask me out without being too obvious about it.

But no—this year was the "Year of Fatgirl," apparently. For the past several weeks, I'd been coerced into adopting an accidental superhero persona in order for my grandmother to find the person who'd stolen her recipe. He'd framed her for its loss, caused her to lose her job, and then disappeared, leaving barely any clues behind.

So instead of hanging out with my friends, I was stuck here, on a road trip to a modern-day insane asylum, on the Saturday before the end of Spring Break, trying to connect with the only clue we had left—a lunatic whose brother headed the Darling Donut company, the same company that'd given my mother her first real modeling job.

I sighed.

I didn't want to think about Mom, either.

I pulled my knees up to my chest, trying to hide my face more, almost hoping I could hide from the rest of the world, too.

After much pushing and prodding, AB finally managed to find a way to visit with Trevor Darlington, the guy who we suspected of sending Karen Bright and her fiancée a pack of radioactive doughnuts in "celebration" of her engagement.

"What's wrong?" AB asked.

There was a now-familiar blend of impatience and concern in her voice, and I almost pitied AB for having to deal with me.

Originally, she'd set out to get her job back, not to actually become my mother-mentor figure as we navigated through my awkward Fatgirl stage. I didn't think she would've stuck around if she'd come during my full-blow puberty days.

I was just about to assure her I was just getting sick from her spastic driving when she added, "Is it Zeus? I told you he's nice enough, and you're not risking anything if you date him."

"Excuse me?" My cheeks burned as I thought back to the last time I'd seen Zeus. He'd taken me to visit his dying mom, and in a weak moment, I'd let him get close enough to nearly kiss me and even prepared myself to let him. "But I would be risking *everything* to date him. There's my reputation, my social status, and my dignity! So don't talk about things you don't know about."

"What's really wrong with him, Kallie? If I don't know what I'm talking about, why don't you tell me what's so wrong with dating Zeus?"

"Where do I start?" I huffed angrily. "He's gross. His clothes are so frumpy, I can't tell how fat he actually is—and what if he's somehow fatter? Next, he's got pimples, his hair's always a mess and oily and slimy. And he's not popular at all. He's a loser, and an ugly one at that."

I felt bad for being so hard on him, but, well, AB wanted to know. So now she knew what my problems were with Zeus.

AB smirked. "Well, according to ZZ, the ugly ones try harder."

I gritted my teeth together. "That's not funny!"

"You're right," AB agreed, surprising me. "It's not funny. And I'm rather ashamed of you, to be honest."

"Why me? Because I know I'm pretty and I deserve better?" The heat in my cheeks increased as my embarrassment burned into shame.

"First, you of all people ought to know that beauty doesn't last," AB said. "Your mother's insecurities alone should be proof of that. Second, Zeus is going through a hard time with his mother's condition and his father's anger and grief. Of course he's stressed out and doesn't take good care of himself. He's busy trying to take care of others. And when he does have free time, he spends it helping out other people, ourselves included. He's proven himself trustworthy and friendly, and even useful to me. He doesn't ask me for much in return, you know."

I thought back to our last encounter with an alternant—Officer Max Powers, who'd consumed a radioactive doughnut of AB's while he was on the job. Zeus had asked AB for a favor, although he hadn't told me what it was.

Maybe he'd asked AB for help in getting a date with me.

I shivered in complete disgust at the thought.

AB pursed her lips together, giving her a smug, morally superior expression. "He's not always going to look how he looks now."

"Yeah, he could look worse." I shook my head. "Anyway, all that stuff doesn't mean he deserves me."

"I agree." AB snorted. "He deserves much better."

"What do you really know about it?"

For the first time, AB flushed over with anger. "I know my son deserved better than the supermodel he married, Kallie. So you'll have to excuse me if I think there's more important things to a person than how he or she looks."

I went quiet at that one.

As much as it stung, AB and I were in agreement there, especially after I'd found out my mom had been working with ZZ during her "retirement gala" last week. Thinking of how much my dad still pined for her only made me angrier.

Still, by all accounts, Mom had married Dad because he loved her, and he was a safe choice after AB managed to get Mom out of the trafficking ring she'd been allegedly unintentionally involved with before.

But if anything, that proved that it wasn't a good idea for Zeus and I to get together.

"You know, if you think you're going to shame or manipulate me into dating Zeus, you're the one who should be ashamed," I finally snapped back. "That's all I have to say about that. I don't want to talk about it anymore."

"Good to know, Kallie." AB sighed and went back to driving.

She seemed sorry she'd said anything, which I could only be thankful for—even if it was nice she cared about me.

Dad had been working overtime a lot in recent weeks. I didn't believe that there was actually a "Darling Donut supply chain shortage" but I didn't eat them, so what did I really know about things like that? All I could think of was how good a shortage would be for all their obese customers. Dad had said that Richard Darlington, Trevor's brother, and the current CEO of Darling Donuts, was planning a new product release soon, and it was all I could do to stop myself from asking if it was "Diet Darling Donuts" or something equally stupid.

"Did you hear from Zeus today?" AB asked, almost as if she'd just remembered something.

"I said I didn't want to talk about it," I muttered darkly.

"I was just asking in reference to our mission here." AB's voice was practical, even if her tone was a little too sweet. "He said he was going to hack into Fairview's records and make sure I was listed on the approved visitor list. Can you check my phone?"

"You can check it yourself," I grumbled.

I didn't need the reminder of my withdrawal pains. I'd left my phone at home since I didn't want to run the risk of being tempted to text anyone. I'd largely left my phone off for the past week, and I was beginning to feel the pains of my withdrawal.

Thankfully, I only had to imagine the pain of picking it up to feel better. Amory was probably still mad at me for blowing up at her over our disagreement about Blake Turner, and I did not want to talk to Zeus at all, and if Dad needed to get a hold of me for some reason, he could call AB's phone.

And as sad as it was, those were the only people who cared enough about me to actually call me.

I sighed. "I don't want to deal with anyone else today, anyway."

AB didn't hear me—or rather, she didn't listen to me, since she tossed her phone into my lap.

"Hey!" I frowned. "This is my phone."

"No, it's not," AB practically sang. "Remember?"

It took me a moment to remember that she'd bought the same style of phone as me. It'd been one of her earliest digs at me, and I didn't appreciate it now any more than I had before.

I stuck my tongue out at her. "Fine, I forgot that you bought the same one as me just to irritate me."

As she rolled her eyes, I looked down at her phone.

I nearly gagged. "Zeus messaged you. He says you're good to go, and that he'll be watching our progress through their system."

"Good." AB nodded approvingly. "Good boy, Zeus."

I ignored that. "There's some other important-looking messages," I said, before describing them. There was one from some lady named Carol, who was asking AB to work for her; there was a message from an attorney about some subpoena, one from a spammer selling tea, and then the one from Zeus. "What's the job offer about? And the lawyer one? Do you know? With all the spam-looking stuff, I can't actually tell if it's real or important or not."

"Oh, those aren't important right now. Carol's been eager to get me to come over to Europe to work for years now. She's the lady at CERN. She was almost suspiciously excited that I'd gotten fired from the NAH," AB said. "But you couldn't pay me to live there, and in Switzerland of all places."

"I thought it was a nice place?"

"A nice place to visit. But not to stay. There's a price you pay when you stay in a place where you don't really belong, Kallie." She frowned. "They might have set the Geneva Accords in place, but that just means they know how to go around their limitations. And even I have some limits."

"Good to know," I muttered, amused at her own admission. "What's the subpoena for?"

"Max's trial," she said bitterly. "He called me as a witness. But I've decided to ignore it for now. I've let it be known that I'll be out of town for several weeks yet. Of course, they'll need to set up a grand jury, so I'll probably show up anyway. If not, I'll make it up to him later."

I didn't say anything to that. AB wouldn't have wanted to go to court. She'd likely easily condemn herself in the process of testifying. I hated that she was sacrificing Officer Powers to protect herself, so I hoped she would make good on her promise to make it up to him.

If such a thing was even possible.

"What's the message here about buying tea about?" I asked, trying to lighten the mood. "Some Welsh prince is offering you a lifetime supply of it. Should I tell him yes?"

"A Welsh prince, huh?" She surprised me by smiling brightly. "I'd reply that he's a bit too old to be a prince."

It took me a moment to realize it was likely a protected message from Agent Grey, of INTERPOL. I'd met him in Fort Lauderdale, too, and he'd seemed interested in AB. I had to laugh at the thought that AB might have a crush on him, too, especially since I didn't think she'd allow herself to be so emotionally compromised.

But then, I guess she's already emotionally compromised because of me.

It was too easy to remember how she'd tried to take care of me, even though she'd lost the lead on her case when she'd lost hold of ZZ.

Before I could ask her if she'd heard any updates on ZZ's semi-memory loss, AB let out a long sigh. "Well, there it is. Fairview Mountain Center."

I looked over at the towering building. I knew it used to be a grand hospital of sorts, but it looked more like a hotel than anything else. It was tall, made of stone and steel, and simple white letters graced a drooping overhang: "Welcome to Fairview, where the views are fairer than ever before."

"It looks both scary and silly," I muttered, suddenly even more unhappy we'd come to see Trevor.

"Hopefully we'll get some answers," AB said as she parked and pulled her purse out of the backseat. "Let's get this over with, darling. We're here."

As much as I'd worried we'd never arrive, suddenly I wished we were back on the road.

Still, I swallowed hard and squared my shoulders. "All right."

The outside of Fairview was tall and imposing, but once we walked inside, I saw that it was just very … clean.

Yes, that was the perfect word to describe it.

Clean.

Clean and square, with rounded safety corners.

There were spotless, white-washed walls, with white-tiled floors, and even more white, rounded molding along the doorways. The bright, overhead lights were pristine, and it almost made me dizzy. Standing in the entrance atrium was like standing inside a magnifying make-up mirror; I felt very exposed, for some reason, as if the lights could pierce right through me, illuminating all my flaws.

I was grateful AB was the one in charge; she seemed to do a lot better about ignoring things like the environment we happened to be in.

"Why did I have to come with you, again?" I whispered. The words were loud and scratchy to my ears as we headed for the visitor's center to sign in.

"You need to learn how to do these things, Kallie." Her voice was soft and sharp, almost like a cat's, as she spoke out of the side of her mouth.

"What things?"

"Anything that might require initiative, definitive action, or creative problem-solving."

"You mean things that are illegal?" I asked, only half-jokingly.

AB's grin only widened ominously. "I can neither confirm nor deny such a description."

"So, yes, then."

"Please, Kallie. We're Americans. If the government found a way to outlaw thinking, we'd rebel soon enough. Besides, you go to public school. You already know how unattractive it already is."

"I'm half Hispanic, too. I'm not just white, like you."

"So what? Being American has nothing to do with any ethnicity, it's a creed." AB snorted. "I guess I shouldn't be surprised at that comeback. It just proves me right, just like how you were the one who thought I was racist for years simply because I didn't like your mother."

"She *told* me that."

"She *lied* to you."

I glared at her. "You know what? Just shut up, and I'll shut up, too, okay? That way, we can call it a draw."

"Fine," AB agreed. "But get ready. We're almost at our first checkpoint."

"You don't have to make it sound like we're on some kind of spy mission," I muttered.

"Why not?" AB smirked. "This is what spying's all about, Spygirl."

I clamped my mouth shut, not trusting myself to say anything coherent in reply.

We made it through the visitor's check in and headed straight for the front desk.

A pretty-ish, middle-aged-looking nurse lady wearing a white uniform looked up at us and smiled. It was a smile that, just like the asylum—rehab center—was perfectly clean and white.

I began wondering if everyone was crazy here.

"Trevor Darlington?" The lady repeated, as AB introduced herself as his great aunt, Prudence McCormick-Darlington. "He's in solitary confinement at the moment. I'm afraid he's not allowed to see anyone but immediate family."

"We are immediate family," AB insisted. "Or at least, I am. This is my personal Certified Nursing Assistant. She's come to make sure I take my own medications on time."

The nurse lady looked over at me again, eyeing my clothes skeptically. "This is your CNA?"

"Yes," I lied, suddenly feeling awkward.

Perhaps I should've worn something a little more professional-looking.

My jeans, tank top, and flat dress shoes didn't help me look like I belonged in the medical field. If anything, my outfit probably made me look like a middle-schooler, especially since I hadn't bothered to wear any makeup, either.

I cleared my throat and hurriedly glanced at the clock. "That reminds me; it's almost time for your Prozac, Mrs. Darlington. You don't want to miss it … again."

AB glared over at me, and I looked at the nurse lady helplessly, as if to say, "You see what I have to deal with?"

Nurse Lady seemed more sympathetic, even if she was still doubtful, but she nodded. "Alright, Mrs. Darlington. I'll put in a call to the ward director and see if he's awake. If he's agreeable, I can see about moving him to the visitor cell."

AB nodded. "Thank you. I've missed my little Trevor darling something fierce, and I know how stressful he's been of late. I figured his Auntie Pru will be able to make things all better."

Nurse Lady didn't look convinced, and I could only cringe.

AB didn't always strike me as the best actress, but she did make up for her lack of talent with an impressive, nauseating amount of passion. While Nurse Lady was on the phone, I nudged her, hoping she'd catch the hint.

Before AB and I could argue again, Nurse Lady hung up the phone.

"You can go on in and head up to the fourth floor," Nurse Lady said. "Richard Darlington is scheduled for his monthly visit today, and he'll be able to approve your visit or not."

The corner of AB's mouth twitched, ever so slightly.

She was not happy.

"Oh, Richard is here, too?" she asked instead. "Why, it's been ages since I've seen him, too. That all sounds great."

"Just great," I agreed, trying not to sound cynical.

AB tugged on my arm and led me toward the nearby elevator. Once we were inside, I pushed the buttons for the fourth floor.

AB pushed the third floor button. "We're going to get off early so I can go to the bathroom," she said.

"They probably have a bathroom on the fourth floor if—"

"It's an emergency," she insisted.

We walked off onto the third floor. Immediately, AB pulled me after her again, and she began walking down the hall at a brisk pace. No one questioned us.

"If you look like you know what you're doing, people are less likely to stop you," AB explained quietly. "I'm going to head up the stairwell to the next floor, but first, I want to see if we can catch a glimpse at this Richard Darlington person. We'll need to split up. You take this floor first, and work your way down to the first floor. See if you can spot him and get a really good look at him. You understand, Kallie? We need a strong description."

I suddenly felt nervous, like it would be a hugely bad thing if I failed, but I had no choice to back out of the assignment. "What do I tell people if they stop me?"

"You tell them that your patient, Prudence Darlington, has gone missing—that you were on your phone for 'only a moment,' while she was in the restroom, and then when you looked up, she was gone." AB winked at me. "You're pretty and you can probably cry on cue, right?"

"Well, duh, yes—"

"Then I'm sure you'll be fine." AB gave me a bright smile. "After all, you're my granddaughter."

Before I could ascertain whether or not that was truly a compliment, she turned on her heel and left me all by myself.

As I watched her go, I heaved a sigh in reluctant admiration; I could only hope that, as her granddaughter, I would be able to move as well as she did at her age.

I walked briskly throughout the halls of the asylum—rehab center—looking around without trying to seem suspicious, and no one was eager to stop me. AB's advice was pretty spot-on. It was actually a little disconcerting by the time I made it down to the first floor, still uninterrupted by any of the numerous attendants, looming visitors, or janitorial staff I saw as I walked up and down the various, white-washed halls.

It was only when I started heading toward the front desk that I slowed down a little.

There was a larger waiting room I'd missed earlier; AB and I had walked right past it, too distracted by our bickering, no doubt.

Nurse Lady was still at her desk. I glanced around, trying to see if there was a way to get around her to another hallway when she glanced up and saw me.

"Did you need something?" she asked, and I could only stare at her, like a deer caught in the headlights, knowing it was over.

"Um … I was … " I glanced around, hurrying to try to think of an idea. "I lost my phone. I just thought I'd come down and see if I'd left it here."

"You left your patient to get your phone?" Nurse Lady was a lot less sympathetic when I didn't have AB bothering her.

"Um, yes, but only for a few moments," I said. "She's very high-functioning."

Nurse Lady picked up the phone. "Director? Hey, it looks like we've got a missing visitor in the building."

"I know where she is," I insisted. "Fine. I'll get my phone later."

"You really need to keep your patient within your sight at all times," Nurse Lady said. "Otherwise, you're in the wrong profession."

"Tell me about it," I muttered under my breath, skipping back over to the elevator.

Before Nurse Lady could chide me again, another voice spoke up.

"Hello there, Ms. Wood. Is Trevor ready to see me today?"

The voice was sweet and fluffy, almost like a doughnut. I caught sight of the man and stared.

He was older, but still considerably good-looking. He had a good tan, and his dark hair was brushed upward and off to the left; there was a small mole on the upper side of his lip, and his teeth seemed very white and straight. He wore a very expensive suit, shined shoes, a crisp white shirt, and a red tie.

He looked like he'd walked straight out of a suit magazine catering to someone my dad's age.

"Oh, Mr. Darlington," Nurse Lady said in a cheery, cultivated tone. "You're here. Excellent. Your brother will be glad to see you and your great aunt, too."

"Excuse me?" The man I'd figured out was Richard Darlington cleared his throat. "Great aunt?"

I swallowed hard. Casually, I leaned on the "Door Open" button but ducked against the panel so he couldn't see me any longer.

"Yes, we just had a Prudence Darlington check in," Nurse Lady said. "I already sent her upstairs with her apparently irresponsible nursing attendant. Hopefully she's there waiting for you. I called up the ward director on his floor to get him prepared in the visitor's cell."

"This is disturbing," Richard said. "My great-aunt Pru died five years ago. I recommend you call security."

Oh, no.

I hurriedly pressed the "Door Close" button and hit the fourth floor button next. I could only hope I'd find AB before they did, and we'd be able to get out of here before it was too late.

Just as the door was about to shut, a man slipped through the disappearing doorway. I almost screamed at the intrusion, fearing that I was done for, that I'd been caught already.

But it wasn't Richard Darlington who was suddenly standing in the elevator with me.

It was another familiar-looking man, though—although I couldn't quite place him at first.

He seemed to have the same issue, because he saw me, and then squeaked out a protest.

"Oh, no!" He covered his face with his hands. "Don't look at me!"

The voice was familiar, too.

Instead of backing down, I stepped a little closer. He was taller than me, with wide shoulders he had hidden under a longer trench coat. He wore a hat, but I could see a thin layer of straight hair peeking out from its wider brim. As I watched him, he leaped over to the corner and tried to pull out a pair of sunglasses.

That's when his hat fell off, and I got a clearer look at him.

My mouth fell open. "Azure? Is that you?"

"No! Never!" He glared at me through his well-manicured nails.

Yeah, it was Azure all right.

Once I saw it, I couldn't unsee it.

His half-shaved head wasn't styled; his hair flopped around like an old, depressed broom. His eyes were beady and sunken into his face without layers of eyeliner to make them pop, and he even needed to shave a little; there was a five o'clock shadow on his normally, baby's-bottom smooth face.

"Don't come near me or I'll call the police and have you arrested for harassment," he threatened.

"I'm not even doing anything," I protested. "I just recognized you. That's all, Azure."

"Shut up," he insisted. "I'm not Azure … I'm … I'm his twin! Yes, that's it. I'm just his ugly, normal, completely heterosexual, too-white-skinned, cis-male twin brother with a boring desk job probably."

"What's wrong with you, Azure?" I asked, unable to stop myself from grinning. "I'm just one person."

"That's all it takes!" he practically shouted as he fixed his hat and put on his sunglasses. "My—I mean, my brother's—reputation is on the line. I don't know where you know me—my brother—from, but I'm definitely not him."

At that, the elevator opened and a woman was waiting at the door. Once she caught sight of Azure, she brightened.

"Oh, Stan, there you are," the woman said. "Your dad is starting to ask for you. He says he'd like to see his one and only son before he passes into the light."

"He's dying?" I asked, suddenly horrified at the thought, although I also picked up that Azure really wasn't telling the truth about his "brother."

And that his real name is "Stan."

For some reason, I had to stop myself from laughing at that one.

"Oh, not yet. Not likely. But he's dramatic, just like his son." The woman smiled as she reached out her hand to Azure. I noticed on her left hand, she was wearing a large ring with a sapphire surrounded by tiny diamonds. "Come on, honey. The kids are eager to see how you'll respond to this round of 'Grandpa's Dying Wishes.'"

Azure sighed. "Yes, dear. Just give me one moment with this young lady. She and I were just talking about Model Middle America."

"She recognized you?" The woman laughed. "Even without all the stage make up and the extra muscle padding?"

I laughed.

He glared at her. "Stop giving it all away, Susan!"

Susan chuckled. "Sorry, honey. It hasn't happened a lot throughout the course of our marriage. You have to admit, it's amusing."

Azure—Stan—glared at me as I began laughing harder.

He shoved his hands into his pockets. "Look, this doesn't leave this building, okay, what's-your-name? What do you want? Money? Connections? A chance to be famous? Maybe my autograph? I'm not going to give you a photo op today, don't even think about it!"

As he grew increasingly hysterical, I was just grateful he didn't recognize me as "Fatgirl."

"Azure, I'm just 'Arlanda,'" I said, interrupting his tantrum-like breakdown. "Remember? The night of the Amphitheatre getting held hostage? I got sick and went to the changing room and … Fatgirl stole your clothes from me."

Azure's now-beady eyes widened, ever so slightly, making him look a little less like a mouse, before they narrowed again.

"What are you doing here?" he asked. His eyes widened in horror. "You're not Gynnifer Stills' niece, are you? The one she loves so very much, but she's always whining about? Is this an undercover op against me? I knew it!"

"Honey, calm down," Susan started to say, as Azure began to frantically pace around in circles. "They're going to think you need to stay here."

"It's bad enough Richard Darlington is here, too, only a few days after he hired me to be his personal fashion consultant," Azure hissed. "This cannot be a coincidence. You're with WACC news as some kind of intern, aren't you?"

His eyes were small, but piercing in the bright, white, overhead lights.

"No," I said. "But if I was, you'd be doing a good job giving me all the details."

"If you print any of it, I'll destroy you," he hissed. "I don't know how, but I will … somehow."

Before I could reply and try to calm him down again, the loudspeaker crackled to life.

"Attention, attention everyone. We have a code white. Thank you."

"What's a code white?" I asked, looking between the two of them.

Neither could give me a solid answer, and then someone grabbed me from behind.

I started to scream and struggle, until AB spoke in my ear. "A code white means there's a visitor in an unauthorized area."

Azure and Susan looked at AB and me, and then AB gave them a winning smile. "If you'll excuse us," we have somewhere else to be."

"Wait." Azure stepped up. "Arlanda, I need you to promise me you won't tell anyone about me."

"Arlanda?" AB asked, but I shook my head to her. I'd have to explain later.

"I don't think you have to worry," I said, trying to reassure him. "We were just here to visit my … I don't know, third cousin? And we couldn't get in I guess."

I looked over at AB, who huffed indignantly.

"What do you mean, 'I don't have to worry?' Are you out of your mind?" Azure practically spit at me. "If the fashion world hears about me, I'm done for."

"You're not the only one who has crazy relatives," I said. "Even Richard Darlington, the owner of Darling Donuts, has his brother stuck here."

"It's not *that*," Azure argued. "My God, you are so stupid and naïve. I'm talking about this."

He waved his hands down his front, and then to Susan. Behind her, I could see two small-ish boys poke their heads out of a door.

"Daddy?" one of them called, and I knew he was one of Azure's sons.

"Your kids are sweet," I said. "I don't see what's wrong."

"You don't know what it's like in the fashion and modeling world at all, do you?" Azure glared at me. "Look, people think I'm outrageously outrageous and flamboyantly flamboyant and super gay and super trendy, frankly. If anyone—*anyone*—found out I'm just Stanley Myers from Pine Bluff, Arkansas, I would lose my job."

I looked over to Susan, who looked down and nodded.

"My wife and kids depend on me to work," he continued. "And I *like* my work. I've been able to make more money at my jobs than King Midas would make playing tag in a crowded New York subway station. And we like our lifestyle. I would never recover from the truth getting out. Never. *Never.*"

"But—"

"But *nothing*, Arlanda!" Azure glared down at me. "No one wants to hire a straight designer. Especially a white male like me. Women, that's fine. They can be straight or bisexual or whatever. But me? They'd never. Not right now, in today's world. It's just not fashionable. Variety will always be in fashion, and so I make myself outrageous. When you're as outrageous as I am, no one thinks to question you on it. And when they do, you can call them a bigot and that's usually the end of it."

"How do you know you're not gay, then?" I looked over at Susan, who was clearly amused by my growing confusion.

Azure drew himself to his full height proudly. "Look, I know who I am and what I like and what I want, no matter what small-minded people say," Azure hissed. "I know truth is terribly inconvenient for others, and the only thing I can do to make it more comfortable for them is to lie about it."

"So you're living your truth, even if you have to lie about it?" I asked, nonplussed.

"Sounds like you and Azure here are best friends," AB murmured behind me.

I thought back to my objections to dating Zeus and blushed. I didn't have room to criticize Azure for his concerns, even if I found them largely silly, if I used the same ones.

Of course, my situation was entirely different, and I was completely justified, while Azure just seemed like a coward to me.

"Anyway, Spygirl, we got to move." AB tugged on my sleeve, pulling me out of my thoughts. Behind us, I saw two white-uniformed orderlies heading our way.

The elevator behind us suddenly opened up, and Richard Darlington himself walked by.

Azure practically threw himself behind me. "Don't move," he snapped.

"You're fine," I whispered. "He's here to see Trevor. He's not here to catch you without your face on."

"Ha, ha." Azure angrily snorted behind me as we all watched Richard.

"Come on, you know I'm right." I shrugged. "People see what they want to, or what they expect to. You know this from your own experiences."

I don't think Azure was listening to me. He was too busy staring at Richard.

"Ugh, I wish he wouldn't part his hair on the left," Azure muttered. "With that beauty mark on his face, he looks like he's going to fall over. Thank God he doesn't smoke or he'd be impossible to properly photograph."

"Beauty mark?" I squinted over at Richard, before I saw the small, brown birth mark just over his lip on the left side of his face. I'd noticed it earlier. "I didn't realize it was fake."

"It's not. Richard's lucky when it comes to brains, but not beauty marks," Azure said. "Trevor's got one, too, but it's on the other side of his mouth. It's an identical twin thing, with only the smallest differences. Too bad Trevor's insane."

"So they're twins, are they?" AB asked, watching Richard with renewed interest. "I thought Richard was older."

"Well, he is," Azure said. "But only by minutes. Of course, he's still that overachieving-first-child-prodigy that Trevor never was."

"Look, can we just find a way to agree here?" I crossed my arms as I looked up at Azure. "I'll keep your secret, okay? Just help me and my abuela here get out of this place without getting caught."

"We're the code white," AB explained, backing me up.

"That's fine," Susan said, stepping forward. She seemed like a very sweet woman, eager to help. She was very welcoming and gracious as she smiled. "We can help you, for sure. Why don't you come and meet my father-in-law? And I'm sure my sons, Patrick and Harry, will love having some new people to play with."

Before I could object, Azure grabbed me by the arm and shoved me down the hall toward his father's room.

It seemed like a long time had passed before AB and I finally managed to get back into her Imperial. The interior red velvet cushions were much more comfortable than the chairs in the elder Mr. Myers' room, and I sagged into them heavily as AB started the engine.

"Well, that was … unexpected," I said, as AB slammed her foot down on the gas pedal, still halfway through buckling up.

"That was embarrassing, you mean."

"They're not mutually exclusive," I replied, thinking about our earlier conversation in the car.

"Hmmph." AB rolled her eyes and then went silent as she sped down the highway.

I knew I should've been grateful for the silence, but I was oddly disappointed she was lost in her own thoughts. Without my phone, I felt almost compelled to talk with her, but I didn't know if she would welcome it or not.

"That was Azure in there," I said a little later, finally giving into conversation impulses.

I owed AB an explanation anyway, didn't I? And even if I didn't, I couldn't imagine she'd turn one down.

"Azure? It was all white in there," AB said. "I'm not sure if it was to inspire thoughts of heaven or euthanasia, but either way, I get a headache just thinking about it."

"Azure is the guy in there—Stan, I mean. He was the original designer for me at Model Middle America," I said. "He's the one who technically designed Fatgirl's costume. The first one, anyway. I know you've made the upgrades since then."

"I guess so," AB murmured. "But bulletproofing the suit and blocking facial recognition tech doesn't require a lot of work. Especially simpler work, like changing colors."

"If you say so."

She frowned, wrinkling up her forehead. "He didn't recognize you as Fatgirl, did he?"

"No," I said. "I said Fatgirl stole them from me while I was sick. He was too busy freaking out over how I'd recognized him to question me."

"Well, that's good, I guess," AB said. "Hopefully that's enough of a cover, and I can let it slide."

"Let it slide?"

AB gave me a chilling smile. "It means I don't have to worry about firing up my memory scrambler. Just yet, anyway."

"Right. I'm sure Azure's a lot like ZZ; he wouldn't want to lose control of his secrets."

AB snorted. "No, and it's best we leave him as is. The bright side about that is twofold. One, we know his weakness, and you've got the necessary blackmail goods on him now, while he's got nothing significant on you."

"I wouldn't use it against him," I insisted. "That's rude."

"You're going to have a hard time when you meet the real world, Kallie," AB said with a sigh.

I rolled my eyes. "What's the other bonus? You said it was twofold."

"Stan is clearly very easily upset," AB said. "It's easier to discredit him by painting him as a crazy person. And he's got a family history to back it up, thanks to your bargaining."

"I still wouldn't tell anyone his secret."

"With the right incentive, people are capable of anything, Kallie. But you're good to honor your word. Just remember, there's some honor amongst thieves, but very little love. They'll protect themselves first, and their honor second."

"I'll keep that in mind," I replied dryly. "What about you?"

"Me? You've known me long enough to know you won't worry about me throwing you under the bus."

"No, not that. I meant, what did you find out while I was 'looking for my patient' on the first, second, and third floors?"

"Oh." AB pursed her lips together. "We might have a problem. The Phi-ger went off while I was looking for a way to see Trevor without the Fairview staff knowing."

"It did?" I looked around, only to see AB's huge pocketbook on the floor behind her seat. "How come it didn't go off sooner?"

"I don't know," she admitted. "But there are only really three possibilities. The first is that the device is on the fritz."

"I doubt that. You seem pretty good at keeping up with things like that."

"Thank you." AB grinned at me. "I didn't think it was that either. It's more likely that there's so little protactinium around that it's not picking up any until we're close to the source, or it's possible that there's something inside of Fairview that's stopping its radioactive signal from getting picked up by my device."

"Huh. Can't help you with that one, I guess," I said. "I'm not sure I know anything about radiation."

"Well, it's possible there's lead in the paint there, and I wouldn't put it past Fairview to have some," AB said with a sneer. "It used to be an asylum."

"I kind of figured that."

"It's also possible, now that I think of it, both are the right answers." AB looked thoughtful as she swerved around another eighteen-wheeler and then ducked between a camper and a large truck.

"So Trevor's being poisoned?" I asked.

"Well, if he's really the one who sent Karen Bright and her fiancé that box of radioactive Darling Donuts, then it's possible he's been affected by prolonged exposure."

"I'm okay, though, right?" I asked, suddenly nervous again. "I've been exposed to these chemicals much more harshly than he has, I'll bet."

"Don't bet on anything less than a sure thing," AB warned. "But I have the cure. The Anti-F serum should strip you of all the harmful residue. I'm not able to get any to Trevor as he is now. We'll have to try another tactic, or wait until he's out of there."

I didn't really like how she was so easygoing with her experiments on me, so I pushed that thought out of my mind.

"What do we do now?" I asked. We seemed to be out of things to do.

ZZ's brain was fried.

Trevor wasn't reachable.

Officer Powers was on trial.

Mom was likely working for the scum of the earth.

Seriously. What do we do now?

"Right now?" AB slouched in her seat. "Let's just get home."

"Good idea," I said. "Dealing with those nurses and those kids was exhausting."

"You can rest if you want, but I need to talk to Zeus."

"What?" I groaned. "Why?"

"Information, Kallie," AB replied. "Knowing is half the battle. Knowing what to do with what you know—now that's wisdom. I had him do some research while we were out here today. So, next we need to talk to Zeus and see what he's found."

"Why is it 'we' and not 'you,' AB?" I asked. "I don't want to see him right now."

"Did you get into a fight with him?" AB asked. "You seem awfully bitter and angry toward him."

"I don't want to talk about it."

"Okay. But you'd better watch it. You can get stress wrinkles if you keep all of your anger inside of you."

"I'm not talking about it." I glared at her. "Anyway, are we home yet?"

This time, she groaned.

I felt better after that.

○ ○ ○ ○

When we got home, Dad was still at work, and I was left all by myself while AB chatted it up with Zeus.

I didn't really want to talk about Zeus, and I didn't want to talk *to* him, but I hated to think AB was right about the stress wrinkles. I almost wished I had a sister or someone else I could talk to, but the only person that came to mind was Amory, and I didn't think she would want to talk to me.

I was okay with that. School was back in session starting tomorrow, so I figured it was time to face the music of Amory's wrath.

She'd left me alone after the Spring Fling, and even before it.

Now that I'd had my week in "Florida" while being off social media and off my phone, I wasn't angry at her anymore.

Glancing over, I saw my phone was sitting on my night table, looking up at me like a neglected pet. I picked it up and sighed.

With AB busy, I picked it up and headed out of the house, heading in the direction of the high school. I didn't think anyone would be there, but it was possible the lacrosse team would be practicing. I cheered at the thought of seeing Blake practice momentarily, before remembering he didn't really even like me, apparently.

Blake had a crush on Amory.

And Amory … Well, I couldn't say how she really felt about him. Maybe she did think he was stupid and silly and no one worth dating. Or maybe she'd just said that so I wouldn't want to date him.

I opened my phone and turned it on.

Immediately, it started beeping like crazy, as hundreds of messages and notifications burst out like virtual fireworks.

Some of the messages I just ignored, and I trashed several emails. I was about to check my messages when I heard Amory call out to me.

"Kallie!"

I whirled around.

I was close to the school now, and suddenly I felt terrible for not wearing more makeup. Amory waved to me from the front stairs of the main entrance, and I tentatively waved back. She was sitting there, quietly and calmly, and I slowly made my way up to see her.

"You gonna yell at me again?" Amory asked.

I put my hands in my pockets. "No."

"How was Florida?"

"It was okay." I shrugged. I didn't mention I'd been home for the last several days, just hiding in my room or hanging out with AB in her bedroom laboratory. "How was the dance?"

"Fine."

I nodded, and then we both looked away. It was probably the closest we were going to come to an apology, and I was fine with that.

What I wasn't fine with was the silence between us. Just like earlier with AB, I felt compelled to keep talking. With seemingly nothing else to do, I sat a little ways down from her on the school steps.

"What are you doing here?" I asked. "I was just going for a walk."

"Same."

"You live a lot farther away than I do," I pointed out.

"So?" Amory's lips flattened. "Maybe I wanted to walk."

"Where are the other girls?"

"I don't know. I don't really care at the moment. I don't really want to see them."

I watched Amory again. She seemed conflicted and upset, and I didn't think it had anything to do with me.

"What's going on? Where's your mom?"

Amory scowled. "I wish I didn't have a mother. You're lucky yours isn't around, you know."

If it had been a week ago, I would've gotten really offended and fought back. But I was actually in agreement. Thinking of Mom working with ZZ, I eyed my arm, where the slash she'd put in Fatgirl's arm was still slightly visible.

"Yeah, you're probably right," I said. "I wish my dad wasn't so hung up on her still."

"At least he's around. I wish my daddy was still around," Amory admitted. She pulled her knees up to her chest. "He left and now my mom's getting remarried this summer."

The words were spoken so matter-of-factly, I knew Amory was actually in a lot of pain.

I reached out and put my hand on her arm. "I'm sorry."

She flinched and waved me away, but I could see her eyes filling with tears.

"The guy she's marrying is just some boring white guy," Amory said. "He's got a boring job in finance, he's pudgy, and he actually likes wearing plaid. He thinks my mom is some kind of exotic princess, and she doesn't seem to realize how typecast and racist it is. She thinks it's adorable."

I didn't know what to say. Somehow saying, "Mom is working for a criminal," didn't seem like it would help.

"I'm sorry," I said.

"My dad used to play college football," Amory said. "He owns his own gym. He's attractive and fit and funny. I can't imagine what my mom sees in Scott."

"Maybe your mom is marrying him for his money."

"Ha." Amory shook her head. "I already accused her of that. She's giving up alimony and child support from my daddy to marry Scott. He doesn't make as much. He's a middleman."

"So she must really love him, I guess?" I realized that Amory wouldn't like hearing that, so I shrugged again. "I mean, I guess it's also possible he's blackmailing her into getting married."

"Use 'extortion,' Kallie. 'Blackmail' is so racist."

I rolled my eyes. "Well, I was joking, anyway. If he's as boring and safe as you say, he's probably not reckless enough to do something like that. Is he nice to you?"

"Of course he is." Amory's voice cracked. "He's very attentive and nice and he even helps me with my homework if he sees I'm struggling. But I don't want him to be my stepfather. I want my daddy to come home."

I scooted closer to Amory. "I'm sorry. I know how that feels with my mom being away."

For awhile we just sat there together. The silence seemed better now between us.

The more I thought about it, the more I suddenly wondered—was Scott the reason she didn't like Blake?

"Well, I don't want to talk about that anymore," Amory finally said. "Tell me about what happened in Florida. I could use a good distraction."

I almost wished I could tell her the real story.

"Well, I went on a cruise with my grandmother—uh, I mean, my abuela," I said. "She's old so she didn't do much. But there was a guy there she seemed to be crushing on. It was sweet, in some ways. But I never even knew my grandpa. He died a long time ago, when my dad was young."

"Did you meet anyone?"

"Um … " An idea struck me. "Kind of. There's this guy that I hung out with some. But he's really not that attractive, and he's kind of fat. He told me he loves me. I don't hate him, but I'm not attracted to him. At least, I don't think so."

"You don't think so?" Amory bristled. "Well, what does he look like, anyway?"

"He's tall. Kind of tan. Nice eyes, with dark hair. Lots of pimples though, and his skin's kind of oily or sweaty."

"Well, you were in Florida," Amory pointed out. "Maybe he'd be more attractive in a better climate. Where was he from?"

"Mexico, I guess. Somewhere like that." I didn't actually know where Zeus had moved from, but his family was Hispanic. Or Puerto Rican. Or Cuban? I didn't know. "I guess I don't know a lot about him."

"But you're not sure you're attracted to him?" Amory arched one of her perfectly-shaped brows.

"I guess he's kind of like my version of Scott," I said. "He thinks I'm beautiful and lovely and I don't understand why all the time. But he's very nice and if he was only more attractive, I'd probably be okay with dating him."

"Well, too bad he doesn't live nearby," Amory said. "Maybe he could date you for real, and you'd stop drooling after Blake Turner."

"But he's ugly," I said. "And Blake is just so beautiful."

"Well, I guess I can't disagree with that. But my mother is unfortunately proof that looks aren't everything." Amory sat up straight again. "I don't want to talk about Blake anymore, though, okay?"

"Okay." I put my hands on my lap. "What do you want to talk about, then?"

"Let's start planning our end of the year summer bash," Amory suggested. "Got any ideas?"

Amory and I talked for another hour before we decided to head home.

We decided not to talk about our fight, or Blake, or anything much else. I didn't need to blame my period, or pretend I'd eaten too many laxatives, or anything else.

We just moved on.

Part of me hoped that when we were older, Amory and I would still be good friends—even if I wasn't sure we would be.

After all, she was right. Looks weren't everything, and that was as true for friendship as it was for love. We were mostly friends because we were the best-looking girls among our peers. But by the time we said goodbye, it seemed to me that Amory were in agreement that our friendship had to mean something more if we were really going to be friends. So, I felt a little more hopeful by the time I arrived home.

And then I saw Zeus's mom's car in the driveway next to AB's Imperial.

"Ugh. Not this." I shook my head and groaned.

○ ○ ○ ○

"Hey, Kallie."

Zeus's smile was both shy and eager as we finally saw each other again, and all I could think of was how I'd almost kissed him—and how I'd been wondering about how it would have felt, if we'd succeeded.

My face heated over, and I pretended to cough to hide my blush.

Stop thinking about it.

"Why are you here?" I did my best not to sound irritated, but I was pretty tired. I supposed I could always blame my lack of southern hospitality on that.

"He found a lurker on my phone," AB said. "So he's going to come and get it and take it back to his house to work on establishing a tracer."

"Oh, okay."

Lurker, tracer … I didn't know anything about computer stuff beyond what I learned in Mr. Embers' class, and I had a feeling he wasn't teaching us stuff that was shady or likely illegal.

"The lurker was pinging your signal while you were in Fairview," Zeus said. "So that means he's found a way to trace you."

"He?" I asked, suddenly more confused.

"Yes. ZZ sold it to a man, and she bought it from one, too," AB reminded me. "Although I think we can probably cross Trevor Darlington off our suspect list after today's adventure. Even if he was the one who sent the ones to Karen Bright, he's not likely the one who's sent the others out."

"It sounds like he's really out of it," Zeus agreed.

"Why?" I frowned as I looked over at AB. "What did you tell him?"

"I told him what I told you. He was setting my Phi-ger off, and he was very insistent that he was Richard. Trevor's not much of a success. It's sad to think that his greatest fear would be that he insists he's the successful one, and no one believes him."

Zeus and I both went silent along with AB. It was sad to think that he would have extra problems, because AB wouldn't be able to cure him without some kind of drastic action.

"Maybe you can make a pill out of the Anti-F formula," Zeus suggested. "I can see about taking it over there and getting it into his prescription mix."

"What? Why would you go?" I asked, indignant. "I could handle it. I was pretending to be AB's CAN earlier."

"It's CNA, darling," AB corrected.

"Whatever."

Zeus gave me a kind smile. "They wouldn't recognize me. And your lurker still doesn't know I'm watching his link. I would be the best one to do the job."

"I'll think about making the pill," AB said. "But I'm not sure it would work. Radioactivity is a powerful thing, and putting it in the blood at once is the only way to ensure it would be potent enough to work all at once."

"Maybe you could do a serum, and I'd be able to see if I can hack into his records and schedule him for a shot," Zeus offered.

"I don't think this is a good idea," I said. "I don't care if you do; I don't."

Zeus gave me a small, cocky grin. "Come on, Kallie. Where's your sense of adventure?"

"I'm all adventured-out, if you really want to know."

"Well, I imagine it's not easy being Fatgirl," Zeus said. "If I could help you, I would."

"Oh, great. I can see the headlines now: 'Fatgirl and Lard Boy, Taking the Fight Against Diabetes to the Forefront' or something." I crossed my arms defiantly. "Gynnifer Stills would have a field day."

Zeus laughed. "She'd finally get her promotion, don't you think?"

"Ugh, I hope not."

"Yeah, Gloria would hate that," Zeus said.

I shrugged, thinking of my mom as much as remembering some of Gynnifer's more questionable actions at the mayoral debate a few weeks ago. "Maybe it would be better for her if her aunt wasn't around as much. You never know."

"Don't say that," Zeus said, surprising me. "Everything gets better when people know they're loved."

It took me a tremendous amount of effort to stop myself from saying, "Ask your mom about that."

Fortunately, I was mature enough *not* to say that. But I still whirled around and stuck my nose up in the air. "I still don't think it's a good idea for you to go," I said. "You should be more careful."

"But what about Trevor?" Zeus asked.

"Please stop this!" I finally broke. "If you just unmask whoever's dishing out the doughnuts, Trevor will be able to go free from his rehab program, right? And then we can ambush him as he's walking out. You don't need to risk your neck for me or anyone else, Zeus, and AB, you don't need to waste our time with more research."

AB and Zeus both looked shocked at my outburst, especially considering I was right on both accounts.

"You know what? Before you get any stupider ideas, I think you should go. We have school tomorrow, and I need to start getting ready for it," I said, pushing at Zeus. He relented easily enough as I headed to the door. "Goodbye. We'll talk later—AB especially, probably."

I slammed the door shut on him and breathed out a sigh of relief.

He's gone.

"You know, I don't know why he's in love with you," AB said.

"I don't know why he is, either." My eyes teared up as I thought about my conversation with Amory earlier.

And I don't know why I care so much about him, either.

Quickly, I stormed to my room and flopped myself down on my bed.

○ ○ ○ ○

The next day, it was practically a relief to go back to school.

I breathed in the smells of the hallways of Cuttingham City High, basking in an odd sense of home.

No—not home. Hierarchy.

That was more like it, I thought.

Here at school, I was one of the popular girls. I was pretty. I had lots of friends.

I waved hi to Uli and June and Lizzy, and then Amory, too, as I passed them on my way to my locker. Boys looked over at me appreciatively, girls looked over at me with a mix of envy and admiration.

There was no dyed-haired-harpy haranguing me for a news interview, there was no Alternant that I needed to sit on, and there was no Sweaty Fat Kid who did his best to protect me even as he celebrated me with the dedicated fan webpage he'd created for me.

Okay, there *was* a Sweaty Fat Kid here, but he was more than my fan; he was my friend.

And he loved me for me, not just for Fatgirl, and not just for Popular Kallie.

No one's ever done anything like that for me before.

I slowed down to a stop, right in the middle of the hall.

All around me, everyone was talking about the Spring Fling and their vacations, and some were talking about report cards and the coming end of the school year next month.

But, suddenly, all I could really think of was how warm and safe I'd felt as Zeus held onto me outside his house. I thought of how I'd lied to his mom about how we were dating, and how happy we were able to spend time with each other.

I hated how I was a better person when I was lying. But as I stood there, I suddenly didn't mind the thought of dating Zeus so much.

I wanted that lie to be the truth. I wanted to be the kind of woman who could look past how a man looked to see how he honestly loved me.

"Kallie?"

My cheeks burned over as I heard Blake Turner's voice behind me.

"Oh, hi, Blake."

I turned around, and when I saw him, I didn't feel anything for him in that moment.

His perfectly perfect face seemed slightly odd, as if it was just a little crooked. His smile was bright, but it didn't have any of its usual dazzle.

"Is something wrong?" Blake asked. "Do I have something stuck in my teeth? You're looking at me with a weird look on your face.

"Oh, I'm sorry," I murmured. "I'm just … getting back into brain-mode for school. What's up?"

"I didn't know you weren't going to the Spring Fling this year, and Amory didn't want you to feel left out if the rest of your friends had dates," he said.

"Oh."

I couldn't have been more surprised if the floor randomly opened up and swallowed me whole.

I remembered Amory saying that she'd turned down Blake's request for dates for my own good.

Is it possible she was serious … like, seriously?

"I hope I didn't make her too upset, and I didn't want you to feel bad, either," Blake said. "I just didn't really know, you know? And then when you were pretty insistent about it, I was kind of hoping that—"

I held up my hand. "Let me go ahead and stop you," I said. "I'm not really looking to date anyone right now. I need to focus on my studies. And work on my modeling portfolio, I guess."

I actually had to figure out what I was going to do with my career choice, period, but I didn't need to tell Blake that.

At that moment, some younger version of me was screaming at me horrendously, demanding to know what kind of drugs I was taking or if I'd hit my head too hard lately. She would be absolutely insane at the thought of turning down a date with Mr. Perfect himself.

"So it's nice of you to be interested. And honestly, I can't blame you. It's been a while since I've dated anyone, and you're very popular and handsome and strong, but … I just don't feel like I really love you." I cleared my throat, realizing how mean that sounded. "Besides, there's more to relationships than how people look. I'm not always going to look like this."

"Well, I'm sure you'll change your hair at some point," Blake agreed. "And I'm sure you'll look even better."

"I still don't think we're a great match."

"I actually agree."

I frowned. "What?"

"I'm sorry," Blake muttered. "I … I kind of really like Amory. I'd love to take her out on a date at some point. I thought I'd see if you could help me. I didn't actually want to date you. Not that I wouldn't be honored to, if we did. You're very beautiful yourself."

Blake kept listing off all my sterling qualities—how I was pretty, popular, and beautiful, all the same things but different words.

And all I could think of was thank God I'd farted that day. Because of that, I'd gotten to meet Zeus.

One fart had destroyed me.

And I was never so grateful for it.

"So, anyway … what do you think?" Blake asked. "Do you think you could convince Amory to give me a shot?"

"I don't know," I admitted softly. I thought about Amory's issues with her mom dating a new guy, and getting married to him. She'd told me before Blake wasn't the kind of guy I should date, and that he would only drag me down.

But as I saw Zeus coming down the hall, I suddenly envied Blake and the challenge before him. Somehow, I knew he'd have an easier time of things with Amory than I would with Zeus. At least he didn't have to fight himself to figure out his real feelings for her.

And at least social media and the rest the world wouldn't have to wonder, either.

Everyone would take two glances at me and Zeus and ridicule me until I couldn't show my face without wearing three bags on top of it.

I thought of Azure and hated how much I was as much a coward about who I loved as he was.

I was almost grateful when my phone went off; AB was calling, and I saw Zeus was approaching me, waving as subtlety and frantically as possible.

That could only mean one thing …

"Hello?" I answered the phone. "Where do I need to go, AB?"

"The Darlington Donut Factory," AB said. "We need to hurry. Your friend Azure is there, ready to jump off the roof."

My hands felt numb at the thought. Zeus came up beside me and took my arm. "I'll drive," he whispered.

I nodded. "Alright, AB. We'll be there ASAP."

The first thing that went through my mind when I saw Azure was that I wasn't sure if getting the antidote to him would help him grow his hair back; transformed or not, Azure looked very much the same as the last time I'd seen him at the asylum—I mean, the rehab center.

The second thought I had was that I hoped my dad wasn't anywhere nearby.

I was on a lookout pass on a nearby road; AB's Imperial had pulled off to the side, and there were plenty of woods that led down to the side of the Darlington Factory. From where I stood, looking on Azure's shadowed figure on top of the large factory, I could see another road leading back to the loading docks. It was there one of Dad's large tractor-trailer trucks would be parked, loaded or unloaded, and then shipped out again.

"Are you ready, Kallie?" AB asked as she looked over me carefully. "You look like it."

I'd stuffed down my doughnut. "All I ask is that you let me skip the rest of the school day for that emergency 'doctor's appointment.' You're going to have to get Zeus an excuse, too."

Zeus gave me a grateful look, while AB only rolled her eyes.

"Fine," she said. "I'll make sure he gets home when we're done with this here. Just don't let him die, okay? That'll cause a lot more trouble for us, and Max isn't able to be much help to me anymore."

"And, you know, because dying's bad," Zeus added softly.

I nodded and tucked the last of hair into my hero suit's hood.

The navy-blue lines of my outfit made me feel like a tight ball of mass, something powerful but still unwieldly.

"Be careful, Fatgirl," Zeus said to me. "I'll get the serum element prepped. You get the blood, okay?"

"I'm getting better about that," I said proudly, patting the small pouch on my belt. Zeus grinned up at me, and my knees felt a bit weak again.

I hated how I had trouble loving him because he was not handsome, but I sure couldn't stop myself from loving that he loved me, even in my current ugly form.

Before I could say anything else to Zeus, Azure let out another scream.

"I'm going to jump!" Azure cried out.

I had to admit, until the day before, I wouldn't have expected him to look as ordinary as he did. Azure's hair was gone, but his skin had gone to its palest shade of white, including his head. He was wearing another long coat, as he had the day before, but there were no shiny shoes, no colorful pins, and no outrageous elements at all.

He was going to be my most boring Alternant ever.

This is probably why he looks normal—that is his greatest fear, isn't it?

Azure screamed again. "I have nothing left to live for!"

"That's not true, Stan!"

There was a new voice calling from behind him. It was Richard Darlington, wearing another similar suit as the one I'd seen him in yesterday.

"Don't call me Stan!" Azure yelled, putting his hands over his ears as he screamed again. "I already have nothing to live for! Don't make my existence worse."

"Azure!" I raced over to the ground below him. "You have lots to live for. What about your wife and children?"

"No! Don't say anything, or I'll jump even faster!"

"But your family—"

"No, don't speak of them. I've been fired because they found out I wasn't as diverse as implied."

I looked back at Richard. "Did you fire him?" I asked, incredulously. "All because he's not gay? Or not super gay?"

Richard shook his head. "No! I just told him I saw him out while I was visiting my brother, and I thought we would go in a different direction with my stylist needs. I didn't fire him; I just released him from the contract."

"How is that not firing him?" I asked. "And the timing does seem bad."

"I'll get my lawyer on it if you need it, but I'm not firing him because he's married or straight or white!" Richard called down to me. "I just wanted to go with a more classic style for my next product launch. It's an issue of branding and style, not personal malice!"

"No, you hate me because I'm straight!" Azure yelled, before he moved to the very edge of the roof.

Nervously, I glanced over at AB, who nudged me forward.

"Please don't move, Azure," I shouted.

"Don't say my name!" Azure shrieked down at me.

"Zeus is going into the building, Kallie," AB whispered in my earpiece. "Keep Azure distracted for a little bit longer, okay? Richard and Zeus should be able to get him."

I moved forward again, trying to keep myself directly below Azure's form. I was about to call out to him as a WACC helicopter came buzzing onto the scene.

"Oh, no," I moaned.

Azure saw it and hollered, curling himself into a small fetal position, still crying out. I covered my ears at the horrifying noise.

He was supposed to be the most boring Alternant, but he and Blake sure like to scream …

A second later, I saw a flash of light flicker off the roof door, and there was Zeus. He came up and stood behind Richard.

I smiled in relief. The two of them began talking, and they slowly began to move toward Azure on either side of him.

"Distract him, Kallie," AB hissed in my ear. "They'll take him down, if they can get him."

I nodded and then cupped my hands around my mouth. "Azure! What would Susan say if you died?"

"I don't know any Susan!" Azure screamed back.

This is so weird, I thought. It had to be the only suicide attempt where talking about family only made him more likely to jump.

Or maybe not, I thought, remembering my own mother.

"The Azure I know wouldn't jump like this," I shouted back. "He'd be appalled at the thought of making a big mess of his body on the pavement."

At this, Azure finally stopped crying and looked down at me.

"This is not outrageous enough of a way to die for you," I added, although my voice was drowned out by the hovering helicopter.

I glared over at them, and I wasn't surprised to see WACC's logo. Gynnifer had a team ready for this kind of thing now, apparently. Maybe Fatgirl was getting more viewers to tune in.

It was then that Richard appeared just behind Azure.

I turned around to see Azure falling, as Zeus cried out, and I hurried into action.

Azure screamed all the way down.

"No," I breathed. Rolling hard against the ground, I slid over the grass and managed to twist my way underneath him.

I didn't catch him, but he flopped hard against my stomach before he bounced off me. My skin seemed to reverberate with the pressure and sudden pain, but I still managed to grab hold of him.

Azure was screaming and screaming and screaming, and I had no idea that a human was capable of screaming that much.

"Hey," I snapped, slapping his face. "Snap out of it."

"He might need the antidote before he stops," AB told me. "Come back to the woody area by the car. Zeus got everything ready; I just need his blood now.

"Okay," I agreed, eyeing the helicopter uneasily.

I picked Azure up and threw his screaming sack of bones over my shoulder and ran for the cover of the woods.

I was grateful for the cover, and I had to admire AB's forethought, if she'd actually planned for it. She appeared behind me shortly with a needle.

"Here we go," she said, sticking the large, sharp end into Azure's thigh.

"You got it already?" I frowned. "I thought we needed blood first, to personalize the cure."

"Oh, that's a sleepy-time drug," AB explained. "Might as well use it, right?"

I wisely said nothing.

○ ○ ○ ○

It took a little time for him to wake up, but when he did, Azure was his sort-of normal, non-outrageous self.

He was also much calmer, thankfully.

"Are you okay?" I asked him, suddenly unnerved by how peaceful he appeared. I really hoped AB hadn't overdosed him on the "sleepy-time drugs." I didn't even want to think about which drugs she'd used.

"Of course I'm okay," Azure said evenly.

"What about your reputation? I know you were worried about it."

"Oh, that?" Azure gave me a conspiratorial wink. "I'll just tell them that the crazy person they saw on the news wasn't me. It was, unfortunately, my twin brother, who's now safely locked up in Fairview Mountain Rehab with Trevor Darlington."

"Somehow I don't think the media will buy that," I said.

Azure scoffed at me. "Please. They'll lap it up like crème. It'll be too outrageous to be anything but the popular narrative by the time I'm done explaining it."

"I guess if it's outrageous enough, no one really questions it," I said, feeling slightly depressed as Azure brightened.

"Exactly!" he said.

Clearly, Azure hadn't learned his lesson. He didn't see that juggling all these lies was only going to hurt more people and cause more trouble in the end.

I looked over at Zeus, who was currently helping AB clean up.

Suddenly, I understood more, and I hoped that Azure was lucky enough to escape his problems.

Especially since I had a feeling that, as I watched Zeus tenderly take AB's arm and escort her back to the car, I wasn't going to be quite so lucky myself.

"Kallie?" AB's voice crackled in my earpiece. "Let's go. I don't know about you, but I'm hungry."

"Are you?" My stomach still ached from where Azure had landed on me. Still, I sighed. "Alright. Let's get some lunch."

○ ○ ○ ○

A few hours passed, and after all that excitement, I walked into my house, surprised but glad to see it was empty.

Dad was at work, and AB had dropped me off before taking Zeus home. It wouldn't likely take that long for her to return, even if she did want to talk to him.

I made my way to the living room and turned on the TV, disturbed to see the news advertisement promising "exclusive footage" of today's "excitement."

"Ugh." I shook my head. I could only hope none of the magazines questioned Azure's cover story, or he'd probably be tempted to actually kill himself.

Maybe he should spend some time in Fairview. He already had some family there, as AB had pointed out before.

My phone rang.

It was Zeus.

Quickly, I silenced the call.

Even after all the excitement with Azure, I still felt bad about how I'd been treating Zeus lately—and I felt especially bad that I'd been thinking of him as much as I had.

At the end of it, Amory and AB were both right.

It wasn't Zeus's fault he'd moved here mid-school year, that his dad had him work with him sometimes, that his mom was dying. The only thing that was Zeus' fault was how much time he'd been spending with me and AB, and I couldn't fault him for wanting to be around me all the time.

I was very popular and beautiful, after all, just as Blake had said earlier.

"I should be nicer to Zeus," I muttered to myself.

Just then, my phone rang again.

It was Zeus—again.

I clenched my fists and gritted down on my teeth. *Is he watching me now?*

Maintaining my death-grip on my phone, I answered it. "Oh my goodness, you'd better have a freaking good reason for calling me right now."

I didn't even bother saying hello; it was time to reassert myself when it came to Zeus. He was the one who'd offered to help me and AB, after all. He should know I was tired after a long day of getting sat on.

That literally never happened to me. Usually, I was the one sitting on people, not the other way around, and not one Alterant had bothered to jump off a building first.

So, yeah, Zeus should've known I was tired. And frankly, it wasn't as if I owed him a date—even if I liked him.

I didn't owe him anything, as far as I was concerned.

"What in the world could be so important that you need to talk to me right now?" I demanded to know.

Zeus sighed into the phone. "Kallie, I need a favor—"

"That's it! I literally can't take this anymore," I snapped, interrupting him. "I won't date you just because—"

"Kallie, it's not that." Zeus seemed just as eager as me to shut down that topic. "We have a problem. A box of doughnuts—Darlington Donuts—was dropped off at my house. And … I didn't notice until it was too late."

"What do you mean?" I asked. "You didn't eat one, did you?"

"Um … I didn't think they were radioactive. I mean, Richard Darlington himself just congratulated me on helping him save Azure."

"He practically killed him," I muttered.

"Well, yeah, but you saved him."

"I'm not going to argue with you right now."

"Good. I don't feel very well."

"Oh, no." I put my hand on my forehead, dreading the oncoming headache. "Alright. Don't move, okay? I'm coming to get you. You're at your house, right?"

"Yes."

"Okay," I replied. "You sound okay. You probably didn't have a lot."

"No, I destroyed the rest of them, after I realized something was wrong."

"Good. Keep talking to me if you want."

Suddenly, I had to wonder what Zeus was most afraid of, though. His mother dying? She was already so far gone. Me not dating him? I mean, we were literally already there. What else could he possibly be afraid of? Dieting? Pimple cream? A comb?

"Kallie?" Zeus's voice sounded scared.

"I'm here." I cleared my throat and softened my voice. "Well, it's good to know you're sane enough we don't have to worry about that. Just stay where you are, and I'll come and get you, okay? Everything will be all right, I promise. I'm already on my way."

"Bring Dr. White."

"Oh, I'm sure she'll be excited for this one."

Before he could say anything else, I hung up the phone.

AB and I were both being targeted now—and I was more than certain of it.

Why else would Zeus and his dad get radioactive doughnuts? And Azure, right after I'd run into him at Fairview? And even Officer Powers had a backstory when it came to AB.

Was it possible ZZ had tipped off Trevor? But then, why go through all this trouble by targeting the people we knew?

Something didn't add up right.

I passed by the living room; the TV was still on, showing footage of my dramatic save. I watched Azure hit me square in the stomach, and I felt sick all over again.

And then Richard Darlington was on the screen, talking eagerly.

Azure was right, I thought, watching him talk. The mole over the right side of his lip made him look a little lopsided.

"I'm just so sorry that this man was so traumatized," he was saying. "And I am so grateful for Fatgirl saving him. I couldn't bear to live with the guilt if something happened to him. I am deeply indebted to Fatgirl and her bravery and innovative methods of saving him. In the last few months, here at Darling Donuts, we've been partnering with Sorra March and her bakery, and I'd love to come out with a new commemorative doughnut in Fatgirl's honor, to thank her for all she's done for our city … "

He kept talking about me, but he was really talking about his doughnuts. Something still seemed wrong about him, but I couldn't place it.

I shook my head. I'd have to figure it out later, if there was anything at all.

"AB?" I called out to her, as her car approached the driveway. "We have an emergency."

She rolled down her window, the Phi-ger already beeping in her hand. "I know. Let's go save your Zeus."

I didn't bother to correct her. "Yes, let's go."

For once, I was glad AB drove like a demon. I could only pray Zeus was okay as we ran off to rescue him.

Fatgirl

LARD BOY

EPISODE 10

○ ○ ○ ○

C. S. Johnson

A horror too beautiful to contemplate …

FATGIRL
LARD BOY

○ ○ ○ ○

"I can't believe Zeus was that stupid!"

I balled up my fists into my lap as AB drove in her usual demon driver form through the streets. "He should've known better than to eat a radioactive doughnut."

AB sighed. "It's not like he would've, if he would've known."

"Well, he should've known." I shook my head. "He's supposed to be so smart, and then he goes and does this stupid kind of crap."

"You did it yourself, if you'll recall."

"That was before we had to worry about city-smashing Alterants, your former job, and now an internationally wanted criminal."

AB slammed on the brakes, and I nearly lost what little of what was left in my stomach. It was bad enough I'd just had a semi-suicidal grown man bellyflop onto my engorged, Fatgirl stomach; AB's driving might as well have been some kind of off-track roller coaster ride of death.

"Would you stop driving like a suicidal maniac?" I hissed. "I want to get there quickly, too, but I'd also like to get there in one piece."

"There's an ambulance," AB said, nodding in the direction of suddenly-loud sirens. "I might be able to fake my government clearance documents, but even I'm not going to trump a medical emergency."

"Government clearance documents?" I asked.

"Never mind. You get them when you reach a certain level in the system. You'll likely never get them now, since you're my relative, and I've been blacklisted."

"Well, I can always turn you in." I relaxed in my seat, grateful for the small break in carsickness, even if I knew it was only temporary. "And maybe I should. You literally just dropped Zeus off at his house right before he ate one of your radioactive doughnuts. Didn't you hear the Phi-ger go off? You're lucky he's not too far away from us or we'd be in more trouble."

"I was on the phone with KP," AB explained through pursed lips.

"KP?" I frowned, trying to remember who that was. I could only remember he was the one AB had gone to see once; she'd forced his plane into an emergency landing after calling in a fake terror threat.

"Yes. My old lab assistant. He's upset with me. Apparently, Agent Grey has been poking around the NAH offices some this week."

"Oh, no wonder you were distracted." My voice was laced with sarcasm as we remained close behind the ambulance. "Agent Grey, huh? Well, no wonder you were distracted, since he's your Lover Boy."

"Hardly." AB wrinkled her nose, before she paused. "Although if things were different, I suppose this would count as flirting, now that you mention it."

I'd been teasing her, but I was a little caught off guard by the vulnerability I suddenly saw in her eyes.

"You know, it's okay if you like him," I said. "You're allowed to have some happiness, aren't you? Or don't you have the right government clearance for that?"

AB gave me a sidelong look, and then said nothing.

Her silence was disturbing; I didn't want to think she was confirming my jest.

I looked back down at my phone, and then looked back up at the street. The ambulance was still in front of us.

"Can't we go around it?" I grumbled.

"I don't think we're going to be able to do that," AB murmured. "In fact, we might be stuck with it the rest of the way there."

"Oh, great. You don't think Zeus was stupid enough to call an ambulance for himself, do you?"

"No." AB's voice went soft before she slammed on the brakes again, and then turned down a different street.

"What're you doing now?"

"We might have to wait a bit, Kallie." Her knuckles whiten as she gripped the steering wheel.

Before I could ask what was the problem, she turned down another street and practically spun the car onto its side wheels. I gripped my seatbelt for dear life, and feverishly, I began praying for death or deliverance. Vertigo overtook me, and my stomach revolted in helpless disgust.

It took me a moment to settle myself after we finally stopped.

"Look," AB whispered.

I opened my eyes. Through my bleary vision, I saw Zeus' house; we were just a small block up and parked near the end of his street. From where I was, I could see the ambulance had parked out in front, and there were a couple of EMTs rolling out a stretcher out the door.

It wasn't Zeus who'd needed the ambulance.

It was his mom.

"Oh, no."

Before I could think through things clearly, I hurried out of the car and ran over as fast as my shaky legs could carry me.

"Mrs. Evans," I called. "Mrs. Evans!"

I was surprised when I saw her eyes blink open. She looked in my direction.

"Kallie." She reached out for me as I came up beside her, walking in line with the EMTs.

I took her hand and squeezed it. "What happened? Are you okay?"

"Probably," she whispered. "My oxygen levels dropped really low and I'll need to get some medication from the hospital, I think, that's all—"

"Who are you?"

The familiar voice of Zeus' dad snapped loudly through the air, and I nearly jumped back in shock. I looked over to see him coming out of the house. Jose Evans was wearing his Cyber Knight Security uniform, and I had a feeling he was either supposed to go to work or he'd been coming home from it.

"I'm Kallie," I said. "I'm Zeus' … uh, girlfriend."

"Zeus doesn't have a girlfriend," Jose said.

"Um, well … " I glanced at Mrs. Evans, and she managed to give me a small smile.

"It's alright, honey," she said to Jose. "She's with Zeus."

"No, she's not. He's not allowed to date anyone. So go home, young lady," Jose said to me. "Get out of here. We don't have time for you right now."

"Where's Zeus?" I asked, before I remembered that he was stuck inside because he'd eaten that radioactive doughnut.

"He's inside, sick in the bathroom," his mom explained. "He probably didn't like to see me faint like I did."

My own stomach tumbled again as Jose pushed me aside and took Mrs. Evans' hand in his own. I would've been more angry with his rudeness if I didn't see the fearful tenderness in his eyes as he looked down at her.

"Kallie. Check on my son, please," Mrs. Evans said. I could barely hear her as the ambulance finished packing her up.

"I will," I promised.

I watched as Jose jumped inside the vehicle and the doors slammed shut; less than a moment later, the ambulance took off, speeding away in a way that would even make AB nervous.

I guess if she really wanted to get a new job, she could see if they were hiring.

I barely noticed as AB came walking up beside me. I was still watching the road, almost expecting the ambulance to come back.

"Well?" AB asked. "Are we going to go tend to Zeus or not?"

"Oh. Yes." I shook my head. "Sorry."

"I know." AB sighed. "You're young yet. You're still not used to losing people."

"No, I'm not."

She gave me a pat on the shoulder. "Believe me when I say it's a blessing, and you should do your best to keep such innocence as long as you can. Once you lose it, there's no getting it back."

I swallowed, feeling glum. "Well, I guess you would know, huh?"

AB smirked. "You have to admit, you'd hate to meet the person who knows it better than me."

"Likely."

Together we head toward the door, AB just a step behind me. Her large, bag-lady purse was on her arm. Inside of it, I could hear the small *ping-ping-ping* of her Phi-ger as it chimed, indicating we were indeed near an Alterant form.

I rang the doorbell, and I was happy we'd finally be able to take care of Zeus.

But he didn't open the door for us.

"Try calling him," AB prodded. "We don't actually know what's wrong with him. He might be transformed to something … largely unnatural."

"I hope not," I muttered as I pulled out my phone. It was too easy to believe that was what had happened though.

"Call him, Kallie, don't text."

I scowled at her as I erased my text message, and then dutifully pushed the call button for Zeus' number. "You know, some people don't like calling."

"That's why some people shouldn't have phones."

Before I could make a super-smart, super-snazzy comeback, Zeus answered the phone.

"Kallie?"

"I'm here," I said. "Well, we're here. AB and I are outside. Come let us in. She's got her stuff."

"I'm glad you're here."

"I'm sorry about your mom, by the way," I said.

Another reason I didn't want to call; I was afraid I'd end up sounding like a moron, unable to do anything but try to comfort him, even though I probably wanted to comfort myself more.

"It's okay. We're hoping she'll just need some medication and that'll be it."

"Well, good." I paused a moment, before I turned back to the issues at hand. "Now, come open the door."

"No."

It wasn't often that Zeus didn't do what I wanted, so I was shocked, and then angry, and then insulted. "What do you mean, no? We're here to get you back to normal."

"That's fine. But I'm lucid enough to do it myself," he said. "I don't want you to see me like this."

AB pulled out a small length of wire. "Keep talking," she told me quietly.

"Why would you be upset if I saw you?" I scoffed. "Look, you get to see me in Fatgirl mode all the day long. I should be able to see you just fine. What happened? Are you Lard Boy now, or something? Fatgirl's new, beloved sidekick?"

I almost laughed at the thought of Zeus as Lard Boy. I could see us now, starring in our own television series, *The Misadventures of Fatgirl and Lard Boy*, where he'd be wearing some kind of blue and green spandex suit to complement my pink and navy one. He'd have to wear glasses, but we'd just look like two hot air balloons trying to joust in air as we took down evil and saved the day.

A small chuckle escaped me, regardless of how humiliating the idea made me feel.

"It's more along the lines of 'something,'" Zeus said. "Still, I don't want to you to see me like this. It's embarrassing."

AB twiddled around with the wire, and then the door opened.

"Look, this is a safety issue," I said. "Is there still a ton of powder on your face? Did you get jelly on your shirt?"

AB and I walked into his house. Thankfully, I remembered the layout from before. As Zeus continued to give us some stupid excuses, we finally caught sight of him in his mother's sunroom.

Her bed and all the pots of flowers were still decorating the room, although the flowers I saw this time were new and fresh.

Zeus was standing with his back to me, looking out into the yard.

"Just trust me," he was saying into the phone. "You don't want to see me like this. You would just have nightmares for weeks."

I cleared my throat behind him. "I already have nightmares for weeks. I think I can handle this. You seem fine to me."

Zeus went still. And then slowly, slowly, slowly … he turned around.

And then I saw his face.

My mouth dropped open in horrified shock. My phone fell to the floor. My knees buckled, and I felt faint and dizzy all over again.

I just couldn't believe my eyes.

"I … I can't believe it's you," I finally managed to croak out.

○ ○ ○ ○

He was … just … so perfect.

Literally.

My cheeks were suddenly scorching hot as I stared at him.

No longer was Zeus the Sweaty Fat Kid I'd noticed that day in Mr. Embers' class. He was still the same height, but all of the bulk of his sweatshirt was gone; he was dressed in a simple, stretched out t-shirt, and his biceps were nice and big; his once-charcoal hair was now a harmonious ebony, no longer so oily and curly. Instead, it was smooth and wavy, with a glowing sheen; his dreamboat-blue eyes were no longer hidden behind thick-framed glasses; and his skin was smooth and perfect, without a pimple in sight.

"You look like you've been Photoshopped by God," I whispered in awe.

Beside me, AB rolled her eyes. "Please, Kallie. Stop being so shallow."

"I told you I didn't want you to see me like this," Zeus muttered, his voice full of bitterness.

"Come on," I said. "After dealing with Baby-Boy Blake, Sore-Loser Sorra, Bad Guy Cop, and Staid-Looking Stan, this should be considered a literal miracle. This is the best thing that ever happened to you."

He cringed and looked over at AB, who gave him a sympathetic look.

What on earth is wrong with him? If Amory or Uli or any of the other girls could get a guaranteed makeover from a doughnut, they'd be stuffing their faces in less than a second.

"Why are you so afraid of looking this good?" I asked. "I mean, you look almost as good as I do, and you see how well I handle it. Being attractive shouldn't terrify you."

"Most of what you do is terrifying to normal people, I'll bet," AB muttered as she got out her purse. "Give me two moments, Zeus, and I'll have the cure ready."

He was clearly relieved. "Thank you, Dr. White."

As AB began to work, I nudged Zeus as quietly as I could. "What's wrong with you?" I hissed. "Don't you know how lucky you are?"

"I don't want to look like this, Kallie. I like who I am."

"But this version of you is so much better." I looked him over again, still gawking over how much of a demigod he'd become.

"Honestly, I was worried you'd turned into some kind of cartoonish sidekick of mine. I honestly don't know why you'd want to change back. You could get anyone in the world to date you looking like that."

Zeus eyed me with a critical look. "Are you saying you'd go out on a date with me if I asked you now?"

"Looking like that? Absolutely, yes." I glanced back at AB's centrifuge, watching as it whirred around in quick, tight circles. A few brilliant ideas struck me, all at once. "In fact, let's go now. AB can make the cure while we get some dinner. I can call up some of my friends and we can hang out."

This is perfect.

I'd told Amory about my trip to Florida, and how I was having mixed feelings about a boy I'd met there. Zeus, in his current form, could be that guy, and I could get her honest assessment of him. Even if he was technically an Alterant at the moment. And even if I didn't completely care what Amory thought.

But she was different from my dad and AB, and my mom wasn't anyone even remotely available or reliable right now. I needed some kind of outside opinion, even if it was hers. And at least I knew enough of Amory's biases, or I could guess them.

"I don't think it's a good idea," Zeus said.

"Come on," I begged. "Please? You have to hang out with me in my Fatgirl form all the time. I should get to spend some time with you this way. It's only fair."

Zeus only looked more depressed. "I can't believe you're begging me to remain poisoned like this."

"It can't be any worse than when I have to deal with it," I insisted, lowering my voice. "But if you want to date me, now's your chance. Take it or leave it."

He hesitated, but I curled a lock of my hair around my fingers and gave him a flirtatious, pouty look. Less than a moment passed before he finally gave in and nodded.

I grinned.

Like he was really, actually going to say no.

"Dr. White?" Zeus turned back to face her. "Kallie and I are a little hungry. Would you mind if we went out to dinner? I can always get the cure when we're finished."

"What?" AB frowned. "What about your parents?"

He glanced around. "They won't be back until tomorrow at the earliest. I don't have to worry about them thinking I'm some kind of stranger."

They discussed different points back and forth, but I didn't really pay attention to anything they said. I was too busy just staring up at Zeus and thinking of how all I needed to do was break AB's plungers and centrifuge.

And then I would get my way, at least until dinner was over, AB had her spare centrifuge out, and finished the cure for Zeus.

I looked up at Zeus again, and suddenly I just never wanted anything more.

I'll do it.

Carefully, as nonchalantly as possible, I scooted backward, and then I pretended to trip over a flower pot between me and AB.

"Whoa!" I yelped as my arms went flying, and I gracefully soared off to the side as I took careful aim.

AB scrambled to get out of my way. "Kallie, what in the world—"

A second late, I was successful.

I landed with my fist square on the centrifuge; it fell to the floor, banged up a bit, and the whirring noises all stopped.

It was dead.

Perfect.

"Oh, no," I murmured, pretending to be embarrassed. "I tripped. I'm sorry, I didn't mean it."

AB's face went flat; she wasn't buying my charade.

But Zeus shrugged. "I guess we really do have the time then, right?"

"AB, you can go back to our house and get the cure mixed, and Zeus and I will just find a place to hang." I looped my arm through Zeus' now-perfectly-sculpted muscular arm. "Just call me when it's finished and we'll come right over."

Unless I can find a way to convince him to stay like this.

"I don't like this, Kallie," AB said. "The doughnuts are mostly stable, but it can lead to terrifying results, even in smaller doses."

"So? I know how it works with Fatgirl." I didn't know why she was bothering me about that. But then, I couldn't seem to think straight around Zeus anyway.

He was just too gorgeous.

I ran my hand up and down his arm, glorying in the miraculous change.

But AB's perpetually unhappy, ugly expression did seem to break the spell, if only briefly.

"Hey, Zeus." I smiled brightly. "Go and start up your car, okay? I'll be out in a moment and then we can get started on our date."

"Sure. I mean, I guess. If you say so," he replied, suddenly seeming a lot more agreeable. He looked down at my hand on his arm, and slowly, almost reverently, he let himself fall out of my reach.

He looked a little dazed as he left the room, almost as if he knew a whole new world had suddenly opened up to him.

Which, technically, it had, since he would be taking me, Kallie Grande-White, out on a date. It was something that so very few people in the past several years had been worthy of, and a privilege only one person in this particular half of the school year, had managed to secure.

Before he could, of course, Amory ruined it for him. And then he ruined it for himself by liking her more than me.

I should get her to go out with Blake.

Amory and I had talked earlier, before Azure's little show that was no doubt still being splattered all over the city's news screens, and since she was unhappy about Scott, her soon-to-be-stepfather, she could use a little distraction, too. And Blake, frankly, could use a little company while I paraded Hot Zeus around in front of him and let him know what he was missing.

That would serve Blake right, for not asking me out in the first place, and it would be nice for Zeus to finally get a chance to one-up Blake by taking me on a date.

I hated how perfectly evil my plan was.

But it was still perfect, so of course I had to do it.

"Kallie." AB shook her head, clearly disappointed. "What's wrong with you?"

"What's wrong with *me*? What's wrong with *you*?" I snapped, suddenly wondering if she knew what I was thinking. "Don't you see him, Abuela? He's so handsome now. And he deserves a nice night out on the town. His mother was just carted away to the hospital, remember?"

"I'm surprised you remember that yourself."

Briefly, I flushed over.

Maybe I had almost forgotten about that, thanks to the light of grand beauty that was now Zeus' countenance. But I'd still recalled that detail when I needed it—when I was trying to convince AB to let us leave.

"Anyway, I've been Fatgirl for hours at a time," I said. "And Robert Cuttingham III was able to last days under the spell of his doughnuts. Zeus will be fine. We can change him back to his old, ugly self later."

"Kallie." AB sighed. "From the sound of things, he didn't ingest much. But the effects could still get worse and things can still change."

"Well, let's hope. He should be as attractive as he can get." I squared my shoulders. "You said we're here to help him. Let's help him live a little."

"I'm only going to let you leave because I do actually need to go back to the house and get a new mixer," AB said flatly. "In the meantime, keep your phone on you and keep me posted. And don't go overboard, Kallie. He might be in love with you, God only knows why, but you shouldn't do anything that he'd hate you for later."

She packed up her purse-bag with a huff.

I don't know why the old bag bothered me so much. I didn't know why she couldn't get a nicer-looking purse, either.

I promised myself I would try to keep everything she'd said in mind.

And I was texting Amory and trying to get ahold of the rest of the girls—and everyone else, too—by the time Zeus opened his mom-car door for me.

"This is going to be great," I said as I sat down.

"Great." Zeus didn't seem convinced.

○ ○ ○ ○

Going to the nearby mall was cliché, but it was cliché enough that it was ironically enjoyable.

Even if I was unironically enjoying it.

"This is embarrassing," Zeus said, trying to pull his hood on for the fourth time.

"Stop it," I said. I pushed down the hood again, firmly but still gently. "This is your new normal now. You're gorgeous, and so I am. And we're two extremely beautiful people, in a public place. Of course other people are going to notice."

"They're gawking at me."

"And as I said, you're gorgeous. So I can't blame them." My own mouth was still more moist than usual, and at that moment, I was literally wishing I could kiss him now. As I was staring at him, I caught sight of a flashing sign at the pet store behind. "Oh, look. It's a sale."

"Unless it's a book store or comic shop, I don't want to go into it," Zeus warned.

"It's a pet shop," I said, pointing. "Let's go pet the puppies."

"But we're not going to buy one."

"That's not the point. The point is to pet the puppies without paying for them. It's how people feel about going to summer camp to ride horses. It's fun while you're there, but you don't actually want to live in a place where you'd have to shovel out horse poop everyday."

Zeus sighed. "I guess I should be thankful that you don't want to spend any money."

"Don't worry, we'll have plenty of time for that later. We just need to kill some time while we wait for Amory and Blake and all my friends to get here."

"Oh, Kallie, tell me you didn't."

I rolled my eyes, tugging on his arm. "Are you going to come pet puppies with me or not?"

Zeus shook his head, but he allowed me to drag him over to the pet shop.

As we walked in, I recognized the store as the one that had announced their support for our lacrosse team because of the "Kitty Eyes" fiasco, and then took back their support once we lost.

Anxiety flared inside of me.

I hope the lacrosse team doesn't remember that.

I was already risking quite a bit. I'd told Amory that Blake had insisted on taking her, me, and all the girls out as a belated Spring Fling apology, and I told Blake that Amory would consider going on a date with him if he did a group date with me and the girls and his team first.

Amory had been a harder sell, until I told her that June and Duncan, one of the team's top scorers, were secretly dating and this was our chance to get her to owe us. This was important, I said, because finals were coming up, and June was the one who led our group "study" gatherings. Her parents expected her to get good grades, and the rest of us were willing to help her along, of course.

Especially since it usually helped us along, too.

I could only hope June and Duncan were actually somewhat attracted to each other. I'd sworn to both not to say anything, so either they would figure out how to "dump" each other graciously, or they'd end up married after high school.

I didn't really care.

I was with Zeus.

And I got to watch him play with puppies.

All while the girls in sales were drooling over him and asking him if I was his sister or cousin.

That part was annoying, and it got worse when the boys in sales began asking him that, too.

That was Zeus' limit.

"Why would you even ask me that? Do you think she deserves someone more like you?" he asked, scoffing at the average-looking, low-to-mid-twenty-something sales guy. "You're not even remotely successful, and if you think you're handsome enough for her, you're delusional."

The sales guy flushed over red. "We were just trying to figure out if you were going to get one as a couple or not; our questions aren't meant to be personal."

I saw the uncharacteristically haughty look on Zeus' face as he balled up his fists. "Good. I won't have to fight you, then. Unless you keep talking to her."

The sales guy looked green as Zeus flexed his perfect arms threateningly.

My eyes went wide, and my amusement turned into horror. Quickly, I took his arm. "Okay, darling, that's enough puppy time, I think. Let's go find our other friends, okay?"

Zeus glared at the sales guy the entire time we walked out of the store.

"He shouldn't have ruined things for us," Zeus muttered as we left. "Next time, I'll save us some time and just punch the guys who look at you."

In the back of my mind, another flare of panic went off.

AB warned me about this …

But I didn't want all the good times to end. We still needed to meet up with Amory and the others.

"Well, hey, all the sales girls were hitting on you, too," I said. "And they were pretty and cute, too. Most of them, anyway."

Zeus went quiet for a moment, and then he nodded. "Well, I guess that's true. I don't think they were more attractive than you, though. You're the most beautiful girl I've ever met. At least, in a conventional way. I guess there are more exotic beauties out there."

I gritted my teeth together, wondering if I could fool myself into thinking he was joking or not.

"You see her?" Zeus pointed to another lady, who was dressed like a model as she strolled through the mall. From the look of it, I would've been willing to bet she was lonely on a weekend night, and she was on the prowl for some amusement. "She's prettier than you, I think."

"Yeah," I said. "What about her? Are you going to go beat her up, too, since she's prettier than me?"

"No, but I'm glad we agree she's prettier than you," Zeus said. "Do you think she'd want to go out with me looking like this?"

I narrowed my eyes at him. "You're too young for her."

"I don't know about that." He eyed her more carefully—practically oogling her. "I'm seventeen."

"Going on twelve, by the sound of it," I muttered.

"Look, Kallie, I don't know why you're complaining about me," he said. "I'm as attractive as you wanted. Naturally, other people are going to think I'm attractive and worthy of their love and devotion, too. And maybe if I get more of their attention, you'd love me."

I did my best to ignore that last part. "You can find others pretty, but you're still supposed to be completely devoted to me."

"I am, but I'm just pointing out that there are prettier ladies out there, and you shouldn't be jealous of me noticing them."

"That doesn't make any sense."

"Sure it does. You're just too jealous to figure it out."

My mouth dropped open. I pulled out my phone, ready to text AB and tell her to get over here with two syringes full of Anti-F serum.

"Kallie! Hey, Kallie!"

But that was when I saw Amory heading in our direction.

She was upset with me, clearly; I saw her pinched lips ready to spew out some kind of verbal passive-aggressive hello, when she noticed Zeus beside me.

"Hello, there," she murmured, immediately putting on her best, flirtatious smile as she faced him. "Are you Kallie's Florida Man?"

"Florida Man?" Zeus asked, glancing down at me. He seemed confused enough to return to more of his usual, nice self, and I was relieved.

Maybe his bad behavior was from the adrenaline rush in the pet shop.

Maybe I was imagining things.

Maybe I was overreacting.

Maybe I could still get us through the evening.

Maybe.

I mean, it's a fifty-fifty chance. Right?

"Well, who is this handsome hunk, Kallie?" Amory asked, her voice brimming with impatience.

"Oh, yes," I said, clearing my throat. "Amory, this is Zeus. He's the one I was hanging out with in Florida, and he came all the way here just to be with me."

Amory's eyes blinked in understanding. "That's why you called all of us and lied to get us to come here."

"Um, well … I didn't lie, exactly … "

"Oh, really? Because we're all more than a little confused about things, except how we got here."

She jerked her thumb to the food court behind her, where June and Duncan were at least eyeing each other with some interest, and Uli and Declan were also chatting nicely. Lizzy was laughing with some of the others, and Blake—my once most perfect, model boyfriend-looking ideal—was just watching Amory as she talked with me.

I saw him look at Zeus and frown, as though he was suddenly worried.

"I didn't lie about everything." I leaned on Zeus' arm. "And you can't blame me entirely, can you? My dad doesn't want me going on dates by myself, and I wouldn't have been able to see my Zeus here at all if I didn't tell Dad you guys would be here."

"Your dad's a pain," Amory muttered.

I thought about reminding her that I still had mine around, but then I remembered how kind most of my friends were about my mom leaving and wisely stopped myself. They'd let me have my space to grieve, even if it was a lot longer than I would've given them myself.

"Well, we're all here anyway," I said instead. "And the mall's still open for another hour or so. Why not make the best of it?"

Amory glared at me. "Fine, Kallie. But you owe us."

I might've wanted to punch her face in, but I gave her my best smile. "Of course."

She turned her attention to Zeus. "I'm Amory, Kallie's best friend," she said, stepping closer to him.

In all my plans and in all my lies, I'd never imagined that Amory would recognize Zeus as Sweaty Fat Kid. And I was right. She took one look at him and couldn't tell she'd seen him dozens of times before.

Zeus didn't appear to remember he'd seen her before, either, because he immediately stepped away from me, took her hand, and gave her a small kiss on the hand like he was out of some old-fashioned movie.

It was so cringe-worthy, I gagged.

But Amory, seeing how attractive he was, didn't seem to notice that. She just kept her eyes on him as he began smooth-talking her.

"It's a pleasure to meet you," he said. "Kallie didn't tell me that you were more beautiful than she is."

"Uh, Zeus, cool it with the flattery," I interjected. "Amory knows when you're trying too hard to win her over."

Amory laughed gaily as Zeus ignored me. "Oh, I can see why Kallie enjoyed meeting you, Zeus. You're definitely a keeper."

"I'll let you keep me for a bit," he agreed, and it was at that point I had enough—and Blake wasn't looking happy, either.

"Amory, Blake is calling for you," I said. "Why don't you go talk with him and the others about what we're going to do here? I need to talk to Zeus for a moment, okay?"

She glared at me, but Blake came up beside her. "Hey, Amory, what do you think about trying out that vegan hut?"

"Ew, gross," Amory said. "It's just pizza and kale."

"But I thought you'd like that," Blake said. "Remember last week when you said you were thinking of going vegan—"

"That was last week."

As the two of them began to argue over things, Amory gradually got more frustrated, while Blake was content to be the loser. And he undoubtedly was.

Zeus watched them alongside me, more amused than I was. "I'd get Amory a full steak instead," he said. "She needs to keep her muscles or she'll lose all her shape."

"Ugh, can you stop?" I groaned. "I didn't want them to end up fighting. If anything, Blake should finally step up and ask her out, don't you think?"

"I don't really care."

I sighed. "Well, good for you."

"You know, I wanted to go on a date with you," he said. "I didn't want to go out with your friends."

"I brought them here so you could see what it's like to be popular and pretty."

"I am 'pretty,' and if you'll love me only if I'm popular, I'll go take care of that, I suppose," Zeus said with a tired sigh. "I guess I'll go challenge the guys to some arm-wrestling."

"No." I tried to pull him back, but he brushed me off. I stamped my foot. "This isn't how a date with me is supposed to go, Zeus!"

"Well, I deserve better then," he said. "Maybe you should worry about your own looks."

"Excuse me?" I huffed as I gave him an angry look.

"Yeah. I've been with you for a whole night now, and I can see your flaws much more now."

My mouth dropped open, and I could only wonder if he was playing some kind of huge joke on me.

"You're getting some wrinkles on your forehead. Probably from how you're always yelling and insulting me and Dr. White," he said. "Or maybe it's a side effect of being Fatgirl, huh? There's no telling how many side effects of that haven't been categorized."

My face burned red. "Would you keep your mouth shut about Fatgirl?"

"Oh, sure," Zeus said, waving his hand dismissively at me. "I'm sure you wouldn't want anyone to think I'm hung up on that kind of enormous, ugly beast of a woman now that I'm dating you."

"You know, Blake once said he'd date Fatgirl before," I nearly shouted, angry all over again. "Don't tell me he's better than you."

"You've been on this date with me long enough to know I am the best-looking guy around here," Zeus said. "But it doesn't really matter what I look like, does it? You didn't love me when I was ugly, and you don't really love me now that I'm not."

His words struck me, hard and fast, and I felt as though he'd punched in the gut. Shame festered inside of me, and I suddenly wondered if this was all my fault.

And it was.

Why did I let Zeus get me to agree to go out on this date?

"You want to know the worst part of all this?" Zeus sighed. "I still want you to love me, though, so I'll go prove I'm good enough for you. If such a thing is possible."

As he left me, standing there shellshocked, I knew it was time to call AB.

I took out my phone and I was startled to see her already calling me.

"What is it?" I asked. "Please tell me you have the Anti-F serum for Zeus."

"Oh, I do," she said, practically purring. "Don't tell me your date ended earlier than planned?"

"Oh, it's over," I agreed. "Now, shut up and get over here so you can help me."

○ ○ ○ ○

AB promised to get there as soon as she was able—which, given her driving skills, was probably going to be no more than five minutes.

With renewed hope and determination, I put my phone away, and set my eyes on Zeus.

He was already arm wrestling with the guys from the team.

And he was beating them.

I watched as Blake sat down for his turn.

An hour ago, I would've relished this scenario. Now, I felt sick to my stomach as Zeus slapped Blake's arm down fast; I could hear a *crack*, and I grimaced as Blake grabbed his arm.

"Watch it!" Blake yelped. "You almost dislocated my elbow."

"Well, maybe if you were a better lacrosse captain, the Cuttingham City Crusaders wouldn't have lost their last games," Zeus replied easily enough. He cracked his knuckles and grinned up at me. "What do you think, Kallie? Do you like me more now that I've shown you that I'm stronger than the entire lacrosse team? Probably not, I know. But I thought I'd ask."

June pulled me over this time. "Kallie, I know you've spent your vacation with this guy, but I have to say, he reeks of toxicity. What were you thinking, dating him? Are you depressed?"

"Um," I murmured, embarrassed. "He wasn't like this before."

"Well, if he's not going to be his real self in front of your friends, you might want to tell him to leave." June sighed as she looked over at Duncan. "I'm worried Duncan might have the same issues, but he's being a lot quieter about them."

Oh.

For a moment, I thought June was concerned about me. But she was really concerned with herself.

"Hey everyone," I said. "How about a movie? We can see the next showing of that … that big movie everyone wanted to see … I think it starts in ten minutes!"

"Movie?"

The rest of them looked at me strangely, as if I had two heads. Silently, I turned and appealed to Amory for help.

She crossed her arms. "No one made any plans for a movie. I wanted to just walk around the mall."

"I'd like to do that, too," Blake added, already whipped.

Amory looked at Uli, who couldn't seem to choose between Amory and me. She eventually shrugged. "I don't have a preference."

Lizzie giggled. "I'm sure the boys would be happy to eat first."

Zeus arched his brow. "We didn't talk about any movie before. But I guess you're just interested in yourself and doing what you want, aren't you?"

His dismissiveness was the last straw for me.

"Oh, you know what? I forgot that Zeus needs to get back to the airport," I said. "He's unfortunately got to go home and get back to Florida to do more … uh, Florida things."

I grabbed his arm and tried to haul him away, but he and his now-perfect, large muscles remained seated, almost mocking me.

"If you love me, you'll come with me now," I hissed through my teeth.

At that, he finally stood up and I hauled him away from the others, smiling the entire way along.

"What are you doing?" Zeus hissed. "I thought you wanted to show me off to all your friends."

"I did," I admitted, still trying to keep my smile as we rounded a nearby corner. "But you're being ridiculous."

"I'm only being ridiculous because I want you to love me."

"That's even more ridiculous," I objected. "Why do you really even love me, anyway? I'm shallow and mean and I enjoy being those things most of the time. Even when I'm being shallow and mean to you!"

I honestly felt like crying after saying that.

The only reason I didn't was because we were walking past an electronics store, and Gynnifer Stills' overly-blown-up, overly-done-up face was splashed onto the bright screen, and she was interviewing Azure.

Not "Stan," his real, normal-person name.

But Azure, speaking of "his twin brother" and his horrific episode of attempted suicide on the Darling Donut factory earlier today.

" … I just can't imagine how terrifying that would've been for you," Gynnifer was saying, leaning in so close to Azure she practically cuddled up to him.

Azure put his hand over his forehead. "I'm just so glad that Mr. Darlington is so understanding," he said. "My brother was just too distraught about my success, and I didn't want to worry about him causing me my new job."

"And you were so concerned he would kill himself over this?" Gynnifer asked. Her eyes were gleaming with fake sympathy, which was probably actually narcissistic ambition.

Gynnifer Stills would be the kind of woman who got excited over someone killing themselves like this. It would mean more airtime and a promotion for her.

"Yes, of course. Thankfully, he didn't die. And of course, Mr. Darlington has his own family issues," Azure continued. "So he's very understanding. In fact, he's given me a nice pay raise to help me afford my brother's counseling."

I snorted at the thought. Azure would probably take the money and use it for "retail therapy."

"Do you think there was anything else involved?" Gynnifer asked. "The video footage WACC was able to record shows he might have been unstable."

"Well, who knows? Drugs, I'm sure, were involved somehow," Azure said. "I mean, no one just randomly starts trying to kill themselves, do they?"

"Not randomly," I muttered.

Nothing was random in this case, or at least, I didn't think it could be. Azure had been affected just after AB and I'd run into him at Fairview. Zeus had already said she had a technological "lurker" on her, some kind of signal that was tracking her and following her around—and the signal's home base was right at Darling Donuts' factory. And then after Zeus had helped Richard Darlington calm Stan down, Zeus had been given some doughnuts, straight from the factory.

I watched Azure continue to talk about his dreams and aspirations, how he'd started off so poor and lonely to go onto winning a designing role on Model Middle America, and then settling into a new role with Richard Darlington and the future of Cuttingham City.

"After that last nightmare of a mayoral election, I wouldn't be surprised if Richard started speaking up more," Azure said with a wink. "He can be very persuasive. I should know. He once got me to eat carbs!"

As the television audience fake-laughed and Gynnifer began to egg him on, telling Azure to show the audience his six-pack abs, a new thought occurred to me.

Azure wasn't likely the kind of person—in his regular form or his outrageously outrageous form—to eat a doughnut for no reason.

Was it possible … Richard Darlington was the one who gave Azure the radioactive doughnut?

Richard was the one who'd sent Zeus some doughnuts. And he'd apparently been working with Sorra March, the owner of a "Divorced Delight" bakery in Cuttingham City before she also became an Alterant.

I was just about to pull out my phone and call AB when I heard Amory call for me.

"Kallie!"

I blinked back to the present moment and blushed, realizing I was standing there, in front of the TVs, all alone.

Zeus had disappeared, and Amory was stomping her way over to see me.

"Look," she started, "I get that you needed your friends to cover for your date, but you could at least make sure that your date is with *you* instead of hurting the rest of the lacrosse team. They're all arm-wrestling again, and now I have to wonder if this isn't some kind of set up to get our team benched."

"I'm sorry. It's not that. I was just … watching the news." I pointed to the television screen, where Gynnifer was once more showing a replay of the helicopter footage. "My dad works at that factory. I was worried about him. Sorry."

That particular lie wasn't so bad; it was only really bad because that should've been the first thing I'd thought of when I saw the Darling Donut Factory.

Amory groaned and then glared at me. "Fine, I'll excuse you this time. But you still need to get that Zeus of yours under control."

"How's Blake doing?"

"Why would I care?" Amory huffed.

"Because you know he likes you … don't you?" I gave her a skeptical look. "That's why you told him not to ask anyone from our group out for prom. You knew he wanted to ask you, but you knew I wanted to go with him."

"It doesn't matter. And I still don't care about Blake, even if you've got a boyfriend now," Amory said. "I can't stop him from acting like a jealous moron."

"Jealous?" I asked.

"Zeus said I would've dated Blake if the team hadn't lost so many games this year."

"They've only lost a few—"

"That's not the point, Kallie!" Amory cringed. "I swear, if Zeus wasn't so good-looking, I would've thrown him out of the mall myself. And if *we* weren't such good friends, I would've left, too."

As mean as she sounded, I knew Amory was right; I had to get Zeus under control.

I made my way back to my friends to see June and Duncan were off by themselves to the side, but Uli and Lizzie were all right up next to Zeus as he and Blake were in the middle of their rematch.

"I'm going to win this one for Amory," Blake declared, leaning into his grip.

"She doesn't want to date a loser," Zeus said. He caught my eye as Amory and I came up to them.

"Blake, stop this now," Amory ordered.

"No, I'm going to win," he declared.

"Zeus, it's time for us to leave," I said, but he ignored me as Uli and Lizzie cheered Zeus on.

"Go, Zeus! You're so strong, you can beat him!" Lizzie practically squealed.

"Come on, Zeus!" Uli shifted away from him as she saw me. "Kallie is watching you!"

The two of them were in the middle of the match, but Zeus didn't even seem concerned. He yawned as Blake was clearly trying much harder to win.

It was, literally, one of the most pathetic things I'd ever seen, ever. I stood there, paralyzed with disgust, as I watched Zeus finally push back against Blake's arm.

He was taunting him, just playing with him, like a cat playing with a fish before eating it.

It was at that moment I had enough.

I pushed past all the lacrosse team members and my so-called friends. I grabbed Zeus by the ear. "Zeus, your mother needs you to go home now."

The mention of his mother—the dear, sweet Mrs. Evans—seemed to knock some sense into Zeus. His eyes briefly cleared, and I was able to distract him long enough to break him free from Blake's grip.

"I'm calling it a tie," Zeus called back as I took hold of his ear and dragged him off.

"No, I won!" Blake turned to Amory almost expectantly. When she flipped her long braided hair over her shoulder, huffed, and walked away, he began to grovel after her.

"Amory, please wait," I heard him whimper affectionately.

"Leave me alone," Amory snapped. "This is embarrassing, and you're embarrassing."

I noticed that without me, Amory, and Blake, the rest of the group didn't seem to know what to do.

But just then, I couldn't seem to care.

I was more than relieved when AB showed up. She was tucked into a side hallway, near a bathroom, and given the amount of crap I had to deal with, I could see it as symbolically appropriate.

"Close your eyes and come this way," I told Zeus, trying to be flirtatious. "I have a gift for you."

"What is it?"

"You'll see. Just close your eyes, okay? If you love me, you'll do it."

"But—"

"You'll do it without questioning me, either."

Once he'd shut his eyes, I waved my hand at AB, telling her to slip out of sight. Zeus was already temperamental at best, and I just needed the syringe.

I was really looking forward to jabbing him with it, too.

As Zeus and I ducked into the hallway, presumably to make out, AB quietly passed me the syringe.

I pushed Zeus up against the wall.

As I held him there, I faltered slightly. He was still really gorgeous. There was a small sheen of sweat on his forehead from all the arm wrestling; his hair was slightly mussed, and of course he was just generally good-looking.

I glanced over at AB; she had her back to us as she played lookout.

It was really tempting in that moment, to just kiss him anyway.

As if he knew what I was thinking, he opened his eyes.

They were still the same ones I'd always known; the dream-boat blue, startling in their clarity and depth.

I leaned in closer to him, and he began to lean in, too. I could feel his hands take hold of my shoulders, and I closed my eyes.

I could only picture Zeus' face—his real one—as we stood there.

Realizing I didn't want to kiss his fake-self any longer, I hurriedly injected him with the syringe full of the Anti-F serum.

"Sorry, Zeus," I whispered softly, as he began to shrink back into his normal form.

He let go of me and sighed. "I'm sorry, too."

Our eyes met, and I couldn't say if either of us knew why we were apologizing.

"I don't want to hear it, AB."

Beside me, my grandmother was obviously quite pleased as the two of us stood by her Imperial, waiting on Zeus to catch up.

"I told you so," AB said, practically singing out her words with sadistic joy. "You shouldn't have let your hormones get the better of you."

"Well, I know never to let it happen again, at least."

"Ha. You're a teenager. I doubt you'll remember it longer than a week. Anyway, consider this poetic justice for what you did to my centrifuge. You can pay me for a replacement, since I'm out of work."

It had taken us some time, but we'd been able to sneak out of the mall without getting noticed by our classmates. Zeus had slowed down behind us as we headed out of the building. He seemed to be deflating back into his usual form and trying to sort out what was real and what wasn't from his ordeal.

"Oh, leave me alone. If you're really bothered by it, I'll get you a new one." After I made a mental note to have Dad give her some money for "another Girl's Night," I crossed my arms and pouted. "Don't you care at all that I'm upset?"

"Not when it's your own fault," AB said. "If anything, you should have more sympathy for Zeus."

I rolled my eyes. "Why?"

"Because, think about it. His biggest fear was that he wasn't attractive enough for you to fall in love with him."

I paused. I didn't tell AB the rest of the truth, that Zeus would've literally become anything to get me to love him. But the part I did tell her was bad enough.

"I don't have any sympathy for him. He actually called Amory prettier than me." I ducked my head to my chest. "Can you believe that?"

"He was under the protactinium's influence, darling. You can tell by just looking at him he's desperately in love with you. Even if you're not as pretty as the next girl."

"You think she's more pretty than me, too?" I couldn't believe AB would betray me like this.

"Kallie, someone, at some point in your life, is *always* going to be more pretty, more popular, more intelligent, or more successful than you. And even if you are the best at all the things you want to be best at, it's only a matter of time before someone else beats you out." She paused. "To clarify, I think you're lovely-looking, and Amory is quite pretty as well. But you're my granddaughter, and she's not. And there's no one who can take that away from you."

I felt my heart swell up with a little influx of joy. But a moment later, I smiled.

"So, you do think I'm prettier than her?"

"Ugh." AB rolled her eyes. "Of course you are, darling. Now, will you please be smarter than a preschooler?"

Before I could tell her off again, Zeus finally came up next to us.

"Kallie?" Zeus hesitated as he approached me. "Do you want me to drive you home? I think I'm all better now. And your house is on the way to mine … but I do understand if you've had enough of me today."

"One moment, please, Zeus." AB pulled me over to the side. "Look, Kallie. Go with him, and be nice, okay?"

"Fine. I'm too tired to be mean anyway."

I pushed past her and headed toward Zeus' car. "Come on, let's go."

I didn't want to do what she told me to do, but I figured if I made her happy now, she'd leave me alone later. And I did want to try to apologize to Zeus in a more clear, meaningful sort of way.

But I wasn't sure where to begin, and I wasn't lying to AB; I was tired. After a long day of Alterants, Amory, and Azure, I was more than ready to go to bed.

As Zeus and I drove home, I began to drift off. Zeus didn't say anything, and I figured if he didn't want to talk, that would be fine with me, too.

Zeus' driving was so peaceful; it was nice not having a lunatic at the wheel. Regular driving was almost like getting rocked to sleep.

I'd nodded on and off a few times when Zeus finally drove past AB's Imperial and parked in my driveway.

"Hey." He nudged me carefully. "We're here."

I yawned. "Good."

He parked the car and came around, opening my door for me.

"You don't have to do that," I said. "Date's over, right?"

I didn't feel like I had to tell him that the date really had been over for some time now.

It's for the best I didn't; he contradicted me a second later.

"The date's over when you're home and I've walked you to your door."

I got out and he shut the door. But rather than walk toward the house, I leaned against my car door. "You don't have to do this. You should go home and get some rest, too. You've had a worse night than I did."

"I still want to apologize and ask you to never bring this night up ever again."

"Why? I was the one who was more repugnant between us, literally," I said, still feeling a bit disgusted with myself—and maybe a little bit with him, still, too.

But it was kind of awful, to know that Zeus' biggest fear was that I would only love him if he was attractive. It was, unlike my biggest fear of being fat, a fear more grounded in reality, and I'd just spent the evening proving it to him.

No wonder he'd gotten progressively worse throughout the night. I did, too.

"Well, I still feel bad about everything. Even all that with Blake and the team, and making Amory have a terrible time, too," he said.

"Amory was supposed to have a terrible time," I admitted. "Blake likes her, but she doesn't want to date him. And since he didn't want to date me, and you were very attractive, I thought it would be a nice way to get back at him for not dating me."

When he said nothing, I gave him a rueful look. "See? I don't know why you even like me."

"I think it's natural to be upset when we don't get what we want," he said carefully. "But in your case, there's a better way to get back at them, and my way doesn't require me to eat a radioactive doughnut."

"Really?" I put my hands on my hips. "And just what is that? I can't think of anything that would work."

"You could've gone out on a date with the regular me," he pointed out. "We could've done everything we just did, without the doughnut."

I fell silent as I realized he was right.

I was a bit of a shallow jerk, I supposed.

"Oh," I finally said. "I guess so."

"So will you go out with me on another date, then?" Zeus asked. "As my regular, not-good-enough self?"

"I … I … "

Honestly, I didn't know what to say. I didn't want to be shallow. I really didn't. Earlier, I'd seen how easily Azure had laughed talked to Gynnifer Stills on her news program, selling her the idea he had an ugly "twin brother" who was his complete opposite.

I didn't want to be like that.

Azure was stupid.

I was smart enough to know you were only ever the person you were—face, body, arms and legs and all. And if you wanted to change to be more attractive, you could only start by admitting you needed to change. A person who didn't admit they were ugly wasn't going to magically become beautiful. And even with intentional, directed change, there were reasonable limits; my amber-ebony hair wasn't going to start growing out as blonde, even if I continuously dyed it.

Of course, Azure had been "beautiful" for so long in his career that he'd probably figured out a lot of other people were stupid, too. And that's probably how he managed to keep getting away with his charade.

Either way, I didn't want to be shallow, and I didn't want to be stupid.

And for what it was worth, I'd had fun with Zeus before. Sometimes I didn't even mind our time together during my Fatgirl outings, even if I was in my angry, awkward blob state of being. As terrible as I was, Zeus was still devoted to me—as every guy should be and would be—and even tonight, he sought to make me see him as someone worthy of my admiration, even if he'd been poisoned into overdoing it.

"I guess that's a 'no?'" Zeus asked, after my long moment of silence.

"No, it's not," I grumbled. "It's just … complicated, okay?"

"What's the issue?"

"The issue is that you're you, and I like you just fine, okay? Really, I do." I tried to keep myself from sounding angry. "I've owed you big ever since I farted in Mr. Embers' class and you took the blame for me."

Zeus arched his brow at me. "But?"

"But my 'normal' world doesn't like you, or at least, it doesn't like the idea of you. Only June said anything bad about your behavior. Amory thought you were a hunk, and the other girls all kept staring at you."

"But that wasn't the real me."

"Yes, I know. But if you were your regular self, they all would've hated you. And that's just one issue we would have. I've known for a while now that you love me, so it just feels like you asking me this, here and now, is wearing me down. Women generally aren't supposed to give into that kind of tactic."

Especially with ugly men.

I left that part unspoken. Frankly, it's something that shouldn't need to be said.

But honestly, after Zeus' radioactive behavior tonight, I didn't find him quite so ugly. AB was probably right about Zeus; the pimples would go away when puberty was past, and he could still grow a few more inches, lose the weight, and get a better shampoo.

But even without all that, I was relieved to see him looking normal again.

"I wasn't using it as a tactic," Zeus said.

"I know. I promise, I know. You wouldn't do that," I assured him. "On purpose, anyway. And then there's the website and how you know some pretty devastating secrets about me. I don't want to wonder if I'm going out with you to make sure you don't tell anyone."

"You know I wouldn't."

"I *know*. I know, okay? But I'd still wonder, especially if our date didn't go well."

Zeus rubbed his forehead. "I guess you weren't kidding when you said it was complicated. But I still think you're making it that way on purpose."

"Look, I'm sorry about that, too, okay?" I looked down at the ground and shuffled my foot, feeling vulnerable. "I didn't think about anything much before all this Fatgirl stuff started, other than how my hair and face should look. I'm trying to make up for it now, for better or worse."

"For better *and* worse, by the sound of it."

"I found out my mother left me to go play top henchmen to a retiring criminal," I reminded him. "Some of it's bound to be for worse."

"So, I guess that things between us would be different if I did everything differently, then?"

He smiled when he said it, but I knew he actually felt bad. All I felt was frustrated; why was he getting sad over the truth?

"It's not all bad," I argued. "Look, tell you what. I have an idea. I'll make a deal with you."

"If I lose the fat, bulk up at that gym, and get rid of my acne, you'll consider dating me?"

He didn't say it in a sarcastic tone, but his words still seemed insulting.

Especially since they weren't bad ideas.

"No," I snapped back. "I was going to say let's wait until after AB finishes up her business. Fatgirl can throw in her enormous towel, and then we'll go out on a real date. Just the two of us. And we'll try to have a nice time. Okay?"

Zeus seemed surprised. "Really?"

"Yes. Really." I crossed my arms over my chest. "That way, we'll get rid of the Fatgirl website, so no one sees it as blackmail potential. And we'll have a real reason to celebrate. I mean, AB's stuff is literally the only reason we hang out now, and it's depressing to think about that. I mean, she's on her quest to find the guy who framed her, got her fired, and sold her recipe to someone like ZZ."

"I like hanging out with you now."

"Yeah, but don't you want to talk about other things than radioactive doughnuts, conspiracy theories, and government secrets?"

"That describes someone's dream date, I'm sure," Zeus said with a smile. "But we can talk about other things now if you want."

"It might spoil our later date if we do. I mean, do you want to argue about which movie to watch? Or where we're going to get food? Or which stores we'll go to?"

"Well, I think we can rule out the pet shop."

I grimaced. "Agreed."

"And I'm not spending any money," Zeus said. "You'd shamelessly clean me out if I did."

I couldn't stop myself from smiling at that admission. "We'll see how things turn out. And that's another good reason to wait for our date, too. It'll give you time to save up more money."

"Okay. It sounds like a good deal." Zeus held out his hand to me, and I shook it. "But don't get any delusions of grandeur about spending money. I'm still a simple guy."

"That's good, though. I'm complicated enough for the two of us."

"Well, you're not wrong there," Zeus agreed, and we shared a laugh.

My laughter faded as I kept my hand in his. It was still kind of sweaty, but I didn't mind it so much this time. There was more warmth, and remembering how cold he'd been to me after he'd progressed into an Alterant, I preferred him this way.

"How long do you think it'll take Dr. White to find the traitor she's looking for?" Zeus asked. "I mean, no offense, but I don't want this to be a deal that goes on hold indefinitely."

"I'm not clever enough for that," I said with a smile. But then I thought about watching Azure on the screen while we'd been in the mall.

Azure wouldn't have eaten a doughnut. I was certain of that, based on what he'd said. Someone had stuck him at the Fairview Mountain Asylum—Rehab Center—and it was too much to be just a coincidence.

"I don't think it'll be long," I assured him. "AB and I agree the targets are getting more personal to us. So someone knows what's going on."

"That reminds me," Zeus said. "I promised Dr. White I'd look into isolating that lurker more. It was coming from the doughnut factory, but if I can trace it to a personal IP address, we might get more answers."

"I have literally no idea what you're talking about, but it all sounds good." I slowly let go of Zeus' hand. "Maybe since Richard Darlington sent you those doughnuts, he's involved in this, too."

"Maybe. He seemed like a nice guy to me."

"Well, put him to the test, then," I said. "See if he'll let you look at the computers in the factory. Maybe since he sent you and your dad those doughnuts, he'll be open to a free security check by you guys."

"That's a good idea." Zeus took out his phone and pulled up a website. After a few moments, he turned the phone around to show me. "Look, he's got his email listed."

I saw Richard Darlington's picture was there, listed as the CEO and President of the Darling Donuts Company. He looked very polished and professional, much as I'd seen him back at Fairview.

Something seemed off, though.

"Are you sure that's him?" I asked. "I thought Azure told me that he's got a beauty mark mole over the left side of his lips. That one is on the right."

"No, it's on the left," Zeus said. "You're looking at it from the front, aren't you, so it's inverted."

"Are you sure?" I shrugged. "I know Trevor's supposed to have it on the opposite side. But we just saw Richard earlier today, and it was on the right side then."

"They're twins. I'm sure it's easy to get them confused."

"But not everyone would … would they?"

Zeus and I met each other's gaze at the same time.

"Time to talk about conspiracy theories again?" I asked, and he shrugged.

"I don't know how I feel about the idea of Trevor swapping identities with his brother and running the company," I said. "What would be the point?"

"To stay out of jail for trying to poison Robert Cuttingham III?"

"But if that's true, he's put his own brother in an insane asylum and poisoned him with the doughnuts, too. Or at least the chemicals. The protactinium or whatever."

"Well, the protactinium would turn Richard into his worst fear. Do you think he'd be upset if he was his brother?"

"Um … yeah, maybe," I said, recalling how Azure had mentioned Richard was the prodigy child between the two of them.

"Let me find the photos," Zeus said. "And tomorrow, I'll go over like you said, pretending to offer him a security check as thanks and a business offer. If it's really Richard, we can put the paranoid conspiracies behind us and work on finding AB's lurker."

I looked back at my house, where I had a feeling AB was watching us. The curtain twitched, just ever so slightly, and I knew it was time to go inside.

Still, I didn't really want to leave Zeus. He'd had a hard night, and it wasn't over yet.

"Will you be alright tonight?" I asked quietly. "I know your mom's still at the hospital."

"It's nearly midnight," Zeus said. "I should be okay."

"Don't eat anything else," I warned him. "I need my sleep. School's starting up soon, and at this rate, I'll have to start wearing Mardi-Gras masks or something to cover the bags under my eyes."

Zeus chuckled. "I'd dare you, if I was sure I'd be at school to see it."

"I could always ask Gloria to get pictures."

"Thank you. But there's no pressure." He gave me a soft smile. "I always knew you were kind, you know."

I paused. "Kind of what?"

"No, Kallie, just kind. Most people just look at you and say you're pretty, I'm sure," he said. "But I remember how you tried to distract Blake from making fun of me when we were at that lacrosse team practice, and I knew you had a good heart. It didn't surprise me—entirely—when I noticed the resemblance between you and Fatgirl."

My heart suddenly sagged as I stared at him, and I felt like I'd just been struck by lightning. I exhaled in a rush, and my nose prickled with the pressure of unshed tears.

"Anyway, have a good night." He pulled out his car keys and shifted back toward the driver's side. "I'll see you tomorrow sometime, okay? And I'll contact Dr. White when I find some answers for her."

I could only nod.

I watched him get in the car, I watched him back up and turn and then leave. Some part of me wanted to call him back and make him stay, but I couldn't seem to move my lips.

Time seemed to stop, and I was just too far taken aback.

When he was finally out of sight, I shuffled into the house.

Dad was still at work—how he did it, I never knew—but AB was waiting for me with her cup of tea ready.

"Kallie?" she looked alarmed as she caught sight of me. "What's wrong? Did he say something? Did he hurt you?"

"No. No." I snapped back to my old self and scowled at her. "No, and it's none of your business what he said to me. Stop bothering me about him, would you?"

AB studied me for a long moment, and then she smiled.

"Oh, Kallie, relax, would you? It's okay if you're in love with him."

"I don't—I mean, I couldn't—I … "

AB's smile only widened at my sudden sputtering.

"Never mind. Good night." I had no choice but to move as the tears finally broke free. I turned away from AB and headed up to my room.

"Good night, darling," AB called after me.

I didn't want her to be right.

I didn't want to believe it.

But she was right.

And it was true.

I was in love.

And I hated it.

Fatgirl

WHITE PRIVILEGE

EPISODE 11

○ ○ ○ ○

C. S. Johnson

"Love is the only force capable of transforming an enemy into friend."

~ Martin Luther King, Jr.

FATGIRL
WHITE PRIVILEGE

○ ○ ○ ○

Can this Monday get any worse?

I was probably jinxing myself by even thinking such a thing, but as I stood just outside Cuttingham City Central High, I felt trapped.

My feet seemed anchored into my immediate surroundings, and I felt sick as I stared up at the school's main entrance. Its looming doorway seemed to be as ominous and inescapable as the gates of Hell.

And perhaps it was.

More than ever, I desperately wished I could go home.

Go home, climb under my covers, and forget about everything. Literally everything.

After missing the Spring Fling and then living through a tumultuous spring break, I was back at school. But instead of feeling like the refreshed beauty queen I should've been, there I was, pretending to wait for my friends, without a care in the world.

Like any good actress, I at least looked the part; I was wearing a flashy, scarlet-red flowing skirt, two-inch heels, a cutsie top paired with a matching choker, and a light jacket. I'd done my hair up in a French twist, and I'd painted on my makeup with the determination of a soldier eager to camouflage herself as she walked into enemy territory.

Which wasn't too far off from the truth.

I told myself I was a model of beauty and a true inspiration to my peers, which was just a nice way of saying I was better than all of them.

No wonder I'm lonely; it is lonely at the top.

But I knew I was lying, and silently admitting my hidden insecurities made me squirm.

The truth was, I deserved to feel lonely.

This is what I get for deciding to help AB.

My jaw tightened in silent fury. It was really all Abuela-Blanca's fault I was even at school; Dad was sleeping off a weekend shift, and

I didn't want to be stuck keeping company with my eccentric, likely insane grandmother.

"Kallie!"

I might not have wanted to be home with AB, but my heart still deflated as I heard Lizzie, my white-girl friend, calling for me.

My smile was fake as it was swift, and I could only pretend to be excited.

I honestly had no issue with Lizzie herself. But as I watched her approach me, I had to wonder why we were even friends. Sure, we shared *some* peripheral interests—makeup, hair, clothes, being popular, and stuff like that.

Today, she was wearing a new pair of glasses, one of her reoccuring motifs. It was an easy revenue of attention for her, but the more she did it, the more she'd have to do it again. I originally appreciated her savvy, but now she was a one-trick pony. People would notice when she stopped; and if she continued it until graduation, what else would she really be remembered for?

I didn't even remember her for much more than that.

Behind her, I caught sight of June and Uli heading my way, too, and suddenly, the collective thought of their company only made me feel more lonely, even if I knew I would be more distracted from my loneliness.

I can't tell the girls anything about me. Nothing about my mom. Nothing about Fatgirl. Nothing about Zeus.

The heat in my cheeks increased exponentially at the mere thought of him. It was like a crack breaking through a dam, bursting forth, followed by a surging waterfall and then a tsunami.

I'd dated plenty of boys before, each of them more insufferably pretty and impeccably petty than the last. But that's all they were, really: pretty faces that would take me places, give me pretty things, and offer me social clout. Honestly, and I mean painfully honestly, as much as I loved looking at someone like Blake Turner, he didn't strike me as the kind of boy I'd follow off to college and marry.

But Zeus … well, Zeus was the kind of boy I could at least see staying friends with past high school. That was something, and something more dangerous than I liked to admit.

"Kallie!" Lizzie cheered as she gave me a quick hug. "Oh, I'm so glad you're here."

Gallantly, I patted her on the back. "Thanks. I wish I could say the same."

Lizzie giggled, unaware of how sad and lonely and depressed I really was. But that was a good thing, I supposed—I'd wanted to pretend as though nothing earth-shattering had happened over break, even though the earth had shattered for me several times in recent days.

"Did you hear from Amory this morning?" Lizzie asked.

"No," I said. "Why?"

"She said she was desperately sick."

"Yeah, Amory's not coming today," June announced as she came up beside us. Her voice lowered as her eyes shifted dramatically. "She sounded so traumatized over the phone; I hope it's not deadly."

"Oh," I said, feeling both sympathetic and jealous.

It seemed that just like I didn't want to be here, Amory didn't, either.

"Well, at least Blake has been calling her, and practically non-stop, too." Uli giggled. "Maybe that will cheer her up. Declan told me he's been in love with her for months now."

"More like it would cheer him up," I said blithely, remembering how Blake fawned over Amory during our disastrous group date a couple days before. "Well, I'm sorry Amory's feeling sick. I hadn't heard from her myself, as sadly, my phone is on the fritz again."

"I thought you lost it?" Lizzie looked confused. "Wasn't that why we weren't able to find you after you took off with your Florida Man?"

"Oh … um, I forgot. I actually found it, but it was broken. I must've dropped it," I murmured.

I didn't actually remember what I'd said happened to my phone after I'd dragged Alterant Zeus away and injected him with some of AB's Anti-F serum. All I knew was that I was content to lose my phone altogether, especially if it meant I never had to think of that particular debacle ever again.

It was my foolish hope that if I forgot about it, everyone else would, too. But everything about my life was an embarrassment and ongoing humiliation, and I was smart enough to know the internet would only get joy from my suffering.

I was just about to change the subject entirely when I saw Zeus.

Speaking of embarrassment and ongoing humiliation …

My mind immediately went blank with horror and fear—and to my disgust, the smallest spark of joy.

Zeus was his normal self, thank goodness, and he was so incredulously normal that he gave me a smile, waved a half-wave, and then ducked his gaze down to the floor as he passed by.

He knew his place with me; he knew he didn't fit into my life.

Which was largely perfect, considering my mom had run off with her terrorist BFFs, my depressed dad was overworking himself half to death, and my PhD-in-radio-insanity grandma managed to manipulate me into being my city's accidental superhero so she could get her job back …

You'd think after all that, falling in love with someone you once knew as "Sweaty Fat Kid" should've been easy.

But no, it wasn't, and I wished so badly—so, so, so, so badly—that I could just will myself out of love with Zeus.

AB had told me it was okay to fall in love with Zeus, but she'd failed to consult literally the rest of my life.

Here at school, I was the popular, pretty girl, who didn't even have to be that mean or put out to be admired. I was smart enough I could go to college, and I probably would, once I figured out what I wanted to do with my life. And I was generally pretty nice, too. Of course, everyone was allowed to have a bad day, and yeah, it probably wasn't the best that Amory and I had a very tenuous friendship … but all of that wasn't enough to make me into the kind of girl who wound up with a guy like Zeus.

Zeus was … well, he was the ugly kid, kind of fat in a teddy bear sort of way, with a crown of oily curls and pimples all over his face, like freckles on a ginger. He didn't have a lot of close friends, and he geeked out over tech without it being his full personality, he seemed to like books, but I didn't really know which ones. I supposed no one really hated him, even if he was the butt of some of their jokes and more hateful comments.

Personally, I knew he was smart and I knew he was loyal and even brave.

"Hey, Kallie."

My thoughts were hopelessly interrupted as Blake Turner suddenly appeared beside me and my friends. I hadn't been paying attention at all while my friends talked about planning a surprise "Get Well" party for Amory.

Still, needless to say, I wasn't particularly happy with Blake disrupting my full-blown, inner-existential crisis.

"Hello, Kallie?" Blake tried again, waving his hand in front of my face.

I whacked it away and scowled at him. "What is it?"

He ran his hand through his perfect hair, and gave me a polite, perfect smile.

Normally, I would have been enchanted …

But now I literally did not care. Blake seemed more like he was trying to placate me, and if he was doing that, it could only mean that he needed me to do him a favor.

"Well, I was hoping I could talk to you for a moment." Blake eyed the other girls carefully. "It's about a surprise for June. From Declan."

"Declan?" June's mouth dropped open. "Why? Duncan's the one who likes me."

"Right, I meant Duncan. Sorry. Both of them are my team wingman," Blake explained. "I get them mixed up sometimes."

"It's an easy thing to do," Lizzie replied sympathetically.

"No, it's not!" June and Uli snapped at her at the same time. "Declan/Duncan is much hotter!"

June and Uli frowned. "Excuse me?" they both chimed at each other.

I couldn't stop myself from smiling as Blake and I left Lizzie to deal with the sleeping giants she'd unwittingly awakened.

It was amusing to me to hear June and Uli debating over which one of their presumed boyfriends was hotter, especially given my own current issues.

Suffering is awful, but I felt better knowing other people were suffering, too.

"Do you think your friends will be okay?" Blake looked back at them dubiously as we walked inside the school.

I shrugged; I was actually okay with their arguing, even if it looked like it would get ugly. Not only would they not miss me now, the plans for Amory's "Get Well" party were likely on hold. "We can worry about them later. We've got your problems to discuss after all, don't we?"

My tone was a little harsh, but Blake didn't appear to notice.

"Thanks." Blake nudged my shoulder in a friendly way. "I was hoping Amory would be here today. After you left us at the mall, we didn't really have that good of a time. I mean, I did, but she said she didn't."

"That's not surprising. Amory's going through some difficult stuff."

"What do you mean?" Blake looked surprised. "What's wrong?"

"Oh. Uh … "

I hesitated. Amory was upset her mother was getting remarried. From what I remembered, Amory's dad owned his own gym franchise, and whether he was wearing his gym gear or a suit, he looked like a walking, talking superhero action figure. He wasn't around very much, and when Amory admitted her parents divorced, I wasn't surprised to hear it.

But from what she'd told me, her stepfather-to-be was an accountant; he was as boring as a textbook, bland as cardboard, and white as rice. Amory had said he was nice, but he wasn't anything extraordinary like her father. She couldn't see any reason why her mother would actually *marry* the guy.

I bit my cheek, thinking of my own mother. I didn't think saying, "Maybe she's part of some kind of terrorist plot and she's marrying him for cover," would help Amory.

Frankly, it didn't help me, either; all it did was make me feel more angry for my dad's sake.

"Kallie?" Blake asked, looking concerned. "She's not dying, is she? I heard someone say she was out sick today."

"Oh, no." I didn't think it was my place to tell Blake about Amory's personal problems. "It's just her time of the month. I'm sure you understand. Being sick doesn't help that."

"Oh. Oh, that's … that's understandable." Blake cleared his throat. "And that's good. I was worried I made her upset because of our date."

"I'm sure that didn't help," I muttered, feeling embarrassed all over again. That group date had to be the worst group date in all of history at this point.

Blake and I reached my locker, and I was grateful I had the distraction of putting up my bag and pulling out my books for math, mentally checking off my list of things to remember; Mrs. Bakersfield was going to review over matrices today, and I still didn't understand them at all.

I mulled this over as Blake kept talking about his problems.

"Well, I was hoping you'd be able to maybe help me understand where I went wrong with things? I mean, I did everything Amory wanted at the mall, even if I didn't want to."

"Everything?" I sighed. "You didn't stand up to her at all?"

"No. I laughed at her mean comments, and some of them were pretty mean, if you want to know, and then I bought her all the things she'd wanted, and then I apologized when she wanted me to … "

"Ugh." I groaned into my locker.

Blake didn't seem to notice my discomfort, and I felt even stupider that I'd ever liked Blake at all.

His voice faded as I saw Zeus again; he was just down the hall, likely heading off to whatever class he was supposed to be in for first period.

My heart began to pound between my ears as he caught sight of me and smiled.

He was certainly not handsome, but Zeus had a nice smile—it was so genuine, especially when I compared it to Blake's.

It was just so nice to see that authenticity, I couldn't stop myself from smiling back, my heart reeling with joy and confusion and crippling fear.

"So, what did I do wrong? Kallie?"

Blake's voice cut through my emotional chaos, and I remembered I was supposed to be helping him at the moment.

I blinked as I looked back at him. He seemed more alien to me than ever before; no longer was he a perfect specimen of perfection. Instead, he was just a boy, and I was no longer captivated by him.

But it was still a little awkward to realize he was expecting a coherent answer from me.

"Well … " I fumbled with my bag and then reached for my lock, trying to buy myself another moment.

"Well, what?" Blake asked, seriously concerned.

My patience snapped. I was rather irritated by his self-centeredness. "Well, why do you think Amory would want to date you anyway?"

"I know I'm not good enough for her," Blake replied. "She agreed with me when I said so."

"You actually said that?" I arched my brow.

Wow, Blake sure is pretty … but he's also pretty dumb.

"Yes."

I sighed. "Well, telling a girl she's too good for you probably isn't going to help your cause."

"But I'm aware of it and I'm working to do better," Blake said. "I thought she'd appreciate me telling her that."

"But telling her that doesn't *actually* change you." I frowned.

"I said I was sorry."

"What is there for you to really be sorry for?" I asked. "And what is there for her to forgive you for, either?"

"What do you mean?"

"I mean, when you say you're sorry, you're supposed to change and be forgiven," I said. "Otherwise, it's just meaningless words."

Blake gave me a blank stare, and I honestly wondered in that moment how he'd even passed kindergarten; this was really basic stuff.

"Look, forget about that, I guess, if that's too hard." I shook my head. "Geez, how many girls have you dated?"

"I haven't dated as many as you think, maybe," Blake said easily enough. "I'm used to knowing when girls like me, and then waiting until I'm sure they'll say yes when I ask them out. This is different. I really am in love with Amory, but no matter what I do, it's not enough for her. She doesn't like me in return."

"It's normal for guys to be unworthy of their true loves," Zeus said.

I nearly jumped out of my skin as I realized he was standing there with us, and I didn't know what to do. I was on the verge of a panic attack when Blake scoffed.

"Yeah, you'd know that." Blake rolled his eyes. "One look at you and any girl would faint, and it's not because of your good looks."

"Hey!" I glared at him. Blake knew he was insulting Zeus, but he was also insulting all the girls who would be interested in dating Zeus, and that meant me.

So, yes, I was going to say something about that.

I crossed my arms over my chest, preparing for battle. "Look Blake, if you only have good looks, then yeah, it's no wonder why Amory won't date you."

"Come on, Kallie, help me," Blake begged.

"Not if you're going to be a jerk to my friends," I said with a snarl.

"He's your friend?" Blake's eyebrows raised, and so did Zeus' as I stood my ground.

"Yes. He's nicer than you. Why wouldn't I be friends with him?" I scowled. "Apologize to him, right now."

Despite my sound logic, I still had to steel myself against the oncoming flood of comments I knew I would hear throughout the day.

I'm Fatgirl; I've stopped terrorist, infiltrated a spy's headquarters, survived a trip to Florida, and regularly deal with AB. I should not *be afraid of society's opinions of me.*

I recited all my Fatgirl accomplishments over and over as I stared down Blake, waiting for him to apologize to Zeus.

"Well, sorry, then," Blake finally muttered unhappily. "Didn't think you'd get along with an ugly … someone like him, that's all."

"Ha," I snapped. "'Didn't think' sounds about right. That's not even a good apology."

"It's okay, Kallie," Zeus said quietly, but I ignored him.

"See, Zeus actually has a real personality," I said to Blake, still infuriated. "He cares about people and making them happy. That's why he was doing the videos for Coach a few weeks ago, so you and the team could develop better plays. Even though you were a jerk to him, then, too."

"Okay." Blake sighed. "Sorry."

I nudged Zeus. "Do you forgive him?"

"What? Oh, yeah," Zeus replied. "But it's not a big deal—"

"Of course it is!"

"Well, I said I was sorry, Kallie," Blake said. "Can we please get back to Amory?"

Blake's grumbling was almost as unbearable as his problems. But since I knew that our group date at the mall was more or less all my fault, I didn't want to completely leave him hanging.

"Well, saying you're sorry for being a self-centered jerk is a good start," I retorted. "Fine. Now, you've got your looks. What else? Why would Amory date you?"

"What about my lacrosse skills? And my general popularity?"

"Good looks, lacrosse skills, and popular?" I scoffed, the rage burning inside of me. "Is that it? How does that even really factor in? What happens if you break your leg? Or get suspended from the team? If that's all that keeps Amory by your side, then she should be able to leave you if you miss a goal!"

Blake looked uncertain, while Zeus was trying hard not to laugh.

It was then I realized all of those reasons were likely the ones I'd deemed Blake the only one worthy of dating me, only a week ago.

"And I got news for you," I continued, suddenly feeling more embarrassed than ever. "Looks fade, eventually. What's going to be left when you're old and ugly?"

"On a practical level, it might help if you share her values," Zeus suggested, and I shot him a warning look.

"Stay out of this," I snapped.

Zeus only laughed, and I felt extra-flustered and silly, screaming at Blake for all the things that were technically wrong with me, too.

I whirled back to Blake. "You know what? I'll talk to her. I'll see if she'll give you a fair shot. One date. Okay? I can't guarantee anything but if I do this for you, promise me you will work on getting an actual personality beyond what sport you play and how you look."

"Thank you, Kallie. Thank you so much." Blake looked relieved and hopeful. "You'll do that for me?"

He didn't seem to get that I still thought he was vapid and awful.

But I didn't want to get the idea that I was the one who was truly worthy of scorn, either.

"Of course." I hid how sick I felt, thinking back to all of AB's teasing and prodding for me to accept Zeus. "That's fair. And I'd want someone to do that for me if I was in your pathetic position."

I didn't have to look over at Zeus to know he was still smiling. Part of me was happy that I made him proud, but I was super embarrassed that I was happy about it, too.

Thankfully, the first bell rang, cutting our conversation short, and Blake had to leave for gym.

"Thank you again, Kallie," he called out, giving me a thumbs up. "You're the best!"

"Ugh." I put my head into my hands.

"That was awfully nice of you," Zeus agreed.

"Shut up," I muttered. "After our group date at the mall, I owe him at least that much. Probably."

Zeus looked horrified. "Was I really that bad?" he asked.

It was tempting to say yes; it would have been nice to blame all my problems on Zeus.

But I shook my head. "No, but collectively it was terrible. I feel like I owe Blake and Amory for all the trouble I put them through, okay? And this is something that'll make them forgot about me and you."

"They don't even know it was me," Zeus reminded me. "They call me 'Florida Man' on the school's internet chat rooms."

"I didn't need to know that." Once more, I was glad my dad didn't let me get on social media that much. Really, I did get on anyway, and excessively so, but if I wasn't on it, I at least had a good excuse for not being there. It was a lot like my phone in that regard; I didn't care anymore if I had it or not. It would only be too tempting to look up Fatgirl's reviews and fandom comments, and it was bad enough I had to deal with Zeus for that.

"Fixing Amory up with Blake will give you something else to help you forget about your promise to me, too," Zeus said. "I guess you'd like that, huh?"

My cheeks burned, recalling that I'd promised Zeus a real date—just one—after AB's mess was all cleaned up.

"No." I bit down on the inside of my cheek, feeling angry. "I won't forget. I promised you, remember?"

"Okay." He still seemed surprised at my sincerity, and I just hated that even more.

I wanted to grab him by the shoulders and scream, "I have integrity, thank you very much!" very, very loudly in his face. It was only the fact that he was a foot taller and a good eighty pounds heavier than me that I refrained from doing so.

"I have to get to math." I swung my backpack onto my shoulder and flipped my hair over my shoulder, grateful it was time to leave. "See you in Embers' class."

"Sure."

I started to walk away and didn't look back. But my heart still skipped a beat when he said, "Bye, Kallie."

It was entirely different from how Blake had called out his thanks, and if I didn't hate myself so much, I might've smiled and waved back at him.

After Zeus had eaten his own radioactive doughnut, he'd looked so perfect it almost hurt to look at him. But it also taught me that if he was prettier, he would be fundamentally different from who he was—and I truly loved who he was, even if he didn't look that good.

I loved that Zeus was a big-hearted mama's boy, a person of goodwill and good humor. He'd been trustworthy and reliable, helping me and AB, despite all the various humiliating, stupid, and highly illegal things we'd had him do. He was smart, too, with computers and geek stuff, and he had a good work ethic, even where his anti-social father was concerned.

And despite all his sensibility, he was in love with me.

So, yeah, so what if he was a little overweight? So what if he wore clothes that looked like they came from a discount thrift store, that his glasses were too thick, that his hair was an oily mess?

He was in love with me, and he was a good person; that alone was nothing short of a miracle.

I might've had to be crazy to love him back, but I wasn't stupid.

I sighed and dropped my head to my chest, so tired with myself, I could only wish the ground would open up and swallow me whole.

"Bye, Zeus." I whispered the words, even though I knew he was already out of earshot.

Ugly ones try harder.

ZZ's rather crass advice on dating rang through my mind right as I sat down in my seat for my first period class, but for the first time, I wondered if I wasn't the uglier one between me and Zeus.

I would have to try harder to be worthy of his love.

Maybe if I did that, I would want to actually tell him how I felt.

My stomach turned violently at the thought of telling Zeus. I was in love with him, and that made me scared enough to feel sick.

He knew me well enough, and I doubted he would believe me. He'd probably think I was playing some kind of cruel joke on him, and given all my collective terribleness towards him since we met, I couldn't blame him. He might not even want to be my friend anymore.

And then, what about Fatgirl? What if he realized how pathetic and petty I actually was, and he fell out of love with me, and then he didn't care about keeping my secret anymore?

Such thoughts were too familiar, and even the night before, I'd turned them over and over in my mind for hours, worrying and fretting and feeling hollow.

I'd never felt so conflicted—and that was truly saying something, as I'd recently found out my mother, who'd abandoned me and my hardworking, now-heartbroken father, was working under an internationally wanted criminal.

Thankfully, before I could worry too much about it, the bell rang, and Mrs. Bakersfield started her lecture, and I could only thank God for advanced algebra.

Between matrices and miracles, it was hard to say which was easier to make sense of—but I certainly knew which was easier for me to stomach.

By the time I walked into Mr. Embers' computer class, the stress of school managed to calm me down—somewhat, anyway. I didn't have to think any further than my dad to know that it was easier to avoid your real problems if you threw yourself into your work.

And then all my suffering and anguish came rushing back as I saw Zeus.

"Hey, Kallie."

I managed to not blush, and even nod to him politely as he waved. Word had gotten around that I'd called him my friend in front of Blake; people knew we were friends now, and that meant we were allowed to be friendly without causing suspicion.

Right?

"Hey," I replied back as nonchalantly as possible, practically forcing my voice not to crack.

But at my acknowledgement, Zeus seemed to take this as permission to come up and talk to me.

"Hey, I need to talk to you," he said softly.

"Um … " I started freaking out as Uli, who was sitting beside me, raised her eyebrows. I could almost see her wondering why I was talking to Zeus, and why I looked so nervous. "Right now?"

"If you don't mind." Zeus gave me a pointed look toward his pocket. "I wanted to show you something I thought you might find interesting."

"Interesting?" I repeated, suddenly torn between dread and frustration and, for some awful reason, irrepressible curiosity. The list of reasons Zeus wanted to talk to me were extremely limited, and I couldn't do anything about any of them just then.

It didn't help that Uli was practically laughing at me now; I could see her cheeks bloating up with contained laughter as I stood there, talking with Zeus like we were real friends—which we were, but I wasn't ready to publicize.

"Yes." Zeus pulled out his phone, and Uli finally laughed aloud.

"What is it?" I barked at her.

"Oh, I was just laughing at this joke I heard before," Uli murmured as she blushed.

"Oh, good, because I thought you were hacking up a hairball just now," I snapped. "Thank goodness you were only laughing."

She scowled, and I didn't even know why I was bothering with her.

"Kallie." Zeus put his hand on my arm.

"I don't have my phone with me," I snapped at him, still feeling like a caged animal.

"I figured that much out earlier," he whispered. "Dr. White did, too."

Nope, not good.

"I don't care," I lied. "I don't want to deal with this now. I mean, we literally can't, either. We have class to deal with. If AB wants my help, she's going to just have to wait for it this time."

Zeus sighed and handed me his phone. "Just look at the emails," he whispered.

Before I could object, he stepped away, and Mr. Embers called us to begin our work.

Uli shifted away from me as I sat down, and I was just glad that we didn't have to do any group or partner work for the day. Uli usually let me take the lead on such projects anyway, and I didn't feel like graciously earning her another A just then.

While I pulled up the class program, I looked down at Zeus' phone as inconspicuously as possible.

But it was hard to maintain the façade when I saw Amory's email address.

The huge, all-caps "FATGIRL: PLEASE HELP" email subject line did not help, either.

The email was just as bad.

Hey Fatgirl

I know you don't know me, but I need your help. I can't tell you what's wrong here, but I need you to come and rescue me from my mom's house. Here is her address. Please come ASAP. You're the only one who can save me.

It wasn't even signed, but I figured that wasn't anything to be concerned about. What was concerning was that Amory was emailing me—well, Fatgirl—at all.

It was a well-known fact that, as one of the most popular girls in school, Amory was out sick today. But I'd been sure she was out of school because she was *actually* sick.

How … why … how on earth did she get herself in a situation where she needed *Fatgirl* to come and help her?

I thought back to Azure, Fatgirl's original fashion designer, and then I thought of Max Powers, the policeman who'd originally helped Fatgirl at the Model Middle America broadcast. I even thought of Zeus, who'd eaten a radioactive doughnut only a couple days before.

Someone *had* to be watching Fatgirl; someone had to be targeting people close to her—and that meant someone was targeting people close to *me*.

Does someone know who I am? Is this a trap?

The thought was paralyzing—but it couldn't be a coincidence. Could it?

I glanced back at Zeus, who was watching me. I could almost read his thoughts.

Even if someone was targeting me, or Fatgirl in particular, it didn't matter.

We had to go and help Amory.

And fast.

I hated myself for it, but I stood up. I gathered my things, walked over to Mr. Embers, and let out a deep, tired, sick-sounding sigh.

"Mr. Embers, I'd like to go see the nurse, please," I said in what I hoped was a hoarse voice.

Mr. Embers was a nice guy—probably the type of guy who was friends with Amory's would-be stepfather—and he nodded.

"What's wrong?" he asked, even though he was already writing out the hall pass.

"Honestly … too much to say," I muttered, shaking my head. "But you know that my bestie, Amory, is out sick, and I probably have what she does."

Mr. Embers nodded. "Well, I hope you both feel better soon. Take care."

"Thank you."

I slumped my way out of the classroom. I kept the "act" up until I felt Zeus' phone vibrate in my hand.

A text message appeared from his dad on the screen, and out of sheer ignorance, I read it.

I stopped in my tracks.

It was written in Spanish, but even I knew enough to see that it said Zeus' mom was out of the hospital and heading home to get comfortable.

My heart sank; I suddenly felt even more terrible than ever.

While I was dealing with all my problems, Zeus was on the verge of losing his mom to cancer.

How did he do it? I wondered. How did he really come to school, help me with my superhero duties, work with his dad, and still act so freaking *normal* when life was just full of all these terrible things?

My only hope was that at the end of all of this, AB would use her memory scrambler machine on me, use some kind of internet bomb to make all the stories about Fatgirl go away, and I could move on with my life.

A new thought suddenly struck me as I stood there: My life now included Zeus. And I couldn't forget all the rest without forgetting him, too.

Before I could rationalize the idea of forgetting him entirely, his phone rang.

I expected it to be his dad, or even his mom. But when I looked down, I saw it was none other than "Dr. White" calling him.

I answered it. "Hi, AB."

"Don't you mean, '*hola, Abuela*'?"

"Don't push it," I hissed. "You're lucky I answered instead of hanging up. Why are you calling Zeus, anyway?"

"I was trying to get a hold of you. I'm coming to the school to get you," AB said. "As you might've guessed, we have a situation. Your friend is in danger, and who knows who else might get caught up in the trouble."

I bit my lip. "I think it's bad, too. I know Amory. She wouldn't just eat some doughnuts."

"We'll talk when I pick you up," AB said. "I'm nearly there."

"I'm heading to the nurse," I said.

"Oh, that's a good idea."

"It is?"

"Yes. It's a better alibi."

"Oh." I rolled my eyes. "I knew I could count on you to make the best of this."

"Of course, darling." AB sounded smug. "Things might be bad, but they're not bad all the time. There's no need to be a complete cynic."

○ ○ ○ ○

AB might not have been a complete cynic, but she was quickly forcing me to become one. The first thing she did as I slid into the back seat of her Imperial was toss me a doughnut.

"Here."

I groaned as AB slammed her foot onto the gas; I barely had any time to shut the door as she sped off. "Can you at least wait till I'm in the car?"

"Well, you're in. Are you going to eat it or not?" she asked, motioning for me to get going.

"I just got here," I reminded her as I buckled my seatbelt. "Do I have to do this right now? What about Zeus?"

"He's coming," AB said, swerving the steering wheel around. "But you'll want some privacy to change into your suit, and we're going to meet him at the other end of the school, anyway."

"He's sneaking out? How do you know?" I held up Zeus' phone. "I still have his phone."

"I emailed him. He's in computer class right now, remember? Now, get in the back. You're going to balloon up fast, and if you get stuck in the front, we're going to lose time."

I hated to do it, but I had to give AB her due. She was crazy, but she was crazy-prepared.

"You know, you could be less irritable while we do this," I said, pulling my Fatgirl suit over my head and tucking my hair down into my hood.

"I'm here to do a job, not make friends."

"Is there a reason you can't do both?" I pulled my arms through the sleeves. My suit wasn't actually that bad. I would've liked it better if I didn't have to blow up like a hot air balloon in it, but the fabric was nice and breezy, yet still warm, and the fit was comfortable, even if it was tight.

"No, but there are priorities when it comes to this business."

"I guess you're right about that," I muttered.

"Of course I am." AB glanced back over her shoulder at me with an irritated look on her face. "Which is why you need to take your phone with you when you go places from now on."

"I don't want it." I sank further back into the red velvet backseat. "The last thing I need is for you to be able to reach me all day long."

"I can do that without the phone," AB reminded me.

"Yes, but there are more barriers in the way now." I arched my brow at her as my body slowly filled out with muscle and fat. "If you're going to do it, I might as well make it harder and more annoying for you."

"You also hurt yourself," AB pointed out. "We're here because of your friend, if you'll recall."

"No, we're only here because of your recipe," I retorted. "This is all your fault."

"*I* didn't steal my own recipe." AB parked the car off to the side of the school.

"But you're the one who convinced me to become Fatgirl!" My earlier silent rage was all too eager to make itself known.

"Only because you ate my doughnuts!"

"They were just laying out on the kitchen counter! You probably left them out there on purpose."

"They're still not yours," AB reminded me. "You should've asked. And then you're the one who had to get all fat anyway."

"You told me that's what the doughnuts are designed to do." I threw up my arms in disgust, and then felt even more embarrassed as the car shook at my sudden movement.

"Yes, but I assume someone who's biggest fear is being fat is someone whose extremely sheltered and shallow."

"Well, here I am!" I crossed my arms tightly over my chest and curled away from AB's sight as I suddenly felt like crying all over again. "So … this is all your fault. Why did you even have to come live with me and Dad? Yeah, we're not perfect, and we're probably going to need therapy over Mom leaving us, but at least neither of us were radioactive at the beginning of all of this! You probably scared her away, too, didn't you?"

Some small part of me knew that AB wasn't to blame for someone else stealing her recipe, nor was it her fault that "Fatgirl" had taken off as much as she had. I was only really reacting to things and stuck in the misery of chaos.

The larger part of me was content to fuss and whine and whimper about all the things that made me upset; I desperately wanted to blame her and yell at her and punish her for all eternity.

"I'm sorry for how complicated things have become, Kallie," AB muttered begrudgingly. "I did not intend for this to happen. I didn't start it. But I am doing my best to see that it ends. That is all I can do for now, and I hope you can understand that."

I barely heard her.

"My friends are being targeted now, aren't they?" I whispered instead, remembering my earlier fears.

"We'll have to see," AB said slowly. She was being uncharacteristically nice, and I knew she was lying.

But it was nice to see she wasn't as tough as she'd said she was.

"What do you mean?" I asked, still hurt and grumbling over everything.

"I mean, we'll have to get to Amory and find out how she got the Protactinium in her system. We won't know anything for sure before we get some answers."

I watched her in the review mirror carefully. She pursed her lips in a bitter frown, and I could only wonder what she was thinking.

I cleared my throat. "What are the chances that someone knows who I am?"

"I don't know," AB said honestly. "But you're right to suspect someone has figured out who you are—and who gave you the Fatgirl serum. There's only a handful of people who have those kinds of resources."

"Has ZZ come forward with more information, you think?" I asked. "Or maybe Agent Grey has slipped up and revealed our identities?"

"No." AB's frown softened a little. "Eugene and I have a rough history together, but he wouldn't betray me like that."

"What about my mom?" I asked slowly. "She might've seen the footage that the news put out about the Model Middle America fiasco and figured out I was Fatgirl."

AB went silent for a moment, and then she shook her head. "Even if she did, she wouldn't know about Zeus, or Azure, or Max. Or even Amory, correct?"

"Well, she would know about Amory," I said. "But I don't think she'd go after the others."

"I don't think we have to worry about Kate. I'm more inclined to think ZZ said something, although she's been under constant watch since INTERPOL took her in," AB told me. "Eugene sends me regular updates."

"Why?" I asked, suddenly happy to tease her.

AB didn't take the bait. "I think he wants to retire soon, and I have a feeling he's trying to get back on my good side before he cuts ties with his protection detail. He sends me some updates about your mother, too. Nothing is in them that indicates she is spying on you or concerned about you at all."

"Oh." I didn't know how it was possible, but I felt even more depressed all of a sudden.

"I meant she's not concerned about you being connected to her work." AB shook her head. "I'm sure she misses you, Kallie."

"Thanks." I looked out the window glumly. My mom had always been a figure of inspiration to me. I always wanted to be the beauty queen she was; I mimicked her in all the ways I could, and even as much as I hated her involvement with all of this, I still missed her.

"I wish she was dead," I muttered.

The words were harsh and stark in the Imperial's interior, and I even flinched at their echo.

Of course that was the exact moment Zeus opened the front door of the Imperial and sat down.

"You wish who was dead?" he asked.

I curled my fingers into my fatty forearms. "Never mind," I said, feeling fully shamed all over again.

"Kallie and I were just talking about who could be behind this," AB explained. "Given our current situation."

"It does seem odd for Amory to be a target," Zeus agreed. "But I've been tracking that link since last week. Inside the Darling Donuts factory, there's a shadow link that's been following us around, bouncing signals off your SIM cards. It's been periodically sending information out to Washington, DC."

"What does that mean?" AB asked.

"It means we've got someone from Washington watching you," Zeus said. "And it's connected to the person who's watching Darling Donuts, and Trevor Darlington, too."

I must have looked confused, because Zeus added, "Trevor's the twin brother of Richard, who owns Darling Donuts. He's the one who's stuck in the Fairview rehab center and sent Karen Bright's fiancé those doughnuts to 'congratulate' them on their engagement."

"I knew that," I muttered, blushing, realizing I'd forgotten some of the details.

"He's also drugged up on Protactinium, too," AB reminded me. "It seems like a good fate for him, really, considering ZZ sold him my recipe."

"But he's not the one who's using the Darling Donut company to make more radioactive doughnuts, then," I said. "Not unless he's a really good actor and using it as a cover."

"I'd be more likely to assume it's the guy who's tracking the factory who's doing that," Zeus said.

"But why?" I asked. "Are you sure it's not the government, or Agent Grey, or another person who's after people like ZZ? That seems more like a government sort of job. I mean, they'd want to watch over AB to make sure she doesn't sell her recipe to anyone else."

"I'm not without my own insurance policies," AB said as she started the car up again. "Hmm. But that's possible. They could be watching me from a different perspective. But it doesn't make any sense that they would be using the factory to do so."

We sped off like a bullet out of a gun, and I felt whiplashed; riding in the car with AB felt more like getting onto a roller coaster, and I was pretty sure I'd never want to go to an amusement park ever again.

"You know, AB, you said the person who stole it had to be someone who knew you very well," I said, gripping the armrest as AB went flying around a tight curve. "What about your friend? That one that you called in a terror threat to the airlines, just so you could talk to him in person?"

"KP wouldn't betray me," AB muttered. "He was checked out by the NAH himself. He was clean. And he was my assistant. Everything he has in life is because of me and my work."

"Wouldn't that give him more incentive to betray you?" Zeus asked.

"Have you ever heard the expression, 'Don't kill the golden goose'?" AB asked. "Well, *I'm* the golden goose. I've worked with the NAH for decades. I've developed over half the inventory in their top-secret file cabinets. I've done things that averted world wars and caused natural disasters."

Zeus and I exchanged a nervous look.

"If I'm gone, there is no future for him. He was shuffled to a new department immediately after I was dismissed." AB shook her head. "There's nothing ZZ could give KP to match that kind of job security."

After a longer, more awkward moment of silence, I cleared my throat. "Well, maybe the person who gave it to ZZ is watching you."

"He could be watching Richard, too," Zeus added.

"Richard?"

"Yeah. Maybe with Trevor down in rehab, Richard is using the donut recipe for himself."

"For what?" I asked. "What's the point in having a recipe that turns people into their worst fears from a business perspective? And I mean other than selling them to terrorists, okay? I'm smart enough to see that."

"Well, the government would hate to have more competition," AB muttered. "But that would be something to look into. Perhaps you're right about Richard, Zeus. Perhaps there's an angle there we're missing."

"I still don't know Richard," I said. "There's no link between me and Amory and Fatgirl that would make them go after her."

"As I said earlier, we'll find some answers." AB jerked the wheel off to the side, and forced her car off the road.

"What are you doing?" I screamed, as we drove through a small cluster of woods.

"Making a shortcut through this HOA park," AB said. "Get your mask on, Kallie. We're getting as close as we're going to get."

I glanced around and saw glimpses of the semi-familiar houses around us.

We were in Amory's neighborhood alright. But we were in the woods that bordered them.

"I can't just drive you to the front of her house," AB explained. "I'll find a good place to park back here and then we can each approach her house from different points."

I groaned. "You mean I have to walk in broad daylight like this?"

"You've done it before."

"That doesn't mean I want to do it again!"

"You'd still do it," Zeus said. "For Amory's sake."

"That doesn't mean I'll enjoy doing it," I snapped. "Do you know how totally humiliating this is?"

"No, I don't," Zeus said quietly. "But I do know Amory is likely very frightened and lonely, and I know you're the best chance she's got to getting back to her normal self."

As AB sped onward, I put my face into my thick, fattened hands and screamed. It didn't solve my problems, but it did help me feel a little better at least.

Until I looked back up and saw the back of Amory's house.

"We're here."

Great.

I wanted to help Amory, I really did. But I couldn't see what was wrong. Her house looked normal.

Maybe she was seeing the "ghost" of her dad, the way that Robert Cuttingham III had with his late wife, or maybe she was as fat as I'd become.

I paused; that actually made sense. She wouldn't think of reaching out to Fatgirl without cause, would she?

I clenched my fists, suddenly faced with the temptation to laugh. After all the remarks Amory had made about Fatgirl and her unfortunate weight and general ugliness, she had finally gotten her comeuppance!

That had to be it!

"Kallie, what's wrong?" AB's voice crackled through the small earpiece woven into my hood. "You look like you're going to throw up."

"I'm … not … going … to throw up," I managed to murmur, keeping my laughter in check as I walked up to the back door. "I'm here for Amory and I'm desperately worried."

Yeah, worried I won't have a camera.

It would be great to have something like that over Amory, I thought. It would be proof that she wasn't perfect.

I rang the doorbell, newly excited by the prospect of my mission here. For all I knew it could be a trap, but there was a slim chance this could be an honest accident of sorts, and as AB said before, there wasn't any point to being a complete cynic.

"Amory?" I called, cupping my hands around my mouth. "Are you there?"

"Fatgirl?" I heard the squeak of a voice that sounded similar to Amory, but not as confident nor as lively.

"It's me," I said, feeling nervous. "I got your message. You said you needed to see me?"

"Yes. I've been watching the business with the Alterants, and I've been turned into one. Everyone knows you're the one who has the cure. And I need it."

"Okay, well, let me in, and I'll give it you."

I was actually really relieved; some of the Alterants lost their minds and acted like uncontrollable monsters. Amory seemed to manage to stay somewhat calm.

"I can't let you see me," Amory said.

"I know being an Alterant is an awful experience," I said slowly, thinking of my own current form. "But I need to make sure you actually need the cure. I know you have a reputation for being beautiful, but getting a few pimples or gaining a few pounds isn't the same thing as … as … "

My words trailed off as the door opened and a girl with big, tear-filled blue eyes and wavy blonde hair stood in the doorway.

She was five feet, seven inches tall, same as Amory. And she was wearing one of Amory's dresses. And she was even standing about where Amory would have been standing, but she clearly wasn't Amory.

Amory wasn't white, and this girl had the skin of a pure porcelain china doll.

I was about to ask her where Amory went when she spoke.

"Okay, I'm here. I need you to fix me now."

At the sound of the semi-familiar voice, my mouth dropped opened.

It was really her.

It was Amory.

○ ○ ○ ○

There was no use being a full cynic, according to AB, and I had to agree with her in that moment. If anything, I knew for sure that life wasn't a complete tragedy; rather, it was a comedy, one that happened to have a lot of tragedy.

I had a surreal desire to just laugh for some reason, probably at the absurdity of it all. I lived in a world where there were super-fat superheroes, doughnuts that could transform you into your greatest fear, my mother was best friends with an internationally wanted criminal, my grandmother invented perhaps the stupidest legitimate biological weapon of terror, and I was in love with Sweaty Fat Kid.

My list of impossible things was getting rapidly shorter.

But even as I faced the temptation to laugh at the absurdity, I also wanted to cry. The radioactive doughnuts activated the fear response, and it was just awful to think of how Amory's worst fear was being turned white.

I mean, *I* was half-white; and yeah, maybe it was cool to hate on it, since being Hispanic made me more like the beauty queen my mom was, and it was easy to think being white was being bland, but I was *still* half-white. It wasn't something to fear. It was something fundamentally part of my genetic make-up, something immutable, something I didn't have any real choice over. It didn't make me a bad person; I was Fatgirl, and I'd just come in my hilariously hideous superhero suit to help my best frenemy, even though it could have been a trap set up by AB's archenemy!

I was definitely not perfect, but I wasn't a terrible sociopath bent on world enslavement. It wasn't like being white made me Hitler's secret great-great-granddaughter or something.

Although …

I glanced back toward the woods, where AB was hiding.

"What are you doing?" AB hissed. "Where's Amory?"

"Never mind."

I shook my head to clear my thoughts.

Maybe Amory was fearing that she was no longer herself, and I could empathize with *that.* As Fatgirl, no one really wanted to be me—not even I wanted to be Fatgirl!

I turned to Amory. "Well, I guess this isn't a pimple issue, huh?"

She scowled at me. "Of course not. I know how to handle those issues; I'm going to be voted Prom Queen next year."

Ignoring her prissy posturing, I pulled out the small pack from behind me to get the syringe. "I'm going to need a blood sample," I said, as I explained the process of reversing her condition.

"How long will it take?"

"Not long," I said. "Um, sometimes it depends on how many doughnuts you've eaten."

"Doughnuts?" Amory asked.

"Yes, that's usually how they're ingested," I said. "Did you eat doughnuts recently?"

"No." Amory scoffed. "A lady as beautiful and thin as I am doesn't eat sugar."

"Uh-huh." I knew she was lying; I'd seen her eat tons of food before and "sugar-free" really only applied to the gum she chewed. But since she let me take her arm, slowly pierce her skin with my needle, and take the sample back to AB in the woods without issue, I decided it was wise to humor her.

Until she decided to follow me out to the woods.

Where Zeus and AB were hiding.

"No!" I said, jumping in front of them. "No, don't go back there."

"What's going on?" she asked, putting her ivory hands on her hips.

"There are people there, with cameras," I said, shuffling her back toward her house. "And there's someone who's making the cure for you. So you'd better get back to the house and wait. You don't want anyone to see you now, do you?"

Amory frowned, and I could see some small freckles on her face. "No one is going to see me like this back here—"

"Amory?"

Amory and I both turned at the same time to see none other than Blake Turner standing in her backyard with a small container of soup in one hand and flowers in the other.

"No!" Amory put her hands over her face and screamed, while I just felt dumbstruck.

"What are you doing here?" I demanded, getting up in his face. "Haven't you had enough experience with Alterants?"

Blake's mouth just flapped open and shut as he stared at Amory.

She stopped screaming. "I swear to God, if you tell that Gynnifer Stills lady about this, I will kill you," Amory growled, before she pounced on Blake.

He dropped the flowers and the soup, and I felt disappointed, since after my long weekend, I hadn't eaten, and I could smell the wholesome goodness of chicken noodle soup as it smashed all over the yard. But since Amory was cat-fight slapping Blake, I couldn't do anything but vow I would get soup later.

"Hey, we need to stop," I said, putting myself between Amory and Blake.

"Why don't you just stay out of this, Fatgirl?" Amory scowled. "This boy has been stalking me, trying to get me to date him!"

"Well … why not just go out on a date with him, then?" I asked. "If he likes you, maybe you should give him a chance?"

"He likes me, but I don't like him," Amory insisted. "Can't you see? He's white."

I gritted my teeth together. "What does that have to do with who he is? Surely there's more to him than his skin color."

"He's a *white person.* He's descended from slave owners."

AB groaned over my headset. "She does know that the white people who bought slaves bought them from other black people, right?"

"Hush, AB," I hissed.

"What are they teaching you in school?"

"Does that really matter right now?" I muttered. "I don't think she'd care, anyway."

"What did you say?" Amory turned toward me. "Are you making fun of me?"

"No, no, not at all. I was … just saying that this boy seems nice. And he's not a slave owner now," I pointed out, feeling really awkward.

"He still wants to be a colonizer." Amory shook her head.

"I don't want to colonize you," Blake said back, finally finding his voice. "I just wanted to date you."

"That's the same thing!"

"Um … no it's not?" Blake looked to me for help, and I wasn't sure I could give it to him.

"We just want to be equal, but it's people like him who will keep us from being equal," Amory yelled.

"Equal how?" I frowned, terribly confused. "What do you mean by 'equal'?"

"You see? Black and white people are just too different to be equal," Amory insisted. She tugged at her arms. "And this is why this is so disgusting. We're not the same and we never will be."

"But no one is exactly the same as another person," I reasoned. "Even twins don't always like the same things. You and I will never be the same, either. Do you want everyone to go around looking like me?" I gestured down to my less-than-ideal self, and Amory turned away in disgust.

"That's not the point!" She shook her head, letting her blonde hair flicker through the air. "Ugh, you just don't understand."

"Help me, then." I reached over and carefully patted her on the back. "Why are you so afraid of turning white?"

For a moment, I wasn't sure Amory would even reply. But a second later, she burst into tears and put her head in her hands, shaking with grief.

"White people have taken everything from me," Amory shouted. "My mom is marrying a white man, and she'll never get back together with my dad!"

Amory fell to her knees, and before I could stop him, Blake fell down and sat next to her.

"I'm sorry," he said. "I'm sorry for all the trouble white people have caused you."

"You're not the people who caused the trouble for her," I said, angry at how stupid he was again.

"No," Amory said, stopping me. "This feels good. Keep apologizing."

"What? He shouldn't apologize," I said. "Your mother decided to marry the white man she's marrying; he's not forcing her to marry him."

At least, so far as I know …

"And as for the white people owning slaves, that's part of history, and we can't change the past," I said. "But Blake's never been a slave owner, and you've never been a slave. Don't make him apologize for something that doesn't affect you. It's like apologizing for the weather."

"It does affect me!" Amory insisted. "There's a certain way people look at black people, and Blake should apologize for that! I want an apology!"

AB sighed. "I can't tell if this is something augmented by the Protactinium or the terrible public schools."

"Shush," I muttered.

"I'll apologize to you for sure," Blake said. He thought long and hard in silence for a moment, and then he took her hand. "But if I do, will you be able to forgive me?"

"Forgive you?" Amory stared at him blankly, almost as if she was confused about all of this, too.

Hope and dread both stirred inside of me.

I was irritated with Blake for even thinking of appeasing her so easily, especially since, as AB mentioned, it might be due to the radioactivity in her system, while Amory seemed to be taken aback by his question.

But I was also hopeful that maybe what I'd said to him earlier had finally sunk in a little, about how he needed to stand up to Amory, and maybe even how he ought to know how apologies were supposed to work.

My earpiece crackled. "I have the serum," AB told me. "I'd come and get it, quickly, if I were you."

At her word, I slipped away from them, watching as they just both stared at each other, still unable to speak.

"Thank you," I said to AB as I took the serum from her hand.

AB nodded. "According to my Phi-ger, there's a lot more Protactinium around than usual. She may have to wait awhile before she reverts back to normal."

"So … she ate a lot of doughnuts?" I asked, and AB nodded.

"Most likely," she said. "While she is changing back, we need to ask her some questions."

"Yes," I agreed. "We need answers."

"I need a break, too," AB said, nodding toward Blake and Amory. "One thing I like about you and Zeus is that you're rather good at keeping your drama away from me."

Behind AB, I saw Zeus blush, and I felt my face heat over, too.

"Alright, enough." I took that as my cue to leave. "Let's get Amory back to her usual self."

I'd never seen someone so happy to get a shot.

Amory's blue eyes began to fade back to their usual golden brown, and common sense seemed to come seeping back into her vision.

"It might take some time to get back to normal completely," I warned her. "So just stick around here until you think you're ready to go out."

"I'll stay with you," Blake offered.

Amory scoffed, and I finally stepped forward.

"Look," I said. "This boy's willing to do a lot for you. He's not your dad, or your mom, and yeah, he's clearly not perfect and he's made a lot of cringy mistakes."

Amory eyed me suspiciously. "Where are you going with this, Fatgirl?"

"I'm just saying, give him a chance. If you're right about him being too white for you, you'll at least have the proof. And if you're wrong … well, it would be great to be wrong about something like true love, right?"

Amory's eyes speckled over with tears. "I don't know. My best friend likes him, still, I think. I don't want to hurt her feelings. And the white thing is just a good excuse, isn't it? I really don't want to be like my mom, just getting married and then divorcing someone great, and then getting married to someone completely different."

I shrugged as I looked away. "I don't know about your best friend, but I do know that divorce hurts, and I'm sorry. All I'm saying here is that you shouldn't take your pain out on this guy."

I nodded back toward Blake, who beamed at me.

Carefully, I leaned forward so only Amory could hear me. "Besides, you'll want to check to make sure he didn't get a video of you in your Alterant form. Just go on a date and keep him happy long enough to make sure he won't tell anyone. Or you might never live it down."

"Well … that's true. And Lizzie will be depressed if she hears about this," Amory agreed reluctantly. "She's my white-girl friend, and I wouldn't want to tell her that even as a white girl myself, I looked much better than she ever will."

I was about to excuse myself so I could gag in private when she added, "And poor Kallie. She's already upset about her Florida Man, and I can only hope she'll understand enough about Blake and me hanging out. I don't think she likes me very much sometimes."

I faltered, feeling sad. While I didn't think Amory liked *me* very much, it was still a little surprising to hear that Amory didn't think I liked her very much.

"I'm sure this Kallie won't mind," I said.

"You're talking about Kallie? Yeah, she said she'd try to get you to agree to one date with me anyway," Blake said as he stepped forward. "She even talked with me about it before school today."

Blake seemed very happy with the results, while Amory at least didn't say no right away.

"I'll think about it," she said instead, and I knew that was Girl Code for "If I can't find somebody better."

But I couldn't blame her, either, not after all the stupid moments I'd had with Blake earlier. The man might have had a good heart, but he needed a better brain.

"Amory, while we're waiting, I need to ask you some questions," I said. "Who gave you the doughnuts you ate?"

"Oh, I didn't eat any doughnuts," Amory said.

AB's voice tickled my ear. "I can get the memory scrambler out again if she's not going to cooperate."

"Please." I gave Amory an imploring look. "I need to know the truth. It's the only way we'll be able to find out who's turning people around the city into Alterants."

Amory sighed. "Okay, fine. But you *cannot* tell anyone about this. I'm not supposed to be eating carbs this month. I need to look good for my mother's stupid wedding."

I ignored that as Amory and Blake walked with me into Amory's house.

On the counter was a small, familiar box.

Darla Donut—a younger version of my mother—stared up at me with evil innocence in her painted eyes.

Inside, all twelve doughnuts were gone.

There was a delivery slip, indicating that there was only one box, and then there was a slew of numbers indicating the time, date, and other information about the order.

"Can I keep this?" I didn't know what to make of it, but I knew Zeus or AB could.

Amory nodded. She was already a lighter shade of tan as her hair turned back into black curls at roots.

"Thanks."

I watched as Blake came up behind her and put his arm on her shoulders. "Well, Amory, how about I cook you something to eat?" he asked.

"Cook?"

Both Amory and I spoke at the same time, and we were both genuinely surprised that Blake had another talent.

"Sure," he said. "I'm not great about soup, but I should be able to handle something simple like some pasta or some eggs, maybe?"

Amory smiled shyly. "Well, I do like eggs. And I've had enough doughnuts to last me a lifetime, so some healthy protein would be good."

"I make a lot of my own food for the same reason," Blake agreed.

As the two of them started talking about food, I had a feeling that things would be okay between them. Quickly and quietly, I slipped out of Amory's house with the empty box of Darla Donuts in hand, holding it up like a prize as I made my way back to Zeus and AB.

○ ○ ○ ○

AB and I dropped Zeus off at his house—well, kind of, anyway. We parked down the street so he could get out and pretend that he was walking home from school. He was still getting home too early, but I didn't think his parents would mind at all. I remembered the text message from his dad.

"Tell your mom I said hi and I hope she's feeling okay," I said.

"Thanks." Zeus gave me a small smile. "I will. I'm sorry you guys didn't need me today. It was still nice to come along though."

"I like having you here," I said. "You're my witness for all of AB's antics, should I ever need to take her to court for anything."

"I'd love to see her try," AB replied, giving Zeus a wink. "I've worked in Washington for years. I know how to get out of a good lawsuit."

We all shared a good laugh, and then Zeus headed out.

"You did good today," AB said as she began to drive like a speed demon again.

"Thanks. I'm as surprised as you are."

"Surprised you managed not to look like a fool in front of Zeus while you were in your super suit?"

"No." I stuck my tongue out at her. "Not for that."

Although you might have a point.

"I meant that I'm surprised I didn't try to get some blackmail items on Amory," I said.

"Oh, I'm not surprised about that at all," AB said. "Give yourself some credit, Kallie. You have more integrity than others might guess, but I know you. And you're very conscientious about keeping your word. Even if you hate doing it."

My eyes welled over. "Thank you."

AB grinned at me.

A few moments passed before I cleared my throat. "Since I do want to do the right thing, I suppose I should apologize to you."

AB stopped the car, hard on its brakes, so she could turn around and look at me. "Excuse me?" she asked, while I was still choking on my seatbelt.

"You heard me," I muttered. "I'm sorry for blaming you for all my problems earlier. I know it's not your fault someone betrayed you, and other people have used your recipe to do bad things, too. Can you forgive me?"

It was hard to say, and my pride was hard to swallow—especially up against the seatbelt as it was—but I knew it was the right thing to do.

It was AB's turn to have tears in her eyes. But she nodded. "I forgive you."

"I don't know how you can," I said. "I seem to be messing things up just as badly for you more often than not."

"No." AB shook her head. "Relationships don't last because the guilty are punished, but because innocent are merciful. Now, obviously, justice must be done. But it can still be done with mercy and grace, and I hate that those things are oddly foreign in today's world."

"Better foreign than forgotten," I said. "I hope Blake and Amory are able to remember them."

"I doubt they can even define them," AB scoffed. "Which reminds me. Next year, we're homeschooling."

"What?" I leaned forward, ready to argue. "But it's my senior year. I don't want to miss prom!"

"Come on, Kallie, you're in school to get an education, not to wear evening gowns."

"That's not the only reason," I insisted. "There are plenty more besides that."

AB and I argued all the way home, and to her credit, she did let me voice all my reasons, even though some of them were quite "shallow" still.

We were in the house when I finally passed her the doughnut box from Amory's house.

"Here," I said. "You can argue with Dad about my schooling, but I'm going to take a nap. I'm going to have so much homework to make up because of all of this superhero business."

"I want a school that teaches you proper history," AB muttered. "Your classmates are severely undereducated, Kallie, and that ought to concern you. There's no telling how far behind you've gotten."

"Dad!" I called. "Dad, Abuela wants to homeschool me next year. Come and rescue me, please."

I almost expected the silence, but when it felt more empty and ominous, I knew Dad wasn't home.

AB gasped.

I turned to see she was looking down at the delivery note. "Oh, no."

"What is it?" I asked, suddenly feeling sick again.

"The name on the delivery slip," she whispered, handing it to me.

I looked it over. "Yeah, what about it? I can see it says 'Amory Franklin' on here."

"No, no, not the recipient," AB said. She pointed to the top. "Look at the delivery man's name."

My fingers went cold.

"John White."

Dad.

"We have to go," AB said. "Now."

"Go where?" I asked.

"To their factory, Kallie, please," AB said, rushing downstairs. "I need to pack more ammo. I'll call Agent Grey while you get another doughnut out of my freezer. Hurry!"

What was going on?

"Hurry?" I repeated, feeling dumbstruck and confused.

"Yes, hurry, Kallie," she insisted. "Don't you see? Amory is your friend, and she was targeted. Now my son, your father, is implicated."

"He's supposed to be home," I said, feeling more dazed than I should have been. "He's supposed to be here."

Here. Safe. Out of trouble.

My dad didn't know anything about AB's work, my superhero duties, or anything I'd learned about Mom.

"Please, Kallie, *move.*" AB looked uncharacteristically shaken as she passed by me and headed out the door again. "He's in danger, and we've got to save him."

I ran upstairs and grabbed my phone.

I'd put it on the charger, and the instant I turned it on, I saw I had a missed call from Dad, and a message, too.

My fingers were shaking as I pushed the play button.

"Hello, Fatgirl. I'm calling to let you know that your father has finally received his promotion at work. Unfortunately, if you don't come to save him, he'll die by the time you get this message."

The voice—one I didn't recognize—was harsh but playful, and as sick as I'd felt several times during the day, I felt like throwing up. I reached for the nearest garbage can when I heard my dad's voice.

"Kallie, this is your father. Don't worry about me; don't listen to him, I'll be fine … I love you."

I fell to the floor, crying.

AB came up behind me, trying to get me to move. "It's only too late if we don't do anything, Kallie," she insisted. "Come on. You can be sad later. Now I need you to be angry and focused."

Reluctantly, I wiped away my tears and nodded. AB was right.

It was time to go.

Fatgirl

FINALE: PART ONE

EPISODE 12

○ ○ ○ ○

C. S. Johnson

This is how the world ends …

FATGIRL
FINALE: PART ONE

○ ○ ○ ○

"This is bad, isn't it?"

I said the words quietly as AB sped down through the streets of Cuttingham City. Her Imperial's engine roared almost gleefully, and if things didn't look so dreary, I might have smiled; for once, I didn't even mind my grandmother's terrible, whiplash-happy driving.

"Things might be bad, but they're not bad all the time. There's no need to be a complete cynic, Kallie," AB replied.

I might have believed her, if I didn't see the grim expression on her face and her white-knuckled grip around the velvet-lined steering wheel.

"Are you sure?" I asked tentatively. "I mean, Dad's been captured by our enemy. The guy's expecting Fatgirl to show up at any moment, and here we are, rushing off to meet him. It doesn't seem like a good plan."

AB didn't respond for a moment. Then she cleared her throat, straightened her shoulders, and glared at me through the rear-view mirror. "Really, Kallie. Don't be like this. And here I thought you didn't want to end up like me?"

"I might be cynical, but you're being delusional."

AB's nose wrinkled. "Did you eat your doughnut yet?"

I noticed she changed the subject, and if we weren't speeding off to a doughnut factory to save my dad, I might've laughed and called her out.

Instead, I pulled out the doughnut. "No," I admitted glumly. I'd grabbed a handful of doughnuts from the freezer before leaving the house; the one I held was a cold, powdery mess, and there wasn't any time to let it thaw like the usual ones AB gave to me.

But as I bit into it, I couldn't help but think how the sweetness of it seemed more like poison than anything else.

And perhaps that was fitting.

After all, AB's doughnuts, the ones she made with her radioactive additives—and not the legal kind—were strikingly similar to the Darla Donuts that had first brought my dad into my mother's life.

He'd been a delivery truck driver for the company, and she'd been the model chosen to be Darla Donut herself. With my mother's large eyes, full lips, and delicate features—all of which I'd inherited—she was the perfect choice to model for them. She was both sophisticated but domesticated, proud yet humble; her eyes were full of wholesome promises, the very picture of a perfect wife and mother.

Mom doesn't even know how to bake! It's so unfair …

I looked down at my half-eaten doughnut as the jelly filling oozed out onto my hand.

I licked it, feeling more depressed than ever.

My dad could die today, and it could be my fault, my mom's fault, *and* AB's fault.

All of us were guilty of bringing my dad into this, and he was the only one who didn't deserve it.

My hands puffed out, and my palms stretched wide; my body transformed slowly into its dreaded Fatgirl physique, and I vowed once more, silently and vehemently, that after all of this was over, I would never, ever eat a doughnut ever again.

"I'm not delusional, you know," AB spoke up suddenly. Her voice grated against my nerves, and it didn't help that I could see the Darlington doughnut factory looming in the distance.

"What are you, then?" I snorted. "Desperate?"

AB gave me a half-smirk in the mirror. "Perhaps. But don't worry. I have a plan."

"Do you?"

"Yes, I do," she assured me firmly. "Mostly."

"Well … what is it?"

AB seemed insulted at my question. "I've already made some calls, Kallie. I've called KP, I've called Max, and I've even called that airhead of a reporter down at the WACC station. I called Zeus for you, too, so you're welcome for that, although he's been a little delayed."

"Delayed? Why?" I felt the blood rush out of my face. Why would Zeus desert me in my hour of need? It made no sense. He was supposed to be in love with me! No way would he ever leave me hanging like this, not when I needed help. "Is something wrong?"

"He'll be a little while, he told me. That's fine. He's working on some stuff from his phone." AB gave me a small smile. "He's pretty smart, even if he is besotted with you."

I groaned. "Well, speaking of smart, I'd like to hear your plan, please."

AB's expression lost its joy. "I said I had a plan. I didn't say it was smart."

"So … what does that mean?" I felt my face balloon out with muscley-fatness as I pushed my hair into my navy hood.

"You'll see."

"I hope so," I nearly shouted. "What did you tell everyone else you called?"

"I told them to get to the doughnut factory, ASAP."

She seemed a little more confident, but I wasn't so certain. I was even less certain when she reached her hand back. "Give that to me."

"What?" I coughed. "Give you what?"

"The rest of your doughnut. If you're not going to eat it, let me have it."

"Oh. Sure. Here you go." I handed it to her, just thinking she was worried about the filling getting on her red-velvet seating.

But my mouth dropped open when she popped the remaining half of the doughnut into her mouth.

"Wait, what are you doing?" I asked, horrified. "Are you insane? We don't need *two* fat superheroes right now!"

"Relax," AB replied, but I obviously wasn't going to listen to that.

"What have you done?" I put my large hand over my mouth in stunned shock, watching as she only pressed her foot down harder on the gas pedal.

This is too much.

I reached for my phone, desperate to call Zeus. I would need his help, I realized. It didn't matter what he was dealing with; he had to get over to the factory *right now.*

I couldn't save my dad and get AB back to normal without help.

This is all just … insane.

It got worse when I realized I'd left my phone at home.

It was probably still on the floor from when I'd broken down over the news about Dad.

"Don't worry," AB told me, her voice low and deadly. "As I said, I've called in my favors. Make no mistake, Kallie: tonight, this will end everything. You can trust me on that."

"You're compromised," I reminded her, nodding at her body. "You'll be bloating out before we get to the next block."

Her blue eyes glittered with an almost demonic light. "My biggest fear isn't that I'll get fat, Kallie."

"What is your biggest fear, then?" I asked, as she suddenly swerved her car viciously to the left; the force was enough to send me flying. I could hear the hinges creek, and somehow I felt another, even more powerful wave of genuine fear.

While I had to admit I'd never been sure my grandmother loved anyone, I knew she loved her car. She wouldn't do anything that would risk it …

Right?

"We're here." AB let out a cackling laugh. "Let the games begin."

Fleetingly, I saw the iron gates to the Darling Donut factory.

Impossibly, AB sped up.

"Stop," I whimpered. I leaned forward, my hands folded next to her. "Please stop, AB. We're not going to get through—"

"Brace yourself," AB barked.

"No!" I screamed as AB drove right into the entrance gate. I only barely heard lock snap free as the gates screeched open; I was screaming, just absolutely screaming, wishing for all the pain and suffering to be over.

My body was flung forward, but thanks to my girth, I didn't move much; AB had been prepared for impact, but I saw her grit her teeth in pain and dark exhilaration.

"Yes, yes!" she hollered out, clearly ecstatic over her triumphant maneuver.

I clapped my hands over my face and huddled my body into itself as the tires popped and the engine sputtered, and we slid further toward the building.

I am an accomplice to destruction of property and domestic terrorism.

Why was that the only coherent thought in my head at that moment?

My thick-fingered hands trembled as the car hit a speed bump and we went flying. The car twisted to the right, and I unsuccessfully flung my weight around to try to steady it.

AB was laughing again as she pulled her sunglasses down over her eyes and aimed for the double-front doors.

"AB, for the love of God, stop!" I yelled.

It was almost like she was deliberately refusing to listen to me.

The Imperial rammed into the glass doors, shattering both them and the windshield. It finally began to slow as the reception desk loomed ahead. I could hear all sorts of alarms going off as lights began to flash, and even though I wasn't prone to epileptic attacks, my head pounded with pain.

"Get ready to get out," AB ordered. "I'm almost fully contaminated."

"You mean insane," I yelled back, brushing all the dusty glass and debris off.

The car skid to a stop, and I was ready to cry again.

Somehow, I managed to sit up, grabbing onto the driver and passenger seat. "What in the world was that?" I screamed. "Are you trying to get us killed? Are you trying to get *me* killed?"

AB coughed and then narrowed her glassy eyes at me.

"I'm a woman who's been trained for years to be as accomplished as I am," she snapped. "My biggest fear is that all I have done for the greater good will be used to perpetrate evil—that everything I've sacrificed for my family will lead to its ruin. I have nothing left to lose, and before the end of the night, no matter what, everyone else will know it!"

She reached down and tugged at her purse, which had been lodged between the passenger seat and the glovebox. With some effort, she finally pulled it free. She reached inside and took out her gun, and then another one—because of course she had two—and then scowled at me.

"Before I'm at full contamination, you should know you'll need to stop me," she said, making my stomach feel even more sick and twisted, especially as she pushed a new magazine into one of her guns. "Thankfully, I'm only a half-dose. My lab bag is in the trunk. We need to save everyone, get the bad guy, and then make our escape."

"*That's* all you have planned?" I gaped at her. "That's *all*? What about actual details?"

"Couldn't do it," AB said with a shrug. "You said it yourself: our enemy knows we're coming, and while he's probably expecting some violence, we still can surprise him—and ourselves, too."

"That's not a good idea!" Before I could harangue her for her terrible choices and demand more concrete direction, the now-smoking engine lit up in flames.

I screamed, but AB only chuckled. "That's my exit cue," she said, shoving her way out of the demolished car. "I'm coming, Johnny!"

I watched her from the backseat as the car continued to burn. For that moment in time, I was certain I would never see anything more absurd and frightening in all my life.

Considering the last several months of my life I'd been forced to balloon up into a super-fat, so-called superhero who sat on people, that was really, really saying something.

The engine sparked again, and I blinked back to reality to see the dashboard melting in flames.

"Yikes."

I moved quickly, feeling like an over-stuffed squirrel squeezing out of her tree after hibernation. My hips and thighs ached with pain as I shuffled my way out the back door, and I rolled onto the floor in pain.

After I straightened myself out and stood up, I looked down the hallway I'd seen AB disappear down.

"Right," I muttered, wondering what to do at first, before remembering AB's so-called "plan."

Save everyone. Stop the bad guy. Get out.

I gulped.

I wasn't sure I would be able to do the first part.

But as the Imperial continued to burn beside me, I knew I had to do something.

Carefully, I hurried toward the trunk; I needed AB's lab bag. I would need to get her to take the anti-F serum and turn her back into her normal, non-murder-happy-granny self.

Sirens were blaring off in the distance, and as I struggled to pull out her bag, I thought I could hear the fire department headed our way.

Fear constricted my breathing; I definitely had to move fast, since AB's enemy—whoever he really was—wouldn't want police or firemen around while he held Dad captive.

Maybe crashing into the building had been smart, maybe it had been homicidal … it was hard to say.

I was just about to slam the trunk shut when I saw it.

Laying there was a Fatgirl-sized belt with two holsters, with two shiny pink Berettas at either end.

I thought back to the "girl's nights" AB and I'd gone on at the gun range, and I almost smiled.

I was still a minor, I reminded myself cautiously.

But it seemed to me that if AB really thought she had nothing to lose, it meant one of two things.

One, it was possible she didn't really love me enough to realize I could be lost in all of this, and she didn't really care if I survived or not.

Or …

Or she trusted me enough to know I would survive, even with her limited training, and she didn't need to worry about losing me at all.

Cautiously, I took hold of the belt and tied it on.

The building's alarms stopped, and a new voice sounded over the intercom.

"Well, well, well … It's nice to meet you, Fatgirl. I've heard so much about you from your father. Why don't you come in and join us?"

The voice was familiar, but it still took me a moment to recognize it.

My eyes went wide.

It was Richard Darlington.

Wait—Richard Darlington … he's the guy behind this? But … why? I mean, really … why? It makes absolutely no sense!

I tightened my grip around my new guns as though they were talismans.

Whatever else, I had no choice.

I had to save my father.

○ ○ ○ ○

I scuttled through the labyrinthine halls of the doughnut factory, turning away from AB's path of destruction and chaos, and started making my own.

My heart was pounding between my ears as I turned down different halls. I felt sick, both from fear and AB's driving, and I would've sold my soul in an instant to wake up and realize I'd been in some kind of violent coma for the last three months, even if that meant I'd missed out on the Next Top Heartland Teen Heartthrob Model audition.

"Kallie … where are you going?" Richard Darlington's silky voice sounded over the PSA system again. "We're in the heart of the factory, if you want to come and see us. Your dad is waiting."

I glanced around, looking for the source of his voice; there were several sound panels along the ceiling, and I realized I was being stupid.

"Well, which way should I go?" I hollered back, hoping he would be able to answer me.

"Follow the signs, of course," Richard replied. "Your father is very smart; I figured that you would be, too. Was I mistaken?"

I bit down on my cheek to keep from snapping back at him.

I had to focus; I had to be smart, disciplined, mature.

I would beat him to a pulp soon enough.

"Jesus," I muttered.

At that moment, as if to answer me, Zeus' voice crackled over my earpiece.

"Keep moving forward, and then go down the hall on your right," he said. I knew he was smiling as he added, "And it's Zeus, like 'hey-Zeus,' not Jesus."

"Zeus?" His name escaped me, just barely, but I felt hope rise up inside me again.

"That's right," Zeus said. "I'm on my way but I'm working on hacking my way into the factory's telecoms in the meantime."

"You're not texting while you're driving, are you?"

"Of course I'm not texting," he assured me. "I'm talking to you now, aren't I?"

Clearly, he'd been hanging around AB too much. He was just as bad as she was when it came to not actually answering my questions.

"Zeus—"

He cleared his throat. "Don't talk to me until I say so, okay?"

That was sure convenient, I thought glumly, but I listened to him.

With AB's bag in hand, I started to juggle-run forward, and then I turned to the right just like Zeus directed. In front of me was another long hallway, but this one was lined with windows. Through them, I could see the entire factory line, as it went from the machines that mixed the ingredients, molded the dough, filled the doughnuts with jelly, and then baked them.

It must've been the nostalgic longing inside of me, or maybe the difficulty of breathing correctly in my huge superhero-body mode, but I stopped running and just stared at the sight before me.

I'd been here before, I remembered; I could see myself in Dad's arms, as he carried me from the beginning of the doughnut baking line. I was a little girl, and I'd seen the whole process as ingredients were mixed, dough was shaped, and then each doughnut rolled down the conveyer belt.

Back then, I'd been just as enchanted.

Now …

Now, nothing was on, or at least, the machines were not moving; I could see lights and all sorts of flashing knobs and buttons, but there was an eerie stillness about the place.

A flicker of something caught my attention; across the way, on the other side, there was another hallway that was lined with windows.

And each one was methodically getting blown out.

Glass shattered through various panels, and I realized AB was making her way to Dad, too.

"There she is!"

I snapped out of my stunned nostalgic trip just as a group of security guards rounded the corner behind me.

"Yikes!" I yelped. I jerked away and ducked down, wincing as a string of rubber bullets rained onto me.

My suit was made of specialized material, woven too tight for the bullets themselves to get through; but my suit didn't stop the pounding pain, and when several of them hit my foot, I ended up stumbling and rolling over.

"We got her," one of the guards called into his radio, as the rest of them raced over to grab me.

I glanced up to see them surrounding me, and I felt nothing but anger as I watched them.

Yes, maybe AB and I had crashed a car through the doorway, and maybe it was possible she was going on some kind of shooting rampage through the building.

But why on earth were these guys here in the first place?

Didn't they know their boss was the guy behind all the Alterants that had been unleashed on the city recently?

"Augh!" Ferociously, I yelled as I grabbed at them. I was too fat for them to secure, even all together, and I wasted no time in fighting for my escape.

After some second-guessing and awkward karate-like movements, I finally sat down on one and rolled onto the others, yanking their guns and other weapons from them as I kicked and swatted and sat down even more.

I felt relatively proud of myself as I stood up, and none of them were able to move without moaning.

One of them weakly grabbed at AB's bag on my wrist; the bottles inside clacked together uncomfortably, and I felt a twinge of fear; I had to protect AB's bag if I was going to be able to save her, too.

"Stop," I ordered.

"No, you stop," the guard muttered back, and briefly, I thought how annoying it was to be disobeyed.

So I knocked him out—mostly accidentally. I punched down at him, and he crumbled, letting the bag go at last.

"Ouch," I whimpered, frowning as I shook the pain out of my hand. "That hurt."

"You shouldn't put your thumb inside your palm when you punch," Zeus' voice said in my ear. "That'll break your thumb if you're not careful."

"If you want to trade places with me—" I shut my mouth quickly, remembering what he'd said. Richard Darlington and his cronies were watching me.

"It's okay to talk to me now," Zeus said. "I managed to hack in and I'm looping the feed now so it looks like you're turning down the next hall, and that'll be it. I'll turn off all cameras … now."

The entire hallway went dark, along with the rest of the factory.

"Whoops." He sighed. "Sorry about that. Let me see if I can fix it."

"Nice work, Lard Boy," I muttered. I reached out my hands and felt along the windows, trying not to be scared. "Are you almost here?"

"Almost," he promised.

A spark of light came on, as the emergency lights ignited inside the factory limits. They weren't as bright as the regular lights, and it was then, without the distraction of all the shiny machines, that I could see where they were keeping my dad.

"Zeus, wait." I squinted through the window. The center of the room was several yards away still, but I could see he was alive. "There's my dad."

I breathed a deep, deep sigh of relief. Dad didn't look too bad; he seemed more uncomfortable and bitter than on the verge of death.

Granted, he was still tied in a chair, and Richard Darlington, for all I could remember what he looked like, was standing next to him, holding a gun to his head.

Thank you, God, that he's okay.

Another loud explosion of glass shouted out from the other side of the factory. The glass shattered as a bullet launched through it.

Richard started screaming, and I started running.

"Stop it," Richard warned, as he whirled around and focused on the windows across from me.

AB was getting closer, I realized.

Richard stepped closer to my dad, cocking his gun.

"Zeus, how do I get down there, and fast?" I gasped.

"I'm working on the lights—"

"Never mind about the lights," I said. "Tell me how to get to my dad!"

"Well, you can go up some and then on your left—"

"My left?" I could barely concentrate; all I knew was it wasn't going to be fast enough.

"Yes, your left," Zeus continued. "There's a staircase … "

Shattered glass rained down from the opposite hallway again.

Inspiration of the worst sort struck.

I grabbed the guns at my side. My hands were shaking; I would have to be careful if I was really going to do this …

And I don't actually want to do this …

But I had to, if I was going to save my dad.

Carefully, but still somehow clumsily, I took off the safety of each gun. There was a small *click* at each movement, and I felt nervous all over again.

After I swallowed hard, I held one in each hand.

I squeezed down on the trigger for both, scrunching up my face as I prepared for the bullets' exit.

Nothing happened.

It was too hard to squeeze it with just one hand, and my pointer finger was too big with the whole Fatgirl schtick, I realized with a grumbling sigh.

"Kallie?" Zeus asked. "What's wrong?"

I ignored him as I put one gun away in the left holster, and then I placed both hands on the other.

Once more, I squeezed the trigger—this time, I was using my pinkie finger, which was a much better fit.

Bang!

I'd still squeezed my eyes shut, and the windows shattered.

I was surprised when there was barely any kickback as I kept shooting in a small circle.

Well, there wouldn't be any kickback, would there? I'm Fatgirl.

Fatgirl didn't have to worry about things the same way regular Kallie did.

"Kallie? Are you okay? Is someone shooting at you?"

I could hear Zeus calling to me, but I ignored him.

Tossing the guns aside, I launched myself through the broken window, rolling in air as I braced myself for impact.

I hated how I almost bounced; the fall, even from an entire floor up, didn't hurt much. Honestly, the guards and their rubber bullets had been harder to deal with—but the shame and humiliation of it all hit me fresh and hard, and I had to quickly catch my breath as I stood up.

"You!" Richard whirled around at my arrival, aiming his gun at me. "Don't move, or I'll shoot."

"It won't work." I slid back into a defensive stance. "Your guards already tried to stop me that way and it didn't work!"

"Well, I'm using real bullets," he scoffed.

"My suit will still block them," I insisted.

He paused, and I could see the mole on the left side of his face twitch, as if he was having trouble deciding what to do.

And then he sneered at me. "You know what? You're right," he said, and he turned around to face my dad again.

"No!" I screamed, running forward. "No, don't hurt him!"

"If you do it, you'll be gone, too, Richard Darlington," AB shouted, and I briefly saw her holding her own gun steady at Richard.

"I'm not going to lose again," Richard shouted. "If I can't win, I'll make sure no one else will, either. I refuse to be a loser for the rest of my life."

"What are you talking about?" I shouted. "AB and my dad aren't here to make sure you lose. We just want to stop the Alterants and get AB's recipe back."

"You're here to stop me. You're here to make sure Karen gets away from me," Richard repeated, jamming his gun into my dad's forehead. "You want to take this all away from me, now that I've managed to steal it."

I was too scared and confused to reply in a smart, logical manner, or even really wonder why he was concerned about Karen. I didn't know why he would be worried about his brother's former girlfriend, and that was if he was talking about Karen Bright at all.

And he still had my dad at his mercy, too.

The stomach-tumbling fear I felt paralyzed me; I could hardly hear Zeus in my ear telling me he was working on turning the cameras back on, especially while AB shouted a stream of expletives at Richard.

"Richard, you will stop this at once," AB called out with a laugh. Even where I was, I could hear the *click* of a newly loaded magazine as she shoved it into her gun. "You don't want to be a loser, and I refuse to lose my family."

"Mother." Dad seemed embarrassed as he stopped her. "Please, I beg you, relax. Come down here, and let's just all talk this through. Can we please try that, Mr. Darlington?"

"No." Richard determinedly stepped forward. All of us went silent in horror as Richard began to pull back the trigger.

Dad's face crumpled, but he knew he couldn't get away. "Tell Kallie I love her!"

"No!" I screamed, once more stomping forward, desperate to save my father, as Richard hesitated.

"I can do this," he muttered to himself, as though he was going insane. "I'm going to kill him. Watch me! I swear I will, I swear I will … I swear … "

Richard seemed reluctant, even unsure, to actually want to carry through with his threat, and I raced to take advantage of his inner conflict.

After all, I wasn't the most popular girl at school for just any reason: I knew when to call someone's bluff, and then absolutely humiliate them if I felt like it.

I only just reached out to grab his shoulder when there was a large, loud rumble.

And it was coming from above us.

"Zeus?" I hissed. "What's going on?"

"I don't know, but there's a helicopter—"

Boom!

All of us—even AB—went silent as the ceiling suddenly ripped open. Shockwaves rained down and jolted me; I could feel the fatness of my body ripple from the explosion's pure surge of power.

"Watch out!" Clumsily, I scuttled over to protect my father as the steel beams and drywall fell down all around us.

As my terror grew and more ceiling tiles fell down around the factory, I heard the increasingly persistent *whir* of Zeus' aforementioned helicopter.

I didn't know what was happening, but AB aimed her gun up at the helicopter and started shooting.

Another enemy? Did Richard call for back up?

I looked at my father, who was watching me with an odd, curious expression on his face.

"Kallie?" He looked down at me, clearly unprepared to realize I was Fatgirl. He sighed a moment later. "What have you and my mother been doing together—really?"

"You can probably guess," I murmured.

"No. No, I honestly can't," he replied, baffled by my transformation.

"Well, right now we're saving you, so maybe you shouldn't distract me," I snapped, feeling awful as my cheeks burned in humiliated shame. I was about to throw AB completely under the bus when the crackle of a megaphone cut through the air.

And then I heard her voice.

"John!"

It was my mother, calling for my father.

"Mom?"

Hearing her voice was like getting slapped in the face with a fistful of sandpaper. I was too dumbfounded and teary-eyed to say anything.

Instead, I watched as Mom descended into the factory from the helicopter on a cable, dropping down through the now-butchered roof.

What in the world is Mom doing here?

She was buckled to a cable, and as she landed on the other side of Richard, I could only stare. She wore a snazzy spy-like suit, with matching leather boots and gloves. She was even sporting some special glasses with yellow lenses, and I felt very … very ugly and young and silly standing there next to her in my pink and navy superhero suit.

I then reminded myself that I wasn't supposed to care about Mom at all, since she'd not only abandoned me for her modeling career, but she'd abandoned my dad to work with an internationally known terrorist.

That night in Fort Lauderdale raced through my memory, remembering how she'd stabbed me and cut my arm, how she'd walked arm-in-arm with ZZ, and how she'd told AB she didn't want to be a mother to me because she had other, more important things to do.

"Kallie? What's going on?" Zeus' voice called out through the dark wanderings of my mind, and I was just stunned that somehow, despite the noise, I was still able to hear him at all.

I still couldn't answer him—I was just too shocked—but I was so grateful he managed to keep me anchored to the real world.

I felt extra-speechless as Mom stepped forward and punched Richard, right in the face, much as I'd done to that guard earlier.

Dad and I both gasped as Richard wailed, and AB started shooting from her location in the hallway again.

Mom didn't seem to notice. She went over to my dad and hugged him. I could see her whispering to him, and I saw him reply.

Without knowing what they were saying, I still knew they were speaking tenderly to each other.

My shoulders slumped forward in aggravation.

Dad had no pride at all when it came to my mom, apparently.

I turned away from them, trying not to cry or vomit, or some combination of both; instead, I brushed my suit off, letting the dust fall as I tried to further compose myself. I pulled out my earpiece, fearing I would break down entirely if I said anything. It didn't help Zeus was practically screaming in my ear, telling me that he was nearly there.

I didn't want him to see me—or my mom or dad—like this.

"Dr. White, would you kindly please stop the onslaught?"

The sound of Agent Grey's voice called out over the megaphone; it was almost as surprising as hearing Mom's. I looked up just in time to see him descending down another zipline into the factory, too.

"It's none of your business if I'm shooting at you or not," AB yelled back, as her shooting suddenly stopped.

"Thank you, madame," Agent Grey called as he deftly landed on his feet and began to unbuckle himself from the zipline cable. He seemed ancient, but he worked through the motions quickly and efficiently.

Not bad at all, especially for an old guy.

"Don't thank me," AB snapped back.

"Giving up, are you?" Agent Grey asked, as he walked over to stand between me and my parents.

"Out of bullets," AB replied angrily.

"Of course," Agent Grey muttered, giving me a laughing wink.

"No, no, no … " Richard started weeping and rolling on the floor.

With nothing else to do, I walked over to Richard and sat on him, making him moan egregiously.

Despite his pain, I almost grinned.

It looked like Fatgirl was going to save the day after all—and while it was humiliating to be known as the hero who sat on her villains, Richard deserved it.

It's still better to be the person sitting on someone than to be the person being sat on. Especially where Fatgirl was concerned.

"Good idea." Agent Grey nodded to me approvingly, before he turned to my mother. "And you've done some nice work, too, Kate. You've done INTERPOL proud."

My eyes went wide, and then narrowed.

Why is Mom here with Agent Grey?

As if he'd heard my thoughts, Agent Grey respectfully bowed his head to me. "Forgive us for the rude interruption to your mission. It is nice to see you again, Fatgirl."

"Huh." I crossed my arms over my lumpy chest, making Richard groan even more as I shifted my weight on his back. "Why are you here? Did AB call you in?"

"No, Margaret didn't, and she won't like that we're here. But we have brought a gift; I'll see if my comrades can manage to get him down here for us." Agent Grey pointed toward the helicopter before he checked his watch. "There we go. Give it a moment."

I looked back up at the sky; in the helicopter, another person was looking down at us while getting strapped to the cable. From where I was, I couldn't see the guy's face; I was only certain that he was very frightened. He struggled to stay still as the zipline ropes were attached to his suit and he looked like he was clawing at the copter's siding.

Watching him, I had a new appreciation for Agent Grey's effortless-looking entry.

"Maybe you should've come down with him," I said. "He seems pretty scared."

Agent Grey smiled. "Well, that and he's detoxing. He had a lot of Protactinium in his system for a long time. It's bound to have some repercussions on his nerves, at least."

I blanched at the thought of my own numerous, overly-massive transformations.

"Don't worry; Dr. White is overseeing your intake with the highest of care, I'm sure," he told me before clearing his throat. "Margaret, come over here, if you would, please. I have a guest to introduce to you."

"Guest?" AB appeared at the other side entrance to the factory, her smoking guns still in hand.

I stared at her curiously; her voice seemed different, but her mood seemed normal. I had to wonder if by some miracle her radioactive doughnuts had fizzled out.

"Hmmm." Agent Grey seemed to notice my concern. "What's the old bird gone and done?"

"She ate one of her doughnuts," I explained.

"Ah, that would explain it," he agreed. "She's not in full control of herself at all, is she?"

"I'm sure that's what she'll tell the jury," I muttered.

Agent Grey chuckled. "You certainly have Margaret's sense of humor, Kallie."

"Kallie?" Mom gasped.

Our eyes met at the same time.

"Kallie!" Mom practically choked out my name, staring at me. She was still crooning over my father, but I could see the absolute horror and disgust in her expressive eyes.

A new round of shame burned through me.

Too easily, I remembered that day when I'd blown myself a kiss in the mirror, dressed in her perfect dress, perfectly prepared for my debut on the Model Middle America Teen Heartthrob Model competition.

Back then, I had been my mother's dream; now I was her nightmare.

"Well, I didn't really change my name to 'Arlanda,'" I snapped. "Not that you'd care either way."

"Oh, Kallie." Her large amber eyes were filled with delicate tears.

"Yep," I snapped. "This is what you get for leaving me with AB."

"AB?"

"AB … you know, Abuela-Blanca." I gestured toward AB as she came up to us, still carrying her guns like the reincarnation of Annie Oakley she obviously imagined herself to be. I sincerely hoped both guns were really empty of rounds, as she'd admitted earlier. "Dad's mom."

Mom looked from AB to me, and then to Dad, who only shrugged.

"We've had a very strange time without you home, Kate," Dad said.

Mom gave him a placating look. "Let me get your cuffs off for you, John."

As she moved to free him, I held my ground. "Well, if you think this is strange, Dad, wait till she tells you about ZZ. Didn't know she was besties with an international terrorist, did you?"

"Kallie … " Mom bit her lip, and I wanted to slap her for trying to use the pretty-faced-victim card; I would've done the same thing in her position, and I felt even worse seeing her trying to manipulate me.

"No, I don't want to hear it," I nearly shouted, making Richard moan again. My body was trembling with anger now that I was done being afraid.

"Please, Kallie, ZZ and I were colleagues in some of her covert operations before you were born," Mom tried to explain. "When INTERPOL asked me to step in and grab her now that she's retired, I couldn't refuse."

I rolled my eyes. "I'm sure."

"I literally couldn't refuse," Mom insisted. "If I didn't help INTERPOL, you and John were going to be in danger. And I couldn't tell you, either."

I felt my resolve against her soften, if just a little. And then I remembered her stabbing me at ZZ's auction. "That's sure convenient."

"What is all this?" Dad asked. "What are you talking about?"

"Why don't you explain things, Agent Grey," I suggested. "Tell us all what my mother is talking about."

"She's talking about one of the largest human trafficking organizations in the world," AB spoke up.

We all turned to look at my grandmother, who held up her guns and aimed them at Mom.

"Margaret." Mom looked even more hurt.

"What?" AB huffed. "Might as well come clean, Kate. You said if you didn't leave them, they would be in danger. Well, now, if you want them back, it's time to tell the truth."

"You won't get me back anyway," I warned, but AB shot me a silencing look.

"What does a doughnut factory have to do with human trafficking?" Dad stood up and rubbed his wrists. "Where does Richard here fit in?"

At the sound of his name, Richard groaned from the floor and began wriggling underneath me, trying to escape.

"No," he wailed. "No, this isn't happening!"

"Believe me, I wish you were right," I grumbled at him, sitting on him even harder. Richard cried out in pain, and I felt only the slightest twinge of guilt for making him suffer.

I needed *someone* to suffer.

At that moment, the man from the helicopter dropped down in the middle of our small crowd. The man waved his arms wildly, trying to catch his balance as he grappled with the cable.

"Careful, now." Agent Grey reached forward and held onto him, while AB remained firm in her defensive stance. Mom and Dad stood together, unsure of what to do with the situation, and I just stayed where I was, sitting on Richard.

Agent Grey steadied the man, and I blinked to see Trevor Darlington.

"What's Trevor doing here?" I asked. "Won't his caretakers at Fairview Rehab Center miss him?"

"I'm sure the owners will, since they were well paid to keep him," Agent Grey said. "But this isn't Trevor. *This* is Richard."

I looked from the man I was sitting on to the man standing between Agent Grey and my mom. They were identical twins, alright, except for the mole. Richard had one on his left side, and Trevor had one on the right—or was it the other way around? I supposed the mole clue really didn't help me, since I couldn't remember which side it was supposed to be on anyway.

"My brother poisoned me to get ahold of the recipe so he could win Karen back," Richard—the real Richard, not Trevor, who I was still sitting on—explained. "He took my place, and tried to use it to poison Robert Cuttingham III."

"No, that's not it," Trevor hollered from underneath me. He wriggled one arm free and pointed at Richard. "Or not entirely, anyway. You *wanted* me to be you, since you were going to use ZZ's recipe to take over the country in time for you to announce your campaign launch! It was a good cover, or so you said at the time."

Richard looked stunningly sober. "Your mind must be rotting with all that radioactivity. I've never heard of anything so preposterous!"

I cleared my throat. "Are you sure? I mean, look around."

He looked at me in ghastly disgust.

"The Alterants started happening after Blake ate the doughnut we had at school," I said. "And that's when Fatgirl's website blew up, and you began to use the Alterants as a way to cover Trevor's tracks, isn't it?"

"No." Richard huffed. "Stop your assumptions. I'm innocent. I've been stuck in Fairview for weeks, thanks to my brother's treachery. Besides, why would I poison someone like Gynnifer Stills? Or Joe Weber or Jim Williams?"

"John Weber and James Walter," I corrected. Thinking of them left a bad taste in my mouth. "And technically they weren't Alterants.

They were just set up—not that you would know that unless you were behind it."

Richard blanched, but jutted out his chin defiantly. "I did not order those doughnuts," he insisted.

It was hard to believe him, but it was clear he knew about the doughnuts, and knew that they hadn't been Alternants.

"Either that's a confession, or you know the person who did order it," I said.

"I do not know what you're talking about." Richard finally shut his mouth.

"I'm sure you boys will be able to fight it all out in your state-sponsored therapy sessions," AB said. She cocked her guns and held them up, aiming for both of them. "Or I can do the taxpayers a favor, and—"

"I think it's time we fixed Margaret," Agent Grey said. "Kate, will you get Trevor while Fatgirl does the honors?"

AB bristled as Agent Grey approached her. She redirected her aim toward his heart next. "What do you think you're doing? You're already in trouble with me, Eugene. You could have told me Kate was under your charge."

"Just like you could've warned me about any other little things over the course of our history together," he replied easily.

I was grateful he didn't seem to mind she was threatening him. I watched them nervously as I walked over to where AB's lab bag had been blown away by the helicopter attack.

As I pulled out the portable centrifuge and readied AB's cure, Mom took care to put Trevor in handcuffs.

I felt a little more nervous as I just needed some of AB's blood. How was I going to get that?

I looked at Agent Grey, who seemed to realize my conundrum.

"I'll keep her still," he offered.

Relief had just washed through me when he pulled AB into his arms, knocked the guns out of her hands, and planted a firm kiss on her mouth.

A fresh batch of shock nearly made me pause.

Everyone else just kind of stared, too, which didn't help.

Belatedly, I heard the police sirens in the distance grow louder as they came closer.

Mom finally spoke up. "I can help if you're stuck," she offered to me.

"Have you handled Protactinium before?" I asked, realizing I didn't need any more surprises for the rest of my life.

"No," she admitted, trying to be cheerful. "But I wouldn't mind getting to stab your grandmother with a needle full of drugs."

"I'm sure the feeling is mutual," I snapped, pushing away from her.

AB didn't even really notice as I took her blood, ran it through the centrifuge, and stabbed the anti-F serum into her again.

She pushed away from Agent Grey almost immediately after that, though.

"What are you doing?" she asked him.

He pulled her hand up to his cheek and nuzzled it gently. "Enjoying myself, if you must know."

She huffed at him, but I could see her eyes were full of sparkles.

"Alright, that's enough," I said. "We've saved everyone, the bad guys are in custody, AB should be back to normal momentarily, and the police are starting to show up. So, let's get out of here, shall we?"

"Good idea, honey," Dad replied, as he reached and took Mom's hand in his.

I groaned. I was about to tell Dad that he'd have to stop groveling at Mom's feet, and that if he wanted her back so badly he would lose me, when Mom shook her head.

"Wait. We have more," she said, turning to Agent Grey.

"What do you mean?" I snapped. "You mean you're not done ruining my life just yet?"

Mom looked hurt again, and I just wanted to slap her. She had been a tool in a human trafficking ring, from which AB had just managed to barely get her out of it, then she married Dad without telling him, and then she had lied to us and left us for an entire year.

Mom might not have had much choice in the matter, but she should've known I was hurting considerably more than she was.

"Kate is right," Agent Grey said as he squeezed AB's shoulder. "There's still one last task we must complete."

I was surprised to see AB nod, and even more surprised when she put her hand on Agent Grey's.

"What is it?" I asked, almost expecting to hear them announce they were getting married or something.

"We need to get the real culprit in all of this," Mom said. She reached into a pocket of hers and pulled out a piece of paper and handed it to AB. "This is for you. ZZ's mind is a bit muddled, but I was able to confirm this with some of her other messages."

AB looked at it. Her lips pulled down in an angry, bitter frown. "I was hoping that wasn't the case, but it does make sense with the documents Kallie grabbed for me in Fort Lauderdale," she muttered. "But there is no other option in all of this, is there?"

"What is it?" I asked.

"The person ZZ used to buy my recipe," AB said, holing up the note for me to see. "Kenneth Pham. My former lab assistant at the NAH."

"Who's that?" I asked. "I've never heard of him."

"You've heard of him," AB said. "I call him KP. He's the one who sold me out and betrayed me, and then gave the recipe to Trevor and Richard—and both of them wanted to use it for their own personal gain, although for vastly different reasons."

"Well … he's not here, is he?" I looked around nervously.

I didn't see anyone, but I felt strange as I looked at the camera on the far side of the room.

It seemed to glisten at me, almost malevolently, and I suddenly wanted nothing more than to leave.

"We'll have to find him," AB said.

Agent Grey took her arm. "We will."

I almost gagged at their affectionate glance, but I held it in. Instead, I opted to take control of the situation myself.

"Okay then," I said. "Let's get the Darlington brothers out of here, and once they're in jail, we'll be able to worry about KP."

If I had been more attentive, I might have noticed no one argued with me, and they were all quick to follow my lead.

But I was too busy looking forward to never being Fatgirl ever again.

○ ○ ○ ○

We all walked together as we went out the factory's side exit.

Thankfully, no one seemed to notice us, even with me in my hot pink and navy super suit.

No one said anything as we looked back at AB's Imperial, which a bunch of firemen were hosing down while police cars were lining the front parking lot.

Trevor was still wining about Karen dumping him, and Richard was grumbling about being held hostage in a rehab center for months while his political and business career were derailed. AB and Agent Grey were a little too quiet for my liking, to be honest; it was so weird to see AB's blue eyes light up with that much wonder and pleasure. He didn't do anything to help, either; he pulled her close when he thought no one was looking and pressed a kiss to her forehead.

"Does this mean we can let the past go?" he asked her. "Did I make up for my past mistakes?"

"No," I nearly shouted, before AB could reply. "You kept my mother from me for a year so she could play lackey to a well-known terrorist!"

"It had to be done," Agent Grey murmured, only somewhat regretfully.

Mom gave me a small smile, and I scowled back at her.

"Doesn't mean I'll forgive you, or her," I snarled.

Mom looked sad again, but I saw Dad squeeze her hand in comfort. I almost lashed out at him, but it was then I saw Zeus.

He's here!

He was just standing before us, breathing hard. I felt a rush of happiness in seeing him. He'd tried to come to my rescue, but the truth was, whether he knew it or not, he'd already rescued me. It turned out Sweaty Fat Kid was just what I needed to be a better person, and I was so incredibly grateful for him in that moment.

"Zeus!" I grinned as I ran toward him, leaving all the others behind.

But just as I reached him, I stopped.

A man I didn't recognize was behind Zeus, and I saw the gun jutting into his back. He had a large forehead, with dark eyes, and an even darker intent shining through them. His black hair was peppered with white and gray at the temples, and his mouth was curved down into a deep frown as he looked at me.

"So, you must be the grand-brat," he said. "Is that right, Zeus?"

He thrust the gun into Zeus' back again, and I watched in horror as Zeus nodded.

"Let him go," I said, my voice suddenly shaking.

"Not yet," the man said.

"KP."

I looked beside me as AB came up next to me. Her eyes were clear, only full of hardness, and her guns were back in her hands. "I was wondering if you were nearby."

Behind me, Mom and Dad had taken cover, and Agent Grey had his watch back out; I hoped he was calling for backup.

"You've ruined everything—again, Dr. White," he said. "You couldn't just go away, could you? Innocent people have always suffered at your hands, and surely it's nothing to you for this kid to join their ranks."

I could feel my heart twisting up inside my chest. I'd agreed to help AB find the man who'd stolen her recipe. I'd sat on a terrorist, faked my way through fashion trends, lost my mom and nearly lost my dad, teamed up with INTERPOL and became a beloved laughingstock of a hero to my entire city. I'd blown up three times my size to sit on Alterants, learned how to inject people with needles, missed out on prom, and even fallen in love with the big fat teddy bear man from my computer class instead of the perfect-looking lacrosse jock.

But now, there was nothing I could do.

"It's time we finished things, Dr. White," KP said. "I finally have nothing left to lose."

Zeus and I locked eyes, and all I could do in that moment was pray for a miracle.

Hold on, Zeus. Hold on. We'll think of something.

As KP tightened his fingers around the trigger, Zeus shivered.

And I could only glance over at AB, desperately hoping I wasn't delusional.

Please, God, let us think of something …

I could barely live with myself as it was. If something happened to Zeus, I would never forgive myself.

I clenched my fists. I had to save him.

I just had to …

Fatgirl

FINALE: PART TWO

EPISODE 13

○ ○ ○ ○

C. S. Johnson

Fatgirl is finished … or is she?

FATGIRL
FINALE: PART TWO

○ ○ ○ ○

Things had been bad before, but now they were undoubtedly worse.

My innocent father had been captured by an insane, desperate lunatic pushed to the edge after losing his girlfriend to a rich man—and now, *another* insane, raging lunatic had taken hostage the one person in all the world who truly loved me for who I was.

I wanted to fall over and cry. I hated how cruel life was. Babies in the womb form in the fetal position, and in that moment, life was just one long, awful sequence of events forcing me back into that posture.

But somehow, miraculously, I was able to remain standing. I had to remind myself to breathe, and my fat-ball body was jiggling like a bowl full of jelly, but I was able to stand.

As KP loomed menacingly behind him, Zeus gave me a pitiful look. I sincerely hoped he wouldn't tell me he loved me, just as Dad had done moments before, or I knew I would be lost.

I was already halfway lost as it was.

AB, almost as if she'd sensed my bewildered helplessness, came up beside me.

"AB," I whispered. "I don't know what to do."

"That's okay, Kallie. I'm the one in charge of the plans, remember?"

I couldn't even look at her. "So you have one?"

"Yes."

I hated how I could hear the catch in her voice.

I gritted my teeth. "Is it a good one?"

"I'm not sure," she admitted. "We'll see, I guess."

Panic flared inside of me like never before. My body trembled with rage and fear, and I felt like puking.

This can't be how things end … It's not fair.

I'd worked so hard to save everyone; I'd only wanted to do what was right, and now I was being punished for it.

And Zeus is paying the price …

"KP, let's talk about this," AB said calmly, shifting her weight as she crossed her arms. "I've known you and trusted you for years, ever since you came to the NAH. Where did all this back-stabbing betrayal come from?"

As I tried not to let any oncoming tears block my vision, KP eyed AB disdainfully.

"You only have yourself to blame, Dr. White," he yelled. "It would have been so easy, if you'd just gone along with my plans—if you'd just let the hunt for the recipe go. But no, you kept insisting that it'd been stolen."

"All of this mess here in Cuttingham City was to stop me?" AB asked.

"Yes." KP nodded. "Once I heard about Frank Whitey's capture and that kid getting turned into a baby, I knew what you were about; it helped that Trevor Darlington was starting to go crazy, and after I ensured his cooperation, it was all I could do to make sure the blame landed on you."

"Yes, I know," AB said, her voice impatient. "I'm wondering *why* you did this, not *how*. That part seems simple enough."

"Why?" KP looked insulted. "Just think of all the riches that we could've had if we just let your recipe slip out."

"Oh, KP." AB's hand went up to her cheek as she moaned in muted disgust. "Please tell me it wasn't about the money."

"Well, it was!" KP snapped.

"That is a tad cliché," I heard Agent Grey mutter behind us.

"Plenty of people do things for money," Mom reminded him. "I've seen it firsthand."

KP ignored them as he stared daggers at AB. "All you had to do was let the recipe 'escape,' and send the other feds running while we sold it off. We could've made a fortune on the black market."

"I'm not a fan of harming my own," AB said. "The NAH is not supposed to be like *other* feds, for goodness' sake."

"You know the truth, and you don't care?" KP said, flustered. "Aren't you tired of the system that they have rigged up for themselves? One where they get rich while the rest of us get poor? Don't you want some of that yourself?"

"There are some things money can't buy," AB insisted.

"Tell that to all my Project: SERUM customers," KP argued. "I had four lined up before you went home that evening!"

"And yet you sold it to Zina Morozova, of all people." AB wrinkled her nose as she shifted her weight again. This time, she nudged me.

She apparently wanted me to do something; I was certain of that.

But what? Seriously, what?

I glanced around, fervently searching for some kind of clue of what to do.

AB sighed softly, no doubt seeing my ignorance.

"Why not?" KP asked. "ZZ's the one person who would've made sure no one else got a copy."

"Unless *she* sold it—which she did." AB gestured back toward Trevor and Richard Darlington, who were muttering at each other under their breath as Mom and Agent Grey held them secure.

KP blushed. "ZZ had a very unique offer at the time," he continued, clearly embarrassed that he'd given into ZZ's charms; I had to swallow a laugh, remembering how ZZ described her customer as a very sad, pitiful man. "When I found out that she sold your recipe, I set out to retrieve it again. The Darlington brothers weren't hard to manipulate."

The two of them continued to talk about ZZ and various governments and mercenaries after the recipe, and I practically grew bored.

So instead, I kept my focus on Zeus.

I didn't know AB's plan, but it was enough to know she had one, right? I just had to wait for a moment when I could save him.

If only I hadn't taken out my earpiece earlier.

At that moment, a shadow appeared behind KP; I squinted my eyes to see, but it was very dark out now, and especially more since the Darlington factory lights were still largely out, the police cars were on the other side of the building, and the fire from AB's Imperial had been doused.

"But that's enough about that," KP said, suddenly more rattled than ever as he looked at me. He wrapped his arm around Zeus' neck and then pushed the gun barrel into his head. "This ends now, Dr. White!"

All of my hope went flying out the window.

"No!" I screamed. "No, stop it. Please, stop. Zeus doesn't deserve this."

"Actually," Zeus said quietly, clearly trying not to whimper, "I do deserve it."

KP paused—and so did the rest of us.

"What are you talking about?" KP asked.

"Yes, what *are* you talking about, Zeus?" I snarled. "You actually don't deserve this, you know!"

Zeus gave AB a solid nod. "Dr. Pham doesn't know it, but I've been recording our conversation. I have a tracker log keeping up with his access to the donut factory's computer logs. He's been able to watch Trevor and Richard for months or last several weeks based on my findings. All I have to do is turn it into the police, and then he's done for."

"Shut up," I ordered, both extremely proud and horrified at the same time. "Don't give him a reason to shoot you!"

"Maybe he should keep talking," KP muttered, tightening his grip around Zeus' neck, and I feared that he would choke him next.

"Stop," I cried again. "Please, stop this. Take me instead!"

"No!"

I was flattered and frustrated as Zeus, Mom, Dad, and even Agent Grey all objected to my offer at the same time.

Only AB said nothing—and I took this as her blessing, whether she wanted to give it or not.

"Let him go, and take me instead," I continued. "I am AB's granddaughter."

I pulled down my mask and pushed it away.

All the Fatgirl shame in the world wouldn't stop me from saving Zeus.

KP's nose twitched, and I had to wonder if he was trying not to laugh at me.

"I know who you are," he said instead.

"If you know who I am," I said, slowly and angrily, but still determined, "then, you know I'm worth more to you alive than that kid is to you dead."

KP eyed me carefully, sneering as he saw the reaction from everyone else around me.

"So, what do you say?" I asked. "Let's make a trade. I insist. I'll do whatever you want. Just don't hurt him."

"Kallie." AB finally shook her head. "Don't give yourself up like this. That won't help us in the long run."

"I'm not interested in helping us in the long run anymore," I argued. "You asked me to help you figure out who stole your recipe. Now you know, and now I want to save Zeus. I can't … I can't let anything happen to him."

Without another word, I walked forward, watching KP carefully.

"What about the kid's recording?" he asked me.

"Come on, he's lying," I said quickly. "Do you really think kids today are capable of doing anything like that? They have to put warning labels on laundry detergent pods."

KP didn't say anything.

"He's probably stuck on his social media sites all day," I rambled on, practically frothing at the mouth as I barely stopped myself from yelling. "I mean, look at all my other friends you targeted. They were dumb enough to eat radioactive doughnuts, weren't they?"

Standing in front of KP, I waited, still not really sure what would happen.

I never negotiated a hostage situation before, and I certainly never volunteered to be one.

But what else can I do?

I couldn't leave Zeus alone and I couldn't leave him to die.

I needed him to stay alive.

Zeus had always been so thoughtful. He cared for his mom, he tried to please his dad, and yet he wasn't above breaking the law or committing fraud to help me. He'd done so much for me and AB for her stupid recipe, and it was about to get him killed; if I could stop it, I had a duty to do just that.

And there was just the simple fact that I loved him. He was a funny, helpful, sweet sort of guy, who loved me for more than just how pretty I looked. He loved me for how I treated people and for what I thought and who I was.

Yeah, he wasn't really that good looking, but in his own way, he was definitely unique, and the more I spent time with him, the less some of that stuff seemed to matter.

"What's wrong, Fatgirl? Having second thoughts?" KP asked.

"In a way," I murmured, before mentally berating myself for losing my focus.

Thankfully, while he seemed to sense my hesitation, he had his own to deal with, too.

I was just about to ask him what was wrong when he grabbed my hand, jerked me forward, and pulled me beside Zeus. He kept his arm around Zeus' neck, but he held the gun to my back.

"I've got two hostages, now," KP said triumphantly, and I about screamed.

But that was when it happened.

The shadow I'd seen earlier popped out of nowhere from off to side. It moved like a blur; I barely managed to make out the outline of a man as he grabbed KP.

I blinked in split-second recognition; it was Officer Powers.

Relief poured through me like a monsoon on steroids. For the first time, I knew we could win.

I knew we could escape.

"Move!" I called out to Zeus as I jut out my big, muscly butt and tore myself away from KP.

Thankfully, Zeus twisted free, and Officer Powers managed to pull KP's gun upward.

KP angrily cried out, firing bullets repeatedly into the air, but Officer Powers bent KP's hand over his arm.

The gun went flying from his hand.

"Grab it," AB ordered.

Desperate to do anything that seemed remotely helpful, I lunged after it.

I wrapped my large hand around the gun. The metal was cool and heavy, and it seemed too easy, really, that I just picked it up, and everything was suddenly finished.

As I held it up to show the others, silence seemed to descend on all of us.

All except for Officer Powers—well, not "Officer" Powers since he was suspended from the force, but rather Max; he was still wrestling KP on the ground.

But behind us, Mom had hold of Trevor or Richard, while Agent Grey had the other evil twin; and even Dad had Mom's other arm, almost like he was worried she would try to escape again.

AB walked toward me, trying to explain what had happened.

" … so Max got so close since your large body had given him enough of a blind spot … "

But I wasn't really listening to her.

I was too busy being happy.

Zeus was fine.

As I glanced over at him, he grinned back at me. "Good job, Kallie."

And at that, I fell to my knees, indescribably grateful he was alive and well, and tried not to cry in relief.

I was already bloated out to the size of a sailboat; I didn't need to add a blotchy face with tearstained cheeks to the mix.

That was when a sharp *prick* of pain stabbed through my arm.

"Ouch!" I yelped, dropping KP's gun and grabbing the sore spot on my sleeve. "What was that for?"

AB gave me a grin as she held up a needle. "You're welcome."

"What … ?" My voice trailed off as I realized AB had gotten ahold of her lab-bag.

"Cuttingham City and I are indebted to Fatgirl. But her services are no longer required," AB said with a bright smile. She reached out a hand to me. "Good job, my darling girl."

I swallowed hard, surprised by the lump in my throat. "Thank you, AB."

I put my hand in hers, almost like we had when we made the deal.

But AB pulled back.

"Oh, I'm not helping you up, Kallie," she replied with a smirk. "Hand me KP's gun, please. You can get up yourself. You might be shrinking thanks to the anti-F serum, but with all the weight you still have, you'll tear my arm out."

"You're so old and fragile it's a wonder you haven't died already," I snapped back.

After all the moments of the past hour where that might have been true, I felt bad about my retort, but I still held back from apologizing as I handed her KP's gun.

Thankfully, AB just laughed. "Here," she said, holding out her bag to me. "There's one last doughnut in there that's still de-thawing if you're hungry."

I reared back from her. "No, thank you!"

AB remained firm. "I have an extra set of clothes for you to change into, too," she said. "So you don't have to worry about dressing like Fatgirl anymore, either."

"Oh." At that, I took the bag eagerly. "Okay. Thank you."

"Don't thank me yet." AB nodded back to where my parents were standing, and Dad was already locked in a passionate embrace with my mom. "I'm sure there's some more fallout that we'll have to deal with before this is all over."

I almost groaned.

But then I noticed Agent Grey was looking at AB, too, and I couldn't stop myself from grinning.

"Well, you'll have your own personal trouble to deal with too, given how much you seemed to like Agent Grey 'helping' to keep you still," I said.

AB surprised me by giggling; the sound of her innocent laughter made me want to tease her more, but KP started screaming louder, shouting all sorts of obscenities, and it was time to get moving.

Max tied him down with a pair of handcuffs Agent Grey had produced from his utility belt.

I didn't feel any pity for KP.

AB had trusted him when he'd said it wasn't him, and he'd betrayed her for money and sex and some kind of destructive chaos plan of action that had poisoned plenty of people around the city, including my friends. It was the kind of motivation suited to a video game villain more than a government scientist.

Well … AB would say otherwise, probably.

If I did have to pity KP, I would pity him for losing AB's trust.

She knew how to use guns and a bunch of radioactive materials, and she had enough contacts to call in fake terrorist attacks to land planes and wiggle out of Interpol's reach; there was no telling just how badly she could punish him.

For now, it was enough to know we were alive.

"Thank you, thank you, God. For saving us," I whispered.

"I think we're about even now, aren't we, Dr. White?" Max asked, giving AB a charming smile. "Or do you perhaps owe me more now?"

"I'll testify to get you out of your charges, if that's what you're hinting at," AB replied.

"I'd like a few phone calls for a new job, too," Max said. "It's hard getting into a new position when 'radioactive contaminant' is on your HR profile."

AB laughed. "Well, I'll see what I can do. It's only fair; you've always been reliable over the years."

"Yes, you were right to pity me back when we first met," Max agreed.

At his comment, I suddenly understood; AB had been counting on her backup all along. And even though she called in all her favors, and KP was one of them, Max was, too. Other policemen were around the corner, doing their job, and Max was doing his, too.

"Thank you, Officer," I said. "I'm so glad you were here to help."

"You're the real hero, Kallie," Max said. He reached out and shook my now-shrinking hand.

"Because I'm a positive role model for overweight superheroes everywhere?"

"No." He grinned. "Because you did what you could to save that kid, to the point you were willing to give your life for his."

Max gestured toward Zeus, who was handing his earpiece equipment over to AB. My grandmother looked like Christmas had come early, and she was actually getting something other than coal.

"I don't feel like it was heroic," I murmured.

"Doesn't matter what you feel; it *was* very heroic of you." Max nudged KP with his foot unceremoniously. "I wasn't sure I would get this guy in time, and you gave me the time and opportunity to take him down."

"Thank you." I mumbled out the response almost reluctantly. But I saw AB as she gave Zeus a few soft words, before she glanced back over at me and added, "Kallie would like to thank you, too, I think."

Zeus looked incredibly happy.

"You think?" I excused myself to Max and then I raced up to Zeus.

It was hard to stop myself from jumping into his arms.

Zeus was prepared, even though I was still shrinking down to my normal size. He clasped me as I grabbed him, and then I held him tight, hugging him.

As I held him, my Fatgirl suit sagged on me like loose skin, and it hit me that everything was finally over—and for real this time.

Thank you, God. Thank you.

It's over.

It's all over!

I could've shouted it from the mountaintop.

As if he knew what I was thinking, Zeus patted my hair down affectionately. "Well, this has certainly been an adventure."

I tried to laugh and nearly choked instead. After clearing my throat, I peeked up at Zeus. "Did you really have KP's recorded confession?"

Zeus nodded. "Of course I did. I've been able to record all the conversations that you and AB have."

Suddenly, my gut twisted. What if I'd let slip that I was in love with him?

Did I? Did I say I was in love with him?

Embarrassed, I tucked my face back down into his chest.

It was too hard to remember with all the fear and the adrenaline eating up my memory, and I couldn't entirely bring myself to care that much. I embraced Zeus tightly, and decided that after I changed my clothes, fixed my hair, and attempted to look more like my usual gorgeous self, I would tell Zeus how I felt.

And *that* would make it official.

Not some dumb recording.

○ ○ ○ ○

The next hour managed to pass by both more quickly and slowly than I would've liked.

There was a lot of commotion, and I couldn't pay attention to all of it completely. I did see Max talking to some of the other cops, I saw the Darlington brothers get shuffled into a police car, and Agent Grey eventually called for his helicopter. In the distance, AB's Imperial was all fried up beyond recognition, and I could already hear the very distinctive voice of Gynnifer Stills complaining there wasn't enough light for her "Breaking News" report highlight.

From what I could tell, my mom and dad were on their way to forgiveness and reconciliation—and I already knew I didn't want any part of that.

Still, I wasn't going to object to Dad standing there holding Mom's hand. It seemed too hypocritical, in some ways, since I was holding onto Zeus' hand pretty tightly myself.

"Are you doing okay?" Zeus asked me.

He probably meant if I was okay with my parents acting like lovesick teenagers from the 1950s, but he could've been asking about any number of things.

So I only shrugged.

I didn't really care that much—not at that moment. I really just wanted run away, change my outfit, and look presentable enough to be able to confidently declare to Zeus that I was in love with him. I hadn't been able to sneak away to change out of my suit, so I put on the spare shirt AB had in the bag for me.

Fatgirl's suit still hung on me like curtains, but it hid enough of the bright, hot pink part of my costume that I wasn't immediately recognizable as Fatgirl.

There was also another part of me, terrified from how close I'd come to losing him, that didn't want to leave Zeus' side.

I was greatly comforted by the fact that he didn't seem eager to leave me, either. His sweaty palms were wrapped firmly around mine, while his moonbeam eyes glittered with contentment.

My heart ached. *Maybe it doesn't matter so much that I'm dressed this way.*

Zeus was probably the last person in the world who would think I was God-awful ugly as I told him I loved him.

Realizing that, I couldn't hold it back any longer.

"Hey," I said.

He looked at me, and I couldn't stop myself from smiling. Zeus had both a hidden strength and a hidden sweetness to him.

"What is it?" Zeus asked.

"I … I want you to know … " My cheeks burned.

I couldn't hold it back any longer, but I also couldn't seem to get the words out, either.

"Ah." Zeus nodded in understanding. "I will take care of it."

I stopped short. "Take care of what?"

"I'll take down the website," he said with a grin. "I'll miss Fatgirl, though. I'll bet you the rest of Cuttingham City will, too."

"Um … "

"You might not think that, but it's true," he said. "You were really brave."

"Me?" I pulled my hand out of his to cross my arms. I was back to my thin, gorgeous, model-ready self, albeit in a shirt large enough to cover a couch and leggings that felt like anorexic elephant skin hanging around my ankles; I wasn't in a position to shake Zeus senseless, but it was more than tempting.

"What's this me being brave stuff? You're the brave one here! You got that recording!"

"You would've traded your life for mine," he reminded me. "We couldn't have gotten here at all without you."

"But you're the one who made the difference at the end," I argued back, but the smile on his pimple-covered face just melted my heart. "You know what, just shut up, okay?"

I planted my feet firmly on the ground and straightened my shoulders.

"Zeus," I said. "I … I—"

Brinnnnnngg!!

Of course, it had to be at that moment that Zeus' phone went off, ringing out an ear-piecing screech, like a banshee rising from the grave.

"What is that?" I yelped, grabbing my ears. I'd never heard a ring so loud before, and I was caught off guard at its timing.

But I was even more ticked off when Zeus answered it.

"What is it?" he asked.

I went still as I heard his dad yelling at him in Spanish. Even though I didn't know what he was saying, I felt terribly sick; Jose Evans would never know his son almost died just moments earlier.

It was so tempting to take the phone away from Zeus and scream at his dad; Zeus had never been good at standing up for himself, and it was time to make some changes.

I was Zeus' girlfriend after all—even if Zeus didn't really think it was real, I was more than willing to make it real, and like any good girlfriend, I would start off by pissing off his dad.

There was honestly nothing more girlfriend-like I could do.

But before I could grab the phone, Zeus let out a long, sad sigh.

"Alright, I'll be there as soon as I can," he said, and then he hung up the phone.

"What is it?" I asked.

"I have to go." He looked back at me apologetically. "My mom's in the hospital again … and it doesn't look good."

It was funny how the world could change so drastically in just a few seconds.

Given everything I'd gone through in the last twenty-four hours, I was lucky I hadn't had a heart attack.

The pain I felt hurt worse than anything I could have imagined—because there was nothing I could do.

My mouth felt dry as I spoke. "I'll go with you."

Before he could do anything else, I took charge of the situation.

I practically dragged Zeus over to AB, who was talking with the others. She'd just wondered aloud if her Imperial could possibly get replaced, while Dad was wondering about his job, when I interrupted them.

"What is it, Kallie?" AB asked, no doubt seeing my distressed look.

Quickly, I explained what was happening, and AB, thankfully, didn't seem as keen to embarrass me for once.

"That's no problem. Go," AB said. "I'll take care of things here."

Agent Grey came beside her and gave her a kiss on the cheek. "*We* will take care of things, Margaret," he corrected her.

I almost rolled my eyes, but I was glad somebody was happy, at least.

"Keep me posted on your mother, too," AB told Zeus. "I know this is a hard situation for your family."

There was something weird about the way she spoke with him, and I wondered if there was some kind of secret between the two of them.

Maybe she'd told Zeus that I was a sucker and soft-hearted and a lot more stupid-headed than I come off, or that I'd come around, or something like that.

I couldn't say, but I didn't want to think about it either.

Not with Zeus' mom in the hospital.

AB nodded toward her bag, which I wore over my shoulder. "There's some cash in there for parking," she said. "You can have it with my blessing."

"Thank you," I murmured, oddly touched at her generosity. I was already grateful for her forethought regarding my clothes; although I was more concerned for Zeus, it was a relief to know I wouldn't go into the hospital dressed up as Fatgirl.

We drove off, largely in silence. Zeus had arrived to the Darlington Donut factory in his mom's car, the one with the flowery decals on the side, but the last hour or so had given me plenty more to think about than how embarrassing it was to drive around in it.

There was Trevor-Richard's stupid decision to make radioactive doughnuts to further their own personal and public ambitions; KP's betrayal of AB for cash and sex with a former KBG agent; Mom working with Agent Grey and Interpol, supposedly to save me and Dad; and Dad nearly getting killed as everything finally came to a somewhat epic battle inside a doughnut factory.

But none of that mattered.

All I could do was bite my lip and try really hard not to cry as I thought of Mrs. Evans.

I don't really want to do this.

Mentally, I berated myself. I didn't want to do this, but I was really still only worried about myself.

"I'm actually glad to see AB's driving has rubbed off on you," I said, using one hand to clutch onto Zeus' and the other to grab onto the armrest.

"Sorry," Zeus murmured.

"No, it's okay," I said. "It'll be okay."

Then we fell back into silence, and I felt stupid for saying that.

Who really says stuff like that?

People that think they're God, I guess.

Well, at that moment, I didn't feel like God.

I felt powerless. Hopeless. Stupid and meaningless.

"I'm sorry," I whispered.

"No, Kallie," Zeus said. He tightened his grip around my hand. "Thank you."

He gave me a kind look, and then pushed his foot down harder on the gas pedal.

I gritted my teeth, but I didn't say anything else.

We only stopped once Zeus found a parking spot and he turned off the car.

But then, he surprised me; he didn't hurry to get out or move.

He just sat there.

"Zeus?" I nudged him. "What's wrong?"

"Kallie." Zeus murmured my name and squeezed my hand. "I'm scared."

I swallowed hard. "I'm sorry."

"Earlier, the thought of dying didn't bother me much," Zeus said quietly. "Dying for someone I love is easy. But … I don't know if I can live without my mom."

"I know." My nose prickled and I sniffed back tears. I tried not to cry; I didn't think that it would help anything. "But, hey … I'll be here for you, okay? Just like you were for me."

I think that was what he was wanting to hear, or maybe it was what he needed to hear, because he was able to get out of the car.

I followed closely, nonchalantly trying to roll up my loose Fatgirl suit as we walked. It was hanging freely underneath my shirt, and I felt very self-conscious as we walked inside.

There were nurses all around, running through their routines. Occasionally, one or two would look at us and ask if we needed help.

When we rushed past them, the nurses only shook their heads and went back to work.

Eventually, we were able to ignore them completely; I got the worst feeling in my gut when I saw their reactions. I forgot how ugly I looked until I caught sight of myself in a waiting room mirror.

I looked perfectly terrible.

But I forgot all that again, too, as Zeus and I arrived at his mom's room.

"Mom." I heard Zeus murmur softly, and he let go of my hand as he raced to her side.

I had trouble breathing.

Mrs. Evans looked pretty bad. In the few short days since I'd seen her, she'd gotten inexplicably worse. She looked like a skeleton; her skin was taut across her face, even as she slept. There was a breathing tube in her nose, and her colorful silk scarf had fallen to the wayside. It was brightly patterned with flowers and I was reminded of her room.

I remained in the doorway as Zeus reached down and hugged her.

On some level, I envied him; he doted on his mom, while the thought of even seeing mine made me feel sick.

"Zeus."

His mom stirred softly, and her arms weakly raised up to embrace him back.

I could practically hear Zeus' heart break. For a long time, they held onto each other, and I felt like a weird stranger for watching.

But, just as my feet were starting to ache, and I wondered how late it was, Mrs. Evans turned to look at me.

"Oh, Kallie," she whispered. "You're here."

"Um … yeah, I can leave if you … " I stuttered badly, but she reached her hand out for me.

Seeing no other real choice, I walked to the other side of her bed. Every ounce of tiredness I'd felt inside of me disappeared as I took her hand.

"Thank God you're here," Mrs. Evans whispered to me.

I tried to give her a smile, but it was too hard; I was starting to cry.

She smiled for both of us in that moment.

We both knew we were faced with the impossible. And yet we were both here, and perhaps that was the only thing I could really do for her, or for Zeus: I could be there, so that they didn't have to face this alone.

Zeus slid back as his mom reached out her arms to me.

I braced myself; her weak arms were chilly and cold, and I suddenly wanted to cry even harder. It was a cold hug, but it was still more than I'd get from my own mother; in that moment, I desperately didn't want her to leave us.

"Remember your promise," she whispered to me. Her voice was so soft, I wondered that she could speak at all.

I held onto her more tightly. It was not the time to worry about how I looked or how I was dressed, or even how little I really knew her; I clung to her, wishing she could be my mom, wondering why this had to happen at all, and praying for some kind of miracle I knew wouldn't come.

"I remember," I whispered back.

I felt awful—really, really awful.

I'd promised her I would be there for Zeus before, and at that moment, heaven and earth would've had to move me away from him.

But in the next moment, it turned out something else could move me.

Jose Evans cleared his throat. "Ahem."

Zeus and I looked back toward the door, where he was standing with some flowers.

"Jose." Mrs. Evans smiled at him; it was a smile reserved for the love of her life, and Zeus and I said nothing as he came over, scooted in front of me, and took his turn embracing her.

"I love you." Mrs. Evans' whisper was even more weak as she held Jose.

She looked at Zeus. With her other hand, she reached out and brushed a lock of his oily hair out of his eyes, and then put her hand on his cheek. "I want you to be strong and brave, and to do your best. And I want you to know it's okay to be happy. I will be at peace when you smile, my loves."

"We love you," Zeus murmured, keeping hold of her hand.

His mom nodded, and then her body went limp. I was about to let out a loud sob when I noticed she was still breathing.

Still, I only barely managed to put my face in my hands and hold back my weeping.

A few moments passed, and I felt a hand on my shoulder.

Jose was looking down at me—and he was clearly angry.

"It's time for you to go now," he said quietly. "You're not supposed to be in here."

"I'd like to stay, if I can," I replied, blushing. I was caught off guard by his sudden hostility. I looked over at Zeus; he was still holding onto his mom's hand. He didn't seem to realize his dad was being a douche.

"No," he said sharply. "You're not family, and you're not paying the medical bills for this. You need to leave and give our family some privacy."

I gave him my best "pretty-eyes" beggar look. "But—"

Jose's dark eyes mutated into something beyond terrifying. "Now."

With his hand still on my shoulder, he led me to the door.

"Wait," Zeus said. "She can stay—"

Jose shot a dark glance over his shoulder, and Zeus gave me an apologetic look.

"I'll wait outside," I promised, glancing back at Mrs. Evans.

I hated feeling like it was the last time I would ever see her alive.

Jose pushed me out into the hall, and then he shut the door behind us.

"What's going on?" I asked. "I know this is a hard time for you, but you don't have to be so mean to me."

Jose ignored me. He whistled, and then suddenly, two big, burly men walked up to us from down the hall.

They'd seemed to be waiting—almost like they were bodyguards.

Jose pushed me toward them. “Escort Miss Grande-White out of the hospital for me,” he said, before speaking to them in rapid Spanish.

Once more, my Hispanic heritage made me feel ashamed I’d never bothered to learn anything more than “white people” Spanish.

Jose then turned back to me. “These men will take you back to the parking deck. I don’t want you near my family.”

“Why?” I asked. “That’s not fair! Zeus and I are dating.”

Jose scowled at me. “What does a pretty girl like you want to do with my son? There’s only one reason that you would date him, and it’s not a good one. He must have told you about our family.”

“Well, I know about his mom, obviously,” I snapped. I felt more than upset.

Jose dismissively shook his head. “You’re a very good actress—fitting for you, since Zeus mentioned you were trying to be a model. But now it’s time for you to leave, so I can spend my wife’s last moments in peace.”

The two bodyguards came up behind me, and I felt more frightened than I wanted to.

Still, I tried my best to appear unaffected. I crossed my arms over my chest and stomped down the hall, keeping at least five steps in front of Jose’s thugs.

They kept following me, and I soon broke into a run—from their leering smiles, I was worried that they would hurt me, and I didn’t see any other alternative just then.

Instead, I ran back to the parking deck and sat down in Zeus’ car.

I sat down and cried, feeling angry and sad and awful.

I didn't know what else to do. All I could do was just stay there—stay there and pray, I supposed.

But as soon as I blubbered out the words, “Oh, God,” I just started crying harder.

Tears ran down my cheeks; I didn’t know what to do.

There was nothing I could do.

For a long time, I sat there and cried.

I only stopped when I realized how cold it was, sitting in that car. Everything was just so cold and dark, and I felt more alone than ever. Maybe I was shocked enough to stop crying, or maybe I was just out of tears.

I had cried a lot in the last several hours, and not even the fake kind that got me attention.

I shivered, hugging my loose, baggy clothes to me even more tightly. I didn't know what time it was; just that it was very late, likely close to dawn, and I didn't even have my phone on me to help pass the time in a distracted way.

"What a strange time to miss being Fatgirl," I murmured.

My voice felt hollow against the silence around me.

But it was then that a new idea struck me.

Jose said I couldn't be with them since I wasn't family, and since I wasn't paying the bills.

And that was true for me, Kallie Grande-White.

But *Fatgirl* had helped with his finances.

Thanks to those rotten politicians, I'd gotten a bunch of people to raise money for Zeus' family and his mom.

Surely that had to count for something.

"And," I said with a small amount of amusement, "Fatgirl wouldn't be afraid of those bodyguards, either. She'd just sit on them."

I looked over to the passenger side of the car, where AB's bag was sitting there.

I lunged at it.

AB had told me before there was one last doughnut inside, and she'd frozen it before, so it was probably ready …

I grabbed ahold of it, and I pulled it out.

It was just like a Darla Donut; it was soft and innocent looking; no one would be able to tell how radioactive it was just from glancing at it. I wondered at it for a moment, that so much of my life had been tied to such a small, stupid, irritating thing.

And yet, here I was again, holding it, ready to put aside my pride and dignity.

All so I could be there for Zeus.

I looked down at myself and sighed. "Well, here we go. One last time. For Zeus."

I stuffed the doughnut into my mouth.

The powder was as sweet as ever, and at the first bite, I remembered AB wasn't around to give me any serum.

Decidedly, I pushed that thought aside as I chewed; I'd worry about it after Zeus' mom … well, after everything was over.

I took another bite, remembering how I'd felt earlier, seeing my dad held hostage and wondering if I was going to lose both my parents after all. My mom wasn't technically dead, but my dad had been half-dead without her here. He'd been lost as soon as she'd left, and I'd lost a good chunk of him as well as her.

I thought about Jose's brusqueness and wondered if Zeus hadn't already lost something of his dad. It certainly seemed plausible to me.

I took another bite of the doughnut and sighed. I didn't know what to expect, but I'd do anything for Zeus.

Hadn't I just proved that? I smiled down at my hands, waiting for my Fatgirl transformation to take place.

But as the seconds passed, I frowned.

What's going on?

My fingers were still in their small, elegantly featured form. My belly wasn't swollen up like an infected hangnail full of puss, and my suit still hung on me like sweatpants twenty sizes too large.

It's not working.

"Nothing's happening." I glanced down at AB's bag, riffling through it. Was it possible she'd had a *regular* Darla Donut in there?

I dumped the bag over, with no real answers. But I doubted it; AB had told me herself she'd grabbed a few from her freezer, and the inside of the bag was still moist …

"What did she do?" I yelled, angry and bitter this time.

My mind raced, thinking over her last injection of anti-F serum. Was it possible she'd given me the wrong dose?

No … that doesn't make sense, either.

I'd deflated like I normally did. Frantically, I ripped open her bag again, searching for another doughnut.

But there were none left.

None.

"Why?" I screamed, flinging the bag away. "What is wrong? Did AB mess up on the recipe?"

I put my head in my hands again, my head aching from all my crying and emotional stress, and I realized that I wasn't even worried about how splotchy my eyes were or how frazzled my hair was.

"Oh, my God." I glanced at myself in the window's reflection, and I realized what was wrong.

I'd ballooned up into Fatgirl's form at the Model Middle America audition because I'd been super scared of about being super fat.

After eating AB's doughnuts, I'd turned into my worst fear—a fat girl—and accidentally became a national laughingstock of a somewhat superhero.

But now, I was no longer afraid of being fat.

"So … the doughnuts don't work anymore," I reasoned. "They won't make me fat anymore."

I clenched my fists, before pounding them on the dashboard while I screamed again.

All I'd had to do throughout the course of AB's mission was *not be afraid of being super fat*, and I would've been able to get out of helping her.

I almost laughed at the absurdity of it all.

But I began to cry instead.

"And now," I cried, "the one time I want to be fat, I can't be!"

I fell forward, crying again, my whole body heaving with sadness.

I didn't even notice when I fell into a troubled, exhausted sleep.

Tap-tap-tap-tap.

I flinched, and the movement was small enough to hit my forehead against the window.

"Ouch," I muttered, before I realized I was asleep, with my face pushed up against the window in Zeus' car.

Tap-tap-tap-tap.

I blinked my eyes open, only to see AB on the other side of the window.

At once, I was disappointed; I'd wanted to see Zeus.

"Kallie," AB said. "Open up. I'm going to take you home."

Groggily, I yawned as she opened the door and sat down in the driver's seat. There was a small beam of light coming through the parking deck, and I wondered how long I'd been there.

But I forgot about all that, and everything else, as I saw AB's face.

Her eyes were unusually sympathetic.

Honestly, it was the worst look I'd ever seen on her face, and I had to remind myself she wasn't the real enemy.

I was the pathetic, stupid slobbering moron who'd fallen asleep in the car.

"What happened?" I asked the question, but I already knew the answer. "Is Zeus … is he okay?"

AB sighed. "He'll be okay. Eventually."

I bit my lip. "Did … ?"

"Yes." AB nodded. "During the night. Shortly after two."

I was surprised when I didn't cry. I just felt extraordinarily numb.

"He and his dad are still taking care of things with the doctors," AB continued, much too gently. "I said I would take you home."

"You spoke to him?" I asked, suddenly angry. "Why didn't he call me?"

"You don't have your phone," AB reminded me gently. "And I saw him only for a few moments. His dad has been expecting this, and he doesn't want to deal with anyone bothering them right now. Zeus only managed to sneak away for a moment when he saw me."

"I'm still out here," I said, rubbing my face. "I've been here all night."

"I know." AB gave me another sympathetic look. "He said to let you know he'll try to call when he's free."

"Is there anything we can do?" I asked. "Anything at all?"

AB sighed. "There's not really a whole lot we can do in situations like these, Kallie. Losing those you love is … beyond unbelievably unbearable."

It was then I noticed for the first time that she had tears in her eyes too.

I don't know why, but the sight of them made me weak. I reached over and hugged her.

AB seemed a little surprised, but she gripped me back. I was tempted to cry more, but no more tears came out.

I felt like a little girl as she held me, and I could feel her weeping, too.

At that moment, I honestly never understood how I could have ever hated my grandmother.

Yeah, it was true that she was white and somewhat disapproving of my mother, and maybe I didn't know her very well, and she was workaholic and obviously she was dealing with stuff that was just way above my paygrade with all her "classified status" stuff from her government work.

But she taught me so many things about myself and about the world, and even if we still disagreed about some stuff, I knew she loved me.

Just like Zeus loved me.

And I couldn't—wouldn't—ignore that lightly.

For a long time again, we held onto each other.

And then AB patted down my hair. "All right, darling. Let's go home."

"What about Zeus?"

"The good Lord will have to take care of him now," AB whispered. "There are some paths we each must walk alone. As much as it pains you, this is one of those times for him, Kallie."

"I promised his mom I would be there for him," I objected.

"And you will be. But later," AB said. "Right now you have to take care of yourself, too. You need to rest after all your ordeals."

Another surge of disappointment suddenly washed through me. I wouldn't get to tell Zeus I loved him.

On the bright side, I can plan it better, and I can look my best.

Maybe that would cheer him up, I thought. Miraculously, a small smile formed on my lips at that realization.

I can make him happy, I thought. And that was something for me to feel hopeful about.

"Okay, AB," I said. "You're right. Let's go home."

"Of course I'm right," AB said lightly, and I appreciated her attempt at levity.

"Tell me what happened after I left you guys with KP," I said, sniffing loudly and wiping my boogers off on my sleeve.

AB gave me a considerable look, and then shrugged. "Alright. You seem like you're able to listen, and this might be good for you."

"I just feel better that you're driving in Zeus' car," I said. "You might feel like driving responsibly. That was the only thing that stopped me from throwing a full-on tantrum earlier."

AB gave me a smile. "I told you Zeus was good for you. He's still making us into better people."

I laughed a little at that.

And I felt a bit better, before I felt worse.

It felt wrong to laugh when so much sadness was in the world.

Almost as if she'd read my thoughts AB shook her head.

"No, Kallie," she said. "Zeus' mother was a very lovely lady, and the world will feel her loss. But one way we can combat sadness in this world is with joy. It's our duty and our privilege to be able to do so—especially together."

"Thank you." I gripped my hands in my lap, lacing my fingers together. I felt like I was trying to keep all the sadness in the world inside my fists, but it kept fighting me, and I would fail at some point.

But at AB's kindness, I relaxed.

AB started the engine, and more responsibly than usual, she sped off.

The trip home was largely uneventful. AB described what happened after I left.

KP was arrested. Max helped AB get ahold of the evidence that incriminated me and her, for which I was extremely grateful. He'd even put out some rumors that Fatgirl was dead from the tragic events at the doughnut factory, and AB mentioned that the new mayor lady might erect a statue in my honor.

I groaned at that thought, but I couldn't really care too much.

AB was expecting a call from her former boss any moment, exonerating her from the recipe's theft, and it struck me that she might get her job back.

That she might leave me.

"Will you get your job back?" I asked, surprised I'd asked the question at all.

"I don't know," AB admitted. "We'll just have to wait and see."

"I hate waiting," I said.

"Some things are worth waiting for. Just like some things are worth working for."

I glanced up to see AB had pulled into my house's driveway.

"Aren't you going to return Zeus' car to his house?" I asked.

"I'm dropping you off first," AB said. "You need to rest. I can tell."

I didn't argue with her. My night in the car had been uncomfortable at best, and at her words, my body ached, screaming for me to go in and sleep.

I decided to listen.

AB let me out, and as she headed off to Zeus' house, I went my room.

Falling on the bed was no leap of faith—it was an act of desperate, undeniable need.

But before I closed my eyes, I pulled out the knife my mother had used to stab me back in Fort Lauderdale.

AB wasn't the only one I would be waiting on, I realized.

But I could wait to hear about what my mom's decisions would be.

I tucked the violet-colored blade under my pillow. Then I closed my eyes and fell into a deep, deep, deep sleep.

He said he would call.

That's all I could think of over the following days.

I waited and waited and waited for Zeus to call me.

But he didn't.

AB didn't want me go and bother him.

"He's grieving, too, Kallie. It would be best for you to give him, and others, some room to process everything," she told me, and I about snapped at her for interfering.

But she had a point about me leaving others alone.

When it was time to go back to school, I quickly realized that I didn't want to deal with other people, either.

I was almost out the door when I suddenly begged AB to give me a few days off to recover more. She seemed to sympathize with me, but despite my pleading and pleading and pleading, she sent me onward.

"Don't be mad at me," she added on my way out, as if I wasn't already hating her for how awful she was making me feel. "You will do better with a distraction."

I didn't want to be distracted, though, and I made sure she knew that in no uncertain terms.

"You're not the only one who's waiting, Kallie," AB said. "Your mom's waiting to hear back from your dad about what they're going to do. I'm waiting to hear from my former boss. KP's thankfully waiting to hear his rights. Max is waiting to hear about his suspension. Please try to go on with your life."

From her tone, I felt like she was suddenly taking things personally.

"Okay, there are lots of things that other people are waiting for," I said. "But really, don't I deserve some special treatment? I was Fatgirl for the last several months, remember?"

"We all suffer, Kallie," AB retorted. "Pain is universal."

"Come on, AB."

"Come on, Kallie." She mimicked my tone. "You ought to go to school and keep your grades up. Or I really will homeschool you next year, and you will *not* like what's on the curriculum."

Reluctantly, I smiled. "I guess you really don't know anything about public school."

She arched her brow at me. "Don't I?"

"Do you?"

When she said nothing, I gave up. I was upset and I was stir-crazy and I couldn't do much anyway. Going to school wasn't going to change that.

But AB was right; I was pretty distracted when I got there.

Blake Turner was there, and I no longer thought he was some kind of perfect specimen of perfection that I was owed, like he was meant for me, and I was gracefully awarded on this mortal plain.

Actually, I found Blake quite irritating. His eyes seemed suddenly too close together, and his hair looked too bleached. I also noticed that he never seemed as smart or as strong or as fast as I thought he had been before.

That was okay, though. I'd let a lot of my delusions about Blake go, and the last of them were eager to go, too.

I did notice that he seemed genuinely happy. I guess he and Amory had come to terms with each other, and she had at least agreed to a date.

And that was nice. Especially for her.

I had a feeling that Amory was more worried about him blackmailing her because of the whole donut incident; I honestly couldn't say if she was more upset about eating a doughnut in the first place, or if it was because she turned white because of it, but she did not mention it.

That was my back-up amusement if I needed it.

It was especially kind of funny because my other friends didn't understand the sudden change in our affections. It was strange to see Amory giving Blake more of a chance, and then there I was, just looking sad.

I wasn't eating, but more because I was sad this time, and not because I was on a diet.

I had to give Lizzie credit where credit was due for that.

"Are you okay, Kallie?" Lizzy asked. She adjusted her glasses frames in a flamboyant manner as she examined me.

"I'm okay," I lied. "Just didn't want to come to school today."

That last part wasn't a lie.

Lizzy gave me a sympathetic look. "I'll hate Amory for dating Blake if you want," she offered.

"No, don't worry about it," I said. "I'm not mad about that. Actually, I'm happy for them."

"You are?" June came up next to us. "Really?"

"Yeah." I put on my best smile for them. "I have someone else I like."

"Oh, yeah?" Uli came up to us now. "Who is it? Is it a secret?"

"Um … "

I looked at all of them, and I didn't care just then.

"No. It's Zeus."

"Oh, you're still hung up on your Florida Man?"

"No, not that one, exactly," I said, grimacing as I thought of Zeus' transformed self. "I'm talking about Zeus Evans."

"Zeus Evans?" Lizzy frowned, while June and Uli exchanged a glance and started laughing.

"What?" I asked. "What's wrong with him?"

June giggled. "Well, you're joking, right?"

"No."

June and Uli laughed harder, and then Lizzy snapped her fingers.

"Oh, you mean that large, sweaty fat kid?" she asked. "Oh, that's hilarious, Kallie!"

"I'm not joking," I insisted, and the three of them went dead silent.

"Why?" June finally asked. "He's not popular. And he's not handsome by any close meaning of the word."

"He's kind of a nerd, too," Lizzy said.

"So?" I looked at all of them, angry now. "He's very nice. And he is smart. He's got a lot of talent. And he likes me, too."

"Oh, Kallie, that's so … sad and hilarious at the same time," Uli said. "He's just so gross, really. Remember that time he farted super loudly in Mr. Embers' class? It was awful!"

"You know what?" I gave up. "*I* was the one who farted that day. He covered for me. So—"

"So you owe him?" June looked concerned. "He's blackmailing you?"

"Don't use the term 'blackmail,' June" Lizzy said in hushed tones. "That's racist."

"He's not blackmailing me," I said. "He's really nice. And his mom just died, so you're laughing at a kid who's basically an orphan now. I know how it feels to lose a parent, remember?"

I didn't mention that my mom was back—I mean, she sort of was—but I kept staring at them.

They were all shocked and silent, and I didn't even care. They routinely insisted they were better than everyone else, and yet here they were, just … just being thoughtless jerks.

"Hey, Kallie." Gloria Stills came up beside me. "I think it's time for class."

"Good." I glared at my circle of fake friends. "I'll see you later. Bye."

I could hear Lizzy whispering, "Do you think she's sorry enough for him that she'd date him?"

I groaned, but Gloria put her hand on my shoulder companionably.

"Don't worry about them," she said. "That was really brave of you."

"Well, I guess so," I said glumly. "That's why I feel miserable now, isn't it?"

"No." Gloria shook her head. "No, you feel miserable because Zeus must be feeling miserable, too."

"He was supposed to call me." I thought about my phone, which I'd tucked into my purse. "If he doesn't call me soon, he's going to be even more miserable."

"He and his dad are working on funeral arrangements," Gloria told me. "It'll be this Saturday at noon."

"What?" I glared at her. "How do you know?"

Gloria gave me a bitter smile. "Aunt Gynnifer wanted to do a follow-up story since Fatgirl raised all those funds for her and now she's … well, gone."

"Oh."

I knew from our past interactions that Gloria's aunt was a piece of work, and I had to admit, it was convenient at times that she worked in journalism.

As we walked to class, I felt bad for Gloria having to deal with someone so selfish and self-absorbed.

That's probably the reason she's good at dealing with me.

The thought wasn't happy, and I vowed I would invite her out for a girl's night or something, maybe.

"Don't worry. Zeus does really love you," Gloria said as we entered into our next class. "I'm sure you'll hear from him soon."

But I didn't.

I didn't hear from him at all.

I tried to call him, and his number was disconnected. I went to his house—walking all the way, so I was truly dedicated—and no one was there.

I started to have a panic attack as I realized I couldn't find him.

"Why do people I love always leave me?" I whimpered as I walked into the house.

As if God wanted me to have an answer, my mom was waiting for me in my room.

"Oh, no," I said when I saw her sitting on my bed. "Get out of here."

"Come on, Kallie. Don't be mean." Mom sighed as she crossed her arms.

It was a surreal sort of experience; I had always looked at my mother and saw her beauty. But just then, I only saw the ugliness in her.

The once flawless nature of her skin was full of small little creases, mostly around her lips and eyes, and there were two small lines by her brows—which were otherwise perfectly plucked and waxed, and even lined with some pencil work. Her eyes, the same shade as my own golden amber, were once full of sparkles, but now their shine was dim and gloomy. Her ebony hair was seamless night, and her nose seemed as straight and small as ever.

Almost too straight and small.

"Did you get work done while you were with ZZ?" I asked.

Mom winced. "A little. ZZ wanted a girl's day after I convinced her to let me back into her newest operation. I was hoping your father wouldn't notice, but I had a feeling you would."

I said nothing about that, since it was then that I noticed Mom was holding the dagger I'd gotten that night we'd fought in Florida.

"This is a very rare, ancient item, you know," she told me. "It's from a secret society of spies. ZZ was wondering where it'd gone after the attack."

"I don't want to talk about that with you," I said, snatching the dagger from her. "And as far as I'm concerned, this is mine, not yours. So leave it alone. And leave me alone, too."

"All right." Mom shrugged. "I came to apologize to you."

"There's no need," I said. "Go away now."

"Kallie, you don't know the pressure I was under," Mom continued.

"Well, you don't know how sad Dad was, or how I felt," I retorted. "So let's call it even and go our separate ways."

"I won't be going," Mom said. "Your father and I have agreed to patch things up."

"Oh, patch things up?" I snarled. "Just like the Titanic, huh? Simple as that."

"I know it's hard to imagine, but I'm really actually surprised myself," Mom admitted. "I haven't been very truthful to John, and I haven't been very nice to you or him lately."

"Gee, I don't know. You've only been gone almost a full year, so you and Interpol could find out that ZZ's got papers on everybody from here to Moscow."

"Kallie." Mom sighed. "I'm not perfect. Margaret can tell you I have a checkered past."

"You liked this adventure," I accused. "I saw you with ZZ in Florida. You didn't mind playing the model and spy at all."

"Oh, of course, I enjoyed myself." Mom surprised me by admitting it. "I had a very exciting life before I stopped modeling. I don't regret getting married or being your mother; but yes, I do miss it at times, too. Missing something isn't the same thing as regretting it."

I wanted to vomit.

"So you threw away the life that you don't regret for the life that you missed," I said.

"I wanted to protect you," Mom corrected.

"'Victory is reserved for those who are willing to pay the price.'"

Immediately, I turned to the book on my nightstand. Glaring back at me was *The Art of War*, almost like it knew I was not the prize Mom wanted, but the price she was willing to pay for her adventure.

"Glad to know my worth," I muttered.

"I didn't mean it like that. I had to leave you to protect you, Kallie." She sighed again. "I just don't know what to say to you sometimes. Let's not pretend that this is easy, please."

"Just tell me when you're moving in," I said. "So I can tell you when I'm moving out.

I expected her to deny me, but she just arched her perfectly shaped brow. "Where would you go?"

"I'll go with AB," I said immediately, knowing I would likely regret it. "She's offered to homeschool me next year."

"What about prom?" Mom asked.

"I don't care anymore."

Mom sized me up, looking for the lie; but I knew she wouldn't find it.

"Fine," Mom said. "Dad and I will talk about it."

I paused. "Really?"

She nodded. "You're almost eighteen, my goodness. Maybe it's about time that you had some real-life experience."

"Really?" I was too shocked to say anything else.

"When I was your age, I was already modeling full time and yeah, maybe it wasn't the best choice, but I hoped by retiring from it, I would be able to give you stability and love and find joy in your journey and giving you something that I could never have."

"And you wanted to stay out of jail," I added.

Mom glared at me. "I hope you realize how lucky you are, even if I'm not the mother that you wanted or the mother that you deserved."

"I don't know if I deserve you or not," I admitted, thinking about how terrible I was at times. "But you're my mother—whether we like it or not, whether you like it or not. You're a spy and working with international criminals … there's no class or TV show script for me to follow on this."

Mom smiled. "I'm sure there is, Kallie. You just haven't found it yet."

She walked toward my door and paused, pulling it back to show me there was a dress hanging up. "I ordered you a new dress and shoes," she said. "Margaret told me that there's a funeral coming up this weekend, and you need to look really nice."

She was right about that.

And for the moment, I felt happy again.

I really did like getting new clothes and new shoes.

Mom saw my smile, and I hated her for that. "I figured it was the least I could do," she said. "I know you'll want to look pretty when you show up for that special boy of yours."

She looked like she wanted to say more, but she bit her lip, and didn't say it.

I could almost hear her thinking it anyway—it was too similar to what my so-called "friends" had said about Zeus earlier.

She was probably thinking, 'Oh, what a shame that he's too fat and too ugly for you.'

But she couldn't say that anymore.

She was my mother, but that didn't mean that I was going to go to her for advice after all of this.

"If you want, I'll drive you," she finally said. "I need to thank him myself, for helping your grandmother. My part of the case with Interpol is finished now, thanks to him."

I swallowed hard and blushed. "No," I said. "Dad's going to drive me. He's not working anymore so he can take me."

After the Model Middle America mess, he owed me, and he was willing to make good on it.

Mom nodded. "All right then. Have a good time."

And then she left, and I breathed out a long sigh of relief.

And *then* I oohed and awed over my new dress, already rehearsing what I would say to Zeus when I saw him.

○ ○ ○ ○

I didn't know if it was because my dad was a man or because my dad was used to dealing with difficult women, but he actually agreed with me when we got to the funeral home and I told him to stay inside the car.

"I can escort you inside," he offered, but I shook my head.

"No, it's fine, Dad," I said.

"You aren't mad at me, too, are you?" he asked. "Because of Kate?"

"What?" I blinked at him, realizing he was worried I was upset at him for taking Mom back. I shook my head. "No, I'm not upset at you."

Frankly, I was still upset at Mom.

"Good," he said. "I love you, Kallie. And I do want you to be happy."

"I love you, too." I looked at the sun shining down on the funeral home—Shady Meadows Funeral Home was just outside the city, and it was full of flowers just peeking out from their blooms in the Southern springtime. "Why don't you go home? I'll get a ride from Zeus. We'll be here for a while anyway."

"Are you sure?" Dad asked.

I nodded.

"Okay. Love you." He waved as he pulled out of the parking lot, and I was actually happy I was here on my own.

I'd been able to do plenty of things on my own, but this was something that really made me feel like a true adult.

Once he left, I walked into the funeral home. The place was packed, and there were lots of Spanish speaking women and men and even some children.

I felt very small and intimidated as I looked around, but I actually felt better as I walked up to the casket.

There were beautiful pictures of Mrs. Evans everywhere, and even with her emaciated form sleeping away for all eternity, I felt like I knew her as a friend. While she'd suffered, I could see the joy on her face.

I looked over at the pictures; she clearly loved her son. There were several photos with Zeus next to her, and it pained me to realize how much of a cutie pie he'd been as a young kid.

His curly hair was more noticeable and charming and looked much better—much, much better, as if he'd been able to be cared for properly. The pimples weren't there; instead, I saw he had freckles, and his eyes were very, very blue without his glasses hiding them.

That must have been from her, I thought, looking at the pictures. His mom was just so bright and cheerful and colorful. She'd had such pretty, curly blondish hair.

I felt sad that I'd never seen her with hair.

From the pictures, I could tell when her diagnosis started; Zeus started to look a little bit more plump as his mom shrank in size, and the pimples started to get worse.

He must've been just as stressed as she was.

In almost all the pictures, he looked at her as if she'd been his best friend all his life. And I realized just then how many pictures were just of Zeus and his mom; he didn't seem to have much time for his dad.

Or maybe his dad just didn't have much time for him.

I knew how that felt.

As if he'd known I was thinking of him, Jose stepped up next to me. "You should leave," he said.

"I'm here for Mrs. Evans," I said, suddenly realizing I'd forgotten her real name.

"I told you in the hospital not to show yourself and I mean this now: If you truly have any real affection for my son, you will stay away from my family," Jose said.

I glanced around at his family, and I suddenly felt their strange looks. I didn't want to feel like an outcast—or a target—but I couldn't stop myself from feeling afraid.

"Leave, now," Jose demanded.

"But I love Zeus," I argued. "He's one of my only real friends. And I promised his mom I'd be here for him."

"Well, you won't be," Jose said. "We're moving back to Mexico now that my wife is dead."

"What?" Once more, the world was torn out from underneath me.

Jose ignored my question. "So you see, you ought to leave—before you break his heart even more."

For the first time in days, tears stung my eyes. "You're lying," I accused, but I remembered how Zeus' phone number had been disconnected, and how his house had been abandoned. The Fatgirl website was down, Zeus hadn't come to see me, he hadn't called …

I closed my eyes, impossibly full of pain.

It can't be possible …

"We're leaving right after the funeral," Jose told me. "Everything's been taken care of."

"I still want to say goodbye," I insisted, feeling myself say the words more than anything.

He has to be lying.

"Go and say your goodbyes then." Jose nodded toward another room, and that was when I knew Zeus was there, waiting for me. "But don't be selfish and cause my son anymore pain. He's been through enough."

I looked at Jose. "You're a terrible father."

Jose surprised me by smiling. "I will not miss you, or your nosy grandmother," he said. "*Adiós, señorita.*"

He nodded his final goodbye to me, and I almost wished I could slap him and feel good about it. But I knew I had to get to Zeus.

If Jose wasn't lying, I only had a little time left with him.

Please, God, let him be lying.

But as soon as I saw Zeus there, sitting down on one of the funeral home's smelly couches, I knew Jose had been telling me the truth.

Which was a real shame.

Zeus had already lost some weight, and his pimples had cleared up with grief. He'd washed his hair and had it styled—perhaps one of his aunts or someone else had taken charge of him—and with his suit and nicely knotted tie, he suddenly made me think of a pudgy prom king.

He looked over at me and stood up, surprised. "Kallie. What are you doing here?"

I was already running up to him. Even in my heels, I happily bore any pain to be there for him, knowing it would be worth it.

"Zeus, you idiot. What do you think I'm doing here?" I wrapped my arms around him, and he embraced me back. I leaned my head onto his shoulder and held him close, and then I pulled back enough to shake him. "I can't believe that you've ignored me all week."

"I can't believe anyone would survive ignoring you for a week." He gave me a small smile before his eyes turned somber. "My dad won't let me call you."

"He doesn't seem to like me very much." I hugged him again, burying my face in his chest. "I'm not the nicest person I know, and I'm not the best at being your friend, either. But I don't know why he doesn't like me."

"Don't talk down to yourself, Kallie. You're my best friend," Zeus said, making me want to cry again. "My dad's probably trying to protect me. And maybe you, too."

"What do you mean by that?" I said, suddenly angry and suspicious, even though I had no real reason to be.

Zeus shrugged. "My dad's not technically an American citizen. My mom was, and I am, but he has to leave now and I have to go with him."

Crushing, debilitating depression fell on me.

Jose hadn't been lying.

"The only reason that we were here in the States was for my mom's care," Zeus admitted. "Now that she's … well, my dad said it's time for me and him to go back home to his family."

"What about his work?" I grasped for any shred of hope I could get. "His security business is here."

"My uncle runs another business down there. My dad will work with him."

Zeus fell silent after that, and it vaguely made me wonder what kind of work his uncle did. But I didn't care about that too much, because it finally, finally hit me—and it hit me hard, like the force of ten thousand bricks falling from the sky.

Zeus was actually leaving.

I fallen in love with him, and now he was leaving.

Stop being so selfish.

He lost his mom and now he would lose me, too.

"So … you're really leaving?"

"Yes." Zeus hugged me close again, letting his hands thread through my hair. "I have to leave, and so … I just wanted you to know how grateful I am for you, and … how we should try to keep this light and not say anything that would make it harder, okay?"

"What?" I pushed back at him; this time, I wanted to yell at him.

"Tell me about school," he said, attempting to lead me down the intoxicating, familiar streets of our usual conversations. "Tell me if Amory has broken it off with Blake yet, or if you saw the scandal Gynnifer Stills legitimately uncovered in the mayor's office, or if Dr. White has a new recipe that needs—"

"Shut up," I interrupted. "Don't you know me at all? If I want to make my life harder, and all the lives around me harder, I will do it. Because I'm Kallie Grande-White, for God's sake. If I want to stand here and tell you that I—"

"Don't say it," Zeus snapped. "Don't—"

"Stop interrupting me when I'm trying to tell you I love you. I'm allowed to say it, and I don't care if it hurts!"

Now, he tried to pull away from me, but I didn't let him.

"Kallie—"

"Stop." I glared at him, and he actually stopped moving, almost like he was too shocked to do anything but stand there.

"You're the best friend and partner in superhero crime that I could've ever wished for. I don't care if you're Sweaty Fat Kid. I love you," I repeated, suddenly feeling like a clingy moron. My cheeks were burning red now, and I was pretty sure my heart was pounding hard enough to set off an earthquake. "I don't know how much time we have left together, but I'm going to spend it with you. And there's nothing you or your father can say that will make me change my mind."

"Kallie—"

I put my hands on his cheeks. "Do you hear me?

As he nodded slowly, I could see that there were tears in his eyes.

All I wanted to do was just comfort him and love him, and before I knew it, I was leaning up on my tiptoes and pressing my lips to his.

Under any other circumstances, I might have enjoyed feeling the jolt of shock that went through him, or I might've realized he didn't know what to do when being kissed.

But just then, I was too happy to do anything but lean into him.

Our kiss was both sweet and salty, and when I pulled away, I saw the sparks of joy and wonder in his eyes.

"You didn't have to do that," he whispered.

"Of course I had to." I smiled at him, even if I was trying not to cry.

"It'll make leaving you harder."

"Leaving me was going to be hard no matter what," I insisted, already feeling guilty that he was right. "But at least you know I love you. And I'm not even lying, if you're worried about that."

"I was just a little worried about that," he admitted sheepishly.

"Jesus, you're a piece of work, aren't you?" I laughed.

I really did love him, and I really did want him in my life, and I knew I would never forget him.

"It's 'hey, Zeus,'" he whispered, before I let him lean down and kiss me again.

It was too short of a time later that Mrs. Evans was laid to rest in her cold, deep, lonely grave. I held on to Zeus' hand as we watched her disappear into the ground. Her coffin was followed by dirt and then new grass patches, and then some flowers.

I didn't think his dad appreciated me being there, but Zeus managed to fend him off and I was allowed to stay. It was likely the last time Zeus and I would see each other anyway.

At that thought, a lump formed in my throat as I stood next to him.

People came up and said their prayers, offered their condolences, and promised to be in touch if Zeus needed anything. Eventually the long line of people dwindled down, and only Zeus and I remained at his mother's grave.

I was glad I'd sent Dad home. I didn't know how long it'd been, but I'd cried at least six rivers worth of tears, and I didn't want him to see me like this.

Jose appeared to the side of us. Behind him was a new car, one I didn't recognize. He motioned to Zeus. "Zeus. *Vamos.*"

Zeus and I glanced at each other.

Impossibly, I felt even sadder.

"Don't go," I begged, feeling stupid for saying anything as I hugged him. I would have closed my eyes, if I wasn't forcing myself to remember every detail I could—how he smelled, how warm I felt, how safe I felt; how tall he was, how cold it was, how hopelessly awful everything was …

"I can't stay." His voice nearly broke.

"You could stay with me and AB," I said, brightening up. "She's going to homeschool me next year."

Zeus let out a soft chuckle. "I'd love to see that," he said.

"You can," I insisted.

But he shook his head. "I wish I could. But I can't."

I hugged him harder as I nodded. Tears slipped down my cheeks again.

"I'll miss you," I whispered.

"I'll miss you, too," Zeus promised, holding me tight against him; his grip on me was almost painful, but I reveled in it.

How could I not? I felt the same way. Any pain was durable, so long as we were together.

When he finally let me go, I felt my heart shatter again.

But I let him go, too.

"I don't want this to be the end," I said.

"It won't be," Zeus said. "You still owe me a date, remember?"

"You're right." I brightened as I looked around. "This certainly doesn't count. No offense to your mom."

"She would be the first one to agree with you." Zeus smiled. He was trying to make me feel better, and I appreciated it.

God knew I needed it.

Rather than cry again, I sniffed back my tears and snot, and merely nodded. "Okay. That'll work. And it'll give us some time to plan it out. So that'll be nice."

Together, hand in hand, we walked to the car, where his dad, as terrible as he was, was at least decent enough to get in the car and give us one last moment of privacy.

Zeus cheered. "That reminds me. I have a gift for you."

"If it's donuts, I'm going to kill you," I warned.

"No, it's not," he said, giving me a heart-wrenching chuckle. He reached into the car and pulled out a package.

It wasn't that big; it wasn't likely a piece of jewelry, but it was definitely not a box of doughnuts, either.

Maybe it was a book? Maybe it was something from his mom, I thought. Possibly a photo book?

"Here," he said, handing it to me. "For you."

I frowned at the postage stamp.

"I was hoping you would be here today so I could give it to you, but I wasn't sure … "

I opened the wrapping. Inside, it was indeed a book. It was a little worn, and I knew at once it was Zeus' copy. The cover did look kind of familiar, but the title was in Spanish and I almost chucked it back at him.

"What is this?" I asked. "*El Senor De Los Anillos*?"

"It's *The Lord of the Rings*," Zeus said. "You told me that you kept your mom's *Art of War* book when she left. I thought this might be a little bit lighter reading for you."

"*Lighter* reading?" I arched my brow at him.

Zeus grinned. "You do need to work on your Spanish anyway, right? And what better way to do it than with this?"

He seemed so happy at my befuddlement.

"Okay. I'll read it while you're gone," I promised. "And I'll think of you when I chuck it across my room in frustration."

Zeus laughed, and then he leaned down and kissed my cheek. "Thank you again. For everything."

Carefully, keeping his gift in my hand, I hugged him again, and then I kissed him one last time.

My heart reeled in despair as he opened the door to his dad's car.

"I love you," I said.

"I won't ever forget you … Fatgirl," he whispered back.

I laughed and cried as his dad drove off.

I watching the window where Zeus was sitting. He gazed back at me, and our eyes never left each other's until the car finally turned away at the entrance to the cemetery, and then drove off out of sight.

And then, that was it.

I was alone.

After a while, I sat down on the sidewalk curve, holding onto Zeus' gift.

I knew he was gone, but I didn't want to believe I'd never see him again, just like I didn't want to believe I'd ever be happy again.

The sun was setting when a pure pristine white Imperial came up beside me and slowed to a stop.

The window rolled down, and AB called out to me from the driver's seat.

"Need a ride?"

Reluctantly, I stood up.

I didn't want to leave. I was still sulking. But considering AB's persistence in irritating me, I decided to play along for now.

"Nice car." I climbed into AB's new car, feeling like a robot. The last of my humanity had been squeezed out of me, and I was more than exhausted. "What happened to the one you ran into the doughnut factory?"

"Johnny's decided to take the Darla Donut company to court, but they've decided to mediate. After the president and his evil twin kidnapped him, everyone agreed it would be the better option—well, everyone except Gynnifer Stills," she said, her eyes gleaming with amusement. "This was part of his settlement."

"Cool." I sat down, and I had to admit, AB had done a good job getting Dad to negotiate well. It was almost the exact same as her previous one, except a lot cleaner.

"I thought it might be best if I picked you up today," AB said as we drove off. "Your mom admitted to me that you two weren't on the best of terms, and after talking to Johnny, I can attest that you're probably not going to like the news you're getting when you get home."

"Mom's already told me they're not getting divorced," I said.

"Yes, but that's only part of it," AB said. "Your dad's settlement with Darla Donut is enough that he's retiring early, and they're moving to Florida. Your mom wants to open up a modeling consultation business."

"Oh, no." I groaned. "Please tell me you're not serious."

"I'm sorry, darling," AB said. "But if I wasn't, don't you think I would've tried to make you laugh?"

I put Zeus' book on my lap, suddenly feeling bad I hadn't brought a gift for him.

"He'll be okay, you know."

I looked over at AB. "How do you know?"

"I'll keep an eye on him for you." She gave me a smirk. "Of course, I can. I've got contacts, remember?"

"Aren't you on some kind of government watch list yourself?"

"Sure I am," she agreed, easily enough to make me recoil. "But the people on the same watch list could be some of our potential allies. Some are even confirmed already."

"Already? What are you talking about?" I asked.

"Kate's doing a new business venture, and I thought it might be a good idea to do one, too," AB admitted.

"So, you didn't get your old job back with the NAH, then?" I asked.

"Not exactly," AB said. "My old boss did call and apologize to me, and I've even got it on tape. But I've decided not to go back to the NAH. If anything, this misadventure has taught me that there needs to be more oversight for these sorts of things. So I am going to start my own business."

"What kind of business? What you going to do?" I asked.

"Well, it's not a question of *me*, exactly." She gave me a smile as she whipped the car around another turn. "I was thinking about it, and I'd like to offer you a job, Kallie. I've decided to start my own private investigation firm. I'm going to tell the world what I find out, too—thank God for the first amendment protecting the press! So you'll be an investigative journalist and private eye."

"Me?"

"Yes," AB said. "I think it'll help you pay for your rent and schooling while you live with me."

"I'm going to live with you?"

"Of course. You're going to be homeschooling with me, remember? And we need to hold people in power accountable. I mean, really, Kallie, look what happens when you don't."

"Alterants and radioactive doughnuts everywhere," I murmured, making her laugh.

"Yes," she agreed cheerfully. "It'll be a lot of work trying to infiltrate different businesses and government locations without an accomplice. So, what do you think? We'll find a nice little office in Florida where we can make sure your mom isn't causing any real trouble. We ought to be on the lookout for ZZ, too, although Eugene says her mind isn't completely back to normal yet."

"Is Eugene one of your confirmed allies?" I asked.

"Hell, yes. He owes me big for not telling me about Kate working for him." AB grimaced, but then she gave me a wink. "I need to make sure he's suffering constantly or he really gets into trouble. On the upside, he'll be able to get some nice gadgets for us. Speaking of, here you go. You left these in the Darlington Donut Factory."

AB reached behind her and pulled out my twin pick Berettas and the holster, and I nearly jumped as she put them on my lap.

"Don't worry, both have their safety on," she assured me.

I carefully placed them on my lap, still careful to protect Zeus' book.

"What about prom?" I asked.

"Well, you might miss prom," she said. "But I think it could be an excellent opportunity for us. Lots of money, intrigue, and some fun tax-write offs."

I thought about it for several long moments. Living with Mom and Dad didn't seem like fun; I knew I'd probably get to the point where I could forgive Mom for leaving us, but I didn't want to rush it.

And moving away from Cuttingham City—and Fatgirl's legacy—did seem very attractive.

It's not like I have anyone left to really keep me here.

"What kind of job does your new firm have lined up in Florida?" I asked.

"Well, there's a couple of retirement homes that need a good going over. Some of them seem to be money laundering dumps," AB said.

"We're always going to have to deal with old people I guess," I reasoned. "So, it makes sense that it would be a good place to try to clean some bills."

"That's right." AB nodded appreciatively. "And I think with you by my side, we can convince them I need a lot of living assistance. What do you think, Spygirl?"

Hearing my new moniker, I felt a little better.

Clutching Zeus' gift and my twin Berettas to my chest, I smiled.

"Just promise me that I won't have to eat any doughnuts."

AB and I looked at each other and laughed, and then together, we drove off into the sunset.

Spygirl

DATE NIGHT

A BONUS EPISODE

○ ○ ○ ○

C. S. Johnson

Comedy time's over …

Spygirl is a serial, episodic work of fiction. It's part cozy mystery, sweet romance, family drama, a little satire here and there, and, of course, spy fiction. As spin-off to my *Fatgirl* series, which is set during Kallie's school years, which contains a blend of satire, superhero fiction, and contemporary genres, *Spygirl* picks up about 10 years later.

<u>SPYGIRL</u>
DATE NIGHT

○ ○ ○ ○ ○ ○

Ricardo was a nice guy.

I'd been working hard and I deserved a nice evening out.

It'd been a few months since my last somewhat-serious boyfriend and I broke things off, and a few good laughs would do me good.

AB and Eugene were having a night in while he's in town, and watching my grandmother and her husband make elderly googly eyes at each other was the very last thing I needed to see tonight.

And Ricardo was a *really* nice guy.

These are the things I tell myself as I turn my car into the Lauderdale Laugh Shack parking lot, but they might as well have been a list of excuses a serial killer keeps on hand when being asked about his alibi.

The Fort Lauderdale heat slams into me as I open the door. I've been living with AB in Florida long enough that I'm used to it, but I'm already looking for things to complain about, so the sudden, whiplash change in temperature doesn't help.

Neither does the look of the place.

I grew up in a small, Arkansas city, and the urbanized, rural, hick-happy aesthetic of the comedy club made me wish I'd worn overalls and cowboy boots instead of my designer dress and three-inch heels.

And I detested overalls.

"Ricky is a really, really nice guy," I reminded myself. I pulled out my lip gloss and applied another bright-red layer; my lips suddenly felt very dry, and it wasn't from the heat.

Just then, I heard someone from across the parking lot calling my name.

"Kallie! There you are."

I smiled brightly as Ricardo—Ricky—headed over my way.

He had recently turned thirty-three, placing him six years older than me, but his black hair had a few streaks of gray at the temples already. I knew that came from the stress of taking care of his parents; Ricky showed me their pictures on our first date, telling me how his mom bought him the dating app for Christmas since his fiancée left him at the altar a few years ago.

That led to more awkward, interesting conversations. I'd learned to embrace them, because it helped me refrain from dating anyone I didn't really like faster, and it also kept us from talking about me.

As the daughter of a former model, a protégé to a former government agent and the step-granddaughter to an international spy, I didn't like to talk about myself that much.

Ricky seemed to need me to listen anyway. Apparently, the ex-fiancée was a very pretty, very smart, very studious girl he'd met during graduate school. He'd showed me a picture of her that only reminded me of Gloria Stills, the most average of all average girls I'd gone to high school with, and that wasn't exactly a compliment. Ricky also assured me she was very nice.

Frankly, she didn't sound very nice to me, not when Ricky mentioned that she'd taken off on their honeymoon with her former boyfriend.

I didn't know if he was lying or not, but when I told Ricky my grandmother made me get the app because she didn't want me to end up basically alone if she got whacked by the KGB or the CIA, Ricky didn't run away screaming or tell me I needed therapy. Instead, he only nodded in understanding, and that was really, really nice in that moment.

Maybe his parents and AB would get along.

All things considered, it was nice to see someone on my latest dating subscription wasn't aiming to sleep with me or get a free meal out of me. And Ricky did seem to enjoy my company. He never pushed me to invite him inside when he dropped me off, he never touched me inappropriately, and he always offered to pay the bill.

He was a really, really nice guy.

I reminded myself of this once more as he came up to me and gave me a small side-hug. I enjoyed his teddy-bear hugs.

Ricky is much taller than me, and yes, he's a little overweight. But I've spent a good deal of my life learning that there are plenty of worse things to be than fat, and most of his weight issue I attributed to the idea that he just needed someone to take good care of him. His mother was struggling with dementia, and his father was on oxygen thanks to his stage three lung cancer.

At that, I let myself linger in his embrace a little longer.

Small, little wafts of his dad's cigars clung to his shirt. He was still in his work clothes, but I knew he'd just come from his parents' house.

I gave him a knowing look. "How are your parents today?"

"Good." He grinned back at me. "My dad's the one who suggested this place."

"Oh?" I looked back at the front of the building, analyzing it more critically, looking for an advertisement for a three o'clock early bird special. "Is he a fan?"

"No," Ricky said with a laugh. "He says you're too sophisticated for me. He wants to see if you can handle a setting that's a little more rustic."

"This is still in the city," I pointed out.

"You're talking about my father, a proud Cuban immigrant straight out of the Castro days," he reminded me. "He thinks if you can't handle getting stuck at sea for four days on a raft partially made out of milk cartons, you're too sophisticated."

"I suppose if I ever offer to cook for you, he'll only approve of me if it's over a firepit, then?"

"You can actually cook, you mean?" Ricky chuckled at my joke and took my hand. "You make me laugh, Kallie. Maybe they'll let you have a chance at the mic, huh?"

"I doubt they're that desperate."

I finally relaxed a little as we walked inside. The club had a stage and there was the small scattering of tables covered with red and white, picnic-style tablecloths. The seats looked comfortable enough from a distance, and the lights were dimmed.

Ricky pulled me along behind him, clearly excited. "Let's sit up front."

"If you want to," I said, secretly hoping he would change his mind.

I liked Ricky. He was a nice guy—a very, very nice guy. But I knew in my freshly pressed dress and pristine heels, paired with his worn-in work suit and his graying hair, he looked like my sugar-daddy.

And *that* would make us a prime target for any comedian able to see us from the stage.

I could only hope the guy we were there to see was an actual comedian, not someone who came just to lecture or insult the audience.

"Who are we here to see again?" I asked, looking at the framed portraits and playbills lining up along the wall. There were a couple of "definitely-douchey" faces up there. I had a sudden, sneaking suspicion that Ricky's dad thought I was a gold digger and this was his idea of a punishment.

At minimal, it's likely a warning …

"We're here to see Will Slater," Ricky said, pulling out a ticket brochure to show me. "He's apparently become very famous on the internet; one of those up-and-coming stand-up comedians."

"Oh, so he's better than me?" I fluttered my eyelashes teasingly.

Ricky blushed.

"What is it?" I asked.

"You're too beautiful to be a comedian," he said. "Any guy lucky enough to date you would either laugh at any joke you give him or he'd take you so seriously, he'd ruin your jokes."

"Case and point, I guess." I gave him a smile even though I was annoyed.

In high school, I was "too pretty" to have "real problems." Now, as an adult, no one seemed to be able to take me seriously or understand me because I was still "too pretty."

I knew I was more than the sum of my looks, but it was irritating to realize others completely dismissed that possibility.

A few moments passed as more people came into the Laugh Shack. Ricky and I looked over the menu.

I resolved just to get iced tea with lemon—my usual. Maybe that would convince Ricky's dad that I wasn't after Ricky's money. "What do you want to drink?"

"I'm hungry," Ricky said. "I'm buying, okay? Get whatever you want."

Ricky's a very, very nice guy.

Polite, thoughtful, sincere.

A very loyal, devoted son.

His parents were never super rich, but they were hard workers. They'd suffered in Cuba and risked their lives to come over to America. They'd made sure he had a good education and that he knew how to make money, and he went to Mass every weekend.

Ricky had a good sense of humor.

I remembered all of these things after we ordered drinks and a few appetizers, and then we sat there making more small talk.

Ricky told me about his day at work, how his father's best friend from Cuba had just married an immigration lawyer, how his mother was calling the dog by the wrong name …

I nodded along and asked the right follow-up questions. I knew he liked the attention. He was used to taking care of other people who relied on him; it made sense he would appreciate my concern, even if I didn't understand all of his references.

I was a little surprised when he asked about my day.

"How about you? Work go okay today for you?" he asked.

"Oh … it wasn't bad," I said, nicely skirting over the extreme lengths I'd gone to in order to serve papers to a serial gambling addict on the run from collections. It was a nice-sized bounty bonus, too, since he was wanted for several unauthorized, pharmacy-related dumpster dives. "Kind of a boring day, actually."

"Your grandmother is still keeping you on payroll, then?"

"Oh, of course," I said with a laugh. "Although you can't expect me to tell a CPA otherwise, right?"

He grinned again. "As long as it's not your taxes I'm working on."

We laughed as the waiter came with our appetizer plate came.

Ricky ordered a plate full of cheese sticks, some fried jalapeños, some chicken tender tacos, and other things. There was also a basket of chili cheese fries, and he eagerly dug into the plate.

I let him; I stuck to my iced tea. Over the years, I'd adopted more of AB's use of hot tea at home, so it was a nice treat to get it iced.

"Here, take some food," Ricky insisted, pushing his plate toward me.

"Oh, thanks." I mustered up a smile as I picked up a cheese stick.

I didn't really want to eat much; perhaps it was an older habit from high school, but I didn't like to eat in front of people. Ricky never seemed to notice; either that, or he didn't want to draw too much attention to himself.

"Something wrong?" Ricky asked, his mouth partially full of food.

In that moment, he was quite endearing in how he cared for me—even with the chewed-up chicken and cheese stuck in his teeth.

I thought about explaining my admittedly strange habit, but I held back; I didn't want to make him self-conscious. After all, it wasn't like I cared how much he ate.

But before I could say anything, the lights dimmed, and the show started.

Ricky put down his chicken taco to wipe his hands and clap. I clapped too, before I quietly rolled my cheese stick into my napkin.

Will Slater came out and did a little lap around the stage.

"Good evening, Fort Lauderdale!" He waved his arms up in the air, and then did another lap around the stage before finding his spot at the mic. "How's everyone doing tonight?"

We all gave him a tepid, happy response, and Will groaned playfully in response.

"Man, I knew coming to Fort Lauderdale was risky," he said. "All these old geezers around, right? That's why everywhere else, I go on at eight, instead of six!"

Ricky chuckled a bit, and I smiled. It was true, there were lots of older people around the city.

Will gave a few good opening liners, mostly complaining about the weather, politics, and the food being made for old farts, both literally and figuratively.

I was checking my phone five minutes in.

"But hey, it's not all bad here! The best part of this is I'm going on a cruise right after this. Woo-hoo!" Will ran around the stage again, then came back to the center. "This is the only place besides LA that I take my victory laps first. Here it's because I get to run and catch my ship—in LA it's because I'm never the right color for the jokes I tell."

Mid-laugh, Ricky started choking.

"It'll be okay," I assured him as I pounded him on the back. Seconds later, a small, half-chewed bit of a cheesy-fried jalapeño flew out of his mouth.

"Here." I handed Ricky a glass of water. "Flush it down."

"Whoa, whoa, whoa," Will said behind us. "My jokes aren't that bad that you're trying to kill yourself to get out of them, are they?"

Immediately, I realized the whole room was fixated on us.

Ricky waved at Will. "No," he said. "Just too excited. Laughing too hard."

"Well, that's awesome to hear, man," Will agreed. He looked at me, and I could've sworn his eyes lit up like he'd just won the lottery. "And it's even more awesome that you got your own hot nurse here with you."

Before I could say anything in return, he waved to the audience.

"Let's hear it for Hot Nurse Lady!" he said, and at once, all the people began to clap for me. "Saving her patient here. Maybe she'll get a nice bonus, huh?"

There were a few cheers for me as I quietly waved back and sat down. Ricky beamed with pride and gratitude, and I felt a bit better about coming.

"I don't know if you can all see it, but she's really, really hot," Will continued. "If I were her patient, I'd pretend to choke on a regular basis, if you know what I mean."

The audience laughed, and I felt irritation stir up inside of me again.

"I'm his date," I corrected Will.

Will's eyes lit up like nuclear Christmas lights. He'd clearly been waiting for me to take the bait.

"What? Did you hear that!" Will gaped at the crowd, looking like a drunken clown. "She's his date! Can you believe it? I mean, really, how much is he paying?"

I arched my brow and crossed my arms over my chest. "Excuse me?"

"Come on, Hot Nurse Lady," he jeered. "Have you seen a mirror, or are you one of those unicorn women who don't know how attractive they are? You're way too gorgeous to be hanging with this loser."

I had enough. I stood up. "This so-called loser has a real job, where he doesn't need to insult people for money and social media clout!"

"Exactly!" Will doubled down, grinning like a moron. "That's why he can afford you, as hot as you are, and how … not hot he is."

"Kallie, it's okay," Ricky whispered to me. "Let it go. This is part of the show."

I didn't let it go.

"I guess that means you don't have a girlfriend at all," I shot back. "Since you're so rude, you'd need to be a billionaire to get any female to just look at you."

As the crowd laughed—much noticeably louder than they had at his previous jokes—Will finally seemed to realize I wasn't in the mood to be laughed at, and I wouldn't let him dump on Ricky, either.

After all, Ricky was a very, very nice man.

He treated me well.

He had a good heart and a good family and even a good job.

Plus, he'd just choked! *And* he'd still played it off for Will, even giving him some encouragement.

Ricky didn't deserve this.

"Come on, lady," Will said quietly. "I'm just ribbing you some. You're the gorgeous mean girl, and he's the sweaty, fat friend from high school that always wanted to date you. It's funny stuff. Lighten up."

I didn't sit back down.

Will narrowed his eyes a little. "I mean, if it's even healthy for you to lighten up," he said. "Now that you're standing up, I'm pretty sure you'd evaporate if you lost any more weight. But don't worry, Chubby here can give you some if you need it."

My ears started to burn. I looked down at Ricky, who was no longer eating his food.

"I don't need to 'lighten up,'" I said. "But—"

"Yeah, no kidding," Will interrupted. "So, were you an anorexic or bulimic in high school?"

"I wasn't either," I shot back. "I just happened to see a face like yours and voluntarily throw up."

Will's face flushed over as people in the audience laughed.

"Well, look at that," I said with a half-hearted, fully-derisive laugh. "I'm no comedian, but I'm doing a better job than you are tonight!"

Will glared down at Ricky. "Can't you control your woman, man?"

Ricky looked over at me pleadingly, but I shook my head.

"You know, I'm not actually his paid escort, and I'm here because we've had several very nice dates, and he's a very nice guy. He takes care of his family. He likes music, and he wants to own his own business one day. The worst thing he's done since we started dating is buying tickets to you show tonight." I held my head high as the audience broke out in cheers. "I'm my own woman. I make my own decisions, and they happen to be very good ones. That's why I'm not on a date with a real loser like you."

"Hot Nurse, Hot Nurse, Hot Nurse!" The roaring chants from the audience cried out happily in support.

Will looked taken aback, and I could see the earlier light in his eyes implode like a dying star.

"All right," Will finally snapped back at the audience. "Well, all right, let's move on, shall we?"

"We'll move on when you do," I retorted.

"Seriously, lady, that's enough," Will yelled at me. "Security, how about you escort these two out? Bring in backup, considering this guy's ass and the giant stick up this lady's—"

Pure, red anger blurred my vision.

"I've had enough!" I walked up to the stage and I snatched the mic right out of his hands. "Hello everyone, I'm sorry to interrupt this performance … oh, wait, no I'm not, because it's awful. Who agrees with me?"

"You're hot!" one of the guys in the back called. "I'd agree with you no matter what!"

"Well, still," I said, "I think I'm doing a better job so far. Right?"

The audience cheered, while Will grimaced. "I haven't gotten to the good stuff," he said.

"I shudder to think what your idea of 'good' is," I gave a derisive snort of laughter. "How can you possibly be a good comedian when all your jokes are based on what people look like? Are you really that shallow? I have to ask, but how much do you hate women?"

A bunch of women cheered for me at that. Men clapped, too, and the guy who'd called out before whistled at me.

I ignored them and pointed at Will. "If you can't find something smarter to comment on, why don't you just stick to troll-posting on social media like all the other edgy children, the tired wannabes, and the hacks and the has-beens?"

Behind me, more laughter poured from the crowd.

I smirked at Will. "Well, I guess you took your victory lap too early today," I said. "But don't worry—I'm sure there's an early bird special waiting for you on your cruise."

"Woo! Hot Nurse, Hot Nurse, Hot Nurse!"

The cheers and the happy cat-calling started up again.

"What's your problem?" Will scowled. "I gave you nice jokes, talking about how pretty and skinny you are."

"Frankly, it's too bad I'm not fat, or I'd sit on you," I snapped back.

"If you want to sit, just go sit down!" Will grabbed for the mic, but I stepped back. "Give me back the mic!"

"No," I yelled.

Will launched himself toward me again, this time snagging the bottom of the mic. I pulled back, but he managed to hang onto it.

While we fought over it, the audience laughed.

"I think Will's the one paying her," a man shouted. "This is the best show he's had in months!"

At that, I jerked the mic back. "I'd have to be brain dead to work with him!" I yelled into it.

"Yeah! You go, Hot Nurse Lady!" The audience stood up, giving us a standing ovation.

Just then, Will elbowed me.

But AB's self-defense training requirements finally paid off—I dodged the full brunt of the hit and slammed my knee into his groin.

"Uh…*eugh*." Will made a painful, unearthly noise, like a chalkboard getting scraped over with spikes, as he fell to the ground, landing on my feet.

That was then I realized the three-inch heels I'd worn were a really bad idea.

"Augh!" I let out a cry as I toppled over, slamming my knees together and twisting away from Will so my dress didn't go flying up.

On the upside, I didn't flash anyone.

On the downside, I landed right on Will's back.

Laughter roared throughout the room.

"Aha, this is awesome," the guy from the back shouted. "She sat on him anyway!"

The whole crowd stood up, cheering and clapping for us, still whistling and calling out "Hot Nurse Lady" happily.

Everyone was enjoying themselves.

Everyone—except Ricky.

My cheeks heated over in humiliation, but when I saw Ricky stand up and push in his chair, a cold wave washed through me.

He wasn't happy.

Quickly, I pushed Will to the side, carefully stood up, and brushed myself off.

"I'll send you the bill for my dress," I snapped at Will. "It's dry-clean only."

Will groaned as he rolled around to look at me. "If I wasn't leaving Fort Lauderdale tonight, I'd sue you."

"Go ahead and try! I know quite a few good lawyers," I shot back. Giving Will one last look of severe, shameful disapproval, I turned on my heels—carefully—and hurried after Ricky.

○ ○ ○ ○ ○ ○

"Ricky, wait." I dashed to his car, where he was just climbing inside. I stood next to him and pulled him into a hug. "Give me a minute, okay?"

"Why?" Ricky asked, his voice low and sad. "So you can embarrass me some more?"

At that, I went still.

Then I pulled back from him. "Excuse me?"

"Kallie, I expect some level of teasing," he said. He waved down at his front. "I mean, look at me. And look at you. You're just too good—and too beautiful—for someone like me. Will's right."

"No, he isn't," I said through gritted teeth. "I didn't date you because you paid me to."

"But it looks like I do."

"Looks?" I repeated. "But you don't! We've been out on four dates. You're a very nice man. You have a lovely family and … you're just so nice."

Ricky gave me a sardonic look. "And I suppose I have a personality, too? Is that what you mean?"

"No! What I mean is that I don't date you for your money *or* your looks. Believe it or not, I have a few really bad memories of being fat in high school."

That admission alone nearly had me throwing up in my mouth. I wasn't going to admit the full truth about *that* particular topic to Ricky, no matter how well I got to know him.

But it was still something I wanted to let him know—because being fat wasn't the worst thing in the world, and I had firsthand experience of that.

"I find that hard to believe," Ricky muttered.

"Even after I defended you to that jerk in there?" I crossed my arms, suddenly even more angry at Ricky than I had been at Will.

"That's part of the show," Ricky insisted. "I'm a fat guy, Kallie. I can take it."

"But you shouldn't have to!" I said, angry and sad and frustrated. Tears welled up in my eyes, but I blinked them away.

"Maybe not, but I can," Ricky said. "And for what it's worth, I think you're very nice too. You're just a little too … much, you know?"

We both fell silent for a long moment, and then I gave up.

I was too defeated to keep fighting for him, especially when he didn't really want me to fight for him anyway.

"You know, you should realize that you're a great guy," I said quietly. "You have a lot to offer a nice girl. You shouldn't sell yourself short."

"I prefer it," he admitted.

That was the closest I would get to an apology.

"I'm sorry that things didn't go well tonight," I replied, keeping the emotion out of my voice.

Ricky cleared his throat. "Me, too."

He didn't actually say the words, "We're breaking up," but he might as well have.

Honestly, I didn't know why I felt so disappointed. I'd only dated Ricky a few times.

He was just a nice guy.

A very nice guy.

He wasn't someone I loved; he was more like … like someone who reminded me of someone I loved.

My heart suddenly began to ache.

I knew it was time to leave; I wanted to find a place to go and cry.

"Thank you, Ricky," I said. "For everything."

I reached out my hand, and he took it; for another moment, I clung to him, unwilling to say goodbye, even though it was inevitable.

Then he let go of me.

And then, he got in his car, and I walked away.

And then, that was it.

I deleted his phone number from my phone, I blocked him on the dating site, and I vowed I would never ever wear three-inch heels in public again.

My blood boiled as my tears slipped free. I hated that I was angry at Ricky; I hated it even more that I was angry at Will Slater, and maybe even more angry at the world.

What is wrong with me?

I wiped my tears off my cheeks. I got back in my car, feeling more tired than ever.

I sat down, stared out of my windshield, and looked up at the cloudy sky.

A long, sad sigh escaped me.

Slowly, I pushed myself, forcing myself to keep moving, no matter how long it took me.

"Well, I'm going to go home now," I whispered, trying to push back the impending loneliness that would invariably set in. "And when I do, I'm going to watch *The Lord of the Rings* again. The extended versions."

Surely nearly twelve hours of engrossing story and beautiful cinema would allow me to forget all the trouble with Ricky.

Wouldn't it?

I studied the sky again, straining my eyes to find just one star, even if it was small. The uncertainty and darkness of the skies overwhelmed me, and I just wanted some small, pin prick of a sign to know that I wasn't alone, that hope was real, and things would work out in the end.

There.

A star glittered through the clouds; and despite the light pollution, the nearby airport, and everything else, I knew it was real.

I smiled—just a little.

It was enough.

For now.

C. S. Johnson is the award-winning, genre-hopping author of several novels, including sci-fi and fantasy adventures such as *The Starlight Chronicles* series, the *Once Upon a Princess* saga, and the *Divine Space Pirates* trilogy. With a gift for sarcasm and an apologetic heart, she currently lives in Atlanta with her family. Look for more books and news at www.csjohnson.me.

Thank you for reading! Please leave a review for this book and check out www.csjohnson.me for other books and updates!

www.ingramcontent.com/pod-product-compliance
Lightning Source LLC
Chambersburg PA
CBHW020532310726
48979CB00014B/2308/J
9781948464949